THE CHRONICLES OF GILLEAN

BOOK 1

A TIME TO FIGHT

DANIEL CLERC

SR

PUBLISHING

THE CHRONICLES OF GILLEAN:
BOOK 1 — A TIME TO FIGHT

HSR PUBLISHING

Visit our website at: www.thechroniclesofgillean.com
www.hsrpublishing.com

ISBN: 9780984886609

Acknowledgements

I have never experienced war. However, through my years of medical practice, I have been blessed with the opportunity to hear stories and learn from those who have. My life has been touched by veterans from World War I, all the way to the men and women fighting in the conflicts of the Early Twenty-First Century. It is here that I thank all of them for their sacrifice, and for their willingness to share experiences of strength and frailty, stories laden with emotion, self-reflection, and observations about life.

I would like to thank those who helped pull *Chronicles* out of the shadows. Several read the manuscript when it was in its primordial form, always an arduous task, and provided valuable feedback; Jude Verzosa, M.D. (medical science, martial arts, and the subtleties of fight sequences), Daryl Clerc, Ph.D. (the exacting world of physics and military technologies), Patrick Muir (military, history, nuances of character development, and hours of conversation), Steve Nelson (a computer science visionary), and Lesley McLaren, M.D. (whose opinion is dear to me). Jackie Tew and Vivien Tucker were ever gracious in reading the manuscript and providing valuable feedback/error correction. Beth Szyperski corrected errors and smoothed out the writing (she diligently hacked away at my penchant for wordiness). Chris Bivins demonstrated spectacular talent in designing the artwork. Diane Mettler is a brilliant editor who helped define the edges of intersecting and twisting plots. She challenged and pushed me until the characters were polished, their quirks of personality were revealed, and their passions and conflicts were exposed. What emerged was *The Chronicles of Gillean*—the story of Jake Gillean's life and a world torn asunder four centuries in the future. It is a gripping narrative with multiple layers of protagonists and antagonists ranging from the concrete to the abstract and a story, which over the course of thirty years, has dually fueled the wheels of my imagination and haunted my waking thoughts.

There are many friends and family who have lent an ear and given moral support over the years. All of you know who you are − THANK YOU. My amazing wife, Janie, has been supportive from the beginning, helped guide the process, called me on my many tangents, and was kind enough to stifle screams of agony when she read the earliest drafts…over and over again. A constellation should be named after her. And my children − thank you for patiently supporting this endeavor as I wrote (then lost everything in a computer crash), rewrote, and then revised the story over and over again. It couldn't have been written you in my life.

To those who sacrificed their lives for a cause greater than their own—for liberty and equality of opportunity. We are forever in their debt.

PROLOGUE

In the recesses of REM sleep, he could see her hand. It was shaking and bloody, he reached for it, it was warm, he could hear her crying, she was alive, thank God she was alive, then there was an explosion. Jake's eyes suddenly opened and he yelled out. His pupils were dilated and his heart was pounding. He was dripping with sweat and his bedding was torn and ruined,. Gradually, once he realized his surroundings, his muscles began to relax. "Not again," he muttered as he put his feet on the floor. He was going to spend another night wandering not only the grounds, but through knots of tangled emotions and violent memories. By this time, the unrelenting nightmares had been torturing him for decades.

The mind of Lt. Col. Jake Gillean was trapped between two worlds. Waiting for him when he drifted into sleep was a world where he was once again fighting terrible battles. He could hear the screams. He could see and smell the carnage. He relived all the anger and loss. In the other world, the one of wakefulness, the great wars had slipped into the past, and he was left a relic, living in a time that no longer belonged to him.

As he quietly moved through the dark hallways, he considered the vile nature of his dreams…what were they? Were they sages proclaiming tumult in the vast oceans of his mind? Maybe they were deep-seated storms that would rip and churn until satisfied that his greatest vulnerabilities had been laid bare. If that was the case…hadn't they achieved their goal a thousand times over? One thing was certain; he always felt the stab of guilt and loss in their wake—and a sense of complete powerlessness.

Jake gripped his cane and carefully limped outside, nursing the frailty and excruciating pain in his hip. The air was still hot, and the high humidity pressed hard against the world. He took a deep breath, feeling the heaviness entering and exiting his lungs. He put the house to his back and began putting distance between himself and its lonely corridors. He tried to distract his thoughts by focusing on the waxing and waning noise of the cicadas as he moved along the path. There was a time, albeit a life ago, when his dreams were altogether ordinary, but he couldn't really remember when that part of him changed. After fighting for so long, after all the death and innumerable hardships, his memory of sleep being a time and place of serenity had completely abandoned him.

Off in the distance, he could make out the silhouette of the guard tower. He still had enemies who longed for the old days. There were threats against his life, and the guards were there to protect him. On nights like this though, he wondered if it was worth it, if it wouldn't be a fitting end to die a martyr while there was still something left.

Jake was a warrior, a fighter, and a leader of the most elite force that had ever existed, but his final battles were being fought in solitude. He shifted his weight off his hip and squeezed the cane as though it was a weapon. He whispered into the darkness, "They're demons." He was referring to his nightmares. He came to regard them as living entities...as demons of madness, as demons of his own creation that peered at him from the edge of consciousness. They were merciless manifestations of his past that, ever so patiently, would bide their time, waiting for him to lose his grip on wakefulness, close his eyes, and drift into slumber. Then, when his defenses were down, they would find traction in the choices he made, their claws would pull on his worst experiences, and their gaping mouths would drool upon the events he prayed most to forget. But despite their never-ending torment, he was still standing. A brutal battle for possession of his soul was being waged, and under the weathered and wrinkled skin, remained the stalwart and chiseled features of a warrior. In his eyes burned the determination of an indomitable soldier who would never give up. In his mind he repeated the vow he made long ago...that he would never again give up hope.

His nocturnal wanderings brought him to the pond. He stopped at its edge. His mind was somewhere else, invested in a memory that had grown old and gray. He was sitting on its bank with his father. He couldn't recall the exact words that passed, but he remembered how he felt that day. It was so long ago and yet so fresh. Jake's mind suddenly ripped at his vestments and roared out with fury against his demons...he hadn't done everything right, but he was willing to bear the weight of his mistakes. The world was a better place because of him. No...he would never die their way again.

Because of the incredible events that occurred in the life of Lt. Col. Jake Gillean, because of the intensity of the fighting and the ultimate objectives that were at stake, there is no obvious beginning to his story. Therefore, the story begins at the moment he lost everything, the moment he lost his soul...the moment he died. This is his epic story.

[*The descriptions within the story are at times graphic and vivid. My apologies to any who may find this disturbing. To understand the journey, it's important to experience the nature of the events as Jake Gillean did, within the proper context, and with the same level of detail that seared them into his soul. At the same time, I have tried to tone down the language as much as I dared. One of those inexorable facts of life is that many people, including soldiers, swear. There are occasions in the tragedy of the moment or in the heat of battle when a guttural word, one that would never be uttered in mixed company, actually serves to capture the essence of a moment more succinctly than a thousand pictures. This being the case, I have left out language that served no substantive purpose and left in place that which is contextually relevant.*]

-Daniel Clerc

I have no hope, but that I have no soul; that death will embrace nothingness.

- Lt. Col. Jake Gillean (his final thought…his first thought)

CHAPTER 1: MY GOD, MY GOD

[DATE: DECEMBER 2, AD 2440]
[HE ARRIVES]
[LOCATION: FRANKLIN, TENNESSEE]

The powder was dry. The guns were loaded. With nervous anticipation, the cannon crews stood ready to fire, waiting only for the order. Across the field, thousands of soldiers clenched their weapons and prepared to march into battle. The day had dawned with unforeseen beauty, and today they would march in honor of the men who gallantly fought so long ago. It was the five hundred and seventy-sixth anniversary of the Battle of Franklin, Tennessee, the last major battle in the Western Theater of the American Civil War.

As Franklin was just twenty miles south of Nashville, the event was certain to bring a fairly large crowd. That little fact notwithstanding, the beautiful weather and intense advertising campaign helped encourage thousands of locals to gather for the festivities. Anyone with a vague sense of historical intrigue found himself or herself captivated by the prospect of seeing what it might have been like to fight an ancient battle, a battle buried almost six hundred years in the past. As most of the souvenirs and assorted items of decorative memorabilia indicated, the original Battle of Franklin took place on November 30, 1864. The date fell on a Thursday this year. Being a day of the week unacceptable for such an event, the reenactment was moved to Saturday without protest.

Some of the spectators were drawn to Franklin with sentiments regarding war and man's relationship to man. Their belief was that, as far back as collective human memory reached, certain truths stood firm against the tests of time. One of these truths was that the most undesirable characteristics of mankind, those aspects most in need of change, are the very characteristics that have remained indelibly intact. As there were no indications that any great evolution was going to take place in terms of man's fundamental nature…the world and its travails, its power struggles and intrigues, would likely continue to plod along as they had in the past. Such being the case, the

1

most useful way to establish a clear vision of what the world is, and what it will be in the future, was to discover what it once was and what it has always been. For those spectators, the central theme of human existence was on glorious display in Franklin. To live was to struggle, and life represented a never-ending cycle of destruction and rebirth. However, for the bulk of the crowd and for the throng of excited children, their motives didn't run near so deep. They were simply looking for fun and a novel experience.

A few people, despite having blended in perfectly with the crowd, had entirely different reasons for being there. They were undercover agents conducting a clandestine operation. They shared fragments of a heavily guarded secret, a secret painstakingly hidden from the world for over half a millennium. They attended the event disguised as mothers and fathers, as nondescript spectators, as security, as newscasters, even as civil war reenactors. As they had rehearsed and trained, each had a specific job to do. Some were engaged in high tech crowd surveillance, some would activate electronic devices that would accomplish a variety of tasks, from disrupting local communications to blocking any image capturing devices such as cameras and/or video recorders, and four different crews were actively collecting scientific readings from the surroundings and uploading the encrypted information to clandestine satellites that circled the earth. Others had the task of spreading innocuous rumors through the crowd regarding what they were about to witness. It was going to be an orchestrated cover-up on a mass scale, at a time when advanced technologies made such an act virtually impossible. To a person, each member of the team understood the gravity of the situation. If everything went as planned, what they were about to witness would change the world. If just one of them failed, everything might be lost.

Parents lectured their children, trying to get them to understand what actually happened during the battle and during the war, an arduous task as most of them had little idea themselves. By late afternoon on that infamous day, the proud soldiers of the Southern Confederacy's last freely maneuvering major field army, the Army of Tennessee, arrayed themselves into massive lines of battle. Not before, or since, have so many men participated in a frontal assault on the North American Continent. In retrospect, one can only wonder if any of those fifteen thousand men and boys truly understood that they were the last real muscle fighting for an exhausted and dying nation…or that more than one in three would fall in the spasm of violence that was waiting for them across the field of advance. Regardless of their fear and trepidation, they solemnly did their duty. They shouldered their weapons and marched across an open, two-mile wide field, and with jaws held firm and resolute of spirit, they attacked into the very gates of hell. Against a tremendous spasm of fire and fury, they relentlessly threw themselves against a well-entrenched Union army. Five hours later, the terrible and futile sacrifice of life culminated in an exhausted wail that reverberated across the Americas; it was the last real gasp of a dying nation. Following the battle, the Confederacy limped on for five months. Only then was the Union of States restored.

The Battle of Franklin would be left to flounder in the wake of failed secession and in the wake of a failed country. Outside of Tennessee, it's a battle that's all but forgotten, not because of a lack of importance, but because of its heartrending tale of sadness and of lives sacrificed for a cause that, argued in retrospect, was already dead. To this day, the events that occurred at Franklin unabashedly display for the world the best qualities of man, and at the same time…some of the darkest aspects of humanity. With so many others, the banner of November 30, 1864 will continue to wave and history will continue to weep for the failings of mankind, for the jaded fabric within us that allowed such a terrible event, but the banner must wave lest we forget.

All the pieces were in place. It was time for the reenactment to begin. The mass of wide-eyed spectators lined up behind the Union fortifications. The crowd consisted of families with children, retirees, students, and the generally curious. Like a great Roman amphitheater, people were spread across the landscape to the rear and to the sides of the troops in blue uniforms. These reenactors represented the fighting men of the North in the devastating war to restore the Union. Just events unfolded so long ago, thousands upon thousands of Union soldiers fell in line behind earthen walls and anxiously waited for the attack to begin. Across the long and wide-open field gathered the forces of the enemy. They wore gray, and butternut, and every other conceivable ragged outfit. These were the soldiers who fought for the South. They fought fiercely against what they perceived was an invasion from the North, an imperialistic war that would deny them not only their Constitutional right to secede, but also their rights as a free and independent people.

With the opening cannonade, thousands of Confederates emerged into full view and began marching across the field. The spectators were immediately sucked into the battle as Union soldiers scrambled. Their actions demonstrated the urgency and seriousness of the task thrust upon them. There were no alternatives for them, they had to fight, they had to repel the attack to survive. Well over fifteen thousand Confederate reenactors marched in unison toward the Union earthworks. The sight was almost as awe-inspiring now as it was frightening on the actual day of battle. The Union cannon were belching fire and fury at the oncoming mass of

Confederate troops, targets too numerous to miss. Controlled explosions out in the field brilliantly decorated the landscape with glorious flashes of bright orange. Reenactors surrounding the site of each blast threw themselves to the ground and large holes began opening in the Confederate lines, just to be filled again as the mass of men moved forward.

Despite the fact that the cannon were shooting only half-loads of gunpowder, mixed with flour for visual effect, and absolutely no ordinance, the noise was deafening. The booming of the guns vibrated the ground with guttural intensity. Raw and unadulterated adrenaline surged. The field filled with a dense cloud of smoke. The massive lines of Confederates, an army that just moments before was completely visible across the field, were now progressively disappearing behind and into the ebbing and flowing white-gray wall.

Children laughed and excitedly cupped their ears as their parents held them up for a better view. For every few people who were thrilled with how marvelous the show was going, another person choked with semi-accurate perceptions of the absolute fear the soldiers must have experienced that terrible day. For at least a few of those in attendance, sights, sounds, and smells of the actual horror that occurred on this hallowed ground five hundred and seventy-six years ago raped the perceptible edges of their sixth-sense. For them it wasn't exciting, it was something more akin to a swirl of sadness and the grotesque realization of how many men actually died…and the inhumanity of man that ultimately lay at its core. Despite this, they simply couldn't avert their eyes. At the same time, the covert agents were doing their work—data was being uploaded, and electronic devices were being jammed.

The Confederates were converging as they closed in on the Union fortifications, their lines of advance moving inward at oblique angles. Some Union forces had been ordered to take up position in the open field, well out in front of the fortification's earthen walls. They were immediately in the path of the Confederates. They were supposed to slow down and hurt the Southern juggernaut. The Union soldiers knew better. For them, it was suicide. For the commanders who put them there, it was murder. At the last moment these men broke and sprinted to the rear, for the safety of their main entrenchment. At the same time the Union troops broke and ran, the advancing throng of Confederates intermingled with them and began running. They were going to ride the wave of retreating Union troops right over the wall and into the Northern stronghold.

Now, the adrenaline of the spectators and the reenactors surged to an even higher pitch. The clatter of small arms fire began to reverberate across the fortification's walls in earnest. Close to twenty thousand Union rifles were firing. And then, as the sheer mass of Confederate men advanced close enough to be within range, Union cannon on the opposite side of the Harpeth River added their ferocity to the fray. The Harpeth River was immediately behind the Union fortifications. Its position explained why the men fought so hard. The Union fought so hard because they had no choice…they couldn't retreat, and the Confederates were determined to get at them for the same reason…because they couldn't retreat.

On the field, the wall of white and gray smoke seemed to churn and breathe as if it were a living entity. From the Confederates' vantage, being inside the cloud was a surreal experience. It was very still in a haunting way. It was pressing and thick and suffocating. It was nothing more than a hellish veil that would keep secret the death and dismemberment that occurred within. The smoke did its monstrous work by pulling a veil over the worst of man's atrocities at the very moment they were being committed. Only later would it nonchalantly dissipate and reveal the human carnage, the mangled flesh, and the shattered lives left in its wake.

In the fractions of time interspaced between the explosions coming from the Union cannon, a strange sound pierced the background. It was competing for attention. It gradually grew louder, yet it was entirely unidentifiable. Something unexpected was happening. Those long dead were woken from their slumber. Unseen by living eyes, the ghostly images answered the cursed call to once again march across the hallowed ground. Hidden within the heavy smoke, there materialized an eerie and ghostly shoulder. Then it was a shoe. A short distance away appeared the image of an Alabama teenager, a boy cut down by a war he didn't fully understand; his life extinguished long before he learned to live. More apparitions appeared within the secret confines of the smoky gauntlet. The dead men were from Georgia, Mississippi, Tennessee, and elsewhere. Hundreds of ghostly apparitions appeared. Then, they lost themselves into the thousands. The energy of their lives preserved forever in the agony, the fear, and the hatred they experienced at the very moment of their death. Silent shrill screams pierced through five hundred and seventy-six years of forgotten time. Once again the men of the South were being torn apart by shot and shell. As before, the brave, the ever so brave men, continued their unrelenting march into the waiting arms of the angel of death.

The battlefield apparitions were real, but only insofar as the memories and the wrenching agonies of the moment were being ripped from the past and were being cast down in the midst of the reenactment. The visions were contained within the conscious experience of one soldier…the man who was the focus and the target of the covert operation. Something unique in the history of man was coming to bear this day. A fragment of the past was converging with the present. Nothing would ever be the same.

Within the cloud of smoke materialized a horse, a majestic black horse. First its hooves became visible in the thickest cloud of smoke, then its muzzle, and then its legs. The animal was mortally wounded. It was hobbling badly, struggling with all its might to stay up, lurching from side to side on three legs while blood rhythmically spurted from where the fourth had been. There was a rider in the saddle. The smoke was too thick, too obscuring. His body tilted backward, flopping with little resistance as the horse tried to steady itself. The soldier's arms were extended outward, at least what was left of them. His dirty gray uniform was stained red with blood. In the throes of death, the rider released a haunting guttural moan.

After nearly six hundred years, the moment had finally arrived. The covert operatives sprang into action, their adrenaline surged as a sickening and blood-curdling scream took ownership of the reenactment. At first it filled the spaces between the booming of the cannon. Then, as the reenactors increasingly took notice, as the field guns and musketry fell silent, left in the hum of silence, only one terrible and twisted sound remained to fill the void.

"He's arrived! He's arrived!" one of the operatives announced. "We have visual."

"Confirmed," another said. "Target is on the ground. Target is on the ground. Bring in the hovercraft."

The sound that took ownership of the reenactment was the sickening cry of a spectacular horse. It was screaming in agony. It was only one horse but it might as well have been a thousand. A horse and rider, although still partially obscured by smoke, emerged in front of the Union fortifications. As the smoke slowly dissipated, the horror of the scene came to bear. Blood was everywhere. The horse staggered dizzily, it was missing one front leg. Blood was pulsating out of the mangled stump. By some ungodly force of nature it remained upright, faithfully protecting and supporting his rider to the very end, to the very moment of death.

"Converge," the lead operative commanded. "Field units converge. Secure target. Go. Go. Go." As all the communications were encrypted, they were lost to everyone except the operatives.

The crowd was confused at first, thinking that what they were witnessing was somehow part of the reenactment. Then reality set in. The Confederate horseman and his mount were real, and they were dying. Gasps of shock and horror quickly spread across the landscape. Parents hid the eyes of their terrified children, shielding their innocence from the horrifying scene that was unfolding right in front of them. First one Union reenactor, then another…they dropped their weapons and rushed forward over the earthen fortifications, to investigate and help.

Blood was everywhere, almost completely covering the soldier and half of his mount. He was upright in the saddle but his limbs were limp, and his head hung downward, as though he was already dead. His uniform was identifiable as Confederate gray, but barely so from the massive trauma. The horse was bellowing and screaming in agony. It was a sickening and haunting sound unlike anything the crowd had ever heard. Children hid their tear-streaked faces as the horse screamed in pain, its agony shaking them to their core. The once majestic animal was struggling to keep its rider. It staggered and bellowed. It was swaying back and forth. It almost went down, but then caught itself, and on three legs it hobbled in a circle. Finally, with an ear-splitting dying bellow, it crumbled to the ground as the Union and Confederate reenactors converged. The limp rider followed his mount down, falling like a rag doll. At the last moment, the closest of the Union reenactors, one of the operatives, got under him just enough to support his head and shoulders, and then he pulled the target away from the horse so that it wouldn't crush him under its weight.

After being lost for so many centuries…Lt. Col. Jake Gillean had finally returned.

CHAPTER 2: THE BEGINNING

[FEBRUARY 6, AD 2441]
[2 MONTHS LATER - 67 DAYS AFTER ARRIVAL]
[LOCATION: NEW WASHINGTON, TEXAS]

Billions of high-tech communications occur each day. Satellites, towers, fiber optic cables, digital gamma relay stations; they function like neurons to interconnect the cells of a large multi-cellular organism called humankind. As a developmental process, it had taken billions of years for the planet to mature to this point. With this as the palate, considered in the grand scheme of things, the hundred-odd communications that took place in the two months following the reenactment, communications generated by the covert group that successfully secured the return of their target at Franklin— communications exceedingly important in every way imaginable—were entirely lost in the background noise of the highly technological world of the Twenty-Fifth Century. Yet, hardly had more important directives ever been relayed. Each message was short and almost exactly the same.

It was 0235 in the morning. Dr. Benjamin Murray fumbled with his alarm clock. For no particular reason, there was a frantic quality in his semi-conscious efforts to reestablish silence. With his frontal lobe still not fully awake and aware, he indiscriminately slapped at the nightstand. His efforts resembled those of a drunken sailor, and the noise continued unabated. His hand missed the alarm and hit the wooden surface. It was enough of a stimulus to pull him further out of the deepest neurological caverns of stage N3 sleep, or what's commonly referred to as deep sleep. He finally managed to grab the alarm, and he squeezed it in the frustration of his semi-conscious state. Just before he acted on the urge to smash the indomitable device into a thousand pieces, he realized that the alarm was innocent. It wasn't the source of the noise he was hearing. The noise was actually coming from his embedded biotech communications device (BCD). He hunched over the edge of the bed and planted his feet on the floor. His head was spinning, and he felt incoherent.

"Display," he murmured softly.

By using an integrated neuro-projector, the exceedingly small quantum computer implanted in the regions of his left frontal and maxillary sinus (a device that eventually became known as a BCD) produced a digital image that only he could see. It functioned by stimulating patterns of neurons in his retina. This produced an image that, in turn, was conveyed through his normal neural circuitry to the back of his brain, the occipital lobes, for visual processing. In a similar way, it transmitted sounds to his cochlea so that he could hear incoming messages. The BCD integrated its functions with those of its host by communicating information through the brain's normal auditory and visual ports. While Ben knew that BCDs weren't entirely safe, and even though he never really liked the idea of having the device implanted in his skull, he loved what it enabled him to accomplish. The devices were capable of receiving and processing a wide variety of coded inputs from the external environment; they could process and record everything the host was seeing and hearing, play it back for analysis, and upload the information to external government computer systems. Further, they could monitor a wide variety of host biometrics, and among its most basic functions…it could function as a telecommunications device.

'Odd,' he thought as he rubbed the sleep from his eyes. The information indicated that the communication was being sent and received from himself. It was originating from within his own BCD. His was a very special government-issue device with highly classified specs. All communications were routed through the agency. That being the case, a communication never got through without knowing exactly from where it was originating. 'Maybe there was a problem with the system,' he speculated. Usually the satellite relays performed flawlessly, but he supposed a glitch wasn't outside the realm of possibilities.

He glanced at his wife, Cecilie. Despite the noise, she continued sleeping. Then he realized the obvious. She couldn't hear the incessant bleating of the incoming call as it was occurring exclusively within his head. She would go on sleeping unless he somehow managed to make too much noise.

He answered the communication in a gravelly whisper. "Murray," he said. "What is it?"

The answer he got in response was a haunting encrypted voice. It had been ten years since he last heard it, and since then, he dreaded the day he would hear it again. Each time his BCD alerted him that there was an incoming communication, his subconscious would squeeze him with the notion that it might be the call, the call that would forever change his life, and potentially the world.

"Dr. Benjamin Murray?" the voice began.

Immediately Ben was fully awake and alert. Hearing the voice was a trigger. His body reflexively surged with adrenaline. His heartbeat quickened, his blood pressure rose, and his eyes dilated. It was the same physiologic response he would have had if there were an intruder in the house.

"Dr. Benjamin Murray?" the voice repeated.

"Yes," he finally managed to answer.

"He has arrived." Click. The voice was gone and the communication severed. That was the entire message. Just three small words–yet they carried with them the fate of the country and the fate of the world.

Ben stared blankly at the shadow-covered wall opposite the large windows in the bedroom as a mountainous wave of nervous anticipation swept over him. He was suddenly lost in a swarm of racing thoughts. Would he survive? What terrible things might happen to his family as a consequence of his actions? How could he possibly fulfill all of his mission objectives while being under the very nose of the tyrannical government he meant to overthrow? The stress was overwhelming. Dropping his head into his hands, he rubbed his face. He became acutely aware of coarse stubble and how tired he actually was. The latter was something he would have to fight through. There was simply too much to do. He considered how the sequence of events in his life led him to this moment. How many of the watershed events of his life were actually of his own making, and how many were manipulated by discrete and unseen forces he couldn't fully comprehend?

Ben watched his wife for a long while. Because of the message, a chasm had suddenly opened between them. It was palpable and completely unwanted by him and completely unbeknownst to her. He was embarking upon a journey that would not include her, and there was nothing he could do about it. She was right there, he could reach out and touch her, and yet she seemed a million miles away. Through a lens of sudden and abject loneliness, his beautiful wife, Cecilie, looked so peaceful. She was the absolute love of his life. He trusted her completely and without reservation, yet he couldn't share with her even the vaguest details of what was happening or the screaming gulf that he felt was now widening between them. In fact, he now had no outlets and no support network for the critical mission that had just been launched. While he was prepared, he was also as alone in this as anyone had ever been.

Ben anticipated that it would be within his lifetime that the sequence of unstoppable events would begin. Through the years, he often visualized receiving the ominous call. He considered what his reaction would be, and how events might unfold. But now that reality had set in and it had actually come, what stood out most in his mind was that incredible forces were being unleashed, and that unstoppable events thus initiated were far greater than any of the people involved. Up until now, there had been an inner conflict. Beyond the sheer confidence that he should be the one to shoulder the fate of everything worth living for, a secret part of him hoped that the responsibility would bypass his life, and the task would fall upon someone else at some undefined date in the future. But deep down, because of his unique skills of interrogation and his position within the Ministry of Public Safety (the MPS), he fully expected that the burden was going to be his to bear.

CHAPTER 3: THE BRIEFING

[FEBRUARY 8, AD 2441]
[69 DAYS AFTER ARRIVAL, TWO DAYS LATER]
[LOCATION: NEW WASHINGTON, TEXAS]

Ben was quick in making assessments of people. His memory was sharp, his attention to detail well honed and hawkish. He was all about the defense of his country. As such, he had no problem interrogating and killing or maiming enemy soldiers, officials, ambassadors, criminals, or anyone else who might represent a potential danger to the well being of United America. For him, when it came to protecting his country, the ends fully and entirely justified the means—at first. After years of work, his idealism began to waiver under the weight of intense internal conflict. One too many times, his targets were little more than political rivals to the Egalitarian Party.

Ben's path to becoming an interrogator was circuitous and rather unorthodox. He was never one of those control freaks or power-trip types destined from the moment the umbilical cord was cut for either law enforcement or incarceration. He was actually more of a stargazer and a dreamer. He spent his childhood fantasizing about piloting military craft into the vast reaches of space. In lieu of schoolwork, he devoured science fiction literature. Eventually, he turned his dreams into reality and became an SAF, Space and Air Force, pilot. However, after an inexplicable visual defect, what appeared to be a laser burn injury to his retina that resulted in a blind spot, he was forced to hang up his flight jacket. He was discharged from the military and found his way into the intelligence service. With an incredible talent for foreign languages and after impressing the right people, he was trained to be a covert field operative. He spent the next several years in the field. It was during that period of time that he was introduced to the art of interrogation. He knew that he had found his calling. Believing that there had to be better ways to apply technology in the process of extracting information from an unwilling subject, he envisioned an unexplored niche and pushed himself to become a physician. Calling in some favors, and as a result of some back door maneuvering that occurred without his knowledge, his entry into medical school was expedited, and he eventually became an interventional neuropsychiatrist.

Soon thereafter, Ben was instrumental in the development of a classified virtual neuro-modulation device. It was an amazing piece of technology that allowed the user to manipulate brain function down to the discharge of a single neuron. His ultimate vision included something else, an added feature that was capable of destroying brain tissue with extraordinary precision. With this tool in hand, he was able to bring together and hone a very unique skill set. Once the highly advanced technologies were fully integrated with the BCD device implanted in the left side of his skull, which effectively coupled the process of interrogating someone else's brain with the function of his own, what emerged was an aggressive and calculating interrogator with little in the way of scruples.

Ben was able to spawn a classified unit within the Ministry of Public Safety. In fact, due to public sensitivities, the nature of the unit and the brutality of its work, very few people outside the elite circles of Egalitarian Party insiders even knew that it existed. Even fewer knew exactly what his team did and the extent of its capabilities. While the Egalitarian Party was concerned with maintaining the pretense of law, there was no point in fanning flames of public dissension. As such, Ben's work remained hidden and would never see the light of day. When it came to the interrogation of prisoners, the process was in violation of just about every ethical statute that existed since the reign of Genghis Kahn. The public would be rightfully outraged should they ever learn of it. While his methods weren't exactly akin to overt torture, the techniques he actually used to extract information from prisoners were not only considered inhumane, they were ethically and morally reprehensible for everyone except the most ardent supporters and philosophically unscrupulous members of the Egalitarian Party. Essentially, what he did was what no one else in history had ever been able to do. He learned to seize absolute and total control of another person's brain. He could control it and get exactly what he wanted. Dr. Benjamin Murray discovered the means to wrest from a person something that had always been regarded as personal and completely autonomous…their conscious mind. He raped their thoughts and destroyed what he wanted, with no judge or jury to counterbalance his decisions.

The MPS was the bastardized grandchild of several national security agencies that merged over the course of the last several centuries. It included remnants of the United States Department of Homeland Security, the Central Intelligence Agency, and counterparts from the pre-merger countries of Canada, Mexico, Nicaragua, Honduras, Panama, El Salvador,

Costa Rica, and Cuba.

While the MPS was the principle out-of-country intelligence operation for the United American Government, its domestic counterpart was the Domestic Security Service, or simply, the DSS. Both organizations functioned to investigate any and all threats against the general welfare of the country, and both wielded exceedingly powerful intelligence and investigative capabilities. Their covert operations included espionage on absolutely every level, occasional abductions, and even assassinations. The actions of the MPS and the DSS were controlled by an umbrella organization full of bureaucrats and political appointees called the North American Intelligence Agency, the NAIA.

When the Egalitarian Party's political movement swept into power after World War IV, a war that ended roughly seventy years ago, one of their first acts was to take over the MPS and the DSS. It was in the wake of a disaffected public mood that they first took over the Houses of Congress and the Executive Branch of Government. Once elected, they steadily stripped away all opposition and replaced the weary and bankrupt, but free country, with one that was more akin to a fear-based police state. In many ways, it resembled an old Marxist regime straight out of the textbooks. They centralized power in New Washington, took over the press corps to stifle dissenting opinions, took over the banking and industrial sectors of the economy either through indirect over-regulation or through more direct means. The Internal Revenue Service, the IRS, became more muscle for the Party, ensuring that anyone who didn't fall in line with the Party's agenda risked being audited. If found guilty of tax evasion by The Panel of Judges, all of whom were Egalitarian Party appointees, the conviction was one of *disloyalty to the citizens of United America*...or *sedition*. In this manner, the Government seized ownership of companies all across the country, many times symbolically turning them over to the workers in exchange for Party loyalty.

The most radical event that occurred in the early post-war years was when the High Judiciary, the most powerful judicial arm of the government, and the only branch that was able to actively oppose the Egalitarian Party's agenda, was destroyed. The Court was in full session when an explosion ripped the building apart. No one survived. It was blamed on a disaffected SAF pilot who was acting at the behest of the Traditionalist Party. He claimed that the computer systems in his plane were compromised and that he didn't have anything to do with the accident, that the guided missiles fired on their own and he couldn't abort the launch. The corroborative cockpit recordings notwithstanding, he was convicted and executed. Three things happened; the Traditionalist Party was destroyed, the High Judiciary was repopulated with Egalitarian Party loyalists, and the military was stripped of all its old guard loyalists. This happened before Ben was born, so he didn't have any direct experience with the tumultuous events of those days. However, he did interrogate an elderly individual who at one time was a Party insider. He had retired and was living in self-exile in the Bitterroot Mountains of Montana. Before Ben eliminated him as a threat, the man claimed that a few high officials within the Egalitarian Party orchestrated the entire event, and most poignantly, that he was one of them. He suffered with guilt and regrets his entire adult life, and eventually he turned his back on the government. His mistake was assuming that a quiet retirement in the mountains would be tolerated.

Ben remembered that interrogation as one of the most disturbing he had ever done. The man acted as though he expected him. He was tearful and told Ben everything he knew willingly and without resistance of any kind, but he issued a dire warning that the information would place Ben's life in danger. He begged for forgiveness for what he did, for the people who died in the explosion, and for what his actions did to a country that at one time embraced liberty and justice. Then, after a more thorough neural extraction, Ben eliminated the man. Memories of the encounter stuck with him from that day forward.

A successful mission involved capturing a person of interest, performing an interrogation, rapidly extracting the target information, and then returning the target back to his or her life with the caveat that there would be absolutely no memory of the interrogation experience. The target would wake the next day and be none the wiser. However, if the interrogation was a bust, the process was not for the squeamish. While he never had any problems sleeping because of the things he had done, some of the things he had learned from his targets scared him beyond measure. Information ranged from abuse and incest, to exploits and fetishes that defy description, to plots against the government. The things he learned were so succinct and disturbing that he occasionally suffered extreme bouts of insomnia. Each of these cases reinforced his belief that the ends accomplished in saving lives fully justified the means he used to extract the information. He considered it his contribution to the defense of the nation. Over the years, the secrets he had extracted from enemies of the Party and the country, information regarding germ warfare and nuclear threats, had saved innumerable lives, and in actuality, the number likely climbed well into the millions. Nevertheless, Ben moved silently and stealthily through his life, appearing charismatic and a bit aloof…and almost no one outside his unit knew about his staunchly aggressive and remorseless alter-ego.

Weaving his way through his mid-fifties and still in good physical condition, Ben was not only energetic, but he stood out as a seasoned veteran well ensconced in MPS operations. That explained why he wasn't concerned when he received an order by way of Director Zimmer's secretary late in the afternoon the day before. He was instructed to clear his morning schedule and report to the Director's office at 0800. The order didn't reveal any details, but they never did. At exactly 0800, punctual and always straight to the point, the Director received Ben into his office. His secretary promptly turned and beat a hasty exit.

Zimmer didn't react. He studied Ben from across his desk and after a moment of awkward silence he said, "Dr. Murray." His facial expression was stern, scowling, and meant to intimidate.

"Director Zimmer," Ben answered. Understanding the psychology and a master of the same techniques, he wasn't one to be intimidated.

Nevertheless, Zimmer's expression was unwavering. Finally he said, "I've been briefed, and I would like to give you an opportunity to explain yourself."

Ben maintained a stoic exterior, but on the inside, his heart skipped. His mind raced, and he felt the cold grip of fear. Was it possible that Zimmer knew about his disloyalty to the Party? How could he know? "Sir," he said. "You have me at a disadvantage." Ben quickly weighed his options. He could easily subdue Zimmer. He could even perform a forced interrogation on him to find out exactly what he might know. All he needed was a few minutes. No. He couldn't do that. The office had to have security features in place.

Before Ben went any further, Zimmer broke his expression and chuckled to himself. Rising to get out of his chair, he said, "You're not as easy as the others. I'm just messing with you. Brought you here to bring you in on a developing case."

Ben played it cool, expressing a slight degree of confusion and hiding away his sense of relief. Zimmer informed him that over the next hour he was going to be briefed on a developing case. Then they were going to have a meeting with the President regarding the matter. Zimmer didn't personally reveal any further details except to say that it was a serious matter that involved national security, adding that it was unlike anything they have had to deal with before. At that point, they exited the office and proceeded into the guts of the DSS building, making their way through the back offices and into the forensics lab. That brought them to Tommy Dahlins.

"I want Dr. Murray up to speed on the John Doe case," Director Zimmer said. "Tell him what you know." The order was meant to help get Dahlins started. Zimmer was the Director of the NAIA, which made him one of the most powerful men in the Egalitarian Party—a man with a direct line to and from the President. His well-earned reputation was for being brusque and aggressive. He never forgot a detail, was acutely perceptive, and was always wary of other people's motivations.

"We're so all over the place with this one, where would you like me to start?"

"The beginning!" Zimmer impatiently directed. He was angry. He made it a point to avoid mincing words and was never the type to suffer fools. He expected all of his requests to be followed fast and to the letter, and most importantly…without question.

"OK. At this point, the subject is proving to be a real John Doe. It's not as if he doesn't exist…he actually doesn't exist," Dahlins said.

Tommy Dahlins was an agent with the DSS's criminal identification unit. He had ten plus years in the service but he managed to tick off the wrong person and his career stalled. He was passed over for several promotions and choice assignments. Once that happened, his personnel file was essentially dead in the water. Further advancement was unlikely, and he wouldn't get a field position. He'd finish his career tucked away in the lab.

"Explain to Dr. Murray just what the hell that means!" Ben could sense the Director's tension. Something was under his skin. Dahlins was aloof, to be sure, but otherwise seemed decent enough. It was unlikely that he was the source of Zimmer's mood.

Dahlins went on, "What it means is that we ran a full DNA match analysis against our entire population database and got no matches.… out of eight billion citizens, didn't get a match. Didn't get a match on his fingerprints, dental records, or retinal scans either. He has an implanted bio-communications device, a BCD, in the left side of his skull, it's military grade with maxillary and frontal predominance. The serial number is a dead-end though. It doesn't exist."

"Whoa," Ben said. "John Doe? A military grade BCD? What are you talking about? What John Doe?"

"Dahlins can only tell you what he knows," Zimmer interjected. "You'll be briefed on the case in its entirety. John Doe is a subject we acquired under an unusual set of circumstances. He was badly injured."

Ben wanted to ask about the BCD. If the device wasn't one of United America's, might it be possible that John Doe belonged to a foreign government? But he decided to hold his question for the time being.

"Give a description of John Doe's condition when he was found," Zimmer ordered.

"He suffered several gunshot wounds," Dahlins continued. He was pointing to different parts of his own body as he explained, "To his right upper chest wall with extensive lung damage. Another to his left shoulder. That one completely destroyed the joint. His right forearm was essentially severed and was hanging on by only a couple of muscles and some skin. His right femur was shattered and there was extensive soft tissue damage. In addition, he had some facial trauma, one ear partially missing and a small fragment of metal in one eye. A couple fingers were mangled or missing, and he took a glancing shot off of his left hip.

"The docs said that besides the major trauma, some other injuries didn't match anything they had ever seen. It looked like he had been exposed to at least a small dose of radiation. But it wasn't associated with any lasting cellular damage. The type of radiation remains indeterminate. He's a mystery to the doctors and the forensics team. But that's not the strangest thing. The surgeons at the hospital pulled these out of him."

Dahlins pulled a handful of plastic specimen bags out of an evidence container. They were neatly labeled, as if being prepared as evidence in a criminal proceeding. They contained bullets of various shapes and sizes. Some of them were misshapen and nearly unidentifiable as bullets. Other bags contained what appeared to be odd types of shrapnel.

"These were all pulled out of John Doe," Dahlins said.

"I thought I knew a bit about ballistics, but I've never seen anything like this. What exactly are these?" Ben asked. He fingered the bags, holding one of them up to examine the contents. Flipping it over, he examined the backside as well.

"You're correct to ask, doctor," Dahlins said with an unbridled degree of excitement. "The projectiles in those bags were used in the 1800s." He waited for the facial expression indicating that Ben was taken aback, and he continued, "We tracked the manufacturer, based on the metal composition, to munitions factories that were located in several states that made up the Union during the American Civil War."

"Wait a minute," Ben said, "are you suggesting that these bullets were actually manufactured in the 1800s?"

"Yes. That's exactly what I'm saying. We've compared these against the current manufacturers of replica bullets, and these are definitely the real deal. You see, each bullet carries telltale signs of the old versus modern manufacturing techniques. That's how you can tell them apart. Plus, the metal composition is different. We then compared them to authentic bullets stored in museums and there was a perfect match. The bullets you're holding in your hand were not only pulled out of John Doe, they were manufactured in the 1800s."

Dahlins went on to discuss the type of weapons that would have been used to fire the projectiles, the muzzle velocities, and based on the condition of the bullets and the resultant injuries, the approximate range that they were fired from.

As Dahlins was talking, Ben experienced the dual increase of excitement and the cold grip of fear. Could John Doe be the one? Was it possible that the man his secret society was looking for, the man he was charged with protecting, that this was the same person Dahlins was describing? Ben was acutely aware of Zimmer. He felt his piercing gaze. He was standing under the watchful eyes of one of the elite members of the Party and one of the most powerful men in United America, and at the very same time he was being introduced to John Doe, the man who was the last great hope to bring it all crashing down—a man who should never have been allowed to fall into the hands of the Egalitarian Party.

As Ben suffered under the heavy burden that was confronting him, he simultaneously felt the sheer weight of the lead projectiles in his hand. It seemed impossible that a man could be shot in such a primitive and barbaric fashion, and that he would survive. The secret society's objective, the lives of so many people, the hope for United America, it was all hanging by the tiniest of threads.

Ten minutes later, the briefing was concluded. Zimmer led Dr. Murray through the maze of labs, and they emerged into another hallway. He was walking next to the Director but about a half step behind. Every move and every behavior was a primitive dance of egos, and in that environment he was content to allow Director Zimmer every nuance of his superior rank.

"What happened to you?" Ben muttered to himself. His mind was awash with vivid images of the trauma, the mechanisms of injury, and the resultant physical damage suffered by John Doe.

"I would ask where the corpse is being held, but he seemed to imply that John Doe actually survived his ordeal." Ben was playing a role and simply making conversation at this point. He suspected he knew more about John Doe than Zimmer did, including his identity. The problem was that his objectives were now making him an enemy of the Party, and in effect...an enemy of the state. He needed to play everything perfectly if he was going to be successful. It was imperative that he discover what Zimmer was planning.

"He survived all right," Zimmer answered.

Ben feigned surprise. "Really! He's alive?" He wanted to ask, 'How is he? Where is he?' but he checked himself as that type of response would have been far outside the MPS norm.

"Been in the hospital since acquisition. He's finishing an extended stint in an inpatient rehab facility at New Bethesda Hospital in Nashville.

Within a couple days, he'll be ready for discharge. They think that going someplace more like a home might do him some good." Zimmer made a curt motion to his head with his thumb as if to indicate there were some mental problems. "Some think inpatient psych would be more suitable."

"Has he explained what happened?"

"When he was first in the hospital, he made some gibberish noises. Most of it was unintelligible though. The only thing that was understandable was he repeatedly said that the paramedic knew him. Then nothing. He hasn't said anything since. He was so extensively traumatized, and then on so many sedatives and pain meds, that we can't really say for sure that he even knew what he was saying."

"He hasn't said anything since?"

"Not a word. You heard Dahlins. He was damn near ripped apart. With his injuries, he should be dead—miracle he survived. One out of a million survives those injuries. Hell, a year ago he would have been dead. I'm told the only reason he stood a chance was because of recent advances in critical care surgery, something about advances in artificial hemoglobin and blood products. At this point, I have far more questions than answers. It certainly doesn't help matters that he isn't talking. I'm told he yells out in his sleep. During the day, he mostly drifts in his own world. He does participate in rehab, and the docs say that they have never seen anyone recover so fast. Real warrior, whoever he is." Zimmer had his own suspicions but didn't want to offer any just yet.

"What's the status?" It was Ben's turn to point to his head.

"Everything seems to be intact. The reason he isn't talking isn't because of a brain injury. All the tests came back normal. If he can make noise, I suspect that he can talk. He just needs the right kind of motivation. That's where you come in, Doc. You know a hell of a lot more about this sort of thing than I do. All I can tell you is that it appears he's not talking because he doesn't want to."

'This is good,' Ben thought. The last thing he should do is talk. He has no idea how much danger he's in. As long as he doesn't talk, Zimmer might not realize the potential danger he poses to the Party. The country is not the way John Doe left it, and he probably won't like what he sees. Should he demonstrate any hint of displeasure, his usefulness will be over as far as the government is concerned.'

"Why am I being involved?" Ben asked, even though he knew the answer.

With a cagey smile Zimmer quipped, "I sense that the good doctor doesn't cope well with anticipation." The nature of his response wasn't lost on Ben. It implied that Zimmer was watching him with the greasy eyes of a savvy and ruthless political survivor.

They headed down the hallway at a brisk pace. They were soon out of the building. Ben wasn't struggling to keep pace, but he did have to consciously avoid actually breaking into a slow jog.

"We have to move," Zimmer explained. "That was a warm-up briefing. Another one is coming. You should be able to put everything into context, and you'll understand what I expect from you. I know you have lots of questions, but believe me," he gave Ben a confident glance, "you're going to have more in an hour. The President does not like to be kept waiting. The last self-important son-of-a-bitch that showed up late had to explain to his family why he was out of a job." Zimmer didn't laugh.

Director Carl Zimmer was a political appointee of President Martinez. With his resume; retired Five Star General with the United American Army, former Director of the United American Security Council, and Presidential Advisor during the last two administrations, he was essentially regarded as a Party favorite and an extreme loyalist. No one of any importance dared question his political appointment to the position of NAIA Director, and he was ultimately approved with well over ninety percent Congressional support.

Zimmer was a hard driving force, a real bulldog. You either kept up with him or, in no uncertain terms, he would find somebody else who could. Of his underlings, he asked the difficult, but never the impossible, and despite his reputation to the contrary, he was always fair. At the same time, he was never to be crossed or disappointed. The mere force of his personality was such that many proud and strong willed individuals buckled under his intimidating stare. Like a predatory animal, he sensed weakness. Always calculating, he would pounce on the weak, if nothing else…because it gave him pleasure to do so.

Zimmer was a true patriot in every sense of the word, and despite being in his sixties, he showed absolutely no signs of slowing. His father, an international businessman, was killed by a terrorist when Carl was nine years old. He carried the extracted bullet in his front pocket ever since. It reminded him of the painful nights he spent listening to his mother trying to quiet her tears in the solitude of her bedroom. As a replacement for his father, he adopted the defense of his country and the principles of equality espoused by the Egalitarian Party.

* * * * *

It was only natural for Ben, and everyone else alive in the year 2441, to take for granted the world into which he, or she, was born. They had no experience with a world, or a time, other than the one in which they lived. Advanced technologies ranging from home robots, to computer-guided vehicles, to genetic treatments for disease, were all indelible parts of the landscape from the moment their first memories were being formed. Little did they realize how different their world actually was from the one experienced by ancestors only a few generations removed.

One of the differences, and arguably the watershed development for mankind, involved the creation of energy technologies that all but eliminated the need for oil. It was one of the greatest success stories in human history and was pioneered in its entirety by a privately owned international corporation called *Mutare Science and Technology Global (MST)*, and its energy sub-division, *Elektor*. *Mutare* was a Latin word that meant *to change,* while its primary energy sector's name was an old Greek word meaning *the beaming sun.* By the Twenty-Fifth Century, energy was being captured in outer space by massive satellites. Several dozen were in orbit above the planet at any one time, circling the globe beyond the outer stratosphere. Others, the primary facilities, were positioned on the surface of the moon. Basically, they functioned by trapping, or harvesting, energy from the sun. They converted the vast amounts of energy into a laser that was projected to large receiving plants on earth. The plants converted the energy and transferred it to billions of discs about half a meter in diameter and ten centimeters thick. The discs were used as batteries. A single disc easily had enough stored energy to power a large home for well over a year in the harshest of climates. It accomplished this without the generation of any harmful pollutants, ozone disruption, or carbon dioxide emissions. It was an environmentalist's dream. But that was only one of the advantages.

With the growing frequency of terrorist attacks throughout the Twenty-First and Twenty-Second Centuries, it became strategically imperative that the electrical grid system, the system used to power the world, but especially the highly industrialized societies, be fundamentally changed to reduce vulnerability. Society learned the hard way, in fact it had to learn the same lesson over and over again before the message drove itself home, that it only took a single, or at most a few, precision strikes to completely disrupt Western Society; to bring life, commerce, and everything else to a screeching halt. The Achilles heel of the technologically advanced societies was that they couldn't function without the technology, and the technology was useless without electricity. Society evolved to become over-reliant on electricity running through wires. If it wasn't a terrorist attack or a deliberate act of war causing the problems, it was a natural disaster. The grid structure, the suspended and buried power lines, the monstrous ongoing cost of infrastructure maintenance, the strategic and market vulnerabilities they represented, the market forces fighting to keep them in place for financial gain, and even the increasingly recognized negative health ramifications of being exposed to powerful electromagnetic fields… all these were now things of the distant past.

MST, the most well known global corporation in the history of the planet, was the agent of change. To date, its inner workings remain shrouded in secrecy. It silently and purposefully maneuvered itself to remain completely independent of any government, a process that required foresight and skilled diplomacy. It functioned as long as it could while based in North America, and as a result of political pressures and financial extortion from lawyers and politicians, it left and set up its primary facilities out-of-country. It did so by literally raising its own private island in the middle of the South Pacific. It was the size of Cuba but shaped like a horseshoe. It had cliffs ranging from one to three thousand feet in height along its periphery, with the only exception being the central harbor. It was relatively impervious to anything nature or man might throw at it, and at the same time, it was oriented perfectly to capture rainfall in its lush interior. After MST developed its energy program through its Elektor subdivision, it gave away the energy at cost. It sold the land-based technologies and sent out teams to teach any interested party how to manufacture the batteries. Its goal was to eliminate the need for oil and nuclear energy as a means of power and to open up the next chapter of human history. In that, it was a resounding success.

Each home, office, factory, and hospital now had its own independent and abundant supply of energy. All things considered, the global power supply was now essentially invulnerable. The systems that evolved over the centuries provided for a clean and essentially limitless supply of power. As a result, technological developments were occurring at such a rapid pace that serious plans were advanced towards permanent colonization of the Moon. Further, the possibility of extending that process to other planets, including Mars, was being considered.

Interactive virtual reality news dissemination was another technological advance that changed the face of mankind. There was a time when information and news dissemination was controlled and manipulated for the masses by the sociopolitical views of a few prominent and exceedingly wealthy media conglomerates. Largely, their motivation was exactly as logic would predict—to advance their own financial self-interests and their own social agendas. Now, television, newspapers, and magazines were as obsolete as clay tablets and papyrus scrolls for the dissemination of news. *Vintel*, or virtual intelligence, based on a combination of Internet search engines, virtual reality, and holographic imagery was the norm. Any individual could select or create his, or her, own virtual person to deliver news or almost any type of information imaginable.

The Vintel units used for information dissemination came in a variety of sizes. They resembled antiquated television sets in some respects, except that they actually created a three-dimensional image. The units allowed the viewer to adjust the viewing angle or rotate an image with ease. Moreover, viewers could increase the speed of the transmission as the brain has the ability to process information faster when allowed to integrate it from several senses simultaneously.

With the development of Vintel units, the news media was forced to go through a metamorphosis. Before World War IV, a war that raged from the year 2374 to 2379 A.D., the content of the news was still created by a variety of large and small media outlets, but full disclosure of who owned the outlet, their financial interests, their sociopolitical agendas, and their pertinent associations had to be fully disclosed with each broadcast. While passage of this Disclosure Law was a watershed moment that did much to change the face of news dissemination, of politics, and of society, it did come at a price. It almost caused a revolution. Eventually, alleged violations and declarations that the government had to step in to promote objectivity and balance, led to a government takeover of the media. The official government takeover of all forms of news dissemination occurred in the year 2382, just a few years after World War IV. Now, in the year 2441, dissenting voices were all but extinct.

The entertainment and sports media market soared, taking full advantage of the new technologies. The days of going to the movies with large groups of people and watching a movie on a flat screen, inside a large auditorium... those days were long gone. That type of experience was the domain of retro-parties celebrating the past. Vintel made every movie and sporting event three-dimensional and fully interactive, and the units could easily be big enough to encompass an entire room. This allowed the viewer to walk into a life-sized movie and personalize the experience. Even the oldest movies in existence had been converted to the new format. A viewer could march with ancient Roman armies, ride on the deck of the Titanic, stand on the stairs with Clark Gable and Scarlett O'Hara in *Gone with the Wind*, or travel into and through outer space. One might even re-experience home movies or sporting events from the actual field of play. The possibilities were wonderfully endless.

Technological advances were occurring in a world that was being swept by massive waves of sociopolitical change. In a process that began in earnest during the Twenty-Third Century, the separate countries that occupied the North American Continent merged into one great, unified, continental nation. It called itself United America, or the UA. A mammoth democratic republic, the UA was formed by the merger of Canada, the United States, Mexico, and the Central American countries of Guatemala, Honduras, Nicaragua, Costa Rica, and Panama. In addition, the island nations of Cuba, the Dominican Republic, Haiti, and several smaller Caribbean nations joined. The last to join, a few years ago, was Iceland. Greenland's status was pending, but all indicators looked as though it would join within the next several years, much to the consternation of Europe.

While the seeds of union were sewn several centuries earlier with the formation of the European Union, the fertilizer that actually allowed the seeds to grow in North America was the North American Free Trade Agreement. This initiated a process that resulted in the breakdown of barriers, the formation of continental financial institutions, and finally, a single North American currency called the Amero. The socioeconomic and political theories of Bradbury Longhart, who lived in the 21st Century, although highly contentious in the elite circles of his time, had largely been predictive of the mass integration of the world's societies. All it took was four hundred years for his predictions to come true. The basic premise of Longhart's macrobehavioral theories of socialism was that harmonious political and cultural integration only occurs after diverse societies are fully and stably integrated both financially and religiously, after relative economic equalization independent of productivity, and after becoming intertwined with one another from a monetary perspective. At that point, war and mass violence, militarily and in the civilian sector, was akin to social self-mutilation and economic suicide.

Modern political theorists added that the advanced speed, ease, and affordability of travel were also exceedingly important factors to consider. The merger of nations was only possible when one could travel from Anchorage to Managua in a matter of hours. In a world such as that, continental merger was not only inevitable, it was impossible to stop.

Arguably one of the most important developments in United America, and one of the factors that allowed the Egalitarian Party to maintain complete control, was the marriage between governmental tax policy and new monetary technologies. It was the utilization of these advanced technologies that allowed for what was initially heralded as uniform tax reform. Individual and corporate taxes were significantly and specifically individualized in a manner so that growth, development, industry, and economy would flourish, with factors and complex equations built in to promote micro- as well as macroeconomic growth, better health, and improved education. The system was supposed to efficiently accomplish a level of fairness in taxation while rejecting outright the promotion of class warfare for political gain, and without surrendering to mass appeals for unearned wealth redistribution. It was supposed to eliminate the ability to hide money in sordid schemes to avoid paying taxes, and at the same time it was supposed to significantly limit the cold squeeze of over-taxation and its resultant destruction of the citizens' innate psychological motivation to work hard as the means to achieve financial success.

That's what the political advocates claimed back when there was a debate. What they didn't predict was that the Egalitarian Party would create an authoritarian government and seize complete power, and would ultimately have the ability to pick winners and losers in the marketplace.

The sociopolitical and economic structure of United America had for centuries been a unique blend of a free-market economy swinging back and forth across the political spectrum against varied degrees of socialism, each acting to counterbalance the other. In the face of extreme circumstances during and following World War IV, the pendulum split and in some ways it moved further to the right while in others it swung far to the left. What emerged was monstrous. United America fell into the unrelenting grip of the Egalitarian Party, and soon thereafter, the Democratic Republic ceased to exist…being transformed into an all-dominant and repressive Fascist state.

United America's transformation into Fascism didn't occur overnight, and it likely never would have occurred if extreme circumstances hadn't made it possible. The Egalitarian Party assumed power in a climate of severe financial stress in a nation left reeling by a series of two brutal World Wars. Soon thereafter, internal fighting occurred within the Egalitarian Party and the movement was hijacked. The end result was that it was purged of its Marxist Socialists and the reigns of power were seized by a group of aggressive and politically savvy Fascists.

Ultimately, the metamorphosis that made Fascism possible in North America began well before World War III. United America's political pendulum at that time, in the Late Twenty-Third and into the Early Twenty-Fourth Centuries, had swung far to the left. As a result, the country suffered horrendous trade imbalances, monstrous deficits, and unsustainable social liabilities. Under the guise of free-trade and environmental protection the manufacturing sector had been all but destroyed, and it was impossible for the country to pay its way and at the same time pay back its debts. In the end, the cost was horrendous; prolonged mass suffering, global economic depressions, and worldwide political instability. The political winds in United America swung hard back to the right and the country recoiled into an isolationist ideology—an act that created an international power vacuum and a world that quickly careened out of control. The nation was only able to resurrect itself after the people threw off the onerous yoke of inflation and high taxation. The country eventually emerged and attempted to re-engage the rest of the world. But it was too late. The result was World War III.

The war began with a clash between China and India, and soon thereafter, Brazil and its South American Confederation of States declared war on United America. The underlying causes were border disputes, long running feuds, state sponsored international terrorism, and a complete breakdown of the diplomatic process. The war lasted from 2320 to 2324 and close to a billion people lost their lives. The nuclear devastation the world suffered was numbing. Washington DC and New York City were hit and over a hundred years later they were still uninhabitable, primarily because of radiation, but also because of the extent of the damage. They, along with several other United American cities, would be unfit for human occupation for an extended period of time, and this was despite great successes in the development of radioactivity clean-up technologies and antimatter infusion techniques. Instead of being a wasteland for thousands of years, current progress suggested a couple more decades, and that timeframe was routinely being shortened. As for now, major cities across the globe were still under the control of deformed rats and cockroaches.

Because of the utter devastation to Washington DC, the capital of United America had to be relocated to a place that was considered safe and highly accessible. Texas was the compromise location, and New Washington was built.

Inconceivably, just fifty years after the end of World War III, the world had to endure the Fourth World War and the worst global disaster of all time. Only then did international relations settle into a period of relative quiescence and coexistence. Approximately seventy-five miles southeast of Shiraz, Iran, was the geographic epicenter of the Great Tragedy. It happened on July 21, 2379. It was the event that forced the conclusion of World War IV. To this day, the exact cause remains a mystery. The party-line position remains that it was a dark comet or a massive meteor. As always happens, vague rumors maintain that it was a cover up, that the real cause was outlined in classified government reports that were collected during the war. These reports purportedly outlined details of dangerous experiments with a new class of weapon that were being conducted deep underground in the area of Shiraz by Persian scientists. It was said that it involved the development of a class of weapon that was so devastating as to make nuclear weapons as useless and obsolete as a smoothbore musket. With the nuclear devastation and inhumanity of World War III and the subsequent development of anti-nuclear weapons, it was hard to imagine what hellish consequences would be necessary to force the conclusion of World War IV; the answer was the Great Tragedy.

On the infamous date of the Great Tragedy, the world was devastated beyond anything in recorded history. Humankind was fortunate only in that it survived. A radius of roughly twenty-five hundred miles around the Shiraz epicenter was completely destroyed. Everything turned to dust; people, buildings, monuments, animals, and even planes flying overhead. The disaster extended in an arc through Somalia, Ethiopia, Sudan, Egypt, Israel, Iraq, Iran, Pakistan, and well into India. However, it was not a destruction that occurred just over the surface of the land, but in three dimensions, stabbing into and wounding the earth's crust. It caused great and violent earthquakes, volcanic eruptions, and continental shifts. Giant tsunamis hundreds of feet high ravaged coastal areas around the world. Then great winds, hurricanes, and tornadoes carried the ruin overland. The next three years saw temperature increases from six to seven degrees Celsius, polar ice caps receded and water levels rose to the point that numerous cities were submerged.

In the end, an estimated twelve to thirteen billion people perished. It took fifteen years for the earth's temperature to stabilize and return to normal. In what was the Middle East, there was a newly formed mountain range extending down what used to be the Arabian Peninsula with peaks reaching altitudes of thirty-one thousand feet. Where the Suez Canal was once located, now a waterway several hundred miles wide exists and the Indian Ocean flows straight into the Mediterranean Sea. To this date, after sixty-two years, there were still several small but active volcanoes. However, the overall picture was optimistic and the trend was moving quickly toward environmental stabilization. While the world's previous weather patterns returned in the western hemisphere, the patterns in Europe, Asia, and Africa were dramatically altered.

At the conclusion of World War IV, United America's political pendulum shattered. Elements of the public's sociopolitical ideology swung hard to the left while other elements moved far to the right. It was the perfect soil for the anti-Marxist Socialist. In the end, what emerged was an authoritarian form of government that quickly and successfully consolidated its power. They made promises of a better more secure future while waving the banner of Fascism. Then the process of remaking society began. Individualism was rejected in lieu of strengthening the individual's relationship and dedication to the community and to the State. Extreme and militant nationalism was held aloft as being of the highest virtue. Social Darwinism and eugenics saw resurgence, and the process of culling the elderly and infirm again reared its ugly head. In order to achieve greater worker equality and more orderly control of the wheels of capitalism, the government seized possession of industry through heavy and burdensome regulations, but without nationalizing them. The mirage of ownership wasn't important to the Egalitarian Party as they unilaterally controlled everything. The politicians were in direct control of all industry, the entire economy, and almost every aspect of the lives of the citizens. It had been an amazing and extremely traumatic transformation that cost millions of American patriots their lives. As time passed, the government of United America, firmly controlled by the brutal Egalitarian Party, steadily bore less and less resemblance to the governments of America's past. In actuality, it was frightening in its similarities to the old style fascism that once emerged in Europe—in Early Twentieth Century Germany.

By the present year—2441 A.D., the Third World War had slipped approximately one hundred and twenty years into the past, and the Fourth World War was sixty-two years into the history books. In the time since, the Fascists had managed to consolidate their control, they eliminated all opposition, and they indoctrinated two generations of citizens to their version of society and history. Only a small percentage of the population remembered the freedom and liberty that had existed before the Egalitarian Party seized power.

CHAPTER 4: WHO IS HE?

The guards stood like statues at regularly spaced intervals up and down the corridors. Their pressed black uniforms were flawless and their pulsars were ready at their sides. Around their upper arms were white bands emblazoned with the symbol of the Egalitarian Party.

"What are the requirements to work security?" Ben asked in jest after seeing at least fifty of the soldiers, "Six foot two, two-hundred forty pounds?"

"And bench press three hundred," Zimmer quipped.

They approached another high-energy force field and its retinal scanner. Security was tight. Zimmer went first and then stepped aside. Over the years, Ben had been through the scanners innumerable times at MPS headquarters, but these scanners were different, much more ominous and intimidating. He put his face in front and stared at the sensor. A line of green light moved across his face while a red light scanned both of his retinas. He heard a beep and the force field deactivated. They stepped through and continued their way through the labyrinth of tunnels underneath New Washington. In total, there were well over seventy miles of heavily fortified tunnels interconnecting the various buildings and nearby military bases.

Ben would have been lost without Zimmer's lead. Not only had he never met President Martinez, but he had never been in the Presidential section of the labyrinth. Because of the nature of his interrogative work, he was usually kept at arms length, answering directly to Director Zimmer. This enabled party leaders to maintain a degree of plausible deniability should political infighting ever make the claim necessary.

Despite abundant confidence in his abilities, Ben felt a foreboding squeeze of nervousness. It grew as they approached their destination. 'I'm just being paranoid,' he thought, 'there's no way they could know about my connection to John Doe.' He tried to rationalize his emotions, but he couldn't help feeling as though he was walking into a trap, that he might never see the light of day again.

They arrived at their final destination with a couple of minutes to spare and entered a plush room roughly five meters by ten meters in dimension. It was skirted on three sides by computers and screens. In the center of the room was a beautiful mahogany conference table. Dr. Murray was surprised to note that one side of the room was a huge window. It looked into a large underground geo-dome. He did a double take and chuckled. In the distance he saw a driving range and people swinging golf clubs.

Some of the most powerful people in the world, the power within the Egalitarian Party, were already in the room. General Toby Wayne, the Director of the North American Security Council, was a great friend of Zimmer's. Their familiarity was immediately obvious.

"Hey, you old bastard. You just keep getting uglier," the General said. His tone was crass and sarcastic. General Wayne enjoyed trading verbal barbs. The problem was that almost everyone was scared of him and wouldn't dare insult him out of fear that they might be putting their career in jeopardy.

"Who the hell invited you?" Zimmer said, shaking his head in disgust. "At least you decided not to wear your dress. Doesn't matter…everyone knows about it. Saw the pictures myself. You looked pretty in the yellow one, you know, the one with the big bow on your backside."

"Dreaming about me again, aye Carl? Shouldn't air your fetishes in public."

"You're as belligerent as ever you old goat," Zimmer said. "Problem is, no one over there at Strategic has the cojones to give you the what for." They laughed and shook hands.

Ben felt like an animal being stalked. He studied his surroundings and took note of the others' reactions. Caroline Chu, the Vice President, was less than amused. Her facial expression failed to hide disapproval of what she considered locker room antics and behavior that was beneath the dignity of their respective ranks. The leader of a faction within the Egalitarian Party that zealously advocated social justice and economic equality, she was highly regarded and popular among her political colleagues.

The man across the table was unfamiliar to Ben. He didn't notice Ben as he was watching the exchange between Zimmer and Wayne. His facial expression was flat and unmoving, completely hiding that he thought they were buffoons. His name was Guy Stuart, Ph.D. He was an astrophysicist and Director of Research and Development at Bunker 12. Bunker 12 was a shadowy facility that had repeatedly proven itself to be the nation's premier advanced weapons program. While it was buried somewhere in the mountains of New Mexico, its exact location was classified.

Zimmer made a round of casual introductions, introducing Ben to General Wayne, Vice President Chu, and Dr. Stuart. Ben began to feel more at ease. Given the powerful people in the room, he would have never been brought into their presence if anyone suspected him of duplicity.

It was shortly thereafter that the President arrived. Secret service agents surrounded him. They swept into the room and scanned it with electronic equipment, looking for everything from explosives, to weapons, to listening devices. Each person in the room stood and was quickly scanned. Party loyalists or not, after the previous President was assassinated just over a year ago, stabbed in the neck in a brutal act that severed both of his carotids, the security details were tightened. It was a conspiracy that brought down a large contingent of Egalitarian insiders, and it ushered in a paranoid era where no one was beyond suspicion.

President Juan Martinez stood broad shouldered and tall, waiting at the door for the security detail to complete their scan. Once they finished they hastily exited the room and closed the door behind them. He turned and smiled, greeting Zimmer. "Good morning, Carl," he said as he extended his hand. His voice was exuberant and effortless in its confidence. "I trust you have something interesting?"

"Yes, Mr. President," Zimmer responded.

"I would like to speak privately again regarding the matter we discussed yesterday."

"Yes, Mr. President."

"I have some ideas regarding how to proceed. I'll have my office determine when it will be convenient, and you can clear your schedule."

"Certainly, sir."

President Martinez shifted his focus to his Vice President. "Caroline! How was your trip?"

"Very good, sir. I think they're coming around to seeing it your way. Should be going back to work as we speak."

"You are amazing. Thank you. I would like to hear about the deliberations."

The President's smile diminished when he turned to General Wayne. It was subtle but enough to indicate that there was an undercurrent of tension between them. The greeting was brief and smooth, and he shifted his attention to Dr. Stuart.

"When are you going to invite me to come see your facility?"

Dr. Stuart laughed, "Sir, it's your facility. We're just keeping the seats warm. I hope that you will visit so I can show you what we've done. I think you'd be proud of what we've accomplished."

"Oh, Dr. Stuart," he said as they shook hands, "I'm already proud of what you and your colleagues have accomplished." He patted him on the shoulder and said, "I'm pleased you joined us."

"Thank you, sir," Dr. Stuart responded.

He turned to face Ben. "Dr. Murray," President Martinez said, warmly extending his hand. "I'm pleased to finally make your acquaintance." He vigorously shook Ben's hand while deftly disarming him with a smile. He looked him straight in the eye and said, "I have heard quite a bit about you from Carl, and I've read your personnel file. The Party owes you its gratitude. I don't know if anyone ever told you this before but on behalf of this country and all of us in this room, thank you. Thank you for the service you continue to provide." He gestured toward the others in the room, "We'll never really know how many of us unknowingly owe our lives to you."

Everyone in the room was impressed. What they didn't know was that the President was referring to Ben's work as a whole, but more specifically, to the interrogative work he performed to discover that there were bombs planted along the foundation of the Arizona stadium hosting the Fiesta Bowl in the year 2432. It was a perfect plan. Tunnels were dug from a privately owned warehouse three blocks from the stadium and explosives were placed at key points under the foundation. It was the perfect act of terrorism. Everything would have happened according to plan except that halfway around the world, Ben was performing a forced neuro-extraction on a terrorist financier who outlined all the sordid details.

Ben remembered that night as though it happened yesterday. It was an extremely dangerous night drop in Central Africa. Ben's group was charged with the task of harvesting information relating to a domestic terror group's financial support network. In the course of extracting the target information, he stumbled across something else. At first it seemed to be nothing more than an incidental and meaningless sentence fragment. With time running out on the mission, he discovered to his horror that it was the key to something much more important. He altered the course of the interrogation, and his target eventually revealed information pertaining to the demolition of the Fiesta Bowl. It led to the arrest of thirty-two terrorist operatives living and operating within the Phoenix area. Unbeknownst to the others in the conference room, General Wayne and his family had tickets to the game. He had no inclination that Ben had actually saved their lives.

"Thank you, Mr. President," Ben said, secretly wishing that the attention would shift to someone else. At the same time, his ego was reinforced.

This was the first time anyone in a Party leadership position, much less the President of United America, had ever expressed gratitude. This was personal. It was the President being genuine and expressing heartfelt recognition for the service he had provided to the country. Then, like an invisible sword with its tip lodged right at the point where he was going to betray his country, a deep stab of guilt ran through him.

Ben was surprised that the President's words would touch him on such a deep level. After everything he had seen and done in his career, he wasn't easily impressed. But President Martinez was different. It was scary how completely disarming and alluring his persona was. One doesn't ascend to the highest political position in the world, even in a one party society, without exceptional talents, and in that, Ben had just been taken to school.

A few more pleasantries were exchanged, and the meeting began. The President asked Director Zimmer to begin. Zimmer cleared his throat and took command of the room.

"The information that I am about to present is extremely sensitive. Due to its…its nature, there are no written reports in existence. Of course, the highest levels of security are in force. Due to the nature of this topic, we have the option of striking this meeting from the record at the conclusion of our discussion." Director Zimmer scanned the faces around the table for reactions. A couple eyebrows were raised, chairs moved closer, and spines straightened. They understood that this had to be big or he never would have made the suggestion of striking the record. "At this time, I am the only person in possession of all the information I am about to share with you. Although there are several dozen people involved at this point, the entire program remains highly compartmentalized. No one has anything more than a very basic and fragmentary knowledge of what I am about to share."

The President cleared his throat. "Gentlemen, I again remind you that this is highly sensitive material and is to be treated accordingly. It will never be discussed with anyone outside the confines of this room, and it will only be discussed within this room." After a powerful moment he said to Zimmer, "If you're ready, Carl." He was busy with the demands of the Presidency and wanted to get to business. He was aware that Zimmer had a propensity for self-aggrandizing pomp and a tendency to embellish moments when he was about to make some startling revelation. As such, it was his gentle way of telling him to get on with the briefing.

The center of the mahogany table lifted and slid to the sides. A Vintel unit rose up from underneath and sprang to life. Approximately one and a half meters in length, width, and height, it immediately analyzed the room and determined the position of each of the six people sitting around the table. By manipulating the refraction of light, each would actually see the same briefing, despite sitting on opposite sides of the table.

A hollow computerized voice and crisp rotating three-dimensional images corresponding to what was being said appeared:

FILE: SEC283HN8S

STATUS: CLASSIFIED - LEVEL IV

PROJECT CODEWORD: BRIDGE

ON SATURDAY, DECEMBER 2, 2440 A.D. THE SUBJECT, HEREAFTER REFERRED TO AS JOHN DOE, A CAUCASIAN MALE APPROXIMATELY FORTY YEARS OF AGE, APPEARED ON THE FIELD IN THE MIDDLE OF A HISTORICAL REENACTMENT OF THE BATTLE OF FRANKLIN. THE ORIGINAL BATTLE TOOK PLACE LATE IN THE AMERICAN CIVIL WAR, ON NOVEMBER 30, 1864 A.D. IN FRANKLIN, TENNESSEE. DUE TO SEVERE TRAUMA, JOHN DOE WAS IMMEDIATELY TRANSPORTED TO NEW BETHESDA HOSPITAL IN NASHVILLE. HE UNDERWENT A SERIES OF SURGERIES AND HIS CONDITION WAS STABILIZED.

With the voice overlay, the Vintel unit showed crisp and flowing images from the reenactment. The troops could be seen marching and shooting. The cannon were firing, and smoke covered the field. Then came the noise…it was the sickening noise of the horse screaming. In the center of the field, in front of the Union fortifications, a horse and rider materialized out of the smoke. The Vintel closed in on the rider until his face became clear.

'My God, it's really him,' Ben thought. His heart was racing. At the same time, he felt like he was going to be sick. Of all places, this John Doe as they were mistakenly calling him, had landed in the laps of the Fascists. The most Ben could hope for was that they wouldn't be able to piece his story together until after he was secured outside their reach. At that point, the wheels would be in motion and it would be too late.

EXTENSIVE INTERVIEWS WITH WITNESSES, REENACTORS, AND SPECTATORS FAILED TO PROVIDE ANY INFORMATION REGARDING JOHN DOE OR HIS SUDDEN APPEARANCE. GUNPOWDER FROM THE CANNONADE COVERED THE FIELD. THIS SIGNIFICANTLY LIMITED VISIBILITY AND NO ONE ACTUALLY WITNESSED THE EXACT MOMENT OF HIS MATERIALIZATION.

SERUM SAMPLES FROM JOHN DOE WERE SECURED FROM THOSE THAT WERE TAKEN ON ARRIVAL AT THE HOSPITAL. HE WAS FOUND TO POSSESS ANTIBODIES SPECIFIC TO THE GENERAL MILITARY FORCES WITH ADDITIONAL IMMUNITY ONLY

SEEN IN THE SPECIAL OPERATIONS FORCES OF UNITED AMERICA. THE PATTERN IS CONSISTENT WITH THAT SEEN IN THE LAST HALF OF THE 24TH CENTURY. MORE SPECIFICALLY, IT MATCHES THE PATTERN SEEN IN THE SPECIAL FORCES DURING WORLD WAR IV. FURTHER ANALYSIS OF THE THREE-DIMENSIONAL STRUCTURES OF ANTIBODIES SPECIFIC FOR HEPATITIS A THROUGH M, HIV1 THROUGH 9, EBOLA, AND MODIFIED SMALL POX, INDICATE THAT HE MOST LIKELY WAS THE RECIPIENT OF THE ELGEN-MAKR #7 COMBO VACCINE MANUFACTURED IN TORONTO. THIS VACCINE HAS NOT BEEN IN USE SINCE THE YEAR 2383. IT HAS BEEN REPLACED BY #8 IN 2384, #9 IN 2401, #10 IN 2431, AND MOST RECENTLY, #11 IN 2437. WHILE THE LAST 58 YEARS HAVE SEEN THE GENETIC ENGINEERING OF SEVERAL NEW GERM STRAINS FOR USE BY BIO-TERRORISTS AND FOR INTERNATIONAL GERM WARFARE, IT HAS ALSO SEEN THE SIMULTANEOUS DEVELOPMENT OF NEW AND MODIFIED VACCINES TO COUNTER THE THREAT. THERE IS NO EVIDENCE TO SUGGEST THAT JOHN DOE EVER RECEIVED THE NEWLY MODIFIED VACCINES.

"Wait a minute," General Wayne said. "Pause this thing." Zimmer stopped the Vintel as the General continued, "Are you telling us that, through blood work looking at antibodies, you can tell what type of vaccine was used for immunization?"

"Yes," Zimmer confirmed.

"And based on that analysis, you think that this guy belongs to United America's special operations forces at the time of World War IV?"

Zimmer didn't respond.

"And he just suddenly appeared at this reenactment? Do you realize the implications?"

"Please," Zimmer said, holding up his hands. "Let me present my case in its entirety." General Wayne reluctantly nodded, but he made it clear that he was uncomfortable.

EMBEDDED IN JOHN DOE'S RIGHT MAXILLARY SINUS AND IN HIS FRONTAL SINUS IS A MILITARY GRADE BIOTECH COMMUNICATIONS DEVICE, OR BCD. HIS IS THE HELDON SUPER SOLDIER INTEGRATION SYSTEM MODEL 11H16. THIS MODEL WAS MANUFACTURED IN 2375, AND THERE IS EVIDENCE THAT HE RECEIVED A FINAL SOFTWARE UPDATE IN EARLY 2379. THIS UNIT WAS DESIGNED TO ENHANCE THE PERFORMANCE OF SELECTED SPECIAL OPERATIONS FORCES IN THE FIELD. THIS PARTICULAR DESIGN, WITH ITS HIGHLY ADVANCED COMBAT CAPABILITIES, WAS LIMITED TO THE ELITE SOLDIERS OF THE GUARD. IT HAS A WIDE RANGE OF CAPABILITIES INCLUDING NIGHT-VISION, TELESCOPIC MAGNIFICATION, TARGETING SYSTEMS, ADVANCED COMMUNICATIONS CAPABILITIES, LASER AND ENERGY WEAPON DETECTION, AND COMPLETE FIELD WEAPONS SYSTEMS ANALYSIS AND INTEGRATION

IN REAL TIME. IT IS ALSO EQUIPPED WITH A SELF-DESTRUCT MECHANISM UPON ANY ATTEMPT TO REMOVE OR ACCESS THE DEVICE WITHOUT THE PROPER CODES. THIS PARTICULAR SYSTEM IS POWERED BY AN INTEGRATED BIONUCLEAR BATTERY AND IS CONTINUALLY RECHARGED THROUGH NORMAL PHYSIOLOGIC MEANS. ESSENTIALLY, AS LONG AS A SOLDIER WITH ONE OF THESE DEVICES REMAINS ALIVE, THE UNIT WILL CONTINUE TO FUNCTION INTO PERPETUITY.

MODEL 11H6 WAS EQUIPPED WITH A CLASSIFIED RECORDING DEVICE. EVERYTHING THE SUBJECT DID AND SAW, EVERYTHING THE UNIT DETECTED, WOULD ALL BE RECORDED FOR PURPOSES OF DEBRIEFING AND TRAINING. DUE TO BUILT-IN REDUNDANCY AND BACKUP SYSTEMS, IT COULD EFFECTIVELY RECORD OVER TWENTY YEARS OF ONGOING CONTINUOUS COMBAT RELATED INFORMATION. WHEN JOHN DOE CAME TO THE ATTENTION OF NAIA OFFICIALS, ANALYSIS OF THE DEVICE REVEALED THAT THE MEMORY HAD BEEN DOWNLOADED AND THAT THE UNIT HAD BEEN ERASED. A FORTY-EIGHT HOUR LOOP WAS IMPLANTED SO THAT IT IS NOW IMPOSSIBLE TO DETERMINE WHO ERASED THE MEMORY, OR EXACTLY WHEN THE FILES WERE DOWNLOADED. THIS BEING THE CASE, AND GIVEN THAT THE MEMORY MODULES WERE SCRAMBLED, NO INFORMATION WAS RETRIEVED. ALL THAT IS CLEAR IS THAT THE SYSTEM IS FUNCTIONING PROPERLY, THE DOWNLOAD OCCURRED WITHIN THE FIRST FORTY-EIGHT HOURS SUBSEQUENT TO HIS APPEARANCE AT THE REENACTMENT, AND IT WAS NOT ERASED AS A BY-PRODUCT OF HIS MATERIALIZATION AT THE REENACTMENT.

The Vintel showed the schematics of the BCD and superimposed the image over the skull of John Doe. Then it showed a demonstration of an elite member of The Guard in action. He was running and shooting a pulsed laser while his BCD simultaneously ran targeting sequences, analyzed communications, and allowed him to coordinate troop movements. The firepower was incredible.

"Do you have any idea how his BCD memory was downloaded and erased? Or who might be responsible?" Vice President Chu asked.

Zimmer paused the Vintel and said, "We don't know. As with all the devices currently in use, his was manufactured by MST Global. To date, no one has been able to reverse engineer the devices."

Ben grew concerned as Zimmer went on. The last thing he wanted was for the group to implicate MST.

"There are proprietary codes that only MST possesses. We can access the data, but they are the only ones who can permanently erase BCD memory."

"Have you contacted MST?" she asked.

"No." Zimmer said. "My belief is that there's too much at stake, and that MST's objectives are not the same as our own." His distrust and dislike of MST was well known among the Egalitarian elite.

"Is it possible," Ben asked, "that the memory may have been erased in some other manner?"

"We don't know…yet," Zimmer answered. He made no mistake in conveying that he would find out. He continued the briefing.

IT WAS COMMON PRACTICE IN THE SPECIAL OPERATIONS FORCES OF UNITED AMERICA DURING WORLD WAR IV TO GET TATTOOS OF A WIDE VARIETY. THEY TENDED TO BE NONDESCRIPT AND NEVER INDICATED LANGUAGE OR COUNTRY OF ORIGIN. WITHIN THE TATTOOS WERE EMBEDDED HIGHLY CLASSIFIED CODES THAT WERE USED FOR SECURITY PURPOSES, TO VERIFY WHO THEY WERE, AND TO IDENTIFY THE BODY IN THE EVENT OF DEATH. NO SIMILAR PROGRAMS WERE IN PLACE ANYWHERE ELSE IN THE WORLD. ON JOHN DOE'S LEFT SHOULDER IS A TATTOO THAT IS CONSISTENT WITH THAT TIME PERIOD. IT WAS PARTIALLY DESTROYED SECONDARY TO HIS INJURIES. THE REMNANT OF A CODE WAS PARTIALLY OBTAINED. IT WAS CROSS-MATCHED AGAINST ALL KNOWN MILITARY AND GOVERNMENT DATABASES WITHOUT A POTENTIAL MATCH.

The Vintel showed what was left of John Doe's tattoo. The flesh of his shoulder was mangled and a large part of the tattoo was missing.

THE FRANKLIN REENACTMENT SUBCONTRACTED LOW BUDGET MOVIE CREWS TO FILM THE EVENT. THESE RECORDINGS WERE REMOVED AND ANALYZED PRIOR TO BEING COPIED AND DISTRIBUTED. A THREE-DIMENSIONAL LAYOUT OF THE AREA OF THE FIELD WHERE JOHN DOE APPEARED WAS CAREFULLY SCRUTINIZED. SEVERAL TEAMS HAVE ANALYZED THE RECORDINGS. SPECTRAL ANALYSIS OF THE FIELD, OVERLAID WITH HIGHLY SOPHISTICATED THERMAL IMAGING TECHNOLOGY, DISCOVERED AN ANOMALY. APPROXIMATELY 11 SECONDS PRIOR TO JOHN DOE BEING VISUALLY DETECTED, THERE WAS A BIMODAL 30 MICROSECOND FLASH OF VERY NARROW FREQUENCY ENERGY IN THE ULTRAVIOLET RANGE THAT WAS ASSOCIATED WITH A LOCALIZED INCREASE IN TEMPERATURE VARYING FROM 98.2 TO 99.9 DEGREES FAHRENHEIT. THE IMAGE APPEARED TO BE IN A PATTERN VAGUELY RESEMBLING THAT OF A HORSE WITH RIDER, WITH A SURROUNDING TEMPERATURE OF 63 DEGREES FAHRENHEIT EXTENDING OUTWARD WITH A RADIUS OF APPROXIMATELY TWO METERS. THE AMBIENT TEMPERATURE ON THE FIELD ON THE MORNING OF THE REENACTMENT WAS 47 DEGREES FAHRENHEIT. REPORTS OF THE TEMPERATURE ON THE FIELD ON THE AFTERNOON OF THE ACTUAL BATTLE OF FRANKLIN, ON NOVEMBER 30TH 1864, DESCRIBED IT AS WARM. RECORDS DESCRIBED IT AS AN "INDIAN SUMMER DAY." IT IS POSSIBLE, THEREFORE, THAT THE TEMPERATURE OF 63 DEGREES REPRESENTS THE EXACT

TEMPERATURE ON THE AFTERNOON TO EVENING OF THE ORIGINAL BATTLE, BUT THERE'S NO WAY TO CONFIRM THIS WITH FURTHER ACCURACY.

RADIOCARBON DATING TECHNIQUES WERE USED TO ANALYZE BLOOD SAMPLES FROM JOHN DOE, HIS CLOTHING, AND EQUIPMENT. THE RESULTS WERE CONSISTENTLY REPRODUCED AND WERE CONFIRMED BY TWO INDEPENDENT LABS. SAMPLES TAKEN FROM HIS KNIFE, CLOTHING, AND SADDLE REVEALED THE DNA OF TWENTY-THREE DIFFERENT MEN. THE SAMPLES WERE BLOOD, BUT IT WAS 600-YEAR-OLD BLOOD. THE CLOTHING ITSELF, ALTHOUGH IT APPEARED TO BE IN GOOD SHAPE ON VISUAL INSPECTION, WAS DATED AND ALSO FOUND TO BE APPROXIMATELY 600 YEARS OLD. OTHER BLOOD SAMPLES ON THE CLOTHING, INCLUDING HIS OWN AS A RESULT OF THE TRAUMA, WERE DATED TO BE A MIX OF OLD AND CURRENT, OF BEING FROM OUR TIME AND FROM THE 1800S.

ISOLATED FROM THE HOOVES OF THE HORSE, GRASS SAMPLES WERE OBTAINED. AGAIN, THERE WERE TWO AGES REPORTED; SOME WERE FOUND TO BE CURRENT AND OTHERS APPROXIMATELY 600 YEARS OLD. THE DIFFERENCE SEEMED TO BE THAT THE PLANT FRAGMENTS THAT WERE STILL GREEN AND LIVING, MEASURED AS HAVING A RADIOCARBON CONTENT SIMILAR TO LIVING TISSUE, OR THE CURRENT TIME PERIOD. HOWEVER, THOSE SAMPLES THAT WERE DEAD AND DRIED AND EMBEDDED IN THE HORSE'S HOOVES WERE FOUND TO BE 600 YEARS OLD.

FURTHER AND MORE SENSITIVE ANALYSIS OF BLOOD SAMPLES TAKEN FROM JOHN DOE AND THE HORSE, WHEN COMPARED TO RANDOM SAMPLES TAKEN FROM THE WORLD TODAY, REVEAL SLIGHT VARIATIONS OR DIFFERENCES. THE SUBTLE DIFFERENCES ARE CONSISTENT WITH A COMBINATION OF LIVING IN THE 1800S AND ALSO LIVING TODAY, BASED ON ATMOSPHERIC CHANGES IN THE LEVEL OF CARBON 14 OVER THE LAST SIX HUNDRED YEARS. THE LEVEL OF RADIOCARBON IN LIVING TISSUE TODAY IS SLIGHTLY HIGHER THAN WHAT IT WAS IN PEOPLE LIVING IN THE 1800S. LARGELY, THIS IS A FUNCTION OF INCREASED CONCENTRATIONS OF CARBON 14 RELATIVE TO CARBON 12 IN THE ATMOSPHERE. THIS INCREASED RATIO IS SUBSEQUENTLY FOUND IN LIVING TISSUES. THIS INCREASE IS A FUNCTION OF ATMOSPHERIC CHANGE AND OZONE CHANGES SEEN IN THE LAST SIX HUNDRED YEARS. SAMPLES FROM JOHN DOE AND THE HORSE ARE CONSISTENT WITH LIVING HERE…THEN SPENDING SEVERAL YEARS LIVING IN THE 1800S, THEN RETURNING TO THE CURRENT TIME.

Ben again felt his heart racing. The briefing was too much to bear. How was it possible that Zimmer found out so much? Did he have some help? Was there a traitor to the cause, an informant who was feeding Zimmer information? Ben understood clearly that all the available evidence his director was presenting suggested that John Doe was indeed the man he first learned about three decades ago. As a result, what he was feeling was fear…real, palpable, blood curdling fear. But it wasn't so much for him as it was for the secret society he was bound to by accident of his birth, and for its ultimate objectives—objectives that were precariously hanging in the balance. The moment wasn't anything like he imagined it would be, or rather, it wasn't what he hoped it would be. He was surrounded by powerful people whose interests in the person they only knew as John Doe, were absolutely and diametrically opposed to his own. Ben reminded himself that he had to be perfect, as any wrong move would jeopardize everything.

THE CONTENTS OF THE HORSE'S STOMACH, AS WELL AS SAMPLES FROM VARIOUS ORGANS AND TISSUES WERE ANALYZED. THEY WERE FOUND TO POSSESS SOME TRACES OF PESTICIDES, HERBICIDES, AND OTHER BIO-ENGINEERED CHEMICALS. THE LEVELS, HOWEVER, ARE MUCH LOWER THAN WHAT WOULD BE EXPECTED IN TODAY'S ENVIRONMENTAL LANDSCAPE. IMMUNOLOGICAL STUDIES OF THE HORSE INDICATE ARTIFICIAL VACCINATION AGAINST ALMOST EVERY KNOWN EQUINE PATHOGEN. THE HORSE'S ADRENAL GLANDS WERE GENETICALLY ALTERED IN SUCH A WAY AS TO GIVE IT MORE STRENGTH, STAMINA, AND AN INCREASED TOLERANCE OF FAMINE. THE HORSE WAS ESSENTIALLY CREATED IN A LAB AND IS A PRODUCT OF GENETIC MANIPULATION UNLIKE ANYTHING EVER SEEN. IT IS BEYOND THE CAPABILITIES OF KNOWN GENETIC ENGINEERS. THE STOMACH WAS FOUND TO BE FILLED WITH GRASS, SOME OATS, A VARIETY OF SEEDS, A FEW PEBBLES, AND A PARTIALLY DIGESTED CARROT. NONE OF THOSE FOODSTUFFS WERE FOUND TO BE GENETICALLY ALTERED AND ARE CONSISTENT WITH REGULAR HORSE FARE IN THE 1800s.
THE HORSE'S SHOES AND NAILS ARE CONSISTENT WITH 19TH CENTURY MANUFACTURING TECHNIQUES. JOHN DOE'S CLOTHING, FIREARMS, SADDLE, AND OTHER EQUIPMENT ARE ALL CONSISTENT WITH BEING MANUFACTURED AT THE TIME OF THE AMERICAN CIVIL WAR.

DNA ANALYSIS WAS PERFORMED ON BLOOD SAMPLES TAKEN FROM THE CLOTHING, KNIFE, SADDLE, AND HORSE. WE HAVE IDENTIFIED SAMPLES FROM TWENTY-THREE DIFFERENT MEN AND TWO OTHER HORSES. THE HUMAN SAMPLES WERE CROSS-REFERENCED TO OUR POPULATION DATABASE. THERE WERE NO MATCHES. MITOCHONDRIAL DNA ANALYSIS WAS PERFORMED AND WE GOT SOME INDICATION OF LINEAGE ON SEVEN OF THE PEOPLE. FURTHER DNA ANALYSIS WAS PERFORMED THAT, ALTHOUGH PRELIMINARY, SUGGESTS THAT DISTANT RELATIVES OF THESE UNKNOWNS MAY BE ALIVE TODAY. WHILE AT THIS POINT, THE STUDIES ARE IN THEIR INITIAL PHASES, THE NUMBERS SO FAR INDICATE THAT THESE ARE RELATIVES SEPARATED BY 22 TO 28 GENERATIONS, OR ABOUT 600 YEARS.

"Good God," Ben heard the President mutter in wonder and amazement. It was meant to be under his breath and discreet, but the shock of what everyone was hearing was just too much. What was being implied, and the case Zimmer was building, was as convincing as it was astonishing. He was suggesting that one of United America's most highly trained soldiers, a member of The Guard during World War IV, was somehow transported back in time, apparently fought like hell during the American Civil War, and inexplicably materialized at a battlefield reenactment in Tennessee. The idea seemed ludicrous at first blush, but the data was hard, it was scientifically reproducible, and it all seemed to point toward that conclusion.

The Vintel continued. It described the extent of John Doe's injuries and detailed the Civil War era bullets pulled out of him and his horse. It was essentially the same information Ben had seen and heard earlier. The briefing concluded with:

AN UNEXPLAINED PHENOMENON ASSOCIATED WITH HIS MATERAILIZATION CAUSED A MALFUNCTION OF MOST RECORDING DEVICES PRESENT AT THE REENACTMENT. AS A RESULT, THERE ARE FEW PICTURES AVAILABLE FOR ANALYSIS.

THE MEDIA REPORTED JOHN DOE'S WOUNDS AS SELF-INFLICTED SECONDARY TO SEVERE PSYCHIATRIC DISEASE. DAY 1 AFTER THE APPEARANCE, THIRTEEN OUTLETS REPORTED THE REENACTMENT. AN AVERAGE OF 2.3 SENTENCES PER REPORT FOCUSED ON JOHN DOE. ON DAY 2, FOUR NEW REPORTS WERE LISTED WITH AN AVERAGE OF 2.75 SENTENCES. THE INFORMATION HAS BEEN ACCESSED ON VINTEL IN UNITED AMERICA 6,874,276 TIMES FROM THE INTERNET CLOUDS, WORLDWIDE 8,793,417 TIMES. THREE DAYS AFTER THE EVENT, THERE WERE NO NEW PUBLIC REPORTS.

The Vintel report concluded at that point. The unit shut down and retracted into the table. The conclusion of Zimmer's collection of information was met with stunned silence.

President Martinez finally initiated a discussion, "So, Carl, you have everyone's undivided attention, and we're all interested. Tell us, what do you believe we have here?"

"In a nutshell, Mr. President," Zimmer began, "There is ample solid evidence to suggest that we are looking at a case of time travel."

"What?!" Dr. Stuart blurted out. "Have you gone mad?"

"Oh," General Wayne exclaimed as he shook his head back and forth. He saw an argument coming, and he sensed that it was going to be a memorable one.

Zimmer was acutely aware of how his articulation of the facts was being received around the table, and he went on the defensive. "Hell, I know this sounds far fetched and scientists, just like Dr. Stuart, have claimed for centuries that it's impossible," he said, "but look at the information we have. We're all aware of the rumors about the end of World War IV and the experiments the Persians were doing…what if this is somehow related?" Zimmer was referring to *The Great Tragedy*, the cataclysmic event that occurred sixty-two years ago, in the year 2379, the event that forced the conclusion of World War IV.

"My point exactly," Dr. Stuart quipped.

"And it would appear," Zimmer continued making his argument, raising his voice to drown out Dr. Stuart's, "that in the current case, living tissue has been transported through time intact at least twice—from modern times to the past and back again. Any dead organic material appears to age during the process. While there's currently no obvious scientific explanation for the pattern, it would certainly be a model that would fit the information."

"Given The Great Tragedy, the implications of going down the road you're leading us are concerning, but that's just me speaking in terms of… planetary survival," Dr. Stuart commented. There was a dagger's edge of sarcasm in the statement. It had its intended effect, like throwing a cold, wet blanket over the room.

"We can't afford to ignore this. It just fell into our laps. Are we supposed to just ignore it and pretend that it didn't happen? It is imperative that we look at this," Zimmer asserted.

Stuart wasn't having any of it. He was very clear in his body language that he thought Zimmer was a self-important bully, all brawn with no brain. He addressed his comments not to Zimmer but to the rest of the room, especially President Martinez. "It's a lunatic's quest." His voice was as sure as the sun is hot, and his rate of speech swift. "If anyone should ever be shortsighted and crazy enough to attempt to reproduce what the Persians were doing, we also run the risk of ultimately reproducing their results. This planet won't survive another event like that. Further, let's say hypothetically time travel was possible, that the technology was developed, in the interim, will human nature develop? No. We're one step removed from Neanderthals. We haven't evolved in tens of thousands of years. If that technology fell into the wrong hands, it would have the worst possible ramifications. It's a Pandora's Box that would end life as we know it. Technology always advances, but human nature has proven over and over again that it always remains the same. The only difference between us and the hordes who committed every act of barbarism ever recorded in the annals of human history is the benefit of our time and place of birth. We consider ourselves advanced only because we have the luxury of flushing our waste, and we can comfortably take our next meal for granted. It's only by an accident of birth that we aren't hunting the mastodon, fighting the Spartans at Thermopylae, or with Genghis Khan, or even being cooked alive as some sort of cannibalistic sacrifice, or maybe even sacrificing a virgin to the fire god." He stared at Zimmer when he made the last comment. Zimmer's jaw clenched as he held back his anger. Dr. Stuart went on, "But don't take my word for it. All it takes is one look at the other side of this planet, at the results of the Great Tragedy. That should be testament enough for anyone that human beings have not, and for the foreseeable future, WILL NOT change." He hit his fist on the table for emphasis. "As a whole, technology like this is at best a self-destructive malignancy. It will destroy humanity if ever given another opportunity. I implore everyone, this line of inquiry should be stopped before it goes any further."

Ben was taken aback. Being buried in the NAIA for so long, and holding Zimmer up as the one man never to be trifled with, he was startled to witness someone with little to no tact taking his boss to task.

"I don't disagree with you, Dr. Stuart, but I also don't think that we can afford to be complacent. This is something that we should know more about than anyone else," Zimmer argued. "Do I understand you to be saying that we would be in a position of strength if we know nothing about this and someone else did? Is that what you're suggesting?"

Ben noticed that Zimmer's rough complexion stayed true, but the subtle redness of his neck betrayed an anger that he was fighting to keep in check. Poker player he was not.

"I remind everyone," Zimmer continued, "that our evidence suggests we aren't the only players in this game. John Doe's BCD, the Heldon Super Soldier Integration System, was stripped of its memory and erased. I believe it happened after he arrived. Whoever is responsible is now light years ahead of us in terms of technological achievement. I don't know about you, Dr. Stuart, but I don't sleep well knowing that we are technologically second rate."

Stuart's face turned red, and he clenched his fist in anger. He started to rise out of his chair. General Wayne moved slightly to the side and squared himself, but Dr. Stuart caught himself. He smiled and sat back down, sensing that he had to salvage his position as best he could.

"Don't misinterpret what I'm saying," he began. "It scares me that I find this area of research so fascinating and addicting. It's the holy grail of physics, and you're asking that it be explored, to hold it in the palm of our hands, and not at the same time be consumed by it. Where do our efforts stop? When do they stop? That's what scares me most because I know where I'd pursue this…I'd pursue this to the very end. It would all be for idealistic purposes; to study the past, to learn from history, to go back and learn from the NSDAP, then to rescue the last mammoth or sabertooth tiger, or help Stalin to die from smallpox, or even to stop Harzi, LinCho, or Tehnjo. Where does it stop? It's a slippery slope. And what about testing? There are grave concerns in the scientific world. I can't overemphasize how much I believe that the past is the best indication of the risks involved."

"Is there any chance that this guy is just some kind of a freak? And that he staged the whole thing?" General Wayne interjected. He had been in enough top-level briefings to recognize the argument as being a waste of time, and he wanted to move on.

"It's not impossible but very unlikely," Zimmer was quick to answer.

"All it would take is a little research overlaid with some sort of psychiatric disorder," the General suggested. "I've seen similar types of things in the past."

"Seems rather far-fetched given all the information we have," Vice President Chu said.

"Would be embarrassing if we wasted resources only to find out that it was nothing more than an elaborate hoax," General Wayne said. "John Doe might have imagined that he would be the center of something, and we're a bunch of monkeys clapping and waving in excitement."

"If I might address your concerns directly," Zimmer said, "we had a team analyze the wounds suffered by John Doe and his horse. It was determined that the trajectory of the projectiles was from a wide front, possibly several hundred yards wide. We have bullets from six different firearms and wounds consistent with projectiles from at least one cannon, maybe more." He looked at General Wayne and with a cagey smile he added, "Now I don't know exactly how they do their reenactments in Tennessee, but I seriously doubt that they use live ammo."

"I have heard about people sometimes getting shot at reenactments," the Vice President commented.

"I've heard of that too," Zimmer admitted. "The world is full of psychopaths. But something like this, with so many people involved, is certainly less likely. In the end, I suppose that it is a possibility, although a minute one. Largely, that is why Dr. Murray is here," Zimmer said, "so we can find out exactly who John Doe is and what he knows."

A few moments of group contemplation followed. Ben felt that it was up to him to say something. He had to gingerly steer the group without drawing any suspicion that he had a personal agenda. "This does fall within my area of expertise," he said. The comment seemed to meet everyone's satisfaction. "Just to clarify, he is to be treated as one of…ours?" His question caused everyone to draw back slightly.

"Please elaborate, Doctor," Vice President Chu said.

"Am I to treat John Doe as a friendly? From the information outlined so succinctly by Director Zimmer, he may be one of our soldiers from around the time of World War IV. Potentially one of our best, being that he may have been a member of The Guard."

"What's the difference?" she asked.

"During a forced neuro-interrogation," Ben explained, we will get the information, but the subject runs the risk of ending up with nothing. The result can be very similar to the prefrontal lobotomies performed in the 1900s. It might not kill him, but there is the risk that he would be left an empty shell with no memories and no personality. The process can take away all of those qualities that make us unique and special."

"Are there any other viable alternatives?" General Wayne asked the question.

"Yes. It takes a bit longer to do a focused memory extraction. Just a couple hours. But in those cases, we know exactly what we're after, the target is healthy and willing, and again, we have absolutely zero concerns about their long term well being. Problems can and often do arise in the months following the procedure. They can mentally destabilize. Any time we muddle with the brain there are consequences." Ben looked from person to person and made eye contact with the President. He added, "To get the information and to also help John Doe in the process, I will need substantial time. To be done right, with his best interests in mind, it needs to be done the old fashioned way."

"And that is?" Zimmer inquired.

"Interview everybody. Get him healthy. Develop trust. Get a beer. Have a chat. You know…all that time consuming psychotherapy stuff," Ben elaborated.

"I don't think it is in our strategic best interest to take a substantial amount of time getting him to talk," Zimmer quipped. "We have to keep in mind the possibility that this could represent time experiments actively being done somewhere else in the world. We still have enemies. If we're caught with our pants down…"

Ben sensed that Zimmer's influence over the group was swaying them toward demanding a forced interrogation. He had to stall for time, to convince them that rushing things wasn't a good idea. Then he realized he didn't have to convince everyone in the room. This wasn't a democracy. All he had to do was convince President Martinez that a slower approach would have advantages. He had to think like a politician. How did they view the world?

"There is another consideration," Ben blurted out. He had directed the comment to the President so he almost apologetically added, "If I might be so bold?"

"Please, Dr. Murray, go on," President Martinez said. Being well aware of Ben's unique talents and the unhesitating manner in which he applied them in service to the Party, he appeared to be amused by subtle behaviors that betrayed nervousness. He surmised that its source was his unfamiliarity with high-level briefings. 'We all have our vulnerabilities,' he thought.

"I don't mean to speak out of turn," Ben said, "and I realize that this line of reasoning is far outside my realm of expertise, but should John Doe indeed be one of ours, and if he comes around, would he not have the potential to be incredibly valuable…to the Party? He could be a public relations asset beyond our wildest dreams." Ben needed them to think of John Doe as a potential asset. If they called upon him to do a forced extraction, he would have no choice but to grab John Doe and run. Their odds of survival would be incredibly slim, almost nonexistent. But if he could legitimately stall for time, it might make all the difference in achieving his first objective, which was to keep John Doe safe until he might fully recover.

Everyone contemplated what Ben suggested. It was an angle they hadn't considered. The momentary silence was broken with, "The world has changed since the war." The quip came from President Martinez. "The United America he was fighting for doesn't exist. There is the potential that he might find this version rather unrecognizable, or potentially objectionable. What then?"

"Then I do a forced extraction, and we find out everything he knows," Ben stated. "After that he won't be able to render an opinion one way or another." There was a cold frankness in his voice that took everyone aback, except for Zimmer.

Vice President Chu suddenly recognized him. It was as though Ben had suddenly emerged out of the shadows, and she finally took a close look. He was the Egalitarian Party's invisible henchman, the one who had been doing their dirty work behind the scenes, and the one who allowed them to go to sleep at night with a clear conscience.

'Look at him,' she thought. 'That smug, arrogant, son of a bitch. He didn't even bat an eyelash. He took an oath to do no harm, and he talks about destroying this man's brain as though it carries no more implication than taking out the trash.'

"My opinion, kid gloves," she said. While she felt incredible force inside, her voice was smooth and silky, "There is no evidence to suggest dire urgency right now, and we have a moral duty to protect and assist another person who needs help." She studied Ben's body language as she spoke. She perceived a remorseless quality to the man, a remorseless quality in his devotion to the Party. In her mind, it no longer was Zimmer who represented a danger to the person of John Doe. She was worried about Dr. Murray, that his terrible work had become enjoyable.

The President slapped the table with the palm of his hand. That was the signal that he had heard enough and that the time for debate was over. "I agree. Dr. Murray, I reserve the right to ask you to be more aggressive in your interrogation of John Doe. But for now, there is absolutely no reason to believe that John Doe won't be cooperative when he's able and ready. He does appear to be, as you mentioned, one of ours. Bring him along at your discretion."

Heads around the table indicated the general consensus. Ben nodded in turn, indicating his understanding.

"Have you located any other recordings taken at the reenactment?" Vice President Chu asked.

"No. If there were any, there is a good chance they would have shown up already," Zimmer answered.

"Should we have the stories removed from the servers, alter the info, or limit access to the information?" she asked.

"My opinion…no," General Wayne offered. "There's no sense drawing attention to something that's dead anyway. Besides, if a single radical out of the eight and some odd million made an off-line copy on an illegal non-system drive, or if anyone starts to suspect something, removing it from the internet mountain is a red flag that will do nothing more than fan the flames of conspiracy. I think we should leave it. Let it die on the vine."

As the conversation developed it was interesting to Ben that the exact concerns that motivated the underground reform movements, and their fears of an all powerful authoritarian government, were now on display and were being nonchalantly bantered around the table, and yet every person in the room was of the opinion that the conspiracy theorists were traitors.

"I agree. For our purposes, John Doe is best treated as a nut." Zimmer glanced at Ben with an odd expression as he made the comment. "However, for the sake of cutting this off at the knees, the story does need closure. I propose a rather innocuous report backdated and linked that confirms the disturbance at the reenactment resulted from the actions of a mentally unstable psychiatric patient, the wounds were found to be self-inflicted, and he died as a result of suicide."

"As far as the public is concerned, the whole thing just fades into obscurity," the Vice President added. "Does anyone have any objections?"

she asked. In the absence of an objection, she finished, "I think it's the prudent thing to do."

President Martinez nodded his agreement. He studied the back and forth discussion as it continued for several more minutes. He had a reputation for being very thorough. He would carefully assess all sides of a situation and find an option that no one else had thought of. Once he made a decision, it was understood that everyone would tow-the-line. The President again hit the table with his palm. He had heard enough.

"The fact of the matter is that we don't have anything yet," he said. "So we don't need to worry about any kind of time travel testing. If our hand is forced, it will be the biggest decision we will ever have to make. But not yet." Dr. Stuart's stated position was absolutely vindicated. "We need more information before we make any decisions. Never make decisions as important as this in a vacuum." He looked at Ben, "Dr. Murray, we need to know what John Doe knows. To start, let's get a name. He's completely in your charge, and you are entirely responsible for his safety. Carl will see to it that all NAIA resources are at your disposal. Director Zimmer, once again I commend you on your excellent work. This is an extremely important find that could have gotten away. Our entire future may be altered in dramatic ways as a result of your prudence." Director Zimmer got his approval for initiating the investigation. The President went on, "We need answers on this, and I want every angle covered. Dr. Stuart, your clearance will equal my own for these purposes. You will look at everything we have in regard to the end of World War IV and the experiments the Persians were doing, and you will search for any scientific links between those events and the appearance of John Doe. Let's look again at everything John Doe has to offer, the carcass of his horse, all his equipment, even his clothing. Carl will share everything he has with you. I think three months is more than adequate time to get something together, at which time we'll meet again, same time, same place. I'll coordinate with Carl, and he'll quarterback the show. Everyone is agreed." It was a statement more than a question. The President rose from his chair, "Gentlemen, Vice President Chu, if you would be so kind as to excuse me."

CHAPTER 5: THE HOSPITAL

[FEBRUARY 10, AD 2441]
[71 DAYS AFTER ARRIVAL: 2 DAYS LATER]
[LOCATION: NASHVILLE, TENNESSEE]

"What? Out of the whole class, only three of them completed the assignment?" Ben was shocked by the revelation.

"Only three," Cecilie confirmed.

"I don't understand. Where are the parents?"

"More often than not, that's the crux of the problem."

Ben shook his head in disgust. "When I was fifteen, we did what our teachers said, and we took pride in our work." He found it surprising that Cecilie was taking it in stride, as though it was expected. "So, what did you say?"

"It doesn't do any good to chastise them, but I did have such high hopes for this class. I want them to actually like reading. The love of literature can be learned. It just has to be done right. So I swallowed hard, tried the best I could to hide that feelings were hurt, and I gave them my usual speech." Ben indicated with facial expression and hand gesture that he wanted to hear the speech so Cecilie went on, "I wanted to try something different, something that might reach them, or at least reach one of them. So we moved the desks, and I had everyone sit on the floor in a half-circle. I sat on a chair in front of them."

"Oh," Ben said. "Good move. Using some psychology." He was referring to the kids being positioned on the floor and having to look up to see her. Subconsciously, it put her in the position of dominance and authority.

Cecilie smiled in agreement. "We had a nice back and forth. I eased them into a good discussion about how important literature is, not only for brain development, but as part of becoming a well rounded person. In order to make my point, I explained that my life was not interesting, and that while they were the center of their own lives, their lives weren't really that interesting either. The sooner they realize that the better they'll be. I tried to emphasize that life can be an incredible experience. It's up to them to make it happen...if they choose to travel the roads less taken. I said, 'Open your eyes, open your hearts, and open a book. Take the opportunity to climb out of your life, and for a time, you can live the life of someone else. Seek understanding. Learn about them, and in turn, you'll find that you are learning about life, and you are learning about yourself.' I think I had everyone's attention at that point so I finished with, 'Learn about yourself in a realistic way, and you'll make better choices with your life. The day will come when you look back on it all, and you'll truly be able to say that it was an incredible experience.'"

"I wish I would have had a teacher like you," Ben said. "But I think I would have failed."

Cecilie was surprised. "Why do you say that?"

"Because you're so beautiful, I wouldn't have been able to concentrate. I do much better with ugly teachers."

She was brilliant in his eyes. She taught literature at the local high school. Helping kids open their eyes and hearts to the wildly different worlds and experiences available through books was her life's passion. She emphasized that each story had the potential to open new worlds full of wonderful experiences, each one just waiting to be discovered. She emphasized that for hours at a time a reader could fight off dragons, live in ancient Egypt, experience life as a serf in Medieval Europe or Russia, or as a slave in Early America, or even as an adventurer far off in the future. Each year, there were one or two special students who were her personal projects. The joy she would experience when they learned how to open their minds, when they would finally 'get it,' was enough to rekindle her enthusiasm and sense of utility.

Cecilie took in the scene. It looked like either Ben was moving out or that the bedroom had been ransacked. She leaned back against the dresser and casually twirled the end of her long sandy blonde hair in her fingers. She knew he liked it when she did that, but her coy smile betrayed what she was actually thinking. "Do you need help?" she asked. Cecilie had often accused Ben of packing like a woman, and his response was always the same...that the only way he could possibly understand women was to experience the insanity.

"No," he replied. "I have it all under control."

Cecilie could anticipate how long he was going to be away based on how much underwear he packed. From the size of the pile she judged it was going to be another extended absence. He had every last pair in a stack that had to be ten inches high.

"Do they have laundry stations in Nashville?"

"I'm sure they do. Why?" As soon as the question rolled off his tongue he regretted it, but it was too late, and he couldn't take it back. He had unwittingly initiated a chain reaction.

Cecilie was in good form. She didn't respond immediately. She made him wait for it. "Well," she finally said, staring at the pile of underwear, making him wait a little longer. "You might consider the possibility of actually doing your laundry." That was her first gentle suggestion. He perceived a little stabbing sensation. Hitting around the edges was her usual modus operandi when stressed, or when she discovered that he wasn't doing things the way she preferred. Then came the second comment, "It only takes a few minutes, and it's really easy to do."

'That wasn't too bad,' he thought. He continued piling his clothes on the bed.

"Or, do you plan on just throwing these out and buying new ones, like you've done in the past?"

That one hurt. He accepted the blade like a man and didn't respond. All he could do was turn to face her and sheepishly grin. Then Ben realized, 'Oh God, there's more. She's winding up again.'

"Those expenses add up over time you know." Then she added, "We spend more on your underwear than we do on the lawn."

It was a double stabbing. Ben grabbed his heart as though he had been wounded. "Don't make fun of me," he said. Then he stretched his arms out and pleaded, "Help me! You don't know what it's like to be completely helpless in this cruel, cruel world!"

Cecilie laughed.

"Hold me. Please hold me. You know I can't live without you," he said. "The stress of being away from you has reduced me to this. The ways I'm forced to cope are private. Please don't go public with this."

Now it was Cecilie's turn to anticipate his response…sarcasm and humor. It was always sarcasm and humor. "This one," he said as he picked up a pair of underwear and feigned tearful sentimentality, "I wore on your last birthday." He picked up another, "This one I wore when we celebrated the end of the school year. This one was our date night when we had that romantic dinner at Bonjour Bifteck. And this one," he looked at it, "oh… never mind," and he quickly put it aside and grabbed another.

"Wait. What was that one?" She demanded.

"Golf game with Joe."

Cecilie couldn't help laughing.

"Don't make fun of my special memories." Ben grabbed his wife in his arms and squeezed her in a long embrace. 'My God, how am I going to keep you safe,' he thought. But what he said was altogether different. "This is hard for me too." Then he offered in a soft voice, "What do you say we leave here and find a deserted island? We'll live our life without all the forces that keep pulling us in opposite directions. We can be together all the time. Every time you turn around, I'll be there. Every time you look up, you can take it for granted that I'll be there. And when you're lying on your side and snoring like you have been doing here, I promise I won't leave to sleep somewhere else."

"What?"

"I'll lay awake all night listening to make sure you don't stop breathing."

"What are you talking about?"

"Snoring should never be regarded as normal. Most breathing problems during sleep actually can't be detected by simple observation. On our island we'll have to take your snoring seriously."

"I don't snore."

"But you can feel good about this because since we'll be together all the time, I'll go with you to all your doctor's visits so you can be properly evaluated for sleep apnea."

"I don't snore."

Ben hugged her in a tight embrace. "On our island we'll do everything together. We'll never be apart. Every day…all day, we'll have nothing to do except hold each other. We'll show each other over and over again how much we love each other."

"OK," she said, pushing him away. "That was nice. Why don't you just go ahead and finish packing."

"What? You don't like our island?"

"Would never work, sweetie. Unless our island has a store where you can buy clean underwear." Cecilie turned to exit the room. She stopped in the doorway and informed him, "I'm going to Nashville next week. I read an interesting book about Andrew Jackson and his wife, Rachel. I'm going to visit The Hermitage. It would be great if you could join me."

It had taken Ben the entire day to clear his schedule and finalize arrangements for what would likely be an extended mission. It would begin in Nashville, and from there, he was uncertain. He already told Cecilie he would be leaving in the morning—it was a matter of national security, and he didn't know exactly how long he would be away.

"Sounds fun, but I don't think I'll be able to join you," he admitted.

Cecilie stopped in the doorway and turned back to face him. "Oh," she said with a curious and hurt expression. "Why?"

Ben sensed that their evening together was about to crumble. All he wanted was to take his time saying goodbye, to avoid all the intense emotions. "The work I'm doing," he explained, "it's very serious."

"Well, how long are you going to be gone?"

"I don't know for sure," he said. "It could be several months."

Cecilie was trying her best to control the sudden sense of loneliness and sorrow. "When will you know?" she asked. It was a reasonable inquiry.

"That's just it. It's a developing case. I won't be as available as in the past. You might not hear from me for an extended period of time." He wanted to tell her to run, to take the children and their families and get out of the country, to find a place where the Egalitarian Party wouldn't be able to hurt them. But he couldn't. His stomach was in knots. The belief that he was betraying his family was real. Once he walked out the door he wouldn't have any guarantees regarding their safety. The only reassurance was the promise from the secret society that a watch would be kept over them, and they would do their best to extract them should the mission become compromised.

The depth of the pain in his eyes was enough to keep her growing frustration in check. He was worried about something that he couldn't share. "I understand," she finally mumbled, failing miserably to hide her disappointment. She looked up and forced a smile. "Don't worry about me. I'll be fine. I have lots of things I can do. You will, if it's at all possible, let me know that you're okay?"

"Of course I will," he agreed.

After twenty-five years of marriage, it was increasingly difficult to be away, especially now that their four children were grown and living on their own. The same house that had been the center of commotion, and so much noise that he occasionally had to wear earplugs, now felt like a place of despair. When alone, he knew it to feel like a morgue full of dead memories, and that's where he was leaving her. The mere thought almost pulled him down to his knees.

Lost in her thoughts, Cecilie helped him arrange the clothing into his large military-style canvas bag. She leaned over and kissed him and said reassuringly, "We'll get through this just like we always do." They embraced for a long time.

'She makes me feel so weak,' he thought. 'How can it be that she is the strong one?'

Ben never talked about his work with Cecilie. Over the years, she grew so fatigued wondering what he did that she simply stopped asking. She reasoned that it was classified, and he couldn't tell her even if he wanted, but that was only half the story. It was true he couldn't share with her the trials and tribulations of his work because of its classified nature, but it was equally true that he didn't want her to know. Most of the people he was forced to deal with were rather unsavory characters. That nuance of information however, would be completely lost when considered against the brutality of what he did to them. His job was to pull out of their brains everything they knew. There were no limits beyond those imposed by his conscience on what he might do…and he was very good at his work.

When he wasn't interrogating specific targets for the Egalitarian Party, he practiced his interrogation techniques on career criminals, death row inmates, and captured domestic terrorists. It didn't take long to discover that, in most cases, criminals had perpetrated a long list of crimes. The pattern became familiar. Often enough, they had problems dating all the way back to childhood. They started small and the severity of their crimes grew, culminating into the crime for which they were eventually caught and convicted. In the process of interrogating them, he pried information out of their neural networks pertaining to crime syndicates, drugs, gangs, prostitution rings, and numerous unsolved murders and robberies.

There were very serious moral and ethical issues related to his work. As such, the creepy shadows of guilt that were playing out in his mind would magnify a thousand-fold if Cecilie were ever made party to what he actually did. She was the one person who had the potential to see his soul, and if she were to ever see him as he really was, her ultimate rejection would be devastating.

Cecilie was a counter-balance for goodness in his life. In a weird way, Ben thought that if she knew more about his work…it would somehow violate her, but not because she wouldn't be able to handle it, or because she was weak. Quite the opposite was in fact closer to the truth. In a nebulous way, the dynamic was more complex. It was more that he found secrecy in his work an absolute necessity in order to preserve his own sanity. He needed to be able to mentally step out of his world and into one that was completely untainted, completely innocent, and completely beautiful. If she knew what he was doing, somehow coming home would lose those intangible psychological qualities that made it an escape from the real world; home would cease being his sanctuary.

* * * * *

Ben found New Bethesda Hospital to be a sprawling complex sitting on approximately four hundred acres of beautifully landscaped Tennessee countryside. It was just on the outskirts of Nashville. It was his first time on the campus. He found that it consisted of a large primary hospital and several surrounding buildings connected by multiple tunnels and walkways. The flanking structures were mostly clinics, surgery and rehab centers, psychiatric facilities, temporary housing for out-of-towners, and parking garages. The uniform white stone architecture gave the buildings a castle-like appearance, but with a modern twist, while the multitude of windows added a warm and inviting touch. It wasn't meant to be, but under the circumstances, he found it to be a foreboding structure.

It was 3:30 P.M. and Ben was in the hospital's administrative office. When he introduced himself and flashed his credentials to the secretary, she nervously called the administrator. Mr. Edwin Kerr immediately appeared in the doorway. He was short, sweaty, and magnificently overweight.

"Come in," he said, indicating that Ben should enter his office. He asked for credentials and began asking questions. "What is your interest in one of my patients?"

While misplaced curiosity was understandable, an inflated sense of self-importance was another thing entirely. It was Edwin's tone and demeanor more than anything that irritated Ben. He didn't answer the question. He stared at Kerr without blinking and stepped toward him.

"This is Party business. Are you standing in my way?"

"Uh, no." Kerr quickly backpedaled. "No, I'm not. I'll do whatever you want."

While maintaining a rigid exterior, Ben found some degree of humor in the show. It was on these occasions, when he made people squirm and emasculated men who thought they were important, that he really enjoyed his work. While he was masterfully adept at getting people to do exactly what he wanted, there were always times when he knew he was being called an ass behind his back. But with all sincerity, it was not possible for him to care any less about the opinions of those he considered inferior or less motivated.

Kerr was tremulous as he agreed to cooperate. "I, I, I will make all the arrangements. Security clearance, hospital privileges—consider everything taken care of. We'll get out of your way."

"Thank you," Ben said. He slapped Edwin on the fat of his upper arm and added, "Sensible move." He turned and walked out of the office.

At an institution like New Bethesda Hospital, the nation's premier military hospital, care often included the treatment of injuries that were obtained under very cloudy or classified circumstances. Special ops soldiers were often brought in for treatment after suffering 'training' accidents. But this one was different. It was incredibly rare that a high-ranking MPS operative with NAIA clearance, which implied Presidential sanction, would personally assume care of a patient. This was an environment where no one involved in the direct care of these mystery patients really wanted to know the sordid details of what caused their injuries. The staff's fundamental desire was to practice medicine. In that, they wanted life at the institution to be as uneventful as possible. As a result, New Bethesda had evolved a culture that fostered a dual *care for the patient* and an *I don't need to know* mentality.

Ben felt a growing sense of unease. At first he simply attributed it to being paranoid. Then he guessed it was because of the danger, danger unlike any he had ever experienced. In the past, his paranoia usually turned out to be justified. As he walked through the corridors and made his way toward John Doe, his unease grew fierce. Finally, he came to the firm realization that the internal alarms were blaring for a reason. He felt like he was being watched, and that he was vulnerable.

Ben's life was at the edge of a precipice. He stared down the corridor. Not fifty feet away was John Doe. A short walk and only one door separated them. For years he planned exactly what he might do if he received the ominous call from the secret society, the call that would alter the course of the world. Then, it did come. *He has arrived. He has arrived. He has arrived.* He kept repeating the phrase in his mind. Sometimes it was loud, almost a scream, sometimes it was full of excitement—a herald's cry—other times it was soft and slow. Regardless, it always came back to the same thing… John Doe had returned.

Ben nervously walked down the hall. He always imagined that he would simply introduce himself. He would casually strike up a conversation and get on with it, but now that he was actually in the situation, he was surprised to find himself scared. How was he supposed to help one of the greatest soldiers United America had ever put on the field of battle, a man of such indomitable spirit that his own steadfastness paled in comparison? It was like a squire trying to rescue a knight. But the die had been cast, and this mission was his.

He stood at the door, ready to meet the man who was going to change everything. He was conscious of each breath as it went in and out. He felt winded. Then he felt like he was breathing too fast. His hand was up. He was ready to knock. He was going to swing the door open and make his introduction.

BANG!

The noise startled Ben, drawing his attention away from the room. A few feet away a little, elderly man was hunched over, leaning against the wall. He was a visitor, well dressed, wearing a coat and a hat that resembled an old-fashioned derby. His cane had fallen to the floor. He was staring at it, debating how he was going to bend over to get it back. Ben picked it up.

"There you go," he said as he handed it over.

The man slowly looked up until the brim of the hat revealed his eyes. His gaze was piercing. He looked at Ben, then at John Doe's room, and shook his head to indicate that Ben should not enter. He followed with a subtle hand motion that commanded him to back off.

"Thank you," he said as he took the cane. He grasped Ben's forearm with his other hand. He squeezed it twice and said in a harsh whisper, "Be very careful, Dr. Murray," pausing before adding, "or you'll end up hobbling with a cane like me."

When the man turned and walked away, he was using the cane on the opposite side.

Something terrible had gone wrong. Ben felt a surge of panic. He cautiously backed away from the room. His mind was racing. His unease had been justified. He was being watched. He had to shift gears and engage in some activity that wouldn't raise suspicion. He focused his thoughts and made the decision to instead sift through the mountains of data on the hospital's computer, reasoning that it was a believable endeavor. If questioned, he could maintain that he believed the more information he had, the better prepared he would be to question the subject.

He found his way to the nurse's station. It had been an extended period of time since he had done any real work in a hospital setting, but once he got started, although distracted, the memories came back. The hospital's electronic medical record system (used to store all the patients' information: lab results, imaging studies, physicians' notes, and nurse and patient entries) was very different from the system he had used during his training. He was impressed at how fast it pulled the information up with a simple voice prompt, or a single touch in the matrix of the holographic screen. He could open several windows, flip them around seamlessly, and pull images away from the monitor and suspend them in air up to ten inches from the screen. He could watch John Doe's heartbeat in three dimensions from the moment of his arrival, through his surgeries, and compare it to his present heartbeat, pulling up the images in less than a second.

As he reviewed the medical history, he transferred the data not only to his BCD, but to a handheld computer that possessed its own memory systems and was equipped with state of the art encryption capabilities, not from the government, but from the secret society. He proceeded to scour every detail, making personal notes and taking down times, dates, room numbers, and the names of nurses, doctors, and therapists. His intention was to cross-reference the information against the work schedules of the ancillary staff. Until he met the subject directly, he decided that he would interview anyone who had come into contact with him.

Ben formulated a battery of questions he would ask each individual. He stored the info in his BCD, and auditory prompts would be brought to his attention during the actual interviews. Starting from the very beginning and with the utmost scrutiny, he reviewed the medical hovercraft (MHC) transfer from the field where the Civil War reenactment was held. He scanned the names and signatures of the crew. Then came the emergency room staff, physicians, nurses, techs, and everyone else involved. After that was the operating room and recovery. It didn't take long before he had well over eighty names. He even included those who were working but had no formal contact with the patient. He knew that he would have to interview a significant number of them, possibly all of them, in the upcoming days.

Ben found a complete catalog of images that were taken of John Doe's wounds. "How the hell did he live through this?" he muttered under his breath. A dire prognosis, or death imminent, was written between the lines of almost every report during the first few days of hospitalization.

Almost overnight, the story of a startling recovery began to unfold. He required dialysis the first couple days. Having shut down because of massive blood loss, his kidneys miraculously recovered function and were completely normal less than two weeks later. He lost the right upper lobe of his lung as it was mangled beyond repair. He had a rebuilt shoulder and synthetic bones in the forearm, thigh, hands, and chest. With the latest biomedical technology, muscles and nerves were regenerated where they had been destroyed, and reattached where they were merely damaged. An exact but inverse copy of his remaining ear was used to replace the missing. The eardrum was rebuilt. Numerous scars had been treated with the latest in growth factor medications and laser treatments, and as a result, they had been minimized to the point where, all things considered, they weren't too bad.

'There's nothing left for me to do now except pray,' Ben thought as he paced his hotel room. He sarcastically scoffed at the argument that was transpiring in his head. 'I don't believe. Why should I? Besides, how noble I must appear. God, if He does exist, hasn't heard from me in decades. Then, out of the blue, in a moment of crisis, I have the audacity to expect Him to help me.'

Long ago, Ben rejected any formal belief in an afterlife. The closest he actually came was being an agnostic in his youth. This eventually gave way to full-fledged, but diligently silent, atheism as an adult. He never talked honestly, or openly, about his beliefs with anyone, including his wife.

Spiritual beliefs were nuanced in Twenty-Fifth Century United America. At one time, the government of the people, by the people, and for the people, was embedded but not wedded to the fundamental constructs of

Christian ethics. It was through that Christian lens that the vision of a free society took shape with vital checks and balances built into government. In this was a formal recognition of the fallibility of mankind, the dark side of man's political nature, and innate lust for power and control over the lives of fellow man. In that society, one could worship as they might choose. Freedom of religion was a fundamental and guaranteed right protected by the Constitution. But all that had changed. From the Eighteenth Century to the Twenty-Fifth, so much had changed as to render society almost unrecognizable as having actually descended from the original thirteen colonies.

The anti-religion movement in North America was complex. It began in the sciences and spread through other disciplines in the universities. It garnered influence and support among the ultra-wealthy and in the entertainment industries. At roughly the same time, there emerged a notable anti-organized religion movement. With World War III drawn largely along lines of religion, and the sheer magnitude of domestic terrorism that resulted, the public clamored for increased government control. It began with the revocation of the tax-exempt status of all churches, and donations to the churches not only lost their tax deductibility, but all donations were tracked under the scrutinizing eye of the government. The idea that was the cornerstone of the movement, the idea that finally allowed the government to seize control, was the idea that when revenues were pulled away from United America's tax coffers, in effect the tax-payers as a whole were subsidizing religion, whether they agreed with it or not. Under the idea that there had to be a complete separation of church and state, this was deemed to be unacceptable. Then, after several churches were put on trial for seditious activities and found guilty, the general public was ready for increased government control. What followed was in the name of complete transparency and in order to prevent the emergence of a new generation of fanatics. The government began openly monitoring what was being taught to congregations across the country. They imposed severe penalties for any violation of strict guidelines. At first, the least affected were the Christian churches, and with sentiments being what they were, few Christians objected when the government clamped down hard on those non-Christian religions who were teaching things that many mainstream Americans found objectionable.

Then fifty years passed. It was a time plagued by argument, strife, and outbreaks of violence. Shortly after World War IV, when the Egalitarian Party assumed complete control, the government officially took over what they referred to as the industry of religion. Then came the panels. They invited religious representatives of every recognized spiritual tradition to participate, but the outcome was pre-determined. Proponents of the Egalitarian Party held the belief that religion was responsible for most of the violence in the world, and that the way it was being practiced functioned to enslave people in chains of ignorance and poverty. The Egalitarian Party, understanding that they couldn't eliminate spiritual endeavors, as they are an indelible and insuppressible part of the human experience, championed the creation of a new religion based on agreed core principles. This new state religion supplanted all others, and the practice of the old ways was deemed illegal. The ministers of the religion were employees of the state, and it was taught that devotion to the state was an essential part of eternal salvation.

Much like a country would hold a constitutional convention and hash out a new framework for the governance of society, this religious convention hashed out a brand new holy book. All previous versions of holy books across all religions were collected, burned, or erased. Ten years previous, in anticipation that they would achieve their goals, a malicious computer virus specifically designed at an NAIA lab had been attaching itself to every digital copy of the Bible, the Torah, the Koran, and every other holy book worth destroying. On the drop-dead date, the day that the government officially unified everyone under one religion, all the holy books were destroyed and erased from every known computer network, and newly downloaded versions were immediately filtered out and destroyed.

The outcry was fierce but ineffectual. The general public was tired of conflict and accepted the government's explanation that the move was necessary as a prerequisite for peace and prosperity. The Egalitarian Party's view was that religion was an opiate for the masses, and that it was healthier for the country if they were in control of the supply. That was over fifty years ago. The traditional faiths that had managed to survive did so by going underground.

Participation in state-run religious activities was not obligatory but guided by the dictates of one's conscience. As Ben never experienced life in a society with complete religious freedom, he had nothing to compare his experience against. Regardless, the point where his thoughts about an afterlife got hung up had much to do, at least indirectly, with his work with the MPS. With his interrogative skills, he could with precision and control, damage very small structures within the substance of the brain. Through his brutal handiwork, he observed that he could reduce the most devout disciple into a morally depraved fiend, an addict, or even a psychopath.

Free will was the key. He didn't think it existed. That in turn, destroyed any notion of an afterlife. Ben couldn't reconcile what he was seeing and doing with a belief that human behavior was dictated by free will. His observations that altered brain function in the form of destroyed neurons and synapses resulted in gross behavioral and moral changes didn't fit with a belief in free will. How could the qualitative state of one's eternal spiritual existence be forever determined by the finite life of a biological form whose spiritual course in life could be indelibly changed with such relative ease? By destroying a few strategically placed neurons in a couple specific areas of the brain, he could turn a rabbi into a serial killer, or a housewife into a raging drug-addict. If he was able to do such work, what about the millions of factors that were completely out of one's control during development and maturation? How much of life was free will and choice, and how much was determined by a combination of inherited genes and developmental processes that one had no control over? Should a person's soul be condemned for eternity based on which of the brain's neural synapses survived and which ones didn't? Or which inherited addictions they might have and how strong those addictions might be? The question he would ask God if given the opportunity was, 'Why should the finite function of our living brain, a DNA driven and carbon-based organic computer, over which we have far less control than supposed, determine spiritual success or failure for eternity? Is that just? How is that consistent with a belief in an eternal and loving God?' The questions haunted him, and he found no answers in theology other than the supposition that he needed to have faith, and in some quarters, that his asking such questions and aggressively demanding answers of God was wrong…that it was self-centered, and that it represented the sin of pride.

After a sleepless night, Dr. Murray spent most of the next morning further reviewing the mountain of data. On occasion he left to seek out some additional information in the medical library. It was uncharacteristic for him, but he got to the point where he couldn't maintain mental focus. In addition to being mentally clouded by fatigue and sleepiness, he couldn't shake the intense feeling that he was being watched.

The interviews, beginning that afternoon, were held in one of the empty medical staff administrative offices. It was nothing fancy, a glorified closet that a former lower-level employee used as an office for purchasing supplies. It had a desk and a couple chairs. He brought in his MPS team, and they thoroughly searched and secured the area. They placed security counter-measures in the room to prevent any eavesdropping, and this made him feel a little bit better about the situation. Back to back, fifteen-minute appointments were arranged by one of his agents, Buck, while two others, William and Trudi, worked the field to bring interviewees to bear.

Having his team assist in arranging interviews was an effort to avoid drawing unnecessary attention. For obvious reasons of secrecy, he wanted to limit the involvement of the hospital administrative staff. In all, it took the greater part of two days to complete the interviews to Ben's satisfaction. In the interim, he repeatedly interviewed the nurses and doctors who were actively taking care of John Doe. Still, he avoided all direct contact with the patient. Until cleared by the secret society, he would not approach John Doe.

During the interviews, Ben's BCD would detect a variety of physiologic signals ranging from pulse, skin temperature changes, alterations in the electromagnetic field, and eye movements, including pupil dilation and constriction. The person being interviewed would have no idea that they were being monitored. All the information, routed through his BCD, would be projected to his retina, and to the parts of his brain associated with vision, the visual cortex. What the BCD enabled Ben to see was the exact same as anyone else in the room with the addition of an image from his left eye that was perceived as looking through a piece of glass, like an old style fighter pilot's heads-up-display. The display included anything he wanted to see, from news reports to weather conditions, to correspondence to and from family. What he displayed for the interviews were the physiological signals from the person opposite him in the interview. Not only would he see the monitors, if he happened to be distracted by something in the environment he would hear an alarm prompting him that the person's signals had altered outside the norm. It was usually a sign that he or she might not be telling the truth. The beauty of it was that they had no idea he was privy to their most private physiologic information.

"Hello. You must be Tom Hutchinson," Ben said as he checked his name on the list. Tom was his twelfth interview that afternoon. They shook hands as Ben introduced himself, "I'm Dr. Ben Murray."

"Ben Murray. Why does that sound familiar?" Perplexed, the paramedic thought for a second. His long, rather slender face demonstrated the effort as he scanned his memory. Suddenly he enthusiastically recalled, "My mom has a cousin named Ben Murray. He's with some governmental agency, in New Washington."

'Hell,' was Ben's first thought. First day of interviews and his identity was discovered by a family member. He kicked himself for not being more careful, but he regarded Tom with an intense curiosity. Could he be? It was possible. There was no real way to confirm at this point so he elected to play it cool. He asked, "Who's your mother?"

"Loribeth Ann Hutchinson. Well, she used to be a Murray. Goes by Annie."

"Because her mother and grandmother are both named Loribeth."

"You know her!"

"She's my first cousin. Bloody hell, you're my cousin," Ben excitedly admitted. "I haven't seen Annie in years. It must be at least twenty years. How is she doing?" Ben was happy to have the opportunity to engage in family pleasantries.

"Great. Healthy as a horse."

"What's she doing these days?"

"She's a few years from retirement. Right now she manages the books and contract negotiations for a construction outfit, but every chance she gets, she's out hitting the links. Absolutely loves golf."

A few more good-natured remarks passed. They scheduled dinner together for later that night in an effort to get better acquainted. After the brief detour down memory lane, Ben began the interview in earnest.

"We got the call that there was an emergency at the Franklin reenactment, and they needed a MHC. That's lingo for medical hovercraft. We were needed for a STAT evac," Tom said.

"Who made the call?"

"There's almost always a basic crew and an ambulance on site for those things. Usually they treat a wide variety of minor scrapes, bumps, and bruises. Occasionally, they might take care of a mild case of dehydration or a twisted ankle. But they really aren't equipped or experienced enough to handle a case like this. One of them called us in."

"Do you remember who took the call?"

"I did. I took the call."

"Do you remember who exactly it was that called in your MHC?"

"No. I don't recall that I asked. We usually don't."

"Do you remember what the voice sounded like?"

"I do remember that there was a lot of interference on the line. I don't know why I remember that. Maybe because it's usually so clear."

"Was it a male or a female voice?"

Tom thought for a moment. "I'm embarrassed that I don't remember."

"What was your response time?"

"Approximately twelve minutes."

Interestingly, Ben had already interviewed the crew from the ambulance service. They denied calling the MHC in. According to them, it just showed up on its own. It was there and on the ground not more than a minute, two at the most, after John Doe appeared on the field. The MHC had apparently been called in anticipation of John Doe's appearance. It had been called roughly ten minutes before he materialized. But how? And by whom?

"What did you see when you arrived on the scene?" Dr. Murray asked.

"As we were coming in for the landing, the crowd was controlled. Everybody stood in place watching the show. There were thousands of reenactors and smoke was everywhere. A cluster of men were crowded around the patient and his horse. We had to announce over the loudspeaker that we needed them to clear the area so we could land. By the time we were on the ground and got to the patient, he was in and out of consciousness. There was blood all over the place. He quickly had an oxygen mask on his face and pressure dressings were being placed on his thigh and shoulder. We sank several lines, including a large bore IV in his left femoral vein. Inside of a minute multiple bags of fluids were being run wide open."

"I remember his horse," Tom went on. "It was one of those poignant things that really sticks out, something you can never forget. It was about ten feet away, lying on its side screaming. It was unlike anything I ever heard. I had no idea a horse could make sounds like that. At one time or another, I've seen just about everything a person doesn't want to see and nothing ever bothered me, but I've had a couple nightmares about that horse. One of its front legs was missing and it had been shot several times. Its head was writhing and jerking back and forth. It tried to get up but couldn't. One of its back legs kicked and scraped frantically. It kept looking toward the patient and was screaming at us. I guess it wanted us to stay away. It was mad as hell. Actually managed to move itself several feet across the ground toward us. It was incredible," Tom paused, obviously disturbed by the scene he was describing. His voice betrayed a crack of heavy emotion as he went on, "The animal was half-butchered and yet it still tried to protect its rider. I remember all this steam was rising off of its body. We could see its breath." Tom paused for a moment. "It's hard to explain. You know how you can see your breath when it's cold out?" he asked. Ben nodded. "It wasn't that cold out, but we could still see its breath. And it was tinged red. Little droplets of blood projected out with each breath. Bloody foam ran out of its muzzle and nostrils. It was hard. With all the distraction, I was trying hard to stay focused on the patient. So I didn't see much of anything else. Toward the end, it gave out this tremendous bellow. It extended its neck and head toward us. Its head was right next to me. Its tongue was sticking out. It gave a few final gasps and snorts. It really sounded like it knew it was dying. And then nothing. Its head fell to the ground, a few blinks and a long drawn out exhalation, and it was dead. The whole thing was really surreal."

"Tell me what was happening with the patient."

"By that time, we had his heart paced and had compressed all the major areas of external bleeding. We had him on the backboard. The holographic display indicated that the left side of his chest was filling up with blood and that the lung was collapsed. We inserted a field pneumovac between his ribs on the left side to suck all the blood, air, and crap out so his lung could expand. We quickly had him about as stabilized as we possibly could in the field, so we began loading him up for transport. He had been in and out of consciousness. Once we got him in the craft he failed to maintain his airway. So we tubed him. In hind site, we probably should have intubated sooner. But it all worked out."

"Was he communicating with anyone?" Ben asked.

"Before we tubed him, he was talking and mumbling some. A lot of it was unintelligible with the oxygen mask on and all the noise."

"Where were you?"

"I was at his head so I had a better vantage than anyone. He said a few words. He called out for someone. I couldn't catch the name. He mumbled out, 'I'm sorry.' Over and over, in fact. "I'm sorry. I'm sorry.' He just repeated it over and over. He sounded delirious. He was weak but panicked at the same time. He tried to look over at his horse and called out something a couple times. I might have imagined it, but I swear that as I was going to intubate him, I took the oxygen mask off, and I thought he said the word 'Balius.' He blacked out and went limp. I think it was the horse's name."

"Why do you think that?" Ben inquired.

"Well? Do you recognize it? It's a famous name." Tom paused and waited for a response. Ben was at a loss. "Balius was an immortal warrior horse that belonged to Achilles," Tom revealed. "I thought it sounded familiar so I looked it up when I got back. Sure enough, there it was, just like I thought."

"Balius...interesting," Ben said as he pondered the name. He was integrating everything he had learned so far. Per Zimmer's report, the horse was a product of genetic modification, an engineered animal designed specifically to be bigger, stronger, and more aggressive...and its name was Balius. The possibilities were endless. What Ben didn't understand based on Tom's knowledge of the case, was how Zimmer's group came to the conclusion that a paramedic knew John Doe's name. Once he was intubated, he wouldn't have been able to talk. It didn't make sense. He asked Tom if he knew anything in that regard.

"No. He never regained consciousness after we tubed him."

The sensors in Ben's BCD indicated that Tom was holding something back. His pulse went up and his eye movements were suddenly irregular from baseline. Ben pried a little deeper.

"You have any idea why the patient might have suggested someone on the MHC knew him?" Ben asked.

"No. And I was with him the entire time," Tom confirmed. "Delirium maybe? He wouldn't have been able to talk anyway with the tube in. That is unless I got it in the esophagus instead of the trachea, and that never happens if I'm the one putting it in. What happened at the hospital, I don't know, maybe they pulled the tube out and he started talking."

"Is there anything else you remember that might be helpful?" Ben decided to leave it alone for now because it was likely immaterial, and Tom's signals had quickly corrected themselves.

"Yeah. The smell. One of the things I remember was the smell. Man was he rank. It was like he hadn't had a bath in Lord knows how long."

Ben wasn't able to learn anything else of consequence from Tom's interview. In fact, there really wasn't much to be gained from the subsequent interviews that he hadn't already learned from the medical records. The patient remained unconscious from the time of his arrival at the hospital through his surgeries, and only regained consciousness days later in the critical care unit.

At the conclusion of each interview, Ben finished with, "I want to thank you for your assistance. As this is an ongoing investigation involving national security, you are not to discuss this case unless ordered to do so in the Regional United American Circuit Court." They got the drift of what he meant and the danger of violating his directives.

That night Ben fell asleep sprawled across the couch. It was relatively small, and the position he was in was decidedly uncomfortable. One foot was on the floor and his upper body was sort of crammed into the corner, propped up by the armrest. Despite his discomfort, he was too exhausted and the accumulated sleep deprivation pushed him into a deep sleep.

BANG! BANG! BANG!

There were three loud knocks on his door. Actually it was more like somebody was trying to kick it in. The hinges rattled, and a picture fell off the wall, the glass shattering in the process. Jolted out of sleep, Ben was at full attention as he rolled off the couch. In a fluid move, his pulsar was drawn. What he heard next was an electrical static sound followed by a barely audible pop. One pull of the trigger would have sent an energy wave through the door, blasting a hole clean through it, and set to maximum, anyone on the opposite side would be killed. He pulled the electrical cord out of the wall, and the lamp went out, cloaking the room in darkness.

"Who is it?" Ben asked. There was silence. He glanced at the clock. It was almost three o'clock in the morning. He grabbed a cushion from the couch. Standing to the side, he waved it in front of the peephole and brushed it against the door. Nothing happened. He eased toward the door and quickly glanced through the hole. No one was there.

Positioning himself adjacent to the inside of the door, by the hinges, he quietly listened. The elevator down the hall opened. He could hear someone walking toward his room. By the rate of the footsteps, it was more than a walk, but not quite a run. He quickly flung the door open as the footsteps approached. His pulsar was out in front of him and he took aim. It was a hotel bellhop, a woman. She had a toilet plunger in her hand. She was right there, moving past the door, at the very moment he flung it open. She jumped to the side, letting out a frightened yelp in the process. Her arms flailed outward and she fell against the opposite wall, stumbled, and fell to the floor.

Ben was surprised and embarrassed. "I'm sorry," he said. "I didn't mean to scare you." Holding his pulsar, he simultaneously scanned up and down the hallway while making an effort to help her up with his free hand.

The woman pulled away and fell again. "No!" she yelled. She kicked at him in a moment of frenzied panic.

"You're safe, Ma'am," he reassured in a hushed voice. "Government business. I'm an agent investigating a case. You're not in danger."

"Are you some kind of nut?" she asked incredulously.

"Someone kicked the door, then I heard footsteps coming down the hall. It was a terrible mistake." He tried to reconcile with her, extending his hand to help her up.

She glared at him, refusing his help as she got up and collected her plunger. She looked at his pulsar and then at him with utter disdain. "Government agent, my ass. You should be investigating yourself right along with this damned government." Her words, spoken to a loyal member of the Party, would have been a crime, but under the circumstances, he could hardly blame her. She turned and marched down the corridor mumbling loud enough to be heard. She called him a "stupid moron" and accused his central nervous system of being composed of excrement. Her exact words were, "shit-for-brains," far less eloquent, but much more direct. Even after that, she wasn't entirely done. She followed up with something about the indignity of having a college degree and having to plunge somebody else's toilet in the middle of the night.

Ben stepped back to reassess what just happened. That's when he discovered an envelope taped to his door. He snagged it and retreated back into his room. It was generic white with the letters *REO*, which meant 'right eye only,' written on the outside. It was common knowledge within the small community of individuals who possessed implanted BCDs that the device only picked up information through the left eye. When something was meant to be completely off the record, the left eye was blocked. Ben closed his left eye and cautiously held the envelope up to the lamp. He could make out the silhouette of a folded piece of paper. He removed it. It read:

SECURITY BREACH: BCD COMPROMISED. CONTACT TECH IMMEDIATELY AT NAIA. REPORT A BCD MALFUNCTION. WE ARE TAKING CORRECTIVE ACTION AND WILL OVERWRITE YOUR SYSTEM SO THE GOVERNMENT CAN'T MONITOR AND TRACK YOU. A FUNCTIONAL DECOY WILL BE PLACED IN THE FIELD. ANTICIPATE YOUR BCD WILL BE ACTIVE AND SECURE BY 1100 HOURS. PROCEED WITH INTERVIEWS UNTIL YOU RECEIVE FURTHER DIRECTIVES.

LISTENING/TRACKING DEVICES: NEW TECHNOLOGY - SOLES OF YOUR SHOES, BRIEFCASE, AND WALLET. AFTER CONTACTING THE NAIA, PLACE THE DEVICES IN THE ENVELOPE AND SECURE TO THE OUTSIDE OF YOUR DOOR. DO NOT COME INTO DIRECT CONTACT WITH THE TARGET UNTIL CLEARED. TARGET'S BCD HAS BEEN TAPPED. WE ARE WORKING TO CLEAR THE DEVICE. PREPARE FOR DEPARTURE WITH THE SUBJECT AT A MOMENT'S NOTICE. AFTER READING, PLACE THIS NOTE IN THE SINK AND ADD WATER.

At first, Ben was taken aback. It was starting already. Although his first instinct was to hastily search for the listening devices, he controlled himself and did as the note directed. He went into the bathroom, placed the note in the sink, and turned the water on. Immediately, the note dissolved and disappeared down the drain. Then he contacted NAIA tech support. He reported that there was a problem with the operation of his BCD. It didn't escape his notice that the auditory interface, having always been crisp and clear, was now choppy and compromised by static. They tried to connect remotely with his system, but when their efforts failed, he informed them he was indisposed, but after his current assignment, he would come in and have them perform a complete diagnostic.

He had to focus his racing thoughts and think each move through. The possibilities were endless, and a series of questions was rushing at him. Who authorized the operation to tap him? It had to be Zimmer. But how much did he know? Did this go all the way up to President Martinez? Was he a suspect in the government's eyes or was this a routine operation? Was his family safe?

Ben searched his personal belongings and found the tracking devices. They were revolutionary in size and composition, the technology cutting edge. There was no evidence of micro-machinery, no metal components, and no electromagnetic signature. Abandoning the typical microchip-based technology, they consisted of a melding of ceramic and self-sustaining organic materials, and in many ways functioned like a living organism.

He placed them in the envelope and taped it to the outside of his door. A few seconds later, he heard the same popping sound in the hallway. Then he heard it again. When he opened the door, the envelope was gone.

* * * * *

"I'm Dr. Benjamin Murray. What's your name?" Despite his distraction, Ben opened another formal interview. Six hours had passed, and it was 0900 in the morning. He leaned back in his chair. He was tired and felt the squeeze of anxiety.

Before jumping into the heart of the interview, he offered the woman coffee, or tea, as a means of helping her feel comfortable. The physiological indices his BCD was tracking—pulse and respiratory rate, eye movements, pupil dilation and constriction—all indicated she was suffering an extremely high level of apprehension. At the same time, her mannerisms were cold and stoic, and she promptly declined his offer.

"Do you mind?"

"No," she replied.

With her permission, he nursed a large steaming cup of black coffee. By this time, he had already had three cups, despite the fact that the hospital's brew smelled odd and tasted terrible. 'Beggars can't be choosers,' he thought. He was tired, and in order to do combat with the chemistries of his central nervous system, he had to resort to the tools on hand. Ben formally began the interview. "Please state your name and your position."

"I'm Lydia Capinelli. I'm a nurse in the surgical intensive care unit."

She was a crusty, unenthusiastic woman in her early fifties. He took note of the deep wrinkles that traversed the entirety of her forehead and her lack of effort in attending to the darkened circles under her eyes, or for that matter, to her mostly unkempt and oily hair. Against her attire, scrubs that were entirely too small, the increased girth of her arms and torso gave the impression that she had recently gained a significant amount of weight. He surmised that she was going through some stress in her life, something far beyond the routine demands of her job. Possibly it was because of an ongoing medical problem. Whatever it was, it caused her to simply stop caring for herself. There was no real way to know for sure, and quite frankly, he didn't care.

Lydia's matter-of-fact demeanor revealed that she had been legally deposed before. She knew the drill and wasn't going to offer much on her own. Ben held his cup, smiled, and took a drink, studying her all the while. While she wasn't the talkative type, leaning more toward stoicism, she was for all intents and purposes cooperative enough.

"Good. Good. You can call me Ben. How do you prefer to be addressed?" He began using a mirroring technique. Every body position she assumed, he subtly assumed the same. It was as if subconsciously she was looking into a mirror. He found it to be a very simple and easy technique that helped to ease the stress of the person being interviewed.

"Lydia is fine."

"Lydia it is then. Okay, Lydia," he also liked to use the name of the other person as much as possible without being obvious. A certain egocentric part of how people are hard-wired makes them enjoy hearing their own names. "I want you to relax. This isn't the inquisition. Lydia, you were recently involved in the care of a patient known as John Doe. I want to find out everything you know about him."

"I came into contact with the patient after his first series of surgeries," she began. It had taken a team of surgeons and a large contingent of personnel well over twenty hours in the operating room to put him back together. He bled so badly and required so much synthetic blood, it was estimated that he didn't have any of his own left. While he shouldn't have survived the surgeries, he did come out and made a right turn into the surgical unit rather than a left into the morgue. Even then there wasn't much hope. It was basically watch and wait. Despite heroic efforts to put John Doe back together, if he managed to survive it wasn't known how much mental capacity, if any, he would have left. The lack of blood and oxygen represented a severe trauma to his system, especially to his brain.

"He was in critical condition, and his prognosis was poor for the first two or three days."

"Would you describe his room for me?" Ben wanted her to talk.

"It's a state-of-the-art intensive care unit," she said. "It went in a year or two ago." Lydia went on to build a visual of walls covered by the latest in medical monitoring devices. Three-dimensional holographic images of his heart and lungs were to the patient's right. Another, of his kidneys and their associated vasculature, was positioned adjacent to the cardiopulmonary monitor. Each of the platforms displayed real time images of his internal organs that ranged from forty to fifty centimeters in height, width, and depth. They could be rotated, enlarged, or sliced into cross-sections, and digital readouts of various physiologic parameters, such as cardiac output, pulmonary pressures, renal perfusion pressures, and even glomerular filtration rates and numbers of functional glomeruli (measures of kidney function), could be analyzed by the team of specialists. At the same time, all of his pertinent biochemistries were being analyzed at a sampling rate of every sixty seconds. This data was fed through a computer algorithm that was integrated with dietary. In this manner, his intake of certain nutrients could be immediately regulated through his feeding tube. All his output...urine and feces, as well as losses through respiration and through his skin, were being closely monitored. On top of that, every thirty minutes, an alarm would sound, the personnel would step out of the room, and a laser pulse would emanate throughout the room to sterilize against microorganisms.

"It was on the third or fourth day when he unexpectedly woke up," she said. "It was on my shift. I was adjusting his breathing tube, and his eyes suddenly opened." After his life had been hanging in the balance for days, John Doe came out of his drug-induced sleep and became responsive. She went on, "I alerted the attending physician, and she, in turn, called in the consulting neurologist, who happened to be in the unit at the time. He examined the patient, and the first thing he did was split the neural monitor into multiple displays. That's routine," she explained, "when they want to simultaneously monitor several parameters all at once, such as the perfusion of blood to various parts of the brain, electrical activity, or glucose metabolism. He did some tests and confirmed that stimulation of the patient's extremities resulted in the appropriate patterns of neuronal firing in the brain, and his reflexes were intact." Lydia added, "Everyone was surprised that he appeared to have normal function."

What Lydia didn't mention was what they weren't able to assess, the state of his brain's ability to process information and his psychological state. The brain was different than other organs in that being "normal" meant far more than normal function on a monitor.

"He has an implant."

"What do you mean?" Ben asked.

"This thing in his skull," she said. "One of the surgeons said he's seen them before, that they're used in only the most elite soldiers." She was referring to his BCD. Lydia went on, saying, "It somehow integrates brain function with weapons systems. Apparently they're extremely rare and very advanced."

Ben thought, 'Yeah, Lydia, they are rare. So rare, in fact, that one of them is looking at you right now.' He had to admit that Lydia, despite her stoicism and flat affect, and his initial doubts about the usefulness of interviewing her, was proving to be a treasure trove of information.

"The surgeon mentioned that it was unlike any he had seen. It was designed to look older, but other aspects of it were more advanced. I don't know what all that means but the next day, when the patient woke up, he turned it on."

"What do you mean?" Ben wanted her to clarify.

"The implant, he turned it on."

"Who turned it on?"

"Apparently, the patient." She paused after making the declaration, then continued, "The neurologist was making his rounds, and several of us were there when it turned on. The patient was looking at us, and we could see the device come alive on the monitor. As soon as it did, his brain activity could be seen increasing on the monitors. I remember what the neurologist said. He explained how the parts of the brain, the occipital, frontal, temporal, and parietal lobes, and how the left and right hemispheres process and integrate information. He commented that we were studying the patient, and he was studying us back."

'Good. This is very good,' Ben thought. The patient's mind was working. It was a very good sign.

"I think he was right," she said, "after a couple minutes the implant turned off, and he drifted back to sleep." What Lydia didn't know was that the neurologist noticed far more than he let on. The BCD, at least from what he could determine from the electromagnetic signature and the overall appearance of the hardware on the monitors, was very different from anything he had ever seen. There were extra components, and it appeared more advanced. He guessed that it was a new prototype and decided to keep his mouth shut.

Shortly thereafter the patient began breathing on his own. After a couple more days, each with an increased amount of time breathing without ventilator assistance, his breathing tube was withdrawn. For several days thereafter, the patient was withdrawn. He didn't speak. It wasn't like he was scared, what Lydia described sounded more like apathy and hopelessness. Finally, in the middle of the night, she said that she was on duty when he spoke his first words.

Ben was taken aback. "He spoke to you?" His tone betrayed surprise.

"Yes."

"What did he say?"

"He asked me a question. He asked... 'What year is it?'"

'Oh my God,' Ben thought, 'it's really him.'

"When I told him, he acted as though he was horrified."

"What happened then?" His heart was racing.

"He asked me to look up some names on the Vintel."

"Do you remember them?" Ben asked. He was ready to explode.

"I remember that he said his name was Jake."

Ben was now being squeezed in breathless apprehension. 'My God! My God! It's really him!' His mind was screaming.

"I don't remember the others. There were several. All of them had the same last name. I think it started with the letter 'G,' but I just don't remember. He said I would find them in Spring Hill, Tennessee."

"And what did you tell him?"

"I got on the Vintel and searched the database. I tried to look them up. But the names weren't real."

"What did you tell him?"

"I told him I couldn't find anyone with those names."

"What did he say?"

"He was getting agitated. He asked me to do something really odd." Ben waited for her to finish. "He asked me to check back over the last sixty to seventy years. He told me a certain year, but I don't remember what it was."

"Did you do what he asked?"

"Yeah. As a matter of fact, I checked back a hundred years and didn't find anything."

"Did you tell him that?"

"Yeah. I told him exactly what I did, and I remember exactly what I told him." Ben's facial expression indicated that she should go on. "I told him that he was confused. That those people never existed."

"What did he do?"

"He just went crazy, screaming and crying. I never saw anything like it. All of his monitor alarms started going off. I remember looking at his cardiac monitor. His heart rate had been in the 60s and 70s, but then it shot up into the 140s. Before I could do anything he threw himself out of bed to the floor. We had to pull workers from the medical floor to help restrain him. It took three large guys to hold him down he was thrashing so much. He was so strong, even after all his injuries. We had to sedate him on the floor. Then we put him back in bed. He managed to pull most of his tubes and IVs out. I had to get everything restarted."

"That was the last time he spoke?" Ben asked.

"As far as I know, yes."

Ben thought about what she said for a few moments, then he added, "It was mentioned by others that when he came out of surgery, there were guards."

"Two of them at a time."

"Round the clock?"

"As far as I know."

"They didn't help you restrain him?"

"They weren't there."

Ben's slightly exaggerated reaction purposefully betrayed confusion.

She explained further, "As far as I know, they were there all the time. At least every time I was there. He had been sleeping for a while. Many of the medications he was given have sedative-like qualities, and it wasn't unusual for him to sleep most of the day. I guess they left for a while. I don't know where they went."

"Did they come back?"

"Yeah."

"When?"

"Within a minute or so after I called for assistance."

"And what happened?"

"They asked me what happened." Lydia looked away. It was the first time she avoided eye contact. Her body language didn't escape Ben's notice. Her level of discomfort escalated and her physiologic signals shot through the roof.

"Lydia, what did you tell them?" He was being as gentle as possible in his questioning, trying to avoid any sense of being a punitive authority figure.

"I told them he just woke up and went crazy."

"Did you tell them that he spoke?"

"No."

"Okay. Lydia, that's all right." He paused and looked away as if stumped by something. "Did you tell anyone that he spoke?" he asked.

"No."

"You didn't tell any other nurses or doctors? And you didn't chart it in the nurse's notes?"

"No," she answered, her tone failing to conceal her agitation. "Look, I thought I did something wrong, that I somehow caused his fit. We were under directives from the guards not to talk to him and to report anything he said. That wasn't unusual. We occasionally have to take care of criminals."

"Did you think he was a criminal?"

"I didn't ask. It's not important. Our job is to take care of the patient. There were guards so I assumed he was a criminal of some sort."

"But you spoke to him anyway."

"I'm sick of taking orders from people," she blurted out. Her pulse, which had been progressively dropping, had by now shot back up. "I take orders all day and at…," she paused. Lydia's lips were quivering, her hands shaking. She closed her eyes, took a breath, and collected herself. "Just once I wanted to be in control. I wanted to make my own decisions. And look what happened."

"Lydia," Ben said, "I assure you that you didn't do anything wrong." Thinking that her breakdown might be related to misplaced fears that she was in trouble he added, "and you're not going to be reprimanded.

The fact that he spoke to you is immaterial. I simply appreciate you being forthright with me." He understood the real reason she was being so cooperative…it was because he was conducting an investigation on behalf of the government, and she was scared. She wrongfully assumed that he knew everything already, and that he was hoping to catch her in a lie. "Remember," he said, "everything you tell me is confidential. I just have a few more questions."

Lydia nodded her head, indicating that she was ready.

"Would you describe the guards for me?"

"OK," she said, trying her best to focus. "They weren't military or regular police, as far as I could tell. They wore nice dark suits, and they had some sophisticated computer devices. They were always very professional." Lydia went on to mention that on several occasions she entered the room to find them hovering over the patient, saying things to him, like they were trying to interrogate him. She scolded them for bothering her patient and made them stand outside the room.

That was when Ben figured out that they must have bugged the room. There had to be a reason the patient wouldn't talk in front of them, so they faked him out. It was immediately after the incident that the guards disappeared. In his gut, he knew that they were Zimmer's men— minions of the Egalitarian Party.

So far, Ben's interviews confirmed that no one at the hospital, other than Lydia, had any knowledge that John Doe had spoken. He was perplexed. In his initial briefing with Zimmer and Tommy Dahlins regarding the case, they said he spoke. How did they know, if she hadn't told anyone? He mulled the maze of possibilities. The only explanation was that Zimmer didn't reveal everything he knew. He'd have to be very careful and assume the Party already knew everything he had learned from the interviews. Further, he couldn't shake his discomfort regarding John Doe's BCD being downloaded and erased. If the data fell into Fascist control all hope would be lost.

At the conclusion of her interview, Ben cancelled the next two meetings and followed Lydia into the intensive care unit. She showed him the room where John Doe was being treated, and she took him to the Vintel unit that she used to search for the names. Ben immediately removed the unit, and while en route back to the hotel, he contacted one of his team members, Oscar. He needed a computer expert to assist him in analyzing the unit.

"You want me to do what?" Oscar asked.

"I'm looking for specific verbal commands that were given at approximately this time and date," Ben showed Oscar a piece of paper with the information written on it and then he put it in his pocket to be destroyed. He added, "This is for my eyes only."

"You got it, Dr. Murray." Oscar was a happy-go-lucky computer whiz. Few were better at hacking through the data mountain security walls. Anyone else would risk execution for hacking the data mountain, but Ben was an Egalitarian Party insider, and Oscar was working under his umbrella. It wasn't the first time he'd been called upon for such an activity, and he assumed it wouldn't be the last. "I'll start thirty minutes before, and the unit will transcribe all the Vintel activity. Are we going to expunge the record?"

"The entire system," Ben said.

"Delete the entire unit signature?" Oscar was surprised.

Ben nodded. "I need all traces of the data and the computer signature gone forever. This Vintel unit never existed."

"Oooh," Oscar said. "Sounds interesting. Consider it done. The data will not only be deleted, it will be cyclically overwritten a million times in a few seconds. This particular Vintel unit's wormhole will be collapsed as though it never existed. It will be impossible to reproduce the search."

The Internet had evolved into something very different compared to what it once was. There weren't separate and individual servers scattered all over the country functioning independent of the State. It was now strictly controlled by the government and maintained in geographically specific data mountains. Each Vintel unit was connected to the data mountain complex by a signature that was somewhat like an umbilical cord. In that manner, the mother knew exactly where all her children were and exactly what was going in and out. In other words, the Egalitarian Party wielded the ultimate power…the power of information and the ability to monitor the activities and communications of its entire population.

Within a few short minutes, Oscar was probing inside the data mountain like a quantum assassin. He isolated the Vintel's wormhole from the opposite side, much like a virtual telescope looking back on itself. "Here we are. Thought you could hide from ol' Oscar did ya? Not today baby. Not today," He was talking to himself, but out loud. He turned to Ben, "Are you in a sharing mood today, Dr. Murray? Sounds spooky."

Ben laughed. "Way below your pay grade. Party business, you wouldn't want to know."

"Fair enough," he said. "It is transcribing from thirty minutes before starting…now." He pushed away from the unit and turned around so he couldn't see the monitor. He said, "All you have to do is function 12 and delete at the same time."

Ben moved between Oscar and the monitor and began reading through the transcription. It was mostly requests for lab results and various intensive care orders. He kept scanning until he got to Lydia's interaction with the unit. On the screen appeared the name - *Jake Gillean*. A wave of emotion swept over him. His heart began racing, and his eyes welled with tears. He couldn't believe it. He was actually seeing in print the name of the last great hope for freedom and liberty. At the same time, he saw a life that, if protected and nurtured, might help destroy the indomitable power of Fascism. He gathered himself and read the rest of the names - *Wendy*, *Bailey*, and *Paul Gillean*. Then he read the year Lydia searched—*2379*, a year that had slipped sixty-two years into the past.

As he tried to absorb what he was reading, Ben felt like he had been punched in the stomach. He deleted the information just as Oscar instructed and excused himself. A moment later, he was in the bathroom flushing his face with water. He leaned against the sink and looked at the image in the mirror. He was struck by the lack of youth. He looked old and overwhelmed. There were bags under his eyes from sleep deprivation, his eyebrows were thicker than he remembered, and the wrinkles traveling across his forehead and erupting at the corners of his eyes were deeper and more pronounced than he recalled. He told himself that there wasn't time. He took a breath and turned to the next task.

The computer was torn apart, and he took the vital components so they could be incinerated. The rest he threw in the trash dumpster behind the hotel. Afterward, he took a long walk around the hospital, taking in every nuance of its layout and character.

So far he had been thorough. No one in hospital administration or security had any inclination who the guards were, or who sanctioned their operation. Frustrated by the lack of information, Ben checked with several of his sources at the MPS. The results came back negative. No record of the assignment was found anywhere within the agency. This left several troubling questions. As complex and important as the developing case was, it was very unlikely that Zimmer would have neglected to post a detail to watch over the subject. Ben also considered that since his interrogation group was highly compartmentalized within the MPS, and operated as an unknown, that there had to be other groups hidden under the auspices of the NAIA. These groups would be under Zimmer's direct control and were likely watching over Jake Gillean since shortly after his arrival.

The communications system in Ben's BCD reactivated. He saw the specs rolling past and then verification that the encryption systems were working. Then he heard the communication. "Dr. Murray?" It was the same ominous voice that had notified him of Jake's arrival. It was the leader of the secret society.

"Yes."

"Your BCD is clear. The breach has been corrected. All communications are now secure."

"What's going on?"

"Director Zimmer has two other teams on the case. One is operating out of the DSS and another is a rogue organization off the radar."

"He ordered that I be tapped?"

"Yes. That was carried out by the DSS."

"Has my cover been compromised?"

"No. Your cover is secure. It was a routine operation. Each group is assigned to watch the other. The hospital is a DSS op. The security chief, Martin Zagger, is a DSS operative and the team leader. Lt. Col. Gillean is being watched. We have men in place ready to move, but we need to know exactly what Zagger knows. You'll have to perform a forced interrogation. Seize the opportunity, but your cover needs to be maintained at all costs."

"How am I supposed to perform an interrogation on a DSS operative and maintain my deep cover?" Ben asked. He was feeling the pressure, skeptical that he could pull it off. The DSS agents were formidable, their training intense. It was also a brotherhood. Taking out an agent would incur the animosity and wrath of the entire agency. It had come down to this moment. Intense internal conflict twisted at his insides. As part of MPS, he had worked closely with the DSS over the greater part of two decades. He had grown to consider them kindred spirits, and now he was being asked to turn on them and commit what they would consider murder.

"They don't know what you know," the voice said. "From their perspective, you don't know that they are on the case. All you know is that Zimmer said an unknown party downloaded the memory from Jake's BCD. The implication is that another interest, hostile to the government, is in the field. Remember, you are a patriot and a loyal member of the Egalitarian Party. You are on a mission and are acting in the direct interests of a government asset against a perceived threat. After he's down, communicate that through his BCD, and then it has to be destroyed." Following a brief pause the voice directed, "After his communications capabilities are destroyed, perform the interrogation and eliminate him. We move on your signal to secure the target and move him to a safe location. The President explicitly put you in charge of his safety. It is expected that you will, under the circumstances, act decisively and aggressively. Given your capabilities they will expect him to disappear off their radar. You have acted alone to move him underground, and everything you have done is for the sole purpose of protecting him in the setting of a possible leak of classified information within the NAIA. Communicate that to Zimmer immediately following the move. You will also tell him that you found a listening device planted by Zagger, you suspect he was a spy, and he died before you could interrogate him. Because of your BCD malfunction, you didn't know he also had a BCD. When you used your pulsar it caused a sudden discharge that resulted in his immediate death. Zimmer is already aware that the previous tracking devices planted on you were compromised. He assumes it was a technological malfunction. He ordered Zagger to plant a new device on your person. That will be your pretext for taking him out."

"Okay," Ben said. He had his doubts, but it was the best chance they had under the circumstances. "What can you tell me about Zagger?" The leader of the secret society actually had more assets on the ground and better capabilities than Zimmer, but the whole scenario remained incredibly risky.

"He's armed—pulsar in an underarm holster and another at his ankle. He was special ops and is a black belt." There was a pause. The leader knew what Ben was thinking, then added, "Pick your moment. Strike hard and fast. Don't give him the opportunity to react. He'll rely on brute strength in a close quarters fight. Strike fast. Go for his neck."

"I'll get it done," Ben said. "I'm moving now." His nerves were firing somewhere between anxiety and panic.

Everything was moving rapidly. The threat wasn't hypothetical anymore, it was real. Since Jake materialized at the reenactment, it was going down very much the way Ben imagined in his nightmares—fast, convoluted in its maneuverings, and no matter what they did, there were no margins for error. As he quickened his pace toward Zagger's office, Ben checked his equipment. His pulsar was unstrapped in his underarm holster and ready when he would need it, his interrogation device was set for rapid application, and in his right pocket was a neural destabilizer. The last device was the key. He had to take Zagger alive, but he had to be completely immobilized and unable to speak. The last thing Ben wanted to do was trade blows with the man, especially in light of his training. He'd have to work the situation and find a way to smash the destabilizer hard into the back of his neck. The key was getting him to cooperate. If everything went as planned, and the device was properly applied, it would do its cruel work to perfection.

As Ben made his way across the campus and approached the security office, he ran through the scenarios. He determined that no matter how things went from here, this was indeed a cause worth dying for. He also recognized that since the briefing, he had grown accustomed to thinking about the subject as John Doe. Now he realized that it was nothing more than a cheap trick, a defense mechanism perpetrated on him by a nervous mind. The man wasn't a John Doe, and he knew it. His name was Lt. Col.

Jake Gillean. His was a name an entire nation knew a long time ago, and if he did everything perfectly, if everything worked as planned, it would be a name that everyone would know again.

A few minutes later, Ben was in the office of the head of hospital security. After flashing his ID the secretary quickly ushered him into the security chief's office. She closed the door and left them to make their own introductions.

"Before I answer any questions, do you mind if I check your credentials?" Zagger asked.

Ben stood in front of the desk while Martin Zagger remained sitting. He agreeably reached into the inside breast pocket and pulled out his ID. Before he handed it over he said, "Please feel free." He tossed it on the desk so that it landed right in front of Zagger. "I think you'll be surprised who I answer to." Ben took note of his reaction. He didn't make an effort to catch it, but instead he followed it with his eyes. The ID ended up in front of him, his neck was in almost complete flexion, and his head was angled downward. It was just a split second, but it was the hard-wired neurologic reflex Ben was looking for. It might prove to be useful later.

"Can never be too careful," Zagger stated. His tone was nonchalant. He played it cool and picked up the ID. If the information Ben received was accurate, and Zagger had been ordered to plant a tracking device, this was the perfect opportunity. He would likely try to find some means of distracting Ben. He asked, "Who did you say you worked for?"

"I'm with the MPS."

"Interesting," he said. He looked at the ID and asked, "Do you mind if I call for confirmation?"

"By all means," Ben agreed.

Zagger routed a contact through his desktop communicator to the Central Office of the MPS in New Washington. Placing the device on speaker so Ben might hear, he was transferred to confirmations and promptly put on hold while Ben's number was being verified. Zagger had swiveled his chair to the side and for a brief moment the ID slipped out of sight below the edge of the desk. At the same time, he looked at Ben and chuckled, "My apologies for the inconvenience. You know how these things go." He pointed at a picture hanging on the wall. "Do you hunt?"

As Ben turned to look at the picture, the voice came back over the communicator confirming that the ID checked out. The picture Zagger referred to was of him and a boy, presumably his son. They were proudly holding up the antlers of a dead buck, suspending the head between them.

"No," Ben admitted. "Can't say that I do." By the time he turned back,

Zagger was handing him the ID.

"Great bonding experience. Do you have children?"

Ben didn't answer. He studied Zagger's expression. He was good, a real poker face. If he hadn't known what to expect he might have missed it, but it was audacious for him to plant the device right in front of him, especially knowing that Ben worked for the MPS and that he would be wary. It bespoke an incredible degree of something, either aggressiveness and confidence, or complete stupidity. Ben smiled and took the ID, nonchalantly returning it to his pocket. "How long have you worked here?" he asked.

"Twenty-seven years," Zagger answered, "the last eight sitting behind this desk."

"Being here that long you probably know where all the bodies are buried?" Ben commented.

"I suppose you could say that," Zagger chuckled. The laugh was a little too contrived.

"Are you from around here?"

"Born and raised." He was exceedingly forthcoming, not seeming to notice that he was being interrogated. He was a loud-voiced man of medium stature, in his mid-fifties. He sported a thick brown moustache and a short beard, styled and groomed with precision. His clothes were meticulously ironed and creased, and his office was clean enough to pass any military inspection.

A few more questions and Ben discovered that the guy certainly liked talking about himself, deviating ever so slightly toward being a braggart. All things considered, he was good. He played the role of being a big fish in a small pond to perfection. He was also a sieve of information, but none of it useful and most of it lies. He claimed he had married a local girl, that they had three children ranging from elementary through late high school, and that he didn't get along with the hospital administrator. Ben noticed that Zagger had deformed ears. In the old days, they were called *cauliflower ears*. It was from trauma, likely from fighting. Usually they were found on one side, but he had them on both. His neck was thick and muscular. Because of his clothes, Ben couldn't assess exactly what he looked like, but all evidence suggested that he was incredibly muscular and fit. Under the circumstances, he definitely didn't want to trade blows with the man. It had to be one strike. Otherwise he'd have to use his pulsar and kill him outright.

A coldness came over Ben as they interacted. He wasn't nervous anymore. His heart wasn't racing. What he felt was a surge of adrenaline, but while his body was being primed for an all out attack, his brain was holding his heart in check, keeping the rate nice and normal. He was a predator stalking his prey, constantly calculating and probing for an opening.

"I would like to look at the hospital's security recordings dating back to early December," he said. As they talked, he very subtly moved in front of Zagger's desk. He'd back away and then, taking advantage of distracting conversation, he'd move closer, always with his right shoulder slightly forward and his approach off angle. Then he'd move back again. The movements were graceful, and if he was lucky, they'd be lost in the background to the point that Zagger wouldn't notice—that is, he wouldn't notice his visitor was getting in position to kill him.

"You're too late," he said. "They've already been taken."

"By who?"

Ben's BCD alerted him to an incoming message. He played through it, continuing the conversation despite hearing another voice. "Dr. Murray. We have confirmation. He has succeeded in planting a tracking device. He is receiving communications through his BCD from his handlers at DSS headquarters. We are rerouting his communications through to you."

"Would expect you to know," Zagger said. "MPS. A woman. Early forties, attractive, with short blonde hair. She had MPS clearance. Flashed a badge to prove it. Just like you."

"When?"

"A week ago."

Ben could hear the voice Zagger was hearing through his BCD. "*Tracking device is functional. Repeat. Tracking device is functional.*"

"Let me ask you something," Ben said, changing his demeanor and hitting the chief with an unexpected question. "Did you verify that this woman was in fact with the MPS?"

"Yes, I did."

Ben detected that Zagger's heart rate slightly increased. "I would like to look at your communicator's log," Ben said. "It should indicate the date and time that you ran the inquiry."

Zagger's heart rate was getting higher, and his pupils were dilating. At the same time, Ben heard the DSS communications, "*Be advised that Dr. Benjamin Murray's BCD is offline due to technical failure. We have no means of communicating with him. He may—*"

Ben spoke louder to distract Zagger, "I can access the record and find out exactly who this woman is."

"*—consider you to be a hostile,*" his DSS handlers warned.

"Tell me, Chief Zagger, does this woman actually exist?" Ben's voice was raised.

"*Be careful. He is a—*"

"Does she actually exist?!" Ben asked with his voice slightly louder. In the process of moving away from the desk, he reached into his inside breast pocket and removed his ID. He grasped it in his left hand and turned slightly so that Zagger couldn't see him check with his right hand the position of the neural destabilizer. It was in his pocket and ready to go. He pulled his hand out and began moving in for the kill.

Zagger was confused. Suddenly there was too much happening. He couldn't participate in two conversations at once. He blinked and mumbled something. It was incoherent.

The communication continued, "—*he is a class one interrogator. He's a real*—" Zagger couldn't process the information. It was coming in too fast. He could hear his DSS caretakers, but he couldn't comprehend what they were saying and at the same time maintain a conversation that was quickly deteriorating.

"Who do you work for?!" Ben yelled. His BCD indicated that Zagger's heart rate was spiking and his muscles were tightening. He was getting ready to push away from the desk and stand up.

"—*killer. Keep your distance. He thinks you're…*" the DSS warned.

"Is this the woman?!" Ben yelled. At the same time he said it, he threw the ID down on the desk. Zagger's head reflexively angled downward. Ben lunged forward.

"—*a hostile,*" the DSS finished.

Ben caught Zagger behind the head with his right hand. At the same time, he grasped a handful of hair and tried to smash his face into the desktop. His action was like an explosion and he spared no energy. But Zagger was fast. He slapped his arms onto the table in front of him, and with a fighter's reflexes and the brute strength of the muscles in his neck he extended his head upward against Ben's efforts. But it was just as Ben planned. In the fraction of a second that it took for Zagger to fight off the first thrust of force he had exposed himself and sealed his fate. His arms were planted on the desk, he was rising up out of his chair, and the front of his neck was fully exposed. Ben's clenched left fist was already plunging toward its target. It impacted Zagger's trachea and smashed it backward—the blow primal and grotesque. There was no resistance as Zagger's body convulsed and fell back into his chair. Just as quickly, his body lurched forward with projectile vomiting. His face was red. All the messages being sent to his brain screamed that he was choking to death. As he fought to take a breath Ben grabbed his head with both hands and with all his might, he smashed it into the top of the desk. The resultant crunch of Zagger's face against the wood was sickening, breaking his nose and jaw. He bounced and lay across its surface. Ben pulled the destabilizer out of his pocket and quickly punched it into the back of his neck. When it activated, Zagger went into a spasm, stood bolt upright, and then fell backward and was writhing on the floor. The cervical destabilizer prevented him from controlling his muscles. He was still fighting, but the response was much like having a seizure, except that he was conscious, fighting for breath, and in tremendous pain.

Ben moved around the desk and stood over Zagger. He slowly extracted the tracking device from the back of his ID. He held it up so that it would be seen and transmitted through Zagger's BCD, knowing the image was going straight to DSS headquarters.

"Oh, no!" came the communication through the BCD. *"Zagger! Get out of there! Get out of there!"*

"Who do you work for?" Ben asked. He was calm and cold-blooded. "What's your interest in the patient? Are you a traitor? Have you betrayed this country and the Party? Do you belong to another country?" Ben looked down at him and with a grin of satisfaction he whispered, "Hmm, is that it? Are you a spy? We'll find out soon enough."

"Hold on! We're calling in back up! Agent Zagger! Respond! Respond!" Zagger's eyes were wide with panic and fear. His nose was smashed sideways and split to the point that is was almost unidentifiable. Blood was streaming down his face while red-tinged foam was spitting out of his mouth.

"Having a little trouble breathing? I need you to relax," Ben said, "After I help you settle down, we're going to find out everything you know." At that moment a low energy blast from his pulsar, which he was holding off to the side, destroyed Zagger's BCD. All communications with DSS immediately went silent.

There was no time to waste. Ben removed his interrogation device and pushed it into Zagger's forehead. It unfolded like a living entity. It grabbed into his scalp, continuing until it covered his entire skull, extending up what was left of his nasal vault and protruding deep into his ears. Ben opened the interface between his BCD and the interrogation device and began probing his victim's neural network, callously ripping away the conscious controls Zagger had taken for granted since birth. Martin Zagger's eyes were wide with absolute fright, and he tried to scream…at first.

CHAPTER 6: TORMENTED

(51 days have passed since the target was extracted from
New Bethesda Hospital)

[APRIL 2, AD 2441]
[122 DAYS AFTER ARRIVAL]
[LOCATION: IN A REHAB FACILITY IN NORTHERN QUEBEC]

Jake Gillean ran through the scenarios, reviewing the files stored on his BCD. He was trying to connect the foggy details of the last several months. He didn't know how he got there or how he leapt through time and ended up in the Twenty-Fifth Century. He was on the battlefield, the year was 1864, everything was going dark, and then his next formed memories, although cloudy, were of being in the critical care unit. He was floating in and out of consciousness, only intermittently aware of his surroundings, of the repetitive and rhythmic noise of the machinery, of the air flowing in and out of his breathing tube, and of the seemingly endless parade of specialists moving in and out of his room. Everything was blurry, but he remembered that it registered in awareness. Jake had been in the intensive care unit for several days when brief spasms of arousal resulted in flashes of dreams intermingled with reality. Images of his imaginations and of his surroundings would fleetingly emerge into focus and then retreat into nothingness.

In the first days, two DSS agents were keeping guard. They maintained their distance, and at first, they observed without interfering. But they were like gargoyles, always watching, biding their time, waiting for the perfect opportunity to ply their trade. Their relative inaction was ultimately determined by two factors, both completely beyond their control—their target's inability to maintain consciousness and the constant presence of medical personnel.

At the same time, an entirely different plot was being carried out, unbeknownst to anyone except the leader of the secret society. Like clockwork each night, the covering intensivist, a physician specializing in the care of patients in the critical care unit, would make a special stop at Jake's bedside. Thoroughly seasoned by years of experience practicing medicine, he had become exceedingly subtle in his movements. His actions were not only reminiscent of the slight of hand techniques used by magicians; they were in fact the same. He would examine the holographic images and scroll through the physiologic data. In the process, he would turn up the volume so that each heartbeat and the flow of blood across the valves and through the aorta would drown out the other sounds in the room – LUB – DUBB...LUB-DUBB...LUB-DUBB. Then he'd overlay the sounds of the patient's breathing. Each mechanical breath in and out was audible behind the indomitable sound of the heartbeat like a great biological symphony. Then he would turn and examine the patient. With each visit to the bedside, he would secretly give an injection. It was a compound designed to speed healing. It worked through a complicated process wherein immune activity and the rate of cellular recovery, growth, and reconstruction were substantially enhanced. There was no record of the compound anywhere in the known world. For all intents and purposes, he was acting unilaterally. If caught, that was his story, and he wouldn't deviate. Although neither knew it, Ben and the doctor in the ICU were members of the same secret society, their dedication to the protection of Jake Gillean were one in the same. It had taken the secret society over fifty years and required an incredible investment of resources to develop the drug that he was injecting. Its solitary purpose was to speed healing and thus enhance the likelihood of his ultimate survival.

Despite the fact that the guards were always at his bedside and were attentive in watching his every movement, the physician administered the drug without arousing suspicion. It was only because of his skill that they remained oblivious to what he was really doing. The injector was around his wrist and was designed to look like a watch. The micro-syringe was on the palm side of the band. While examining the endotracheal tube and opening the patient's eyelids with one hand, he would brush the band along Jake's shoulder and make the injection with the other.

Included in the list of unintended consequences, the medication promoted nightmares, making them substantially vivid and disturbing... and rendering it harder, almost impossible, to wake up.

"Aaaauuugghh!" he would scream out. "NO! NO! NO!" In a panic he would fight and claw. The imagery was always horrifying, yet he couldn't wake. It was vile death and disgust, and it was everything cold and callous. It was the brutal reality of what Jake's life had become.

What the staff witnessed was the patient crying in his sleep, or suddenly jerking and gesturing like he was going to scream…but nothing came out, at least in the beginning, as the breathing tube extended down his throat. His movements were interpreted as nothing more than basic reflexes and were dismissed from concern.

Once the breathing tube was pulled out, due to the combination of laryngeal swelling and soft tissue damage, as well as generalized weakness, Jake wasn't able to speak. That's when he first discovered someone had pulled the memory out of his BCD. They erased the quantum drives, but whoever did the work failed to recognize its redundant back-up systems. All the memory was still there, hiding in deeper secondary and tertiary vaults within his device. He reformatted the primary systems and repopulated them with all the information he collected over the course of almost eight years of fighting. It was during his review of what happened when he was unconscious that he discovered DSS agents were guarding him. He listened with great interest to the recording. They were having conversations at his bedside without any inclination his BCD had the ability to record when deactivated. "Tell us what you know. Who are you?" they asked. They chuckled as they outlined methods they might employ to get him to talk. That's when Jake decided to remain silent. He would do so until he regained his strength and sorted everything out.

What Jake's plan succeeded in doing was getting his physicians to suspect he suffered a brain injury; that areas of the brain controlling speech had been damaged. They speculated that it was the result of trauma and blood loss that in turn resulted in decreased blood flow and a lack of oxygen delivery to the sensitive neural tissue. While his brain scans came back normal, he simply appeared to have no ability to communicate verbally. He was either too weak, or the injuries prevented him from communicating through writing.

Three days before discharge from the critical care unit, Jake found himself awake and alone. He was in tremendous pain. His right upper chest and right thigh were the worst. 'It must be pain medication,' he thought, recognizing that his mind was sluggish and that the urge to sleep was heavy. He felt a throb in his right hand. His fourth and fifth fingers were aching as though pliers were squeezing across each digit. He slowly raised it up. The hand was wrapped in a clear dressing that went across the base of the ring finger, revealing that it was missing, and only a small stump of the fifth finger remained.

'It's not mine,' he thought as he looked at the hand. 'It can't be. I can feel my fingers. I can move them.' He didn't remember that he had been through this process already. He moved his thumb and the first two fingers. They followed his commands. Then he got to the missing fingers. 'Oh no.

What happened?' He pondered the morose discovery and then gingerly laid the hand down. He studied his surroundings. The guards who had been hovering were gone. He had an opportunity.

"Nurse," he called out. His voice was hoarse and weak, and the effort made his chest hurt. The room felt like it was floating, and the walls were giving subtle hints that they were breathing. "Nurse."

Nurse Lydia swore she heard something. She looked around. Maybe it was just her imagination. Then she heard it again. She stepped into John Doe's room whereupon her expression betrayed surprise. He was awake, looking at her with inquisitive, almost pleading, eyes. He gestured for her to lean in. There was a sense of urgency.

"What year is it?" he whispered. Jake felt a wave of building anxiety choking at his words.

Lydia was confused. "It's 2440." She answered as though it was a queer thing to ask.

"2440?" Jake was shocked. The monitors indicated that his heart rate and blood pressure were increasing. 'NO! NO! NO!' his mind screamed. 'It can't be! What have I done!'

Lydia studied his reaction with detached curiosity. He had grown sullen and his strength seemed to weaken. The whole thing struck her as strange. "Is something wrong?" she asked.

Jake fought against the panic and again motioned for her to lean close. "Will you find someone for me?" His voice was barely audible.

"Sure," she agreed. Lydia thought it might be an opportunity to help him find someone important, maybe a family member.

"Look for the name Gillean. Wendy, Bailey, and Paul Gillean. My name is Jake. Jake Gillean."

Lydia returned to the bedside a few minutes later, after running a search on the Vintel. "I couldn't find anyone by those names," she said.

Jake's panic was escalating. "Please," he said, his voice beseeching her to help. "Check back. Check the year 2379. Spring Hill, Tennessee. We lived there." When Lydia turned and walked away he felt the urge to pray. It was nearly overwhelming. But he couldn't. He couldn't pray, not now, not after everything that happened and after everything he had done.

'That was sixty-one years ago' she thought. 'There's no way he lived there. He has to be delirious.' Lydia returned to his bedside and announced, "I think you're confused. I looked everywhere, even went back a hundred years. Those people never existed."

"No. no," Jake cried out. The room began spinning, and the walls were bulging in and out as though gasping for air. As he fully comprehended the horror of what he had done, he screamed out, "NO! NO!" Several bedside alarms began bleating as the monitors tracked his out of control systems. Tears were streaming down his face. Losing all sense of reality he bolted upright, into a sitting position. He lurched to the side, screaming out in misery as he hit the floor. Wires and lines ripped away and several pieces of equipment toppled as he fell. Tangled in the bedding his feet were momentarily suspended and he landed on his shoulder. He was shaking and screaming on the floor and began coughing up blood that smeared across his face and streaked the white tile. The suffering he experienced was so deep that he had no realization of the trauma the fall had caused.

Lydia punched the alarm and the announcement, "Mr. Strong to the ICU. Mr. Strong to the ICU," blared over the section loudspeakers. Within moments several employees converged and Jake was subdued. Once they pinned him down, Lydia used a pneumosyringe to administer a sedative in his neck. He went limp. They lifted him into bed and secured his wrists and ankles to the side rails.

Assessment indicated that he reinjured his left shoulder, and a fractured rib that hadn't healed pierced his lung. An operation was required to fix the damage, and he eventually recovered uneventfully. The DSS agents returned briefly after his exchange with Lydia and then disappeared. Thereafter, because of the emotional trauma, Jake wouldn't speak.

True to the known side effects of the compound that the secret society was clandestinely administering to speed healing, Jake's dreams became an inescapable horror. It began in the critical care unit, increased in intensity after transfer to the medical floor, and continued after Ben secreted him out of New Bethesda Hospital and transferred him to the rehab facility. Then seven weeks passed. Although the injections stopped when he was transferred, the side effects proved resilient, and the nightmares kept up their vicious assault. They usually embodied the same general themes...

The stench of death was so thick that the air felt greasy going in and out of his nose. It was overwhelming. It was suffocating. A lone Confederate soldier dismounted his black steed at the edge of a worn and abused battlefield. He breathed the gasses emanating from human flesh that had been left unattended and forgotten, the corpses of men who were left to rot in the open air. His brain bathed in the milieu of noxious chemicals. It permeated all his senses. It was nothing less than the odor of hell.

There wasn't any noise. Complete silence sliced through the stillness until it was deafening. Only with that realization did the incessant hum of flies doing their work slowly rise to the edge of perception. Gradually, at its own pace, it became more intense. A random, revoltingly engorged specimen, fat from feeding on human flesh, would land on his face. He'd flick it away without giving it any thought.

Bodies of dead Union and Confederate soldiers were lying in a variety of contorted positions. Most remained in the positions in which they fell. Others held in their dead hands chunks of earth they had inadvertently collected in the process of pulling themselves along the ground. Trails of dark blood bore witness that they were crawling when they died, crawling to a safety that eluded them, a safety that didn't exist. Many had spilled their entrails. The rapidly drying organs trailed behind, giving the appearance that they were anchored to the earth. All the men were without shoes. Their shirts and coats were laid open. Mostly it was postmortem bloating. For some, their fellow soldiers had rifled through their pockets, taking any possessions that had worldly value. The less fortunate lived long enough to see their friends and foes rummage through their vestments, robbing them not only of their valuables, but their dignity, and the last vestiges of belief they had in the good will of their fellow man. Their last waning hope before joining the ranks of the dead was that their families might find release from the prison of loss and loneliness, that they might learn of their loved one's death. They died, anonymous and alone, knowing that news of their death, news of their bravery, would never be delivered.

The men and boys lay on the field, their lives spent for such a great cause. It was the cause of their generation, a cause perpetuated by the few. They made the ultimate sacrifice for something they would never realize. Their lives were actually gone. Most never expected it to happen to them; as horrible as their experiences had been it was always the other guy who was wounded or who died. They naively thought they would somehow be spared death's eternal grasp.

Did their mothers foresee such a thing? When they were born, when they held their beautiful and innocent babies in their arms and pondered their futures, when they prayed to God for the blessings of health and guidance; was it even a passing thought that they might die like this, that a life cut short would be their lot? Did their mothers know? Did the mothers know that as their children's hearts beat their last that they cried out like babies...that they pleaded not only for God and for forgiveness, but that they called out for their mothers? This was the cost of man's folly...the gift of life auctioned in exchange for the illusion of power. In the end, the call of the auctioneer would prove irresistible, and payment could only be made in the smothering embrace of death.

As Jake made his way through the maze of entangled bodies, he could hear ghostly voices crying out. He perceived flashes of their dying moments. He saw their faces. He heard the sounds of their final moments. The haunting images were chaotically attacking his mind. He was lost, surrounded by dead men as far as his eyes could see in every direction. He could feel his heartbeat. He could hear it pounding...pounding...a regular incessant pounding. He wanted to fall to his knees and scream so loudly that it would all go away; but he couldn't. He didn't know why he was there, why was he subjecting himself to the horrors of the battlefield when every other creature valuing life had so obviously fled. He suffered the realization that every experience he had in life had irrevocably changed him, but was this all that was left...death? What was he doing there? The shadow of a vague memory whispered that he was searching for something... but he didn't know what it was. There was a deep emptiness within him; a void that he *guarded yet longed to fill. He would recognize the object of his search if he would just see it.*

A deep moaning sound pierced the still air. He turned in a quick panic to search out the source. In the midst of several destroyed cannon and caissons, a body lay sprawled over the wreckage. The dead man's head was hanging off the edge of a broken wheel, Jake was suddenly paralyzed with fear, yet he couldn't avert his gaze. The corpse seemed to be looking directly at him, staring right through him, peering into the depths of his soul. The skin had a copper color, but darker over the cheeks. Long blood-soaked hair pulled downward as if the ground was attempting to reclaim its child. A sickly beard and moustache clung to his lip and chin. Pressurized gas escaped from the bowels, finding release through the corpse's throat, producing a baritone gurgling moan. The face was covered with flies. They penetrated the ears, the nostrils, and the mouth. They covered the eyelids, frantically trying to fight their way inside. Gluttonous maggots crawled over one another giving the impression of continuous writhing movements in an open neck wound.

The corpse's head seemed to move. It was a subtle, very slight movement. Jake was absolutely terrified, paralyzed with abject fear, yet he was unable to move, unable to turn and run, unable to wake from his own tortured thoughts. He felt hands on his body, dozens of hands. They were powerful and cold. They grabbed him from behind, pinning his arms to his side, squeezing the sides of his face. They prevented him from turning. They pushed him closer to the corpse. Now he was screaming. He could hear it inside his head, but nothing came out. The grotesque face of the corpse was getting closer. It was only inches away.

Suddenly, at that very moment, he recognized the corpse as himself, as his soul. That's when the dead man's eyes opened, and he turned his head. In a hellish expiration the corpse called out, "WHY!?" The flies immediately attacked him. They covered his face and head. He broke free, but the flies were undeterred by the slaps of his hands. The harder and faster the slaps came, the more flies there were. They covered his eyes, were in his nose, his mouth, and his clothes. Again and again he heard the long drawn out "WWWHHHYYYYY!" He panicked. He was being suffocated. He couldn't breathe. He felt the flies in his throat strangling and gagging him.

Despite Jake's closed door, his whoop-like scream echoed down the hall. He jolted awake in a pool of sweat and panic. He was in a sitting position, his heart pounding rapidly, hyperventilating. His face was sore and his nose bleeding from hitting himself. He reoriented to his surroundings, he was in rehab, in his room.

'Dammit! Dammit! Dammit!' his mind screamed. He was powerless to stop the nightmares and was fatigued beyond expression. He clenched his fists tight, basking in the desire to strike out against the incredible tension.

Within a few moments, his nurse appeared in the room. She found him sitting on the edge of the bed. He was wet with sweat, and blood was oozing from his right nostril.

"Another nightmare?" she inquired, her voice delicate and careful.

Jake didn't respond. Her voice sounded like an echo from a distant land. He felt numb. 'I can't do this anymore,' he thought. 'I'm broken. I don't belong here.'

The nurse hummed a tune while gently wiping his face with a damp cloth. She was at ease, and he felt her acts of kindness penetrating the foreboding darkness of his ruminations. Jake looked ahead, his mind still reeling from the shock of the nightmare.

"If you ever want to talk about them…" she said, recognizing that he was silent by choice. That much was common discussion around the nurses' station. For some reason, he was choosing to live in hell all by himself. She held one hand under his chin and wiped the blood from his mustache. 'It's sad,' she thought, 'the other patients invite everyone to join them in versions of hell, but he won't. He's so different.' She refreshed the cloth and wiped his upper lip and nose again. "I brought you a fresh gown and linens. If you get up, I'll change the bedding for you."

Jake did as she asked, and she replaced his sweat soaked linens. The next two times she looked in, he was standing, staring out his window, position unchanged. Ten minutes later, she peeked in again. He was lying on his side and had drifted back into a restless slumber. She would keep her distance when he was sleeping. One night he startled, and with reactions like a predator, he grabbed her arm. The sudden move made her scream. The look on his face was one of horror when he realized what he had done. His eyes welled with tears, and he immediately recoiled, refusing to look at her, and again refusing to communicate in any meaningful way.

His recovery was progressing ahead of schedule. It had been an hour and Lt. Col Jake Gillean was still running on the treadmill. Sweat poured off of him, but his pace remained the same…fast.

"Look at him," one of the assistants commented to the therapist.

"I know. Remember when he first got here? He could hardly walk."

"I've never seen anything like it. Why is he still here?"

"Oh, I suspect he'll be leaving in a day or two. Have to squeeze the last drop out of his benefits," he chuckled sarcastically.

Jake was more akin to a machine than a man. Week after week, he continued to live in silence, and other than his nurse, no one pretended to care. The overworked staff actually wished more of the patients would simply stop talking and emulate Jake's audacious motivation to recover. In the first week, despite tremendous pain, he walked with the therapist in the hall. At first it was only a couple steps. Then it was more, a hundred yards or so. He started going off the floor to physical therapy. The walking eventually evolved into an exceedingly arduous mile. Then it was several miles. Soon thereafter he was jogging on the treadmill. Then he was able to speed up to an actual run. His new legs and bones were, for all intents and purposes, as good as the originals and better than most others. In the last two weeks, his run times were down to less than eight minutes per mile, and the distance steadily increased from there. Through lifting weights and eating everything that was put in front of him, he quickly regained much of the muscle mass he had lost.

While no one understood his inspiration, strenuous physical activity represented the only means through which he could gain respite from the demon torment of his mind. Left idle, his thoughts would remind him that he lived in a new world, and the inner voices would lure him back into the dank prison of unremitting depression. Exercise and physical recovery were the only things he could control, it was the one way for him to quell the thoughts and temporarily escape the incessant punishment.

There was more to his motivation than just that. Things had gone wrong in his life, terrible things that he had to find the means to rectify. The first step was to recover physically. Then he would try to figure out how he came to be in the Twenty-Fifth Century and how he might fix the things that had gone wrong. He couldn't give up. He had to keep fighting.

Jake found that the other patients increasingly annoyed him. Most of the workers actually fit nicely into that same category. Part of the reason was that shortly after being transferred to the rehab facility, and once he began regaining his strength, he rejected the medications that were designed to keep him calm, perceiving that they were clouding his thoughts. He minded his own business and worked hard, hiding behind an aura that warned everyone to stay away. One day rolled into the next and behind the stoic façade he had to fight harder and harder to maintain control; the growing monster within was raging and clawing, straining at the end of its chains. With each passing day it took more strength and determination to keep it under control. There was an inevitable breaking point. With the sheer level of anger lurking just beneath the surface...it was only a matter of time before Jake would lose control.

The breaking point involved a minister who volunteered his services at the facility. He was doing his job, spending time with everyone, helping them nurture the spiritual aspects of their recoveries and their lives. The mere sight of him triggered something in Jake, something deep and very dark. He sensed that he was going to erupt, and that his rage would push him to the psychotic edge. It was uncontrollable, like a reflex. He'd hear the minister talking about God, about love and compassion, and it made him boil. He wanted to grab him and yell, 'Where was He? The caring God you're talking about doesn't exist!' The day came when the minister ignored the warning signs and brought his message too close.

"Do you mind if I sit here?" he asked. His name was Quinn. His highly energetic and talkative nature was complemented by the black suit and white clerical collar.

Jake tensed up as Quinn pulled out a chair and sat down across from him. He purposefully sat at the farthest table so he could eat alone. Company, especially Quinn's, was unwelcome.

"Good grub today." He seemed sincere and enthusiastic about his food. He shook the saltshaker over his meatloaf, said grace, and dug in. He tried to make small talk and was masterful at filling every last moment with noise. He was relating something about an aunt's recipe for peanut butter pie. Jake ignored him. He thought about getting up and moving but decided instead to eat his food. Once he shoveled in the last bite, he promptly pushed away from the table and stood up. The sudden effort caused the table to shift and a large piece of meat fell from Quinn's fork. His mouth was open and the metal clinked against his teeth. "What the...," he exclaimed. His disappointment was unmistakable, like the opportunity of a lifetime was slipping away. "Was it something I said?" There was no response. All he could do was watch as the hulking figure turned away, placed his tray on the conveyor, and left the room.

Ten minutes later, Quinn came back for round two. Without bothering to knock, he opened the door and invited himself into Jake's room. He seized a chair and sat down. "I've been trying to be nice to you for weeks," he said, "and you keep ignoring me. What gives?" He was trying to reach out to Jake with a message of salvation but frustration was getting the better of him. "There's a lot of anger in you," Quinn said. "I see it in your eyes. I find that anger most often is a natural response to loss."

Jake's agitation was boiling over. He envisioned picking Quinn up and throwing him through the wall. His muscles tightened, begging him to do it.

"Whatever the source of your anger is, I would be happy to help you explore it," Quinn held up his Bible and added, "and we can seek understanding through God's eternal love and forgiveness."

Jake pointed at the Bible, indicating that he wanted it. Quinn handed it over. Jake quickly took note of its front. It wasn't a Bible. It was titled, *Holy Book of the New Age*. He promptly ripped it in half, cover included, and left the destroyed pages dangling haphazardly at the spine.

"Oh my," Quinn gasped. His eyes were as big as pancakes.

Jake handed it back, thrusting the mangled book into Quinn's chest.

"Why would you do that?" He was incredulous. He gazed at the book with an equal mix of shock and disgust. "How can you be so angry? Are you mad at God? Just because you're mad at God doesn't mean He's mad at you."

While Quinn was talking, Jake grabbed his chair.

Quinn was suddenly frightened. There was no way he could defend himself. Fearing that he was going to be hurt, his words grew rapid and his tone panicked. "Why won't you talk to me? I'm just trying to help. I didn't mean any harm. We can work through this."

Jake picked the chair up with Quinn in it and carried it out of the room. His jaws were clenched and his face was lit with fiery anger. His arms and chest loomed ominous and large, dwarfing Quinn in every way. With the adrenaline rush and his loss of control, the physical act of carrying Quinn out appeared to require no effort whatsoever.

"You don't have to do this! I can help if you'll let me!" Quinn squealed.

As he carried the minister into the common area, a shocked hush came over the onlookers. Jake smashed the chair down on the floor, bending one of the legs. Quinn jolted harshly in the seat, but otherwise was unhurt. Jake's face was an inch away. The intensity of his glare conveyed the intended message—stay the hell away from me.

Jake turned and walked away, leaving Quinn motionless in the chair. No one said a word as Jake returned to his room and closed the door.

He was furious. He curled his right hand into a tight fist. Intoxicated with anger, his heart was pounding and his mind screamed. His thoughts focused on God. 'I hate you!' The thought screamed over and over. The rage of what his life had become consumed him. He had to find an outlet. He balled up all his strength and let it loose. His fist smashed through the wall. It felt good. He did it again and again. Each time there was a pop that sounded like an explosion. Pieces of plaster were flying as his mind screamed, 'I hate you! I hate you! I hate you!' Then it changed to, 'Why? Why would you let this happen?' He punched again and again in quick succession. 'Where are you? Where were you?' He stepped back, and in a blur, he kicked the wall. It was a martial arts kick with incredible blunt force. The stud splintered and cracked under the force. His outburst was cathartic and addictive in every way, but he had not yet reached his crescendo. Workers huddled outside, hearing the noise as the room was being destroyed, but too scared to enter. As the bathroom door and its frame were being brutally destroyed with blunt force Jake's agonized mind vented the agonies of his life with each impact. 'You don't exist. You can't.

A just God would never allow so much suffering.' His rage unleashed in a fury of punches and kicks.

After it was over, Jake took a step back and took in the scene. The room was devastated. It looked like a bomb exploded. Blood dripped from his knuckles. He leaned against the wall, sank to his knees, and then held the sides of his head. He was gently rocking back and forth when he felt his soul shudder…the gavel pounded down and a guilty verdict was rendered. 'It's my fault,' he admitted. 'It's my fault. They're gone because of me. It's my fault. I wasn't strong enough.' He was weeping, but there were no tears. 'I won't stop. There has to be a way. There has to be a way to fix what I've done…I have to bring them back.'

* * * * *

Jake wasn't in Tennessee anymore. He had spent the last seven long but productive weeks of recovery in a rehab facility in Northern Quebec. As Ben was interrogating Martin Zagger, Jake was evacuated from the hospital by operatives of the secret society. Afterward, Jake fell off the grid. Ben sent a one-way communication to Director Zimmer reporting that there was a leak somewhere in the NAIA. As a result, he took John Doe underground in order to ensure his safety. Ben discovered from the interrogation that Zimmer ordered the DSS operation and that he knew Jake's name. If Zimmer managed to connect all the dots, which he eventually would, the Egalitarian Party's objectives would change. They wouldn't want Jake for the purposes of investigating time travel…they would want him dead.

Jake was admitted into a rehabilitation facility under the alias, Larimore Johanson. During his years working in the field as an MPS operative, Ben used a multitude of covers. For personal protection and for plausible deniability on the part of the agency, only he knew what they were. He created them early in his career, complete with birth certificates, hospital records, diplomas, tax records, and postal addresses. Larimore Johanson was one of them.

The facility was under constant surveillance by the secret society, and several members of the staff, including his nurse, were members of the group. Jake was as effectively underground as anybody had ever been, and he would be safe until his physical rehabilitation was complete. Then he would be ready and would have to leave in order to carry out the rest of the plan.

By Presidential Order, the case of John Doe wasn't to be discussed outside the confines of the briefing room until the next scheduled meeting. Even so, Ben had to keep Zimmer simultaneously informed and at bay. He reported on a regular basis with brief non-specific updates, detailing only that John Doe was safe but unable to talk, likely because of extreme psychological trauma, and that there were very positive signs he was stabilizing. With each of Ben's reports, Zimmer sounded increasingly distracted...and for good reason.

Once Jake was extracted from New Bethesda Hospital, the secret society had to distract Zimmer and focus the Egalitarian Party's wheels of power in other directions. If John Doe's case might become a lower priority, or possibly fall off the radar, it would increase their likelihood of success. In order to accomplish this, the society unleashed teams of assassins. They began systematically eliminating and abducting undercover DSS and MPS agents, regional politicians, and foreign ambassadors. Their plan was working. Everything at NAIA headquarters was in chaos. Days went by when Zimmer, in addition to having no sleep, hadn't even thought about John Doe and the whole issue of time travel. The Party and United America were under attack, and he didn't know who was behind it. He hinted at one point that he might recall Ben in order to help conduct widespread interrogations, but for the time being, he was utilizing other interrogation teams, and no real suspects had been developed. Rather than contradict the directives outlined by President Martinez, he decided to leave Ben on his current assignment.

CHAPTER 7: THE SECRET SOCIETY

"Who are the MPS moles?" Ben asked.

"Hardy, Mullenberg, Sanchez, and Pang."

"Who handles them?" Ben was at MST Global's headquarters interrogating one of the MPS agents who was extracted from the field.

"I do," agent Rosario said. His voice was analytical, without inflection or emotion. That's usually the way it was once the extraction process began. The agent was secured with leather straps to a chair, while the interrogation device covered his face and skull.

"To whom do you report?"

"Director Zimmer."

"What are your objectives?" At first there wasn't an answer. Ben navigated through the widely variable patterns of neurological discharge. He isolated a series of neural circuits likely corresponding to the question. 'He's good,' Ben thought. 'Rare that I have someone this deep who can still resist. He's had intensive training.'

"What are the objectives?" he repeated. This time, he stimulated pain neurons in agent Rosario's brain. As they discharged, he emitted a deep groan. Immediately the pathway containing the information declared itself. Ben stimulated it.

"Several objectives," he mumbled. "Encryption codes. Anti-laser and exo-suit technologies. Time travel."

Another neural pathway was teetering, but Rosario was still able to inhibit it. Ben destroyed the connections that were turning the pathway off and Rosario said, "A black box project called operation *Aperio*."

Ben had never heard of it. He accessed the word "Aperio" through his BCD. It told him that it was a Latin word meaning *to reveal* or *uncover*. "What is Operation Aperio?" he asked.

"We don't know. All the agents we sent disappeared."

There was no indication he was holding anything back, and a few more questions failed to elicit anything useful. Ben continued, "What are MST's connections to time travel?"

As Rosario talked, Ben was using the interface with his BCD to see exactly what was happening at the cellular level in his subject's brain. With another device—highly sophisticated gloves with quantum computers imbedded in the palms and in each finger—he was able to manipulate the patterns of neural firing in his subject's brain.

"A research division buried within MST Global has been researching time travel."

"Have they had any breakthroughs?"

"We don't know," he revealed.

Ben fished around for another ten minutes. He further outlined NAIA's capabilities in terms of infiltrating MST, and fully defined their regional operations infrastructure. Then he killed Rosario. He sliced a high-energy beam through his brainstem, his body jerked, and he was dead. Ben detached his interrogation device and started to clean it off. He nonchalantly directed the guards to dispose of the body. MST's leader would be given the names of the four operatives who had successfully infiltrated the company. They would be used as tools as long as it was advantageous, and then they would be eliminated.

Ben didn't feel guilty about his work. He was cold to it, completely unemotional and detached. The key was to dehumanize the process and store it in a separate mental compartment. It was the only way he could do what he did and maintain sanity. He viewed the brains under interrogation as nothing more than an organic computer. He'd extract the information he needed and discard what was left in whatever manner was advantageous. They were inanimate objects masquerading as people.

Ben was learning everything he needed to know about the secret society, an organization hiding in plain sight…a company known around the world as MST Global. Preparations were being made for the second phase of the mission…putting Jake's mind back together while, at the same time, discovering every detail of what happened to him. If MST was going to have any chance of achieving its objectives, it was imperative that Jake be convinced to cooperate. Despite the great care MST took in influencing his early life something had gone terribly wrong. Lt. Col. Jake Gillean had been lost in time. Somewhere in the past a mistake was made. Ben had to find out where. In order to do that, MST needed to know everything about Jake's life up to the moment he inexplicably materialized at the reenactment. Ben's task was to get him to talk.

Ben's BCD indicated an incoming message. Overcome by a wave of anxiety, he said, "This is Ben."

"It's time." It was the ominous voice of the leader of MST. "Lt. Col. Gillean is ready. Our watchers report he's fit for duty physically."

"And mentally?"

"Bring him along at your discretion." The lack of a direct answer likely meant that the situation wasn't good. From everything Ben learned, he guessed that his target would be volatile in the extreme. "Move him out of the facility," the voice said. "We'll be watching and will alert you if there's any danger."

"What about Zimmer?"

"United America is threatening to declare war on Europe, Brazil, and China. There has been a complete breakdown in diplomatic relations. For the time being, Zimmer is distracted and his interest in Jake has been re-prioritized. You will be able to move around freely. We will continue making reports directly to him as necessary."

"Understood," Ben said. "I will leave immediately."

Ben often wondered how it came to this, how United America fell under the despotic rule of a Fascist Government, how he ended up being in dual positions with MPS and the organization that would soon rise up in opposition to Fascism, and how Lt. Col. Jake Gillean became central to their plans. It was a complex process and there were many different things to consider, but it all started with MST.

In the world of shadow organizations, the most elusive usually avoid giving themselves a name. But the most formidable, the ones that wield the most power, they're the ones that hide out in the open. The organization that had claim over the life of Dr. Benjamin Murray actually had elements of both. The secret society, of which he was an integral member, saw its inception well over five hundred years ago, in the 1870s, with a seed that was planted in the United States. That seed took root and eventually grew into the company that took the name...*Mutare Science and Technology Global, or MST*. But the story was far more complex than that. From its inception, MST had ulterior motives that reached far beyond the acquisition of wealth and technological achievements. Its aim was to fundamentally change the world and act as a force that would launch mankind into the next great era of human existence.

The ominous voice that periodically communicated with Ben through his BCD was the voice of AF20, the internal codename given to the leader of MST Global and its de facto secret society. AF20 was the twentieth such person since the company was born, AF1 through AF19 having played their roles to perfection in preparing for the ultimate fight.

MST's story was an incredible tale of success against formidable odds.

At the forefront were its many economic achievements, including the development of a device that could detect and accurately identify elemental contents and mineral deposits hiding within solid rock up to a hundred meters below the surface of the planet. This allowed them to drag the oceans and discover vast quantities of the universal currency...gold.

The next achievement for their scientists aimed at the manipulation of matter. It had long been held that an atom was unalterable. In other words, that an atom of calcium could not be changed into an atom of say...iron. But those assumptions were disproven through the steady march of scientific development. Based on the presumption that at the moment preceding the inception of the universe, right before the Big Bang, there was no such thing as calcium or iron, that every element was instantaneously created from a primordial swirl of quarks, of pre-electron, pre-proton, and pre-neutron mass, there had to be a way to deconstruct and then reconstruct matter. Once MST scientists discovered how to do this and perfected the means to create large quantities of anything they wanted—gold, platinum, silver, copper, etc.—their power to achieve AF1's objectives took a giant leap forward.

Despite being the most powerful corporation in history, the rest of the world wasn't about to abdicate power and influence without a fight. Powerful interests within the international banking community, within the Egalitarian Party, and in United America's military-industrial complex believed that MST Global was a threat. Increasingly, the company was under attack by the media and was forced to endure a series of public relations fiascos. Workers in several manufacturing facilities were paid by banking interests to mount a very public strike, and environmentalists were up in arms over government funded research that claimed the company was destroying the environment. At the same time, the academic community was proselytizing that MST's activities were causing global cooling...even though temperatures were actually trending toward a natural upswing as a result of natural sun cycles.

The attacks were being mounted on all fronts and political extortion ran rampant. The United American Government filed a barrage of antitrust suits claiming MST was a monopoly and guilty of unfair business practices. On the backside, there were efforts to force an audit of the company. This was done through the Internal Revenue Service. What ensued were explosive court hearings in the International Court wherein the Egalitarian Party repeatedly tried, without success, to investigate the inner workings of the company. Nevertheless, they continued to file subpoenas for classified company documents. MST endured sabotage of their manufacturing facilities, espionage, and the latest...an interstellar incident where a commercial flight mysteriously strayed into the path of one of Elektor's high energy lasers, killing several hundred people.

MST continued to stand strong despite recurrent challenges. Each attack on its independence as a sovereign company was anticipated, and its responses were orchestrated with perfect precision. As a result, its inner functions continued to be shrouded in secrecy, and men like Carl Zimmer were left angry and frustrated.

Beyond the legal victories, the developments that most ensured MST's survival were in the hard sciences, quantum computers, espionage and counter-espionage technologies, and their weapons development program. They perfected many new concept weapons including pulsars based on fusion-driven flywheel technology, new generations of weaponized lasers, laser-delivered biological weapons systems, counter bio-terrorism technologies, magnometer propulsion drives, supersuits, or exo-suits, for specialized military personnel, human DNA manipulation and genetic engineering technologies, antimatter weapons, energy absorption and shield systems, cloaking devices and holographic warfare systems, and dark matter technologies. They were at the forefront of research and development and actually provided most of the advanced technologies used by United America's military, but only after perfecting more advanced versions for their own protection.

The secret society not only operated out of MST...it was MST. Its tentacles infiltrated governments across the globe, and their agents held key positions in industry, militaries, and legal institutions. They also held high positions within widely divergent political organizations. Ben was just one of those agents. While he was a key player in MST's ultimate plan, he was in fact just one among thousands.

While the first chapter of the secret society's existence took five centuries to mature, the second, in which Lt. Col. Jake Gillean was the central focus, would unfold in a matter of months. Only if MST successfully achieved all of its objectives would there be a chance to write its third chapter...a chapter that would change life on the planet forever.

CHAPTER 8: WHO ARE YOU?

[APRIL 9, 2441 A.D.]
[129 DAYS AFTER ARRIVAL]
[LOCATION: QUEBEC]

Keeping careful watch while posing as rehab facility staff, MST's agents reported to AF20 that the target was ready. The report came immediately after he carried the minister out of his room. That made it evident enough that he had recovered sufficient physical function and would be able to defend himself. It was time to set the wheels in motion. Ben was secreted back to the facility from MST's headquarters in the South Pacific, he flashed credentials, and the discharge process began.

"What the hell did you say to him?" Ben was coming unglued. He shook his head in disgust as he watched the surveillance video of the incident with the minister.

"I, I…" Quinn didn't know what to say.

"You weren't supposed to initiate the approach. Dammit!" Ben exclaimed. "You broke protocol. Your orders were to make yourself available and let him come to you. It was supposed to be his choice."

"I know but…" Quinn knew he screwed up.

"You stupid son of a bitch! Do you have any idea what the ramifications are?" Ben was so angry he felt his hands shaking. His goal of getting Jake to talk was now going to be far more difficult.

"Look, I'm sorry. I know it was the wrong thing to do, but I thought that if I applied a little bit of pressure he might start communicating."

"A little bit of pressure? On him?! About God?! You stupid, stupid son of a bitch! You have no idea what you've just done!" Ben yanked the tattered Holy Book out of Quinn's hands. It was two inches thick and had a leather cover. He tried to duplicate the tear. It was immediately apparent that it was far beyond him, that it took tremendous strength. He pressed it into Quinn's chest and hissed through gritted teeth, "It wasn't your job to think. You were supposed to do what you were told. You're lucky he didn't rip your head off."

"I'm sorry."

"Dammit!" Ben exclaimed. His stress was at its apex as he shifted his attention back to the recording. He watched Jake slam the chair down and Quinn bounce in his seat. It was obvious that Jake was fighting to control the bulk of his rage. What they saw was the tip of the iceberg in terms of his capacity for destruction. His face was tight and his eyes murderously intense. It was the jawbone though that was the most intimidating. It was like that of a proud and defiant Germanic warrior, like those who fought against Caesar in Gaul.

"Leave," Ben said pointing to the door. He turned toward the Vintel Unit and closed his eyes, waiting to hear the door close behind Quinn. Once he was alone, he changed security camera footage and followed Jake's movements. He went down the hall and returned to his room with mannerisms that were altogether unremarkable.

Jake didn't slam the door to his room, but it was closed with force enough to carve out a wide berth. Once alone, he paced a couple times and then leaned his shoulder against the wall. He brought his hands up to grasp the sides of his head. They were shaking. He held that position for a moment, then he clenched his fists and destroyed the room. When he finished he slid to his knees on the floor.

"Oh," Ben muttered. "What happened to you? How am I supposed to put you back together?"

While Ben was reviewing the footage and trying to figure out how to navigate an already complex situation, Jake was taken to an unused office. There was a light-brown rectangular table flanked by four common office chairs. The walls and ceiling were painted an antique white, blending it in bland perfection with the rest of the facility. There was an empty set of shelves positioned in the corner with a few computer cords thrown on the top shelf. The window, having earned the wrath of avian hordes, was covered with purple and white droppings. Otherwise, it afforded a wonderfully unobstructed view of the most colorful scene afforded any window in the place—a red brick wall approximately three meters away.

Jake suspected that this day was coming. He couldn't live in a rehab facility indefinitely. What he didn't know was what, or who, to expect. He sat alone in the room for a long ten minutes. His mind raced, wondering who was going to come through the door and how the scene might play out. At the same time, his external features more closely resembled that of a statue; a tired and catatonic, yet proud statue. Logic suggested that whoever came in would likely want him to talk, to tell his story, but that was something he swore he wouldn't do, something he couldn't do. He couldn't reopen the wounds.

Ben approached the door, ready to go in, but he felt compelled to back away, rethinking how best to establish a relationship. The incident with Quinn kept running through his mind. It was a warning. The last thing he wanted to do was make the same mistake. Jake was a lion, a lion who had been badly beaten, who had been irreversibly changed after being immersed in the death and destruction of war for the last eight years of his life. He would lash out at anyone and anything. While his body was back together, his mind had been all but destroyed. That's why he spent seven weeks in the facility. It was to allow for not only his physical rehabilitation, but the time was absolutely required to achieve some semblance of mental stabilization, to get to the point where Ben might be able to reach him. The last thing he wanted to do was misplay his approach and destroy the relationship before it got started. He had to throw Jake a lifeline, something he might willingly grasp, something worth fighting for.

On the other side of the door, Jake's thoughts were focused on his nightmares. They were coming every night. His sleep remained severely fragmented and was of such poor quality that he lost any concept of what it felt like to be awake and alert. During the worst of it, he admitted that he was already dead, that he was in hell…and that his eternal punishment was to not know the difference. Other times, he yearned that finding himself in the Twenty-Fifth Century was nothing more than an illusion cast over his mind at the moment of death, an illusion that would play itself into darkness once the last bullet finished ending his life. He was grasping for sanity while falling ever deeper into madness.

Without warning, his mind instantaneously blinked into another reality. He was running through the forest. There was a gun in his hand. He felt its uneven weight, the callousness of the metal, and the smoothness of the wooden stock. He experienced the branches slapping him in the face. Unrecognizable voices were all around, they were whispering and laughing, taunting and screaming. Then he saw them—blue-clad Union soldiers. His muscles tensed up. He was an animal, a predator. In an avalanche of fury he began fighting. Suddenly, there was a knock at the door. It was enough of a stimulus to pull him out of the flashback and back into the reality.

Ben stepped into the room. He noted that Jake didn't bother to look up. He was wearing new clothes Ben had purchased for him; a nondescript black T-shirt, denim jeans, and comfortable hiking boots. Ben realized he had misjudged the size of the shirt. He picked out a large but it was too tight over the shoulders, chest, and upper arms. His subject had put on almost thirty-five pounds of muscle since initially hospitalized, thirty since he moved into rehab. His hair had grown in and revealed itself to be mostly blond with some light brown, and a few grays preaching for converts along the sides and back.

Ben pulled the door shut behind him and stepped forward. "Never trust someone who starts off by saying that you can trust him," he started. He made an effort to hand Jake a cup of coffee, but when he didn't react, Ben placed it on the table in front of him. "I assume you drink it like a cowboy." It was an old expression. It referred to the coffee being black, unmolested by cream or sugar.

Again, Jake didn't react.

"I will be forthright, open, and honest with you," Ben said. "I'll answer all of your questions in the best way I can, but you'll have to decide whether or not you want to trust me."

Ben noticed that Jake's ear was taking shape nicely. It was still detectable as being biosynthetic but only to the trained eye. He studied Jake's face. Each scar begged to tell its story. His reconstructed forearm and missing fingers on his right hand spoke of incredible pain while his knuckles and muscular hands were frightening in their capacity for destruction.

Ben took a seat on the opposite side of the table. Despite the relatively cool temperature, beads of sweat shimmered across Jake's forehead. The next things Ben noticed were the carotid arteries just above the neck-line of Jake's shirt. They were pulsating rapidly. He surmised that Jake had just emerged from a flashback. The physiologic turmoil occurring inside the man stood in stark contrast to his external appearance. He was absolute and unmoving.

"You're having flashbacks," Ben commented. "I can give you some medications that might help." Trying to be casual and straightforward, he explained who he was, taking care to mention his military background and tours of duty. As he talked, he again waged the same internal debate he had been having for weeks, about how much to reveal during the initial meeting. The determining factor was the decision to go with his gut. He told Jake everything he knew as outlined in the two briefings with Zimmer. He pulled up at the end, choosing not to reveal anything about MST, or the other things he knew about Jake's ultimate connections to the company.

"First and foremost," Ben said, "I'm here on a mission to help you, as a doctor, and if you're willing, a friend. Anything you say remains confidential." He spoke with absolute sincerity, but he was also careful to avoid sounding contrived in the process. It was a good sign that Jake hadn't thrown him out—he had already lasted longer than Quinn.

Jake still didn't react. Hardly a blink had occurred since the conversation began. He was inclined to be careful with the newcomer as he had a lot to say, and he was being useful in that he was revealing a volume of information. It allowed Jake the opportunity to piece together events that he didn't understand. Until that moment, he had no knowledge of the Great Tragedy at the conclusion of World War IV, the event that destroyed the entire Middle East and large parts of South Asia. Further, Jake had no real memories of his reappearance at the reenactment in Tennessee or of his first days in the hospital. Ben was allowing him to connect the dots. Part of him wanted to dislike Ben, but enough rationality remained to allay judgment.

Ben added, "You have no reason to trust me, but at this point, you have no cause to distrust me either. Based on the information I have…I believe that you are one of ours. That being the case, it is my intention to do everything I can to help you, and I am the best game in town."

Jake finally made a move. He reached out and took the coffee, the cup disappearing in his grasp. He took a slow methodical drink. He considered Ben's words while at the same time he noticed the stark contrast between the white of the cup and the darkness of the fluid and how weak it was, compared to the stiff and rank coffees he had grown accustomed to in the throes of the Nineteenth Century. This time there weren't any unidentifiable substances in the liquid. It was finely filtered, clear, and pure, made from coffee beans, not acorns or tree bark. His thoughts once again spiraled out of control. He realized it looked exactly the same as the liquid in a latrine; a latrine containing the waste of a thousand dirty and filthy soldiers, men suffering from every form of foul disease and dysentery whether non-communicable or contagious. It didn't matter what walk of life they came from, if they were rich or poor, proper or disgusting, in the end it all came out looking and smelling the same. With that dank thought he lifted the cup to his lips and took another slow and methodical drink.

After a long period of tense silence Ben said, "I know you can talk." His comment had an unmistakable edge to it. It was a challenge. "I also know that you have nightmares and scream out in your sleep." After a flash of anxiety, he added, "I also know that you asked your nurse in the ICU about several people. Wendy, Bailey, and Paul."

As though he had just come under fire on the battlefield, Jake snapped into complete focus and awareness. For the first time, he looked directly at Ben.

"I'm guessing that your name is Jake…Jake Gillean. Wendy, Bailey, and Paul are important to you," Ben said, purposely repeating their names. "I assume they are your family."

Jake didn't react, but under the stoic shell he was like an animal on the hunt. To actually hear the names being formed and coming off the lips of another person was impossible. It couldn't be real. He was sizing Ben up, studying every subtlety of expression and movement. For the first time since the agony of that day in the ICU when he was told there was no record of his family, that they were lost, he chose to activate his BCD. His mind was sharp and fast, causing the world around him to shift into slow-motion. The first thing he detected was that Ben had a BCD, and that he was being scanned.

"I can't find any records of them, or you, anywhere," Ben said. "Can you tell me why that might be?" He regretted it as soon as the words finished rolling off his tongue as in mid-sentence he detected Jake's BCD was springing to life. Now there was another BCD staring at his. Jake's jaw clenched and his eyes transformed into a glare. Ben detected a rapid increase in Jake's pulse and an acute dilation of his pupils. The electromagnetic field around his upper body changed, indicating substantial increases in muscle tension. He was ready to explode, to launch himself across the table in an attack.

Ben had to shift gears quickly. By all appearances he had lied by not telling Jake that he had a BCD. It was a terrible oversight on his part. Now that it had been discovered, he felt the stabbing loss of integrity, like all his words were now regarded as being predicated on a lie.

"My apologies," Ben said. He held up his hand to indicate that no offense was meant. "I should have told you from the beginning, but until you activated yours, I didn't think about it." His heart was racing as he pushed away from the table. "It was an oversight in etiquette, nothing more," he said. In his quest to get Jake to talk, Ben had blinders on, and he made the blunder of focusing only on his volatilities. He forgot that he was pitting himself against the perfect combination of speed and strength, and a man of incredible intelligence. While Jake was a mystery waiting to be unlocked, Ben's sudden fear for personal safety helped him to recognize what was right in front of him, what he already knew...that Jake was a superior specimen in almost every way imaginable.

Jake eased back. It was enough of a signal that Ben could continue. He needed to change the subject. "When you were in the hospital there were several agents watching you. They were from the DSS. I consider them hostile," he said. "The op originated out of a back door channel, and I didn't discover it until right before we evacuated you." He forcibly exhaled. It was an outward expression of his stress. "There's so much I have to tell you. You disappeared sixty years ago. You were fighting for freedom and liberty. You and soldiers like you sacrificed everything for a country you loved...not because of the country, but because of the ideals it embodied within the fabric of its society. The United America you were fighting for no longer exists. The Democratic Republic you knew is gone. It has been transformed into a Fascist State. Everything is controlled with an iron fist by the Egalitarian Party." Ben let the revelation settle before adding, "I think you'll find that there are those within this system who do not have your best interests in mind, and there are others, like myself, who are willing to fight to restore society to what it once was."

Ben was satisfied that he had revealed everything Jake needed to know or could possibly find out on his own. Now he needed to convince Jake that it would be in his best interest to cooperate. He turned off his BCD. Jake saw the electronic signature disappear. Ben finished, "We need you. You're our last hope. Whatever happened to you, please let me find a way to help. Tell me your story. There's a possibility I can help put things right. There is always hope."

Jake's lack of response, the absence of any feedback, was unnerving. He was trying to make sense of everything Ben said. When he looked up, the anger was gone. His eyes weren't pleading. In fact, they weren't even sad. They were just empty. He had an agenda. He needed to understand how he came to materialize at the Civil War reenactment in the future…in the year 2440. The world around him wasn't his. He didn't belong. Things within his control and far beyond his control had gone terribly wrong, and he had to figure out a way to fix the mistakes he made. Without intonation, he spoke his first word.

"Hope?"

It was a forlorn and unanswerable question. He had spent countless hours contemplating the word. With fists clenched in rage and his spirit destroyed, long ago he screamed out in utter submission and despair until his only remaining hope at the moment of death was that he would close his eyes and his existence would blink into nothingness.

Ben was conflicted. Part of him wanted to jump up and scream, to celebrate that Jake actually said a word. Another part wanted to weep. The angst and despair of that single word…*hope*. To have things go so terribly wrong, to wreck the human spirit to the point that even hope had been destroyed…what was he supposed to do? How was he supposed to fix it?

Ben got up and looked out the window. As he leaned on the sill he was embraced by the acute sensation that time was running out. He could protect Jake for a short period of time, but once Zimmer put everything together, there were no guarantees. Ben turned back to face Jake. "Tell me what happened. I will help you. Behind me are thousands who will do everything they can to help you. And behind them are hundreds of millions who are scared into submission, people who need someone to show them the way, someone to lead them."

Jake subtly shook his head. "You can't help me."

"I can try."

"You don't understand. You can't help me."

"You're right," Ben said. "I don't understand."

Jake again shook his head. "What's done is done. There's no changing that now. You can't help me."

"If you're sure I can't help you, will you help us?"

Jake didn't react.

"I realize what I'm asking is difficult. You fought for a flag sixty years ago that I'm asking you to fight for again."

"Americans don't fight for flags," Jake commented. "They fight for beliefs and ideals."

Ben smiled. It was the response he was looking for. He said in as poignant a tone as he could, "You materialized on that field in Tennessee at the moment you did for a reason. I can't explain it, but I have to believe it. I believe in you Lt. Col. Jake Gillean. All I'm asking is for you to believe in me. I have the ability to help you in ways you can't even begin to imagine."

Jake noted that Ben called him by his rank. 'How did he know? He slipped it in as a sign,' Jake thought. 'He knows more than he's letting on. But if he knows that...then...no. It's not possible.' Jake considered his options. The building tension was like an overpowering storm. There were so many reasons to leave, to just walk away and bury forever his cursed life and all his experiences. But then Jake's mouth began moving and he almost unwillingly said, "What do you want to know?"

"Everything," Ben answered. He experienced a wave of dual relief and excitement. "In order for me to help you I need to know everything about your life, from your earliest memory onward."

Jake's tension played through with his fingers unconsciously curling into tight fists. He burst, "Do you have any idea what you're asking me to do?" The proposition was difficult beyond measure. He was being asked to open wounds that were still fresh, and others that were festering and rotting inside. He studied Ben, considered his face. There was something oddly familiar and comfortable about him. But why should he trust him? Why should he trust anyone? All he knew was that there was a whispering hint at the far reaches of his battered sixth sense that told him it was okay. Despite everything he had been through and the mountain of anger he maintained, he still nurtured a primordial shadow of hope, but he was scared that if he looked for it directly and discovered that it was gone, it would be more than he could bear.

Ben remained silent. His body language and demeanor suggested a complete presence of mind. Jake was his entire focus and nothing else mattered.

Jake cleared his throat and began. "I am…" He stopped. Under the suffocating squeeze of stress he brought his hands up to his face. He rubbed his eyes and momentarily held his fingertips across his forehead. He forcibly exhaled, fighting to control memories that were screaming out in protest. "My story?" he questioned in frustration. He looked back up at Ben and began, "My name is…Jake Gillean."

CHAPTER 9: THE
FOOTBALL GAME

(Jake Gillean's story unfolds. It begins seventy-three years in the past.)

[DECEMBER 2, AD 2367]
[ARRIVAL DATE MINUS 73 YEARS]
[LOCATION: SPRING HILL, TENNESSEE]

Festive lights from the Spring Hill High School Memorial Football Stadium illuminated the night sky as a blanket of low riding clouds worked to smother the occasion. It was a contrast of forces; one a celebration of life and excellence, the other a morose and unstoppable balm against things worth enjoying. For those in attendance, it was an escape as the world's problems took pause and faded into the shadows for a few hours. The level of excitement was palpable, rising and falling in direct proportion to spectator fantasies of catching the winning touchdown and achieving football glory. Cheerleaders jumped and yelled, performing their routines with exacting precision. The dull booming vibration of the deep base music rattled the stands in a manner reminiscent of a primitive religious ritual. Somewhere within its notes were buried hypnotic blueprints that caused the younger kids to visualize incredible athletic futures and the adults to dust off their memories and relive the glories of yesteryear.

The visiting team, the Franklin Lions, had two superstar players, Drew Jackman and Wayne Biggs. Drew, the tight end, was also mean enough to play defensive-end. He was big, fast, and agile. Accustomed to racking up yards and being a dominating force on the field, he had been taken out of the game by the Spring Hill Titan's defensive scheme. While he hadn't been much of a factor, at least on the surface, by being on the field it forced an alteration in the coverage schemes. The Titans had to utilize Jake Gillean to cover him. This, in turn, freed up Biggs to run with reckless abandon. Until there was a means to create two Jake Gilleans, it was a lopsided chess match.

Along with the college scouts, agents from MST Global were in the crowd. They were always in the shadows watching. From the moment of Jake's birth, they were always there, silently studying him like ghostly apparitions, hidden from view unless they wanted to be seen. This was one of the occasions when they determined to intervene in his life.

"What's your name?" the agent asked.

"Dent."

"You handle all the water for the team?"

"Yes, sir," he excitedly agreed. "Sometimes I help with the first aid too."

"Wonderful," the agent said. He was dressed in a sweatshirt and was wearing a hat, both proclaiming him to be a Spring Hill Titan's football fan. "Did you see the recruiters?" Dent nodded his head. "I counted seven of 'em."

"No. There are three more on the other side. Right behind the bench. They came from all over the country so they could check out Jake, Biggs, and Jackman all at the same time."

"Can I see one of those bottles? No. Not that one. The one right there." Dent took the indicated bottle out of his rack and handed it over. "Holy smokes," he exclaimed. "These are the same bottles we had when I played. This was my favorite bottle. It brought me luck. We won the State Championship that year." Dent's eyes were wide with excitement. "It was crazy," the agent went on, "we were all superstitious and each of us had our own bottle." Unbeknownst to Dent, the agent laced the drink with a designer drug created by MST. "Put some extra ice in this one and make sure Jake gets it. It always made me the fastest and strongest player on the field."

"Yes, sir," Dent said. "Extra ice."

"Make sure," he yelled. Dent stopped and turned back to hear the last of his instructions. "To let him rub your head. That always gave me good luck."

"I will," he agreed.

The agent had been to every game. He knew that Jake always took the last bottle and that he rubbed Dent's head. The purpose of his statement was to seed Dent's mind and ensure that he would give the bottle to Jake.

MST designed the drug to unlock Jake's potential, so to speak. If anyone else took the drug nothing would happen. With Jake it would be different—it was the key to a lock. As his brain matured, he would eventually learn how to open the lock himself, but until then it took incredible circumstances and intense stimulation of precise neurologic circuits in his brain to unleash what had been living within him. The drug would, for a brief time, make it easier for him to tap into what was already there.

The whistle blew, marking the two-minute warning. As Jake ran off the field, he looked back at the scoreboard. It read: 4th Quarter, 2 minutes remaining, Titans 34, Lions 32, 3rd Down and 3. It was the Lion's ball on the Titan's 28-yard line.

As the Titans crowded around their coach, Jake took a moment to watch the opposite side of the field. The Lions were doing the same thing. He made eye contact with Biggs. Both nodded in acknowledgement and turned toward their coaches. They had played against each other for years and had generated familiarity both inside and outside the world of sports. They shared a mutual respect.

The teams' uniforms were filthy, splattered with a combination of sweat and dirt. The occasional player sported bloody smears across his jersey, a proud testament to smashed noses, crushed fingers, and the fighting spirit. Despite the herculean efforts, there was only a slight sense of exhaustion among the players. With the help of a huge surge of adrenaline, they were ready to let it all hang out for the final two minutes of gladiatorial struggle.

The Franklin Lions' coach was an ex-professional player. His wasn't the typical career-cut-short story. He played for twelve seasons as a running back in the North American Football League and was famous. He wanted to give back to the sport and his community, so he volunteered to coach the team. He was excitedly yelling at his players. Every so often, when his heart rate was up, spittle would fly from his mouth. As he yelled at his players it would sparkle in the stadium lights like a fireworks display.

"Drew! I want Gillean out of this play. You hear me!" The coach's demeanor was approaching the level of a tirade, "Hit him hard off the line, then a twenty-yard out. Gillean better be on his back or down the field. Are you hearing me Drew?!"

The coach took a swig from his water bottle and shifted his attention to Biggs. Wayne Biggs was the running back. He was an absolute superstar, the consummate athlete. College scouts from all over the nation were actively recruiting him as one of the top talents coming out of high school. He played aggressively and could shift with lightning fast speed from being a freight train to running as agile as a deer, and he had the rare talent of being able to shift directions without telegraphing any of his moves. The defenders were usually left somewhere behind, stumbling over their feet. Biggs broke nearly every record in the conference. While his coach was accused of running up the score on defeated opponents, no one doubted Biggs' potential. He was a likeable mound of eighteen-year-old muscle who was absolutely determined to succeed.

"Wayne! It's all you!" the coach said as he smacked his shoulder pad. "You're a tank! You hear me! You've got the ball! Off tackle! Up the middle! YOU'RE AN ANIMAL!" He shifted his attention to the rest of the team. "This is it! Just like we practiced. Now go out there and get that conference title!"

Physically, the Lions were larger than the Titans, but despite the discrepancy the first three quarters had been fairly evenly matched, and at one point, the Titans established a sixteen-point lead. By the time the fourth quarter rolled around, the size difference was expressing itself. The Titans were losing the fight on the line and were being manhandled. The Lions notched fourteen points in the fourth and were threatening to score again. While the Titans were still playing with enthusiasm, the grind of the game was taking its toll.

On the Titans' side of the field, they huddled around their coach. Jake took several bottles of water and handed them to his teammates, then he chose one for himself.

"Jake, no," Dent said. He handed him a different bottle. "This one's for you. I put some extra ice in it for you."

Jake smiled and switched bottles with Dent. He rubbed his friend's head and messed up his hair. He took a big swig. Dent smiled, satisfied as he watched Jake drink from the special bottle.

The game had been a highlight reel of athletic effort and endurance. Every player on the Spring Hill Titans knew that Jake was a successful player because of them. They believed it even though it wasn't true. They believed it because that's what he said. Jake would bust a fabulous run and carry three or four tacklers several yards before finally going down. Afterward, his first priority as he approached the huddle was to tell his friends what they did to make it happen. Not worried about records, he was an example of pure and unselfish athletic talent, as well as athletic leadership. As a result, the team won. They won against teams that they had no business beating. The difference was that they played as a single unit, as a team. "There's no *I* in the word *TEAM*," Jake would say.

His friends would occasionally yell, "There's no *I* in the word *Titan*." Then they'd laugh at the joke. Eventually it became a mantra, but everyone got the point.

"Okay guys. Crunch time," Coach Rucker said. "Biggs is killing us. They're going to jam it up the middle. We're going to stay with the 4-3 formation. But I want everybody to move up a bit. Play it tight. Jake, you're going to plug the center with everything you got. Pull coverage off Jackman as soon as the ball is snapped. Eddie and Steve, I want double coverage on him. Don't let him get behind you! Keep your eyes on the rest of the field. Got it? Let's go! Get back out there and win this thing. Remember, this is for the conference title!"

Excited by the daunting task in front of them and the reward of a conference title, the players hollered as they broke from the sideline huddle. They enthusiastically ran back on the field, yelling and smashing each other's shoulder pads. The coach grabbed Jake's uniform at the shoulder and didn't let go, holding him until the others were on the field. Jake understood that his coach had something to say.

Jake took another big drink and tossed his empty bottle to Dent. He was beginning to feel a little strange, like he could jump ten feet in the air. He wasn't concerned, chalking it up to the rush of the game.

The coach wrapped his fingers through the bars of Jake's facemask. He pushed him several yards onto the field, away from the sideline, away from the other players and assistants. At that point Coach Rucker transformed into a frenzied tyrant. His face scowled and eyes squinted. A deep furrow formed across his brow. It was a side of the coach that Jake had never seen.

He shook Jake's helmet back and forth and said through half-gritted teeth, "Jake! It's all up to you. You have to plug the middle. If they get a first down, they are gonna eat the clock and kick. Do you understand me?! You're responsible for winning or losing this title!"

Jake was taken aback. He didn't know how to respond. What came out was, "Yes, Coach!"

Rucker's face was pressed into Jake's facemask. "GET MAD, DAMMIT!" He screamed. "GET MAD! I WANT YOU TO HIT HIM WITH EVERYTHING YOU GOT! KNOCK HIM INTO NEXT WEEK! DO YOU UNDERSTAND ME?!"

"Yes, sir!" Jake said. His heart was racing. He felt wild with excitement.

Rucker was hitting the side of Jake's helmet. "PLANT HIM! IT'S ALL UP TO YOU! GET MAD, AND THE TITLE IS OURS! NOW GET OUT THERE AND GET IT DONE!" Coach slapped his back and pushed him toward his teammates.

Jake was acutely aware of the screaming crowd. Across the line, he saw Biggs moving amongst his teammates, his shoulders were wide, his legs were muscular, and he was a helmet taller than his teammates. They gathered around him as if they were elfish underlings worshiping his athletic prowess.

Jake felt the resentment rising. Biggs was no bigger than he was. He began envisioning his adversary not as a person, but as something inanimate and loathsome. He was running over Jake's friends, and he had been doing it the entire game. Biggs waved to the crowd on his side of the field. Then he made the wrong move…he mockingly waved to the fans on the Spring Hill side of the field. The insult, the disrespect, it was unconscionable. With a sudden and perceptible thump Jake wanted to kill him. Biggs grabbed Jackman's facemask. They screamed some primitive yell and moved out of huddle. Jake perceived their movements as though they were in slow motion.

Jake felt real rage. He felt powerful as he paced in the defensive backfield. He felt his heartbeat quicken. It was pounding. It felt amazing. He willfully pushed for a little extra adrenaline. He loved the feeling. Then, like a switch being flipped, it happened. Primed by the neurologic stimulation, the centers in his brain that controlled rage exploded with activity. It was beyond his ability to control. What he felt was a wondrous mix of anger and hatred. All reason was gone. The higher centers of his mind gave way under the surge of absolute primal aggression. A Pandora's Box had been opened, unleashing something that was buried, a capacity for violence that was waiting to be discovered.

Jake took the position of outside linebacker on the right side of the field. Drew Jackman lined up across from him. Wayne Biggs set up in the running back position. Like a Homerian epic below the walls of Troy, Biggs and Jackman loomed ominously as the largest of the onrushing aggressors. Opposite them, Jake was the only one equally capable and proud, a lone defender fighting against the odds.

Completely owned by his anger, a sudden realization gripped Jake. It was a thought he would never have entertained. He was resentful, feeling what could only be described as absolute disdain for his teammates, their shortcomings, and their inability to step it up to a higher level. Jake snapped his chinstrap and dug his feet into position. The next instant, something even more primal and animalistic snapped. His eyes dilated. His right hand developed a slight tic or quiver as a gluttonous surge of energy cloaked in sheer hate and anger flowed through him. For only the second time in his life, Jake had unwittingly unleashed something that consumed him, and he fell under the control of a true and absolutely murderous rage. The sensation was overwhelming, it was terrible, and it was absolutely pleasurable all at the same time. All sense of right and wrong was gone, replaced by primitive instincts and primordial urges long buried under the fabric of the mind. Insanity was wielding his strength and speed as weapons of war. His muscles were unsheathed and unbridled from the limitations of the mind. He was a lion stalking its prey, but not a defenseless deer, this was the ultimate adversary…another lion.

In his mind, the crowd fell into a muffled silence. He perceived the field in such a way that it seemed to contract and expand. His peripheral vision widened, and he saw everything in slow motion. As his brain processed the situation, he heard background noises. They resembled high-pitched screams of madness and vengeance, of terror and agony. They grew in intensity to reach an uncontrollable zenith.

The ball snapped. Jackman lunged forward, and with all his speed and might, he tried to plant a massive hit on Jake. He was right there. He was unloading a rib-crunching blow. Jackman closed his eyes at the point of impact. But there was no collision. He hurtled uselessly through the air. With lightning fast reflexes, Jake had sidestepped the impact. He was running to plug the hole that was developing in the center of the line. Just as Coach Rucker predicted, his teammates were being flattened. Like the parting of the Red Sea, the defensive line opened and a lane was revealed. Jake followed Biggs' movements behind the line. He barreled into the lane with the ball tucked under his right arm. He was like a great anatomic model, every muscle in his thighs bulging with each powerful step.

The rest of the field faded into a blur as Jake and Biggs ran at each other. The high-pitched screaming in Jake's head was deafening, like hundreds of people being torn into thousands of pieces. He directed his absolute hatred and aggression toward Biggs. He wanted to hurt him, to run through him in such a way as to break him in two. The feeling at that moment was beyond pleasurable. There followed a crunch of tremendous force as the two collided. Above the sound of the impact, and over the sound of the crowd, was the sound of ligaments giving way under the sudden pressure. Despite the crowd noise, the grotesque snapping sound triumphed over all. It immediately silenced the crowd. It was a knee. It was Biggs. In the fraction of a second the impact lasted, the football hurtled loose. It flipped through the air and into the outstretched arms of one of Jake's teammates. He ran down the field with the ball.

Jake didn't know what happened. Everything went black. He didn't know where he was. His bell was rung, and when the field came back into focus, it was spinning. The screaming in his head beat a disorganized retreat, and as the chaotic noise faded into the background, one abandoned cry was left behind. That was all that remained, a low-pitched guttural scream, a scream of fear and loss as much as a scream of pain. Jake was dizzy. He became increasingly aware of the stadium, and then the crowd. At first he didn't make the connection between what he was seeing and what he was hearing. The field continued to spin. He staggered to the side, almost falling. His legs weren't obeying his commands. He went down to a knee, holding the sides of his helmet, still basking in the grip of utter hatred.

When he processed the site and realized what happened, he snapped back to reality. The feelings of hatred and anger abandoned him as other parts of his higher conscience regained control. The anguished screaming he was hearing superimposed itself on Biggs. It was Biggs who was screaming. In that moment Jake comprehended the reality of what he had done.

Jake was overcome with fear. He couldn't talk. He felt nauseous. Biggs was on the ground screaming, his left leg bent grotesquely backward at the knee. It was bent almost to a reverse 90 degree angle. Tears rolled down Biggs' face. He was on his side screaming. He tried, as much as his helmet would allow, to bury his face in the turf. He was holding his thigh, frantic for someone to make everything better, to tell him that his knee would be okay.

Jake's teammates were initially ecstatic in their celebration of the fumble and subsequent touchdown. It essentially amounted to a conference title. But, as they realized what happened, the joyous moment turned into something more suppressed. In the name of sportsmanship they quieted themselves and went down to a knee on their side of the field.

At first, Biggs' mother didn't know what was happening. Then it all came together for her as well. She ran from the stands, her face a testimonial to the pain and worry only a mother can express. Off balance and the world spiraling out of control, Jake witnessed her agony as she ran onto the field to her son. He felt a terrible stab and the blade twisting within his soul.

Jake and his coach made eye contact as the paramedics arrived. Jake was terrified by what he had done. Just a moment before, he had wanted to hurt Biggs, but now that it had actually happened, he wanted nothing more than to take it back. He felt suffocated, like the world was pressing in, preventing him from taking a breath. Jake swore to God. He swore to God that he would never allow that to happen again. He prayed for Biggs first, and then he prayed for help. He told God he was sorry, he was sorry, he was sorry.

As the paramedics wheeled Biggs off the field on a gurney, Jake approached. The crowd chanted, "Biggs, Biggs, Biggs," as a sign of respect and admiration.

"Wayne, I'm sorry," Jake said. He didn't respond as his emotions were careening in other directions.

Jake turned to his mother, "Mrs. Biggs, I'm sorry. I didn't mean for this to happen." He was almost pleading for some acknowledgement that his apology was being heard and accepted.

She looked at him with a distressed stare but otherwise didn't respond.

Jake turned and began walking back to his teammates. Several had followed him over and were standing behind him.

"Gillean!" The voice boomed from the Lions side of the field. It was their coach.

A wave of tension swept over the field and through the stands as Biggs' coach approached. He was known for volatile moods, and no one knew exactly what was going to happen. He walked up to Jake and put his hands on his shoulder pads.

"It was a clean hit," he said. "These things happen in football. It's not your fault."

Tears were forming in Jake's eyes, and one ran down his cheek.

"You're a hell of a player. One of the best I've seen. This wasn't your fault." He patted the shoulder pads and nudged Jake around toward his teammates. Then he turned and walked away.

After the game, there was a trophy presentation and everyone celebrated the glorious conference title. The level of enthusiasm heightened in the locker room as the guys caroused around, talking about the big party but not so loud as to be overheard by the coaching staff. Jake tried not to be a wet blanket so he feigned enthusiasm.

He lingered behind so that by the time he approached the coach's office, nearly everyone was gone. Coach excitedly motioned for Jake to come in. Jake dropped his bag at the door and took a seat. He noticed the conference trophy on the desk. It was shiny, silver and black, and shaped like a football. The coach picked it up and held it, sporting a permanent grin and beaming with pride.

"Great game eh, Jake!" Coach Rucker exclaimed. Jake didn't respond. His demeanor was subdued. "Hey, what's the matter with the star player?"

Jake gathered his thoughts. His relationship with the coach had always been predicated upon absolute hierarchy; the aggressive and assertive coach and the diligently obedient player. "I wasn't playing football," Jake said. He was frightened. It was a poignant experience for an eighteen-year-old, and he was having trouble sorting it out. "When I was running toward the line," he said, "I was trying to hurt him. I didn't care about the game or making a tackle. I meant for it to happen." He looked his coach square in the eye, hoping to find help, some reasonable explanation. "I feel guilty about what happened because...because I meant to do it. I wanted to hurt him. I lost control."

"Jake, it's okay," the coach chuckled, "it's part of the game. It was a great play, one of the best hits I've ever seen. You probably just got your bell rung." He smiled and slapped him on the shoulder, "I'm sure you'll feel better in the morning."

Jake wanted to scream, 'You're not listening to me!' But what came out was, "It's all my fault. Biggs deserved better."

Coach Rucker was taken off guard. He hesitated, not quite knowing how to respond. "Do you know him?" he asked. He wasn't really interested in going down this road, but given the circumstances, he had to put his celebration on hold.

"I've talked to him a couple times," Jake said, "mostly at games. He lives next door to my cousin. Did you know that when he was in grade school his dad made him watch as he killed himself? The family was left with nothing. Biggs ran a milk route and mowed lawns as a kid, and he gave all the money to his mom. He worked harder than anyone I know and was about to get a football scholarship. It was his ticket for an education and a better life. Because of me, his life is ruined."

"That's not true," the coach interjected. "He lost his nerve, Jake. If he had taken the hit head on instead of trying to cut at the last second, this wouldn't have happened. Besides, if it didn't happen tonight, I promise you, it would have happened in the near future. When defensive backs faster, stronger, and a hundred pounds heavier than you plant him in the turf in college, his knee would have busted then. Facts are facts—he doesn't have the genetics to play football at a higher level. This was his end of the line. Tonight was his night to be culled from the herd. Yeah, it sounds harsh, and it sucks. I know that. It doesn't seem fair either, but fair has nothing to do with it."

"Do you really believe that? Is that what you're going to tell his mother? That it was his time to be culled?" Something in their relationship changed, an intangible element of respect and adoration was gone. "Look at that," Jake said pointing at the trophy, "I'm ashamed at what it cost. And for what? It's a stupid trophy. In a year, nobody's going to care. In fifty years, it'll have a layer of dust on it. It's nothing more than a meaningless piece of plastic, a piece of plastic that ruined Wayne Biggs' life."

"Come on Jake, everybody's happy. Everybody's proud of you."

Jake rose to his feet and shouldered his bag in the doorway. He paused and said, "No…not everybody, coach." He turned and walked away.

In a moment of introspection, Coach Rucker held the trophy. He stared at the inscription. It struck him as generic and cheap. He set it down on the desk and examined his collection of trophies. He thought about why he started coaching. As he noticed his reflection in the glass case, a forgotten truth returned home. He saw someone who, despite the best intentions, had turned into what he despised.

He hurried out of the room in pursuit. Rounding the corner, he saw the exit door coming to a close as if it had suffered a great yawn and was now slowly closing. The outside lights had been turned off, allowing the darkness of the night to press in. A slow drizzle and misting rain added to the contrast between the bright and dry interior and the outside world. It was an amazing contrast of forces with only very simple and transient things working to separate the two worlds… a roof, walls, and electricity.

"Unbelievable," Jake muttered. His hood was pulled over his head, and he walked toward his pod. At that moment, all he wanted to do was go home and talk about the game with his father. He'd certainly help him sort it out and would provide some degree of comfort.

Suddenly, Jake stopped. The hair stood up on the back of his neck. He felt afraid, like he shouldn't take another step, like he was being watched. He looked around, first to his left, and then to his right. No one was there, just the darkness. He remained motionless until he heard from behind…

"Jake!"

The silhouette of Coach Rucker in the doorway. Jake shook off the feeling and went back to see what he wanted. He was still exposed to the rain when he pulled off his hood. The coach remained planted in the doorway.

"Listen, Jake," he said, "I've been here for a lot of years, and you are by far the brightest and most athletically talented student I have ever had." The coach had been humbled and was finding it difficult to look Jake in the eyes. He went on, "But more important, beyond anyone else I have ever known, you have this quality, this gift; you are absolutely adored by your family, your teammates, your community, and your coach. It's something that can't be taught, Jake. You are a leader and a blessing to everyone around you, and it emanates from in here," he pushed his index finger toward Jake's heart. "Part of the reason you're liked by so many people is because you are exactly the type of person who would feel bad about what happened tonight. I didn't teach you that. That's something you taught me."

Jake didn't know how to respond.

The coach continued, "I don't understand exactly what happened, and I don't think I ever will. Jake, I shouldn't have pushed," he paused looking for his words, "I used you. And you're right. It is just a stupid trophy and it isn't important in the grand scheme of things. I'm sorry, Jake. As your coach I failed. I have a responsibility, and I took advantage of you. I hope you will be able to forgive me." He extended his hand.

Jake contemplated his coach's outstretched hand. He grabbed it but then hugged him, giving him the customary three pats on the back. As he turned to walk away, he felt better, his feelings had been validated. He said, "You know coach, minus that play, it was a great game." Jake stopped, was lost in a brief moment of thought, and added, "And the coaching scheme was excellent."

The coach grinned, and the door slowly closed. He again noted the contrast between the brightness and warmth of the interior versus the cold and dark world, and the real fragility of the barriers between the two. Walking back to his office, he reveled in the strength of character exemplified by his star player and acknowledged the glaring defects in his own.

Jake pulled his hood tight. The rain was coming down harder. Taking notice that the feeling of being watched was gone, he made his way toward his pod. It was the only one left on the lot, waiting for him under a rather archaic and dim fusion-driven lamppost. As he got closer another pod that was parked along the street flashed its lights, twice slowly and twice fast. Then it started rolling toward him, completely silent. Jake smiled as he recognized not only the pod but also the behavioral pattern. It came to a smooth stop in front of him. When the window began to open music blared from the interior. The interior light came on and exposed several of his friends. They were lively and festive, laughing and carrying on. A familiar head popped out in front of him.

"Hey, where you been Jakey-boy? We've been waiting for you," Tom Wilson said from behind the wheel. Tom was one of Jake's best friends.

"Just going over the game with Coach."

"Are you coming?" Tom was referring to the big party. It was going to be a wild time. Everybody who was anybody was going to be celebrating the conference title.

"I don't know, Tom. It sounds like fun, but I don't think I'm gonna make it."

"What? The star of the game? The star of the whole friggin season isn't going to cut loose for one night?"

"I would like to be there, if nothing else just to see you throw up after half a beer."

"Hey, that only happened those eight or nine times." The girls in the car were laughing and poking fun at Tom. "Hey, hey," he said to the girls, "be gentle. It's a shell, I'm not so tough on the inside." He said to Jake, "What are you doing?"

"Going home. Dad hasn't been well. Since he couldn't come, he and mom will be anxious to hear about it."

Jake noticed Wendy in the back seat. She seemed out of place and uncomfortable. Parties weren't really her thing. When they made eye contact, he didn't look away but smiled instead, casually noting her beautiful brown eyes. If a momentary facial expression could halt time, if it could express itself in outright words, his would have shouted for her to get out of the vehicle…to come with him, to be with him. If only they could escape the rest of the world for a few minutes, he would finally tell her how he felt, how he had quietly loved her for years, and how his mind couldn't escape the joy, but also the pain, of constantly thinking about her. He'd confess that the joyous wonder of something as simple as seeing her smile made his knees go weak and his heart palpitate…that she had rule over his heart without even knowing it. In the mere moment that their eyes met, his facial expression screamed all those things, if only she could be made to understand what he had been feeling for years.

'Hi, Wendy,' he was just about to say…but Tom interrupted before the words took form. Jake shifted his attention back to Tom but not before Wendy detected a flash of disappointment.

"Dude, I'm sorry," Tom offered. He was a good friend, and as cavalier as he tried to be, Jake knew him to be sincere and loyal to the end. "I'll tell you what. Feel free to totally downplay my contribution tonight. It'll make your effort look better. I'll play along if they ask. If you change your mind and want to go out, call me. It'll be a special date. Just me and the star football player, together at last." He was talking in a singsong feminine voice and was making exaggerated kissing noises. Tom engaged the pod, and it pulled away out of the parking lot, the computer piloting the vehicle by voice command while Tom was goofing off.

"Nice. Real nice." Jake half-heartedly chuckled. Tom was always good at making him laugh.

He watched as the pod pulled out of the lot and onto the street. What he was unaware of was the exchange of words occurring on the inside.

"Wendy," Tom said. "What are you doing with us?"

"What do you mean?" she said, failing to hide that she was caught off guard by the question.

"I mean, you shouldn't be in here with us."

Wendy was shocked that Tom would say out loud exactly what she was feeling. Not really knowing what to say, she asked, "Where should I be?"

The other girls laughed. "Oh, Wendy," one of them said, "how can you not know? Everybody in the world knows except you."

"What?" she asked, beginning to feel like they were ganging up.

"Don't you see how he looks at you?"

"Who?"

They laughed again. "Jake," Tom said incredulously. "Hot pants, stop the pod." That was his voice recognition name for the pod, which he publically claimed was a beautiful, insanely jealous, and very affectionate woman who was madly in love with him.

"AFFIRMATIVE BIG BOY. COMING TO A STOP." The pod's sultry female voice responded. It pulled to the curb.

While the pod was in the process of stopping, Tom continued, "Look, since you apparently don't get it, let me help. Jake Gillean has been in love with you for years. You're in here, and he's out there. We're going out to celebrate, and he's going home to be with his dad. What does that tell you? I don't know what it tells you, it tells me that he's better than all of us. He deserves better than us. And he absolutely loves you."

If what Tom was telling her was true, what a fool she had been. For years, she thought the attraction was just hers, never dreaming that it was mutual.

"Can I take you back?" Tom was grinning. The other girls began chanting that he should.

Wendy turned and gazed out the rear window. She could still see Jake in the parking lot. She looked back at Tom and her girlfriends, but now she was smiling. It was a nervous smile. She nodded her head in the affirmative, unable to subdue feelings of excitement.

"Hot pants," Tom said. "Go back to the parking lot and stop with Jake on the driver's side."

"AFFIRMATIVE YOU INCREDIBLE STUD. BACK TO THE PARKING LOT. JAKE GILLEAN TO THE LEFT SIDE." The sexy voice confirmed.

The other girls giggled. "Oh Tom, you incredible stud," they teased. The computer was in complete control of the pod and executed the maneuver to perfection.

From Jake's perspective, he watched the pod pull away, then come to a stop half a block away. He thought something was wrong, but then it circled back and came to a stop. He expected Tom's window to open, but instead, Tom casually waved and gave him a thumbs-up. The back door on the opposite side raised up. When it retracted he saw Wendy. Tom pulled away, and they were alone.

When Jake saw her, he forgot his worries, time stopped, and he felt his heart patter.

"Do you mind some company?" she asked.

"Yes. I mean, no," Jake said. There was an awkward pause as he collected his thoughts. He laughed at himself and said, "Company would be great."

She walked toward him quizzically. "If I didn't know better, you seem a little distracted."

'Oh God, she is so beautiful,' he thought, 'and her smile.' Wendy was athletic and stood at five foot eight inches tall. Her legs were lean and her hips perfectly feminine to the extent that for years, he couldn't get them out of his mind.

"I kind of got the feeling you might want to talk to me," she said. It was more of an innocent statement than a question. She smiled and took a step toward him, angling a little to the side. "It's been a long time, since we've spent time together."

As confident as Jake was in every aspect of his life, he felt incredible pangs of nervous discomfort when he was around her. He had stumbled over his dialog with her more times than he cared to remember. The bottom line was, beyond anything else, he really wanted to go out with her, but for some reason he couldn't bring himself to ask. Now he felt like there was some invisible force pushing him toward her. It was irresistible in its effort, somehow forcing him to break the ice. He didn't want to be nervous anymore. It was time to conquer his boyish anxieties. He had to ask her out.

"Wendy, let me ask you something. How come we're not boyfriend-girlfriend?" He slowly moved toward her, cutting off her angled movement so they were face to face. He was absolutely mesmerized by her long dark hair, and how her deep dark eyes blended perfectly with her olive skin.

"Well, let's see." As Wendy spoke, she inched toward him, closing the gap at about the same rate. "I've known you since kindergarten. In the 1st grade, I watched you pick your nose and wipe it on Billy Myer's coat. In the 5th grade, you beat me in the spelling bee. Of course, I kicked your butt every year after that. It gets better though. I believe you have the record for being the most flatulent 8th grader in county history. And for at least the last two years, almost every time we're around each other, you get all weird and uncomfortable.

"Oh, that…I was hoping you hadn't noticed."

"I thought it was because you were going to ask me out, and you were nervous, but you never asked. It just makes a girl think you're more into sports, that's all."

'She's so amazing,' he pined.

"Well, there's a reason for that. You see, I think that, well." Jake's nervous anxiety was racing back. It was already challenging him for the throne. But not this time, he was too proud and sure of himself for that. He fought through it and answered in the best roundabout way he could. "There's this girl you see. I just can't get her out of my head. Don't get me wrong, I don't really want her out of my head. The problem is she doesn't know she's in there." He moved toward her.

"I think she knows," Wendy said. She moved toward him in turn.

They were about a foot apart. "Okay, I'll make a confession." He made a subtle hand gesture exposing his heart. "I have this medical condition. Every time I'm around this girl I'm madly in love with, my mind explodes, and my heart starts racing. I can't put words together without tripping over my tongue. I've been to therapy, but…" Jake smiled. "But I think my original question was to you…something about why we're not boyfriend-girlfriend?"

"The obvious answer, Jake, is that we've never kissed. I think that by definition, you can't be boyfriend-girlfriend without…"

It was the opening he dreamed of, and there was no way on God's green earth he was going to let it slip by. He moved in and grabbed her by the shoulders, briefly gazed into her eyes, took her into his arms, and pressed his lips against hers. The world faded away as he kissed her. Nothing else mattered. He found her embrace entrancing and warm in ways he couldn't explain.

Wendy felt her knees weaken. His muscular arms were holding her up. She found his kiss to be absolutely honest and unpretentious, completely masculine and yet gentle, and she perceived something else…a feeling of complete safety and security.

Since early childhood, Wendy experienced odd sensations when she was around emotionally charged people, sensations that mirrored what they were feeling. It was both a gift and a curse. While it would eventually develop into something incredibly powerful, for the moment, she basked in the feeling of being in Jake's arms, sensing the depth of his unwavering confidence and his complete awareness of her.

They talked and kissed, and kissed and talked, completely oblivious to the fact that it was raining. Jake asked all about her and what was happening in her life. He laughed when she revealed that she would be the class valedictorian because he was the next in line, and unless something happened, he would be the salutatorian. They talked about Jake's father and his illness.

They talked superficially about the game. She thought he was interested in talking about it. At the same time, he thought she wanted to talk about it. Regardless, Jake chose not to talk about what happened with Wayne Biggs or with the coach. He couldn't shake his melancholic feeling about the game, so he hid behind a smiling and extroverted mask. As bad as it made him feel that he was connecting with the girl of his dreams at the same time that Biggs was in the hospital, there wasn't anything he could do about it.

Just as they were approaching the point of being soaked, the rain finally got their attention. Jake didn't want the moment to end, but prudence won out. He showed her into the passenger side of his pod. They continued talking, but something was different; an inexplicable barrier had been shattered. They weren't just friends anymore.

CHAPTER 10: HIS FATHER

"It's too low," Thomas quipped.

"Okay." Janet was supporting most of his weight as she pulled him forward in the chair. She repositioned the pillow, sliding it a little bit higher behind his back. "Is that better?"

Thomas didn't answer. "Where do you think he is? It's almost 2100."

She glanced at the clock. "I don't know. Maybe he's out with his friends. You know how teenagers are." Her comment had an unmistakable edge to it.

"No," he scoffed. "Not my son. He's not like the others." His comment was followed by a coughing fit that in his weakened state was getting the best of him. Thomas Gillean was in the final act of an arduous nine year battle against multiple sclerosis. Over the last year, its course had been progressive, and his central nervous system was left reeling from the ongoing barrage. Finally, two weeks ago, the damage to his brain and spinal cord had reduced his quality of life to the point that he decided to forego further treatments. He accepted hospice into his home for comfort care and was preparing to die.

"That's not what I meant," she said.

"I know what you meant." He was aggravated. "Jake is a good boy. I don't know what more he can possibly do to prove it to you, or why he even has to."

"I'm not having this conversation again." Her voice was irritatingly calm and patronizing. She knew that annoyed him.

"No, you're not," he jabbed back, "It takes two to have a conversation." He was going to add, 'You're about as motherly as a fencepost,' but the effort wasn't worth the outcome. Thomas could still talk, but his voice was hoarse and the effort was exhausting.

"If you need anything, just ring that bell like I told you." She turned to exit the room.

Thomas grabbed the bell and gave it a sharp ring. When she turned back, he shot, "For the thousandth time will you go see the doctor and fix your depression? Why do you have to be so bull-headed?"

Janet snatched the bell and placed it back on the end table. "This is for medical needs, not for your commentary."

"I'm home!" Jake yelled from the kitchen.

The sudden elation in Thomas's eyes spoke volumes. His pride and joy was home. Now they would be able to talk football.

"I brought someone with me," Jake announced as he made his way down the hall. A moment later, he appeared in the doorway, did a quick visual check to make sure everything was okay, and he stepped into the den. That's when Thomas saw Wendy, who came bouncing into the room behind him.

"Wendy!" Thomas exclaimed as loudly as his voice would allow. For him, the sight was as immensely pleasing as it was expected. He had known for years she was going to be his daughter-in-law…but that it would happen several years after his death. Regardless, he felt incredible joy that he was witnessing the beginning of what would prove to be an incredible journey.

"It's so nice to see both of you again," Wendy said. "It's been a long time." She sensed the tension in the room. She also hid her dismay at how much Jake's parents had changed. Thomas was only a fraction of the tall muscular figure she remembered. And Janet looked twenty years older—her blond hair had turned gray, and she appeared completely exhausted. Her effort to smile was telling, like she unwillingly channeled her strength to pull her face into a pleasant expression that wasn't real and one that she didn't mean.

Thomas ignored his wife and addressed Jake, "Tell me that you got up enough nerve to ask her out?" He furrowed his brow on one side and raised it on the other. It was a quirky expression that he developed over the years.

"Well," Jake paused. He was confused as to what the official status of their relationship was. He looked at Wendy. "I guess so," he said sheepishly.

"No," she declared. "No, he didn't." She addressed her answer directly to Thomas. "Hit all around the edges, but he didn't officially ask. I was waving him in." Wendy started making exaggerated gestures with her arms. "Lights and horns were blaring, I even had a banner that said 'YES, I'LL

BE YOUR GIRLFRIEND' but he didn't officially ask."

Thomas' laugh turned into a cough. 'She is such a breath of fresh air,' he thought.

"Okay, okay," Jake said. "Wendy, will you…" Her facial expression stopped him in his tracks. "Oh," he laughed. Getting down on one knee, he held out his hands and took hers, and said, "Wendy, will you please be my girlfriend?"

Thomas made an exaggerated effort of clearing his throat. When they turned their attention to him, he said, "Make him promise he'll always treat you right."

When she turned back to Jake she was beaming.

"I promise to always treat you right, with honor and respect." He went to kiss her hand when Thomas cleared his throat again.

"Make him promise to obey."

Wendy loved this game.

Jake laughed. "I promise to obey your every command, my princess." He hurried and kissed the back of her hand before his father could add anything else.

"I accept," Wendy said.

"Good for you," Thomas said, thrilled by the development. "Janet," he abruptly shifted, "Why don't you go find something to do. I want to spend some time with the kids." His tone was harsh and unwavering.

The moment was awkward. Numbed by the experience of being a spouse turned caregiver, she absorbed the hurt and exited the room.

Despite the fact that his last setback with multiple sclerosis left him nearly blind in one eye, he still had enough vision in the other to see that he had embarrassed Janet. "Jake," he said, "would you check on your mother? With your permission I would like the honor of talking to Wendy alone."

"Whoa," Jake said as he entered the hallway. "Sorry, Killer." He darted around the robot as it busily tracked its target into the den."

"Oh my goodness," Wendy exclaimed. "Is that the G model?"

"It is," Thomas confirmed.

Killer entered the den. He walked just like a person, but his gait was wide, more like that of a toddler. His head was following a mosquito, tracking it with his sensors.

"He's bigger than ours," she commented. "We still have the E model with the rollers."

Killer locked onto his target. The mosquito made the fatal mistake of landing on the wall. Even though it was six foot high, it wasn't out of reach. Killer stood about two feet tall, but his weaponized arm extended up to six feet. That meant his targeting systems could reach all the way to the ceiling. The tip of his arm approached to within six inches and there was a sudden zap. The mosquito fell dead to the floor. Killer raised both arms over his head, let out a whoop, and did a dance.

"He's so cute!" Wendy exclaimed.

Killer picked up his victim and said in a deep baritone voice, "I told you and your fool friends to stay out of my way."

They laughed.

"Did Jake program him?"

"He did," Thomas said. "Killer, what's the count?"

"I have accrued 2,342 confirmed kills, Master Thomas."

"Very good. Please close the door on your way out."

"We really need to upgrade," Wendy said as she took the seat next to Thomas. She reached over and embraced his hand in hers and was immediately seized by an overwhelming wave of peace and contentment. Even though he was in his fifties, his physical appearance resembled someone approaching ninety. But there was something else far more poignant about the man. Despite his frailty there was incredible strength.

"I am blessed," Thomas said. "I can still sort of smile, see." He motioned toward his face. It was held in a sagging grin, identifiable only after he pointed it out. "And I got to see you," he added as he squeezed her hand.

"I'm happy I got to see you too," she agreed. "Do you mind if I ask you something?" Despite his facial expression being flattened due to diminished control of his muscles, she was able to discern a quizzical expression. "I hope I'm not being impolite but I couldn't help noticing the tension between you and Janet."

Thomas dropped his head slightly and closed his eyes. "I know," he admitted. "It's hard even for me to understand. It's even harder to explain." He looked back up. He was completely open, welcoming the opportunity to remove the veil. "I'm going to die." He sensed for a fleeting moment that Wendy was uncomfortable. "It's okay. It's not a secret we have to tiptoe around. This body was always temporary. It won't be the MS that kills me. It'll be pneumonia most likely. There are far worse ways to go than that."

The doctors told him that because of his lack of control of the muscles in his throat, it would be very easy for the food and juices in his stomach to come up his esophagus and aspirate down into his lungs. It would cause a terrible pneumonia and would be a merciful end for a weary soldier.

"Is there anything you want?" she asked. "Anything I might be able to do?"

"No," he said. "Sometimes the disease is delivered from the person, sometimes the person from the disease. I think my destiny is the latter. What I want is…I want to soar. I want to be free. There are a few things I have to do here, but otherwise I want to spread my arms and soar into eternity. I want to meet my maker. But I can't do that if there are all these chains holding me here. Janet…she keeps pulling me back. She makes me worry."

"Have you talked to her about it? Maybe she would understand."

His eyes were tearing up. "I've tried, Wendy. She doesn't listen. To think that one of the things I fell in love with was her strength. I took pride in her aggressiveness. I used to brag about it. She was the perfect military wife. I never had to worry when I was deployed. But all things change with time. Now she's as stubborn and ornery as a constipated mule."

Thomas was trying to contain himself, but the tears were slipping down his cheeks. Wendy handed him a tissue. "I'm sorry," he muttered. "You didn't come here for this." He forced a smile and added, "It's a time for celebration."

"Are you afraid?" she asked. The question was sharp and unexpected but not unwelcome.

"Yes," he admitted. "I am, but not about the things you might think."

"Can you tell me?" She was curious and felt completely at ease with Thomas. For inexplicable reasons, all the barriers that normally would have prevented her from asking were absent.

Thomas smiled. While it would have been comforting to tell her, to reveal what he knew about her and Jake, he couldn't share the details with her. So he gently changed the subject. "Years ago," he said, "I was hoping for a cure, to return to the carefree days when I expected to live forever, but eventually that changed. One day I woke up and something clicked. I came to understand and accept that life is a death sentence. It's finite. We live out our lives, and then we die. That's when I found new hopes and dreams. I can't put it in words, but I feel liberated."

"That makes me happy for you," Wendy commented. "Sounds like a nice place to be," then she quickly added, "under the circumstances."

Thomas chuckled, amused by her swirl of extroversion and compassion.

"Is there anything about your life that you'd like to do over, something that makes you sad?

"What makes me sad," he said, "is that I won't get to enjoy your company. You are an amazing young lady, and you bring so much joy into Jake's life." He looked away in thought before adding, "I can't remember the last time I've seen him so happy."

"Really?" A blush swept across her cheeks.

"I've been telling him to ask you out for a long time. He's so confident and sure that I confess I found it amusing to see him stumbling over himself when it came to you."

She laughed.

"We would go through role play sessions so he could practice. And tonight...he seems so much at ease. Like something changed." Mystified, he went on, "Other girls never caught his attention. His heart is yours. He loves you, Wendy. If you let him, he'll give you the world. But he's going to need you."

"What do you mean?"

"Don't ask me how, I just know that you are going to have an amazing life. There will be ups and downs and challenges that will force both of you to grow. He will be a pillar of strength, but before everything is said and done, there will be a time when he will need you. He'll need all of your strength."

She looked puzzled, but before she could ask anything more he said, "But that's for another day. Wendy, I'm so happy you're going to be part of Jake's life. Do you mind if I have a few moments with him?"

"Sure, I'll go visit with Janet." She was genuine and energetic to the extent that he felt an immediate and lonely void when she left the room.

"Congratulations," he said when Jake returned. "Great game. You won tonight in two respects. She's a...," his exclamation turned into another coughing fit before he finished with, "...wonderful young lady. Do we need to have the man talk again?"

"No," Jake said. "I remember." He took a wad of tissue and wiped a strand of drool that was running down his father's chin.

Thomas looked at him, his expression demanding a more complete answer.

Jake elaborated, "I remember. Discipline. Maintain control of myself. Respect her and honor her always. She is the daughter of parents who love her, she is a gift from God, and she is to be treated accordingly... always."

"Good man," Thomas nodded. "Jake, I'm sorry I couldn't be there tonight. You know I would have if circumstances were different."

"I know, dad," Jake said.

Jake took the seat next to Thomas's recliner. It was his mother's favorite antique Queen Ann chair. She had the ornate woodwork restored and the chair reupholstered with expensive, white fabric. It had been in her family for more generations than anyone besides her could recall. She could recite its entire history and relate anecdotes about each of its owners, all the way back to its original purchase in the mid-1800s. It had been passed through the generations for over five hundred years and was her prized family heirloom.

Thomas felt strong, like he had more energy than usual, and like this was going to be the last council he would have with his son. "I sense something's amiss in Jake's world," he commented. "You want to tell me what's bothering you?"

Jake didn't want to talk about it. Wendy was in the other room, and he already talked to the coach about it. The last thing he wanted to do was talk about Wayne Biggs, but it was right there, bubbling under the surface. He proceeded to describe the details of his hit on Biggs and extended the story through the expression on his mother's face when she ran onto the field.

Thomas listened intently as Jake went on. He mentally tried to place himself in Jake's shoes as his son described how ashamed he was and how he didn't feel joy in winning the conference title. Jake questioned whether or not he was supposed to be happy, if he was supposed to celebrate with the rest of the team. He felt guilt to the point of being nauseous, and on top of everything else, he couldn't wrap his head around the intense and murderous rage. He didn't want it to be there. It made him feel ashamed, like he had a deep and serious defect of character.

Long ago Thomas recognized in Jake a degree of self-reflection that went far beyond the norm. He was a bit of an enigma in that his emotional introversion was wrapped in the cloak of a highly controlled and obligate extrovert.

"Jake, I want to share something with you," he said. "You must admit that everything that is happening to me gives me," he paused to clarify the exact words he wanted to use, "a perspective, of sorts. If you choose, you can disregard what I'm about to say as the rantings of a young man who woke up and discovered that he was old."

"Dad, I've always listened to everything you've told me," Jake offered in self-defense.

"I know you have, Jake. You've always made me very proud that way. Let me tell you first off that I don't know how many more talks like this we're going to be able to have. So I'm going to lay everything out."

Feelings of sadness and fright swept over Jake. "What do you mean?"

"It's okay," he said. His voice was confident and reassuring. "It's important for you to understand what I think about my son." Thomas knew some things to be true; first, if he didn't say what he needed to say now, he might not get the chance. Secondly, if Jake didn't hear them from his father, he'd never hear them, because his mother would never participate in an open emotional exchange with loved ones. "From the time you were little," he went on, "you have somehow managed to maintain an image of being easy-going while in reality, you're incredibly aggressive, both athletically and academically. Your moods are consistent, you're an optimist, you're popular among your friends, and you never make excuses for yourself. That's quite a balancing act isn't it?"

"Yes," Jake agreed.

"You work really hard at it don't you?"

Jake again agreed.

"Why?" Thomas asked. "You never let up. Why?"

"I don't know," Jake said. He felt like he was being put on the spot. "I guess I'm not happy unless I've done my best."

"Is your best good enough?"

Jake thought about the question. "No." Deep down, no matter how hard he tried, for some reason he always felt like he could have tried harder, like he was a failure.

"That's a lot of pressure to put on yourself." Thomas considered this an intrinsic characteristic of a leader. Regardless, he slightly raised his voice and pointedly said, "Jake, I want you to remember to give yourself a break. You're human. The sooner you realize that the better."

"I know," Jake said. "You've told me that before." He knew his father was right, but he couldn't help being his own harshest critic.

Jake's circle included everyone, and he made efforts so that no one was left out. Thomas was beaming with pride as he reminisced about the times he saw Jake teaching his academically gifted and socially challenged friends how to fish and hunt, and as they got older, how to talk to girls. At the same time, he encouraged his athletic friends to work hard and make good grades.

"You know something else I love about you?" Thomas said, "I love that as good as you are in sports, you understand your brain is more important than your biceps. It's easy to forget that during the teen years. And I love that you've developed talents in music. You're quite good you know."

Jake agreed with his father on that point. He was good with music. He could see the music taking shape like three-dimensional structures in his mind. It came easily, and he loved jamming with his friends. He could play the guitar, piano and flute, and he was fairly good with vocals.

Thomas took note of how good looking his son was. He inherited from his father the relatively small joints at the elbow and knee, along with a narrow waist, broad shoulders, and a thick chest. He had the appearance of the consummate athlete, and his Germanic ancestry showed in the sandy blond hair and a strong jaw.

"Jake, you're mature beyond your years," he said. "You're loyal to your friends and a natural leader. You understand right and wrong, and you're willing to stand alone, if you think it's the right thing to do. You have a well developed sense of spirituality."

Jake knew it was coming. When his father was about to reprimand him for something big, he always started by telling him what he was doing right. Then he'd let him have it. He sensed they were getting close.

"Remember all those talks we've had about testosterone and what it can do to a person?" Thomas asked.

"I remember."

"You've done a good job." Thomas laughed, "It wasn't always easy to maintain your dignity was it?"

"No, it wasn't," Jake agreed.

"It'll get harder. Believe me, it'll get harder. Though, by the time you're thirty it'll begin to taper off." Thomas looked away and didn't say anything.

"Dad, are you okay?" Jake asked. He felt a wave of fear that something bad happened. His father was unmoving, staring off with a blank expression. "Dad?"

Thomas suddenly turned back and blurted out, "You know what won't taper off? Your anger." The statement was stabbing. "There's a viciousness to it, Jake. I've only seen it a couple times, like that time on the playground. Do you remember?"

"I remember," Jake said.

"Your anger will get the best of you."

Jake didn't know what to say. His first inclination was to defend himself, but he knew the depths of the struggle he had endured to control his temper.

The playground episode his father was referring to happened in the sixth grade. Jake remembered it as if it were yesterday. He was eleven years old. For several months, two bullies had tormented him. They were several years older and quite a bit bigger. He silently endured their abuse until one day he finally snapped.

"Oh, look at the little baby," they laughed. "Is the baby going to cry?" Basking in the power, they shoved Jake back and forth between them. He was the perfect target, a head shorter and thirty pounds lighter.

Jake's expression was flat, completely without emotion. He didn't say anything and didn't respond. If he didn't give them anything maybe they'd go away. As the weeks and months rolled by, his strategy was proving to be a miserable failure.

Then something different happened. They turned from Jake and set their targets on Tommy, his best friend, the same friend who dropped Wendy off in the parking lot.

"Hey, Tommy," one of them grabbed him from behind and held his arms while the other grabbed his chest and pinched him hard. "You like that?" He grabbed his nose between his fingers, laughing while he squeezed and twisted it. "Oh look! Now you look like your daddy!" They laughed and shoved him. "Have you been drinking again? Are you a drunk like your old man?" They pushed him to the ground and were kicking dirt and rocks on him.

Jake was in shock, frozen in place as he took in the scene. The anger was building inside but there was nothing he could do, he was scared.

"Did you get kicked out of the army like your daddy?" they taunted. Tommy was hysterical and sobbing uncontrollably. The predators had their prey on the ground. They were pulling at his collar and laughing, spitting in his face, and kicking more dirt and gravel on him. Tommy was in a fetal position emitting a high-pitched cry. The emotional pain of the violent fights he witnessed between his parents, the abuse he endured at the hands of his drunken father—it was all too much for him to bear. While they taunted and laughed, what Tommy saw was his father. He could feel his giant fist twisting his collar to the point of choking him. He could feel droplets of spittle raining down on his face. He could smell the wretched alcohol and see his father's gnashing yellow teeth. In the moment of stress, in the moment of utter humiliation, he decompensated and began sucking his thumb.

Jake was stuck in place until he caught site of Tommy. When he saw his thumb in his mouth something burst. A rage was unleashed which absolutely consumed him. Like an unguided missile he screamed and lashed out at the two bullies. He smashed one in the face with his fist as hard as he could. The blow sent him flying backward, his nose broken and blood smeared over his face. Jake grabbed the other by the hair. He rammed his face again and again into a wooden plank that was part of the playground equipment.

"Stop!" the boy screamed.

Other kids gathered around cheering as he kicked and gouged and punched with the only thought being that he wanted to kill them. He threw the boy backward and he fell to the ground. He stomped his face and kicked him in the stomach. Then Jake jumped on top of the first bully, who was still on the ground, holding his nose crying. Jake smashed him in the face with his fists screaming out with every furious blow. Then he was kneeling on the boy's arms, and clenching his hair in one hand while smashing him in the face with the other, over and over again. He suddenly found himself being lifted into the air from behind. He continued to fight, yelling and flinging his arms and legs out in every direction like a rabid animal. He wrenched free and was momentarily on top of one of the bullies again. He punched him several more times and was in the air again, seeing nothing but sky. This time the school superintendent had a better grip, and Jake wasn't going to get away.

Moments later, the fit passed. Jake swung hard in the other direction, as though he was riding an out-of-control emotional roller-coaster. He began to cry. All he wanted was for his father to rescue him and for his mother to not find out what happened.

Both of the boys had bloodied noses (one of them fractured and bent sideways), bloodied mouths, there was a chipped tooth, black eyes, multiple bruises and cuts, and their egos were destroyed.

When the school notified Janet, she flew into a rage. She set about severely punishing Jake. Without asking for an explanation, she hit him repeatedly across his backside with a belt. Jake endured tirades from his mother before, but this was the worst he could recall. She was carrying on and yelling, and continued until late that afternoon. When Jake's father got home, she would demand that he punish Jake the same way.

An eternity later, when Thomas finally did take his first step into the house, it was like he entered a war zone. Janet was yelling, and he found Jake shattered.

"Both of them had to get medical attention! They had to go to the hospital!" she screamed. "We told him fighting was unacceptable!" She pushed the belt toward Thomas, "You need to reinforce the punishment."

Thomas had never raised his hand in anger against his child, but Janet was digging in her heels. She insisted the punishment be administered.

He remained calm even though everything around him had descended into chaos. "Did you ask him what happened?"

"You should have heard what the superintendent told me." She pushed the belt toward him until he took it.

"Did you ask Jake what happened?" he asked again.

"It's important that we be together on issues of discipline."

"You hit my son!" Thomas erupted. "And you didn't even ask him what happened? What the hell is wrong with you?! What kind of parent are you?"

A wave of relief swept over Jake. His father was going to make everything right. He was a huge looming figure, absolute and indomitable in every way. From Jake's perspective, the more the world started to press in, the bigger and more stalwart he became.

Thomas put up his hand indicating that he wanted Janet to be quiet. He looked at Jake with an expression of concern. "Let's go talk."

Jake followed him outside, the dog following, and they walked in silence to the back side of the property, to their favorite pond. They sat on the bank for a good while before they began talking. Thomas was throwing pebbles into the still water while Jake became slowly mesmerized by the circular waves flowing outward.

"You've had a rough day," Thomas finally said. "You want to tell me about it."

Jake started crying.

"It's okay," he said, rubbing Jake's head. "I'm not going to hit you. Why don't you just tell me about it and maybe we can figure out what happened."

"Okay," Jake sobbed. As he talked he found it easier, and by the time he got to the part about the fight the tears were gone.

"Really?" Thomas exclaimed. "You beat up both of them? And they were how many years older?" He looked away. He tried valiantly but was unable to hide the pride he felt in his son.

"I'm sorry, Dad," Jake said. "I didn't mean to let you down."

"I'm going to tell you something, Jake, and I want this to stay between us," he said, "just between us men. Sometimes in life you don't have any options. You have to fight. You have to defend your friends and stand up for what's right. I've been in those situations more times than you can imagine. I think you did the right thing. You conquered your fear and fought against the odds for something that was right. I'm proud of you for that."

Jake smiled. A great sense of relief came over him as this wasn't what he expected to hear.

"There is something that concerns me." Thomas threw in another pebble and handed some to Jake, inviting him to throw a few in. "What worries me is your anger. You had them down. They were beaten. But you stayed on top of them and didn't quit. Why?"

"I don't know," Jake answered.

"What were you thinking?" Thomas asked as he pointed to his head. "What was going on in there?"

Jake thought about it for a moment and said, "You won't be mad?"

"No, Jake. I won't. This is just two men talking, trying to figure things out."

"I wanted to kill them," Jake blurted out.

"You didn't want to kill them before. But once you got mad, you wanted to kill them."

"I guess so," he sheepishly replied.

"Oh boy," Thomas muttered. His expression suddenly changed to one of intense worry. "It's the anger Jake. You're a young man, and you're going through a lot of changes. We have to learn to control your anger." He thought for a moment and added, "I'm going to talk to some people and figure out what we might be able to do. Then we'll talk about this again. There might be some things I can do to help so that it doesn't happen again. Is that okay with you?" he asked.

Jake nodded.

"I do want you to make me a promise." He messed up Jake's hair. "If anything like this happens again, I want you to tell me before it gets out of hand. I think I can help you because the same things happened to me when I was a kid."

"Okay," Jake agreed.

Jake was basking in the warmth of the relationship he shared with his father when they returned home and entered the house. What followed was confusing. After their discussion about anger, what he witnessed was the only time he ever saw his father nearly lose his mind.

As soon as Thomas laid eyes on Janet and saw the scowling expression on her face, he erupted with a white-hot anger. He threw the belt at her. Or to be more accurate, he retained just enough control that when he threw it down, it landed with a snap in front of her. He stuck his finger in Janet's face, yelling, "You will never strike my child again! You're his mother, not some sadistic tyrant! What you did to him is abuse…it's sick! I expect you to make things right!"

Her mouth fell open in complete shock.

Thomas took a breath and finished, "I will not have him psychologically destroyed because of your pathologies."

The memories of that day were fresh even though seven years had passed. Now, even though so much had changed, Jake found himself engaged in another conversation about controlling his anger. He swallowed hard, trying to focus on what his father was saying, but for long periods of time his voice faded out of focus. Jake contrasted the man who sat on the edge of the pond with the one sitting next to him now—inside he was crying at just how much his father's health had deteriorated.

Jake's coping skills wouldn't allow him to confront the mental imagery of his father dying. On some level he wanted to ask him what it was like to touch the face of death. Was he scared? What did he think would happen after death? But fear and discomfort denied him the opportunity to initiate the discussion…a discussion Thomas would have welcomed.

"If it's our prerogative," Thomas said, "we can live out our lives and in the process let life slip aimlessly through our fingers. We waste so much time grasping at illusions. You see son, I simply refuse to believe that our lives can be reduced to being nothing more than a complex arrangement of organic chemicals. There's something very special about us, something that enables us to appreciate sunsets, poetry, and love. We can look up and contemplate the cosmos and the afterlife. For me…therein lies the great mystery of life. I think it has something to do with awareness; awareness of good things and bad."

A violent coughing spell interrupted Thomas's thoughts. Jake was taken aback. His father was choking; his face was red and panicked as he fought for breath and struggled to bring up the thick secretions. Finally, he managed to cough up a thick bolus of mucus, his foul expression indicating that he tasted its wretchedness. Jake handed him some tissue. Thomas's hands were shaking as he deposited the dank glob into the tissue.

Jake found the conversation growing increasingly uncomfortable. His father was expending all of his energy. It was too much.

"Dad, we can talk later," he suggested.

"No," Thomas shot back. "We need to have this talk now." He easily could have said that it would be his last chance, but he chose to hide that from Jake. After he emerged from the coughing fit his color fled. He appeared ashen, and exhaustion from the effort made him sink deeper in his chair, giving the appearance that he was being swallowed.

It took a minute for him to gain enough energy to begin again. "You know right from wrong," he struggled to say. "You are aware. You have the ability to control yourself, your thoughts, your feelings, and your emotions. That's what sets you apart from other animals. Evil exists Jake. Think of yourself as a conduit for the expression of good and evil. The difference is predicated upon your intellectual capacity to know the difference between the two. You have free will. You choose what you express. You choose your own path, your unique destiny."

He reached for his water, but Jake grabbed it. He positioned the straw and held it up to his father's lips. He took a small amount, barely enough to wet his crusted lips.

"Jake," he said, "I'm comfortable with my relationship with God. I believe all the questions I have will be answered when I die, or the questions and unknowns of this life simply won't matter any more."

Thomas took a few uneasy breaths and was seized by another paroxysm of coughing. Jake was powerless to do anything except watch. Given the opportunity he would have willingly exchanged his health for his father's. But such thoughts were summarily rejected as being irrational and infantile.

With each coughing fit, Thomas felt the essence of life slipping away. It wouldn't be long before he would leave his wife a widow and his son without a father. Until then he would channel all his strength to communicate things to Jake, things he believed were important and might help him along his journey. Jake's foundation had to be strong if he were to survive the challenges awaiting him. He leaned forward and feebly reached for Jake's hands. He held them in his.

Jake was scared. His father was talking about dying, yet he was so casual and fearless. As he held his father's hands, he noted how weak and boney they had become, with the expanding diameter of each joint resembling a snake that swallowed a large meal. They used to be so strong. In the not so distant past, the sheer mass of muscle he carried had the effect of disguising the same joints from any casual notice. Jake was about to mention that he could remember when his whole hand fit into the palm of his father's...

"You see, Jake," he began again, his voice having grown progressively more hoarse, "that's part of the mystery of life and the message of spirituality. There is so much that we simply can't understand, but on our journey, we have the unique ability to be aware. Take the time to study. Become aware of the forces that are driving you. Life is a wonderful journey filled with ups and downs, with triumphs and failures. Along the way, you have the right to choose what's living in your heart. You are blessed with free will. You have the right to make good and bad choices," he said, emphasizing by squeezing his hands, "I want you to understand that I'm trying to put into perspective what happened to you." He guided his finger toward Jake's chest, "In here," he said, "There is a lot of anger. I've seen it come out before, and it will come out again. This is going to be your struggle. Please understand," Thomas was summoning all his strength to continue, "that anger, hatred, envy, greed, lust...they are all very similar in some respects. They are expressed by choice. There may be times when they are completely normal responses to things going on in your life. But given the opportunity, Jake, this anger of yours will consume you. Each time it happens, the more blind you will be to it, and the harder it will be to change things." He stopped for a moment to allow the message to take hold.

"Each choice you make," he said, "is part of the ultimate test. It's okay to make mistakes. That's called being human. What's not okay is to keep making the same mistake over and over again. That's emotionally and spiritually immature and self-destructive. Learn from bad choices. God demands emotional and spiritual integrity. He has high standards. Don't lull yourself into the belief that those standards are lower than they really are just because you want to feel good about yourself."

The room fell into a heavy silence. Jake was trying his best to understand. Thomas slumped in the chair, dramatically weakened from the effort. While the body was giving out, the mind was strong and his eyes determined. The experiences he endured in his life, both wonderful and brutal, had matured under the cloak of his progressive illness. Now he looked at his son and felt the weight of a trust pressing down on him.

"Jake, there is a reason I wanted to have this talk with you. I've come to know some things. It's impossible for me to explain how I know, just understand that I do. You are going to have an incredible life. It's going to be filled with challenges. Promise me that you will guard against this anger Jake. Don't ignore it or try to avoid it. You must learn to control it. You can find a weakness in everybody. Yours revealed itself on that football field. It will make you feel powerful and invincible. It's a false shield against loss and sadness that will destroy everything you hold dear. The guilt will eat at you for the rest of your days."

Thomas had never talked like this before. As such, the warning had a sledge hammer-like effect. It was immediate and powerful, each word being indelibly stamped in Jake's mind.

"Jake, you have a free will," he said. "No matter what happens, don't let circumstances control you. If you find yourself on the wrong path, get off and find your way. Ask God for help."

Jake agreed without responding.

"Now," he said as he slumped back in his chair. "I have a question for you. Are you sure you want the military life?"

"Yes," Jake said. He was surprised by the sudden change of discussion.

"Why?"

"I want to be like you."

Thomas contemplated the response. "What is it about me that you want to be like?"

"Your strength," Jake said. "You're controlled and even-keeled. When you're with your friends, you're all so proud—you have relationships with them that Mom and I can't share. I guess I want to live a life that makes friendships like that possible, and I want to serve my country."

Over the years, Jake witnessed his father's military buddies dropping by to catch up and tell lies, and he watched them reminisce about the old days. Theirs were the deep bonds of brotherhood only soldiers could share, bonds forged in the flames of war. They endured hardships they could never speak of…except with each other.

After a pause Thomas continued, "There is something else I want to tell you."

"There's more?" Jake blurted out. It wasn't a sarcastic comment, nor was it inappropriate. It was more an expression of exhaustion, and of being overwhelmed by everything his father had already said.

"Yeah, but I saved the best for last."

"Okay."

"I was going to wait, but something tells me I should tell you now. Earlier today, Richard…do you remember General Richard Morgan?"

"Yes." Jake said with a sudden nervous anticipation. General Richard Morgan was the superintendent of Special Forces Military Academy in Shiloh, Tennessee, the nation's premier training academy.

"Richard, the head honcho?" Thomas quipped.

"Yes." Jake said.

"The big cheese? The top banana?" he kidded. Jake's eyes were wide and eager as his father laughed. "Can you say, four-star General Morgan? You know he and I go back a long way; we're old friends. I remember one time when…"

"Yes! Yes!" Jake was excited. He was at the edge of the seat, half-sitting, half-standing.

Thomas laughed. "He said they got over ninety thousand applicants for the four hundred slots. He personally reviewed your application and found you to be the most impressive applicant they have had in a long time."

"Yeah?"

"Now it's not official yet, as things have to go through the regular bureaucratic channels…but you got in Jake. He is giving you his personal stamp of approval."

Before he jumped up to celebrate Jake arrested his excitement. He asked, "Dad, are you okay with this? That I chose a military life?"

"Yes," he answered.

"Are you proud of me?"

"More than I can put into words."

"Yes!" Jake yelled, jumping out of his seat.

"Official notice will be here in a few days," Thomas said as loudly as his hoarse voice would allow. Jake was already whooping and doing a dance across the room. Janet and Wendy hurried to investigate what the excitement was all about. Jake danced, twirled, and dipped his mother, and followed that with a kiss on her cheek. He took Wendy by the hand and did the same, except that he missed her cheek and took the opportunity to kiss her squarely on the lips.

As Jake danced with Wendy and sang, "The Academy! Woohoo! I'm going to the Academy!" Thomas and Janet made subtle eye contact. A silent message was conveyed between them. It contained joy for their only son and the realization of his dreams, but it was also laden with worry that the life he had chosen for himself was one that would be hard for his family and terribly dangerous. Their brief glance also conveyed that they understood far better than he the difficult times that lay ahead. Given the state of the world and the increasing aggression the Persians were showing in Africa, there was an increased potential for conflict in the not so distant future. Jake's acceptance into the Special Forces would likely place him in the center of it.

Thomas secreted away his swirling emotions. As he knew how the events of Jake's life would play out, he tried his best to be optimistic that he would, in the end, be able to carry his burden.

Later that night, in the sanctum of his thoughts, Jake was on top of the world. He lay in bed staring at the ceiling. He thought about what his military life would be like. He thought about his father and how happy he was. Then he thought about Wayne Biggs and felt a deep pang of guilt. He focused momentarily on the sensation. It felt like a smoldering vacuum in the middle of his chest that was steadily pulling at his lungs and stomach. There was a simultaneous tightness around the sides of his eyes as the muscles involuntarily contracted. He thought long and hard about the things his father said. He took a deep breath, rolled over, and moved on to happier things. He fell asleep thinking about Wendy and the absolute joy she brought into his life.

CHAPTER 11: THE MAN WE'VE BEEN LOOKING FOR

"I like your father," Ben said. "He was special ops?"

"He was," Jake answered. "Cut his teeth in the South American drug wars."

"Those campaigns were ugly. Lost a lot of good men and women."

Jake nodded in agreement. His empty coffee cup had been refilled twice. He didn't know what to expect but was now feeling especially anxious to get out of the rehab facility. He had been feeling like a prisoner. Now that he had progressed physically, he wanted nothing more than to get out and see the sky, and because of some of the things Ben had mentioned, he wanted to discover what was going on in the world. There was something else…he wanted to go home, to see Spring Hill, Tennessee.

I'm curious," Ben said. "Thomas really gave you the what for that night…what was that all about?"

Jake pushed away from the table and leaned back in his chair. He eyed Ben and said, "There's a lot more to the story. When I think about what he told me, it was like he had a crystal ball and could look into the…," he drew back slightly and finished, "like he could look into the future. He was right. Everything he said was right."

"What do you mean?"

"I mean that everything he said about anger and learning to control it, and free will. He was right. I didn't learn. I let it get the better of me, and now it's just like he predicted. All I've got is guilt. He was right in another respect…guilt never lets go. It keeps eating until there's nothing left."

"What do you feel guilty about?" Ben asked.

"I can't talk about it," Jake said. "Wouldn't make any sense," he was looking at Ben with a degree of suspicion, "at least until I tell you what happened…up to the point that I'm here talking to you."

"I understand," Ben agreed. He wasn't quite sure what he was supposed to say so he said the first thing that popped into his head. "I reiterate that I think I will be able to help you. Until then, I'm hungry." He got up and threw the empty cups in the trash. "Want to get out of here?"

"Not so fast." Jake motioned to the chair, indicating that he wanted Ben to have a seat. "Before we go any further I have some questions." He agreed to tell his story, but he was in a strange land and a strange time. That didn't mean he had to play patsy to someone he hardly knew.

"By all means," Ben responded. He took his seat and looked quizzically at his charge, ready and willing to answer any questions.

"Activate your BCD," Jake said. He was coarse and matter-of-fact, like he was issuing an order on the battlefield.

"Umm, okay." Ben was confused by the request.

Jake detected the electromagnetic signature as it sprang to life. Within a couple seconds he hacked the system and wrested control of the unit away from Ben.

"Hey. What's going on?" Ben was confused and flustered. For the first time in his career with the MPS he was at a complete disadvantage.

"Like I said, I have some questions. Now I'm getting the answers."

"What the hell!" Ben protested. He pushed away from the table. He backed toward the far wall while attempting in vain to shut his BCD down. "What's going on with my system?"

"I have control of it." Jake's voice was easy and calm.

"You can't do that!"

"I just did."

"How? It has the latest encryption technologies."

"You only know what you've been shown or told, Ben. You have no idea what I know. Bunkers, buildings, or quantum BCDs…there's always more than one way in. I happen to know all of them."

"But why?" Ben's tone betrayed extreme discomfort. While he was accustomed to having the upper hand, Jake was clearly demonstrating that wasn't going to be the case. Jake was establishing the hierarchy, and he was in command. "If I would have known it was possible to link systems I would have given you access, right through the front door."

Jake laughed. "Sure you would. If we're gonna be sharing, I want to know what you have in there before you do a purge." He was scrolling through the system files in Ben's database with amazing speed.

"What? You can do a purge?"

Jake chuckled. "When you came in here, you said I didn't have a reason to distrust you. I'm just making sure. There they are," he said as he accessed the buried sub-directories.

Ben could see everything Jake was doing. The information from his BCD was streaming out at an incredible rate and was uploading into Jake's unit. All of his security systems were breached, and the locked files were being stolen. He failed miserably in his attempts to regain his poker face.

"Your heart rate's up a bit," Jake commented. "Something you want to tell me about?" His mood was controlled and purposeful while his physical actions were extremely subtle. The speed and ease with which he commandeered Ben's BCD, and his ongoing maneuverings within the system, were completely hidden from casual observation to the point that an onlooker would have been completely oblivious to what he was doing.

"Yes!" Ben exclaimed. He was getting a small taste of what it was like to be on the wrong end of an interrogation. It was his turn to lose control of something precious, and he didn't like it. "There are some things in there that I need to explain. And other things I was going to divulge at the right time."

"Let's get a couple things straight," Jake said. "First, I don't appreciate being at a disadvantage. Can't play chess if you don't know where all the pieces are. Second, don't make the mistake of underestimating my capabilities. You've done it twice now." He continued to eye Ben's reactions. "And lastly, I expect you to shoot straight. Don't divulge things piecemeal on my account."

Jake was amused with Ben. 'He's going to cry,' he thought, 'No, he'll get over it. Should play with him a little bit though…no. No sense rubbing his nose in it.' He released Ben's BCD. "It's all yours. All the files are right where you left 'em." Jake intended to peruse the files at his leisure. "If there's anything I find objectionable I'll let you know."

Ben's face lost its color. "There are some things on there no one was meant to see."

Jake didn't react.

"Her name is Cecilie," Ben said. "She's my wife, and I care about her dearly. Some of those files…"

Jake held up his hand to indicate Ben should stop. "Don't worry. I'm not a voyeur. Your secrets are safe." Ben was squirming. "Besides, we don't have anything to hide." Jake said. He chuckled at Ben's discomfort. "Don't worry. The sanctity of your marriage is safe."

"What you did wasn't fair."

"Fair's got nothing to do with it."

"Bloody hell," Ben defiantly exclaimed. There was nothing left to say. If

MST was going to rely on someone to fulfill its objectives, that person had to be good…actually the best. So far Lt. Col. Jake Gillean was living up to expectations. Ben clearly understood that much, and in a way, he was happy that Jake had handled him so roughly. "Are you ready to go?" he gruffly asked, making an effort to communicate the level of his frustration.

"Yeah," Jake said.

Before exiting the room Ben exclaimed, "That's crap. What you just did."

Jake laughed.

As they were leaving the rehab facility Ben pondered the momentous events that transpired. Everything so far had proven true. He glanced at Jake and thought, 'This is the leader we need, bull in a china shop for the time being, but a leader nevertheless.'

There was something gnawing at Ben that he couldn't explain. There was no record of Jake anywhere. He didn't exist. At least, he shouldn't exist. That carried with it the greatest degree of consternation.

CHAPTER 12:
HIS FATHER'S DEATH

[DECEMBER 21, AD 2367]
[ARRIVAL DATE MINUS 73 YEARS]
[LOCATION: SPRING HILL, TENNESSEE]

The town of Spring Hill, Tennessee, was abuzz with the excitement of high school football. Three weeks had passed since Jake injured Wayne Biggs, and the incident was all but forgotten. Two more hard fought victories had put the Spring Hill Titans in the State finals. It would pit the Titans against a heavily favored team from one of the Memphis suburbs.

It was two days before the game when Jake's world fell apart. He lay awake, gazing toward the ceiling. The game was the farthest thing from his mind. His father's condition had taken a dramatic turn for the worse. He developed severe pneumonia and was in and out of consciousness. The glowing red lights on Jake's clock showed 2:07 A.M. The death vigil was going into its fourteenth hour. Pain medications and sedatives appeared to be making him comfortable, at least from what they could tell, while other medications were controlling his fever. The most important thing was that there were no indications he was suffering.

The stillness was broken by a wailing scream. It was Janet. Jake jumped out of bed and ran down the hallway. When he rounded the corner he froze in the doorway. His mother was holding his father's lifeless body. He reached out and clutched the frame, digging his fingers into the wood. Under the weight of paralyzing grief his legs felt weak, like he was going to fall. The bedrock of his world was mortal…and he had finally fallen.

It didn't matter that Thomas had struggled for years. Now that he was actually gone, it was as though his death was sudden and unexpected. The finality of the moment struck Jake with emotional brutality. Seized by a sensation of overwhelming vulnerability, he was hyperventilating.

Janet was overcome with grief. Tears of anguish were cascading down her cheeks. She was sprawled halfway in the bed, her head resting on her husband's chest, her hands were at his shoulders pressing and squeezing as she screamed out. The dam that had been holding everything back for nearly a decade burst and a wave of emotion exploded outward.

There was little left of the proud and stalwart man she married. The mass of muscle that decorated his frame had long since vanished. His broad and rounded shoulders were reduced to nothing more than their skeletal underpinnings. Now that his spirit escaped its worldly confines and was finally free she was overwhelmed by loneliness. Her Rock of Gibraltar was gone.

Janet had tried to be a pillar of strength. Through all their ordeals she continuously held her tongue in check and on innumerable occasions, as she witnessed the sequence of little deaths that occurred with each new day, she maintained a façade of calm control. The last thing she wanted was to appear weak, not for her own sake, but for that of Thomas. She believed he had enough worries, and that he took comfort in knowing his wife was strong, that she would be okay after he was gone…or at least that's what she assumed. Now that it was over there was no reason to contain her emotions.

The next two days were difficult beyond measure. Janet hadn't slept. Her hands were tremulous. Deep circles outlined the lower reaches of her eyes. The evidence of her compromised state was further declared by the blood red color of the margins of her eyelids.

In the face of major depression and sleep deprivation, she was task oriented tending to the details of the funeral arrangements. It was going to be a military funeral with full honors. Numerous military brass and some regional politicians would be in attendance. Thomas made only one specific request that Janet knew of—that Jake be given the option of being one of the pallbearers. Otherwise he left the details to Janet and the military.

Jake tried to talk to his mother about what was happening, but she was distant. It was almost as if she couldn't hear him. She would converse with relatives and family friends through the Vintel, or by videophone. Her conversations progressed as if they were scripted. She would briefly describe how the last few weeks had been, then in greater detail she would explain his last days, then the story would culminate with his death. In return, whomever she was talking to would convey how sorry they were, and they'd say what a great man Thomas was. Janet would provide details regarding the times and locations of the viewing and funeral. She would terminate the connection, stare for several minutes with an empty expression resembling that of a depressed sleepwalker, and then she'd contact the next person.

Since his death, Jake leaned heavily on Wendy and his friends. While he prided himself on being emotionally controlled and strong (which for him meant doing everything he could to avoid crying in front of anyone) he was comfortable sharing his feelings with Wendy. They cried together, laughed together, talked for hours about Thomas, and shared wonderful memories.

Jake was trying his best to navigate the maze of tangled thoughts and feelings. But the process was far more complicated in light of Janet's behavior. He was worried about her. He made numerous attempts to initiate conversation, to let her know he was concerned, but mostly she didn't reciprocate. She either had a short answer or didn't bother to respond at all. He loved her and wasn't going to give up.

"Dad said he was going to see me graduate," he said. The comment was offered as another place to initiate a dialogue. High school graduation was a milestone that would have given his father cause for celebration.

Janet pushed away from the table and, without warning, slapped him across the face. The blow was hard. Then she struck him a second time and a third.

"Mom?!" Jake exclaimed. Shocked and horrified, he backed across the room with his arms up to defend himself from repeated blows.

"Shame on you! Shame on you, Jacob Gillean!" she was hysterical. "Your father is dead. Do you get it? He's dead!" she shrieked. "Do you have any idea how much he suffered?! How is it possible that you could live in this house and not realize that? Your father wrapped all his hopes and dreams around you. YOU!" she screamed. "He only lived as long as he did for YOU, Jake! A lesser man would have died years ago! It was all about YOU! YOU! And all you can think about is that he didn't live long enough to suit YOU!"

"That's not what I meant," he pleaded. Jake was overwhelmed. The sting of her words was worse than the physical blows.

"I know what you meant you selfish, self-centered BOY!" Janet wasn't giving in. Her whole body was rigid and her demeanor was absolute in its antagonism. She had a twisted hold on his shirt, just below his neck. "You know what, just go. I can't stand looking at YOU! Go to your room. In two hours YOU have to leave for your game."

"What? I can't play." Jake was incredulous.

Janet shoved and slapped at him again. She stuck her finger in his face, stabbing him hard in the cheek. The quality of her glare was something he had seen before. It was pure hatred.

"I can't," Jake repeated.

"I'm only going to say this once. You ARE playing." She pulled his shirt and shoved it back into his chest, hitting him as enunciation. "No son of Thomas Gillean is going to let his teammates down. Didn't you learn anything? You saw his friends. Do you have any idea what they went through so you'd have the freedom to play your damned football? They didn't have the luxury of taking time off if they got their feelings hurt. When you look at your father in his casket tonight, are you going to tell him you were too sad and selfish…THAT YOU LET YOUR FRIENDS DOWN?!" She slapped him again as she hysterically screamed, "THAT YOU DIDN'T EVEN BOTHER TO SHOW UP FOR THE GAME?!"

"Mom. Stop!" Jake pleaded.

Janet raised her hand as if she was going to strike him again. "You're not a child. It's time you stopped acting like one. Go to your room. I don't want to see you again. When you come back out of that room, so help me God, you better be the man your father claimed you were!" She slammed her fist against his chest and pushed him toward his room. She gave a final shriek, "GET OUT OF HERE! I DON'T WANT TO LOOK AT YOU!"

Jake was at a complete loss as to how he was supposed to process what had just happened. He fell in bed and cried. When the tears wouldn't come anymore, he stared at the wall. He held his father's cross necklace in his hand. He slowly and methodically fingered it. His mind was mysteriously calm. In fact, it was as completely quiet as if he was hypnotized. There were no thoughts, just complete mental silence. The last thing he did before leaving the room was put the chain around his neck. He pulled out the neck of his shirt and let the cross fall into place against his chest. It was positioned at the exact spot his mother had hit him.

Janet was stoic. Beyond asking if he was ready to go, she didn't have anything to say. The ride to the Tennessee State High School Championship Football Game started and concluded with the same heavy silence that dominated the entire time between.

Wendy was with a large group of students traveling to the game in the fan buses. When the caravan arrived in Memphis, it was almost two miles long, and easily half the town of Spring Hill made the trip. They formed a gauntlet of cheering supporters outside the stadium. The players dashed off the team bus with their arms high in the air. They were enthusiastically hooting and hollering as they made their way through the crowd and into the guts of the stadium. As Jake wasn't on the bus, the players accepted his absence as an indication that he wasn't going to play. While none of his teammates dared verbalize the fact that the Titan's star player wouldn't be there, as it would have brought down their morale, there were hushed murmurs of disappointment in the crowd when they discovered Jake wasn't with the team. All Coach Rucker knew was that Janet said he would be there.

Because the rest of the team disappeared into the locker room twenty minutes earlier, Jake's late arrival was unexpected. Janet dropped him off and disappeared. He was alone and his world was spinning. He was on the sidewalk in front of the stadium's main entrance. There were signs with arrows pointing in every direction, but they didn't make sense. He was aware that people were staring. They were whispering, but were otherwise out of focus. Where were the locker rooms? Where were his teammates? Where was Wendy?

Only a few surprised and muted cheers from the mostly dispersed fans were raised. They didn't know how enthusiastically to react, given the death of his father, a man they all knew and respected. The awkwardness was predicated upon social mores and the desire to not have their excitement misconstrued.

"Has anyone seen Wendy?" he asked. The question wasn't directed to anyone in particular. He asked three or four times before someone said they would find her.

Jake felt a hand on his shoulder. "You look lost." The words came from his Uncle Vince.

Pastor Nolan from their church was with him. He smiled and said, "We'll take you. I think the tunnel you're looking for is over here around the corner."

"Wendy! Wendy! Jake's here!" one of her friends excitedly said.

"Where?" She was confused. She had been trying to get in touch with him all day. She even stopped by his house. Janet said he wasn't taking any visitors and then she closed the door in her face.

Jake was heading down the ramp and into the tunnel. He stopped and looked back. There was an open square of bright sky casting its light into the shadows. She was coming. He knew it. He waited, staring at the brilliance of the sky until Wendy's form appeared at the top of the ramp.

She ran down the ramp while he was coming back up. She threw her arms around him and kissed him. When they first touched she was struck by the sensation of something pressing against her temples, while at the same time she found it difficult to breathe, like something was squeezing her chest. Her immediate reaction was to slightly wince and withdraw, pushing him away but keeping her hands on his shoulders.

"Jake, what's going on? Are you okay?"

"I don't want to talk about it." His lower lip was quivering. He was on the verge of tears, but he fought hard to maintain composure.

"I've been worried," she said. "We haven't talked since yesterday."

"I know. I'm sorry."

"What's wrong? Has something happened?"

"It's Mom." He took another deep breath. "Can we talk later?"

"Did she tell you I called several times?"

Jake shook his head to indicate that she hadn't.

"And that I dropped by this morning?"

His response was the same.

Wendy was confused. She kissed him. "I love you," she said. She smiled and grabbed his cheeks, kissed him again and said, "It's just a couple hours. You can do this. I love you."

"I love you too," he said.

"Do it for your dad." Her eyes were filled with tears.

Jake nodded. "See you after the game?"

"I'll be right here waiting."

They kissed again and Jake disappeared down the tunnel. Wendy watched until he was out of sight. Then she left on a mission to find Janet.

When the locker room door opened and Jake appeared, there was a deafening silence. All movement stopped.

"Sorry I'm late," he said. No one moved, but he saw smiles and expressions of sheer elation.

Coach Rucker cleared his throat to get everyone's attention. He pointed and said, "Your locker's over there." He continued reviewing the game plan so Jake could get prepared for the game without being made to feel like he was under a microscope.

His teammates were first and foremost concerned friends. While they wanted to win, they weren't willing to play for the title at the expense of one of their own. One by one they filed past his locker. They slapped his shoulders and said a few words, and then made their way to the field.

Tom stayed behind and helped Jake get suited up. He didn't ask, he just started helping with the pads, the joint supports, and the cleats. "I'm glad you get the chance to see me win State," he said. Under his breath he added, "and the MVP."

"Me too," Jake couldn't help chuckling. "What is that?"

"I want to look mean." Tom's face was decorated with far more black paint than usual. It was smeared at odd angles under his eyes. He boasted, "They need to know what they're up against." He made a clawing motion and a sarcastic roaring noise that sounded more like a sick kitten. "Are you going to wear that?" he asked, pointing at Jake's cross.

"Yeah," Jake said.

"Well you can't wear it loose like that." Tom knew what it was because he saw it yesterday, and Jake explained how special it was. "Do you mind if I tape the chain into the neckline of your shirt so it won't get ripped off?"

"Good idea." After that they threw on the posterior neck stabilizer, the shoulder pads, spleen and liver shields, and then the jersey.

Twenty minutes later, Jake was in the end zone getting ready to receive the opening kickoff. The lower sections of the immense professional stadium were mostly filled, and the energy was rocking the stadium. The vibrations from stomping feet could be felt across the field. Jake paced, lost in his thoughts. Despite all of his efforts to suppress his grief, tears were streaming down his face. He and his father dreamed together what it would be like to play in the State Championship. They imagined the crowd and the energy. But now that Jake was there, his emotions were altogether different. He kept his head down to hide what was happening. His teammates knew but pretended not to notice. Jake took deep breaths. He felt the cross under his jersey and held it as he mumbled a prayer. "God, please help me. Please help me get through this. Please help me." And then he added, "And mom. Please help mom." He prayed for his dad, for his teammates, and for the safety of all the players. Satisfied he was ready, he dedicated the game to his father, took a few more deep breaths, and prepared to receive the kickoff.

The players and coaches watched Jake nervously. From his side of the field it was out of concern for his wellbeing. For the other side it was out of athletic apprehension.

The opposing players began a slow run and then sprinted as fast as they could as the kicker launched the ball in the air. The game was underway. The crowd was screaming as the ball floated in a slow casual arc. It finally came down at the two-yard line. Jake was already running forward when he caught it. At first he was aware of the crowd and their excitement. He was moving fast. He dodged a few players. He did a spin move and broke out of a tackle. Seeing the field clearing in front of him, he dug deep and found a gear that even he didn't know he had. The crowd noise became something of a high-pitched scream. Tears streamed down his cheeks as he ran. His feet and legs moved with such power and speed that they were little more than a blur. He was running for a purpose; for the next two hours he gave everything he had as a dedication to his father. It was the game of his life and a stunning victory for Spring Hill.

CHAPTER 13:
THE UNFOLDING STORY

[APRIL 12, AD 2441]
[132 DAYS AFTER ARRIVAL; THREE DAYS LATER]
*[LOCATION: NEW WASHINGTON, TEXAS; THE OFFICE OF THE PRESIDENT
OF UNITED AMERICA]*

"You look like hell, Carl," President Martinez commented. He didn't really care. All he was concerned about was whether Zimmer could do his job.

Zimmer looked exactly the way he felt. He hadn't slept for two days, and the situation at NAIA headquarters had been going from bad to worse. "We've lost our information networks," he said, "first in Europe, then Brazil, Russia and China, and the latest, Japan. To date we have lost through arrest sixty-three undercover agents and forty-eight level I contacts, and another twenty-seven agents are missing."

"Missing?"

"Meaning we have lost contact, but bodies have not been recovered."

"Who's behind this?"

"We don't know."

"Haven't you picked up any chatter or financial anomalies?"

"No. We have no suspects."

President Martinez clenched his fist and struck the top of his desk. "How is that possible?!"

"I'm sorry, sir. I don't know."

"I'm sorry?" he scoffed. "Do you realize what this means? It could mean war. International incidents like this can't be fixed with diplomacy. The military is on high alert, and I've got brass from every branch pushing for clarification of orders, for rules of engagement. The situation has forced me to consider first strike options."

"Sir?" Zimmer was taken aback by the revelation. He knew the international situation was serious, but even as aggressive as he was, he hadn't fathomed they were actually teetering on the precipice of something that could turn into another World War.

"Look, Carl, we've been friends for a long time. You're one of the few people I believe I can trust."

"I appreciate your confidence, Mr. President."

"This has to be an inside job. Have any of the usual groups on the domestic map been making any noise?"

"Not much...the usual hushed rumblings about imperialism and increased fears about another war, too much government control, and civil liberties, but for the most part we've been able to keep a lid on things."

"What about the Libertarian groups?"

"They stay in the shadows, sir. Eliminate one and two more come in to take their place."

The President was gravely concerned and increasingly bullish, "All these NAIA operations were classified. Do you have any idea how the information was relayed and ended up in the hands of, hell, seems every government on the planet?"

"No, sir," Zimmer answered. "We're covering every angle. I have the world's finest team of forensic computer scientists and quantum physicists working night and day on it. So far there is no evidence that the systems were hacked from the outside. All the encryption systems are intact and have not been compromised."

"Does anyone else have access to the codes?"

"No sir."

"Are you absolutely positive?"

"I'd stake my life on it," Zimmer said, digging his heels in on the point.

"Tell me about the system. Who created it?"

"MST."

"What?!" President Martinez was ready to come unglued. "MST designed the system we're using for all our classified communications... for all our files?!"

"No, sir," Zimmer defended, "not exactly. They designed the foundation of the system and worked out the mathematics as part of a government contract ten years ago, but we created the actual codes, or the key to the lock, so to speak."

"So there's no way that MST could be behind this?"

"It's not outside the realm of possibilities. As you know, we've had differences with MST over the years, but the fact they designed the system in no way gives them an advantage in cracking our codes."

"In your opinion, is this an inside job?"

Zimmer hesitated. "Mr. President," he was shaking his head in the negative, "we don't have anyone with universal clearance. Not even me. No one person had access to all the operations that have been blown. We keep everything compartmentalized to prevent just this sort of thing from happening. To have enough people in place to pull this off would easily make this the greatest case of espionage in the history of man."

"Espionage? They would call it counter-espionage," the President sharply retorted. He was frustrated at the lack of answers. "Dammit! We don't have any friends left, Carl. The whole world is unifying against us." His expression touched the edge of being a glare. "Is there anything you need that I haven't provided?"

"Right now, no sir," he responded. Since the crisis began, Zimmer had been yelling non-stop at everyone worth yelling at, but his efforts so far had borne no fruit. His fears that he was losing favor within the Egalitarian Party's inner circle of power were justified. It was a precarious and potentially deadly situation as the whisper campaign for his replacement had already been launched. If he were replaced, he doubted that he'd be allowed to simply walk away.

"These are serious times we're living in, Carl." The President leaned forward, his eyes ablaze like he was giving one of the Party's choreographed public relations announcements. "For years we've had the Chinese pushing us on human rights, the Europeans accusing us of market manipulations, and the Russians hating us just because they're so damn good at it. They were mad as hell before all this started. Now all of them have discovered, among other things, that we have operatives embedded in their governments and militaries. Hell, the Deputy Marshall of the European Defense Department was one of ours. And just like that," he snapped his fingers, "in just over two months, it's all come crashing down…a damned house of cards. There will be hell to pay."

"Do you think it's possible?" Zimmer was referring to the countries uniting in a formal coalition against United America.

"Possible? It's already happening. And it gets worse. The South American coalition is clamoring for war. Their delegations are promising unconditional support for anyone willing to take action against us. They still haven't forgiven us for the drug wars."

Zimmer was going to say, 'Can't blame them for that. How many millions of people ended up dead?' But he wisely elected to remain silent.

"I've been dealing with screaming Heads of State for two months now," the President said. "Quite frankly, I think it would be easier to just declare war and be done with it."

"Sir? Are you seriously considering…?"

President Martinez waved his hand, brushing off Zimmer's question. He said, "We are in a very good position. We came out of WW4 with our military and industry intact, and in comparison, we've maintained our technological advantage. More importantly, Carl, strong Fascist movements are taking root around the world. Industry, private enterprise, and even the social fabric and religion, are increasingly falling under government control through regulation. It's happening all across Asia and South America." He sneered, "Ownership is a mirage. That's one of the big differences between our system and the idealistic visions of the Marxists…we give the people their mirages. But make no mistake, we control everything wrapped in the perfect cloak of nationalism. Given a choice, I'd prefer to take advantage of the useful idiots within their governments and media, and take them over from the inside, rather than by war. Far less messy." The President chuckled, "Tell you what…you take the military and I'll take an army of liberal lawyers. I'll win every time. It's inevitable…just takes more time. I'll turn your society upside-down. Create an excess supply, and they start looking for things to do. It creates increased regulation and then more are required to monitor and enforce the regulations. The process marches in lockstep with increasing power of a central government. Further, it's cheap to train a lawyer. That's why we have so many law schools. In the last decade, we've educated in excess of seven hundred thousand foreign lawyers, all indoctrinated with our vision, and we promptly sent them back home. The fools in those countries have no idea what they're in for."

"There are still those who long for the old days," Zimmer said, careful how he chose his words…"less regulation and more freedom."

"More choices lead to instability and inefficiency. It's people who hold those views who stand to gain from dealing a blow to Fascism. I want you to start rounding up Libertarians as we find them. Press them hard. Let's see if something develops."

A flashing icon on his Vintel indicated there was an incoming message. He activated the prompt and said harshly, "Yes?"

"Mr. President." It was the voice of his Chief of Staff. "I'm sorry to bother you, but there is an urgent communication for you on matrix 72."

"Thank you." He swiveled in his chair, turning to the Defense Department Vintel unit that was recently installed in his office. It was equipped with all the latest security features. He looked into a device that looked vaguely similar to a pair of old-style binoculars. It scanned his retinas and allowed him to log into the system. He accessed matrix 72 and read the communication.

URGENT: APRIL 12, 2441; 1830 HOURS

1400: NEW WASHINGTON - THE SOUTH AMERICAN EMBASSY WAS EVACUATED AND FOREIGN STAFF RECALLED.

1630: RIO DE JANEIRO - AMBASSADOR WALLACE AND MEMBERS OF THE UNITED AMERICAN STAFF HAVE BEEN DETAINED ALONG WITH THIRTEEN ALLEGED ASSOCIATES, POSSIBLY MORE, WITHIN THE BRAZILIAN GOVERNMENT, MILITARY, AND BANKING SYSTEM. THE PUBLICALLY ISSUED INDICTMENT IS FOR ESPIONAGE SPONSORED BY THE GOVERNMENT OF UNITED AMERICA.

1645: BOISE, IDAHO – THE BODY OF GOVERNOR JULIA MELTON WAS DISCOVERED IN HER HOME. AUTOPSY RESULTS PENDING. PRELIMINARY EVIDENCE SUGGESTS ASSASSINATION.

* * * * *

[APRIL 12, AD 2441]
[132 DAYS AFTER ARRIVAL; (THE SAME DAY)]
[ALASKAN WILDERNESS]

"What are you doing?" Jake asked.

"It's called fishing gear. I rent it, and we go fishing." Ben was struggling. His arms were loaded with high-tech laser sites and a sub-surface marine identification sensor. They were out of balance, while one was falling to the left, the other was tipping over and flipping to the right. As he reached for one of them, the sites on the energy pulsar swung around and hit him behind the ear. In exasperation he managed to tuck it under his arm, but both hands were immobilized so that if he let go of anything it would risk falling to the floor. That's when he noticed Jake's amused expression. They were facing each other in the aisle.

"What is all this?"

"Well," Ben explained, "This is an underwater sensor. It can identify fish out to a thirty meter radius. It gives information on species, gender, and weight. The other two devices are fishing pulsars. They interface with the sensor, and through a process of triangulation, it targets the lasers under the water. When the beams cross it causes an immediate burst…kills the fish we want to eat." Ben's feathers were on full display as he proudly demonstrated proficiency with outdoor living. From the story so far, he assumed Jake knew how to fish. But given the question, Ben logically concluded that fishing technologies must have changed since he was a kid. He briefly entertained the idea that it was going to be fun bringing Jake up to speed.

Jake laughed, "That's not fishing."

"What do you mean?" Ben was taken aback. He had been fishing lots of times and this was how he had always done it.

"It's not a sport if the fish doesn't have a chance." Jake's amused tone carried with it an edge of sarcasm, and he shook his head as though chastising a child. It didn't take long for him to discover Ben's habit of getting defensive when his manhood was called into question. Jake casually asked, "When you rent that stuff, does it come with a dress and a fancy umbrella?"

"Oh, you're so full of it," Ben scoffed.

"Come on, let's put that stuff back, and I'll show you how it's supposed to be done." He emptied Ben's arms and nudged him toward the cashier saying, "Watch and learn."

Ben accepted that Jake was running the show and stepped to the side. Before he knew it, Jake and the cashier were speaking another language. It was English, but about fish in such detail that Ben had no idea what they were talking about. The elderly cashier's excitement indicated he had been waiting a long time for a customer who could keep up with him. Jake nonchalantly posed the question.

"What are the chances of getting our hands on a couple of old fashioned rods and reels?"

"Oh, you're real sportsmen," he exclaimed. "Don't get many folks who like to do it that way. The big city dandies come out here, and all they want to do is cheat with all the technology. There's no sport in it, I say. When I saw your friend here picking up all the equipment, I thought you were a couple of beginners."

"No, not a beginner," Jake said. He glanced at Ben with a 'see I told you so' expression.

Ben rolled his eyes.

The man didn't notice the exchange, as he was busy shaking his fist in celebration, "I had a hunch I would meet some true fishermen today. Follow me," he said. He happily limped down a hall and into a back room, where he proudly showed them his personal collection. He outfitted them with poles, waders, and all the other supplies they would need.

Three days had passed since Jake began telling his story. He started in the rehab center, continued in Albany, New York, and now they were in the deep forest in a remote region of Alaska. Ben guessed that given Jake's background, fishing would be a good vehicle through which he might reveal more of his experiences, and at the same time, they could enjoy the outdoors.

The day was overcast and there was a light misting rain. A local ranger said that grizzly bears were in the area, and she gave them the spiel about safety. By late morning they were fishing.

'What is it about him?' Jake thought. Ben was about thirty meters downstream, casting and reeling, and casting again. There was some strange familiarity. Ben reminded him of someone. It was a distant primordial memory, but despite all his efforts, he couldn't pull it out of the shadows.

For his part, Ben was reveling in the fantastic discovery of a new way to fish, one that teased the brain with what it couldn't see, with the great unknown regarding exactly what marine vertebrates were lurking beneath the surface, and the realization that if he did everything right…that nature might actually lead one of them to take his hook. When he got his first bite, he leaped with excitement. The fish pulled his line with incredible strength, and he had to fight it, not just with brute muscle, but with grace and agility. At one point, it actually came out of the water and flipped in the air. Finally, with Jake's guidance in the proper way to let the line out and bring it back in, he successfully scored his first catch. He was immediately addicted. With an ear-to-ear grin, he imagined how he would share the experience with Cecilie and his children.

As Ben was living in the moment and enjoying every nuance of the experience, Jake was suffering under the weight of unyielding sadness. The coldness of its embrace overpowered any pleasure he might have found in what they were doing or in the majesty of the surroundings. He focused on the year. It was 2441. He could feel the world pressing in. It was screaming that he didn't belong. The time belonged to other people. It was their time to live out their lives. He was an unwanted interloper.

In the cabin that night, they began another poignant exchange. It began with Ben describing how United America initially yielded under the sway of the Egalitarian Party, how the voters succumbed to the empty rhetoric of the suave and persuasive politicians, and how, when a substantial percentage of the populace realized what was happening and rose up in protest, they were smashed. The country was trapped in the indomitable grip of a Fascist ideology, and the Egalitarian Party had spent the last sixty years consolidating power.

"All this happened after World War IV?" Jake asked. He was struggling to come to grips with the fact that after six hundred years of embracing and nurturing the evolving constructs of equality and freedom, the foundation laid by the Founding Fathers had suddenly been abandoned… that everything he and millions of soldiers were fighting for during the war was abruptly abandoned so soon after he disappeared.

"It did," Ben confirmed.

"How is it possible that the country could change so radically in such a short period of time?"

"It hasn't been a short period of time," Ben said. "Think about it. The year is 2441. What year was it when you disappeared, 2379?"

Jake didn't respond.

"If my math is right, that makes sixty-two years. Considering that anyone under ten years old at the conclusion of World War IV probably didn't understand what was going on, it's only those who are now well over seventy years old who have any idea what it was like before the Egalitarian Party came into power," Ben said. "One of the first objectives of the Fascist philosophy is to take over education and the dissemination of information. Control the mind, and you control the person. Control the youth, and you control society."

"How did it happen?"

"In a word," Ben said, "complacency. It's a long and insidious process but cultures change over time. In America there was a progressive abdication of personal responsibility in exchange for increased reliance on a central government. I think that when it's given more and more power, eventually any government has the capacity to become omnipotent. I don't know," he admitted, "but there are probably a thousand different ways of looking at it. In the end, it doesn't really matter, does it? What does matter is what we're left with–a government that doesn't answer to the people."

"Most bad government grows out of too much government," Jake said, "and the natural progress of things is for liberty to yield and the government to gain ground." He watched for Ben's reaction. When none was forthcoming he asked, "You do know who said that?"

"No."

"Thomas Jefferson."

Ben's face was blank.

"He was one of the Founding Fathers, the third President of the United States," Jake said, "the author of the Declaration of Independence." In the absence of a response he added, "Widely considered the most intelligent President ever elected." He thought about mentioning President James Garfield, but then elected to avoid going down that road.

Ben shook his head and confessed, "I'm not familiar with early United States history."

Jake was disgusted and felt compelled to say, 'Apparently. If America had been educated and had shown due vigilance, the Egalitarian Party never would have been allowed to take over.' But he kept the accusations to himself. "Jefferson was a gift and a thinker. He had some things to say about the future of democracy and how it might be destroyed. He said, 'When the government fears the people, there is liberty. When the people fear the government, there is tyranny.'"

Jake couldn't help but to shake his head in disappointment. When Ben detected the reaction, he was pleased. It indicated that on some level, Jake was still emotionally invested in the country he fought for sixty years earlier, and more importantly, it represented hope that he might be convinced to fight again.

Jake mused, "If Jefferson could see what happened to his country… after six hundred years of freedom. It's hard to imagine that it was thrown away without a revolution."

"I never said there wasn't a revolution," Ben corrected. "Whole segments of society tried to resist, mostly outside the large urban areas and in the agricultural belts of the Midwest. But they didn't have the means. One of the first things the Egalitarian Party did was take away all their weapons. By the time the uprisings started, one side was armed and the other wasn't. The outcome was predetermined. Even so, millions of people died fighting."

"Millions? Of United Americans?"

"That's a conservative estimate."

The revelation was utterly shocking.

CHAPTER 14: IN THE WAKE OF THE DEATH OF THOMAS

[DECEMBER 24, AD 2367]
[ARRIVAL DATE MINUS 73 YEARS]
[LOCATION: SPRING HILL, TENNESSEE]

To the east, the sky was hinting toward morning, while in the opposite direction darkness still reigned. It was the following morning, and the men were leaving the cabin for another day of fishing. The air was vibrantly cool and each breath announced itself against the stillness of a landscape relatively untouched by man. After several hours, with the sun cresting over the mountains and bathing the valley with the first rays of warmth, Jake picked up the story where he left off…following the death of his father.

Thomas Gillean died three days earlier, in the early morning hours of December 21, 2367. In the wake of his life, he left behind his wife and his son. They loved him with all their hearts and his passing left a void that would never be filled.

In the weeks before he died, the head of Thomas's hospital bed was kept elevated at about thirty-five degrees. It was thought that the postural modification would decrease the odds of aspiration. The combination of a weakened diaphragm, near inability to forcefully cough, and the risk of having a damaged gag reflex, all combined to make his situation extremely tenuous. He deteriorated to the point of being so brittle that there was little left to do beyond comfort measures. Near the end, his condition was considered 'day-to-day.' His epiglottis, the protective flap over the top of his airway, wasn't working properly when he swallowed. It left the top of the trachea vulnerable and exposed his lungs not only to foods and liquids, but to the contents of his stomach if refluxed. There were stimulator devices that could have been implanted, but Thomas refused on the grounds that he was tired. He said his good-byes and closed himself off from the rest of the world. His final days were spent fluctuating between the privacy of his thoughts and prayers, or in a state of unconsciousness.

When Thomas died, he was hunched over on his side. It wasn't immediately clear exactly what happened. Sometime during the night he might have had an event and then twisted himself over in the throes of dying, or maybe he hunched over first in such a way that his head ended up lower than his stomach. Regardless, the end result was the same. Thomas Gillean had aspirated enough gastric fluid into his lungs to kill someone three times his size. He died at the young age of forty-six, after a nine and a half year battle with multiple sclerosis.

Janet had borne the emotional weight of surviving the thousand little deaths her husband endured during his long battle. Each time his disease worsened, each time he lost some additional function, she saw a part of her husband die. While this made the moment of his actual death a short leap intellectually, it also made it the nidus for a tremendous explosion of pent up emotions. After giving everything she had for so long, all that remained was exhaustion and emotional emptiness. She was drained spiritually and mentally, and depression pushed her toward complete instability.

During the viewing and funeral she mostly stared off into space. Her thoughts weren't dark and foreboding, nor were they wrapped in a cloak of self-pity. They were actually non-existent. Her mind was just blank, completely numb. There was nothing left for her except the undulating feel of loss and despair.

During the viewing, Jake knelt in front of his father's casket. He prayed to God on behalf of his father and asked that blessings be placed upon his soul. Wendy was at his side with her arm around him as he gently caressed his father's head. In his mind he was telling him about the game and how he dedicated it to his lasting memory. He took off the necklace and with absolute deference he placed it in Thomas's folded hands, positioning it so the cross dangled outward.

"I miss him so much," he whispered to Wendy.

"I know, me too," she said, choking back tears. Wendy understood Thomas's suffering was over and that he was in a better place, but she couldn't help feeling sad. She watched Jake struggling to keep it together, fighting to maintain control under the weight of emotion, and it made her cry.

The funeral took place the next morning…the morning of the 24th. In addition to the stress and blur of the event, with relatives and friends coming and going, Janet still wasn't speaking to Jake. It added a smoldering darkness that worsened an already somber occasion. Then came the regimented decorum of a military burial.

They were at the cemetery, the bagpipes were playing, the twenty-one gun salute had just been fired, Janet had the folded flag on her lap, and the casket was being lowered into the ground. Suddenly, Jake realized he had left the necklace in his father's hands. "The necklace," he whispered to Wendy. His eyes were panicked. There was nothing he could do. He was helpless as the casket disappeared into the ground.

"It's just an object," Wendy whispered. She squeezed his upper arm and leaned in close to his ear, "He already gave you everything that's important. We'll try to get it back later."

Jake felt sick, but he knew she was right.

What he didn't know was that one of his father's closest friends, and an undercover operative from MST, had taken the necklace out as the lid was being closed. It was going to find its way back to Jake later that night.

At the gathering that followed the funeral, a stranger introduced himself to Jake and his mother. He said he was a close friend to Thomas. He handed each of them a package.

"In the event of his death, Thomas asked that I give these to you. It was his intention that you open them in private. They contain very personal letters and a recording." With that, he promptly turned and disappeared into the crowd.

Later that night, after Wendy went home, Jake was alone in his bedroom. He held the package and examined it closely, contemplating what it might contain. There was a sense of mystery and intrigue. He unsnapped the ends and lifted the seal. Inside he found a holographic recording and two envelopes.

He plugged the chip into his Vintel unit, and a projected image of his father appeared.

"Hello, son," Thomas said. "If you're watching this it means that I have died." He smiled. "I don't want you to be sad. I'm in a much happier place and God has seen fit to deliver me from my disease." Thomas's image was younger and appeared stronger than Jake remembered, indicating that it had been recorded a year or two earlier.

As the recording went on, Thomas recalled the joy he felt when he first found out that Janet was pregnant. He recalled his excitement the first time he saw Jake walk, describing it like a newborn gazelle absolutely determined to get it right. He confessed that the memory was etched in his mind in such a way that it made his extended deployments painful to endure. At the same time, it strengthened his resolve to make it through the Drug Wars in South America, so that he might come home to be a father and a husband.

"Jake," he said, "your life will be filled with challenges and incredible experiences. Along the way, your resolve will be tested in ways you can't begin to imagine. The obstacles you will encounter and what you will be asked to endure will go far beyond what would break an ordinary person. You are anything but ordinary. You are exceptional in every way that matters. I need you to remember that and remain strong."

Jake was confused and couldn't fight the feeling of being afraid. Was the message a warning of some sort, or possibly a premonition? What exactly was his father trying to tell him? Jake sensed that his father knew more than he was saying.

Thomas instructed Jake to open the smaller envelope. He felt something jingle inside as he tore the seal. He reached inside. When he pulled out the contents he felt tears welling up. It was his father's cross-necklace. 'But how?' he thought, 'how did it get in there?' He squeezed it and swore he'd never lose it again. He noticed there was something else in the envelope—photographs. He examined each one carefully. They were of his father, his grandfather, and his great-grandfather. Each photo was taken when they were deployed. They were decked out in battle gear with all the accoutrements. In each photo, they were wearing the cross-necklace.

"The necklace has been in our family for four generations," Thomas explained. "I wore it on every one of my missions, as did your grandfather and his father before him. It is a symbol of a faith, a belief in something bigger and greater than we can fully understand. In the vacuum of disbelief it's just a meaningless piece of shaped metal. But it meant something dear to those who wore it before you. The cross is a symbol that in the worst of times, reminded me of my belief that there is some ultimate meaning to all the suffering in the world. It's a reminder that honor, integrity, and discipline serve as silent guides, especially in the many trying times of doubt, times when you feel lost, when you lose your direction. More than once," he admitted, "it helped me find my way, reminding me that humility and generosity were lifelong endeavors, that life is a series of tests and that it was up to me whether or not I passed, and that at the start and the end there is a loving and forgiving God."

Jake paused the projection. He was immersed in the solemnity of the moment. He embraced the experiences of the men, the soldiers and warriors, who wore the cross that he held in his hand. They carried it through battles and kept it as they endured hardships he could scarcely imagine. While the mystery of how it got into the envelope remained just that—a mystery, he expunged it from his mind and accepted the cross as his. Because of the memories it embodied and what it represented on so many levels, it was now his most valued possession. He put the necklace over his head and tucked the cross into permanent place under his shirt.

At the moment Jake restarted the projection, his life changed forever.

"I don't want you to open the second envelope yet," Thomas said. "I would like the opportunity to explain how its contents came into my possession. I found it," he bluntly said. "It was under an odd set of circumstances. Its label indicates that it's for you. I don't know what it is or what the implications are for your life. When I first met Janet, and we were dating…"

Thomas went on to explain that he spent several uninterrupted weeks with her family on their farm located between Spring Hill and Franklin, Tennessee. Jake knew the place well. It was about two miles up the road from his home. It had been in his mother's family since the early 1800s.

Being a purebred city boy, Thomas was learning the ways of farm life and trying hard to impress Janet's family, or at least not embarrass himself. The flexion of his masculinity was butting up against Janet's three brothers, who were all hard-working to the point of being wild with it. After proving he could keep up, Thomas was accepted into the family circle.

Thomas made it a point to spend as much time as he could doing chores around the farm. This pattern continued well after he was married, after Jake was born, and continued when he was active in United America's special operations forces. If he had a week or two leave, at least several of the days would be spent on the farm. He alluded that it was one of those days when he discovered the second envelope.

The family was having the property lines surveyed because a neighbor on the backside of the farm was selling to corporate interests. They were planning to develop the surrounding countryside with an ultra modern golf course and an attached resort community. For centuries the honored property lines between neighbors were old wandering fence lines, streams, and large rock markers. Usually, in an effort to avoid feuding and to remain neighborly, the lines were left alone. Property lines were accepted as passed down by the previous generations. However, since this time a corporate interest was involved, the family felt that it was prudent to have everything officially and legally surveyed in order to clearly establish the lines.

Thomas described how he was given the task of digging up a large rock marking a distant corner of the property. It was distinctly out of place in the local area in that it was red, a result of high iron content. The rock had marked the property line for over half a millennium. It had passed the quiet centuries deep in the woods, adjacent to an old neglected fence. The plan was to have the stone dug up. A satellite-guided survey would reestablish the line to within a thousandth of an inch. Permanent large orange metal posts with embedded lasers for sighting would be used to mark the true lines and outline the entire farm. Thomas was left alone with the large rock, while his brother-in-law, Vince, trekked through the woods looking for the other markers that would have to be replaced.

Thomas described his plan. He was going to dig up the rock and move it as fast as possible. As part of their ongoing competition, he wanted to be resting comfortably under a nearby tree by the time Vince returned.

"I dug at the side of that rock, actually it was more of a boulder, like there was no tomorrow," he said. "Once I was able to get my fingers under the bottom edge I heaved and lifted. It was huge. When it rolled over, I remember feeling proud. I was sweating profusely, but the job only took me a few minutes. I wanted to thump my chest and shout out like Tarzan... but before I did I noticed something rather odd. When I rolled the rock over, there was something buried underneath. It was an urn."

Jake was enthralled with the story. His first wonder was if it was the same urn that was on the shelf in the den. All his father ever said was that he found it.

"I cleared away the dirt and lifted it out. Except for worn paint, it was perfectly preserved. There were remnants of black paint and a fancy gold-laced design. I looked carefully, but there were no indications of a name or engravings of any kind. Morbid curiosity got the better of me, and I opened it. The lid was frozen tight. I had to place it between my knees and use both hands until it finally gave way. I expected it to be filled with the ashes of some long departed soul, but it wasn't. It contained an envelope. I pulled it out and examined it. Jake...it had your name on it."

Jake was taken aback. He didn't understand. How could the envelope have his name on it?

What his father didn't reveal was that there were two envelopes. The second one had his name, Thomas Gillean, printed on it.

"I want you to open your envelope now," Thomas said.

Jake paused the hologram and opened it. He found inside an old brittle envelope. It appeared ancient, like it belonged in a museum. The edges were tattered and frayed, the color faded to a dull yellow. He carefully opened the envelope with a letter opener. The aged paper crinkled and slightly tore at several points when he pulled it out and unfolded it. There were three pieces of paper. Only the center was written upon. Its message was worn and faded and barely readable in places. Jake sensed that there was something vaguely familiar about it. The letter read:

JAKE,
YOU'RE ALONE IN YOUR ROOM WATCHING DAD'S FINAL MESSAGE. IT IS DECEMBER 24, 2367. THE CLOCK SAYS 9:43 P.M.

Jake looked at the clock and caught it just as it turned from 9:42 to 9:43. 'How can this be?' he thought. His mind was racing. He stared at the clock, firmly establishing that it indeed said 9:43. His heart was pounding as he continued:

I AM WRITING THIS LETTER TO YOU, TO MYSELF, FROM THE CONFINES OF THE PAST. IF OUR EFFORTS ARE SUCCESSFUL YOU WILL BE READING THIS LETTER FIVE HUNDRED AND THREE YEARS IN THE FUTURE.

IN AN ACCIDENT I CAN'T EXPLAIN, YOU WILL BE TRANSPORTED THROUGH TIME – BACK TO THE NINETEENTH CENTURY. YOU WILL LIVE THROUGH THE AMERICAN CIVIL WAR. LEARN EVERYTHING YOU CAN ABOUT THE FARM AND YOUR FAMILY'S HISTORY… THEY MUST SURVIVE. IF THEY DON'T, EVERYONE YOU KNOW AND LOVE WILL CEASE TO EXIST. JOIN GENERAL NATHAN BEDFORD FORREST'S ESCORT AND YOU WILL BE WHERE YOU ARE NEEDED.

PROTECT JOHN AND ELIZABETH.

JAKE GILLEAN
NOVEMBER 30, 1864

"What is going on?" Jake mumbled in a swirl of shock and amazement. Confused questions multiplied out of control. Was this some sort of joke? Was it a test? Because the letter came from his father he was compelled to think it wasn't…that it was real. There was something about the writing that was odd. It was familiar. He jumped from the desk and rushed to his bookshelf. Where was it? His mind fought to stay focused. He couldn't find it. It was right there, right where he always put it, but now he couldn't find it. Feeling panicked, he ran his fingers across the spines. There. He found it. He yanked his journal out, lost his grip, and it fell to the desk. He grabbed it again, flipped it open and examined the handwriting. He held the letter next to it. "Oh my God," he mumbled. The writing was a perfect match…it was his.

Jake sank into his chair and read the letter again, and again, stopping only when he had done so several dozen times. He examined the envelope. His name was scrawled across the front. Again, it was his handwriting. When there were no further clues he started the projection.

"By now you have undoubtedly read the letter," Thomas said. "You are the only one who knows its contents. I want to direct your attention to the back of the envelope. You will notice that a small section of the flap is missing." He was right. The edges were sharp, appearing as though it had been cut away. Thomas had carefully cut the piece away in order to have it analyzed at a lab. "The paper," he said, "was found to date to the mid-1800s. However, the chemical composition, with some slight variations, is consistent with modern manufacturing techniques. The paper is from our time, but the letter is five hundred years old. I do hope the contents of the letter are such that one day you are able to make sense of this."

When Thomas found the urn and discovered its contents, he was as confused as Jake and far more distraught. It was a hot day in August. He was sitting alone in the woods with the urn between his thighs. The lid was off, and he laid it to the side. He wiped the dirt off his hands and carefully pulled the envelopes out. The first one had the name Jake Gillean written across the front. When he examined the second, his heart skipped a beat...it had his name on it and the exact date. He carefully opened it and unfolded the letter. There were several photos. They were of him when he was younger, one of his wedding, and others that caused him to take pause. They appeared to be him...but he was older, much older, and there was a child with him. What did it mean? Thomas was confused. He looked around the woods to see if anyone was watching, thinking that he was the butt of some sort of joke. No one was there. He was alone. His hands were shaking as he began reading the letter. It was several pages long. It began.

THOMAS GILLEAN

DEAR FATHER...

As he read its contents, each word pulled him in deeper. The story it told absolutely captivated him and, at the same time, profoundly disturbed him. By the time he finished reading, tears were streaming down his face. He was angry and felt completely alone and powerless in a world that suddenly collapsed around him. It couldn't be real. He threw the letter and the urn on the ground and paced. At first he was afraid to touch it. He needed time to sort everything out. Eventually, he put the letters back and secured the lid. With the urn tucked under his arm, he ran through the woods. His mind was racing, and he had no idea where he was going. How could it be? The letter was written by Jake Gillean...his son. But the year was 2441. Its contents were so disturbing he couldn't accept the cruelty of it. There had to be a reasonable explanation.

Thomas ran until he was deep into the property that was being developed by corporate interests. Winded and overheated, he pulled up to catch his breath. He decided to turn back, to go back to the farm. He'd hide the urn until he could sort everything out. When he turned he stopped dead in his tracks. He was face to face with two men and a woman. They were dressed in business attire and appeared to be expecting him.

"Thomas Gillean?" the woman said.

"Yes," he answered, confused by the development.

"My name is Josephine Stuart." While Thomas's appearance was exactly what she expected, wide-eyed, scared, and lost, her voice was calm and reassuring. She introduced the men and said, "We are part of an organization that would like to help you…MST Global. You have heard of us?"

"Yes," he said.

"Please let us help you." She pointed to the urn. "The contents of that letter are disturbing. If you come with us, I think we will be able to help you."

That was twenty years ago. Since that time, Thomas read the letter thousands of times. It was haunting, it was enchanting, it was everything that should and should not have been. He was directed in his letter to keep its existence secret. The one with Jake's name on it would be delivered unopened after his own death. The directions were honored in their entirety.

The urn was an antique dating to the mid-1800s. He had it professionally cleaned and restored to its former luster; it found a new home on the shelf in his den. Over the years, Thomas would find himself holding it late at night. In deep thought, he would run his fingers over its surface. He imagined that he could perceive some aura of energy emanating from within its interior. As he held it in his lap, he often thought about what must have been happening at the time it was originally buried. In those moments, he found himself experiencing the deepest of agonies. But he was alone. There was no way he could share his burden.

Thomas kept his letter hidden. As with the envelope of Jake's letter, he had his letter analyzed. Its carbon dating indicated that it was buried in the 1800s. At the same time, the chemicals within the paper indicated that it could not have been manufactured prior to the Twenty Fourth Century. The correlation between the scientific results, and the written date in the letter wouldn't have made sense were it not for its contents. Finally, late one night about one month before his death, he burned it in the fireplace. It was a burden that seemed to give him the strangest combination of both great joy and violent sadness.

Thomas was a powerful and stalwart warrior. He had endured hardship and tragedy, and experienced war and the destruction of more lives than he could count. His missions and what he did to survive remained the same as with most soldiers…locked away in a quiet place in the mind. While he humbly asked God to help him understand and continually asked for forgiveness, no one ever saw him cry. For Thomas, weeping was a deeply private process. In the middle of the night, when he finally placed the letter in the fireplace and watched it burn, he was so completely distraught that he shielded his face in his hands and bitterly sobbed. He felt alone, just as he did in the woods the day he discovered the urn. Between him and God, no one else knew. It was his private hell to endure while his innocent family slept.

Now that Thomas did everything that was asked and fulfilled his mission, Jake's journey was just beginning. As the holographic projection played through the remainder of his father's final message, it was one of encouragement and love. "Jake, you have made me a proud father in every way. I will be watching over you. Remain strong and remember to guard against anger and pride. Remember our talks. I love you. Good bye." He smiled and finished, "One day we'll see each other again in another world."

The projection disappeared and in its place came the announcement… MESSAGE DESTRUCT IN 5…4…3…

"No, no, no, no," Jake yelled as he tried to pull the chip out of his Vintel.

2…1. And then there was nothing.

Jake was upset. Why would he have made the message destruct? It had to be a mistake. What was the purpose? His father never would have meant for that to happen.

From that moment on, the cross was permanently affixed around Jake's neck. He hid the letter and spent every moment he could spare on the old family farm. It was still active and owned by his Uncle Vince. It didn't take long for Jake to become familiar with the lay of the land and its history, and he became the local authority on his family's ancestry. He accumulated pictures of the old homestead and figured out exactly where everything was.

He found information that was collected through the years relating to the major life events and the general personalities of various deceased relatives. He was especially interested, of course, in John and Elizabeth Stuart. John was described as adventurous and fearless. He turned eighteen and joined the Confederate cavalry in early 1864. He rode under the command of General Nathan Bedford Forrest. He was wounded and had to sit out the last several months of the war.

Elizabeth Reynolds would eventually become his wife. She was the same age and grew up on an adjacent farm. She was remembered as being purposeful and nurturing and having a brilliant talent for music. After the war, John and Elizabeth lived out a long life on the farm. They had one child, a boy they named Jacob. He subsequently took over the farm and raised his own family. So it was that the farm came to remain in the family through the generations.

CHAPTER 15: YOU KNEW

"So you knew you were going to travel back in time," Ben said.

"I don't know," Jake answered. "Reckon I thought it was a possibility. As I got older and learned more about science and physics, the more it seemed impossible. I pushed it out of my mind." He extended his pole behind him and gracefully cast his line, dropping it next to some logs. He added, "There were distractions. We were at war. Wasn't time enough to entertain fantasies."

Over the next two days, Jake detailed his experiences at the military academy and his acceptance into Alpha Group of The Guard, the most advanced fighting force the world had ever known. He described his marriage to Wendy and the birth of their two children, Bailey and Paul. His story advanced twelve years, and he outlined world affairs leading up to World War IV, a conflict that pitted the immense Persian Empire against the rest of the world.

"Jake," Ben said, "I need to know absolutely every detail of your experience during World War IV. I need to know where you were, what you did, the details of the weapons, and how the battles were conducted from your perspective."

"You want to know about the war." Jake was shaking his head. He had doubts. He had already been talking most of the morning and it was now around noon. They were done fishing for the morning and were hauling the gear back to the cabin.

"I need to know the soldier," Ben said. "I know you when you were eighteen years old. I know you when you went through your training at the Special Forces Military Academy. I know your devotion to Wendy, and that she became a pediatrician. But you went to war. Jake, I need to know what happened, what you experienced, and what those experiences did to you."

Jake exhaled. It was a sigh of frustration. "Do you realize what you're asking?"

"I do," Ben said. "But there's no other way. I don't know how much time we have. The world is falling apart as we speak."

Jake was fighting his inner demons and didn't hear Ben's response. He clenched his fists and felt the muscles tightening across his temples. "Those wounds run deep. They shouldn't be relived."

Ben tried a different angle. "You realize that most of the weapons you used were manufactured by MST Global, or one of its surrogates?"

Jake didn't answer.

Ben was looking at a man who had been brutalized by war and nonstop fighting. At the same time, the fate of the world depended upon his willingness to pick up his weapons and wield them again, to sacrifice everything he might have left for a cause…to rescue the people of United America from the tyranny of the Egalitarian Party and its hordes of Fascist disciples. The pendulum was already swinging and there was going to be another war. MST needed Jake to be the leader of the free world. Until Ben made a formal push to convince him that the people of United America were worth fighting for, he would have to hit around the edges, plant the seed, let him think about it.

With his voice and mannerisms purposefully nonchalant, Ben said, "You're unique in that you're the only one alive who has actual experience using the weapons in the field, and you've led men in battle," he carefully added, "and you're still capable."

The comment caught Jake. His reaction was swift, as though he had come under fire. "I did my fighting," he answered. "This one's not mine." His voice was cold and unyielding. He had another agenda and fighting for a world that didn't belong to him wasn't included. He only trusted Ben insofar as he needed help figuring out how to undo the mistakes of his life and set things right.

Ben wasn't discouraged. It was early. He didn't know how much, but there was still time. He went back to his original request. "Will you tell me what happened during the war?"

"I don't know," Jake said. Tired and grief stricken, the act of reliving his youth and young adulthood was ripping deeper and deeper into his most guarded vulnerabilities. The stories were being pulled from a very distant part of his memory, a remote land to which he could never return. It was agonizing for him and talking about it didn't help. It was only magnifying the loss, making the weight heavier to bear. With each story, he peeled back another layer. Underneath was a heavily guarded core. He was risking its exposure, an act that frightened him but had an unspeakable allure. 'No!' his mind screamed. He couldn't face what he had done. It was all his fault…all of it. The accusations were pounding, and he could feel the omnipresent gavel, the shock waves reverberating from his subconscious to the point of physically shaking him. The demons were coming again. They were emerging out of the fog, descending upon him, gnashing their teeth, and salivating on the memory of the man he once was and the life he had. Jake was ready to explode. He had to leave, to focus on something else. With single-mindedness of purpose, he changed clothes and threw on his running shoes.

"You coming?"

"How far?" Ben didn't want to go but felt compelled to pretend.

"Twenty."

"See ya," Ben sarcastically responded. He understood what was happening and wanted to give Jake some space. As he was leaving, Ben yelled after him, "Hey! Better take this!" He tossed his pulsar. When Jake caught it he commented, "For bears and such."

CHAPTER 16: WAR

[APRIL 14, AD 2441]
[134 DAYS AFTER ARRIVAL; (TWO DAYS HAVE PASSED SINCE
JAKE AND BEN BEGAN FISHING)]
[LOCATION: ALASKAN WILDERNESS]

"These are the poles they used," the old man croaked. He was scared. The agents were from the government. Their badges indicated they were from the DSS. Their mannerisms were aggressive and accusatory. He pleaded that he had done nothing wrong. What had he gotten mixed up in? He was scared senseless for himself and his family. They would be ruined, the government would see to that. In a Fascist society innocence wasn't an obstacle to imprisonment. Or, if he said one thing wrong he and his family would lose their jobs and would be left destitute, outcasts in a land controlled completely by the Egalitarian Party.

The officers made him sit on a stool with his hands pinned underneath. He was crying. The woman kept her eye on him while her partner scanned the poles. He used a strange device. It was unlike anything he had ever seen. He carefully waved it over the poles.

Its screen indicated: Analysis complete – DNA detected. A list of eight names appeared. Included in the list were the names the officers were looking for: Benjamin Murray and Target Primary, which was their code for John Doe…or Jake Gillean.

"When did they leave?" she asked.

"Early this morning. They were already waiting when I opened up."

"Where did they go from here?"

"I don't know." She took a step toward him, and he blurted out again, "I don't know. I don't know. They didn't say. They just brought my poles back and left. I swear."

* * * * *

Despite extreme misgivings, Jake came to agree with Ben. He began the difficult process of relating the epic events of World War IV and his personal experience of the fighting. To put everything in context, he began by outlining the rise to dominance of the Persian Empire, a development that took place over the course of two centuries. They were the world leaders in technology and manufacturing, and while foreign competitors were sleeping, they came to dominate the arms race. Eventually, the combination of their sociopolitical system, economic structure, and cultural underpinnings, gave birth to an unbridled quest for world dominion. By the time war broke out, a fully integrated and fervently nationalistic empire with an inexhaustible supply of manpower and an eye for expansion had spread across the Arabian Peninsula, through the Asian Sub-Continent, and came to encompass almost the entirety of Africa. Fatigued and in many ways still reeling from World War III, the rest of the world followed the path of appeasement. When numerous peace overtures failed to diminish their aggressive expansionist policies, it was their military conquest of the African Continent's last holdout, South Africa, that finally caused the world to descend into the terrors of its Fourth World War. For United America it was good versus evil, freedom versus tyranny, and cultural independence versus assimilation. The year was 2374.

Given his position within Alpha Group, Jake experienced the war in brutal fashion. He was constantly engaged and saw action in every theater of a conflict that raged across the globe. It didn't take long for the primary lines of battle to grind into a deadly stalemate reminiscent of the trench warfare of World War I. Hundreds of millions of soldiers were fighting in the field, and every year, tens of millions were dying across Africa, in Southern Europe, and in lines that extended north and east, chewing up vast portions of Southern Russia, curling through Mongolia, ripping through Western China, and finally back to the sea near the Bay of Bengal. While those were the primary lines demarcating friend from foe, with kill zones that exceeded the horrors of human imagination in between, the fighting was in fact occurring in some capacity on every continent.

Bloody tale after bloody tale, and after suffering the loss of more friends in battle than Ben could count, Jake's story progressed to the fifth and final hellish year of the war—the year 2379. He was relating the events of the Battle of Corinth, and as he talked, Ben reeled under the weight of the hardships Jake had endured physically, mentally, and spiritually. Ben found that Jake wasn't the same person he had first gotten to know. War had made him increasingly hard and callous, but at the same time there was something else—something intangible. Underneath the brawn and the perpetual purposefulness of action, there was a well-preserved core of vibrant humanity within him that was fighting against the odds for survival.

Ben was also weighing the prospects of a war to free United America from the tyranny of Fascist control. The prospects of MST gaining victory over the Egalitarian Party were progressively decreasing as the realities of the modern battlefield were being laid out. Further, as he was coming to see it, the likelihood of Jake agreeing to take up arms again after everything he had already endured was increasingly unlikely.

* * * * *

[July3, AD 2379 (12 years have passed since the death of Thomas Gillean)]
[Arrival date minus 61 years]
[Corinth, Greece]

In just over a decade, the blur of athletic shoes racing down the football field had been transformed into military boots pacing between the lines of fighting men in the cargo hold of an ultrasonic transport. They were flying in the upper stratosphere high above the Alps, headed toward Greece and the Corinthian battlefield. Lt. Col. Jake Gillean examined the men of Alpha Group. While he was only thirty-years old, they were his to command. He was impressive beyond measure, and the youngest ever to rise to his present rank.

"Run a final diagnostic," he ordered. Over the roar of the engines it would have been impossible for everyone to hear him, but the command went through the biotech communications device, the BCD, embedded in his skull and was transmitted to theirs. It was MST's most advanced system yet—the Heldon Super Soldier Integration System Model 11H16.

The transport shook from turbulence. One of the men lost his balance and fell toward Jake. He grabbed him by the shoulder, kept him from falling, and steadied him back in line.

"The objectives have been defined," he announced. "The latest schematic on the building has been uploaded, and as we speak, the diversionary attacks on the ground are underway. Everyone knows what you're supposed to do. Is there anything det you don't understand?" His Tennessee accent was unmistakable.

With the exception of a few casualty replacements who had recently been added to the unit, they were all familiar. To a person, they were hardened veterans. Raw recruits didn't make it into The Guard, much less Alpha Group. A soldier had to earn the right to wear an exo-suit and a Guardsman's uniform. They earned it by being braver, more capable, and smarter than everyone else. As a result, they understood each other, they trusted one another, and they knew what they had to do.

Jake made eye contact with his superior officer, Colonel Alexander Fisk. He gave a subtle nod.

"Initiate systems check," Jake commanded. All the BCDs and the weapons systems went through a final integration check, and the links with the remote handlers stateside were solidified before the drop.

Increasingly, Col. Fisk had been hands-off, allowing his second in command to run Alpha Group. It was an unspoken sign that Jake was being groomed for independent command.

Alpha Group was one of five units, each comprised of eighty men, that collectively made up a special operations force called The Guard. The perfect integration of man, quantum computer systems, and modern weapons, they were the Panzers of United America's Twenty-Fourth Century war machine. They were wearing the latest in military grade exo-suits manufactured by MST. The coal black uniforms were covered with a thin layer of pliable but impenetrable metal alloy, while under that was an amazing bio-alloy designed to augment the soldiers' physical capabilities. They functioned like muscle fibrils, but were far stronger, responding, contracting and relaxing, in unison with the soldiers' muscles. The brain was the computer interface. Its signals were intercepted at the level of the muscles through the natural alterations in electrical activity and electromagnetic fields of the fighting soldier, and the suit would, with a delay of only microseconds, exponentially magnify the Guardsman's capabilities. The fully-outfitted soldier was extremely agile, was capable of running at speeds up to and exceeding 60 miles per hour, could jump higher, could punch through walls, and could lift incredible amounts of weight. As it responded to the natural abilities of the soldier wearing it, the more physically fit the soldier, the more the exo-suit would respond.

The exo-suits were loaded with every high-tech enhancement available for use on the battlefield. Built-in energy shields deflected incoming fire, while propulsion capabilities allowed them to jump from incredible heights, out of transports or tall buildings, and land nicely on their feet. The propulsars weren't generally powerful enough to allow sustained upward flight, but they did work in unison with other specialized features of the exo-suits. In particular, the suits had the ability to work in much the same way as a parachute—a powerful energy field could be emitted outward. The field functioned to trap air under its umbrella, or wing-like, projections. The soldiers could jump from transports several miles above target and free-fall or glide to any drop-zone with pinpoint accuracy, and with the propulsars fully engaged during the final moments, when boots hit the ground the soldier would feel an impact no greater than walking down stairs.

Their helmets were encased computers, and the facemasks not only protected against poison gas and biological warfare, they also monitored and manipulated oxygen delivery based upon the Guardsman's level of physiological activity.

Jake was inspecting their equipment, their weapons, and their suits, to make sure everything was in order. It was routine, but he was far more diligent than any officer they knew. He was responsible for their welfare, and a man lost in battle was his personal failure. He threw out words of encouragement and addressed all the final details. He discovered a defective propulsar on one of his men. He detached it and threw it to one of the support orderlies. He caught the replacement as it flew through the air and quickly secured it in place.

"You'll be needing that, Edgar," he said. "Otherwise you'll beat all of us to the target." He punched him in the shoulder with the side of his fist.

"Roger that Lt. Col.," Edgar responded.

They were now over the battlefield. The transport banked hard, circling to get in the perfect position for the men to jump. Since all the old-style orbiting satellites were destroyed early in the war, aircraft had to rely solely upon on-board navigation. It was just before dawn, the sky was terribly dark, and below them explosions were lighting the night sky. Hellish orange and white flashes were fighting their way through a thick encasing layer of brown-gray smoke and cloud. From the transport it looked like an orgy of lightning, like an apocalyptic wrath of the gods.

Hidden underneath the shroud that hung a couple hundred feet above the ground were horrific scenes of fighting. From the vantage of the infantry on the ground, the battle zone had the appearance of being under a shell, a sadistic shell designed by the gods of war to secret away the abject horrors of war. Pulses of laser guided munitions flashed from air to ground. Others answered from ground to air. At the same time, older style conventional weapons and exploding munitions flashed in an orgy of violence. Energy shields protecting strategic targets were absorbing and redirecting accumulated energy outward in controlled bursts, each discharge shaking the ground with a baritone rumble.

The fight for Corinth centered on a key position—a beautiful ten-story luxury apartment complex. It was a site of grotesque carnage, the building now a place of demonic horror. Behind the structure lay a large, open, and relatively indefensible city park, and beyond that was a wide and raised causeway that bisected the city. From that geographically elevated position, the Allies would be able to effectively split the Persian lines and expose nearly the entire city to Allied fire. It would render the city's Persian defense untenable, and they would have to pull back and reform their lines. The Persians understood this, and as a result, they fortified the apartment building to the extreme, using the strategic location to bottle-up and bludgeon United American forces.

The Persian defense was not only technologically advanced, it was barbaric. They knocked every window out of the building and out of each, they mounted civilians as human shields. They tied straps around prisoners' chests and secured them to the structure. Then they threw the infidels out. Captured soldiers, old men and women, girls, children, even babies…it didn't matter. In effect, a shield of innocent lives cloaked the outside of the immense complex. Their screams and cries for mercy could be heard echoing across the battlefield. The Persians didn't care. Corinth wasn't their city, and its sub-human inhabitants didn't merit moral consideration. Their objective was for the enemy to hesitate while they gathered enough strength to repel the repeated Western attacks, but in a few days they would launch a massive counter-offensive along the entire sector. The Persian high command was bringing enough men and material to Greece to destroy the Allied armies and their ill-advised Grecian expedition.

From the Western perspective, if the strategic location could be taken from the Persians, a ripple would be created in their formidable line of defense—a concerted push would take place all across the front. They also understood that the Persians weren't accustomed to backing up. Every inch of ground would be paid for in blood…but that was war.

In the hour before Alpha Group would launch their attack, easily five thousand United American soldiers had been chewed up in the meat grinder in front of the objective. The mile-wide field between the lines was littered with entire divisions of dead bodies and destroyed machinery, and now five thousand more were added to the sacrifice. Persian robots and hovering sentries (which were remote-controlled floating battle stations about the size of a basketball), every modern laser and energy weapon in their arsenal, and biological agents, were being used to check the advance of Western forces. It was a brutal stalemate.

The domestic press was having a field day with the story. Never burdening themselves with standards of truth, they accused the Western troops of mass murder. They sent out-of-context footage back to their respective news outlets who, in turn, screamed for investigations and trials. They were pushing the agenda of the Proletariat Party, a political movement that would be swallowed up by the Egalitarian Party after the war. It was a fringe socialist party that secured a left-wing appeal predicated on being anti-war and advocating class warfare and wealth redistribution.

One of the reporters, a prominent and nationally known personality, crossed the lines and was taken to the building in the hope of interviewing the Persian commander. It was an ill-advised move catalyzed by a dangerous combination of ignorance and mistaken self-importance. She was promptly beaten, raped, interrogated, and injected with a drug that would enhance the perception of pain. Her slow beheading was broadcast for the world to see. Her terrible screams made an impression…an impression that the war was far from over, that the Persian Empire was the incarnation of evil, and it had to be defeated at all costs.

While the press screamed that their constitutional rights were being violated, they were forcibly extracted, by Presidential Order, from the sector at the point of pulsars—so the military could do their job without fear of public indictment and prosecution. Because attempts to take the site failed as a result of the advanced defensive technologies being used, Alpha Group was called in for a surgical strike. Civilians were going to die. They were already dying in large numbers, but if enough force could be applied to take the objective, in the end far more innocent lives would saved.

The transport dipped in fast from the upper stratosphere. It would briefly level off its descent at approximately ten thousand feet and go ultrasonic to get out of Persian controlled airspace.

"Stand at ready." Jake ordered.

The men of Alpha Group were lined up in five rows of sixteen, all facing the rear of the craft. After pouring over every nuanced detail of the operation, everyone understood that the primary objective was to take the building and eliminate all Persian resistance. The secondary objective was to take advantage of the temporary gap in the Persian's high-tech defense and lead a rapid advance of allied forces. They were to seize the initiative and push through the park and along the elevated causeway, securing the position for the army. The preservation of civilian life was a distant tertiary objective.

The men of Alpha Group weren't callous, quite the opposite; they were disciplined enough to do their jobs and mentally strong enough to look past civilians as though they weren't there. To a person, they were experienced and had seen almost every horror there was to see on a battlefield. As a result, they understood that hitting the enemy hard and fast was the only viable means to increase the odds of civilian survival, but many would be killed by friendly fire.

"Sixty seconds." Jake announced. They heard his command through their BCDs. "Final check and sound off."

Each man checked the straps and equipment of the Guardsman to his front, making sure everything was secure. Their weapons had already been inspected several times and were in excellent working order. "One, okay." "Two, okay." "Three, okay." The second line simultaneously began, "Seventeen, okay." "Eighteen, okay." Each line sounded off in this manner while Col. Fisk checked the men at the rear of the lines.

Jake would be the first man out. Col. Fisk would be the last. Just as they finished sounding off, the transport's ramp lowered out of the belly of the craft. An energy shield protected them from the incredible wind shear along the sides of the ramp. At the end of the ramp, at the appropriate moment, the energy shield would de-activate, allowing the men a window of opportunity to jump. At the same time, the transport would pull into a climb with incredible acceleration. They would essentially be sucked out of the cargo hold.

Jake took his position in front of the men. His back was to them, and he took in the scene of what they were jumping into. The sky was black except for a distant hint on the horizon that morning was on the way. Below, as far as he could see in both directions, the flashes of war extended along a wide line. He took a deep breath and secured his mask. He fleetingly thought about the cross hanging around his neck and said a quick prayer, but mostly he focused on the fact that they were jumping into hell and would be landing on the enemy's side of the line. It was high risk and dangerous as hell. He maneuvered his boots so he had a good grip on the ramp and waited for the signal.

* * * * *

"Pick out some good ones," the Persian lieutenant said. "The last ones didn't last long enough."

Private Abdulla backed away from his post at the window and left the room. A few minutes later he returned with four prisoners—a woman cradling a baby in her arms and two old men.

"Is this all they had?"

"Yes, sir. More are being brought up from the rear, but this is the best of what's left."

Lt. Syed Hapatra spat on the floor in disgust. "These Westerners are weak. They're not going to last long, but we have to use the refuse that's on hand. Throw them out." The Persian soldiers were posted on the top floor of the apartment building. The other two soldiers stationed in the room grabbed one of the old men. He was taken to a window, a strap was placed around his chest, and they threw him out. He screamed when he went over the edge. The strap jerked tight and he careened into the masonry. He was secured so that from the inside of the apartment just the top of his head could be seen sticking above the windowsill.

From the prisoner's perspective, the outside of the building was completely covered with a shell of bodies; some writhing, some moaning, some crying for mercy, and still others stinking with the foul stench of death. The allies were keeping up a steady attack. The energy shield in front was reverberating and bouncing as it absorbed everything that was thrown at it. Occasional arcs of electrical discharge danced from the shield to the building, cooking the flesh of random unfortunate souls. The old man extended his arms outward, attempting to find something to grasp onto. What he found were the remains of other people. One of the bodies turned toward him. It was his beloved daughter. He screamed out in agony, his voice blending with the hell around him.

The second old man was secured and thrown outside another window. Then they reached for the baby. The mother shrieked and attacked one of the soldiers, clawing at his face with her nails. Lt. Hapatra anticipated her move and hit her in the face with the butt of his pulsar. She fell back with a fractured cheekbone. When she regained her bearings she wailed as Lt. Hapatra was holding her baby up by one of his legs like a useless rag doll. He threw the baby to Abdulla. "I want this one hanging down in front of us so we can see him." He kicked the woman. "You are weak, just like the rest of Western women. One of ours would have never given up her child so easily. You dog, you infidel, you spawn of the devil. I've got something special planned for you."

After they finished raping her, she was hung upside-down in front of an adjacent window. Her straps were secured so that she could see her baby hanging helplessly in front of the apartment's main gun emplacement.

* * * * *

Jake was always the first man out. He led by example, and among his men, he had a reputation of being absolutely fearless. What they didn't know was that he was afraid. Every single time he was confronted with an open ramp, he questioned why he would ever jump out of a perfectly good transport. The questions would start ripping through his mind… what if his exo-suit failed? What if he was lost in freefall all the way to the ground? What if he froze? What if in the grip of fear, he couldn't make the jump? It had happened to good men in the past. They just froze up. He had seen it. The pressure he felt was intense because the men shared the same unspoken fears, and they depended on him to set the tempo. Despite fear extreme enough to cause his hands to shake, once the light changed to green he always had the perception that something else took over—an incredible and addictive rush of raw adrenaline. Even though the fear was still there, even though it was still palpable in every way, a different part of his mind would take command and he would run down the ramp and dive like a wild man, with nothing between him and the earth except the confidence that modern technology would not fail.

Well-rehearsed after hundreds of drops, the pilot counted off the last five seconds. The Guardsmen heard through their BCDs, "Go in five. Five, four, three, two, one, GO!" The energy shield de-activated at the same time that red lights running along the surface of the ramp turned green and began flashing. The nose of the transport pulled up toward the heavens and accelerated. The men sprinted and jumped. Inside of a moment, they were in the air, the ramp retracted back into the belly of the craft, and the transport roared away.

Once the transport was gone there was complete silence. But it wasn't peaceful. They were in the eye of the storm, hurtling into the gaping mouth of hell. Gravity did its work until the last two thousand feet. During that time, Jake experienced a complete and complex level of mental awareness. The world around him slowed to a crawl as he fell toward his destiny, and potentially toward his death, an outcome that he forced from his mind. There were worse ways to die than fighting for one's country.

The living flashes of light and deep grumblings of the war under the gauntlet caused the clouds that were rushing toward him to roll and churn like a black ocean under duress. As they got closer, he could feel the turbulence violently rocking him up and down and tossing him to the side. Once they entered the cloud, he could feel impacts across his entire body. He was being pelted by tiny particles that in the battle below had been blown into the sky.

In pairs, the men clustered with their respective teams while in free-fall. It was standard procedure in case anyone had problems. The patterns were designed to limit disruption to the attack sequence once on the ground. Jake assigned Edgar to link with him, and they would be attacking the building at adjacent sites. Edgar was less experienced than the others so Jake wanted him close.

While pulsar rifles were strapped to their backs to prevent them from being ripped away with the trauma of hitting the atmosphere at incredible speed, Jake and four other Guardsmen were also equipped with probe launchers strapped across their chests with elastic straps. At the designated cue, he pulled the launcher and shot downward, canvassing the area above the target. The probes were designed to hover at designated heights. They would sample the oscillations in the Persian energy shields and route the information to a central processor. The processor worked the equations and would adjust the energy shields of the individual Guardsmen so they would match. The adjustments occurred in the order of microseconds, and the soldiers would slice through the fields like a hot knife through butter. That is, if everything worked perfectly.

While still falling through the covering canopy, they deployed energy chutes to slow and control their descent. They navigated through seams in the energy shields, and once cleared they aimed their descent at their designated point of attack. When they hit the energy shields, Jake felt a static electricity sensation. It was normal. What Edgar felt was not. His energy shields didn't adjust appropriately and his system failed. He yelled out as flashes of blue electricity arced across his body. The Persian shields violently ripped through his systems and burnt out his shield generator. It finished with an explosion across his back.

"Malfunction! Malfunction!" he yelled. He didn't lose consciousness, but the experience was similar to having his heart shocked with a defibrillator. Now in free-fall because of the system failure, Edgar did exactly what he was trained to do. He spread out his arms and legs to slow his descent.

Jake dove after him and caught him by the belt. "Got you," he said.

Edgar was calm, mechanically doing everything he was supposed to do. He pulled the pulsar off his back and, holding it in one hand, he climbed on Jake and piggy-backed it the rest of the way down. "BCD operational. Pulsar good. Shield systems down. Propulsars down," he announced.

"We hit your DZ," Jake said. "When we hit, I'm going right, through the interior wall."

"Roger," Edgar confirmed, "Lt. Col. to the right."

"After we clear the rooms, you stick close to me until you get a replacement," Jake ordered.

"Yes, sir." Edgar understood that since his shields were down, he was exposed and vulnerable; he might as well have been fighting naked.

In all, the adjustments and exchange only took a few seconds. They burst through the cloud cover and took in the full specter of war. Heavy suppressive fire was coming in from United America's ground forces. The primary objective, the building, was shrouded in thick smoke and arcs of electrical energy danced about with each absorbed impulse. The infantry had stepped up their firing and an assault was in progress all across the front, supported by tens of thousands of holographic projections of Allied soldiers. To the naked eye they looked like real soldiers. They were different and had unique movements. They would even fall as though hit and killed. With rudimentary sensors, something most of the Persians had, it was obvious that they were nothing more than mirages. What the

Persians didn't anticipate was that the distraction was for the purpose of an assault from the air.

Every energy weapon in the Allied arsenal was targeting the front of the building. It had the affect of distorting the Persian energy shields and bending them away from the roof. It created an oscillation gap and made it easier for Alpha Group to get through. At the same time, in every sector up and down the line—the European sector, the Russian sector, and the Australian sector—a similar and well-timed assault was underway.

Alpha Group would simultaneously attack the upper floor and the top of the building, as well as the top of the surrounding buildings. Teams One and Two would go directly into the side of the structure. They would blast through windows and walls and leap through the openings into the guts of the building...into the teeth of the Persian forces.

Jake was personally leading Teams One and Two, a total of thirty-two men, on their part of the mission's first objective. Because of the problems with Edgar's descent he adjusted his trajectory one apartment to the left on the top floor. Once they hit, he'd immediately blast his way to the right, moving back into position, into what was supposed to be his point of entry.

"Here we go," Jake said. "Hold on." The building was coming fast, and their angle of descent shifted abruptly, like they were being flung out of a sling. His pulsar was ready, and at the last moment, when they were no more than fifteen meters from the stone wall and ready to smash into it at nearly a horizontal angle, Jake discharged his pulsar rifle. It was on maximum. The blast blew away a hole four meters in diameter. Their momentum carried them directly through the opening and into the structure, into the middle of the apartment's large living room. Immediately all hell broke loose inside.

Edgar disengaged from Jake's back and killed the Persian soldiers left in the room while Jake twisted to the right and blasted through the interior wall and into the adjacent apartment. The shock of the sudden attack left the Persians reeling.

Jake leapt through the wall and took stock. There were three enemy soldiers. One was killed outright by his first blast, his body nearly turned inside out. Another was lying on the far side of the room with half his body pinned down under a heap of rubble. A piece of rebar had impaled him, sticking through his shoulder and preventing him from reaching his weapon. The third Persian had been knocked into the hallway. While his head was spinning he was trying to crawl away. After shaking off the blast he was certain to make a fight of it. But that wasn't going to happen.

Through the thick smoke, the Persian soldier's image appeared on the heads-up-display generated by Jake's BCD. It was Private Abdulla. Jake shot him. The blast went through the back of his skull. A single-kill energy pulse was enough. It transferred enough energy at nearly the speed of light to cave in the helmet and the back of his skull, and it blew both out the front of his head. Without hesitating Jake followed the targeting cues relayed from his BCD. He swung his weapon around and took out the Persian soldier skewered with the rebar. It was Lt. Syed Hapatra. He smiled slightly as blood dripped from the corner of his mouth. He wanted to say something. Jake's blast was to his heart. It exploded into an unrecognizable mass of shredded tissue. There was no hesitation. No lingering. Jake killed him and moved on, denying the Persian officer any last words.

With the initial blast into the building, remote hover cameras entered the breach. They were flying at incredible speeds through the structure and streaming live information into Alpha Group's BCDs. They showed the Guardsmen where the enemy soldiers were positioned and in which direction they were moving.

With Alpha Group's initial blast, a violent shock wave rattled the building. The Persians on the lower floors and in the interior rooms understood that it meant something had breached their defenses. They didn't know what it was until calls began coming in from Persian soldiers in positions further back who saw enemy commandoes hit the building.

Everything was moving fast. Jake adjusted the settings on his pulsar, setting it to laser and flipping to constant cutting mode. He aimed the pulsar downward. Holding it vertically to the floor he pulled the trigger and made a rapid movement around the edge of the room. The laser cut like a knife. It cut through every tile, subfloor, ceiling, joist, and support the building had to offer, from the tenth floor all the way to the ground, and into the foundation. He made a quick cut around the room, jumped into the hallway, and turned back to the room to finish the job while standing outside the cut. The entire room, in the footprint of his blast, tipped to one side. Furniture, rubble, and dead bodies with limbs flopping, slid across the floor and spilled downward onto the ninth floor. The entire room slipped away and collapsed. Then the ninth floor fell onto the eighth. All ten floors, in the footprint of the rooms taken by Teams One and Two, pancaked downward, leaving behind an empty shaft from the roof all the way to the ground. All across the front of the building, thirty-two rooms in all, the same thing happened. Close to a thousand Persian fighters and nearly an equal number of civilians were trapped and died in the mayhem.

Thick gushing smoke filled the structure and erupted outward through the windows. The visibility inside was reduced to less than one tenth of a meter. The men had no trouble breathing with their masks in place, and for the time being, they would operate exclusively under BCD guidance.

Jake didn't linger to gloat over his handiwork. He was already making his way down the hallway leading away from the room. However, as the officer in charge, it was imperative that he keep track of his men. A coordinated attack with overwhelming force and absolute speed was the key. His BCD rotated the image of the building in three dimensions. He could see the outlined images of Persian soldiers and what were presumably civilian prisoners in the rooms and hallways on each floor. He crouched low, searching for targets. His pulsar was adjusted to pulsed energy and set to kill. His men, having successfully secured their positions, and after eliminating any Persians they could find, were now in the hallway.

"Teams One and Two," Jake announced through the BCD, "objective one - phase one complete. Initiating objective one-phase two." In a highly choreographed maneuver the thirty-two men peeled off into eight four-man search and destroy units. As three main corridors led through the structure, one unit would push down each hallway. The remaining five units adjusted their pulsars to cutting laser with a narrow pattern, in 1.5 second pulses. They integrated their BCDs to target enemy soldiers on the lower floors. If the Persians kept moving they were harder to hit, but if they stopped, just for a moment, the coordinates of their location would be locked in by the system and they would be targeted. From the vantage of the tenth floor, Alpha Group would eliminate them. The pulsed cutting laser would cut a path through everything to the depth of the targeted individual plus one meter. Persians all over the structure began falling in this manner, killed and wounded in every sort of grotesque manner, the lasers indiscriminately cutting swaths through their flesh, taking off limbs and dissecting through their bodies like instant guillotines. Many fell in half so suddenly that their brains took several seconds to realize what had happened, and for moments before death, they would contemplate that the body they were looking at, the one cut completely in half, with internal organs spilling out on the floor, was their own.

Teams Three, Four, and Five landed on the roof of the building proper and two surrounding structures. They had a heavy fight for a few moments as the Persians were able to mount stout resistance and return fire, but the shock and awe of Alpha Group's firepower was too much.

"Teams, Three, Four, Five. Objective two, phase one complete." It was Colonel Alexander Fisk's voice over the BCD. "Initiating objective two, phase two." Objective two, phase two actually had two components. The first, carried out by Team Five, was to prevent any Persian reinforcements from hitting the building from behind. The second, carried out by Teams Three and Four, was to destroy the Persian energy shield that protected the front of the building.

Inside the structure, Persians were streaming down the corridors from the rear of the building to investigate what was happening. Jake and his men waited until the last possible moment, until they were no more than a few meters away. Still hidden in the thick cloud of dust, the men of Alpha Group crouched low along the outside edges of the corridor. Through their BCDs, they saw near perfect unobscured images of the Persians. Jake would give the order to fire. With perfect discipline his men waited, allowing them to be drawn closer, and for more enemy soldiers to fill the length of the corridor. Then, at the very last moment, when the lead Persian began raising his weapon, Jake gave the order and fired. They opened up with everything they had. The pulsed energy waves that hit the Persians churned and boiled their flesh. The entire corridor became a killing field draped in red and stinking with burnt flesh and human waste.

Inside another few minutes, the building was secure. Persian resistance was destroyed and all of Alpha Group's initial objectives were met. Jake didn't have the luxury of lingering, but what he did see was a scene of complete and hellish butchery. Thousands of civilians had been tortured and killed in the weeks leading up to the assault. Their bodies were dumped in empty rooms. It was obvious that they had been starved as emaciated skeletal forms littered the rooms off the main hallways and were piled four and five deep. Unfortunately, this wasn't the first time Jake had seen this. In fact, he had seen worse. The Persians were brutal to the very end.

'They were already dead. They were already dead,' Jake repeated in his mind. He knew that each man under his command was thinking the same thing. The first dozen times he had trouble navigating his way through the psychological trauma. He didn't do that anymore. Enduring scenes like this had the effect of solidifying his ability to compartmentalize his emotions. It was clear that the men, women, and children who died as a direct result of Alpha Group's attack would have been murdered by the Persians. In effect, they were already dead. The only ones who required convincing were those who were already determined to despise Western society and United America in particular.

Jake took a brief survey of the hundreds of United American infantry who were streaming in from below. They would take over security and begin the evacuation of survivors. What Jake saw around him pushed reality into the surreal landscape of insanity. There were dead bodies everywhere, in every sort of grotesque posture, with unabashed evidence that they endured sadistic torture at the hands of the enemy. There were people of every age. The scene reminded him why United America was fighting and why the world was screaming under the weight of its Fourth World War.

Past experience had proven that there simply was no other way. Too many times the Persians had demonstrated their talent for destruction and death. They wanted no refugees except for those they might push back into their enemy's lines with the objective being that they would divert resources away from the military in order to care for them. Otherwise they took great pride in their ability to strike fear, a well-earned fear, in everyone. How these same people could turn around and treat their own kind with such admiration and respect, with gentleness and caring, it was all lost on Jake. He just couldn't climb inside their heads and understand the dual nature and behavior of the Persians. He didn't revel in hating his enemy, but because of his experiences he had grown to hate them with every fiber of his being. He wanted to kill them all and only then would the world's future be safe.

Given the circumstances, none of the Persian soldiers saw it prudent to surrender, not that they would have in any other setting. They were among the hardest and most fervent fighters the world had ever seen, and it was not only their duty to die fighting, but their prerogative to take as many enemy lives with them as they could. In their paradigm, this wasn't limited to the lives of soldiers. Girls and women were breeding stock, children were future fighters, the elderly financially supported the war, and they were all part of the enemy's fighting infrastructure. All of them deserved to die. Once and for all, the Persians were determined that the world deserved to experience a clear and true victor. This was a war to the death…a war of cultural extermination they were determined to win.

A small fraction of the civilians survived. The ones who were rescued were pulled from isolated holding rooms within the structure or were plucked from the horrors of serving as human shields. Of those who didn't survive hanging on the outside of the building, most died from a combination of friendly and enemy fire, from exposure and dehydration, or suffocating as a result of the chest harness. Among those who survived there wasn't much life left. After enduring the ordeal, their eyes were devoid of all the intangible qualities of being alive…they were the living dead. When it was over, four hundred and twenty-three civilians left the building.

Five hours had passed, and Alpha group spearheaded an impressive advance through the park and along the causeway. They fought perfectly as a team, as though they were a single entity with a single nervous system. That was the advantage of the BCD system. They engaged and destroyed everything the Persians could throw at them.

"We have in-coming," Jake announced. He was at the tip of the spear as Alpha Group pounded its way through the banged up Persian defenses.

"We've got movement on both flanks and in front. Sensors are picking up large concentrations of hovering sentries moving fast. I've got several clusters coming in low and another coming down from topside." He fired a sensory drone in the direction of the Persians. They were diverting forces and bringing up reinforcements in an all out effort to reform their lines and contain the breach. The drone would pierce the front and transmit everything it saw as it zigzagged at near supersonic speed a few meters above the ground, for at least as long as it managed to survive. "Teams Two and Four to the left," Jake commanded. "Teams Three and Five to the right."

"Team Four in position," came back the first response. Then came, "Team Two in position." Teams Three and Five sounded off their confirmations as the Guardsmen took position.

Col. Fisk was in the rear, commanding the fluid movements of battle like a great chess master. Lt. Col. Gillean, his most powerful weapon and a lord of war whose skills he watched mature to the point that he considered them superior to his own, was in front where he would wreak the greatest degree of destruction. Fisk took in the quickly changing scene and commanded, "Converging fields of fire pattern delta three. One hundred meter intervals." With reactions that were quick and automatic, the Guardsmen scrambled to their designated positions. "Lock and load," he said. "Fire on my command."

"Team One advance behind me. Stay fifty meters back," Jake said. "Pattern kappa six at one hundred meter intervals." Within two seconds, the men were formed in a semicircle behind Jake with one hundred meters separating them, seven in front and nine behind. They would take out the hovering sentries that were coming in from above.

The hovering sentries were remote controlled battle stations roughly thirty to forty centimeters in diameter. They moved fast and were capable of being armed with a wide variety of weapons, sensory devices, jammers, and electromagnetic pulse bombs.

When Jake engaged the first hovering sentry to hit his advanced position, the feed from the drone he fired began coming back. It transmitted for four seconds before being eliminated by a Persian soldier. How long it lasted wasn't as important as the information it relayed. Less than a thousand kilometers away and converging fast was a full regiment of Kabul Class T7 Robots. They were deadly and almost invulnerable.

"Brace yourselves. They brought some muscle. T7s coming in fast all along my front." Jake already shot down three of the sentries and his position was getting hot.

"Fire at will," Col. Fisk commanded. Both flanks were now under heavy attack.

Laser blasts and energy pulses were chewing up the streets, the neighborhoods, and all the other surrounding structures. Jake ran from side to side and leapt through the air, his exo-suit performing flawlessly. His targeting systems allowed him to take out the sentries, occasionally two at a time. Coming in fast from left to right, one of the sentries was pouring in laser blasts that glowed bright red. Jake reacted in the split second it appeared and knocked it down with his pulsar. It careened into another that exploded in a massive fiery ball. The flames engulfed him, and the explosion brought in a fragment that struck him hard in the left upper arm. An electromagnetic shock jolted his entire body and his BCD signal blinked. The exterior shell of his exo-suit was badly burned but the underlying bio-components remained fully functional. He regained his bearings and calmly moved toward the Persians with his pulsar at his side.

As the engagement unfolded, the chatter among the men was minimal, and transmission over the BCDs was limited mostly to announcement of injuries. Three men had to pull out of line and drop back because their suits were severely compromised.

'Suit temperature above normal.' The announcement was routed from the suit's control module to Jake's BCD. 'Cooling systems operating at 90%.'

As the sentry attack waned and the last was destroyed, Jake emerged from the wall of flames. He was face to face with the advancing line of Persian T7s. The entire region behind him was blanketed in fire. It burnt blue in places, and thick black smoke rose up in the air giving the appearance of a monstrous funnel cloud.

"T7s in pattern beta four with a five hundred meter front, two hundred meters out," Jake announced.

Fisk immediately altered Alpha Group's position. "All teams pattern epsilon 1, seven hundred meter front, refuse the flanks." They redeployed into a large flattened half circle with the Guardsmen at the ends of the line taking positions that bowed outward in a reverse half-circle. They would accept the T7 attack while protecting against a sudden attack on their flank. "Attack protocol Omega 1," Fisk added. That meant that Jake and five other Guardsmen would get behind the line of T7s while the rest of Alpha Group absorbed the brunt of the attack.

Jake knew what was expected. It wasn't the first time he had been asked to perform the maneuver. The T7s were offensive weapons designed for the attack. They were weak in the rear, but they could also turn on a dime. If some of the Guardsmen could get behind them while they were heavily engaged in front, they could take them out one at a time. It was risky but he had done it before. The robots' only real vulnerability was the fusion module, located behind its weapons array. They had to be destroyed or ripped out. Jake felt a surge of adrenaline. They'd have to move fast because United America's artillery battalions were slow in coming up and Alpha Group wasn't designed to trade blows with Persian heavy weapons.

The T7s were only a hundred meters away and were chewing up everything in their front. Jake blasted a hole in the ground and climbed in. The tension was overwhelming. He powered down his systems to avoid detection. It was a moment of complete vulnerability. He'd wait for Col. Fisk's signal and then spring into action. The ground quaked with each step the robots took. As one of them stepped on the edge of his hole the dirt and rock gave way. It tumbled into his oversized foxhole.

"Engage," Col. Fisk commanded. His voice was calm and purposeful. Each of the Teams in
line opened up with everything they had. Jake and the five Guardsmen sprang into action behind the T7s. Jake powered up and lunged out of the hole. He leapt onto the back of the closest T7 and with a laser knife arcing from a weapons array at his wrist and hand he stabbed into its fusion module, twisted, and then pushed the large machine toward the hole. The T7 started to tip and then exploded in an arc of intense orange-yellow flame.

The fighting was fierce. Rear guard Persian soldiers were keeping up a steady barrage to the point that the only way Jake and the other Guardsmen could approach the T7 was to pulsar blast their way into the earth and trench their way to get behind each robot. They would leap out and make quick work of it. So far they had knocked out seventeen units.

"I'm hit!" The call came from Lieutenant Bill McGuire. His voice betrayed panic. He was leaping toward one of the T7s when it suddenly turned and fired, catching him at point blank range. His shield systems were unable to absorb the full measure of energy and were overwhelmed. He was thrown backward and smashed into the trench he had just emerged from.

"Suppressive fire to the rear," Jake ordered. The four other Guardsmen who were fighting behind the T7s turned and laid down fire to quiet the Persian infantry. "Mark position. I need mortar fire plus two hundred meters. Lay it in heavy." Jake emerged from his trench and was running in the open behind the T7s. The United American artillery was coming into line and the energy mortars began falling. The ground was shaking under the intense pressure, and the cacophony of the blasts almost knocked him off his feet. McGuire was one hundred and fifty meters away. The T7 that got him was bearing down. It was straddling the trench and brought its weapons array to fire point blank.

"Oh hell," McGuire mumbled.

A fierce blast hit the T7 from the side. It lurched and then came back down in its original position. It was spinning to meet the attack when Jake physically hit it. His pulsar was on his back and his laser knives were glowing red a meter long from each hand. In order to use both knives, Jake had to divert all of his shield strength to weapons. He was vulnerable. He twisted in the air and sliced the barrel off one of the energy cannons. His other knife went through the control module, knocking out its communications systems. It was now operating with only its onboard computers. It fired into the air but missed, the blast hitting a nearby T7, causing it to explode. Jake was on the ground, behind and under the unit. He plunged his knife upward and took out the right hip joints. He spun and severed off its right leg. It toppled toward him while firing continuously in a wild arc. He reached up and grabbed it as it fell. His exo-suit bulged and strained under the incredible weight. In a fit of rage, he threw all four tons of it to the side. It hit the ground and rolled. He was immediately on top of it. He sliced into its fusion module and leapt through the air toward McGuire. In flight, he deactivated the knives and diverted his systems to maximum shields. The T7 exploded just as he covered the fallen Guardsman, shielding him from further injury.

"Two units bearing on your position," one of the other Guardsmen reported.

Jake was out of the trench and two more explosions followed. He reappeared, flames burning across his shoulders and back. He was standing over McGuire.

"Dammit, Mac, what'd you do?" McGuire's suit was burnt and smoke wafted out in places where the organic components had been singed. His facemask and helmet were off. His right arm was missing just below the shoulder. Blood was spurting out. He was pale and confused.

"I'm sorry, sir," he mumbled. He closed his eyes and added, "You're on fire."

Jake ignored his comment. The flames would go out on their own. "Let's get you fixed up and get you out of here," he said. He routed an order through his BCD. "Gurney to my coordinates." He grabbed the suit at the stump of Mac's upper arm and commanded, "Tourniquet." It tightened and cut off the blood flow. Jake made quick work of patching the holes in McGuire's exo-suit. He replaced his helmet and his mask, programming his system to increase oxygen delivery. Jake grabbed Mac's good shoulder and squeezed. "I think you're going to make it buddy. It'll take more than a T7 to do you in. There's fight in you yet."

McGuire smiled.

A medical gurney flew across the field. As it hovered next to McGuire it unfolded. With six propulsars to support its flight and an onboard heavy shield system, McGuire would be safe on his return trip through the gap in the T7 line. After he was loaded and strapped into position, Jake issued the command, "Go." The propulsars roared and rotated. The gurney took off at a speed that quickly broke the sound barrier. It darted and weaved through the lines and around buildings until it arrived at the designated field hospital behind United American lines.

Jake turned his attention back to the action. It was increasingly evident that United America's heavy artillery was coming into action. The busted line of T7s was beginning to fall back. The Persians were weakening. Now was the opportunity to strike hard and push them out of the city.

"Col. Fisk." The voice came through Fisk's BCD. It was routed through a secure back-up channel. The source of the incoming message was indicated as being the United American High Command. "Col. Fisk," the voice repeated.

He responded without taking his eyes off the fluid battlefield, "This is Fisk."

"Col. Fisk. Alpha Group is ordered to disengage for immediate redeployment."

"Repeat," Fisk said.

"Alpha Group is ordered to withdraw for immediate redeployment."

"Under whose authority?" he asked. Energy bursts were thundering overhead and the ground was shaking under the bombardment.

"The President of United America," came the response.

"Extraction is to begin immediately," he confirmed. Col. Fisk issued the appropriate orders, and the process of withdrawing Alpha Group began.

The highly coordinated extraction progressed like the movements of a caterpillar turning itself inside out. The men in the most advanced positions pulled back to take position in the rear and turned to lay down withering covering fire for those who were in the front. In this manner the entire unit worked to safely extract itself from the heart of the action. Jake remained in the front issuing commands while Col. Fisk commanded troop placement in the rear.

With unmatched poise and discipline, Jake backed up while laying down an impressive barrage of pulsed energy and laser fire. He had issued another command and was delivered a Patton H1 fusion cannon. He was one of the only men strong enough to carry and effectively wield the weapon in battle. Weighing half a ton, it was far too heavy to carry in a fluid engagement that required agility and the quick delivery of precision force, but in a steady fight it was perfect. The ground around him vibrated with each successive discharge. There was an earthquake and he was its epicenter.

The Persian forces seized the opportunity and began pushing forward. They threw in everything they had and the fighting grew particularly intense. At the same time, the men and women of the United American infantry were coming forward with their complement of heavy equipment, but they were comparatively slow and awkward in coming into line.

"TEAM THREE! GET OUT OF THERE! THE BUILDING'S COMING DOWN!" Jake yelled. He ran toward the building while Team Three moved to get clear. In the two to three seconds it took him to react and position himself where he needed to be, he changed the settings on his Patton H1 from pulsed blast to constant, and he widened the spread to maximum. The fusion generator was opened up to 100%. He braced himself for the massive recoil. He slid to one knee and aimed the cannon up as the massive structure was collapsing toward him and his men. With a pull of the trigger it emitted a deafening baritone roar. It shook the ground with incredible force, its reverberations being felt hundreds of meters away. Any glass that had so far been spared within a wide radius immediately shattered into thousands of pieces. The energy field from the weapon hit the collapsing structure and forced it back on itself. A few bricks fell through but otherwise the entire structure was pushed in the opposite direction. Team Three maintained its poise and completed their extraction while continuing to lay down covering fire toward the front.

Col. Fisk had his hands full in the rear. Persian soldiers had taken to wearing United American uniforms and were on suicide missions to slow the United American advance. Corinth wasn't a hot-zone; it was hell on earth. That's why Col. Fisk was concerned—if there was ever a place for Alpha Group this was it. His role was not to question, but he couldn't help wondering why the hell they were being pulled before the area was fully secured. Something very big had to be happening. He'd find out soon enough, but until then, it was his duty to follow orders.

The advance elements of Alpha Group were now behind the infantry. They brought with them heavy pulsar tanks and mobile energy shield systems. The repeated thumping of United America's energy mortars dominated the field. Under all of that, there were the yells of troops as they ran forward to take position in line.

Despite everything that was happening, an event that was evolving off to the side, about a hundred meters off the causeway, grabbed Jake's attention. In the rubble of a blown out building was a little boy. He couldn't have been more than two years old and was covered with dirt and filth. He was crying, his body naked, and his belly bloated and protuberant. One of the GIs, no more than a kid himself, probably eighteen or nineteen years old, was making his way through the rubble toward the child.

"NO!" Jake yelled. "GET OUT OF THERE! GET AWAY FROM HIM!" It was no use. His BCD wasn't integrated with the infantry's communications systems, and they were too far away. With the sounds of battle there was no chance the GI would hear him. Several Guardsmen heard Jake yelling, turned, and witnessed what was about to happen.

Jake dropped the cannon and pulled the pulsar rifle off his back. He brought it up and took careful aim. The child was in his line of site. The pulsar's targeting module had the range. He only had a fraction of a second. All he had to do was pull the trigger. The boy's face appeared in the targeting module, a red circle flashing over his image. Jake's finger was at the trigger, he knew what he had to do. He thought he knew what to do. His mind was screaming. He hesitated…what if he was wrong? He couldn't do it. His brain wouldn't let him do what he knew he should. Suddenly, the child disappeared from his sites. The GI came between them. It was happening too fast. Then, the thought flashed that if he wounded the soldier he might be able to save him. He retargeted his pulsar, aiming at the GI's leg. At the same time the GI bent down to pick up the child. Jake discharged the weapon. At the exact moment his finger pressed the trigger an explosion occurred. Intermingled pieces of soldier and little boy flew through the air. He was too late. He had just done what he had berated his men to never do…he had hesitated.

"Goddammit!" Jake yelled. His knees lurched with weakness. The child was wired by the Persians to explode. All it took was a fraction of a second. He was in Jake's sites and he hesitated. The GI was dead because of his indecision. Shook by the realization that he could have saved him, the muscles down the length of Jake's spine momentarily refused to hold him up. He took a staggered step forward and for just a moment he went down to one knee. In anguish he muttered, "That stupid son of a bitch! Damn all of this to hell!" Explosions were everywhere and the sounds of battle were screaming all around, and as always, there was no time for sadness. Like flipping a switch, Jake forced his mind to regain composure. He reigned in his emotions and turned away, the terrible experience being pushed away and at the same time added to the army of others that haunted his dreams.

His men saw him go down to one knee and assumed he had lost his balance. He immediately came back up, was processing everything in his surroundings with a clear presence of mind, was coordinating movements and directing fire, and without further incident he successfully completed the work of extracting his men.

In the minds of the Guardsmen, Lt. Col. Gillean wasn't human—he was a machine, an absolute and unconquerable machine. He didn't appear to suffer emotions as they did. What they didn't know was that behind the clenched jaw and aggressive demeanor, despite his incredible ability to process battlefield information, behind his selfless dedication toward the safety of his men, and no matter how many times he threw himself into the thick of the fighting to save their hides—what they didn't know was he was being torn apart on the inside. He cared deeply and in private, he wept for his soldiers who were lost in battle, and he screamed at the inhumanity and the violence he witnessed around him.

It took approximately twenty minutes to pull Alpha Group from the fray once Fisk had received the order. It was possibly more dangerous to extract a unit from a hot-zone than it was to embed one in the first place. But this was Alpha Group. They were the elite of the elite and the best equipped of any fighting force in the world. The transport arrived at the designated spot behind the lines of the United American infantry, just beyond the apartment complex that had been their first objective at the beginning of the day. As the men raced past, they noted that its exterior remained decorated with the corpses of dead civilians. It stood as though frozen in time, a ghastly testament to the vicious nature of mankind and the reason they needed to defeat the Persians.

Col. Fisk took position to the side of the transport, at the bottom of the ramp. On one knee, he prepared himself to lay down suppressive fire. He, along with the first Team to arrive at the transport, scanned the surrounding buildings and piles of rubble for any evidence of enemy snipers.

"Sound off!" Fisk yelled.

The roaring noise from the engines was tremendous as the men hit the ramp and boarded the transport. Hovering ten centimeters off the ground, the only part of the plane that actually made contact with the ground was the far end of the ramp. The men hit it hard, raced on board, and strapped in for the rapid vertical acceleration that would carry them out of the warzone. They knew only one thing…wherever the next objective, it was going to be dangerous as hell.

CHAPTER 17: THE MUSEUM

[APRIL 14, AD 2441]
[134 DAYS AFTER ARRIVAL]
[LOCATION: CALIFORNIA]

Jake spent hours reviewing the files he robbed from Ben's BCD. He reviewed every detail of the government and how the Fascists had taken over. He was disgusted. Everything he and his men had fought for, every American who had sacrificed his or her life for the proposition of freedom and equality of opportunity...it had all been squandered. The citizens of United America were living in abject bondage. He was dismayed to discover that people couldn't even travel to the next county without government sanction. They couldn't speak out or resist without being expelled from the societal collective. Salary, finance, investments, lifestyle, careers, even where an individual might live, were all controlled by Party bureaucrats and their banking consortium. Dissension was considered a familial crime against the State. If anyone protested or resisted Egalitarian Party dictates his or her entire family would be punished. All of the immediate relatives would be left destitute. In the history of the world, few governments ever exerted so much control.

Jake's muscles tightened. It was a reflection of underlying anger. This time it was because he realized everything Ben said about the government was accurate and without exaggeration. He had to believe that the populace simply didn't realize how much power it had. Since World War IV, one of the world's shining societies had been reduced to a shaking quivering mass of cowardice. Within it were those who benefited from government tyranny. There had to be beneficiaries. In every society there were groups of people who, for personal gain, would grind their heels into others. As expected, he found them in Twenty-Fifth Century United America. Less than ten percent of society controlled the rest. They were the ones favored by the government, the societal henchmen, the brown-shirts of the modern era. They included the military brass, the labor unions, and government employees ranging from police to firemen, and from doctors to schoolteachers. The Party controlled every aspect of rule all the way down to mayors of the smallest towns. One of the earliest moves the Fascists made when they achieved a Congressional majority after World War IV was the takeover of education. Once entrenched it was impossible for the emerging resistance to dislodge them. Political indoctrination began when children entered pre-school and continued throughout their lives. Across the board, ideas and beliefs outside the dictates of the Party were not tolerated. Jake asked himself how it ever could have come to this.

Their travels across the country, through the countless checkpoints, were only possible because of the advanced technologies Ben brought to the table. As such, they were able to slip through the Egalitarian net without raising any apparent red flags. Alaska was behind them, and they were making their way toward Lake Tahoe.

Ben understood that agents from the DSS were on their tail, and he was taking every precaution. When they passed other pods on the national grid he'd randomly swap identification signatures with them. Tracking based on the pod would be difficult, but not impossible. As such, the plan was that they'd hike through the forest and then pick up alternative means of transportation.

"I want you to see this," he said to Jake. "I need you to tap back into my BCD."

Jake was surprised. It was the ultimate act of trust to open the door and allow someone into your BCD, and despite having hacked the system, he was now being invited in.

Ben indicated the appropriate feed and once Jake was seeing what he wanted he explained, "I planted sensors in Alaska, at the store where we rented the fishing supplies and at the cabin. The first feed is from an hour ago. Those are DSS agents. We're being hunted." The image showed the old man being interrogated. It was somewhat grainy and the voices were distorted, but it was clear what was being asked.

"Zimmer?" Jake asked.

"I don't know. I doubt it. They wouldn't be two days behind if he were controlling the op. I took out a DSS agent back in Nashville. My guess is that he had friends." Ben flipped the feed. "What you're seeing now is the cabin. This is live."

The agents were turning the place upside down. They missed Ben's sensors and the triangulating laser system. He bored holes into the molding and overhead rafters, planted the devices, and disguised the sites so they wouldn't be visible.

"They brought some toys," Jake said, referring to their equipment.

"I think they've seen enough," Ben said. "I'm initiating the targeting protocol." Three lasers all locked onto the female agent. She was moving at first, and they couldn't establish a lock. "Hold still," Ben muttered, "all I need is…there." Once she stopped moving it took two seconds to measure her face. After a process of mathematical extrapolation, the lasers targeted the region just deep to her pituitary gland. It was highly vascular. He was targeting the anatomic location of an artery, the basilar artery. Once the three beams crossed paths it caused a burn. It ruptured the artery. It hemorrhaged and began spewing blood.

Jake watched as the woman suddenly dropped her equipment and grasped the sides of her head. She fell to the floor screaming. Her partner was confused at first. He didn't know what to do. Then he dragged her out of the cabin, and they disappeared off sensor. She could be heard screaming the entire time.

"That should slow them down a bit," Ben nonchalantly commented.

Jake was studied in his response and surprised at Ben's aloof nature about the whole thing. "You took out the woman," he said.

"Far more deadly," Ben answered. "Women don't hesitate. They are cold, calculating, and vicious adversaries. They have the capacity to hold a grudge for decades and then slit your throat while you're sleeping. I'd rather fight a man. Better chance of me and you surviving."

"Won't they know you did it?"

"Eventually. At first it'll look like she ruptured an aneurysm. I'm sure Zimmer will find out about it, but he's been distracted with other more pressing issues. My defense will be that I'm protecting you, and I don't know who's chasing us. By the time they put everything together it'll be too late…hopefully."

"And if you're wrong?"

"Then our lives just got far more complicated." Ben's grin was matter of fact and deadly. "Now, what happened after Alpha Group was extracted from Corinth?" Jake was communicating freely and his story was unfolding in fascinating detail. Ben didn't want to risk losing the momentum.

At the same time, Jake found that the world he was living in was emerging out of the fog. While he didn't like what he saw, it wasn't his problem. All he wanted to do was fix what he had done and restore things to the way they were. It wasn't about his own well being, it was about those he loved the most, the family he left behind. He nurtured a distant hope that Ben might be able to help. He obviously knew more than he was ready to admit, for the time being.

* * * * *

(Jake's story continues. Alpha Group has just been extracted from the
Battle of Corinth)

[July 3, AD 2379]
[Arrival date minus 61 years]
[Portland, Oregon]

There were roughly four hundred of these elite commandoes deployed
around the world. The entire program was collectively referred to as *The
Guard.* Their sworn duty was to function as the ultimate guardians of
freedom, liberty, and equality of conditions. They were protectors of the
innocent and the infirm, and they represented the most stalwart line of
defense protecting the sovereignty of the United American Government.
The men were clearly the most capable of the military's elite Special Forces.
As such, they were in the best of physical and mental condition. It was often
boasted that any of them could play reasonably well any professional sport.
But it wasn't just brawn. The minimum acceptable intelligence, as verified
through a battery of tests, was four standard deviations above the average,
or an IQ in the range of 180. They had to have excellent hearing and
vision and be of upstanding character. They studied hard and in addition
to science and mathematics, they learned computer skills, engineering,
and foreign languages. To a man, they were skilled across martial arts
disciplines and were trained to operate almost all pieces of modern high-
tech weaponry. They were afforded the best in cutting edge equipment
and were generally the first to bring new technologies into the fight. The
caveat to this was that they were incredibly expensive to maintain, and the
budget for the program was often politically contentious.

Members of The Guard came from the enlisted ranks, from the pool of
academy-trained officers, from officers coming out of traditional colleges, but
primarily from the Special Forces Military Academy. It was a brotherhood
with its own internal command structure elected from within based on ability,
experience, and leadership skills. Its commanding officers were promoted
to leadership positions by a combination of the opinions of their fellow
Guardsmen and through United America's High Command.

Alpha Group was one of five groups in existence; the others were Beta,
Delta, Gamma, and Omega Groups. The missions they were assigned
usually included precision infrastructure demolition, pinpoint personnel
strikes, high-risk reconnaissance missions, hot-zone personnel extractions,
night strikes, and as the deciding factor in high-risk stalemates similar to

Corinth. They generally weren't utilized as front line fighters slugging it out from dug-in positions against an equally determined and entrenched enemy force. Their purpose was different. The Guard was designed to be a lightning fast and nimble force capable of striking with surgical accuracy in the chaos of battle. It had to be light on its feet and highly mobile. The men had to get in fast, move even faster, and have the ability to think and adapt to changing circumstances under fire. On top of that, they had to carry enough weaponry to unleash hell. The Guard was an offensive weapon. They simply weren't equipped to survive if pinned-down. As such, their missions were usually quick deployments with fast and furious action, constant movement, and quick extraction. Despite the dangers inherent to the mission, with careful planning and perpetual training they managed to keep casualties to a bare minimum. As one would predict, there were the usual broken bones and superficial flesh wounds, but the number of action-related deaths was low. Mostly this was because the enemy targets were usually dead before they realized they were being attacked. Regardless, newcomers were constantly being trained and equipped at incredible government expense to replace those lost in combat, and there was always the option to form new units, although the political and financial realities of war made this a less likely scenario. At this point in the war, the slow but steady influx of new men pretty much matched the rate of casualties. As a result, the number of active Guardsmen remained fairly steady.

In Alpha Group, the most decorated and accomplished unit of The Guard, Lt. Col. Jake Gillean was second in rank and the point man on most missions. He earned the respect, admiration, and trust of his fellow soldiers. Gillean was the Viking warrior; the strongest, the fastest, the most determined, and the most controlled. If there was ever a fight when every soldier on every side succumbed to fear or exhaustion, or made fatal mistakes in the mental climate of anger or fatigue, the last man alive and the ultimate survivor would most assuredly be Lt. Col. Jake Gillean.

Jake's commander and one of his best friends, Alpha Group's leader, was Col. Alexander Fisk. He was the most experienced warrior, and his skills in command were beyond measure. His meticulous planning and instincts would get them through their ordeals alive, or he would die trying.

Alpha Group completed its extraction from Corinth. As they boarded the ultrasonic transport, Jake was the second to last to get on, with Col. Fisk pulling up the rear. They strapped into their harnesses, and a team of exo-suit specialists began frantically working to repair the damage. Hoses and cables emerged like tentacles from the walls of the hold and attached to various parts of their suits and helmets, and into the shield generators on their backs.

Before the transport's ramp finished closing, the men began receiving a briefing through their BCDs. The men were shocked when they discovered their destination—Portland, Oregon. More specifically, they were going to a museum in Portland that had been taken by Persian SS. By the time the transport was flying through the upper stratosphere, the soldiers discovered just how ugly events were on their home soil.

The Natural History Museum in Portland was a typical museum in every way. It had its geological and earth life collections, displays of dinosaurs, primordial man, and an impressive array of interactive three-dimensional educational activities in holographic chambers. It was not the typical terrorist target, except that children routinely overran the facility on school field trips.

The situation was more ominous because in the last several months, eleven schools in Europe and North America had been destroyed with a devastating loss of life. This was just the latest chapter in a clash of cultures that had persisted in various forms for well over three thousand years, even pre-dating the sacking of Troy. On a grand scale, it was a battle for survival between two cultural species. Both were bent on power and influence, and now it seemed certain that with the advance of technology and better, more efficient, ways of killing people, that the pendulum of dominance was going to move in only one direction.

With the outbreak of World War IV, five long and hellish years ago, the overall volume of death and destruction, the sheer measure of human carnage, grew to become nothing more than statistics, mind numbing and maddening statistics. It is impossible to fully comprehend, either mentally or emotionally, the loss of hundreds of millions of lives when the first, the last, and almost everyone in between were complete strangers. When there is no direct or indirect personal connection, it's easy to move on with near total indifference. The ones who generally took pause were those who had a personal tie or emotional connection with someone who was killed. People all across the globe responded in predictable fashion. Vast numbers turned to their spiritual beliefs for guidance and comfort. Not always, but usually, they were reminded of the spiritual importance of not forgetting about love and forgiveness in this life, as opposed to the easily perceived hunger for revenge. But forgiveness be damned, revenge is what the West clamored for in the wake of so many civilian murders. The interesting paradox was that as some discovered a new sense of spiritual calm and meaning, many looked at the same scriptures and found something else entirely. In their minds, it wasn't about money or power, it was all about religious imperialism and domination. As a result, there was an explosion in the sheer intensity of hatred and anger and its ultimate emotional mass grew beyond measure. The hatreds fed back and catalyzed their own growth, feeding on American, European, Asian, and Persian populations like a great parasite. At that point, most didn't really care how the war started or why…all they wanted was complete victory, one that would leave behind no trace of the enemy or their causes.

The war began five years earlier in Africa. The Persian Empire was actively supporting groups of fundamentalist rebels who were launching cross-border attacks against the sovereign nation of South Africa. Their objective was to support a minority faction of Persian sympathizers who wanted the country to join the Persian Economic Community, a move that would necessarily forfeit the country's economic, legal, and political sovereignty. Once South African forces launched an attack to destroy the rebel bases in the Persian State of Botswana, the Persian Empire officially declared war. South Africa lasted three weeks before its military was completely destroyed. The members of its government who managed to survive eventually ended up in England.

The destruction of South Africa led to a domino effect the Persians didn't anticipate—the West and East had had enough and declared war. They had stood idly by while the Persians took over one country after another in Africa, as they had pushed their influence across the Indian subcontinent and also northward into Eastern Europe and Southern Russia. The pacifists screamed for peace. "The Persian leaders are reasonable," they screamed. "They don't want war. Give peace a chance. Make love, not war." Every slogan ran its course while the Persian Empire grew stronger. Finally, with the attack on South Africa and the consolidation of Persian power throughout the entire Continent, it was time for war. The first declaration came from the European Union, followed by Russia and China, and finally, after a year of fighting, United America. Mostly, it took so long for the world to stand unified against Persia because it was still reeling from the horrors of World War III. After that war, the Persians were left in a dominant position in their corner of the globe. But that was a different Persia, a Persia that could live in peace with its neighbors. Since then the radical fundamentalists, a fringe political and social movement that no one had taken seriously inside or outside of Persia, had filled a political void and gained power. They moved fast, consolidated their gains, halted national and local elections, declared martial law, and ruthlessly eliminated any and all internal opposition. Once they were in complete control of Persia the die was cast. Conflict was inevitable.

Prior to these events, a long series of staunchly secular governments in the Middle East had formed a coalition of states, joined them into one country, and formed a Persian Empire. It was an impressive and complex process that had taken nearly three hundred years. Some wanted to call it the resurrection of the Ottoman Empire. They weren't entirely wrong. To call it a rebirth of the Persian Empire of Xerxes and Darius was however, a stretch. Regardless, by the time war broke out, their vast political, economic, and military dominion encompassed the entire African continent and reached northward into Eastern Europe and to the borders of Greece and Germany. They controlled the entire Indian subcontinent, and they reached well into the western half of China.

The only real thorn in the Persian side, prior to South Africa, was Afghanistan. The tribal nature and fighting spirit of the people who lived there led them to resist with vigor, but the Persians didn't make the same mistakes that every other culture made with Afghanistan; they cordoned the area off, swept the country foot by foot with millions of troops, and exterminated everyone. It was the most complete and absolute genocide in recorded history. As they did their killing and afterward repopulated the country with loyalists, the world watched and did nothing, pretending that it wasn't happening. Everyone wanted to believe that the new Persian leaders were rational and that they could be reasoned with; but wanting something doesn't make it so. Their aggressive expansionist policies and absolute assimilation of divergent cultures into one of their own narrow vision could no longer be ignored. That's when the world finally went to war.

In the grand scheme of things, the overall percentage of the population that had been killed, wounded, or displaced so far was no greater than other conflicts throughout world history. The difference was that developing technology had allowed the world's population to reach approximately thirty-five billion people. This meant that the sheer numbers of dead were staggering beyond the imagination. The first two years of the war had seen more deaths than all three previous World Wars combined, and with unlimited human resources, there was no clear indication which side was going to prevail.

The Atlantic and Pacific weren't wide enough to protect North America, and the Natural History Museum in Portland was only the latest target. Seven hundred forty-two children and ninety-three adults were being held in a large domed holographic theater. In the previous attacks there had been no warning, just sudden and unexpected explosions. The killings were usually without any tangible benefit or purpose, except that from a strategic perspective the strikes fomented fear. They drew the vital military resources of men and material away from the front. But this time things were unfolding differently. They were taking their time. The Persians had a holding force on the ground and were making demands while simultaneously broadcasting political and religious rants. They wanted the release of Persian prisoners and the withdrawal of United American troops from Eastern Europe, Greece, and Africa. A hostage was being killed every ten minutes by slow decapitation with a long curved knife that looked like it came out of some ancient Persian armory. It was of no consequence if the United American President chose to meet their demands as it was understood that all the hostages were going to die. The demands were a psychological ploy designed to undermine the war effort and the authority of the President. The soldiers of the Persian Secret Service were more than happy to sacrifice their lives for a glorious cause. They knew from the beginning that Portland was a suicide mission. They believed there were far worse ways to die than in service to their country.

What the Persians in fact accomplished with their strategy of deliberately targeting civilians, was the generation of more hatred and anger, and they galvanized the public's will to see the war through to its ultimate end, no matter the sacrifice. Theirs was a complete misreading of Western culture in almost every respect, and the ultimate ramifications of their policies were to unite a previously divided nation and make palatable the hard-war strategies it would take to win. With every terrorist-type attack, they increasingly muzzled the pacifist elements within the media and the government. Further, the Persian tactics caused the Proletariat Party, the precursor to the Egalitarian Party, to take a beating in the election. As a result, the Proletariat Party, the only anti-war advocates in United American politics, lost their majority in the Lower Commons, or The House of Local Representatives.

For Jake, the Persians in the museum weren't soldiers. They weren't even guerrillas. There was only one acceptable word to describe them— terrorists. They were called that only because there wasn't a more fitting or disgusting word available in the English language. The deliberate targeting of the weakest and most innocent by soldiers on the ground was looked upon with revulsion and disdain. Repeatedly, the terrorists would avoid direct confrontations with military personnel only to aggressively murder unarmed civilians as opportunities arose. As a result, in the West they were regarded as something less than human, something lower than the animals. Jake believed the only solution was to eradicate them from the world the same way one might eradicate a pestilence or a virus that caused the most revolting human disease.

As events in Portland weren't developing like previous attacks, and because the museum hadn't been blown up, it presented an opportunity. Without hesitation, the President made her decision and issued the order. It raced its way through the military high command and to Alpha Group. She wanted the nation's most elite Special Forces to intervene. It was their only hope.

In flight the soldiers focused all their attention on the briefing. Large military grade Vintel units positioned up and down along the length of the craft raised holographic images of the museum and real time imagery of events on the ground. The image showed a crisp and clear outline of the hostages sitting in the domed theater and the terrorists as they moved throughout the structure. While they couldn't be entirely sure as some of the Persians were certainly hiding amongst the hostages, the images were progressively color-coded as the living were classified as hostage versus Persian. The hostages were labeled in green, and the terrorists were tracked in red. Several dead bodies were lined up in a row on the auditorium stage while their severed heads were piled in the corner. The scene was horrific. Their heat signal images were variably weaker than those still left alive.

Similar to what was done in Corinth, the Persians mounted hostages along the edge of the roof. As the windows were huge vertically oriented monoliths designed to let in the sunshine, they didn't offer the same opportunity for the display of hostages, so they were placed only along the top of the building. They strapped some of the smaller children to their own bodies with a harness similar to what a mother uses to carry a baby through the park. Utilized as human shields, the children were harnessed to their chests facing outward, presumably with a trip wire that would set off an explosive if the soldier should die. Saving these children was going to be impossible.

"Did you see that?" Jake said. Col. Fisk gave an inquisitive look that suggested he wanted to hear what Jake had to say. While Fisk was talking Jake had been rotating through alternate scan sequences and detected an anomaly. "Stop image," Jake commanded. "Image run through subprocessor 4, overlap heat signature with dual electromagnetic sensors—filters at 35 and 150 Hertz. Reverse five seconds. Forward one-quarter speed. Two hundred time magnification sector 17A, second level, at my mark."

As the holographic image reversed and slowly rolled forward with Jake's specs, everyone recognized what they would have missed. Fisk glanced at Jake as though to say, 'how the hell did you find that?' He addressed the men, "Right there. This just got more complicated."

In the second level hallway leading to the auditorium, away from all the others, there was a brief flash of a signal, once magnified it was obvious that it was in the shape of a human hand. Its brief detection coincided with the actions of one of seventeen terrorists who were wearing highly specialized stealth uniforms. The Persian had removed his glove for a brief moment so he could use his bare hand to adjust his mask. It meant part of this was going to be a visual firefight. Guided munitions were useless if they didn't have a signal lock. More civilians were going to die if Persians, cloaked and undetectable, lurked throughout the building.

"Everybody understand what we're up against?" Fisk said. "We have, count them, fourteen targets and at least one stealth. This is Persian SS. They're well trained and very good. We don't know how many more we are dealing with."

"There's going to be hell to pay today," one of the soldiers muttered under his breath.

"Here's the plan," Fisk announced. "We'll have four points of entry, two in the auditorium and two in the museum proper. We make our own doors by blasting through the walls. We can not use our pulsars to gain entry as we don't want to kill everyone on the other side. Understand our primary objective is different this time. We have to save as many of our civilians as we can. Teams One and Two will take the auditorium. With the curve of the building they will be oriented at a 45-degree angle relative to one another and will be separated by about sixty meters. With converging fields of fire, every inch of the place will be covered from those two positions. The outside wall is at least eighteen inches thick. Inside those walls are hostages and terrorists. Choose your targets carefully, but DO NOT hesitate."

Upon hearing the words, Jake's thoughts immediately flashed back to Corinth. He hesitated and, as a result, an American GI was dead. He had berated the men just as Fisk was doing, preaching to them to never hesitate. A stab of guilt ripped into him. He pushed it out of his mind and focused on the briefing.

"Innocents will be killed by friendly fire," Fisk said. "I repeat, DO NOT hesitate. Right now they are all dead. If we save one, just one, our mission will be a success. The museum proper as you see," he went on, "is a large rectangular open room as long as two football fields and five stories high. There are several smaller display rooms along each side on each level. Teams Three and Four will secure the building including the floor and side entrances. They will be responsible for sweeping and clearing all the rooms." Fisk scanned the room. The tension was intense. They were fighting on home soil now.

"Lt. Col. Gillean is once again the point...you'll have Team Five. Your objective: secure the roof and structurally stabilize the interior of the auditorium." He directed his attention to Jake, "It's Team Five's responsibility to get in first. We move after you. Fail and everybody dies." Fisk let the thought sink in before continuing, "The three-dimensional structure has been imprinted on an SSD (structural support device) that is being delivered from Offutt Air Force Base. It is in transit and will meet us on the ground. The device will give us, at most, about two or three minutes after they blow the thing. That means we are working against the clock. We have to neutralize the enemy and get everybody out. After that, anybody left inside is going to be buried under hundreds of tons of rubble. The SSD needs to be planted in the center of the room. Lt. Col?…" he waited for Jake's opinion.

"Right here." Jake pointed to the outer wall, between the projected blast sites for Teams One and Two. "We blow the wall here. Coming from above or below isn't possible. On my mark, simultaneously we blast and move. I will personally deliver the SSD. My team will be divided into two unequal units. One ten-man unit will secure the roof, eliminate hostiles, and extract the children being used as shields. The other six-man unit will target the auditorium. We will imprint the known targets in the room using guided munitions. Listen up, Teams One and Two!" He surveyed the group of men. "I'm moving fast! I'd prefer not to catch one of yours on my way across the room! Visual rules apply. Identify your target. Is there any part of that det you find confusing?" Jake's drawl again betrayed his Tennessee roots.

"All right," Fisk ordered, "You heard the Lt. Col. We hit the ground running. We will be shielded behind the contours of the ground and surrounding buildings. Because the museum sits on a hill, the best we can do is land this bucket three miles away. It's clear in Portland today. As such we can't do a jump. We will come in on the ground. Locals are clearing a path for us. The designated route for each team is uploaded to your BCDs. On my command, once we are all in place, the local sharps will clear the roof and any targets at the windows. They have assured me that the explosives linked to the human shields have been deactivated by the Portland PD's local hostage unit through the use of some new robotic equipment. On my command, Alpha Group…balls to the wall. We've trained for this. You know what is expected of you. You have ten. Look to your team leader. Check your neighbor's equipment." Fisk turned toward Jake in a gesture telling him to finish, "Lt. Col.," he said.

"It'll only take one second for them to kill all those kids," Jake said. "The building will come down. All those kids will die. As Col. Fisk said, if we save one, the mission is a success. Keep in mind they are afraid and won't want to move. Motivate them. Whatever it takes," Jake emphasized. "Yell and scream if you have to. Shock their brains into reality. Have the older children help with the younger. Adults that are still alive may be able to help. Colonel Fisk will be delivering an atmospheric vac-device into the auditorium. This will clear the air enough to preserve visibility."

An atmospheric vac-device is a weapon that when fired releases ionic-sweep mortars. The devices attach to the ceiling or walls and immediately become activated. High-energy ion beams sweep the room while integrated quantum computer driven detection systems simultaneously target the areas with the greatest amount of obscuring dust. They also prevent the beams from hitting people. The ion beam creates a negative charge on the dust particles, and because the device itself emits a strong positive charge, the negatively charged particles move out of the air and collect around the devices. A single device would go a long way toward clearing the air in the auditorium for at least a couple minutes under the worst of circumstances. Fisk would be firing several.

Alpha Group broke down into its five designated teams, each containing sixteen men minus McGuire who was lost in Corinth. They rapidly checked their weapons and then their partner's weapons and equipment. The exo-suits that were beyond immediate repair were set aside until they could be sent back to the MST weapons lab, so several of the men were wearing shiny new black suits. A death-like seriousness permeated the cargo hold of the transport. The stress was palpable and thick. There was a reason they were being transported halfway around the world for the job. They were the best. They were the only ones who could hope to salvage life from this seemingly impossible scenario.

Lt. Col. Jake Gillean and Col. Alexander Fisk shared vast similarities of personality. To the novice observer, they were nearly clones, but to the trained eye, there were differences that were anything but subtle. While both were intelligent far beyond their peers, Col. Fisk nurtured an innate and scholarly brilliance. He was exceedingly gifted in the art of debate to the extent that he could tell someone to go to hell in such an incredible variety of ways that they would smile and hope to enjoy the trip. He wasn't manipulative, but he knew how to work the system to get what he needed for his men; and they always came first. He would advocate their interests as long as it didn't compromise military protocol or mission success. In his spare time, when he stepped out of his uniform and enjoyed a breath of non-military air, he was an avid and scholarly bookworm who could rip through the densest material and retain almost everything he read.

Jake was special in his own unique way. His traits of personality were by now far removed from the youth who paced the end zone crying after his father died. Largely as a consequence of World War IV, he had, to a degree, grown emotionally hard. His was an impenetrable shell tempered by experiences in combat. He chose to lead by example. As a commander, he never failed to help the soldiers who put their trust in him, even if it was for something as trivial as covering them for a latrine break or sharing care packages of cookies that Wendy sent on a regular basis. His absolute dedication toward the welfare of his men was even more evident when it was important, like carrying a heavy pack or a weapon or giving up a clean pair of socks—or risking everything to come to their aid under enemy fire. He was a soldier's soldier, and his men raced to line up behind him. In every engagement, he always managed to embed himself in the heaviest fighting. He was the strongest, the fastest, and externally the most fearless. He was one of the rare men who thrived on the adrenaline of battle. As a result, he had become the consummate warrior. Powered by aggressive and lion-like natural instincts that were tamed and channeled through an unending allegiance to duty, honor, God, and country, he became an Alpha Group commander because every one of his troops, these proud men-of-men, all secretly wanted to be like him.

Jake still possessed a compassionate and caring core, but he maintained a façade of being harsh and absolutely masculine in mannerism when dealing with military personnel. On the numerous occasions his men witnessed him interacting with refugees or the downtrodden, they saw a complete metamorphosis. He had no qualms about transforming instantaneously into someone who treated others with the gentleness and care that a shepherd might show an injured lamb. He was confident enough in himself not to care if the soldiers in his charge witnessed moments of tenderness. He once saved an orphaned boy and carried him two hundred miles to a secondary extraction point when the first was aborted. He would bark orders one moment and sing silly songs to the boy the next. Had the boy been a little older he would have taught him how to properly herd the men of Alpha Group and the proper way to issue orders correctly, and he would have taught him how to do it with a gravely baritone delivery punctuated by a Tennessee accent. The bottom line was painfully clear to the men of Alpha Group, if they followed his every example and instruction they would have a far greater chance of completing their objectives and staying alive to tell about it.

"Okay girls, just like we practiced," Jake said as he checked and rechecked each member of his team. He was thorough, inspecting their boots, exo-suits, helmets, straps, and weapons. He briefed them again and outlined what was expected. "Run a BCD diagnostic, make sure you verify the integration channels, and run an interface check with your weapons. Absolutely everything must check." The diagnostic only took about 30 seconds. It would alert the soldier to any problems with his system, and if caught early enough, the computer personnel at central command could fix the defect.

Jake proceeded back through the ranks rubbing heads, smashing fists and forearms, and making a few jokes. He told several men to contact their wives or mothers, mentioning their loved ones' names with fluidity in the process. "You better contact, Molly. Have you heard from Sara? How's

Angelique doing?" He paused in front of Raul. He was a member of the more handsome variety; single and proud, the type of guy who leaves a trail of broken hearts in his wake. "Damn you're ugly," Jake said. Raul laughed. It was a compliment.

He was still the same old Jake in some ways, but things were admittedly very different now. He was grown. He wasn't a kid anymore. On the rare occasions he had the opportunity to return home, his family and friends instantly took notice of the thick tough exterior where there previously had been softness and happiness. There was an edge to Jake that spoke of an unrelenting aggressiveness. But it wasn't a hyper or lashing-out type of red-hot aggressiveness; it was more of a black and powerfully durable type of aggressiveness, the consistent and unyielding type, calculating and probing as opposed to loud and boastful. His wasn't a demeanor inclined to whistle through the graveyard…but it was one that would stake out the place in the hope of witnessing something disturbing.

After he tended to his men, Jake sat by himself in front of a computer console. Unlike the rank and file of the military, whose communications with family were delayed for two to three days for security and screening purposes, Guardsmen ranked a special screening program that resulted in only a 3 or 4 second delay. The rule was they had to exclusively communicate through a secure dedicated channel with a secure and dedicated receiver placed on the other end. It was absolutely prohibited to communicate with family through the implanted military grade BCDs, as doing so would allow the enemy the opportunity to hack the system.

The Gillean family's receiver was in the kitchen, mounted on the wall. It had a flip down keyboard and a no frills screen approximately thirty centimeters wide by twenty centimeters high. Attached to the device was a loud chiming ringer designed so that the crescendo signal could be heard throughout the house and would get loud enough to be heard outside.

For a moment Jake froze. He wanted to communicate with Wendy, but his mind was tense, ready to lash-out like a predator. While the obscene details of this mission made it absolute in terms of being non-routine, and while the anticipation was eating at him just like all the other men, there was another element to what he was feeling. It wasn't the usual hatred of the Persians, nor was it the fear of dying as that was by now an omnipresent feeling perpetually swirling within his emotive background. It was something else entirely. The whole situation, the whole world and everything in it, had collapsed into insanity. At times like this it seemed as though there were only four consistent and unwavering facets of life; devotion to God, to country, to the soldiers around him, and to his family. While it was sure to be one hell of a fight, a damnable contest of wills with the ultimate stakes hanging in the balance, this was different than Alpha Group's other missions. Dammit! They were on American soil, in the middle of an American city, and they were killing American children. This was more than a strategic point on a map, this represented defense of the country, defense of home soil, and more importantly…the defense of lives innocent in the absolute. The sadistic murderous intentions of the enemy were in violation of every precept of humanity, and as a result, he no longer afforded them the honor of being regarded as human. He regarded them as primal, a subspecies, Neanderthal-like in every way except appearance. Because of that, not so deep down, he enjoyed killing them. Or was it the other way around? As Lt. Col. Jake Gillean absolutely always kept his thoughts to himself, no one knew, and certainly no one would ever dare to interrogate him on the matter to find out which came first—his hatred of the enemy or the enjoyment he experienced when killing them. Was it a reaction or a rationalization? Was it in reaction to the world around him, or was it a self-preserving rationalization masking a deep defect in character? 'Am I a killer?' he often asked himself. Regardless, Jake believed the increasing ease with which he could extinguish human life, at least those defined as the enemy, was unquestionable in being justified.

Where Jake's thoughts and spirit had been driven since the carefree days of his childhood, days he spent fishing with his friends, playing sports, and learning under the tutelage of his father, had rendered him by now, by the time his boots would touch the ground in Portland, almost unrecognizable as actually being the same person. Yet somewhere hidden underneath, there was a compartment where he held in check all those human aspects of life, his emotions, his love for his family, his sense of gentleness and patience. Everything was divided and kept separate. Just as he couldn't allow thoughts and feelings about his family to interfere with his work as a soldier, he couldn't let the terribleness of war seep into his family. Now as he stood in front of the computer console he was all warrior. He couldn't shift gears quickly. In his mind he couldn't find his family. They were buried deep, drowning under an ocean of strain. The tension was too great, the seriousness and risk they would be facing in Portland owned every aspect of his mind. He couldn't communicate with Wendy. He closed his eyes and forcibly exhaled, trying to access the mental files for his personal life, the non-military life he so rarely had the opportunity to experience. He had been engaged in one high-risk action after another for so long he felt numb. As time passed, and the world plunged ever deeper in the chaos and brutality of an unending war he felt as though he was increasingly losing himself, losing a grip on his other life, his normal life, a life he so longed to regain.

With his eyes closed he smiled. It was so slight as to have gone largely unnoticed by anyone stupid enough to be watching, or shallow enough to care, but under the circumstances it held firm to the claim of being a smile. A brief, a very brief moment of unbridled calm swept over him. He held the vision of his home, his wife, and his children. They stood in such stark contrast to the hell he had been living in. In so many ways it was that contrast that actually lit the fires of his motivation. It was a reminder of exactly what he was fighting for. He keyed into the console: WENDY, I LOVE YOU BABY. MISS YOU SO VERY MUCH. HOLD THE KIDS TIGHT AND TELL THEM I LOVE THEM. KISS THEM AGAIN AND AGAIN. PRAY HARD. WATCH THE NEWS ON THE VINTEL. WE'LL TALK LATER. MY LOVE FOREVER AND ALWAYS, J.

He sent the message just before the link shut down. Wendy would not have the opportunity to respond. His mind was again racing through the details of the mission. When he turned away from the console he found himself face to face with Fisk.

"Col." he said with a nod. He took a breath and asked in a hushed voice, "What do you think?" As they were best friends, he usually called Col. Fisk by his first name, Alex, but never, absolutely never, when the other men were present.

Alex was distracted. He said in a voice low enough so the other men wouldn't hear, "High probability this turns into a cluster. If the building's still there, and if everything goes as planned, I think there is a chance we'll get a few out. I do not like relying on an unknown. Those kids," Fisk shook his head in deep dismayed contemplation, "their survival depends on the snipers already on the ground. Before we can get near the building, they have to take out all the Persians on the roof and any who are visible through the windows. We're looking at highly coordinated action from 360 degrees by a group of people with questionable experience and training. At the same time, I understand the Persians are beating up the surrounding buildings pretty bad, and they set up an energy shield around the entire perimeter. Any snipers in position won't be there for long. Their positions are too hot, and with the shield, they'll have to use precision mortar rounds. That's not easy even under the best of circumstances."

"Mole charges in place?" Jake asked.

"So I've been told." Mole explosives were burrowing grenades. They could burrow under the ground by remote control. Several of them were positioned directly underneath the shield generators. If everything went as planned they would explode a fraction of a second prior to a deluge of sniper fire. Redundancy was the key. That's why several mole charges were being used for each generator, and multiple snipers were targeting each hostile.

"I have every confidence," Jake said. "I've reviewed contingency plans with Teams Three, Four, and the ten-man extraction unit from Five. They each have their back-up assignments if the forces already on the ground fail to achieve their objectives. They'll be going in hard and fast on sniper cue. In the contingency scenario, the rest of us move when the shields go down. We may take some heat from the hostiles on the roof, but their fire will presumably be drawn as parts of Three, Four, and Five will be on the roof. It'll take roughly thirty seconds longer to take them out at the extreme. It's the best chance those kids have."

"Good," Alex said.

"Cameras?" Jake inquired, concerned that if friendly fire got some of the kids on the roof it wouldn't play well in the media.

"I was informed there has been a complete lockdown. Every recording device and uplink in the area has been scrambled." Fisk knew the inherent risks they were running. Good men had been court-martialed for making hard choices that meant the difference between surviving and dying in the heat of battle, just because someone captured the activity on a recorder. It was easy for some behind the scenes soft-in-the-middle pansy who never experienced combat and who never had to endure the experience of a weapon being fired at them in anger to raise hell with complaints and objections that the soldiers weren't smothering the Persians with hugs and kisses. It was a dangerous situation and self-preservation from foreign, and unfortunately, domestic enemies had to be accounted for.

"Beer afterward?" Jake's suggestion was an offering of hope in the midst of a terrible situation, hope that they would live through it and that there would be a positive outcome. It wasn't a cavalier attempt to downplay the danger.

"You buying?" Alex asked. He failed to grin at his own inside joke. He often managed to be short on resources when they went to the officers' club. Jake usually bought, and it had evolved into an expectation.

"I'm buying," Jake said.

The pilot's voice came over the loudspeaker, "Buckle down. Initiating descent in five...four...(the men scrambled to get their harnesses on)... three...two...one." Jake buckled himself in and watched out the window. They were one step from floating away into outer space and in four minutes they would be on the ground in Portland. The transport nose-dived at a near vertical. The speed was outrageous and pushed the men to the very edge of losing consciousness. Their exo-suits compressed their extremities and torso to keep oxygenated blood flowing to their heads. That was the only thing that allowed their brains to remain awake and alert.

"Ground in mark...four minutes," the pilot abruptly announced.

The craft traveled out of site relative to the museum, approached ground level some thirty miles away, and traveled at supersonic speed about twenty feet above the beautiful Columbia River. Behind the transport huge waves flew outward, spraying a mist into the sky and leaving a deep wake to be filled in by crashing water. Any boats unlucky enough to still be in the river after the Coast Guard and local authorities were told to clear the way were just out of luck. Portland was ahead, positioned on the south side of the river. The transport went exceedingly low and turned nearly sideways to hug the river's edge. There was a distant line of site from the museum to the water. It needed to be handled carefully to avoid detection by the Persian SS. The contours of the ground and the buildings would bounce the sound waves clean over the museum so they wouldn't be able to hear the transport's approach. Regardless, no chances were being taken and Alpha Group's drop point was three miles away as the crow flies. As the transport slowed, Fourier anti-sound devices were activated. They folded out of the wings just above the engines and immediately the craft became completely silent. The sound waves emitted by the engines were cancelled out by anti-waves generated from the Fourier devices. The craft's wings were folding in as it slowed. By the time they were completely retracted the transport was floating between two enormous green glass buildings that stood like sentinels at the water's edge. With expert skill the pilot guided the craft through an abrupt 180-degree rotation so that the cargo doors would open in the opposite direction, toward the city. The craft hovered silently in the air, and the pilot cut the engines when it was still six inches above the pavement. It crashed down, its weight cracking and tearing the asphalt under the landing gear.

The city was gorgeous. The buildings were coordinated in a variety of architectural styles that seamlessly flowed together. All the masonry was green, a deep forest green. The sidewalks were gray and the streets an unblemished black. For miles it seemed there wasn't a single building less than twenty stories in height. It was quite possibly the cleanest and most beautiful city any of the men had ever seen. Through their fighting eyes, they also recognized it for what it was…an absolute deathtrap if attacked.

The buildings immediately surrounding the museum had been thoroughly swept for Persian elements, and all possible communications between those inside the museum and any potential outside support had been jammed. However, the uplink between the inside of the building and the broadcast of the Persian demands across the world's Vintel system was intact despite all efforts to close it down. In an expanding radius around the museum, civilians were being evacuated. Against the flow of the fleeing masses, emergency crews of every variety were making it into place. They were out of site a couple blocks away but ready to speed into action at the specified time.

The ramp lowered and Alpha Group was on the move. The local police cleared a wide path through the streets so they could move fast in making their way to the museum. Because they needed to shield their movements from the Persian SS who were scanning outward from the museum roof and through windows, and because each team had a separate objective in terms of the exact area of the structure they were going to attack, each team had to follow a different route through the city. They would have to snake their way up a street, turn, go a few blocks in another direction, and then turn again.

The level of tension and panic was exactly what the men had witnessed in Corinth, maybe even more so as this kind of attack and the overt killing of civilians were new to the people of Portland. They weren't just reading about it or watching it on the Vintel…they were living it, experiencing it first-hand. The realities of a far off and brutal war had found their way into a peaceful sanctuary, a sanctuary filled with lives that just hours ago were completely detached from any real understanding of the actual price being paid for their freedom. But that was a few hours ago; it may as well have been a thousand years ago. Everything was so very different now. The dark side of nature was at work, and it was base and remorseless. On this day, there were predators and prey, and so far, the predators in the museum had had it their way, but now the prey had brought forth their own warriors…they were mean as hell and wanted revenge.

Sirens were blaring everywhere, the sounds colliding and echoing off the buildings and up and down the corridors of streets. People were everywhere, all trying to get away. They were in every state of distress, from yelling and screaming to blankly staring in utter disbelief. The police, fire-crews, and other emergency personnel were doing everything they possibly could to maintain order. Then Alpha Group arrived. From the people's perspective, the transport looked like it came from another planet. Its landing gear crashed down into the pavement, and the earth shook under the force of its incredible weight. Next the ramp lowered, and then…they appeared. The soldiers looked like giants with their black exo-suits and helmets. Most were dirty and worn from their action in Corinth, making it obvious that they had come from some far away battlefield. They were absolutely sure and powerful in every movement they made. Because of their appearance, a wave of salvation-like calm began sweeping outward like ripples on a pond. While some of the people just stared ahead with wide eyes, their blank stares hiding any indication that they were actually perceiving what they saw, most let loose a loud emotional eruption of cheering, of deliverance.

The soldiers carried massive weapons unlike anything the civilians had seen, and they did so with near effortless precision. With the incredible technology of the exo-suits they were able to sprint through the streets at incredible speeds, reaching up to sixty miles per hour on the straight-aways. The people were in awe as the five teams of sixteen men, the very best that United America had to offer, raced without hesitation, with complete deliberateness, toward the very location they were trying so desperately to escape.

Alex and Jake were running in front of their respective teams, guided through the twists and turns of their predetermined route by information streaming through their BCDs. They were the first of the teams to reach their first objective—the launch point. From their vantage, there were three Persians clearly visible on the roof of the large green stone building. Their weapons were trained on the surrounding buildings and they were randomly firing. It didn't matter to the Persians if the targets were real or imaginary. The idea of destroying anything American was cathartic and sheer ecstasy. The guts of each of the buildings surrounding the museum were fully exposed in the most primal fashion. Steam shot outward and water drained from ruptured pipes, small fires burned on numerous floors, and dark smoke rose ominously into the Oregon sky. Within the wide radius of the Persian strike zone, not a single structure was left untouched, not a single window was left intact. Shattered glass blanketed the entire area, and the buildings were completely eviscerated of their contents. The sidewalks and streets were littered with debris—desks, computers, and other odd pieces of office furniture. Papers fluttered down from the buildings, turning this way and that, as though it was confetti celebrating a parade…a morose parade honoring death and destruction. Amongst the smothering blanket of rubble, of property that could be easily replaced, were the remains of people who couldn't; innocent and unsuspecting men and women who were going about their usual activities moments before the Persians struck. Without warning, their lives were torn apart by an enemy who they not only didn't expect, but who they didn't understand. Their corpses, in varied degrees of mutilation and dismemberment, were scattered on the ground around the buildings. At least one body could be seen dangling upside-down from a building, about ten floors up, the person's legs somehow tangled in exposed rebar, the body swaying back and forth like a demonic pendulum ticking off the march of death.

Jake took in the site with objective coldness. The clarity of his mission was resonating in his mind. As a result he wasn't distracted in the least. The sites of a battle zone were not new. He had seen it all before, just different versions of the same thing in different lands with different people. There would be time to sort through emotions later, in a psychological debriefing. For now he, along with everyone else in Alpha Group, had to function more like machines than men.

With the sheer level of devastation being wrought on the surrounding city and the incredibly high rate of fire coming from the museum, it was apparent there were far more Persian SS on the roof than he could see. At least some of them were firing from windows, but most of the fire was originating on the roof. That much was apparent from what Jake could see. The pulsar blasts and percussion mortars were coming out hot and heavy. Near as he could figure, from the sound and the level of destruction, it had to be the work of at least fifteen to twenty highly trained soldiers.

The museum was perched on top of a hill and was surrounded by a park. On three sides the park provided a buffer roughly one hundred meters wide between the museum proper and the buildings of the city. That accident of urban planning resulted in at least some diminishment in the damage, and so far had resulted in fewer casualties than the Persians hoped. The main entrance into the museum was on the opposite side of the structure and extended out into the main body of the park. With huge oaks and fir trees, the park was at least five or six hundred meters deep and half again as wide. It was brilliant in its greenery, and from appearances, no expense had been spared in beautifying the location with splendid bronze statues and vibrant fountains that had achieved world renown. These brilliant artistic creations, completely ignorant of what was going on around them, continued to spray water upward in majestic patterns as though pronouncing an era of peace and serenity. It was crass in this ultimate contradiction.

Jake took in the entire vision, processed everything like running a movie in fast-forward, eliminated everything non-essential, and blocked out everything except his job. He took possession of the SSD. As promised, it was waiting for him at the launch point. He indicated that the sergeant holding it should shout out quick instructions on how to activate the device. He already knew how to use it as the manual was relayed to his BCD. All the men did this with the equipment they were using as a universal rule prior to every engagement, no matter how familiar they thought they might be with the device.

"Sir!" The sergeant was yelling, as the noise was loud. "It has to be vertical when activated!" A large chunk of glass and debris fell in front of them. "If it's not," he continued, "you could kill everyone in the building, including yourself! The field emits from the sides in a near horizontal arc for the first three feet and projects upward at the specified angle!" He was pointing to the top of the device, indicating the energy field projection site. "The activator switch is on the base. Hold this button and smash the trigger pin into the floor! Keep your head low and out of the way sir, or the unit will take it clean-off!"

While Jake was getting the SSD instructions, Alex was communicating with the local authorities. There was no time to waste. "Are the snipers in place?" he asked. He paused, listened to their response, and commanded, "We move on my mark." He waited an agonizing forty-five seconds longer until the last team achieved its launch point on the far side of the museum.

Prior to the arrival of Alpha Group, local sniper teams, several units from Salem, a fast mobilizing team out of Seattle, and two military companies of the 82nd out of Fort Lewis, had gained footholds in the surrounding structures. They were brave beyond reproach, finding places to shoot from in the buildings being devastated by the Persians. Without being detected, they had to carefully work their way through the destruction, the smoke, and fires, and make it to a good spot with a direct line of site to the targets on the museum roof. Then they had to accomplish several things: bring their heart rates down and control their breathing in a situation where at any moment they could be killed by random pulsar fire, coordinate fire between all the various units so that all of the Persian targets were covered with acceptable redundancy, and they had to maintain careful and precise aim at their targets until the order was given to eliminate them. So far these men and women had sustained thirty percent casualties while their minds screamed about why the order hadn't been given to open fire, yet they stayed in their positions, locked onto their targets.

"Team Three in position." That was the last of Alpha Group's Teams. The announcement seemed an eternity in coming.

"Acknowledged. Team Three in position," Alex said. "Teams Three and Four mark entry points."

"Team Three marked."

"Team Four marked." They divided their teams in half. On each side of the museum proper, an eight-man group would converge on a single entry point, and a wide opening in the wall would be blasted with their respective vac devices. At the same time, the other eight men would pick individual windows and use their energy pulsars to launch themselves off the ground like catapults. Steadying themselves with the exo-suit propulsars, they would blast through the museum exterior on the upper floors. Their momentum would carry them through the openings and land them in the center of the Persian resistance. It was to be an attack of sudden and overwhelming force, complete shock and awe. The major variable hanging in the balance was whether the snipers would be able to clear the roof. If they didn't, these men would alter their entry points and would instead land on top of the structure and take them out themselves.

Alex made the command. "Snipers mark your targets. Go in five seconds. Mark...five...four...three...two...one...GO! GO! GO!"

At exactly the five-second mark, the Persian's energy shield generators exploded. The museum was now fully exposed to American fire. At almost the same moment, the Persian SS on the roof and any who were visible through the windows fell. As the snipers outnumbered the SS on the roof by a ratio of six to one, many of them were completely dissected by several shots hitting from different directions at once; all were headshots. It was the only way to prevent an errant shot from accidently killing the child hostages. Despite wearing top of the line Persian gear, the shots instantaneously turned their brains into jelly. The snipers targeting the windows eliminated several other Persian SS. While the Persian terrorists were in the process of dying, the eighty men of Alpha Group, with all their high-tech armaments, were sprinting toward the building as fast as their exo-suits would carry them.

The ten men whose objectives, as assigned by Lt. Col. Gillean, were to secure the roof and rescue as many hostages as possible, detached from the remainder of Team Five. With a downward blast from their pulsars that tore up the ground underneath, and steadied in the air by their propulsars, they catapulted up to the roof of the five-story building. They worked as fast as they could to get the children clear, concentrating on the dome first. It was going to blow, and they had only been allotted twenty seconds before the rest of Alpha Group would forcibly blast their way through the walls and attack the main building. Each of the dead Persian soldiers had a child strapped to his chest. Another twenty kids were mounted along the top of the building, hanging over the edge as human shields. The commandoes worked quickly. With laser blades they slashed away the straps holding the kids in place, slapped propulsar bracelets around one of their wrists, and threw them as far as they could off and away from the building. With the exo-suits' incredible power, the screaming kids were launched high into the air and in a long arcing pattern. They gained altitude until well clear of the structure, and when their momentum failed, they began falling. The kids were wild with panic, but they were getting away from the structure. Once they began falling, the propulsar bracelets activated and pulled their arms upward, slowing their fall until they came to rest gently on the ground.

The dome was clear and the Guardsmen were making quick work of it, progressing their way down the rectangular part of the building when their time ran out and the rest of Alpha Group launched their assault. The dome exploded upward with a level of devastation far beyond what anyone expected. The children who had already been rescued but were still in the air were launched far outward by the wave of concussive energy. Most of the ten Guardsmen on the roof were knocked off their feet by the blast. Two didn't get up, hit by large blocks of stone flying through the air. One got struck from behind. It hit him in the head and shoulder…death was immediate. Another, Gibson, had his leg fractured. It was bent grotesquely sideways at the mid-shaft of the femur. Maintaining complete discipline and awareness of his surroundings, he began crawling to the edge of the roof. He announced to the other men through the open BCD channel that he was wounded. A moment later, one of his fellow Guardsmen, Raul, grabbed him behind the knee with one hand and by the belt with the other. He quickly pulled outward on the fractured limb and straightened it in the most barbaric fashion. Gibson yelped out in pain. Raul touched Gibson's thigh and made a command. Through his BCD he tapped into the control module for Gibson's exo-suit. "Left thigh mid-shaft fracture activate splint!" Gibson's suit tightened over the areas that Raul touched, and his hip, knee, and the fracture site in his thigh became immobile. Gibson was essentially in a cast. Raul touched at the upper thigh, "Activate tourniquet!" he commanded. The suit squeezed tight at the upper thigh, cutting off the flow of blood to the limb, preventing internal bleeding in case an artery was severed. Raul picked Gibson up by the belt and the back of the neck. "Hold on Gibs! This is going to hurt like hell!" Gibson drew in his arms and his good leg. Raul spun around as though throwing a discus and heaved. He threw Gibson off the structure with all his might.

Gibson gritted his teeth and didn't make a sound. The pain was excruciating. He twisted a few times in the air and his leg flopped somewhat out of control at the hip joint, his exo-suit unable to completely immobilize the joint. His propulsars activated, and he landed softly about forty meters away from the building. Forty meters wasn't far enough for safety, and he immediately started crawling away, toward rescue personnel that he ordered to pass him by so they could help the children.

When Alpha Group made their move on the building, one man from each Team pulled up about twenty meters from their entry points. It only took a moment and the mobile vacuum explosive devices (MVEDs) were on the ground. They cast a twenty-foot wide rectangular laser image on the side of the brick wall. The other soldiers crowded against the wall next to the outlines. Other members of Teams Three and Four oriented themselves toward the museum windows they were going to use for entry. Jake was positioned immediately adjacent Team Five's MVED image, with two men behind him and two men opposite. His weapon was strapped to his back, and he carried in his hands the SSD that would support the roof before it fell in on everyone. It was pulsating with lights. Its base was a fusion generator and at its bottom was a spike that would implant deep into the concrete when struck with sufficient force. The others in Jake's group calibrated their guided munitions with images of the targets known to be Persian SS inside the auditorium.

"Team Four in position."

They heard, "Team Three in position."

Jake was counting in his head. The team on the roof had been allotted a few more seconds to do their job clearing the roof. Jake was peripherally aware of several children flying through the air screaming. When the allotted time passed, Jake gave the command.

"Mark...three...two...one...GO!" he yelled.

The BCD relayed the command to every member of Alpha Group. It took a fraction of a second and all five laser devices emitted a pulse that sounded like intense static. Bright light filled the door-like images the lasers made on the side of the building. This was followed by a loud pop that sounded like a lightning strike. The bricks, mortar, underlying electrical circuitry, pipes, vents, wood, tile, and plaster, were instantaneously vaporized. The gases and debris were sucked outward with incredible force and speed. In all it took half-a-second.

Jake sprinted through the opening with the SSD. He was moving with amazing clarity and speed toward the center of the auditorium when he discovered one of the Persian SS standing in his path. He was facing the room with his back toward Jake. He was in the process of turning when Jake's elbow impacted the side of his neck. Jake felt the crunching sensation of the soldier's cervical spine being fractured. It didn't matter much because at the same time he was being riddled with shots from Team Five. It mattered only in that he be out of the way so Jake could reach the center of the room.

He cleared the obstruction, had to mind his step over several dead hostages, and he continued running toward the center of the structure. Having to navigate a rail, he hurdled it and jumped up two tiers of three steps. His ears picked up the shots behind him coming in a continuous barrage while at the same time, his eyes beheld the horror inside the auditorium. It was far worse than even he imagined. Hundreds of tiny guided missiles were streaking by him. As the missiles found their targets, they penetrated the flesh approximately two to three inches and then exploded. Dozens hit each of the terrorists before they realized what was happening. The barrage of internal explosions and heat turned most of their flesh into clouds of vile gas. What little was left flew across the room, splattering over the hostages and against the walls.

Colonel Fisk shot several rounds from his atmospheric vac-device. The specialized cartridges attached to the walls. Their function could best be described as causing a visual vortex of sorts, with the air being mostly cleared while the smoke and dust swept toward the devices and collected like filth-balls in an ever-expanding radius.

One of the guided missiles ripped through the leader of the Persian SS, but only after passing through an electronic device strapped to his chest. It was a device that sent continuous signals based on his vital signs to the explosives planted throughout the dome of the museum. It was designed so that if the signals were disrupted by anything, including but not limited to his death, the explosives would detonate. The boom of the subsequent explosion shook the ground with an intensity that knocked many of the onrushing emergency crews to the ground. The concussion rendered most of those inside temporarily deaf and frightened beyond measure.

Jake was in the center of the room by the time the explosion occurred. He kept his head low, dove through the air, and with an outstretched arm, he spiked the SSD into the floor. A downward explosion from the base of the device shot an anchoring support deep into the concrete while, at the same time, the top of the unit successfully activated. A pulsating field of high-energy beams illuminated the room, casting a bluish image on the dome and extending partially down the walls. Several things were happening at once. The SSD bombarded the surrounding structure with high-energy beams, the molecular collisions transferring momentum to the dome, pushing it upward. As large pieces of the crumbling dome fell downward, the computer systems within the SSD detected the movement and increased the force of the beams acting against the falling objects in order to keep them aloft. Computer-guided lasers shot upward, and the pulses from the incredibly high-energy beams broke up the biggest objects, making them more manageable. Essentially, the SSD formed a barrier that would, for a short period of time, support the structure and hold the dome up before it collapsed and killed everyone left inside. With the force field in place, a window of opportunity had opened during which lives might be saved.

After the dome exploded, an extensive amount of gravel-sized debris fell throughout the room. While the crumbling building fought to fill the air with thick dust, the atmospheric vac devices helped…but not entirely. Although Colonel Fisk kept shooting the rounds, they weren't entirely successful given the extreme circumstances. At ground level the dust was mixing with the stench of burning flesh, rendering a sickening sticky quality to the air. What they witnessed from the inside was that in places the roof folded over on itself, revealing windows to the open sky above. In the aftermath of the explosion, the dome was increasingly like a great boiling cauldron, tossing and turning, churning under the weight of opposing forces of incredible energy. Lasers from the SSD ripped through the churning mass of steel and stone and glass, and pulses of bright red light shot skyward. While the energy field temporarily supported pieces of debris larger than a marble high above, smaller pieces rained through and pelted the survivors and soldiers. It took a vast amount of energy to sustain the field and time was extremely limited. They had to hurry to get the survivors out before the device failed.

The sixteen men of Team One, the sixteen of Team Two, and the six of Team Five were securing the auditorium. Within a few seconds they had eliminated the remaining Persian personnel, including several wearing stealth gear.

Teams Three and Four were canvassing the museum. Several firefights broke out. The Persian SS were fighters and they weren't going down without shooting back, but they were being systematically eliminated.

One of the Persian soldiers in the auditorium was wearing civilian clothing. He was sitting with the hostages. He tried to intermingle with them on the way out. He picked up a boy and acted as though he was a surviving adult trying to rescue the child. His ruse was discovered as the boy was vigorously fighting in an effort to get away. The man was knocked unconscious with the butt of a pulsar rifle…Alex's gun, firmly delivered squarely to his forehead with enough force to cause ten men's brains to bleed. He picked up the boy and carried him out, dragging the Persian soldier by the ankle, and then throwing his body clear.

Team Five was the first to switch roles. They began evacuating the survivors as fast as possible. "GET OUT! GET OUT! MOVE IT! NOW!" Jake yelled as he guided the kids toward the gaping holes in the side of the building. He saw children in every state of distress, some were crying, some screaming, others hid their faces and curled up in their seats, and still others stared ahead with blank expressions, their eyes empty of comprehension. One boy in particular caught Jake's attention. He was about five years old and was squeezing the armrests with a white knuckled grip. Blood was smeared over his tear-streaked face. Jake picked him up. He grabbed a girl in his other arm. He was yelling the entire time. "COME ON! LET'S GO! WE HAVE TO GET OUT OF HERE!" They saw him yelling but couldn't hear anything. They were like spooked cattle. He carried the kids to the hole the teams had blasted in the wall. They stepped from the pit of hell into the sunlight, a war-torn sunlight but sunlight nevertheless. He put them down and pointed to the onrushing emergency crews. "RUN!" he said. "RUN! GO TO THEM! THEY'LL HELP YOU! Jake turned and went back in the auditorium.

Once a few of them found the exit, the rest quickly began to herd behind. The emergency crews grabbed them away as quickly as they could emerge from the smoke. The children were in shock. Even the adults were crying and screaming. They were a vast throng escaping from what was supposed to be their grave, covered in thick layers of dust and blood, forever changed, but alive.

It seemed an eternity, but it was only a minute or two, and the structure was cleared of survivors. Several Guardsmen from the Teams that cleared the auditorium were injured but none seriously. While most of the surviving civilians were able to get out with little direct assistance, others were severely injured and required immediate medical attention. Two captured Persian SS had to be dragged out. They had been fitted with neural deactivators, which latched around their necks and caused paralysis. They were thrown into a security vehicle under heavy guard.

Teams Three and Four eliminated terrorists through the rest of the museum. Most of their targets were wearing stealth equipment. Despite Alpha Group being equipped with the best state-of-the-art protective equipment, securing the museum cost the Teams two severely wounded and one dead. Four others had minor injuries. The museum was secured. The wounded soldiers and three more wounded terrorists were taken out. After they completed a final sweep for survivors, Alpha Group hastily exited the building as it was going to come down.

With its impending collapse, the building was being given a wide berth. Personnel of every sort moved away from the museum as fast as their legs would carry them. Paramedics, policemen, firemen, and Guardsmen with children under each arm raced to get away.

"THERE'S MOVEMENT. DAMMIT!" Alex yelled. "MOVEMENT IN THE MAIN HALL. I REPEAT: MOVEMENT IN THE MAIN HALL. LOOKS LIKE A KID!" The anger and frustration in his voice erupted like a volcano. He demanded absolute excellence from his men, and with their technology, no one should have been left behind. It represented a failure. Each Team leader was supposed to run a thorough sweep of their designated area once the structure was cleared of Persian resistance.

Jake was the last to emerge from the auditorium. He was carrying the final survivor, seriously injured but alive. He handed her off to one of the firemen. "RUN!" he said, pointing in the opposite direction. "The building's coming down." Then he turned back. "I'VE GOT IT! TELL ME WHERE!" Jake sprinted back through the auditorium. The SSD was screaming. It was elevated twenty feet in the air, surrounded by a pulsating green and red glow. It was failing. The floor rumbled and large pieces of debris were falling. The entire building was shaking.

Jake yelled as he ran, "I'll NEED AN EXIT! SOMEBODY MAKE ME AN EXIT!" Under the power of the exo-suit he was moving fast. He leapt nearly all the way through the auditorium. It would have taken an extra second to navigate the doorway so he blasted through the wall with his pulsar.

"TEAMS THREE AND FOUR. MAKE HIM AN EXIT! MAKE HIM AN EXIT!" Alex yelled. The Teams were moving fast. Guardsmen from Teams Three and Four, with MVEDs in hand, raced along the length of the building. They were discharging the devices on the run. They were heavy and the recoil was bone breaking, but they persisted. The sides of the museum were being riddled with large holes to accommodate Jake's escape.

"ABOUT 150 FEET DOWN THE MAIN CORRIDOR. UNDER SOMETHING. WHAT IS THIS? WHAT IS THIS? A WHAT?" Alex was looking at a holographic image of the museum. He asked one of the museum officials who had been kept at hand just in case something like this occurred. "LOOK FOR A DINOSAUR JAKE! A TRICERATOPS! UNDER THE TRICERATOPS DISPLAY!"

"GOT IT!" Jake had already cleared the auditorium and was sprinting through the museum. He hurdled a rope barrier, and as he did, there was an explosion. The SSD failed. It exploded, sending out an intense wave of electromagnetic radiation. It caught Jake and propelled him across the floor. He slid along the display reaching for anything to stop his movement. He clawed outward and what came into his grip was the display's skirt. It ripped off as he was thrown across the floor. His exo-suit was destroyed. Small blue arcs of electricity two to three inches long jumped from one location to the next over his entire body. It only lasted for a moment. The circuitry in his exo-suit was fried. At the same time, his BCD went down.

Jake was slightly dazed. He shook his head and re-oriented to his surroundings. He couldn't breathe. He wrestled with the straps and pulled off his facemask. His BCD flickered and then sprang back to life. It picked up a heat signature. It was the child. Then he saw her under the display—20 feet away. Ripping away the skirt had inadvertently exposed her hiding place.

"I'VE GOT HER! I NEED THAT EXIT! MY SUIT'S MALFUNCTIONED!"

"DAMMIT!" Alex yelled. "GET OUT OF THERE! GIVE HIM AN

EXIT!" He was nearly jumping out of his skin with intensity, racing toward and parallel to the museum as he barked orders.

The six-year-old girl huddled under the display in a fetal position. Her eyes were big and full of tears. She was crying hard and had been for some time. Nasal secretions were smeared over her face, and her left thumb was in her mouth, her right hand grasping the left. The building was coming down around them, the roar was deafening, and from her perspective he was scary as hell.

"I've got you baby, come here! We have to go!" His voice was excited. He meant for it to be calm, but that wasn't happening. Everything he was saying could be heard by the other members of Alpha Group.

The little girl was frozen, scared beyond measure. As he reached in and made a grab for her she let loose a high-pitched scream. It was bloodcurdling in quality, sounding like an animal about to be devoured. She kicked him hard, her heel catching him in the face, impacting his left cheek and eye.

"COME HERE!" Jake yelled. He grabbed her ankle and yanked her out. She reached out and clutched at the railing under the display, but the force of his pull broke her grip. Enduring the fright of listening to the screams of people being brutalized and tortured, and with no one to comfort her, she completely decompensated, psychologically regressing to an infantile state. It was a natural defense mechanism built into the circuitry of her brain. In the process she lost control of her bladder and there was urine soaking her pants and the surrounding floor. That was what caused Jake to slip to one knee as he wrestled to control her flailing limbs.

Bricks and rocks the size of small boulders fell behind them as the roof was collapsing in earnest. The architectural design was such that the traction of the collapsing dome was pulling down the rest of the building like a series of dominos. The original openings blasted by Teams Three and Four when they attacked the building were already overtaken by the collapsing structure.

The two commandoes from Teams Three and Four didn't realize that as they blew holes in the side of the building they were actually opening them into side rooms. In the excitement, and with decreased visibility, Jake had no way of seeing them, much less the ability to snake his way through the rooms in time to escape.

Jake held the fighting and flailing girl tightly in his left arm. He felt a surge of adrenaline kick in. He sprinted as fast as he could down the center of the long central hall. Directly ahead of him, over a hundred meters away, he could see an emergency exit. But it was so far away and he was running on his own power, without the benefit of the exo-suit. He knew he'd never make it.

"I GOT YOU! I GOT YOU! I NEED AN EXIT. GET ME AN EXIT! THE FAR END! I'M RUNNING TOWARD THE END!" he yelled. "I SEE EXIT DOORS IN THE CENTER!"

As he sprinted, the building crumbled behind him. The large skeletal Brachiosaurus collapsed and was consumed by the rubble. Models of the Tyrannosaurus and the Triceratops fell into each other as if they were reenacting some prehistoric duel. Then the figures disappeared in the gauntlet of thick smoke and dust.

"WE'RE GONNA MAKE IT! WE'RE GONNA MAKE IT!" His words were meant to comfort the girl, but he was yelling it so loudly, it had the opposite affect.

Jake ran as hard and fast as he could down the center of the building, picking up speed as he went. The girl had stopped fighting him and was tightly clinging for dear life, her legs wrapped around his waist. Her arms squeezed around his chest and neck, her hands clenched around straps on the back of his exo-suit. His left arm supported her underneath and his right swung back and forth, helping as much as a single arm could to create forward momentum.

Like a sentinel riding in advance of a demonic army, the dust cloud coiled in front of the collapsing structure, rolling and chewing up everything to Jake's rear. Its leading edge was like a horizontal tornado churning and roaring as it raced down the length of the museum, riding roughly three feet off the floor and gaining on Jake. Trailing right behind this beast was an exploding cloud of hulking black smoke that filled the building. Jake was racing as fast as he could toward the exit, but it was futile, he wasn't fast enough. He was overtaken. At first it was just the leading edge of the dust cloud. It flirted behind him, nipping at his back and legs as he ran. With a lurch it enveloped him. His legs disappeared in the blackness. He ran faster across the rumbling floor as his torso disappeared in the cloud of swirling dust. The last vision before he entirely disappeared into complete blackness was the red glow of the exit sign mounted above the doors forty feet away. He dug deeper and ran even faster. Jake and the girl were both screaming. He would keep going as far as the fates would allow. If they found his body it was going to be right at the door, with the girl huddled in his arms. Until then, he would run as fast as his feet would carry him. As debris fell at his heels, he shuddered at the unrepentant weight of the crashing stone and steel girders. It was as though the universe was collapsing, folding in on itself in an orgy of violence. Something hard and unforgiving slashed down like a guillotine, scraping the outside of his right arm. It was a two-ton piece of masonry.

Team Four's leader sped to the rear of the building. When he rounded the corner he propelled himself high into the air with his pulsar and aimed his MVED unit at the rear doors. He opened it up to maximum and activated it in midair. The machine popped, the recoil violently throwing him backward. The museum doors disintegrated and a forty-foot wide hole blew outward.

With their screams lost in the complete chaos of the moment, in the roar of the collapsing museum, Jake experienced a heightened burst of adrenaline. The surge, complexed with a sudden seething anger, pushed him to run even faster than before. Huge chunks of brick and mortar were smashing holes in the floor, uprooting and rippling the tile in the process. He was screaming at the moment of his death, running as fast as humanly possible. The monster had him in its clawed embrace; all that remained was for its cold scythe to strike home.

When he guessed that he was no more than one or two steps away from the doors, an exit completely obscured in the thick smoke, he prepared himself to jump and spin at the point of impact. He would absorb the impact with his back, rather than the girl bearing the brunt of the force. Not that it really mattered at this point…he fully expected that running into the closed doors would be their last conscience experience.

Jake's thoughts raced from Wendy, to Bailey, to Paul, and to the little girl in his arms. What would her life have been like? What had she done to deserve to die like this? Without breaking stride Jake prepared for an impact with the doors. He extended his right arm up to protect the girl against the impact and started to turn his right side toward where he thought the doors were. Maybe, just maybe, they could smash through and land outside. Then, in the roaring chaos, he recognized a sound. It was the familiar popping-type explosion of the MVED. It was the most beautiful sound he had ever heard. He straightened his gait and lunged forward with all his might. For a few microseconds, just long enough to form the conscious perception, light flashed through the darkness. It formed what looked like a cross just as the doors exploded outward. It may have been his imagination, but he didn't care. It was enough for him to cling to the experience as some sort of a sign. Another step…then another. There wasn't an impact. The doors had indeed vaporized a moment before. Jake and the girl burst through the opening from the darkness into bright sunlight. Just as he cleared the building, its walls completed their fall inward with a deafening thunder.

"HE'S OUT! HE'S OUT! HE'S OUT!" the Team Four leader announced as several of the other Guardsman arrived at the back of the building.

Alex had been yelling the entire time. He briefly closed his eyes and went to his knees, emotionally exhausted and relieved. Then he was immediately back to the business of command. "Secure the perimeter," he ordered, adding, "Lt. Col., I can't believe how fast you can run, you crazy bastard."

Jake broke stride and slowed to a walk. As the quaking noise behind him began to die down, it unmasked the girl's high-pitched screams. She continued screaming for some time. Jake didn't stop her, choosing instead to just hold her in a protective embrace. His right hand was at the back of her head. The adrenaline rush persisted for a short time and then choreographed its withdrawal in unison with her screaming. Then she started sobbing. Jake continued caressing the back of her head. She buried her face in the nape of his neck. Several minutes passed before her sobbing diminished to whimpering. He kept walking into the park, putting distance between them and what was left of that god-forsaken museum.

"It'll be okay. You're safe now." He whispered the words over and over. "God isn't done with us yet. He still has work for us to do." She didn't respond. Jake added, "God was watching over you today. He was watching over both of us." After another few moments, when it seemed that she might be able to talk, he asked what her name was.

"Tess," she whimpered.

"My name is Jake." He made some small talk, told her he had a daughter about her age, and a son a little younger. She revealed that she was on a school field trip. He finally asked her if she wanted to go back and look through the crowd for her friends, or possibly her teachers. Tess said she didn't want to and started lightly sobbing again.

"I peed in my pants," she cried. She was worried they would laugh. Jake was amazed and overjoyed by the beautiful and complete innocence of her distress. The human mind was indeed an amazing thing. Realizing the importance of her dilemma, he looked around to see what resources were available. A large fountain was a short distance away.

"You know what?" he said. "I think I did too."

"What?" She was surprised.

"I was so scared I think I peed in my suit."

"Really? But you're a grown up."

"Yeah. But it's okay because it can't be helped. That's what people do when they're scared. Soldiers do it all the time. We're both safe now, that's all that matters." They were at the edge of the fountain. "Are you ready?" he announced.

"For what?" she asked with her face still buried in his neck.

"It's gonna be cold. We're gonna get wet," he said as he stepped into the water. "We'll both be soaked and guess what?" he whispered softly in her ear, "No one will ever know we had an accident. It'll be our little secret." He took a big step and they were under the water. It was dazzling and blue. They both gasped, as it was far colder than they expected. It rained down over Tess's head until she was completely soaked. The thick dirt washed off to reveal a beautiful blue-eyed girl.

She delighted in the experience. While they were under the water, she still couldn't see what he looked like because of the dark black grime and dirt that was caked all over him. She undid his chinstrap and took off his helmet, dropping it into the fountain. She wiped his face with her hands. At first it did nothing but smear the thick blackness. Soon however, she discovered an actual person, someone completely new. There was pale skin across his forehead, his nose, and around his eyes. She was unmasking her soldier. Tess wasn't satisfied until she had a good look at the man who rescued her. Then she was happy. It was as if the two people who went in the fountain were replaced. In washing away the ugliness of the world, they disappeared and were replaced by two others who emerged to give the world another try.

* * * * *

Media-types were buzzing around the area. At first, there had been an ongoing live report. Then false images were broadcast to minimize the panic and to mask the developing rescue operation. However, so many rogue reports were breaking through that the dam burst and the full extent of the disaster was revealed across the whole of United America. When Alpha Group landed, and the men began moving into position, regional authorities regained control and a complete blackout was instituted. It was enforced until Alpha Group's assault on the structure was complete and the evacuation was well underway. Half the world was watching when the images re-appeared on the Vintel units.

In Tennessee, Wendy Gillean was glued to the family Vintel. Bailey and Paul were at her side. When she heard the chime indicating that Jake was sending a communication she raced to the unit. By the time she got there the link was already down. She read his short message and gathered the kids. They nervously watched the Vintel as the drama unfolded. The entire system went dark. It was several minutes before it came back on. When it did, the museum had already been assaulted. Smoke was everywhere, and kids were streaming from gaping holes in the side of the building. Others were being carried. They saw the ambulances and rescue personnel scrambling to clear the area. She immediately recognized the exo-suits. The announcer said it was Alpha Group.

'Oh God, please!' her mind cried as she watched the images. She fought to control her anxiety. Bailey and Paul felt her tension. 'Please let Jake be okay, God please let him be okay!'

A commentator was describing the scene. He was excited, talking fast, "MY GOD! MY GOD! THE BEAUTIFUL CITY OF PORTLAND HAS BEEN TURNED INTO A KILLING FIELD. THE SCENES UNFOLDING HERE ARE HEARTBREAKING. IT'S AN ABOMINATION AGAINST HUMANITY—THE DELIBERATE TARGETING OF CHILDREN BY THE PERSIAN SS. THEY ARE TERRORISTS, NOT SOLDIERS. BOYS AND GIRLS ARE RUNNING FROM THE MUSEUM. THEY'RE LIMPING, THEY'RE HELPING EACH OTHER, OTHERS ARE BEING CARRIED AS THE BUILDING IS THREATENING TO CRUMBLE TO THE GROUND. JUST MOMENTS AGO, THE BUILDING WAS STORMED BY A SPECIAL FORCES UNIT FROM THE GUARD—A UNIT CALLED ALPHA GROUP…"

"That's Daddy!" Wendy exclaimed. She stood up. There was an urge to pace, but her feet felt as though they were in concrete. "Those are Daddy's men."

"Where?" Bailey asked. "Where's Daddy? I don't see him."

"I don't know, honey. He's there somewhere. Those men in the black uniforms, the ones with the helmets on and the guns, those are Daddy's men," she said. Wendy pulled Paul up into her arms. He stared at the Vintel, trying to understand the images.

"THE WORD IS THAT THE BUILDING HAS BEEN SECURED. BUT THERE WAS A SERIES OF VIOLENT EXPLOSIONS ALL ACROSS THE TOP OF THE DOMED STRUCTURE. WHAT? OH NO! GET BACK! GET BACK! GET BACK! WE'VE BEEN TOLD THE BUILDING IS COMING DOWN! GET BACK! EVERYBODY NEEDS TO GET AWAY. AS YOU CAN SEE, HUNDREDS OF RESCUE PERSONNEL, FIREMEN, POLICE OFFICERS, AND SOLDIERS ARE CARRYING CHILDREN. INJURED ADULTS ARE BEING DRAGGED ACROSS THE GROUND AS EVERYONE IS TRYING TO GET AWAY…"

"Where's Daddy? Mommy, where's Daddy?" Bailey asked again. She was scared. The images were disturbing enough, but knowing her father was there somewhere in the thick of the danger, made it frightening beyond measure.

"I don't know. I don't know." Wendy couldn't think. She didn't want to cry, but tears were streaming down her cheeks.

"Is Daddy okay?" Paul asked.

"WE'VE JUST BEEN TOLD THAT ONE OF THE SOLDIERS FROM ALPHA GROUP HAS JUST GONE BACK INTO THE BUILDING." The newscaster's voice was panicked, almost to the point of hysterics. His speech was rapid and loud. "WHAT? WHAT? A CHILD? THERE'S A CHILD STILL IN THE BUILDING. A CHILD WAS LEFT BEHIND. ONE OF THE SOLDIERS HAS JUST GONE BACK INTO THE BUILDING TO RESCUE THE CHILD. LOOK AT WHAT I'M SEEING. SOLDIERS ARE POINTING THEIR WEAPONS AT THE SURROUNDING BUILDINGS AND SCANNING THE CROWD. THERE MAY BE MORE ENEMY SOLDIERS IN THE SURROUNDING STRUCTURES. IT'S CHAOS. OH MY GOD! EVERYONE IS IN A PANIC TRYING TO GET AWAY FROM THE MUSEUM."

Wendy pulled the kids close to her. She was in shock, completely helpless to do anything except watch.

"IT'S COMING DOWN! GET AWAY! GET AWAY! THE BUILDING IS COMING DOWN! THERE HAS JUST BEEN A LOUD EXPLOSION! THE DOME IS CAVING IN! LOOK AT THE IMAGES! THE DOME IS COLLAPSING! IT'S ENTIRELY GONE! IT'S PULLING THE ENTIRE STRUCTURE TO THE GROUND! IT'S COLLAPSING IN ON ITSELF!"

The broadcast temporarily went out, replaced with static. This gave way to images of smoke and dust slowly dissipating to reveal the structure. The voice came back. "SMOKE IS EVERYWHERE. THE MUSEUM HAS COMPLETELY COLLAPSED. DID THE SOLDIER GET OUT? DID HE GET OUT? DOES ANYONE KNOW? REPEAT THAT. THE NOISE HERE IS DEAFENING. YES! YES! EVERYONE, HE'S OUT! HE'S OUT! HE'S OUT! HE HAS THE CHILD! HE HAS THE CHILD! OH, THANK YOU GOD, HE HAS THE CHILD! WHAT? WE HAVE IT? WE HAVE IT? SHOW THE IMAGE. SWITCH TO THE IMAGE. I CAN'T SEE WHAT YOU'RE SEEING AT THE MOMENT. I'M TOLD IT'S THE SOLDIER RUNNING OUT OF THE BUILDING AS IT COLLAPSED AROUND HIM.

The Vintel unit showed an image from a remote controlled hover camera in the park at the far end of the building. The museum was collapsing toward the camera. As the building disappeared in a cloud of smoke a soldier appeared. He was running as fast as he could with a child in his arms. The camera stayed with them. Once clear of the building, the soldier slowed to a walk. He just kept walking into the park away from the rubble that used to be the museum.

"NOW WE HAVE IT. THEY'RE BACK UP. THESE ARE THE

IMAGES OF THE SOLDIER AND THE LITTLE GIRL HE RESCUED. THEY HAVE BEEN WALKING IN THE PARK AFTER AN OBVIOUSLY PERILOUS RESCUE. ONLY THE LORD KNOWS THE HORRORS THEY SHARED IN THE MUSEUM. WE SEE THEM STEPPING OVER THE WALL AND INTO THE FOUNTAIN. IT'S WELL-DESERVED, WELL-DESERVED, AN ESCAPE INTO THE BEAUTIFUL BLUE WATER. GET A CLOSEUP. ZOOM IN THE CAMERA. IT'S OBVIOUS SHE HAD BEEN CRYING, BUT NOW SHE'S LAUGHING. IT'S NOT MUCH OF A LAUGH BUT IT IS ENCOURAGING. TAKE IN THESE MOVING MOMENTS OF THIS SOLDIER HOLDING A LITTLE GIRL. SHE LOOKS SO TINY IN HIS ARMS. SHE'S TAKING OFF HIS HELMET. HE'S COVERED IN DIRT, HARDLY RECOGNIZABLE AS A PERSON. SHE IS WIPING HIS FACE, OBVIOUSLY TRYING TO GET THE DIRT OFF SO SHE CAN SEE WHAT HE LOOKS LIKE. THESE MOVING IMAGES OF A CHILD, THE INNOCENCE OF A LITTLE GIRL TORN BUT NOT DESTROYED. AND FOR WHAT? WE HAVE TO ASK OURSELVES THAT SIMPLE QUESTION…FOR WHAT? IS THE WORLD OUTSIDE OUR BORDERS SO BARBARIC? ARE THERE PEOPLE ANYWHERE WHO CAN ACTUALLY BRING THEMSELVES TO BELIEVE THAT THIS WAS JUSTIFIED?"

Everyone watched as the little girl pulled at his chinstrap. Once it was unsnapped, she pushed the helmet off by pushing it over his head. It dropped into the water. The only thing alluring, the only thing non-frightening in the soldier's appearance was his smile, a smile that stood in stark contrast to every other aspect of his appearance. The camera zoomed in to capture the moment as the girl wiped his face.

"WE'RE SEEING THE IMAGES OF THE AFTERMATH OF THIS TERRIBLE ATTACK ON INNOCENT LIFE, A VICIOUS AND BARBAROUS ATTACK THAT DELIBERATELY TARGETED CHILDREN. THE IMAGES CAPTURE BETTER THAN ANY WORDS CAN DESCRIBE THE INNOCENCE OF A SMALL DEFENSELESS GIRL AND THE CONTRAST BETWEEN HER AND THE SOLDIER WHO RESCUED HER; THE MOST HIGHLY TRAINED SOLDIER THE WORLD HAS EVER SEEN, A MAN WHO REPRESENTS THE VERY BEST WE HAVE TO OFFER, A MAN CAPABLE OF TREMENDOUS SACRIFICE, OF TREMENDOUS STRENGTH, WHO IS CAPABLE OF DISPLAYING LIMITLESS COURAGE IN DEFENSE OF ALL OF US…AND YET DESPITE EVERYTHING WE DEMAND OF HIM, HE IS STILL CAPABLE OF A MOMENT OF SUCH TENDERNESS, OF SUCH GENTLENESS

OF SPIRIT. FOR THE WORLD THAT'S WATCHING, THIS IS THE AMERICAN SOLDIER. THIS IS JUST ONE OF THE MEN WHO WILL SACRIFICE EVERYTHING FOR THE SAKE OF YOUR FREEDOM AND LIBERTY. SHE REVEALS TO THE WORLD THE FACE OF THE SOLDIER WHO RISKED HIS LIFE TO SAVE HER…"

"That's Daddy!" Wendy screamed. "That's Daddy! Oh God, thank you. That's Daddy!"

"Where?" Bailey asked.

"Right there. In the fountain. That's Daddy! That's Daddy!" She was jumping up and down with Paul in her arms.

"Dat's Daddy?" Paul asked.

"Yes, honey. That's your daddy." Tears of joy were streaming down Wendy's cheeks. She pulled both of her children to her and squeezed them. All across the nation, parents did the same.

* * * * *

Jake searched the crowd until Tess recognized one of her teachers. She went happily and seemed to be okay when Jake turned and walked away. He surveyed the people around him. There was a woman with a civilian communications link pinned to her collar.

"Do you mind if I use that?"

"Um, sure. Here," she didn't hesitate. She pulled it off and handed it to him.

Jake hadn't seen Wendy in what seemed a lifetime. Although modern technology had enabled them to communicate almost every day, and sometimes several times each day, it wasn't the same as being there. His children were growing up with an absentee father. You couldn't hug a computer image. You couldn't toss it in the air and get laughter in return. Nor could you tuck it into bed at night after reading a story and receive in return a lifetime of unconditional love.

He routed the communication to his home. With the noise and sirens it was difficult to hear so he walked away from the crowd.

"Hi, baby," he said when he heard Wendy's voice.

"Are you okay?" she gasped. "We saw you on the Vintel."

"Really?" he was caught off guard. "On the Vintel?"

"In the fountain. We saw you in the fountain."

"Oh," he said with surprise. "I'm fine. I'm fine. Wendy, is everyone there? Are they safe?"

"Are you sure?" Wendy asked again. She was emotionally exhausted.

In some ways it was worse to watch it unfold at home because it forced her to confront her powerlessness to change anything.

"Really, I'm fine. Are you okay? And the kids?"

"Yeah, we're all just so happy you aren't hurt." Her voice was tearful and yet so soothing and disarming. "We've been so worried." Her voice was starting to crack in earnest. The years had been hard on her, and this was just the latest in a long series of high stress situations.

"I know, baby. Me too. I can't tell you how good it is to hear your voice. Are the kids there?"

"They're right here."

"Would you put me on speaker?" He heard it click. A hollow sound indicated that they could hear him. "Hey guys. It's Daddy."

"Hi, Daddy!" they excitedly proclaimed in unison.

"I saw you on the Vintel, Daddy!" Bailey squealed.

"That's what Mommy said. What are you doing?"

"I was gittin marker off Mommy's nice table," Paul said. He was four months shy of his fourth birthday.

"You got marker on Mommy's table," Jake exclaimed, half laughing and half breaking down in the swirl of emotions. "The nice wooden one?"

"It's not nice anymore. Mommy said so."

"I saw you on the Vintel, Daddy." Bailey said again. She was seven years old and in the second grade. "Who was that girl Daddy?"

"Her name is Tess. She would like to be your friend, honey."

As the conversation went on, he was struck by a longing to leave the military behind and run to his family. He would run away from all the terrible things he had seen. He would run so hard and so fast, he'd run until he could forget all the awful things he experienced. In a moment, he would run to his family and leave everything behind. He would have a normal life. Every day he would enjoy the absolute innocence of his children and hold Wendy in his arms…and he'd never let her go.

"Hey guys, give Mommy lots of big hugs and kisses, and when I come home…"

"You'll help us," they both yelled.

"Love you guys. Be good, okay."

"Okay."

"Is your mommy still there?" He heard the phone click off speaker. "I miss you so much," he said.

"Are you sure you're okay?" She was worried, and she had spent more nights than she could count wringing her hands and praying for his safe return, but the one thing Wendy knew was Jake's voice…it carried with it an unbending confidence and strength. That wasn't the voice she was hearing. There was an edge of shakiness, a fatigue beyond what she had ever heard before.

"Really, I'm fine," he said. "Today has been a really long day. We lost a couple men." He was pacing, feeling dead inside as he took in the scenes of destruction and human carnage. He wanted to tell her that a few minutes ago he almost died, that for the first time in his life he almost failed. Had it not been for another member of Alpha Group coming to his rescue and blowing the hell out of the museum doors, he'd be dead. Tess would be dead. Tidal waves of emotion fought to find some sort of manifestation, any form of physical outlet, but he refused. All they got was a momentary cogwheeling weakness in his legs. The desire to go down to his knees and buckle over was strong, but he pushed the urge away and took brisk steps, drawing in a deep skyward breath. At all costs, he had to shield Wendy from this horror. That included shielding her from his experiences, his feelings, and his worries. If the Persians could hit Portland, and just a handful could cause so much devastation, there was no reason to believe this war couldn't extend its deadly reach all the way to Tennessee. "I'm fine. Look, right now I have to go. I just…I just needed to hear your voice, and I wanted to let you know I'm okay. I love you."

"I love you so much, and we miss you. It's been so long Jake." As soon as the last words passed through her lips, Wendy wished she hadn't said them. It was true, but there wasn't anything either of them could do about it, and now wasn't the time to add another burden.

"I know," he agreed. "I'll call later tonight, and we'll talk some more."

"I'll be waiting," Wendy said.

CHAPTER 18: AFTERMATH OF THE DISASTER

[APRIL 15, AD 2441]
[135 DAYS AFTER ARRIVAL; (ONE DAY AFTER LEAVING ALASKA)]
[LOCATION: DEEP FOREST LAKE TAHOE, CALIFORNIA]

"How is he progressing?" AF20 asked.

"He is cooperating fully," Ben answered as he strolled through the woods. He had left Jake back at the camp so that he might communicate freely with AF20.

"Soon you will need to tell him everything."

"I understand. With your permission, I think we should wait until he describes the Great Tragedy and his first time leap. What we tell him is going to be traumatic. We risk him walking away. It makes much more sense to wait until that point."

"How much longer?"

"We're almost there. He just described the attack on the museum in Portland. A day or two at most and we'll be there," Ben responded.

"Agreed," AF20 said. "I don't have to remind you of the importance of what you're doing. Something went wrong either before or after he went back. He wasn't supposed to materialize at the reenactment or in the condition he did. We have to figure out what happened and fix it."

"Understood," Ben said. "How are things…progressing?"

"Major breakthroughs with some setbacks. The scientists tell me they won't be ready for him for another week, two at the most. Then we move. We'll need everything before then, everything that happened when he was living in the 1800s."

"Understood," Ben repeated.

With Ben gone for a while, Jake navigated through the multitude of files stored in the memory systems on his BCD. He scrolled back to the year 2379 and selected one that he had tagged as a favorite. The BCD launched the appropriate program. He was with Bailey and Paul, sitting on the floor in her room. As he watched it, he experienced a rush of memories and their associated emotions. He remembered that he wanted to escape the violent and chaotic world he was living in, to leave that world behind and enter hers—to see what it was like from her perspective. There was no mistaking that it was the world of a little girl. Her walls were brilliant pink, and pieces of games and little articles of clothing were all over the place. She introduced him to her stuffed animals and dolls, and he quickly discovered that each one had its own personality, some were more huggable than others, and there was one who was downright bossy. She named that one after a mischievous witch from one of her books.

Forgetting his forest surroundings Jake concentrated on the sound of the sweet and innocent voices. It was painful to endure, seeing and hearing his children, yet he had to experience it over and over again. Despite the fact that the results were always the same, that he would experience an intensity of loss and loneliness beyond measure, he couldn't help himself. The memories were alluring in every way and kept drawing him back in. His family was the only reason he had to go on living, to go on fighting.

The interaction in her bedroom evolved and eventually he was painting Bailey's toenails. She would wiggle the toes and fan them out expectantly, knowing that her father was going to do a perfect job. Then Paul tried to help. He successfully managed to smear the polish all over her toe. Bailey protested, "No, Paul!" It wasn't so much the polish as it was that he was interfering with her bonding experience. Jake navigated the dilemma by allowing Paul to put some polish on one of his fingernails. What would it hurt? He'd be happy and it would wash off easy enough.

Bailey watched with interest until an idea, a frightening and dreadful idea, came to her. "Daddy, let's paint yours," she suggested.

"No, no, no," Jake insisted. "Just the one."

"No. All of them."

"I don't think that would be a good idea."

"They will be so pretty," she said, ignoring his objections.

Paul was all smiles and giggles, thinking it was his idea all along.

After they finished with his fingers, they demanded that the toes be made to match. When that was accomplished Bailey said, "I'll be right back." She excitedly ran from the room. Moments later, she returned with one of Wendy's bras. It was light blue with some lace.

"Whoa," Jake said. "What are you doing with that?"

Bailey's face was red with laughter. "Beautiful princesses wear bras."

"No. No. I'm a boy. I'm not comfortable with this," he protested.

Jake was a prisoner to his children's pleasures. She ignored his pathetic pleas for leniency and slipped it over one of his big arms. She lifted the other and worked it through the opening. He exhaled in frustration as she wiggled the straps up and pushed them over his shoulders. It was tight. The garment was far too small across his chest. After careful assessment Bailey determined there was no chance it was going to connect in the back. But it was okay because it was sort of where it needed to be.

"The princess needs a crown," Paul said as he worked the comb of an ornate silver and purple crown into Jake's hair. It previously belonged to one of Bailey's dollies.

"Is anybody hungr…?" Wendy's sentence cut off when she rounded the corner and took in the scene. She froze with a gaping mouth and then roared with laughter. The funniest part was the pleading look in Jake's eyes. It was pathetic, reminding her of a basset hound.

"Mommy, Mommy, we're playing dress up," Bailey announced. The matter of fact way she said it gave the impression that 'dress up' was a regular game in the Gillean home.

"Daddy is a princess," Paul added.

"He certainly is," Wendy said. "You know what…I think the princess needs some make up."

"What?" Jake exclaimed. "I don't think so. I don't play that."

Wendy kissed him on the cheek and said, "The fairy princess must allow her ladies and her boy in waiting to prepare her for the wedding." It was three against one and resistance at this point was futile. They giggled and laughed, having a fabulous time as they applied a base. They added color to his cheeks, making them obnoxiously red. They added eyeliner and mascara, and finally finished with mousse and glitter accents in his hair. When the task was completed they stepped back and took in the scene.

"Daddy, you're a pretty girl." Paul could hardly speak he was laughing so hard.

"I think we've unlocked one of your secrets," Wendy teased. Jake was quite possibly the most homely princess she had ever seen, but at the same time, he was an absolutely wonderful father. She couldn't remember being more attracted to him than at that moment.

"We need pictures," Bailey squealed.

"Oh, no,' Jake mumbled. Her act of immortalizing the memory was the final brushstroke, completing his portrait of absolute humiliation. He did the quick calculation and decided that the joy and togetherness of family was worth the sacrifice. He smiled with each pose until the photo shoot ran its course.

Jake was lost in solitude and hadn't moved for the time it took to relive the file, but he was unconsciously smiling. On a deeper level, he was being tortured by the experience. He missed them so much. Then guilt hit him again. He had been given a responsibility and he had failed. His wife and children were precious and beautiful in every way, and their lives had been wiped from existence. It was his fault. The stab of his crime was deep and relentless. But he couldn't give up, not while he had strength left to fight. If his leap through time happened in the first place, there had to be a way to undo what he had done. There had to be a way to bring his family back. For just a few moments though, he needed a break…a brief respite from the grief. Watching the file was supposed to take him back to a happier time—it just wasn't supposed to hurt so much.

"What's going on?" Ben interrupted.

Jake jolted back to reality and looked around. "Oh, uh…nothing," he offered. His voice was subdued, and he suppressed a sudden wave of irritation.

"You were smiling. Care to share?"

Jake pondered the question and casually shook his head. He muttered, "No. Reckon not." He added, "If you were trying to sneak, I heard you a mile away."

"I was, and no you didn't," Ben said. He nonchalantly set a bag on the ground.

Jake casually shook his head, giving the impression that he was dealing with an incompetent recruit.

"What?" Ben was getting defensive again. Jake didn't answer, secretly reveling in the predictability of Ben's reactions. Ben opened the bag and motioned for Jake to take a look. It contained three pulsars and two top-of-the-line energy shields. They were military grade but much smaller than the ones Jake used in his days with Alpha Group.

"Where'd you get this?"

"It's not what you know, it's who you know. I think we should be prepared."

"From the looks of it, you're planning for quite a fight."

"Actually, that's exactly what I want to avoid. That's why we move around so much."

The energy shield went under their clothes. Jake showed Ben how to put it on and helped him strap it in place. With their clothing worn over the device, it was small enough to not be easily noticed, fitting like an old style bulletproof vest, but thinner, more pliable, and much lighter. They strapped the pulsars in place. Jake preferred both to be under his arms. As Ben already had one, he strapped the extra one around his ankle.

"Now you know we can't turn on the energy shields unless absolutely necessary," Jake said.

"Why?"

"Because on satellite they light up like a Christmas tree. If you want the whole world to know where you are just go ahead and turn it on."

They settled around the campfire. They were traveling on foot. The pod they had been using was taken offline, the global positioning sensors were re-routed to another vehicle, and the onboard systems were deactivated. Ben seared the interior and abandoned it in a deep ravine. It was a ten-hour fast-paced hike behind them. Tomorrow they would emerge on the other side of the forest and pick up another vehicle for the next leg of the journey.

Ben shifted their conversation back to the events in Portland. "Why did you go back in? I mean, why risk it? The mission had already been extremely successful, and the building was collapsing." Ben was amazed with Jake's story. Everything MST had secretly done to him had worked perfectly. It went far beyond his physical prowess. His protection instincts were strong, and his leadership skills were obvious.

Jake contemplated the question. "It's what we do."

"I don't recall any of the other Guardsmen racing back in. Just you. Why? What were you thinking?"

Jake felt the press of the question. "I don't know," he answered. "I guess it was a reflex. When I heard that it was a child…I had to go."

"So if it had been an adult you might have reacted differently?"

"Hard to say. Possibly. You have to live with yourself afterward. I felt like it was my responsibility to help. It's a terrible thing to fail when children are in distress, either through action or inaction. The split second decisions haunt you forever."

"What are you talking about?"

Jake shook his head. He was in distress. His internal dialogue had transformed into something resembling more of a scream. He was thinking, 'I should have killed every one of them. I could have helped, but I walked away. I made the wrong choice. They were looking at me. They were pleading. I was the only hope those kids had, and I failed. I wasn't good enough.' Jake felt the press of extreme guilt. The line of questioning was suffocating. "No," he finally said. "I can't talk about those things yet."

"Okay," Ben agreed. "Everything in time. Let's go back to the museum. When you were running toward the exit and the building was crumbling around you, what were you feeling?"

It was a stupid question, but Jake would play Ben's game. "I was scared."

"About what?"

"What do you mean?"

"What exactly were you scared of? Were you scared of dying?"

"No. That wasn't it," Jake said.

Ben wasn't going to give it a rest until he finished dissecting the event to his satisfaction. "If you could have dropped her and guaranteed your survival versus keeping her and dying?"

"I would have chosen to die."

"If that's the case and you were so resolved to rescue the girl or die trying...what exactly were you scared of?"

"Failure," Jake finally admitted. "Failure. I was scared of failing her, of failing to fulfill my mission as a Guardsman. I don't like failure. I've never been good at it...and that's what makes..." he abruptly stopped. His jaw was clenched tight.

Ben considered the answer with a wry smile. He had successfully peeled back another layer. He changed the subject. "When you were out of the building and had Tess in your arms, when you were in the fountain, what were you feeling?"

"Joy."

"Joy?" Ben furrowed his brow. "Joy? Okay, we've just graduated from the fourth grade. Come on, Jake. Dig a little deeper. What exactly was happening inside you at that moment?"

"I was happy," he said. "Emotions were running strong. I was coming down from a high. I had an urge to cry after what she'd been through, after what both of us had been through."

"A little deeper," Ben directed. "The happiness...why exactly?"

"It was directed at her, at least part of it, that she would live."

"And the other part?"

"It was mine," Jake admitted. "It was for me. I was happy for me. Is that what you want to hear...that I'm selfish, or self-centered?"

"Wrong turn," Ben quickly interjected. He was waving his hands in the air. "Back up. Back up. Go the other way." They were right there, on the cusp of a breakthrough, and he didn't want to lose momentum because of a natural self-defense mechanism. "You felt happy for you...peel it back... why? What exactly made you experience happiness? What reward were you getting?"

"I didn't fail. I was successful. I did something no one else could. I proved again that I was the best damned soldier in Alpha Group. When they looked at me I could see the admiration in their eyes. When the people looked at me I could see it. It made me feel ten feet tall."

"Did you deserve it?"

"Yeah," Jake answered, "I deserved it."

Ben smiled with satisfaction. It was the answer he wanted, but it was also the one that he hoped he wouldn't find. In the process of discovery, in learning everything he could about Jake's life, he originally assumed he was looking for a single event when a choice or action was made that changed everything, a single moment in time that caused everything afterward to go wrong. It suddenly struck him as they were talking that his paradigm might be wrong. It might not have been a single mistake that altered the timeline and resulted in Jake showing up near death on that battlefield. The problem might actually be much more subtle and abstract…a defect that played itself out slowly over time. If Ben was right, it would not bode well. It would be much harder to help Jake, and it would be almost impossible to make things right. He recognized Jake as being a perfect specimen in so many ways, and while his volatile anger and his difficulties controlling it had obviously gotten worse to the point that it was distracting, he was struck by the potential for something deeper and far more insidious–Jake was an exceptional soldier, husband, and father, and he was also a man living in a prison, with shackles that were formed as a result of his perfection… each link forged in the fires of pride.

✳ ✳ ✳ ✳ ✳

[[July 5, AD 2379 (2 days after the museum rescue)]
[Arrival date minus 61 years]
[Portland, Oregon]

After the big pile of rubble that used to be the museum was deemed secure, and after what remained of the terrorists and their local support elements were handed off to agents from the MPS, Alpha Group was temporarily transferred to Hummings Air Force Base (AFB) for refit and debriefing. The name was a misnomer. Hummings AFB was really nothing more than a few small buildings and a single medium length airstrip that, as rumor had it, was well maintained at some point in the past. It had been a civilian enterprise on the outskirts of Portland. Two hundred years ago, it was in the open countryside. Now it was completely surrounded by suburban housing. When it fell into complete disrepair, the military took it over and began using it as a staging area for small operations and border patrol flights. Unbeknownst to anyone with just a casual knowledge of the base, its underground facilities were surprisingly elaborate.

On the night of July 5th, Alex and Jake finally had their chance to enjoy a cold beer, a cold domestic microbrew on home soil. It seemed forever since the men had actually had the opportunity to take a breath and relax. The fighting had been nonstop, and the opportunity to cut loose and have a drink proved to be a rare prize. They were perpetually focused on staying alive, keeping their men alive, and completing each of the never-ending missions thrust upon their command. It was grueling and dangerous work. Death was a daily experience and as hard as Alpha Group fought, and the closer they got to the Persian homeland, the more futile their efforts seemed to be. The only territory that they ever held secure was the ground under their boots. Even that remained secure only so long as they remained in place with ample firepower. As soon as Western forces redeployed to another area, Persian forces would pop up out of nowhere and start fighting again in the rear. The process was frustrating in every way imaginable.

The Officers' Club was a civilian enterprise about a mile from the base. It was by external appearances a dilapidated warehouse, but the inside was different. It had been retrofitted with the appropriate plumbing, flooring, windows, and insulation. The bar and booths were donated from a large restaurant franchise that was updating one of its nearby locations. All things considered, it was fairly nice. The most important thing was that the beer was cold. Neither objected to the cellar- or room-temperature beers served overseas, but they preferred their beer served the American way…cold, in a frosted mug, and with a hint of foam on top.

Regardless of what branch of the armed services other soldiers were from, once they found out that a member of The Guard was on hand, they treated them differently, with complete deference. This was even more obvious if it became known that they were members of Alpha Group, the most elite unit within The Guard. It wasn't intimidation as much as it was respect. This night was no different. One of the Air Force pilots, Major Sparks, sauntered over to their booth. He introduced himself and politely informed them that he would be picking up their tab. It wasn't an isolated event. Most pilots realized that if they had to be rescued, The Guard would most likely be doing the rescuing. Although computers did most of the flying and drones had supplanted pilots on most bombing missions, the pilots still flew some of the most complicated missions. They tended to be high risk, and when pilots went down behind enemy lines, they prayed for The Guard first and salvation second.

The waitress in the establishment was an absolute bombshell. She flaunted her assets; cleavage half a mile long and legs that refused to stop until they disappeared into beautiful swaying hips that were failing miserably in their effort to hide under a very short skirt. Every guy in the place was fumbling in distraction. Her figure was absolute perfection, and her smile…it would stop traffic. She was confident and flirtatious, toying with the men without giving them anything beyond frustration and unfulfilled fantasies. From the moment Alex and Jake walked in, she had her eye on the latter. At first it was subtle. When Jake ignored her, it had the effect of increasing her determination. She changed tactics until the obvious flirtation was painful for Alex to endure. At the same time, Jake seemed completely ignorant, absolutely oblivious to what was happening despite her shockingly forward innuendoes. She would lean way over the table so that he would have the opportunity to look down her blouse if he chose. Her hand was on his shoulder as she rattled off the variety of beers that were available. She even ran the back of her fingers across his jaw like a romantic scene in a movie. Jake didn't react; his radar either didn't pick up anything unusual or he was the master of self-control, and this was from a woman who likely had never experienced rejection...until now. It was as if she was totally invisible.

Alex studied the dance as if the two were brightly adorned birds engaged in some sort of wild and bizarre mating ritual, and the whole of the dynamic was being recorded for study in some wacky ornithology course, where all the students wore plaid suspenders with matching shorts, and hats that were altogether too small for their bulbous and sweaty craniums. How he would have loved to provide the commentary, it would have been sarcastic and hilarious. 'Here we see the female of the species twirling around, doing knee bends and squat thrusts, and an occasional jumping-jack, all in an effort to reveal her beautiful plumage to a potential mate. We see here the male of the species. He's distracted, oblivious to her efforts. He's searching all over for something. His eyes are out of alignment and he has a bucked beak. He's trying in vain to find the elusive navel that he's convinced is hiding under his features. He's found a flea. He's staring in deep contemplation. With his head sideways, he appears to be wondering if he's found it. Oh look, now she's yelling and squawking, and holding up a sign. What does it say? It reads...*my cloaca is right here.* Under that is an arrow pointing to the vacation destination. He notices the sign. The expression on his face is empty. He's completely dumbfounded. I don't think he can read. Wait a minute. He seems to understand now. With a look of amorous seduction he approaches her. He takes the sign away. He's going to seize control, toss it to the side, and complete the mating ritual. No. Class...is everyone watching? He just took the sign. He's running away with it. He's biting off little pieces. She is squawking in protest while he finds contentment in eating her sign.'

Alex laughed at the hilarity of his own thoughts. While he found the woman's futile attempts to capture even a remote hint of Jake's attention comical, he also found the whole scenario primitive and pathetic.

Going for broke, the waitress went nuclear. She dropped the menus on the floor, and without bending at the knees, she bent over to pick them up. While she wanted to look back to see if he noticed her prized assets, the art of the move prohibited such a rearward glance. She looked away and kept walking. As Alex gawked, fully appreciating everything she had to offer, Jake casually looked away without an indication that he noticed anything amiss.

The first time Jake and Alex met, they became friends. At some point, maybe it was before, most likely it was after, there developed a deep mutual respect. It was professional as well as personal. They trusted each other with their lives and with the lives of their men. Privately they were free to interact on a level entirely different than when the others were around. They knew the behind-the-scenes aspects of each other's life and had intertwined them in many respects.

"I've been meaning to ask you about that." Alex nonchalantly pointed to his cheekbone. Jake sported the remnants of a large black and brown welt below his left eye. Alex had noticed it before, but until now, he hadn't said anything.

"Oh," Jake said as he felt his own face. He ran his finger across the area in such a way as to assess the severity of the swelling. In fact, it was the thousandth such assessment. "The girl at the museum. She kicked me."

"She kicked you?" Alex chuckled at the thought.

"I know," Jake admitted, lightly rubbing the area. "I think she must have been a soccer player or something. When she got me, she hit hard enough that my head spun."

Alex laughed. "Amazing. This whole mess, and over a year of constant hell, and your only injury beyond a blister and a scratch is from getting kicked in the face by a little girl. A little girl you were trying to help, no less." He laughed out loud, finding the irony amusing. "Did she draw blood?"

"No."

"Too bad, Jake. I could have gotten you a medal. A Purple Heart if she had drawn blood. If you want I'll fill out the appropriate paperwork. Maybe the review board will make an exception. Technically it did bleed… just under the skin. Who knows? Maybe bad bruises count now?"

"Hey, it's not funny." Jake leaned back, eyeing Alex across the table. His weird sense of humor was poking its head out of the closet. "A couple centimeters over and yours truly could have lost an eye."

Jake knew Alex to be an enigma of sorts. On the outside, he was serious beyond compare. He'd study people in quiet contemplation, intimidating them to the point that they'd get nervous, and he rarely said more than was necessary. When it came to things military, he was aggressive and succinct.

His mind was always a step ahead of everyone else. But underneath it all, he had a sense of humor that was quirky as hell. It ran completely contrary to his aggressive persona. As far as Jake knew, he and his family were the only ones privy to the slapstick side of the illustrious Col. Alexander Fisk.

Alex took a slow drink and seemed perplexed. His brows ruffled and he said, "So Nancy, was it a front kick like she was kicking a ball? Or was it more of a stomp with the heel?"

Jake laughed. If Alex liked someone, he'd occasionally call him Nancy. If he didn't like you, he'd get real close, and in a most articulate and refined manner, speaking slowly so every syllable would be heard, he'd call you a 'dumb ass.'

Jake took a swig from his drink and pondered the question. "More of a stomp. Yeah," he said after thinking it over, "definitely more of a stomp. I guess I didn't think about it. You know, I guess I figured wrong. I assumed she'd be glad to see me. When I was navigating my way through the auditorium, I sort of expected her to lunge at me when I found her. When she didn't, I reached in and grabbed her by one ankle. Before I could react, she smashed me in the face with the other. Can't say I blame her though, after everything that happened."

Alex sarcastically looked him over and shook his head. He wasn't going to have anything to do with a serious conversation. It was time for another beer. He needed to unwind and de-stress. Serious conversation about things military was not going to happen, not tonight. "Let me see something." He held up his beer menu and positioned it in front of Jake's face. First he held it to one side and slowly moved it across. Then he moved it from below and slowly raised it. "Yeah, just as I expected…definitely an improvement. I have to tell you Jake," Alex took another drink and dropped the menu so that it would slide off the table to the floor, in the hopes that the waitress would come back. "I'm of the opinion that our whole conversation should be considered classified. I think this represents an unexpected weakness in The Guard's capabilities. I think its root cause is an unforeseen gap in our training. If our enemies hear about this, there's likely gonna be hell to pay. Potentially, we could be overrun by armies of little girls. All of them trained to kick us in the face. I'm sorry, not kick…more of a stomp. You said it yourself—one of us could lose an eye."

Jake was dumbfounded. "You haven't even had one beer," he exclaimed.

"A whole army of little soldiers, little soccer players, coming at us from both flanks, the ground shaking in unison with their stomps."

"You're gettin' to be a cheap date."

"We better get another round," Alex said. "I can already tell the nightmares are going to be haunting. I'll have to sleep with a helmet on to keep from getting kicked…I mean stomped. Oh hell, that won't work either. You had your helmet on, didn't you?"

The waitress came by with a couple fresh beers. She grasped Jake's beer, half grabbing his hand in the process, and looking him straight in the eyes, she flashed her pearly-whites with a 'come hither' expression. She didn't bother asking him if he was done, she just relieved him of his warm beer, even though there was about an inch of the brew remaining at the bottom, and she replaced it with a chilled mug fit for a Viking king. She moved her hand to his shoulder and asked, "Is there anything else I can get for you?"

"Thank you, Ma'am," Jake nodded. That was all he felt obliged to say.

His southern accent and masculine manners caused her to swoon even more. She hesitated, wanting to hear him say something else, and then she turned to Alex. Without taking her hand off Jake's shoulder she asked, "Colonel, is there anything I can get for you?"

Alex feigned a sigh and said, "We've been in the field and haven't seen a single woman in eight years. In an effort to avoid sounding forward or bold, all I need is for you to stand there for a moment longer, just to remind me what it is we're fighting for."

Jake tried not to laugh.

"Colonel, you're making me blush," she said. She was smiling as if he had given her exactly what she wanted…a reason to stay for another moment. She squeezed Jake's shoulder. "If you need anything…" She picked up the menu and sauntered off to attend to the other patrons.

As soon as she was gone Alex asked in an incredulous tone, "How can you ignore that?"

"What?"

"What do you mean…what? Her. Bloody hell, she wants you in a bad way. It's obvious she has terrible eyesight and poor taste in men, but other than that she's perfect. And she wants you. You? I have no idea why, but she wants you."

"You think so?" Jake acted surprised.

Alex didn't know what to make of Jake's aloof attitude. He had seen it often enough before. Jake's response to women was always the same. Alex shrugged his shoulders and offered, "I have an idea. It's totally innocent; I bet she'd let you take her to see an ophthalmologist. She'd think it was a date, but you…you're just being a nice guy. Problem is that afterward she'd get a good look at you." Fisk took a drink and added, "Hey, maybe at some point she got stomped in the eye by a little girl and that's why she can't see. The fates brought you together. I wonder if she was wearing a helmet." Alex was amused by his own wit, chuckling to himself. "Seriously Jake, she's all over you."

"Never noticed."

"Never noticed? For crying out loud, most guys would give their left arm or more for a fraction of the women who throw themselves at you. Hell, it happens to you all the time. And you never seem to notice!" Alex was emphatic about it. "You can't tell me you haven't ever...you know, in a moment of loneliness," he made a subtle hand gesture to complete the insinuation.

"No. Reckon not."

"Come on," Alex was in disbelief. "Never?"

"Never," Jake confirmed his response without hesitation. "Not even close. Never."

"Never? Really?"

"A guy's eyes play tricks. Don't trust 'em," Jake said. "They connect right up into the stupid parts of the brain. So...no. Not in a million years. I have Wendy. I have a beautiful wife who hands-down is a hell of a lot better looking than her or any other piece of eye-candy, and a hell of a lot smarter. There are also two wonderful kids who put their trust in me. While I assure you, I have the same urges as you, I would never consider throwing that away for something so meaningless." Jake went on, "Look at the potential consequences of acting on such a primitive biological urge. Sex...I can't think of a more pathetic or selfish reason to ruin everything I have that's good. Wendy, Bailey, and Paul...their whole view of the world, their whole life is based upon a foundation of trust and fidelity. I won't be the one responsible for yanking that out from under 'em. It's actually much more about self-respect and a promise I made to Wendy and to God than it is about self-control." Completely satisfied with himself, Jake nodded as if he won the big hand at a poker tournament. He took a drink. Alex seemed deflated so he figured he'd throw him a bone. "Of course Alex, there's no rule stopping you from scoring and telling me all about it."

Alex laughed, "I can see it now. Trust me—with her the lights are on. There are clown shoes, stilts, two of those big foam cowboy hats, and peanut butter, lots of peanut butter, the crunchy kind, not the creamy. Hell, Nancy, no way am I going to tell you about it. I'll let you watch the movie."

"You are hilarious."

"In all seriousness, let me ask you something." Alex took a drink and searched for his words to make them sound as profound as possible. "Do you think something more like a motorcycle helmet with a visor would help?"

"What?" Jake was confused.

"I'm still working this equation out in my mind. You know, a motorcycle helmet. To protect us from little feet trying to stomp us." He pretended that he was being repeatedly kicked.

Jake laughed and pulled Alex's beer away. "Barkeep, Col. Fisk has had enough."

* * * * *

Later that night, Jake was headed back to his quarters to get some shut-eye before reveille. He noticed that the lights were on in the recreation center. As he passed the window he glanced in. First Lieutenant Jim Horner was sitting on the military press machine. He was sitting, but he wasn't lifting. He was leaning forward with his elbows on his knees and his head resting in his hands. Jake watched for a minute, and when Jim didn't move, he decided to go in to check on him.

The sound of the door opening caught Jim's attention. He looked up, saw Jake, stood at attention, and said, "Lt. Col. Gillean."

Jake nonchalantly held up his hand, "As you were, Lieutenant." It was obvious the man had been crying. His eyes were red and his facial expression grim. Jake pretended not to notice, casually walked by, and looked around the room, taking stock of where everything was.

Just like everyone else, Jake struggled as he experienced new torments. He often responded with anger and directed it outward during combat and when exercising. Others, like Jim, coped in their own ways. Some would sneak off to be alone and then they would cry. If they were in the field Jake would follow them, always staying hidden. He would watch over them like a guardian, making sure they were safe and didn't do anything stupid. They would return and everything would be okay for a while. It wasn't his place to judge, and he never let on that he knew. It was essential that everyone cope in his or her own way, so long as it wasn't self-destructive. Jake was always there to support them. There were no guarantees in life—including the ability to remain sane in a world that clearly was not.

Jake grabbed a flat bench from the free-weight area and deposited it on the floor in front of the military press machine. He took a seat facing Jim. "Little late to be lifting," he said. "What gives?"

"Just a little trouble sleeping, sir. Nothing I can't handle." Jim was determined and tense. He was fighting hard but at the same time he was losing control. He was decompensating under the stress. His gaze was focused down at the floor, but he really wasn't looking at anything, wasn't seeing what he was looking at.

Jake didn't say anything for a long time. When he felt the timing was right, he asked, "You want to talk about it, Jim?"

"I can't Lt. Col., I just can't."

"My name's Jake," he said, "I'm from Tennessee, and just like you, I've been through hell. For the time being let's forget about rank. We're just two guys trying to make it through this damn war the best we can. Fair enough?"

"Fair enough," Jim said.

"Now, talk to me."

Jim brought his hands to his face, rubbed his eyes, and took a deep breath as he ran his fingers through his hair. "I don't know. Every time I close my eyes I see their faces. What they did in that auditorium, the things those kids had to endure, what they were forced to watch." He shook his head as he talked. Now he was looking at the wall over Jake's head, his eyes were glassy, and he continued to fight the urge to cry. "There was this little boy. He was maybe six or seven years old. He was screaming. His mouth was open, and he was screaming. But the funny thing was…there wasn't any noise. He was screaming as hard as he could but no noise was coming out. His eyes were darting all over, from left to right and back again, and he just kept on screaming, without ever making a sound. Everything we saw in there was terrible. Absolutely everything. He was just one of hundreds of kids. All of 'em have a story, all of 'em horrible. I don't know why, but I can't get that little guy out of my head."

Jake listened patiently as Jim went on describing how the boy wouldn't move, how he picked him up and carried him out of the auditorium. He found out later that the child had been forced to watch the Persians brutally murder his father. He had taken the day off work to spend time with his son, to be a chaperone.

As the discussion progressed, Jake did his best not to suggest to Jim that he was handling any of it in the wrong way, but he validated Jim's emotional response to the experience. He asked him what he would have done differently, what he thought might happen to the child in the future, and he dug to find what it was that bothered Jim most about the whole experience.

After he had talked himself out, Jake offered, "Jim, you are one of the best soldiers we've got. But you have to remember to give yourself a break. Don't be so hard on yourself. You're completely normal. You're human. Your troubles and your responses are completely normal, and you aren't alone."

Jim contemplated Jake's words for a moment, indicated that he understood with a subtle nod of the head, and asked, "Do you ever have bad dreams?"

Without hesitation Jake admitted, "Yeah. Yeah I do. All the time. With the things we've seen, it would be impossible not to have nightmares and flashbacks. I'm just like you…just like everybody else. Everybody in Alpha Group is going through the same thing. Everybody does it in their own way. You've got to pay close attention Jim, because injuries and casualties aren't always seen. This war has been hard on everybody, and we all carry wounds on the inside." He stood up, extended a fist toward Jim, who hit it with his own. "But we're a team, and we'll make it through this together."

"Yes, sir," Jim said.

"We'll talk more tomorrow," Jake said.

CHAPTER 19: ZIMMER

[APRIL 15, AD 2441]
[135 DAYS AFTER ARRIVAL; THE SAME DAY]
[LOCATION: NEW WASHINGTON, TEXAS; OFFICE OF NAIA DIRECTOR
CARL ZIMMER;]

"Have you seen it?"

"I have."

"And your conclusion?"

"An unfortunate mistake," Zimmer said. "It was a tense situation." His attention shifted back to the incoming reports streaming in from NAIA offices around the world. In an hour, he would be in a meeting with the President and the Joint Chiefs of Staff. He was under intense pressure and felt as though he was living under a microscope. Until the source, or sources, of the information leaks were discovered he was being deemed the one responsible. The breach had to be coming from somewhere within the NAIA. He was in survival mode and didn't have time to waste on trivial matters of peripheral concern.

'He's going to sweep this under the rug,' she thought. Jerica Drum was the Director of the Domestic Security Service, the DSS. She blurted out, "I'm not ready to close the book."

Zimmer raised his eyebrows.

"Zagger was one of my more capable agents," she said. "I've watched that recording more than a dozen times. I've had it analyzed and re-analyzed. Something doesn't add up. I think Benjamin Murray knew Zagger was one of our agents. He knew Zagger had a BCD, and he deliberately killed him."

"I've been briefed. I personally talked to Murray. He's working another case, and at the time, he didn't know Zagger was one of ours."

"Logic dictates that would be his response."

"Do you have something material or is intuition driving this?" Zimmer's tone was dismissive.

"Intuition didn't kill my agent. He was participating in an operation that you authorized, and he was deliberately targeted. He was assigned to monitor a John Doe. May I inquire what the government's interest is in the patient?"

"You may," Zimmer responded. There was an awkward moment of silence.

Drum shifted her weight from one leg to the other. 'The bastard's not going to tell me,' she thought. 'So be it. I know a lot more than he thinks.' She broke the silence by adding, "One of my resources was killed. I think I deserve to know."

Zimmer's stare was like ice. It conveyed the intended message…that she was treading in a dangerous place.

'I probably know more about John Doe than he does,' Drum thought. 'I answer to people far more powerful than he could imagine.' She gloated as she made mental calculations. 'My resources have been tracking his Murray and this John Doe all across the country. By the way, I know his name is Jake Gillean and that he appeared out of nowhere at the Civil War reenactment. It's only a matter of time. I'll find out who he is and what they're running from.' Determining that the silence had gone on long enough to convey a message of her own, she said, "It would have saved both of us some time if you'd simply said you weren't in a sharing mood."

Zimmer continued his icy stare, pretending he either didn't hear her or didn't care. With a subtle movement of his head he communicated that she should get out of his office.

'Go ahead Zimmer, try to stare me down.' Drum was smiling. 'They're good, but so are we. If I were in a sharing mood myself I'd tell you that they're only a few days ahead of us. What are you up to?' Her casual silence rebuked his stare. 'He figured out young that most people would cower if he behaved aggressively,' she thought. 'Probably learned it when he was an adolescent…the Neanderthal hasn't learned anything new… he actually thinks he's scaring me…would be amusing if…'

Director Drum was conducting her own investigation, using only loyal DSS resources. The autopsy on Zagger revealed that he didn't die from the pulsar blast. While it destroyed his BCD, he had in actuality lived on for at least a period of time. The microscopic lesions found in his brain were consistent with having been interrogated with some sort of neuromodulation device. Zagger's brain was denuded of information, and he was executed. Whatever he knew was important. There had to be a reason. Now the

DSS had another agent down. This one was in Alaska. No…there was far more to this story.

Satisfied that Zimmer's blood pressure was up, Drum nodded and said, "Thank you for your time. This has been most productive." She turned and walked away.

* * * * *

Later that afternoon, after slamming his fists on the table in agitation and admonishing his Regional Directors over the fact that they weren't developing viable leads, Zimmer carved out time for a private meeting. His secretary had seen the woman come and go before but didn't know who she was. Her boss arranged the meetings on his own, and she wasn't included in any of the details. She knew well enough to avoid asking.

"Sally," Zimmer said to his secretary, "under no circumstances am I to be disturbed."

"Yes, Director Zimmer," she acknowledged. He closed the office door and the lock clicked.

The stranger's name was Pricilla Kyte. She was one of the most capable agents in his arsenal of *off the record* employees. She wasn't really an assassin, but then again she was. She functioned as a covert operative but was part mercenary. She mastered the art and psychology of developing personal and intimate relationships with her targets. Once inside the circle of trust she extracted the desired information and got out in a style all her own. That was one of the reasons Zimmer used her. It was clean. When she completed a job there were no loose ends for him to clean up. While he regarded her as an asset, he recognized her as the dangerous enigma that she was.

Pricilla was a gorgeous redhead who could morph into any role she desired. She could easily persuade her targets that she was prudish, highly educated and articulate, or if it better served her purposes, she could cultivate an image of being an unintelligent and hard-partying purveyor of wild times. No one ever suspected her of having ulterior motives… much less NAIA funded espionage.

"I trust you're not wasting my time," Zimmer said as he walked around his desk and took his seat.

"I don't recall ever having wasted your time."

"I'm very busy."

"I assumed as much." Her quip was nonchalant, with an edge that suggested he was wasting hers. When he looked at her with a curious expression she elaborated, "War rally in the park. Everybody's on edge, screaming for blood."

"I know. The situation is bad."

"Bad?" She smiled. "I'd say it's good. Everywhere you go it's the same. All across the country people are glued to their Vintels. It looks like the whole world is uniting against us. We need a good war. It's been a long time."

'Idiot,' he thought. 'She has no idea how close we are to actual war.' Despite being a loyal Fascist, he clearly understood what no one would dare say out loud…that United America was all military and little else. Because of government policies, its non-military manufacturing capacity had been all but destroyed and the agricultural sector was reeling. Innovation and output had diminished so much since World War IV that it was forced to import food and manufactured goods from abroad. It couldn't even feed itself much less successfully fight a Fifth World War, and on top of that, despite all the saber rattling, this time America would be standing alone.

Zimmer got to the point. "Were you successful?"

Pricilla's modus operandi was simple. She'd target a specific male, flatter him, engage him intimately, and extract as much information as he'd willingly give. She'd ply her trade and her real passion…interrogation under torture. She was capable of using knives and other brutal means to exact as much pain as possible, if that was what was dictated by circumstances, but she actually preferred staying clean. She loathed having to launder or replace clothing soiled with blood. She was a neat freak, and in lieu of having a high-end wardrobe, her preferred method of torture was to use something she fondly referred to as *my little cutie*. It was a band a few centimeters in width that went around the neck of her target. Few refused when she seductively clasped it around their necks, even fewer when she learned to disarm them by putting a similar appearing device on herself first. By that point, they were usually begging to join in what they thought was going to be a very special experience. The difference was that her collar was a fake. Theirs was a torture device.

My little cutie would create impulses in the pain fibers in her victim's cervical spinal cord. The violent discharges would travel up into their brains. One good jolt would render them completely helpless. They would fall to the floor feeling simultaneously burned alive and ripped apart. She'd toy with them, taking them to the point that spittle would be flying out of their mouths as though they were having full-blown grand mal seizures. She'd laugh with child-like giddiness, keeping score, clapping as they writhed, seeing just how much punishment they could take relative to her previous victims. Then she'd push them into unconsciousness. Once satisfied, she'd stop, allow them to regain consciousness, and then she'd start asking questions.

"I found some success. Some things," she mused, "that you might find to be significant. They have a keen interest in a case that's apparently known to this office. Something about a John Doe who appeared at some military reenactment."

'What the hell?' Zimmer thought. In his mind he was smashing his fist on the table in frustration and yelling. It was a classified case and now it appeared that everyone knew about it. He held her stare. While the shock of what she said caught him off guard, he had no intention of betraying surprise with an inadvertent facial expression. After a moment of mental maneuvering he pointedly asked, "This case as you call it…what exactly is MST's interest?"

Pricilla's assignment was to find out what she could about any secret projects being developed by MST Global. The NAIA had failed miserably in its efforts to plant operatives deep enough inside the company to learn anything of consequence. As a result, Zimmer had to turn to his more unpalatable resources. He was convinced MST was a threat to United American security, and his suspicions were running deeper as he suspected they were involved in the run up to what was threatening to be another war. But what did it have to do with John Doe?

"The research they're doing involves time travel," she said. "There's a connection. They have an interest in the John Doe."

MST was researching time travel? He considered the implications. How did they know about John Doe? The highest levels of security were in place and only a few people knew about his unexplained materialization, or about the investigation he launched. Was it possible that MST had a mole within the NAIA? Was it actually possible that MST was already doing experiments in time travel…that his suspicions about John Doe being a victim of time travel were all true?

Zimmer corrected himself. He had spent so much time thinking about him as John Doe that he had slipped back into the habit. He wasn't a John Doe. His name was Jake Gillean. The name didn't mean anything to him, and there was no record of anyone by that name. The report from Martin Zagger first suggested the name, and one of Murray's clandestine reports from his hiding place corroborated the information. His name was indeed Jake Gillean. Apparently MST didn't know that much. That was good. He took comfort in knowing that Dr. Murray had taken him underground so completely that MST didn't even know his name.

"Pricilla, you're being coy," Zimmer stated. His tone indicated that he didn't appreciate it. "What exactly does John Doe have to do with their research?" There was no way around it. Given her paucity of speech he had to ask. 'She has to have a personality disorder,' he thought, 'something on top of an obvious antisocial personality disorder, something that jaded her beyond being a traditional psychopath.' Zimmer's internal dialogue went on, 'sure, I take care of business too, but what I do is justified. I do it to preserve the integrity of the country and the Party. I benefit in that I remain the Director of the NAIA, but I believe in what I'm doing, and I'm better than anyone else. Besides, no one else could be trusted with this much power. Hell, I'm more powerful than the President. But I'm not like her. She's a murderous little wench who enjoys doing what she does, and she does it for psychopathic thrills and money. She does know a lot... too much in fact. Does she realize how dangerous she is? One of these days, she'll have to be eliminated. I should have it done now; save me the trouble of doing it later. No. I have a feeling. She's dangerous because of what she knows, but I think I'll need this spawn of Satan again. She did mention our little project with John Doe. If she knows too much I'll have to have her eliminated.'

"I don't know what the connection is exactly," Pricilla said, "only that he is somehow related to work they're doing; he is important."

"How did you find this out?"

"The old fashioned way." Her expression was remorseless, sadistic in its underpinnings.

"Reliable source?" Zimmer asked

"He was," she replied.

"Tell me."

"His name was Tyler Kingston, a technician in one of MST Global's material science labs."

"What exactly was he working on?" Zimmer asked.

"Lightweight titanium alloys—strength testing at extreme temperatures for utilization in spacecraft."

Her assignment culminated in Tyler's murder. She kept the relationship going longer than usual in hopes of seeing the legendary MST Island. Once that was achieved, Tyler's days were numbered. They spent the weekend in one of Argentina's coastal resorts. She checked out–he didn't.

The most difficult part of Pricilla's work was covering her tracks and making her victim's death pass as being an accident of nature. Her planning started a couple days before. In this case, Pricilla convinced Tyler to arrange to have dinner with a friend. After he was down and his brutal interrogation complete, she used a voice replicator and contacted his friend. Using his voice she said, "I broke up with Amy last night." Amy being the alias she was using. "I found out she's been cheating on me. She was sleeping around...Yeah, the entire time. It's my fault. I should have seen the signs." She cancelled the dinner saying, "Not a big deal but she left. Anyway, I don't think I'd be good company right now. I don't feel up to dinner, besides I seem to have come down with a bug of some sort. I have a headache and feel like I might be getting the flu. I'm going to stay here for another night and go to bed."

Once that was taken care of, the next step was to kill Tyler. Pricilla used a long slender tool to deposit a pellet high up in Tyler's nasal cavity. The pellet was placed underneath the cribriform plate, or the roof of the nasal passages. It contained a highly lethal form of the bacterium *Neisseria meningitides,* bioengineered to be highly aggressive and completely resistant to every known antibiotic. Prior to dissolving, tiny projectiles from the pellet wormed their way through the roof of his nasal passages, and the overwhelming load of bacteria was deposited directly into his central nervous system. Tyler's immune system didn't stand a chance. To complete the picture, she tucked him into bed and administered a sedative that would be metabolized long after death...rendering it toxicologically invisible. Her final touches included the placement of tissue paper and a wastebasket next to the bed. No one suspected foul play. The autopsy confirmed meningitis as the cause of death.

Pricilla unabashedly laid out for Zimmer the sordid details of her relationship with Tyler, his interrogation, and the particulars of his ultimate death. She went into greater detail regarding what she learned about MST. Historically, the information she produced was as accurate as it was expensive. Zimmer appreciated her for that. In fact, he had long considered women to be better assassins than men—none of the moral hang-ups, and they didn't hesitate. In Pricilla's case that much was true. From the first time they met she struck him as a proud and spoiled cat, domesticated and groomed to perfection, but as soon as the lights went out she'd begin the hunt. She had to have something to kill. She'd stalk and capture her mouse, play with it and torment it, reveling in every moment, knowing that she was going to kill but taking her time. She'd bask in the pleasure, the absolute power, taking extreme delight in the mouse's fear, and killing it while enjoying the experience of sheer primal satisfaction.

Zimmer leaned back in his chair. He studied her from underneath a furrowed brow, calculating the pieces of the puzzle and how they might fit together. He went back to the connection between MST and John Doe. "MST wants him dead?"

"That's not what I said." Pricilla smiled, relishing that she was getting under Zimmer's skin. She was absolute in her confidence. He needed her. She was one of the most valuable assets in his arsenal. "I said that he's important. Not that they want him dead. Believe me, if they wanted him dead, he'd be dead. There are very few people on our little planet that they couldn't eliminate if they wanted."

"Your opinion of MST's capabilities is rather high," he said.

"With good reason." While her expression was sinister, like she was in possession of information far beyond anything Zimmer might imagine, her voice carried an element of being carefree and unconcerned. "I've seen MST from the inside."

"Tell me what you saw on the island." Zimmer was impressed. He'd sent his best people against the island, but their security services usually rooted them out. 'How she of all people managed to get a look at the inside,' he ruminated, 'I don't know. I have to downplay it or she's going to break my bank. Or I could have Dr. Murray interrogate her. He'd pilfer her brain and find out everything she knows.' Zimmer simply didn't like her. The thought made him smile.

Pricilla didn't respond at first. But after a moment, she smiled in response to his. "I saw lots of things."

"Such as?" Zimmer said.

"Their capabilities from a technological perspective are far beyond ours. There's not much more to say than that. One might extrapolate as one wishes. Should MST choose to apply their technology in an adversarial way, I don't see that there's much we could do to stop them. But I'm not an expert in matters such as that. Those determinations are better left in the hands of people of power and strength within the Party. People like yourself."

'Back up and retrace your steps, you evil little tramp. You're not stupid,' he thought. 'I'll give you that. But you know all too well when you've gone too far.' Zimmer knew the score. He understood there were places even Pricilla Kyte wouldn't dare to tread. The Egalitarian Party had taken on a power and might of its own, far beyond any of the individuals who ascended its internal hierarchy. It demanded absolute devotion in every way, and Pricilla had just bowed down in acknowledgement of its power.

"Tyler," she continued, "was far removed from MST's administrative circles, but he did overhear conversations. He was embedded in the thick of the cafeteria gossip mill. He reported that the next generation of energy weapons and shield technologies had been perfected for quite some time, that there was a next generation exo-suit far superior in every way compared to the last, and that there were several ultra secret projects—one of which was time travel, another gravity manipulation, and another that was so secret even their own scientists simply disappeared…never to be seen again. Rumors were that it was the greatest breakthrough in the history of mankind, and that it would change life as we know it on this planet. But he didn't know anything beyond that. Like I said, he was removed from the inner circles."

Pricilla's body language indicated that she was done. Before she got up to leave, she added, "Does the name Murray mean anything?"

'What the hell did she just say?' Zimmer's internal alarm was blaring. 'Did I hear right? Did she say Murray?' He took a breath. "No. Why?" he asked. Zimmer acted dismissive, like the meeting was over and that he was ready to move on. He was busy and didn't have time for idle chatter. He handed Pricilla a hefty sum of money for her *off the record* services, placing the payment on the desk in front her.

"Just something he said. Actually, it was more of a mumble. He was having trouble talking at that point." She giggled slightly. "Something about someone by that name trying to get information from John Doe, information crucial for their program."

She accepted the payment and got up to leave. Zimmer held up his hand to halt her exodus. She backed into her seat. A long moment of silence smothered the room. He began strumming his fingers on the desk, piercing Pricilla with an all-knowing stare. What was her motivation? Did she know Dr. Murray? Was there a history he needed to know about? Did she view him as competition? The questions came in rapid succession. She was a master of deception and manipulation. The unique talents that made her so useful were the same reasons he couldn't trust her. It was this conscious realization that made Zimmer extremely cautious. If the behind-the-scenes politics were bad in a two party system, they were far worse in a single party system. The fewer alternatives available to Party loyalists meant the stakes were higher. The fights were more intense, and one had to be extremely diligent to survive. In that arena, Zimmer was the master. He wasn't prone to making rash judgments, and he didn't make decisions in a vacuum. Every decision he made was part of a much larger and highly fluid chess match. That being the case, he needed to know exactly where all the pieces were.

"Tell me again, exactly, what was said about this person named Murphy?"

Pricilla suddenly felt her heart racing. For the first time in years of interactions with Zimmer, she felt real fear. She had inadvertently gotten herself mixed up in something far more serious than she anticipated, and it frightened her. How had she not seen the potential for danger before? It had never occurred to her that she might one day find herself a liability to Zimmer rather than an asset…simply because of something trivial she learned during an interrogation. Zimmer was dangerous. She could see the potential for ruthlessness in his eyes, and it was obvious it exceeded her own. She would have to be extremely careful.

"Murray," she said, "the name was Murray, not Murphy." She knew that it was a mistake Zimmer made on purpose. It was his way of telling her that he knew far more than he was letting on. He was scrutinizing everything she said, and she should tread with extreme caution. "It was toward the end of the interrogation. I was trying to get him to expand on the connection between John Doe and MST. All he knew was that there was a connection to their time-travel research. He didn't know the specifics though, just rumors. There were rumors that his appearance at some military function..."

"Function? Or was it a reenactment? A few minutes ago, you said reenactment. Which is it?" Zimmer interjected. He leaned forward, his gaze stabbing her, scrutinizing her every nuance.

"Yes. Yes. A reenactment. He said it was a reenactment." Pricilla was doing her best to maintain composure. "There were rumors that his appearance at the reenactment was somehow related to experiments being done in the time travel laboratory. Something apparently went wrong. Somehow there is a connection between John Doe and their ability to fix what went wrong."

"They need the person, or information from the person?"

"I don't know. He wasn't clear on that matter. He implied only that they needed to secure John Doe—that they were looking for him. He mentioned the name Murray in relation to getting information."

"Who is this Murray?" Zimmer asked.

"I don't know." Pricilla's complexion had grown somewhat pale. She knew that it was an important thing to know, and that's why she pushed so hard to get the information. In fact, that's why she pushed too hard. Caught up in the thrill of the moment she should have known better. "The interrogation," she continued, "had been going on for longer than usual at that point. He came to the conclusion that he wasn't going to survive. He stopped talking. I kept up the pressure, expecting him to tell me what I wanted in exchange for ending his pain. He was strong, a lot stronger than I supposed. I kept shocking and he kept resisting. Unfortunately, he lost consciousness, and I couldn't revive him. I failed to get anything else."

Zimmer kept up his psychological pressure. His jaws were clenched as though he was ready to unleash one of his infamous tirades. "Do you know anything about Murray, or anyone named Murray who might possibly be connected to MST?"

"No."

"Is Murray part of MST?"

"I don't know."

"Is Murray an obstacle to MST?"

"I don't know. I assumed from the manner he said it that Murray was an obstacle to MST. But I don't know for sure."

"Why don't you know anything more?" He slammed his fist on the table.

"The son of a bitch died on me," she blurted. "I wasn't able to learn anything else."

"Nothing else? You've got nothing else for me?"

"No. I'm sorry," she said. "I failed. I couldn't find out anything else." She nervously looked away, searching for what to do next. "Director Zimmer, if you feel that I have not performed to your satisfaction?" She put the payment back on his desk.

Zimmer studied her. He reached forward and took the payment. He rolled it in his fingers, staring at her the entire time, and tossed it up in the air. After it completed the up part of the arc and began falling back down, he snatched it out of the air. His entire demeanor changed to something far less threatening. He stood up, sending his desk chair rolling backward until it bounced off the other furniture, and he tossed the payment at her. "No. You'll get paid." He headed for the door, but before he opened it he added, "Don't ever tell me again that you killed your subject before getting everything. Sloppy. Sloppy as hell. That was an amateur mistake. If you're going to be paid like a professional, I fully expect the work to be commensurate. Now if you don't mind, I have work to do."

"Yes, sir. Thank you, sir," she said as she moved past him.

"Don't go too far because I anticipate I'll need you again. And I want a full report in the morning on absolutely everything you saw on that island." He closed the door and locked it after she left. With the fear and insecurity he knew he instilled in her, he was sure that she'd generate a report about MST's island that would be worth reading.

"Murray?" Zimmer mumbled the name under his breath. Was it possible? It couldn't be. Dr. Murray was a Party insider and a loyalist in the extreme. The odds of him having duplicitous loyalties were beyond a reasonable person's comprehension. Could he have some sort of connection to MST? It didn't make sense. There had to be another explanation. Was MST simply aware of him? Were they watching him? Was he in danger? Or had he actually betrayed his country? Was there another person named Murray? The questions were coming in rapid succession. Was Director Drum right? Did Murray take out Martin Zagger with knowledge that he was a DSS agent? The possibilities were endless. And beyond all that, there were MST's secret research projects…what exactly was MST working on? Zimmer took pause. Research. Was that the connection? It struck him that the equipment Dr. Murray used for his interrogations was exceedingly advanced technology. Where did it come from? Did it come from MST?

That was an angle he'd have to investigate.

Zimmer checked his door a second time to make sure it was locked. He went behind his desk. Mahogany cabinets covered the entire wall. He opened one of the doors. Hidden behind the horizontal framing under one of the shelves was a keypad. He punched in the proper sequence and it identified his fingerprints. Only after it detected blood flow through his fingers and accurately typed his blood with a laser for additional identification, did the back wall open up to reveal an elaborate titanium-alloy safe. A series of four old-style dials adorned its front. Along the outside of the dials was a series of numbers going to ninety-nine, the entire alphabet, and also a series of Greek symbols. He carefully turned one dial, then another, came back to the first, and rotated another. It took several minutes before the safe accepted his code and opened its door. Inside was a large stack of paper files and a stand-alone quantum computer.

Zimmer regarded the contents as sacred. He kept all the files updated and completely offline. They were for his eyes only. Should anything happen to him, his successor would be able to access the files and continue his work. MST Global was the key. He hated the organization and in those sentiments he wasn't alone. It represented a real and viable threat to his country's survival. It didn't matter what analogy one might choose, be it feeding wild animals or taking something earned from one working group and giving it unearned to another, the end result was always the same—dependence. MST provided energy through its subsidiary Elektor for little or nothing in return. The world was dependent upon them for its ongoing supply and for ongoing survival. Dependence…it was a basic principle of politics, and it was the most important element that the long-term politician needed to embrace for survival. It was also a vital aspect of gaining leverage over foreign adversaries…and that's exactly what MST had done to United America and the rest of the world.

When MST successfully launched its energy harvesting operation in outer space and began giving away access to the energy at a price that appeared to be below cost, it completely altered world markets. At the same time that they destroyed whole industries, they won the battle for the hearts and minds of people all over the globe with their promise to end energy-based international conflicts, and they largely did it in an environmentally friendly way. That was almost a hundred years ago. Without competition MST became a monopoly, a benevolent monopoly, but a monopoly nevertheless. Regardless of MST's track record, it operated outside the control of the Fascists. That's what made it dangerous.

Now, nearing the middle of the Twenty-Fifth Century, it appeared that until cold fusion technologies became cheaper to produce and maintain, they weren't going to become a viable alternative to MST's energy plants. Besides that, fusion drives were created and patented by MST. The corporation cornered the market on fusion drives, and thus far, government labs had been unable to successfully reverse-engineer the devices. While the quagmire of international patent laws protected everything MST developed, it was also the convoluted morass of scientific and economic obstacles that functioned to prevent any real competition from developing. Further, there had been a major brain-drain, with MST scooping up all the major talent from around the world.

As far as large corporations were measured, MST was something much more. It was actually its own country. It had possession of its own landmass in the expanse of the South Pacific, its own internal governmental structure, hospitals, prisons, and most importantly, it had its own currency. By having its own currency and its own landmass, it had effectively extricated itself from Egalitarian Party control. That's what made it a threat and why it was the primary target of Party animosity. But at this point in time, MST had never hinted that it had anything other than a positive and close working relationship with United America. They shared a wide array of common interests. Nevertheless, should the relationship sour, the people of United America would quickly discover that the country had become second rate. They couldn't provide for the energy needs of its population, and they no longer had the scientific or industrial expertise to develop energy alternatives.

In Zimmer's mind, the most dangerous aspect of the relationship was United America's dependence upon MST in the arena of military technologies. Thus far the trade off was defense. United America provided for the global defense of the corporation in exchange for all the other benefits the alliance brought to the table. But Zimmer wasn't optimistic that the future would be guided by the dictates of the past.

About a year ago, Zimmer learned that MST began developing its own military. Vague reports emerged regarding the use of novel technologies far beyond those currently available to United America's military. MST claimed that the programs were simply part of an internal research and development program and that they were working the bugs out of the next generation of weapons and defense technologies. Once the bugs were worked out, they would roll out their creations for the world to see. At the same time, according to the fragmentary reports Zimmer held in the safe, they had a vast amount of men and material with substantial offensive capabilities in outer space. This was the most immediate and most grave threat. Within an hour MST could effectively reduce the fighting efficiency of United America's armies to that of the early Twentieth Century, simply by knocking out orbiting satellites, disrupting communications across the Internet clouds, and by destroying the data mountains.

Almost all the reports in Zimmer's safe were about MST. He perused through them again in the futile hope that he might find a clue that would tie everything together. He made another entry, effectively updating the file.

Zimmer set about contacting those Party insiders he believed he could trust, the loyal soldiers of the Egalitarian Party and those in positions of power at the MPS and the DSS. He would launch several very quiet investigations. He ordered every aspect of Dr. Murray's life thoroughly investigated. If there was cause for concern, any hint of treason, any suspicious relationship with MST, he'd find it. He also determined that Pricilla be investigated. Should there be any connection between her and Dr. Murray at any time in the past, he was going to know about it. Was she just out to get him? Was she guilty of treason? Zimmer slammed his fist on his desk in frustration as another flurry of questions pressed in. Was there another connection between Pricilla and MST? Was it possible that she was on their payroll? And then, there was MST itself. The corporation had been under intense investigation for years, and despite every effort and untold resources, it remained an organization shrouded in secrecy. That alone brought Zimmer's blood to a boil. Once all the investigations were launched he would schedule a private meeting with President Martinez and inform him of his progress. As he began issuing orders he decided to assign a team to investigate Dr. Murray's family and conduct a clandestine search of his home.

CHAPTER 20: AFTERMATH OF THE ATTACK

[JULY 6, 2379 A.D. (3 DAYS AFTER THE ATTACK ON THE MUSEUM)]
[ARRIVAL DATE MINUS 61 YEARS]
[LOCATION: PORTLAND, OREGON]

It was understood that although Alpha Group had their boots on American soil for a couple days, it was an illusion of sorts as there was war on a massive scale in progress on the other side of the planet. The trip back to their home country was a fluke necessitated by unforeseen events. It was mental poison to entertain even the slightest thought of seeing family. One thought would turn into two, and it would completely preoccupy the mind. It would result in distraction and depression, diminish morale, and lead to mistakes.

The morning of the 6th began with a brisk ten-mile run without exosuits. It quickly swelled to fifteen because of the beauty of the Cascade Mountain Range. When the men returned to base, some weight training followed. In the field, they didn't often get the opportunity to lift weights in a gym, so they took full advantage. After a quick cleanup, they assembled for a midmorning meeting. Orders for the next assignment would be given and they would soon be back in the war zone.

"I have our orders." Col. Fisk held a piece of paper in front of the room. He bent the paper and snapped it tight in his hands. "This comes straight from the desk of our President."

The Guardsmen exchanged glances. They had never seen paper used for orders. Something unusual was happening.

"It reads:

ALPHA GROUP, SPECIAL OPERATIONS DIVISION

UNITED AMERICA OWES YOU A DEBT OF GRATITUDE. YOU HAVE ONCE AGAIN EXEMPLIFIED UNSURPASSED VALOR IN SERVICE TO YOUR COUNTRY. AS A SMALL TOKEN OF OUR OVERWHELMING GRATITUDE, YOU ARE HEREBY GRANTED TWO WEEKS LEAVE TO COMMENCE IMMEDIATELY.

EVELYN MORGAN
PRESIDENT OF UNITED AMERICA

The group collectively jumped for joy. Hats flew into the air. Soldiers hollered out. Alex waited a few moments before getting everyone's attention.

"There is more! Listen up!" he yelled. The room gradually emerged from pandemonium. "The Secretary of Defense, Admiral Percy Bernard, has arranged for everyone's immediate transportation. There are nine transports assigned to take you to designated jump points across the country. To expedite your travels," he continued, "each of you will have secondary flights or vehicles waiting to transport you to your final destination. You will inform us where that is, and you will check in daily through your BCD. The two-week rendezvous point, 0600 on July 20, is yet to be determined. We will let you know. Enjoy yourselves and don't do anything stupid." The room broke into near chaos with yelling and whooping, and several of the men were anxiously moving toward the door. It had been two years since the veterans had any time off. "HOLD ON!" he yelled above the noise, "Before you leave, Lt. Col. Gillean has an important announcement!"

Jake picked up where Alex left off. "Is everyone ready to get out of here, to go home to your families?" They yelled again. "No one has earned it more than you. Prior to learning of the two-week leave, I obtained permission from the High Command and took the liberty of making arrangements," he held up his hands in a gesture that indicated it was voluntary and no way compulsory, "for anyone who might be interested to visit some of the kids in the hospital. It was going to be a surprise for you. They know we're coming and special preparations have been made to receive us. There are two trucks and an escort waiting out front." He pointed toward the door. "The timing is bad." From the expression on the men's faces he gleaned that they agreed. "It's been a very long time for all of us." He wanted to say that it had been two years since he'd last seen his wife and kids, but personal revelation wasn't his style. "That being the case, I completely understand if you decide to go home right now. As you are officially on leave, you may do as you choose with honor. If you choose to come with me, know the place of respect your country has for you. The transports will wait because you are Alpha Group; you are individually and collectively the most valuable and most dangerous weapons this military has."

"Hoo-rah!" one of the men yelled. The room erupted with cheers.

"The transports," Jake continued, "will take off when you're ready. As for me, I can spare a couple hours as there are some kids and parents at the hospital who have been through hell. They're waiting to meet some of the soldiers who helped save 'em."

Jake went out the door after addressing the men. He turned to watch. Were they going to leave on furlough, or were they going to do the right thing—visit the kids in the hospital? He knew they would follow. They were more than companions. They were more than brothers. They were Alpha Group. When nobody else would, a Guardsman always did the right thing. The doors hadn't finished swinging all the way back on their hinges when they flung open again. There was no hesitation. The entire command emerged from the building and jumped into the back of the trucks.

Alex was the last one out the door. He made a quick assessment of the escort and the trucks and said, "I'm only aware of two people in history who could pull this off." He motioned toward the trucks filled with the world's toughest and most highly trained commandoes. He was referring to the fact that they had been in constant action for roughly two years, and on the moment they were granted leave, they voluntarily and without hesitation agreed to another assignment. "You and Alexander the Great," he said, "but with some obvious differences. He promised his men gold and plunder in return. Man for man, with the right place to stand, your eighty would whip the hell out of his forty thousand." Alex didn't attempt to conceal his amazement. "For you, they'd go to hell and back." He slapped Jake on the back and added with a grin, "You're a leader among leaders. Let's stop wasting time and do this thing." He finished with, "Hoo-rah!" and jumped into the back of one of the trucks.

In the throes of introspection and experiencing a keen sense of the present, Jake considered Alex's comments. The caravan was making its way into Portland. The guys were telling jokes, trading insults, and laughing. Jake felt detached, like he was looking in on the scene from the outside. Yes, he was their leader, but he didn't start off that way. He remembered his carefree life before the military. So many things had changed. In order to endure the hardships and tragedy of war, he had been forced to find new ways to mentally cope. It was the only way his mind could survive. He recognized that he had created a protective shell. He perceived all its contours and the nuances of the filter it used to allow him to function. He flashed to Corinth and to Portland. In combat he felt like his physical body was a robot, doing what it was commanded to do by the analytical parts of his mind while at the same time being fueled by anger. The other emotional parts were simply overpowered and left somewhere in the background.

Jake recalled when the protective shell was created. Its birth and his acceptance into the inner circle of special ops commandoes came after he and his squad were captured on their first mission. After several days of torture that included a variety of chemical, psychological, and physical techniques, he was reduced to the point that he lost his grip on reality. He chose to die rather than betray his country or his fellow soldiers. It seemed so long ago, but at the same time it could have been yesterday. His mind continued in its detached state. He didn't want it to end. It was a beautiful day and the air was whipping through his hair in the open bed of the truck. The men were jocular. He studied their behaviors while at the same time he re-experienced the moment, the sheer agony of the moment when he activated the self-destruct sequence built into his BCD. When he had been thus reduced, his training was officially complete. The soldier who emerged after a few days of vigorous debriefing was strong…very strong, and also very different from the naïve child who grew up in Spring Hill, Tennessee. One of the primary differences was that an impenetrable shell emerged to protect his mind, yet he perceived that there was a fire of vibrant life and hope, and an unconquerable faith that continued to burn somewhere deep inside. He smiled as the truck bounced along. They were still several miles from the hospital but small crowds of people were holding signs and cheering on both sides of the roadway. While the Guardsmen were waving, Jake remained detached, engrossed in the privacy of his thoughts. He felt good, like he was being embraced by the warmer aspects of life, by the touch of a loved one. Those parts of him weren't supposed to be there. They were supposed to have been destroyed by war, but they simply refused to be extinguished. They were patiently waiting for him within the protective shell. That made him happy. They were still there waiting for him so that he might resume his life once the fighting was over. As he took the moment to get reacquainted with himself he recognized that his inner spirit had been whispering in his ear all along. It was the part that wanted him to jump in excitement the moment an arduous run would crest a mountain to reveal the majesty beyond. It was the part that was begging to spend the entire night playing his guitar and flute. It was also the aspect of his conscience that reminded him to look at the world through a lens other than war.

Jake took a deep breath and basked in the rare moment of inner peace and contentment. He thought about his personal, and often losing, fight against harboring hatred for all Persians, or labeling all their citizens as evil and all those of United America and the West as good. While psychologically, that would have been an easy thing to do, morally...he felt it would be reprehensible. He recognized that his mind was programmed not only by his experiences but by how he chose to deal with them, how he sorted them out. As a result, he found himself understanding the war in varying shades of gray. He saw man's unending cruelty to man. He saw monstrous suffering and pain, and mankind's shielded indifference. He witnessed first hand the effects of greed, of ignorance, and of the damage poisonous ideas can wreak upon humanity. But he also saw things that were hidden away, things that were easy to miss if one didn't look for them. He saw acts of unbridled charity and sacrifice, and the wonderful perseverance of goodness and love among those hardest hit. Along the way he discovered a theme—the more simple the life, a life without the clutter of possessions and inordinate material desires, the happier people tended to be. When facing their most trying times, those people didn't pray for their suffering to be taken away. They asked God for the blessings of strength and the wisdom to persevere. In those people, Jake saw hope...a vibrant hope that the world would one day be a better place.

"Sir. Sir. Are you okay?"

Jake was startled back to reality. It was Captain Benejo. He was standing over Jake with a grin that ran from ear to ear. "Um, yeah," Jake said. "What is it?"

The Captain pointed. "You're missing it, sir." They were in the middle of a full-fledged parade. The trucks and their escort were navigating their way through the streets of Portland with incredible fanfare. People crowded along the sidewalks to catch a glimpse of the heroes. Police blocked off streets while horns of every variety blared excitement and appreciation. News crews were on every corner, and hovering cameras filled the sky. Confetti streamed down from the buildings and a band from the university belted out marching tunes in front of the convoy. Jake was amazed. All he did was contact the hospital to ask if it would be okay if the troops visited the kids. They settled on a specific time and that was that. Word had obviously spread, and it had grown into something he never would have wanted. The focus should have been on the kids. At the same time, the men had earned a moment of fame, and they were enjoying themselves.

The commotion abruptly stopped about one block from the hospital. It was like entering the eye of a hurricane. City police blocked the street and were only allowing emergency vehicles through the cordon. The band divided and lined both sides of the street so the trucks could pass between their ranks. The police waved the trucks through and then blocked everything else from passing. For the sake of the patients, the hospital didn't want the press or hordes of onlookers in the building. In achieving that objective, they were flawless.

Once inside, the hospital arranged for the soldiers to break up into smaller groups. Each group was assigned a nurse who escorted them to see the children whose conditions prevented them from attending a gathering that was planned in the cafeteria. Pictures were taken at every turn. They would serve as cherished mementoes for the children. Jake brought several boxes of military berets specific to The Guard. They weren't supposed to hand them out, but under the circumstances, he gave clearance and no rear echelon bureaucrat in New Washington would say anything about it.

Jake and three others were taken to the neurosurgical intensive care unit. There were tubes, IVs, and computer equipment everywhere in the room. A photo on the wall was of a boy, about eight years old. He had brilliant blond hair and was posing with a baseball bat. Jake examined the photo carefully, taking note of the boy's huge smile. It betrayed a wonderful and enigmatic personality. Other than the freckles, the boy in the photo and the one lying in the bed were unrecognizable as being the same person. Covered in dressings, his head was massively swollen. The neurosurgeon explained his situation as critical. He suffered a depressed skull fracture and significant underlying brain trauma. He was being kept asleep with medications for the time being, and the respirator was doing all his work of breathing.

His parents took up station at his bedside around the clock, and their ragged appearance was testament that they had hardly slept since the tragedy began. They introduced themselves and thanked the soldiers for all they did.

"Would you tell us what happened?" Jake asked as he held the boy's hand.

The boy's father answered. "From what we have been able to put together, he got scared and tried to run. Everyone was taken to the auditorium, and when the Persians began the process of…" his eyes were welling with tears, "of torturing and killing, Joey got scared and tried to run away. One of the soldiers hit him in the head with his pulsar. We were told he fell on the floor. Other than a few twitches he was motionless. After you took the auditorium, two of his friends picked him up and carried him out."

"I'm so sorry," Jake said. "Is there anything we can do?"

"No," he said. "You've already done so much." He had his arm around his wife. She was staring with an expression absolute in emptiness, the muscles on her face flat and inattentive.

"Ma'am," Jake said. "I'm so sorry."

She turned toward him. There was a quick confused smile as though she was working to process his words. Then, with a voice that barely managed to fight past the press of sadness, she asked, "How could you have let them come over here and do this to my baby?"

"No," her husband snapped. He put his hands on her shoulders and gently turned her away from the Guardsmen. "Honey," he said, "we talked about this." He turned back to address the Guardsmen, saying, "I'm sorry." Fresh tears were flowing down his cheeks. "We appreciate everything you have done. We wouldn't have Joey if it weren't for you. This has been a very difficult time. We haven't slept in days. I hope you understand."

The nurse stepped in at that point and expertly massaged the rest of the visit. A couple minutes later they backed out of the room and went to the next child on the list. The hospital was filled with numerous gut-wrenching stories. Several dozen children and adults, out for a wonderful and educational day at the museum, were now dead. Four more had died in the hospital. Nineteen were currently in the intensive care units, and a total of seventy-four were still hospitalized. All they wanted to do was learn about the long extinct dinosaurs, the great reptilian monsters that once roamed the earth. What they got instead was a lesson about modern day monsters who attack and sadistically murder the weakest.

Following the bedside visits everyone gathered in the cafeteria. It was the largest open room the hospital had. The tables and chairs had been cleared to one side to make room for everyone. A small minority of the parents thought that it would be too psychologically traumatic for their children to see the soldiers so soon. A significant fraction of those sent a representative parent. Others came as a family group. The room was filled with kids. Some were in wheelchairs, and others were on crutches. There were balloons, several clowns, and a couple jugglers, all of them utilizing unique and wild holographic imagery as part of their acts. On the whole, it was a festive and upbeat atmosphere.

The Guardsmen were swarmed by autograph seekers and smothered with hugs and kisses and other diverse expressions of appreciation. Several received on-the-spot marriage proposals from random women. As the event morphed into something he hadn't envisioned, Jake suffered mixed feelings. It was supposed to be about the kids, not about Alpha Group. He struggled to wrap his head around what he was witnessing, trying to comprehend the needs of the kids and their parents. He came to the conclusion a natural part of their recovery had to include an opportunity to express their emotions, and that was true of his men as well.

Jake extracted himself from the event as much as he could and quietly observed from the side of the room. What he witnessed was humbling. The kids were far more resilient than he anticipated. Some were laughing with the clowns while others were transfixed, completely mesmerized by the jugglers who were engaged in wild acrobatics in conjunction with visual distortions generated by their holographic imagery. He felt the touch of joy and couldn't help chuckling as he watched their expressions go from eyes-wide anticipation to giant smiles. Then there were the interactions with his soldiers. The children weren't shy. Across the room they were slapping hands and pulling on pant legs. At that moment, Jake felt the intense stab of being alone and homesick.

"Quite an event."

Jake turned. It was Alex. He nodded. "Reckon it turned out well."

"That has to be the understatement of the year. I'm proud of you. It was the right thing to do, and you're the one we have to thank for making it happen."

"You know," Jake said, "Seeing the kids with their families…it brings perspective back doesn't it?"

"That it does. We'd do well to remember it. It's a good reminder what we're fighting for."

"Can I have everyone's attention?" The announcement came from Beverly Ashton. She was speaking into a microphone from the front of the room. She introduced herself as the hospital's Chief Operations Officer. She thanked everyone for coming, expressed some profound words, and then went on, "We have a special treat for everyone. I was personally informed that we have a musician among us. One of these amazing Guardsmen, one who has touched all of our lives in so many ways, has another talent that he might be willing to share with us." She was handed a guitar. "I'm told he loves playing the guitar, he sings, and he's quite good. I was also told that if we put our hands together and clap, we might convince him to sing some of his favorites for us." Everyone clapped enthusiastically.

Jake didn't want to entertain the thought of what might be coming. He figured he was being paranoid and blew off the notion. Beverly asked, "Is Lieutenant Colonel Jake Gillean here?" When he heard his name actually mentioned in association with singing songs for everyone, he was taken off guard. Jake's dumbfounded expression turned Alex's face red with laughter.

As Jake was being encouraged to the front of the room, he saw more military teeth than the division dentist saw in a month as his laughing men joyously encouraged him. They were delighted to see, for the first time ever, a surprised expression on Lt. Col. Gillean. Despite his lack of preparation, he was absolutely confident. Jake wasn't a novice when it came to playing in front of people and once his mind settled around the idea, he was determined to put on a good show.

To the delight of everyone, he began strumming the guitar and broke into a popular country song from Tennessee. His deep voice was smooth and confident, and his choice proved to be a big hit. When he finished, he dedicated it to the memory of everyone "who was now in a better place… holding hands with God." He named the Guardsmen who were killed and those who were wounded. As he talked, he conveyed the message that what they would want most is for everyone to cultivate happiness and choose to live the best life possible.

While strumming the chords of the next song, Jake explained that the Guardsmen of Alpha Group had loved-ones waiting for them at home, that many were married, and many of them had children. He explained they were terribly homesick as they hadn't seen their families in a very long time. Earlier that morning, they were finally granted leave by the President, but before they left, being the true soldiers they were, his men chose to visit the hospital, and that they believed the kids were the greatest heroes of all.

Jake was completely at ease entertaining the group. After he finished the song, he introduced the next as being a piece he wrote for his children. He guessed out loud that they wouldn't object if he shared it with them. "This one," he said, "is dedicated to Alpha Group. It's a song about them, and now I offer it for them. I hope you like it." The song started out with a catchy swinging beat. He was humming and then broke into song. His voice would build up to a crescendo and drop down for the chorus. The lyrics were hysterical. It was about a big, ugly, sweaty, and smelly Guardsman who could only scratch and grunt, "*Uh-huh* and *Hoo-rah!*" Everyone loved it.

CHAPTER 21: HEALTHY BODY/ UNHEALTHY MIND

[APRIL 16, AD 2441]
[136 DAYS AFTER ARRIVAL, ONE DAY AFTER LEAVING LAKE TAHOE AND ONE DAY AFTER DIRECTOR ZIMMER'S MEETING WITH PRICILLA KYTE]
[LOCATION: RENO, NEVADA]

The incredible city of Reno was the latest stop in their move through the underworld. Ben secured visitors' passes at a local back-alley gym. Jake stretched and got on a treadmill. He found a pace he liked, about seven minutes per mile, and knocked off a ten-mile run. For the last mile, he sped up to a pace of five minutes per mile. This was still significantly slower than he once was and required a greater effort, at least in comparison to his days with Alpha Group. Nevertheless, he was getting back his old form.

The series of clandestine injections he was given when he was in the New Bethesda Hospital ICU were responsible for the rapidity of his recovery. Thanks to MST's biomedical research and their covert operations, he was approaching peak condition. However, he continued to be haunted by the terrible flashbacks and nightmares. While Jake wasn't given a choice, his mental torment was a price MST had to pay to achieve their objectives.

After running, Jake was throwing the weights around as though gravity had little to do with it. He was doing something called the nonroutine routine, meaning he would shock his body by bouncing between very different routines. Today's workout was heavier weights and lower repetitions. He had three hundred and eighty pounds on the bar and would crank out five bench presses followed by a series of five to ten reps of lat pull-downs. He'd take a drink and a minute later, repeat the whole series. After he did that a total of four times, he would move to a different set of lifts that focused on the opposing muscle groups–biceps and triceps, hamstrings and quadriceps, and abdominals and low back.

The previous day, Jake told the story about the museum and visiting the children in the hospital. He hadn't said much since then, and Ben found him difficult to read. The only real conclusion Ben had come to at this point was that Jake was fundamentally different in dire ways compared to the person being progressively chiseled out of his life story. As they hammered away the layers Ben couldn't help thinking about the statues left unfinished after the death of Michelangelo, figures that appeared to be emerging from blocks of marble, blocks that had imprisoned them, hiding them from view. He considered Jake to be like those statues and he was determined to set him free.

"Can I get a spot?" Ben asked. Jake moved behind the bench and Ben cranked out his set. Jake reached in and helped him get the last two reps up, and after the bar was secure in the rack he went back to his own bench.

Ben had to consciously fight the urge to skip ahead, to ask Jake about his experiences in the 1800s and what had happened to him right before he materialized in Franklin. His directives from MST were clear...Jake had to tell his story from the very beginning. Clues to what ultimately went wrong may have developed years, or even decades, before he took his leap through time. The stakes were too high, and AF20 explicitly stated they couldn't risk missing something important.

Ben sat on the end of his bench resting between sets. He contemplated what might be going on in Jake's head. Jake's disposition indicated that he was in a foul mood. He appeared little more than a machine—a stoic unfeeling machine. Yet this was the same person who wept in the end zone when his father died, the same person who put his life on the line to rescue the little girl and stood with her in the fountain, and he was also the same person who sang for everyone at the hospital. Jake indicated he used to have strong spiritual convictions. But now, Ben wasn't quite so sure. After the incident with Quinn, the minister at the rehab facility, and the anger that talk of God had caused, he chose to avoid bringing up the subject. It appeared Jake had rejected everything he believed in. 'He's so angry,' Ben mulled, 'and I get the impression that a lot of it is directed at God. What possibly could have happened that would have pushed him to this...to the point of such utter coldness?' For now though, he decided to keep his thoughts to himself. There'd be a more appropriate time to address those issues. Whatever the conflict was, Ben could see it swirling right under the surface, tearing at Jake in cruel ways.

"Spot," he said. Jake moved behind the bench as Ben laid back and did another set of presses. For now he'd be patient and let Jake tell his story.

A couple of the regular meatheads at the gym were getting their feelings hurt. "That's our bench," one of them commented under his breath.

"I know. I don't like waiting," the other said. "He's been on it for a long time…too long."

They were in good shape and took pride in the physical prowess they had over the regular gym crowd. Having staked out their place at the top of the food chain, they weren't taking kindly to having some stranger challenge their alpha status. Jake had entered their world and was turning heads. He was lifting more weight and with good form. On top of that, his appearance was intimidating. He had grown a moustache and goatee. Just like the hair on his head, his facial hair was blond with some brown and a few grays mixed in, and was neatly trimmed. With the remaining scars on his face that hadn't been completely treated, the ones across his shoulder, forearm, and lower extremities, and his mangled right hand with the missing 4th and 5th fingers, he looked every bit the Viking warrior. Everyone wondered what his story was, but no one dared ask. His demeanor was unmistakable, warning that he wanted to be left alone. That much everyone noted…except the two meatheads.

Behind the façade, Jake's mind was in a constant battle for control. He lay on the bench and positioned himself for the next lift. He found the proper place for his hands, tensed up under the bar, and just before he lifted it off the rack his mind suffered another flashback. He was on a battlefield during the Civil War. His heart was racing and he broke out in a sweat. Just as quickly, he flashed back to the gym. He was under the bar and squeezing it with all his might, unsure just how long his mind had been gone.

After completing his set, Jake walked away to get a drink. As soon as his back was turned, the two meatheads swarmed his bench and started unloading the bar. They began putting on their own combination of weights.

"Hey, I don't think he's done with that," Ben interjected.

"He's done," one of them sneered.

"Oh, boy," Ben exclaimed. He knew what was going to happen. Jake had only been gone for a minute when he returned to discover that the local muscle had commandeered his bench. From the expression on Jake's face, Ben knew it wasn't going to be pretty.

Jake walked up to the meatheads and said, "Reckon you didn't see me using that." He waited to see which one of the two would answer.

"When we got here no one was using it," one of them responded. They continued setting up for their workout.

"I suggest you put the weights back like I had 'em." Jake wasn't in a negotiating mood.

The bigger of the two turned toward him. He was large, slightly taller, and bigger around the belly than Jake, but otherwise in good shape. He puffed up and moved in close. His eyes were aggressive and his face only a few inches from Jake's. He staked his claim and wasn't about to back down. "You're done. Take a walk," he said.

It happened so fast Ben almost missed it. As soon as the words came out of the meathead's mouth, Jake had him flying through the air. He smashed him down on the rubber mat and after kicking the other in the mid-section, sending him flying backward, his foot ended up on the side of meathead number one's face. His arm was extended outward and Jake had a vice-like grip on the man's wrist. He was twisting it with one hand while pointing at meathead number two with the other. He remained calm and in control, shaking his head to indicate that the friend would do well to keep his distance. "Like I was saying, I suggest you put the weights back like I had 'em." As he said it, he gave the wrist a sharp twist. The big man screamed. He was kicking and trying to get out of the hold. Jake twisted the wrist again, saying, "Squirm again and I'll break it." At the same time the meathead let out another higher-pitched scream. He was in agony and the harder he tried to get away the worse the pain became. Activity in the gym came to a screeching halt. Everyone was watching. Jake said, "Best tell your friend to get moving." He gave the wrist another twist.

"OOWW!" he yelled. "Hurry! Hurry! Put them back! You can have it! You can have it!" He screamed again, feeling the ligaments starting to tear. His friend was scampering to change the weights back to the way Jake had them.

"You got a little bit of bully in you don't you?" Jake said. He appeared calm and purposeful on the outside but on the inside he was furious. He was fighting the urge to kill. He twisted again, eliciting a loud scream. "Am I right? You a bully?"

"No! No!" he squealed.

Ben kicked away from his bench and stood as a sentry, making sure no one was coming to the meathead's defense. It was the first time he witnessed Jake in action. He had subdued his opponent as though it was nothing, and was fast beyond anything he had ever seen. Now he was in complete control.

Jake brought the man to his feet, had the arm twisted behind him with one hand and had the scruff of his neck secure in his grasp with the other. "My guess is that this isn't the first time you've stolen someone's bench. You're going to apologize to the good people in this gym," Jake said. He leaned in close and said something in the meathead's ear.

"I'm a bully!" he yelled. Jake said something again. The meathead screamed out, "I'm sorry! I'm a bully!" Jake was forcing him to apologize to the gym regulars. "I don't know my manners!" he yelled. Jake said something else and simultaneously twisted his wrist to the point that the ligaments were ripping away from the bones, the man screamed out. As he crumpled to his knees he cried, "I wear pretty little dresses! I wear pretty little dresses!"

The thirty people who were watching laughed and started clapping. "He is a bully," one of them proclaimed. "He deserves it," agreed another, "he's always pushing people out of the way." Still another chimed in with, "He's a jerk. Make him cry."

Jake felt the edge of his fury back off. There wasn't a challenge in this anymore and he was bored. He wanted to get back to his workout. He gave the wrist a final twist and leaned close. He whispered, "You made a wrong choice. Don't make two. I'm gonna turn you loose. I suggest you leave. Next time I'm going to kill you." Jake shoved him forward.

The meathead fell face first into the floor. His arm was behind his back. It was numb and he couldn't move it. He had been completely humiliated in an environment where he was king. His friend untwisted the arm and brought it to his side. He helped him up saying, "Come on. Let's get out of here." He struggled to his feet, staggered a few steps and turned toward Jake. For a moment his anger almost got the better of him. He contemplated going in for a second round. "No. He's crazy," his friend said. He pushed him away and they left the establishment.

Jake acted as though nothing happened. He unceremoniously went back to his bench and cranked out another set. The crowd of onlookers slowly dissipated, laughing and talking amongst themselves about what they had just witnessed.

Ben was ticked. He was staring with an incredulous expression. "What the hell was that?" he asked.

"Just a little horseplay," Jake responded.

"Horseplay? That's what you call horseplay?" Ben couldn't hold back his frustration. "You could have left it alone. I can't believe it…horseplay." He threw his hands in the air. Ben turned to walk away and whirled back. "Besides, what kind of jarhead uses the word horseplay?" He shook his head and said under his breath, "Dammit. How is that consistent with keeping a low profile?"

Jake casually shrugged his shoulders and chuckled, "I've always had a problem with bullies."

CHAPTER 22: GOING HOME

[JULY 6, 2379 A.D. (3 DAYS AFTER THE ATTACK ON THE MUSEUM)]
[ARRIVAL DATE MINUS 61 YEARS]
[LOCATION: PORTLAND, OREGON]

When the gathering at the hospital was over, the men loaded up and headed back to Hummings Air Force Base. They were emotionally drained after seeing what was left in the wake of the attack, but they were glad they went. What was most important was that the kids seemed to enjoy it.

After everyone departed and the two commanders were left alone in the hanger, Alex slapped Jake on the shoulder and said, "Does a turtle well to stick its head out once in a while." The comment was unexpected and abrupt. He added, "There's more to life than fighting. The songs you sang were good." He reached into the chest pocket of his coat and pulled out a thick envelope. He handed it to Jake. "Hope you don't mind. I took the liberty."

"What's this?" Jake looked inside. "You didn't have to do this," he said. There were four tickets to a large amusement park outside Nashville. It was expensive and had a well-established reputation across the entire country. There were also several dozen photos of the various rides. In addition, there were two tickets to a musical, a romantic comedy, in Nashville.

"I know. But I wanted to. Now don't feel obligated to go. I just thought it might be a fun thing for the family to do. Besides, Wendy deserves a night out with a gentleman, and since I won't be there I thought you might take her."

Jake laughed. "You put this together fast." He was referring to the fact that they were just informed they were getting two-weeks off.

"Rank has its privileges. Outside of hanging with you barbarians I happen to rub shoulders with some high-rollers and people of culture."

"You want to join us? Wendy would love to see you again." Jake asked knowing that Alex wasn't particularly close to what was left of his own family. A couple years back he actually took time to visit for a couple days when Alpha Group was on leave. So, the request certainly wasn't without precedent.

"No," Alex answered, "I have plans."

"Let me ask you something," Jake interjected. "I just spoke to the regional clinic administrator who manages Wendy's office. She already arranged a locum to cover her for the next two weeks. Said she was contacted earlier today by someone from the High Command. You wouldn't know anything about that would you?"

Alex smirked, holding back a grin. "Like I said...rank has its privileges."

Later that day, Jake's feet finally touched pavement in Nashville, Tennessee. It was approximately 1800 hours, and he was elated. The surprise and excitement in Wendy's voice when he told her he'd be home in time for a late dinner, and that she was off for the next two weeks, and all the arrangements had been made, just added to his anticipation.

The southern air was nothing less than exhilarating. It was hot. The temperature was in the mid-90s Fahrenheit. The air was so thick and sticky that everything was visibly blurred in the distance. The air smoldering above the pavement gave the illusion that the horizon was underwater. He was definitely home. His first breath conjured wonderful memories from his youth and young adult life. While he was ten thousand miles closer to home than he had been in almost two years, Jake was also now more homesick than ever before. He wished he could blink and be there. In that very instant he would leave the rest of the world's problems behind, Wendy would be in his arms, he would be swinging the kids through the air, and life would be normal.

The general policy was that members of The Guard ranked a vehicle and driver for their travels. It was a privilege representative of, but hardly commensurate with, the increased risks inherent to their jobs. His driver met him as he got off the plane. Looking every bit of sixteen years old and struggling valiantly to fill out his starched green uniform, the youth scanned the offloading passengers until he spotted his assigned Guardsman.

"Lieutenant Colonial Gillean?" he questioned. When he realized he had the right person he snapped a salute. "Sir." He had escorted generals and politicians but had never been more nervous than when he first laid eyes on the distinctive black uniform of an actual Guardsman, moreover, one wearing the Alpha Group insignia. Jake returned the salute.

"It's my pleasure to be your driver, sir."

"Take a deep breath, son." Jake strode past him carrying his military bag over his shoulder.

"Sir?" the young man asked, turning and trying to keep up with Jake's brisk pace.

"Take a deep breath," Jake repeated.

Though confused, he did as ordered.

"Do you know what that is?" Jake stopped and addressed him directly. "That there is Tennessee air. Enjoy it. There's nothing else like it in the entire world."

Jake took off his sunglasses and stared at the RG-43 Transport, the military pod that would be carrying him home. Private Robberson had the top up and the air conditioning on. "Son, this is completely unacceptable. Turn off that AC and take the top down. It's a sunny day, and I have every intention of enjoying it."

It was a standard military transport, green with rugged external features that were reminiscent of both its ancient ancestors; the truck and the jeep. But the interior features were more comfortable than one would expect for a vehicle of this sort. Resembling the inside of a sedan, it was visibly and palpably softer than its predecessor. Jake threw his gear in the back, where the passenger usually sat. He relaxed in the front passenger seat, contacted Wendy, and updated her regarding his progress toward home. His commanding exterior completely masked his internal excitement and nervous anticipation.

Once they started moving, Jake called the florist in Spring Hill. He ordered a dozen roses to be delivered to Wendy. He put an absolute rush on the order so she might get them before he arrived. When they discovered who it was on the other end of the communicator he heard high-pitched girly screams of excitement. Jake was confused by the behavior and even more so when the owner broke into the conversation and refused to accept his payment. He assured Jake that Wendy would be pleased, and he should trust them to take care of everything.

Jake ordered the driver to make a quick stop at a toy store on the outskirts of Nashville. He wanted to pick up some things for the kids. The manager noticed him immediately. She recognized him from the Vintel footage of the tragedy in Portland. She approached and asked if he was involved in the museum rescue. He said, "I was." She asked if he was the soldier with the little girl in the fountain. When he again confirmed her suspicions she screamed excitedly, jumping up and down in short little hops, flailing her arms and flopping her wrists. Jake was taken aback, not realizing what a national sensation he had become. She rushed to make an announcement over the store's PA system. Everyone forgot what they were doing and rushed to see the famous Guardsman. Then she had the store employees scatter to pick out the most popular age appropriate gifts for his children.

Once Jake made it to the registers, the manager refused to allow him to pay for the toys, informing him that one of the customers, someone who wished to remain anonymous, had already paid for everything…as a small token of appreciation for Jake's service to their country. The crowd clapped, and he signed several autographs. Jake was embarrassed and didn't know what to make of it, but it felt good. He played along, shook hands, and posed for pictures.

"Thank you," he said. "I appreciate your kindness." He smiled, waved, and shook a few more hands as he exited the store.

Soon thereafter he was on the road. The back seat filled with toys.

"You're famous sir," the driver said. By the expression on Jake's face it was obvious he had no idea what Private Robberson was talking about. "Don't you know sir? You're all over the Vintel. First it was you in the fountain with the little girl. Haven't you seen it?"

"I haven't," Jake responded. It was unusual for a Private to be so talkative with a superior officer, but being the hyper type of guy who enjoyed filling every last second with jabber, Private Robberson found his groove. Jake wanted to tell him to shut up, but he was in a good mood and what the young soldier had to say was interesting.

"You should see it sir. It's actually very moving. Everyone's talking about it. And now everyone's talking about the other footage."

"Other footage?" Jake asked.

"At the hospital, singing songs. It's all over the Vintel. The funny song about the soldier…I laughed out loud. You're famous."

Jake was speechless. He didn't expect there to be any recording devices there, he certainly didn't see any, and it was only a few hours ago. His frustration was mounting. The military had rules about this sort of thing, and although he was completely innocent, there would likely be hell to pay back at Central Command. Some rear echelon wuss who never heard a pulsar fired in anger was likely going to raise a complaint. He'd be asked questions about the whole affair, and while he was sure he'd be exonerated from any wrongdoing, it was going to be a headache, and he'd have to put together an official report. Documentation of the whole thing was going to make its way into his personnel file.

By now they were heading south, and the historic city of Franklin was disappearing behind them. The next stop was home…Spring Hill, Tennessee. Between Nashville and Franklin, Jake had ordered Private Robberson to observe some silence, and now he instructed him to lock the computer guidance system at 50 kilometers per hour. He wanted to soak up the scenery. He sat back and gazed at the passing countryside. To him, it was the most beautiful place in the world. But he couldn't fight the nagging sensation that something very important had been irretrievably altered. Something just didn't feel right. There was a vague weight of sorts that was progressively pressing down as he got closer to home. He couldn't exactly describe it. It was new to him. He definitely wasn't the same person who grew up here. For that matter, he wasn't even the same person who last made it home two years ago. After everything he had seen and done, he felt as though he was somehow contaminated, and he was about to bring something home that was going to infect the purity of his family. Something within him that was good and innocent had been lost, while something cold and callous had been gained.

As the houses rolled by, he recollected how naïve he had been about the rest of the world. He recalled the unbridled optimism he once had when he looked out from his protected perch in Spring Hill. Now that he had actually experienced what the world had to offer, his perspective was different. He had become hard and unbending. He wondered if people in his hometown were still as naïve as he had been. All of his beliefs except one had been destroyed by the long series of traumatic and violent experiences. Only one remained solid and found constant reinforcement—that it was a glorious blessing to be born and raised and have a beautiful family waiting for him in the great State of Tennessee.

Some things were different than he remembered. The greens were just a little bit greener. The fields seemed bigger. Even the road was wider. The sky was not only bluer….but bigger and more expansive. Was it that things had changed? Or was it him? Had military service altered his memories, had it so skewed his perspective that he could hardly recognize the world of his youth? Regardless, a progressive joy and permanent grin softened his chiseled features as he got closer to home.

"Look at that Lieutenant Colonel," the driver exclaimed.

Large banners and posters were in place along the sides of the roadway. Everyone had discovered he was coming home. In large brilliant letters: WELCOME HOME JAKE, WE MISS YOU, THANK YOU LT. COL. JAKE GILLEAN. Other versions of the same message lined the roadway. One read: OUR FOOTBALL TEAM NEEDS YOU!!! Two sets of aunts and uncles, several cousins, and dozens of old friends were waiting along the edge of the road in front of their respective homes. When they saw the military vehicle approaching, they waved frantically. The kids added immensely to the excitement, frantically jumping up and down. Feeding off the enthusiasm and energy of the adults, they had no qualms about jumping, screaming, and shouting for someone they had never met.

Their imaginations went wild as the driver laid on the horn and the great homegrown soldier and hero whom they had heard so much about waved at them. They were in a state of awe as the vehicle went by, and they stared until it disappeared over the horizon.

Wendy and the kids were on the front porch anxiously waiting. They weren't waiting for a soldier or a hero…they were waiting for a husband and a father. Wendy got several quick calls notifying her that he had just passed a certain neighbor's house up the road. All of a sudden, in the very great distance, the kids could make out, albeit very faintly, the intermittent blowing of a horn. Each time it gradually grew louder.

Wendy wasn't going to cry. She scolded herself over and over; Jake didn't want to see her cry, especially right when he got home. But the instant she saw the RG-43 pull up the drive, there was an explosion of such overwhelming joy that the tears were freely streaming. It had been almost two years, and he was finally home.

The vehicle wasn't even close to stopping when his door flew open. He was out on the ground running toward her, and in another instant, she was in his arms. They embraced and kissed, again and again. The surrounding world faded into nothing and exploded into everything. They were at the epicenter of the universe with everything swirling around…time stopped in their embrace. The driver didn't bother to stop the engine. He unloaded Jake's gear and the presents, placing them on the sidewalk. He sheepishly waved at the kids and left.

Bailey and Paul patiently waited. On one level, Paul wanted to know his father, but on another level he was scared. Sure, there were the conversations on the phone and the video feeds on the Vintel. There were photographs and mailed presents. But this was altogether different. This was real and very personal—his father was a stranger. From Paul's perspective he was huge and scary, and he was kissing and hugging Mommy.

Unable to contain herself any longer, Bailey rushed forward and wrapped her arms around their legs. For a moment, Jake held Wendy tightly in his embrace, then he hugged Bailey. He spun her through the air and kissed her again and again. He told her how much he missed her and loved her. He blew bubbles on her neck and spun her around again, He kissed her some more while she laughed and giggled. For her, it was almost as though he had never left.

Wendy noticed Paul's fidgeting confusion. She picked him up and whispered, "It's Daddy, Paul. It's Daddy." Usually the outgoing type, he was overcome with apprehension. When Jake was ready for him, Paul chose instead to bury his face in Wendy's neck.

Jake halfway expected Paul to be overwhelmed. He didn't want to get in his personal space right away. He smiled at Wendy, knowing exactly how to handle the awkwardness of the situation. "Do you know where Paul is?" he asked. He turned to Bailey, "Do you know where Paul is? I have something for him, but I don't know where he is."

"He's right there."

"Where?"

"Right there," Bailey exclaimed. "Right there in Mommy's arms." She was excitedly pointing and jumping up and down.

"No way. Paul isn't near that big. Look at how big those muscles are. That can't be Paul."

"That's Paul," she excitedly repeated.

"Are you sure?"

"Yes, Daddy. He's all grown up. He's almost four."

"Okay," Jake finally agreed. He laughed and kissed Paul on top of the head, before ruffling his hair, messing it up like only a father can. "Paul, would you like to help us? You see, I have that big ol' bag and all these presents for you and your sister. I can carry the bag but I need help with the rest."

Paul's head shot up. He saw the other soldier stacking the boxes up, he thought they looked like toys, but now it was official...and they were for him.

"Some are kind of heavy and might take both of you." Jake grabbed his bag, throwing it over his shoulder.

Bailey scampered to grab one of the boxes. She looked at the front with wild excitement and said excitedly, "Paul look! Come here! Come here! Mommy look! It's the Hologram 3 game system!" She went to another box, "It's the Molly Holly Dolly!" She was excited beyond measure.

Paul scampered down from the protection of his mommy's arms. He was still growing into his head and as a result of his load being rather top-heavy, his head appeared to be leading him down the sidewalk, with his body following along behind as though it had no choice in the matter. His momentum changed only when he distinctly planted one foot far out in front, at which point he executed a seamless pivot. He eyeballed the pile of toys and then joined Bailey in the excitement.

Inside the house, Jake discovered that the florist had delivered five times more flowers than he ordered. Ornate displays of roses, tulips, daisies, orchids, and some others he couldn't identify covered the dining room table and overflowed onto the kitchen island.

"Wow!" he exclaimed when he saw the extent of the flowers.

"You are amazing," she said as she moved into his arms. They embraced and kissed again.

"I've got news," Jake said.

Wendy looked quizzical.

"I talked to your clinic administrator. You have the next two weeks off work."

"I know!" she exclaimed. "Did you think of everything?"

"To tell you the truth, arrangements were already made when I called. We have Alex to thank for that. But I did think of a few things." He reached into the chest pocket of his officer's dress coat and pulled out a box. "This is a little something for you."

"Oh Jake," she exclaimed when she opened it. "You shouldn't have." It was a necklace, beautiful and ornate, black pearls set in gold, elegant but not pretentious or ostentatious.

"It comes apart so the black pearls can be changed out with white. I've been carrying it with me for over a year. Hope you don't mind that I didn't send it. I wanted to put it on you myself." He took it in his hands and motioned for her to turn around. He carefully put it around her neck and fastened the clasp. He gently grasped her shoulders and turned her around so he could see it. Jake smiled, "You make it absolutely beautiful." She swooned as he kissed her again.

By this time, the kids had brought several of the presents into the house and were anxiously trying to get them out of the boxes. Jake stopped them. He gathered everyone around. Getting down on his knees to be eye level with the kids, he produced the amusement park tickets, along with pictures showing how much fun they were going to have. Jake told them it was a gift from their Uncle Alex. They squealed in excitement.

Thirty minutes later, the opened presents were all over the house, and the living room was a wreck. There were two spectacular dolls, books, and holographic characters were running and dancing through the house. There were ball gloves for both of them, baseball bats, and a starter set of golf clubs. However, despite everything they had, Paul was fixated on a drum. He was banging it with both sticks and making a thunderous racket.

Wendy's eyes opened wide when she first saw the drum. "Oh Jake, you are so out of practice," she laughed. Very soon the drum would disappear into the far off land where all noisy toys went, never to be seen or heard from again, but for the moment, everything was wonderful.

Jake watched them from the comfort of his favorite chair. There was a time when Wendy wanted to get rid of it because it didn't match the rest of their furniture. But Jake successfully made an emotional appeal in its defense. It was granted a fortuitous reprieve based upon being re-upholstered to her specifications. It was the favorite chair of his father and a prized family heirloom from Janet's side of the family. In fact, Thomas endured some of his toughest battles with multiple sclerosis while sitting in the chair.

Nobody was allowed to sit in it because it was Jake's special chair. Wendy thought it would be good for the kids to realize that the chair belonged to their father. It served as a tangible reminder that he was coming back home and that the family was incomplete without him. After telling the kids about it so many times, it was surreal to actually see him sitting in it. It was like King Odysseus returning to sit upon his throne. Wendy sat on his lap for a long time, talking for what seemed hours. The kids would look up occasionally from their play and spy them kissing. They had no previous experience with their mother being so deliriously happy. Their world was finally awash in feelings of complete safety and family togetherness.

Wendy momentarily vacated her spot. She hadn't made it entirely out of the room when Paul seized his opportunity. He didn't say a word and made a conscious effort to avoid eye contact, but he climbed up on Jake's lap. With a locomotive from a train set in his right hand and a boxcar in the other, he was no longer interested in playing. After nestling in he stared off, sinking into the deep thoughts of a three, almost four, year-old boy. Once in a while, he would reexamine the train engine and work its wheels with his finger. With one of his arms wrapped around his son, and his hand resting on Paul's knee, Jake kissed his head and told him that he loved him. He asked him some questions about the trains. Paul answered cautiously. He would emerge from his shell at his own pace.

To Paul's chagrin Bailey climbed up and sat on Jake's other leg. In return she got the same affection. Both were safe and comfortable and neither could ever imagine getting down.

When Wendy returned to the room, she took pause. There was an aura around her husband. She could perceive it around the children as well, but theirs was healthy and vibrant, Jake's wasn't. His was tired and dark. 'He'll be okay,' she said to herself, 'we'll get him back.' She went to the chair and knelt on the floor, leaning against his legs. Their world had achieved absolute perfection. She had her husband. They had their father. And he had his family.

CHAPTER 23: RELIVING THE EXPERIENCE

[APRIL 17, AD 2441; EARLY MORNING]
[137 DAYS AFTER ARRIVAL, ONE DAY AFTER THE ALTERCATION AT THE GYM IN RENO]
[LOCATION: SOUTHERN CALIFORNIA]

After the altercation in the gym, Ben didn't think it would be prudent to remain in Reno. He plotted a trip south to Phoenix, keeping off the main roads and maintaining a speed just under the limit. He closed his eyes and fell asleep in the driver's seat. It was about 0400, and they were in the vicinity of Death Valley National Park, just skirting the west side of the park.

'There has to be something here. What am I missing?' Jake thought as he reviewed the files stored on his BCD. He was looking at November 30, 1864. He was reliving the Battle of Franklin. There were explosions all around him, the cacophony of the blasts was swirling in deadly concert with screams from the wounded and dying. It was a bloody nightmare. He concentrated, working hard to remain detached from an experience that completely consumed him just five short months ago. There had to be a clue buried somewhere. If he was going to have any hope of finding it, he would have to stay focused. He adjusted the spectral overlays and replayed the scene, searching for some unknown anomaly.

Jake winced as he watched the recording. It was an unconscious reaction. He was being progressively pulled into the experience. He was no longer in the pod. He was on horseback. He was riding Balius and could feel the rhythmic motion and the hardness of the saddle. They were approaching the Union entrenchments. As the battle recording was unfolding, Jake succumbed entirely to the experience and was drowning in the emotional trauma he felt that terrible day. It was unrelenting and unmerciful. He was

298

struck by a bullet. He felt it searing through his flesh. It happened again and again. Balius was struck. A cannon ball took off one of the animal's front legs and he lurched to the side. He was struggling and bellowing, but miraculously managed to stay upright. Despite terrible wounds, Jake's loyal warhorse supported him, refusing to go down.

While Ben was sleeping, Jake broke out in a sweat. His heart was racing. The anguish he felt was overwhelming. He had failed. His mission to save his family had failed. They were gone. They would never get a chance to live. They were lost to humanity forever. Jake's mind screamed out in pain and agony. He was powerless and alone. At the moment he should have died, the BCD recording registered a glitch of unknown origin, some sort of electromagnetic or static pulse. He was suddenly at the reenactment… in the Twenty-Fifth Century. He had inexplicably leapt forward across six hundred years of time. He replayed the scene over and over again. It always ended the same…with no clues as to why or how.

Jake couldn't take it anymore. His mind was exploding from the trauma, his heart was pounding the drumbeat of war, and his soul was screaming out to the heavens. It was building to a crescendo when the experience suddenly burst. He grasped the door handle and squeezed. He couldn't quell the raw emotions or the intensity of his loss. He felt exactly as he did that terrible day…the day he lost everyone he ever loved.

"Pull over!" Jake yelled. His tone was one of panic.

Ben jumped, startled out of a deep sleep. "What?" he blurted.

"Pull over!" Jake had to escape the confines of the pod.

Still not comprehending, Ben hit the manual override and abruptly slammed on the brakes. The pod screeched and lurched sideways, fishtailing in loose gravel. It finally came to a halt after skidding off the edge of the unkempt rural roadway.

Jake jumped out and in the cloud of dust began pacing. 'No! No! No!' his mind screamed, 'What have I done? What have I done?' He was losing his grip on reality, intermingling with the edges of insanity. He wanted to scream. The tears were ready to burst. He'd collapse to his knees and weep. But instead he felt a surge of anger. It was upon him, racing in to protect him, to help him redirect a terrible pain that had to be unleashed. He felt like he was in the very pit of hell. He had to strike something, or someone, anything to relieve the pain. He directed the intensity of his rage on the front of the pod. He yelled out and smashed his fist down against the metal, the blow leaving a deep dent. He punched it again and again, pounding his fists and forearms against the shell that encased the battery compartment, the pain and agony of his loss and the torture of his conscience coming out in the wrath of each blow.

By the time he finished, the entire front of the vehicle was rumpled and caved in. The intensity of the moment began retracting and the reality of Jake's surroundings began taking form. He leaned across the hood. All he could think about was his family. Wendy, Bailey, and Paul. They didn't exist. They were wiped from the record of humanity. They never existed and it was his fault. The reality of the crime cut with incomprehensible cruelty. Jake's next realization was Ben kicking the side of the pod. It was rocking back and forth and the door on the driver's side was covered in little dents.

When Jake recovered enough to speak he asked, "What are you doing?"

Ben stopped and gazed at Jake with a confused expression. He blurt out, "Whatever this pod did to you, I'm going to kick its ass!"

Jake ignored Ben's comment and sank onto the hood. He put his face in his hands. "What is wrong with me?" he muttered. "How could it have come to this?"

He felt the pod shake as Ben gave it a final kick, "Bastard!" he yelled.

Jake found the intended edge of humor. "Okay. I get it," he said. "I want some answers."

"Ask away," Ben said. "But do you mind telling me what set you off?"

"Was reviewing some files."

"Heavy stuff?"

"You could say that," Jake answered.

"Fair enough. If you don't mind, if you do that again, would you give me some sort of warning? I can't help you if I don't know what's going on, and you almost gave me a heart attack."

"Fair enough."

"Good," Ben said. "Now, you want some answers. I'll tell you everything you want to know." Ben wasn't surprised. He knew Jake had a personal agenda. As a matter of fact, at this point in time that's all he had. But Ben wasn't ready to reveal everything he already knew about Jake, his travel through time, and his ultimate connections to MST. He needed just a few more days before he'd lay everything he knew on the line. He'd reveal secrets that were going to shock Jake into the harsh reality of what his life really was and what it had become.

"How are you going to help me?"

"What do you want?"

"What the hell do you mean…what do I want?" Jake said. "I want my life back!"

"Is that what you really want?" Ben asked. He kept his voice calm and soothing. "After everything you've been through, what you want more than anything else is to have *your* life back?" Ben was careful. He had to make a play for time and make Jake think that it was his choice.

"Dammit!" Jake said, still feeling volatile. "Do you have to psychoanalyze everything? Yes. I want my life back!"

"Come on, Jake. Look who you're talking to. The year is 2441. Be realistic. You leapt through time, not once, but twice. No one can explain that. It can't be duplicated. You're the only person in the history of the world who has ever done that."

"I'm not the only one," Jake commented.

Ben felt his heart skip a beat in excitement. It was the first time he heard Jake directly admit that he wasn't alone. But it wasn't time to discuss that… not yet. Ben calmly redirected, "I go back to my original question…what do you really want?"

"You're right," Jake finally confessed, his tone turning calm and introspective. "I don't want my life back. Not anymore. There was a time when that's all I wanted. But everything changed. Now my life doesn't really matter that much. It's theirs that matter. All I want is my family to have the opportunity to live out their lives." He paused, struggling to find the right words. "Every single night," he said, "I have nightmares. During the day, all I can think about is the life I was supposed to live sixty-two years ago. It's the same thing—just one long nightmare. My family is gone, Ben. Do you understand what I'm saying? I loved them with everything I've got and now they're gone. They never existed because of me, because of what happened. I'm exhausted, and I want some answers." The muscles in his cheeks were rhythmically bulging with tension. "How can you possibly help me fix this?"

Ben held up his hands in an effort to calm Jake down. "Okay," he said. "Here's how we'll play this. I'll tell you the plan as I've formulated it, and if you disagree, we'll do it your way."

Jake didn't respond.

"I think you somehow managed to take a leap through time," Ben began. "You went back to the 1800s, you lived in some capacity during the Civil War, and you somehow took a second leap through time and boomeranged back, but you overshot your own time and landed here. I don't know why or how it happened, but something went wrong either before you went back in time or when you were living in the 1800s. There are clues in your story, and if we piece together all the details of your life and your experiences, it'll help us find the mistake, or mistakes as the case may be."

Ben kept his voice as smooth and persuasive as possible, "Jake, I would sacrifice my life to help you but my motivations aren't necessarily the same as yours. My intentions from the very beginning have been to tell you exactly what I'm after and what others working with me might be able to do to help you, but I want to tell you everything else I have at the right time. All I can do is ask you to tell me your story up until the point that you took your first leap through time. At that moment I'll reveal everything and you can make your choice, and you can walk away if you want. I'm part of an organization Jake…a secret organization completely separate from the Egalitarian Party and the United American Government. I understand what you're after. You want to restore your family back to their rightful place in history. I think we can help you. In fact, I give you my word that we will help…or we'll die trying."

In an outward expression of his inner turmoil, Jake brought his hands up to the sides of his head. "Just until I traveled back?" he asked.

"Yeah," Ben said. "Then I tell you everything."

Jake hesitated. He knew he couldn't fix things on his own. He needed help. At the same time, in the deepest recesses of his sixth sense, he was being prodded by the thought that Ben was trustworthy. There was something vague about him, some primordial memory, or maybe he reminded him of someone. He couldn't quite put a finger on it. "Okay," Jake agreed, "I'll tell you what happened."

CHAPTER 24: RIPPED APART

While World War IV was spiraling out of control on the other side of the planet, unseen eyes in Spring Hill, Tennessee, were watching Lt. Col. Jake Gillean. They quietly observed, always there, always watching. Jake had a crucial role to play in a grand performance and MST was determined that he see it through.

It was Jake's tenth glorious day with family. When the incoming message flashed in his BCD, he had no reason to suspect that anything was amiss. The auditory alert and the projected digital display indicated that its origin was Central Command in New Washington. That wasn't unusual. It was protocol. They contacted him daily. The last thing he expected, considering everything Alpha Group had endured and what they had done for their country, was that his two week reprieve was going to be cut short. Fourteen days. Two weeks. It was that simple…but in a world being torn apart by war, it was far more complicated than that. Now more than ever United America needed its most elite soldiers. In terms of the military's priorities, the well being of the Gillean family just was not that important. More sacrifice was needed.

The implications of Alpha Group's immediate recall registered subconsciously a split second before he fully comprehended what was being ordered. In the mere moment between, Jake's mind went on a journey and he relived the wonder and merriment of the previous ten days.

* * * * *

"It doesn't get any easier," Wendy said. Her answer was in response to Jake's inquiry about how his absence was affecting the family. "I thought it would, but it doesn't. Being your wife is a challenge."

"Tell me," Jake said. He was fingering the brass base of one of the candles as they spoke. The kids were asleep. Except for the flickering of the flames, the room was dark. They were deeply immersed in what Wendy referred to as a *marital status report*. They had a right to know exactly what was going on in the heart of the other so they might steer the marriage through all its challenges. As such, a marital status report was a time of openness between husband and wife, a time to reveal and a time to be completely genuine.

"Looking back," she said, "I don't think I really appreciated how hard it was going to be. So much of our life is being spent apart that I feel like a single parent. At times I feel so lonely, but when I hear from you, and especially now that you're here, I feel this incredible spasm of happiness."

"And when you don't hear from me?"

Wendy extended her fingers and put her palms down on the dark surface of the dining room table. "I worry. I wonder what you're doing and where you are. I worry about your safety." Despite almost a decade of loneliness, Wendy bore her crosses with dignity and resilience, and she didn't take her blessings for granted. She went on, "Every day there's the stress of not knowing how you are and fear that something bad is going to happen. That you might die." Jake didn't react to her revelation. She went on, "It's always there. We pray all the time. But the time between our conversations is very hard for me...it's hard for all of us. I try to fight the fear that something bad has happened, but I'm not always successful."

"Are you keeping the faith?" he asked.

"I am. I do my best to help the kids along. We pray every night at dinner and again before bed. We talk about God quite often, and we talk to God in our own ways."

"Do you mind if I ask what you pray for?"

Wendy smiled. "We pray for you, of course. For your safety and your faith. We pray that, with all the terrible things you must be seeing and the things you have to go through, that you stay strong...that you don't get lost and lose your way. And we pray for the strength and wisdom to make it through each day, and for this war to end and all the suffering to give way to something else...like healing."

"Are there times when you cry?" Jake asked.

"I do," she admitted. "Sometimes more than others. I try to hide it, but there are occasions when I break down in front of the kids."

"How do they respond?"

"We cry together. I think they cry because they don't like to see me cry.

But we talk about it, about how we're feeling and why, and afterward we do okay for a while."

As his wife spoke, Jake was reminded of the true depth of her strength. She had never been afraid of embracing her emotions, yet she was steady, unswerving, and rational. She would always see her way through. He understood that while he was the brawn, Wendy was the family captain. She would fight, claw, bite, and do whatever it might take to see the family through stormy waters.

Jake wanted to reach across the table and touch her hands, to hold them, but physical contact was against her *rules of engagement* whenever they were having a session. She maintained that it interrupted her ability to accurately communicate what she was feeling. "What do you want?"

"I want you. I want you to be here and for you to be safe."

"I know that," Jake said, "but why? I mean what is it exactly that you want, you know, on a deeper level?"

It wasn't from a position of weakness that Wendy wished for Jake's return. What she longed for was the existential joy of being with her husband, best friend, confidant, and soul mate. After considering his question she answered, "I want Bailey and Paul to fall asleep at night and wake in the morning feeling completely safe, knowing that both of their parents are in the next room. I want this family to have its father and husband. I want you to be a greater part of our lives. Do you understand the true depth of what I'm saying?" Wendy leaned forward and emphasized, "We're opening the most vulnerable and intimate parts of our lives, and we want to invite you in. We want to share our lives with you, and we want you to share yours with us."

Jake reached across the table and intertwined his fingers in hers. Wendy accepted his affection, but her expression indicated she knew good and well that he remembered the rules. He sheepishly smiled and withdrew, caressing and patting her hands before pulling away.

"Are you still getting a sense of people and seeing things?" He asked.

Jake was referring to tendencies Wendy had since she was a child. They were best described as psychic type skills. She experienced vivid dreams, or premonitions, that often came to be. There were times when she could perceive an aura around people, but it wasn't a purely visual phenomenon. She described it as an amalgam of several senses mixed with a powerfully strong sixth sense. The combination gave her perceptions that were reassuring and comforting, and at other times disturbing. In close proximity she could feel others' emotions, especially the deep and powerful ones, the ones secreted away from the rest of the world.

"I do," she answered.

"What do you see now?" he asked.

Wendy hesitated. "I see a brightness around you," she said, "but it's like a shell. In here and here," she pointed to her chest and head, "I see what looks like a swirling darkness, a heaviness that's pressing in on you. It wasn't there so much before."

Jake slowly dropped his gaze. He knew what Wendy was talking about. He had been feeling it for a long time.

"Do you want to talk about it?" she asked.

"No." He shook his head. "I can't. Besides," he quickly perked up and said, "it's still my turn to ask questions." She recognized his reaction as being forced and fake,

Wendy hoped he wouldn't ask her about her dreams. He was fascinated by dreams, and if he asked, she'd have to tell him. Lately they were increasingly nightmarish and had taken on disturbing qualities. She would wake abruptly with visions of his death that were so vivid she had to wander the house searching for proof they were only dreams, that he was still alive. On other occasions, when she was awake, she would have to fight off the perception that he was calling out, calling out her name, but that he was already gone—he was somewhere else and couldn't return. In those moments, she could sense not only his presence, but she could feel the strength of his emotions and his agonies. It was unlike anything Wendy had ever experienced and it frightened her. She felt like a widow, yet her husband was alive.

Jake asked his final question. "Is there anything that I can do to be a better husband and father, to make things easier for you?" His question was sincere. He knew that pointing an accusatory finger at the terrible times they were living in as an excuse wasn't going to make anything better so he avoided being patronizing.

"You mean besides ending this war and coming home?" Wendy said.

"Yeah, besides that."

"Then no," she said. "Just listening and trying to understand is enough." She quickly tacked on a final, "Knowing that we're as important to you as you are to us really helps."

"That's all I got. Your turn," he said.

Wendy again felt relieved that he didn't ask about her dreams. For the last several months, the disturbing imagery was nearly always the same, but increasingly defined—Jake was badly hurt and alone, abandoned to his own devices in the aftermath of some terrible battle. He was on the ground, staring at the sky, slipping in and out of consciousness. In the throes of utter dismay, he was grabbing at his scalp, pulling at his hair. As his consciousness faded into delirium his thoughts formed as though underwater. In his final moments he was drifting toward home. He envisioned Wendy, Bailey, and Paul. They were waiting, motioning for him. Overtaken by the mirage and the joyful fantasy he struggled to get up. He rolled onto his knees, and against the pain of his injuries, he fought his way to his feet. He staggered toward the vision. At first his expression was one of elation. But as one arduous step turned into two, the gulf between them grew. As Wendy's nightmares progressed Jake's expression changed into one of panic and hysteria as he realized the depth of his loss. He staggered and fell. He did it again and again until he fell for the last time and couldn't get up. Up until that moment, Wendy was an outside observer, experiencing the sequence of events from a position of detachment, but then she was instantaneously cast into the nightmare. She experienced the raw brutality of emotion. Racing toward him, she was screaming for him to get up, to keep fighting. In the next instant, she was cradling him in her arms, his body emaciated and bloody, broken beyond repair. She squeezed him and cried out. As she held him, he transformed into someone very old. His hair was gray and his face wrinkled and worn out. He was covered in scars. They were all over his arms, his face, and his chest. Each was a testament to a life of endless struggle. Jake stopped breathing and died. At that moment, Wendy would awaken from the nightmare and jolt upright. Often she would scream out. Tears were always cascading down her cheeks. Alone and confused she repeatedly suffered the loss of her husband with all the passion as though it actually happened.

"I have so many questions for you," she said. Jake smiled and waited. In the past, their talks proved therapeutic, but it was difficult. Communication of emotions was something he struggled with and that was where Wendy always wanted to go. She was less interested in what he did than how it made him feel.

"Are you happy?"

"At this very moment…yes," Jake said, "since I got home."

"Like stepping into another world?" she inquired.

"Yeah."

Wendy perceived something entirely different. He appeared happy on the surface, but there was more to it than that. The deeper emotional and spiritual parts of him, parts far deeper than all the superficial trappings, those parts were suffering. It made her uncomfortable. Something had come home with him that was dark and foreboding. The fact that he was home represented only a temporary reprieve from demons he was choosing to keep secret.

"Do you want to talk about what's bothering you?"

Her question was soft and gentle, but that's what made it strong, powerful enough to break down Jake's defenses. He froze. His eyes were beginning to well up with tears, but he fought hard to suppress his emotion. To do what he did, they had to stay buried. If they weren't, he believed he'd go insane. "No," he finally said. "I can't. I'm sorry but this is the only place left in the world where things make sense."

Wendy wasn't in a hurry to respond but finally said softly, "I understand."

"I don't think anyone could understand unless they went through it themselves," Jake blurted out. "The experiences I've had, I wish they weren't part of me. But they are. I can't change that. All I can do is put them out of my mind and try not to dwell on them."

"I meant that I understand you don't want to talk about it. It's probably natural for someone who has seen so much of this war to not want to talk about it."

"I didn't mean to be short," he apologized.

Wendy tried a different approach. "I think I have a right to know how my husband is doing. I remember taking a vow…in good times and in bad? I would like for you to give me a status report. I think you respect me enough to understand that any man I'm married to…that I deserve to know what's going on in his heart, and I need to share his struggles. As his wife I refuse to be shut out. Guess what, Jake—you're that man and we're in this together."

"Okay," Jake said. He felt a little pinched. "I'll tell you, but you might not like what I'm about to say. When I'm out in the field, blowing stuff up and killing people, I don't think about home. I push thoughts of you and the kids out of my mind. Not because I want to, but because it's too painful. I can't concentrate. If I can't concentrate people die. My sense of duty and honor, my obligation to my men, and my hatred of the Persians are so overwhelming that at times I feel guilty for even having personal desires. When you spend so much time fighting, the idea that you can go on leave and just walk away from it like you would walk away from a job… it's just not the same. It's not possible. I hate the fighting but love it at the same time."

Wendy was taken aback by his statement. It wasn't coming from the same man she married. 'What has happened to him?' she thought. 'What have his experiences done to his mind?'

Jake was feeling a twinge of anger prodding him along. "Being away for so long," he said, "and coming home has made it painfully obvious to me that being away has created not only a monumental change in my life but a void in the family. It makes me feel guilty, like it's my fault. Then, after being in action for so long and the adrenaline rush of everything

moving at a thousand miles an hour, and living on the edge all the time…
it's hard to come off that and take a moment to ask myself how I feel.
Wendy…I don't know how I feel. I'm completely numb. I get pointed in
a direction, and I just do what I have to. I follow orders and I get things
done. I'm like a robot. I'm not afforded the opportunity to think about
how I'm feeling. You ask me to share, and all I feel is anger. Maybe it's just
a defense mechanism. The point is, I don't know who I am anymore."

Wendy remained motionless while Jake vented his frustrations. Her
hands were folded on the table in front of her, and she hung on every
word, encouraging him to go on without responding. She sensed that Jake's
muscles were tightening. He was becoming increasingly tense and his tone
sharp.

"I've seen things so terrible," he said, "and so inhumane that I don't want
to bring them back for a second go around. I can't. It was hard enough the
first time without having to talk about it again. Not to mention, Wendy,
you're innocent and completely untarnished. You and this family are the
only beautiful things left in this world. I don't want to ruin that. If I lived
to be a million, I would never burden you with the unspeakable things I've
seen and done."

What Jake wouldn't admit, but what Wendy now understood, was that
the war was destroying him. The boy she grew up with and the man she
married were only small parts of the person sitting across the table. But
she also recognized that the vibrant spirit she knew was still there; it was
being smothered but it was still there.

As Jake spoke, his mind was flashing through images of lives uselessly
butchered and thrown away. He saw orphans everywhere. He saw women,
from the very old to the very young, even mere infants, brutally raped. He
saw people killed in almost every unnatural way and in the end for what?
A perverted Persian quest for world domination.

Jake also harbored a secret beyond terrible. When it flashed in his
thoughts, prompted by his own mention of unspeakable things, he fell
abruptly silent. He was too agonized and ashamed to bring it into the light
even for self-examination. In the past, when the thought would tease at
him he would push it away. He couldn't face the truth. The real secret that
haunted him was that he actually enjoyed killing. It was a complete rush,
a pleasure of inexplicable dimension. When he fought and killed enemy
soldiers, in a deep dark place, he enjoyed it. But his pleasure wasn't because
he was helping to win the war or that he was making the world a better
place. His pleasure was something else entirely, something primordial and
savage, predatory and orgasmic, something shameful and loathsome in
the absolute. Because he wouldn't talk about it, he had no idea that many

others, many good and normal soldiers, had the same experience.

It was Jake's duty to kill enemies of United America. He was cold to it. It was his job. Survival was impossible if he had to carry the weight of everyone he killed. For the sake of mental stability they were dehumanized. The closest he came to rationalizing the Persian soldiers as a people with unique hopes and dreams, or even fears, was when he referred to them as *poor bastards*. A modern battlefield was a hellish experience, and his mind had to cope with the horrid sights and the ghastly smells.

From an ethical perspective, Jake often wondered what fine line actually distinguishes a murderer from a soldier. There certainly was a chasm separating the two, but he couldn't really put his finger on it. He thought he could recognize it when he saw it, but he couldn't verbally define the exact line of demarcation. Under what circumstances was it ethical to kill? Was it limited to self-defense? Certainly when the enemy was threatening your territory, it was justifiable, but what about when they were defending their own? What about the people behind the lines, the workers making the weapons that were intended to do you harm? What about the politicians who started the war? What if a person was simply sewing socks for the enemy or writing love letters that might raise their fighting spirit? How far should total war go? When was the extension of killing in a war the moral equivalent of murder?

Wendy could sense that Jake was immersed in some internal conflict, bogged down in a fight to find his words. She elected to break what had become an awkward silence. She asked if he still wore his cross. It was her manner of inquiring about his faith, but in an indirect way.

"I do," Jake said. "I wear it all the time. There are times though when I take it off. I hold it and think about Dad and Grandpa. I wonder if it helped them keep it together." When he looked up, Wendy noticed that Jake's eyes appeared tired. "My beliefs are still strong if that's what you're asking," he said, "but I have to admit that sometimes I don't understand."

"Understand what?" Wendy asked.

"Why. I don't understand…why. If I'm supposed to believe in a God who's all-powerful and all-loving, why would He for an instant tolerate the existence of so much suffering and so much evil? I just can't find any obvious answers. I figure that's just part of the mystery. You know, this might sound stupid, but sometimes I ask God how He's doing," Jake chuckled to himself as though the revelation was embarrassing. "I figure that He's pretty busy, and if He feels all the accumulated sadness and loss that we experience, that it would be…let's just say self-centered for me to complain or ask Him for anything. No sense in piling it on. So we just dialogue."

"I think He probably appreciates that," Wendy said as she leaned forward to grasp Jake's hands. As she rose from her seat, she finished, "And I'm sure He enjoys hearing from you."

* * * * *

Jake's leave was filled with a grueling schedule of activities as they attempted to create as many memories as they could. Jake considered it boot camp for parents, and Wendy was completely exhausted, but in a good way. On consecutive days they went to the amusement park, compliments of Alex, boating, and to an afternoon baseball game. On that particular night, Jake sat on the floor and played dolls with Bailey without interruption for two hours. With hands on her hips she took charge and directed the activity, bossing him into playing the role of the evil hair stylist, and the multicolored unicorns were his crazy henchmen. While she took delight in the funny voices he gave to the characters, she had to keep correcting him because he wasn't playing the game properly. He discovered that playing dolls was not as easy as he thought. It was complex, and multiple layers of etiquette were in force. As far as childhood games went it was as nuanced as any he had ever played.

The next day was particularly exciting for the kids. They went to the zoo and enjoyed so many animals that they simply couldn't keep them straight. They watched the lions, penguins, giraffes, snakes, tarantulas, and everything in between. That night Jake paused outside Paul's room and listened as Wendy tucked him in. He was excitedly recalling all the wonderful things he had seen.

Wendy straightened the sheets under his arms and nestled his stuffed puppy in next to him. She asked, "What was your favorite part of the whole day?"

In his three-year old voice he said, "When Daddy held me on the wall so I could see all the monkeys. He held me for a long, long time so I could see all of them. He lifted up Sissy too."

"That was your favorite?" Wendy said. "The monkeys are my favorite too. I like it when they make those funny faces."

"No, not the monkeys!" Paul protested. "Daddy holding me. I said, 'Daddy I'm gonna fall.' He said, 'You're not gonna fall, I got you.' And he hugged his arm around me. That was my favorite part of the whole day, when Daddy was holding me so I didn't fall."

Jake rested his head against the wall. The simplicity worked its best to break his heart. It was simultaneously beautiful and painful. All they wanted was time—time he didn't have. He closed his eyes and leaned against the wall, hearing but not listening to the rest of their conversation. What he was feeling was guilt as he remembered his own father, his unhurried nature, and the time they spent together. He took a breath and entered the room to kiss Paul goodnight.

The next day began with an early morning hike to one of Jake's favorite childhood fishing holes. The kids learned how to bait hooks, cast their lines, and clean their catch, and they experienced the joy of eating it.

"Gross!" Paul exclaimed. He covered his mouth with both hands.

"Can I have it? I'll eat it. Can I? Can I?" Bailey asked.

Paul's eyes were as wide as they were defiant. Once he saw the plate, he determined that fresh catch was his mortal enemy.

"Mommy, can I have it?" Bailey asked again.

"Hold on," Wendy interjected. She sat down next to Paul and with her cheek pressed against his she examined the fish. She poked it with a fork. "It does look gross doesn't it?" she admitted. "But anything that looks that gross has to be good. It smells good. Besides, you remember the rule?" Paul's eyes grew wider and he vigorously shook his head. Wendy took a bite and exaggerated, "Mmm, this is so yummy."

"It's not gross, Pauley," Bailey chimed in. "Show it who's boss. Show it who's boss."

Jake remained an amused observer as the scene unfolded. When it was apparent that Paul wasn't going to budge, Wendy said, "The rule is that you have to try it. If you don't like it, you don't have to eat it." Wendy came at him but as soon as the fish touched his lip he pulled away, position unchanged. "Okay. The rules state that now you have to eat the whole piece." Before she completed the pronouncement of consequences Paul's mouth opened up like a yawning hippo. She deposited the bite into the gaping hole.

Paul's expression morphed from looking like he was going to throw up, to puckering like he had eaten a persimmon, to one of utter surprise. "It's not gross to my mouth," he happily exclaimed. He ate two whole pieces and declared it to be his favorite food.

After enjoying the day outdoors, the timing was perfect when the children went down for a nap. Jake seized the moment. He directed Wendy to sit on the couch. He looked at his watch and made his eyebrows go up and down.

"What? You're being silly," she laughed.

It was going to be one of the most exciting days of her life. "I have a surprise."

"What?" Her eyes lit up.

"Do I tell you, or show you?"

She thought about it for only a moment and said, "Show me."

Jake couldn't help noticing how entrancing her eyes were. "Holy smokes. Have I told you in the last five minutes how beautiful you are?" He bit his lip in an exaggerated expression. He looked at the ceiling as though he was talking to the heavens and exclaimed, "She's so beautiful it hurts... and it feels so good."

"Stop it," she laughed.

"Okay, I'll show you. We're going to have some fun, but you need to know about the rules."

"Rules? Like what?"

"Well, for starters, you have to promise not to get scared. You have to trust me." She didn't appear the least bit apprehensive. "I mean it," Jake said. "Crybabies and wussies are strictly prohibited." Wendy was all smiles.

Jake led her out the front door just in time to meet Wendy's mother, Heather, as she was coming up the walk. When she noted Wendy's surprise she said, "Jake told me to be here at exactly 4:00p.m." She was otherwise clueless.

Jake activated his BCD and accessed the outgoing message protocol. "Hawk 17. Do you read?"

A female voice came back, "Hawk 17 copy."

"This is Alpha G2RT85. At the rendezvous. Do you read Hawk 17?"

"Copy. Alpha G2RT85. At the rendezvous."

"Bring it in with show."

"Hawk 17. Coming in low with show."

"What was that?" Wendy asked. She only heard Jake's part of the exchange, but she was jumping with excitement.

Jake pointed toward the horizon to the east. "Over there. Keep your eyes on the horizon."

At first there was nothing. Then in the distance came a deep guttural rumble unlike anything she had ever heard. At first it grew in intensity only very slowly. She couldn't tell where it was coming from until a tiny object appeared in the sky just above the horizon's edge. It didn't move left or right but kept getting larger. All of a sudden the rumble turned into a roar, and it ripped past not twenty feet over their heads. Wendy's mouth dropped as it thundered from left to right. It made sharp turns over the fields around the house. It looked like a motorcycle. It was silver and black. As it alternately sped up and decelerated its shape contorted and contracted.

It went by a few more times, went vertical, did a flip, and came in low over the roadway. When it touched down, the side rockets deactivated, and it rode just like a motorcycle. It pulled into the driveway and stopped in front of them, the ground vibrating and a deep baritone rumble dominating the scene. The next moment the engine was off. The pilot dismounted and took off her helmet. With crisp military mannerisms she snapped a salute and said, "Lt. Col. Gillean. Lieutenant Tammy Crotizsky, Third Division, Army National Guard. Flight Wing Hawk 76."

"Lieutenant." Jake returned her salute.

Wendy walked around the bike, examining its sleek chrome wheels and the shiny black tires. They were so black they almost looked purple in the sunlight. The black seats were made of synthetic leather so real in appearance and feel that it was nearly impossible to distinguish it from the real thing. The body of the aerocycle was covered with a deep gray and black metal alloy. Each piece of metal under-lapped the piece in front and overlapped the piece behind, giving it the appearance of feathers on a bird's wing. The windshield wrapped in a concave fashion around the pilot, giving it the look of a cockpit. It was designed to change shape during flight in order to cut drag and protect the pilot from wind shear. It was clear to the naked eye, but with the helmet on it was a fully functional heads-up-display.

While Wendy saw an amazing flying motorcycle, what Jake saw was altogether different. The vehicle was one of the latest products to come out of the military division of MST. He'd seen them perform and they were impressive. He admired the innovative propulsion technologies and shield systems. The aerocycle was designed for low level air support in an urban combat zone. It was formidable in that it could pick up and carry a large payload and could bring weaponized-lasers and four different types of missiles to bear. By combining advances in ion field technologies, smart shape-memory alloys, and some novel applications of defensive laser technologies, it didn't need a thick polymer shell for protection. He did know from experience that it had a major weakness, but that was classified.

Out of a side compartment, Lt. Crotizsky produced two flight suits with helmets and four propulsar wrist bracelets. With quick keystrokes on the virtual control panel the aerocycle elongated. A second control panel and handlebars folded out of the body while the windshield enlarged and extended further back. In less than thirty seconds it completed the transformation and was ready for two riders.

"Mrs. Gillean, Ma'am. Would you like to go for a ride?" she asked.

"You're kidding? Really?" Wendy exclaimed. She looked at Jake and excitedly repeated, "Really?"

"Let's do it," Jake said, taking immense enjoyment in her delight.

Lt. Crotizsky helped Wendy into her flight suit. It was unlike anything she had ever seen. The material was soft and comfortable but when she touched something else it turned into a hard exoskeleton on the outside, much like an insect's. But it remained soft and supportive on the inside. When she zipped it up to her neck, it contorted and wrapped snuggly around her entire body, creating a form-fitting suit. Jake was stunned silent. His wife wearing a flight suit was the most incredible thing he had ever seen.

With the Lieutenant's prompting she banged her arm against the corner of the house. It sounded like she hit it with a bat. But she didn't feel a thing on the inside. She approached her mother. "Mom, you have to feel this," she said.

"It's hard," Heather announced.

"I know, but when I touch it it's soft. It feels like silk. This is amazing." She whirled around and punched Jake in the chest. What she got in return wasn't the blunt thump she expected. His suit didn't harden with the impact. Her fist dug into his pectoral muscle and her knuckles thumped his collar bone.

"Hey," he said in surprise. "What's going on?"

"I'm sorry, honey. Did I hurt you?" She rubbed his chest. "I'm sorry," she said, her face betraying embarrassment.

"Geez," Jake laughed. "The suit can sense when another suit touches it. It won't harden." He rubbed the spot, "I forgot how hard you can punch."

"Love taps, honey, shows how much I love you."

Before they could take off, Lt. Crotizsky had to explain the basic principles to Wendy. "Don't worry. It is very safe," she said. "If you fall off, the wrist bracelets have propulsar technology built into them. Try not to panic. You'll fall until you are about thirty meters off the ground, then the bracelets will kick in. They'll slow your rate of descent, and you'll land at a slow walk. The aerocycle will boomerang back and you climb back on board. It's as simple as that. I took the liberty of locking the flight computer. Once aloft it won't let you go below an altitude of fifty meters unless Lt. Col. Gillean inputs the override. So don't worry. There's nothing to run into up there. Have some fun. It senses your movements so all you have to do is lean to turn and work the throttle for speed."

Appropriately briefed, Wendy took the controls. Jake sat behind her. They cruised down the main road in front of their home. The sheer power of the engine caused Wendy's adrenaline to pump. The aerocycle growled and bellowed as she opened up the throttle.

"Whenever you're ready. Left thumb, orange button." Jake said through the headset.

Wendy, nervously keeping her eyes on the road, quickly glanced at the button. She lightly put her thumb on top of it. Feeling the bike change shape beneath her, she punched it. The jets fired and the bike lifted off. The rush she felt was incredible.

"We're flying! We're flying!" she exclaimed.

The aerocycle was ripping past the trees. Just as quickly it was above them and climbing. For several minutes she cruised mostly in a straight line enjoying the view. She was cautious, attempting only gradual turns and keeping the speed constant. They flew over Franklin and turned back south toward Spring Hill.

"Okay, grandma," Jake said, "feel free to get out of the slow lane."

"Can you handle it?" she challenged.

"Give me your worst."

The virtual display indicated a constant speed of ninety miles per hour. She abruptly pushed the throttle. The engine quaked as though awakened from a deep slumber. The speed shot up to four hundred twenty-five miles per hour. The trees, fields, and towns were flying by in a blur.

"Dear," Jake said, concerned that their speed was still climbing.

"Are you scared?"

"Yes."

"I seem to recall something about wussies." She laughed and pushed the throttle further. The engine roared, surging past five hundred miles per hour and screaming over the hills of Eastern Tennessee. Wendy climbed to several thousand meters, only to dive back down to the fifty-meter floor. It was sheer excitement with no limitations, a feeling of being released from the earth and the constraints of gravity.

They had been flying for almost two hours before they decided to head home. "You got it?" Jake asked.

"I got it. I got it." Their flight path was perfectly aligned with the roadway.

"Careful. Ease it in," Jake said.

"I got it," she repeated. While her eyes were glued to the pavement and the markers on the heads-up display, her hands were white-knuckling the controls and her heart was racing. The ground was racing upward and she was feeling the squeeze of fear.

"You're doing great. Now just ease it down. Hold on to the handlebars when we touch. There's going to be a little bump and a jerk." Just as he finished saying it the wheels touched.

"I did it!" Wendy yelled. She nailed the landing, or at least that's what she thought. At the last second Jake momentarily took control. It was an act of protection that she would never know about.

Wendy's entire outlook was different. If somewhere on top of the world there was a throne…that's where she was. She repeatedly thanked Lt. Crotizsky and Jake for the incredible experience.

Before making her exit, the Lieutenant looked twice and blurted, "Holy Moses! Do you know how fast you were going?"

Wendy beamed.

Once the aerocycle moved a sufficient distance from the house it came to a stop, lifted off the ground vertically, hovered ten meters in the air, spun around, and tilted back and forth like it was waving. It blasted away, did a flip, and disappeared over the horizon.

"It hovers. I didn't know it could do that," Wendy said. "How come we didn't land like that?"

"One thing at a time," Jake said. "Besides, that was enough scare for one day."

Wendy couldn't sleep that night. She lay on her side, her thoughts restless. Moonlight was penetrating the bedroom with just enough strength to make out Jake's chest. She watched as it rhythmically rose and fell with each breath. She couldn't help imagining what he might have seen and done, things so disturbing that he couldn't talk about them. It was like there were two Jakes—one a loving husband and father, and the other a soldier…a complete stranger.

* * * * *

The following day marked the tenth day of Jake's fourteen day leave. It was also the day of the much anticipated family barbeque. Jake's mother, Janet, and Wendy's adoptive parents were under the large umbrella sharing stories. Other family members, including Jake's maternal uncles, and a cadre of friends rounded out the edges of the scene. The Gillians were lucky in that it turned out to be a beautiful day, and their back yard was big enough to support the antics of roughly two-dozen energetic kids. They were running and playing, limbs were flailing about, shouts and squeals were emanating from every direction, and a copious amount of laughter filled in the gaps like a wonderful symphony.

"Turned out to be a great day." The statement was from Tom Wilson, Jake's best friend from childhood.

"It has hasn't it," Jake agreed. "Can I get you anything?"

"I'm good," he said as he held up a bottle of water. "Haven't had a drink since that day."

"You're not missing anything."

Tom was referring to the night of high school graduation. He was inebriated and decided it would be a good idea to go skinny-dipping in the lake with his girlfriend. When she came back to the party screaming, Jake dove in and pulled him out. He performed CPR until emergency crews arrived. Tom woke up in the hospital a day later, and from then on, he was a changed person. He was now a trauma surgeon and head of the department at New Bethesda Hospital.

"I'm glad you came. It does me good to see you," Jake said.

"You kidding? I wouldn't miss Jakey-boy's return. I was thrilled when I heard."

Jake opened the lid and the barbeque pit flexed its muscle, throwing large plumes of white smoke into the air, announcing to the world that a celebration was underway. It was the centerpiece of the festivities, a part of Southern culture that had been preserved across hundreds of years.

By cultural convention, the man of the house assumed the place of absolute masculinity. Accordingly, Jake was the master of the barbeque. The expectation was that everyone would compliment the chef. Even though the other food took much more time and effort to prepare, it simply didn't matter. They were mere garnishments and would bow down before the power of the meat. Part of the nuance was that it didn't matter if the meat came from a cow, steer, pig, buffalo, chicken, or whatever else was acceptable to kill, butcher, and eat, no consideration or moment of silence was observed to honor the animal that donated its hindquarters to the celebration. Typically, honors weren't bestowed upon the farmer who raised it, nor were any relegated to the butcher. All honors went to the one who stood before the barbeque altar; the one who put the slab of dead animal on the grill, flipped it, put sauce on it, and decided when it was done.

"It smells good, Uncle Jake," Fredericka said.

He squatted down to meet her at eye level. "Are you hungry?" She nodded her head in the affirmative while pulling on the sides of her dress, wrestling with being coy and silly at the same time. "I've got a very special one that I'm cooking just for you."

"Really?" she beamed.

"It's almost ready. Why don't you go play and I'll come get you when it's done."

He laughed as she excitedly ran off. Even the kids knew the rules and all the customary manners. Typical and acceptable things to say included, 'Great job on the meat! Compliments to the chef!' or 'That was great!' and 'Is there any left?' The most magnificent compliment, which interestingly was actually more indirect, was to ask the master of the barbeque about his technique, the sauce that he used, and how he prepared the meat.

"Mom, is everything okay?" Jake asked. She was previously mingling but was now sitting alone.

"Fine."

"Do you need anything?"

"No," she responded. "My legs are tired, and I just want to sit."

Jake was happy she came but their dynamic hadn't improved since Thomas died. While they never enjoyed a close mother-son relationship there remained a place for her in his heart. He loved her, but the relationship disintegrated to the point that they held very little sway over each other.

The timing was perfect. Jake flipped the meat and stepped into the house to get another bottle of sauce. He was digging in the refrigerator, trying to get behind the mounds of food. He had just put his hand on the elusive bottle when his BCD activated. The signal indicated there was an incoming message. He pulled the bottle out while navigating through the prompts to accept the link. He was nonchalant. It was about the right time for the daily check-in. When he connected, through his BCD's neural relays, he heard a male voice.

"Lt. Col. Jake Gillean." It quickly repeated. "Lt. Col. Jake Gillean."

"Gillean here," Jake said.

'Lt. Col., this is Captain Zachary Cox, Strategic Command Center, New Washington. I am to inform you that Alpha Group has been immediately recalled. A transport will pick you up at your present location at 0600."

"What?" Jake was stunned. "I have four more days! This can't be right!" He was furious and was yelling, restraining himself just enough so that no one would hear.

"I'm sorry, sir. Those are your orders."

"Why? Why are we being recalled?"

"National emergency. I am not at liberty to discuss the details. You will be briefed tomorrow."

"The President authorized this leave." Jake knew it was futile. His life wasn't his to command, and he was grasping at straws that didn't exist.

"I'm looking at her signature right now," the Captain said.

"GODDAMMIT!" Jake yelled through gritted teeth. "Lt. Col. Gillean has been notified and will report for duty at 0600."

"I'm sorry, sir."

The connection terminated.

Jake needed to lash out. His blistering rage was like that of a thousand madmen screaming at the moment of condemnation. The noose of war was tight around his neck, the supports were being pulled away, and now more than ever he was strangled by the realization that his life was not his own. As the ferocity of his anger reached toward its crescendo he had to find an outlet. He envisioned letting loose a terrible scream, spittle would fly, and he would launch the bottle through the patio doors with all his might, exploding both into thousands of pieces. He would unleash the rest of his pent up rage on the table. He would smash his fists down on its center. It would collapse, splinters flying everywhere. He pictured it so vividly that it was like it really happened. But it didn't. He fought it back and didn't lose control. Other than the vice-like grip on the neck of the glass bottle, his clenched jaw, and a slight tremor that emerged in the muscles of his right hand, there was no outward sign of his white-hot anger. Everything remained tightly bound within his mind.

As his thoughts calmed, he focused on Bailey, Paul, and Wendy. How was he supposed to explain it to them? How would they react? They were so excited about the experiences they were supposed to share over the next several days. Now their plans were shattered.

If he told everyone what happened, it would kill the day. He couldn't do it. They didn't deserve it. What they deserved was a day of joy. The words 'SUCK IT UP!'—words that he yelled at the men under his command— repeated in his mind. This time the order was self-directed. He took a deep breath, faked a smile, and went back to the barbeque pit, pretending nothing happened.

Through the remainder of the day, Jake found himself stealing looks at his wife, his gaze flirting with being a frank stare. He longed for her in ways he couldn't begin to explain. He just knew what he felt. It was good, it was painful, and it was everything in between. He longed for the world to simply disappear and leave them behind. Wendy would periodically make eye contact. They would smile through the crowd of oblivious partygoers and with the slightest movement of their lips say, 'I love you.'

Surrounded by family and friends, Jake felt the weight of intense loneliness. Cutting short his leave was like promising someone who was starving a plate but giving only a morsel instead. It was the cruelest act imaginable, making everything all the more agonizing. Yet he would endure the pain ten-fold if it meant preserving the time they spent together.

Wendy was so beautiful, but now she seemed so far away. He felt strange pangs of nervousness flittering in his stomach. It reminded him of high school, when he would watch her from a distance. In simply looking at his wife when she was unaware, Jake found himself drowning in the duel experience of pleasure and pain. He could never get as close to her as he wanted to be, even if he could merge with the very essence of her soul. What he wanted went far beyond primitive desires. What was it about her that so captivated him? Was it her long dark hair? Her strong jaw and prominent cheekbones? Her lean build? Was it possibly the hint of maturing crow's feet? Her inviting smile? Or was it her energetic and positive spirit and captivating thoughts? It didn't matter. Jake found everything about his wife so intriguing and so entrancing that he wished she could occupy all of his waking thoughts. He didn't want to just look at her, he didn't want to settle for burning her image into his retinas; he wanted to hear her, to understand her, to feel her, to possess her in every way possible. He wanted to tell the world that when he wasn't thinking about her, he wished he was; if he wasn't dreaming about her, he wished he was. He was willingly under her spell.

Heather managed to get everyone to leave by late afternoon. She announced that Jake and Wendy only had a few more evenings and that as much as they loved everyone, they wanted to spend time alone. Wendy's brother, ever the clueless one, wanted to know why. He loudly asked, "What are you doing tonight that requires you to be alone?" There was a moment of silence and awkward glances all around. Embarrassed laughter followed. After a twenty minute mad dash of cleaning, the place was spotless, and everyone said their goodbyes.

After a few minutes of quiet conversation Jake said, "I have to go."

"What?" Wendy was confused. "Go where?"

"Alpha Group has been recalled," he said. "Some sort of emergency. I don't know the details. There will be a transport here to pick me up at 0600."

"What? NO! NO! NO! NO!" She cried. "You have four more days! You only have to be back on the 20th! They can't do that!"

"I'm sorry." Jake didn't know what to say. He couldn't console her.

"It's been twenty-three months since we've seen you," she screamed. "Do you know what that is?" Jake didn't respond. "It's six hundred and ninety-four days. It's one fourth of your daughter's life. It's two-thirds of your son's."

"It's not my choice. I have to go," he said.

"I know. It's just that…" Wendy burst into tears. Through bitter sobbing said, "You just got here. This war…this damn war. What am I supposed to tell the kids? What do I tell them Jake? What am I supposed to tell them?" Tears were streaming down her cheeks, "What do I tell them when they wake up crying in the middle of the night? They miss you, Jake. Children need their father. I need you. Dammit, Jake! Who do I turn to when I wake up crying?!" She hugged the couch pillow to her chest. Unconsciously, her fingers were tightly kneading the fabric. There was nothing left for her to say. She sank into despair and wept. The kids, hearing the change in their voices, came to investigate. Jake quickly ushered them to their rooms.

Wendy took about twenty minutes to gather her composure. She found Jake sitting on the floor in Paul's room. He already explained that he had to leave in the morning. Bailey was sitting on his lap, crying. She was clutching her doll. The expression on her face was that of a child lost in a crowded market. She couldn't understand why he had to leave. Why would her dad have to leave when he just got there?

Paul distracted himself with his train set. The cars were held together by remote-controlled magnets, and he was connecting and disconnecting them as they moved around the track, but the play was mechanical and unimaginative.

"Mommy!" Bailey wailed. She began crying anew and ran into her mother's outstretched arms. "Mommy! Daddy's leaving!"

"I know, honey."

"Why? Why is he leaving? Why is he leaving us? Did I do something wrong?"

"No, Bailey. My goodness, no, no, no, that's not it." Wendy was gallant in her fight to be strong, but under the circumstances, her composure collapsed and she started crying again.

"Daddy, don't go away! I'll be better!" Bailey was wailing.

The tension in the room was growing, and in their heartbreak, no one noticed Paul. He was standing now, taking in the scene. He had a train car in each hand. His eyes were wide and his face turned crimson red. His arms began shaking and he screamed, "STOP!" The hysteria in his voice brought everything to a halt. "GO AWAY! I HATE YOU! I HATE YOU!" He threw one of the cars at Jake. It hit the window, cracking the glass. He lunged at Jake screaming, "I HATE YOU! I HATE YOU!" Over and over again he screamed out in anger while trying to hit his father.

Jake picked him up. Paul's arms and legs were flailing. He clawed Jake's face and grabbed a handful of hair and yanked. He arched his back in an effort get away. He twisted and Jake lost his grip. Paul fell to the floor, only to come up fighting and yelling. "I HATE YOU!"

Jake didn't know what to do. "Paul, no." He tried to reassure Paul that everything was okay. Keeping his voice calm and soothing he tried again to explain, "I love you. I don't want to go. I don't want to go." As his efforts failed his patience ran out and he yelled, "KNOCK IT OFF!"

Wendy jumped between them and picked Paul up. She hugged him in her arms, and he quit flailing. She turned back in time to see a horrific pain in Jake's expression. He was shaking. Tears were flowing down his cheeks. He couldn't talk. His voice was gone. While his eyes were pleading for understanding, he was lost and didn't know what to do.

What Wendy witnessed next was a transformation unlike anything she had ever seen. Jake pulled back and she could see the emotional wall going up. He buried the immensity of his hurt, his eyes dried, and his facial features grew rigid and militant. He stood larger and the size of his frame increased. He turned his attention to Bailey and said in a tone that was soft, but stern and unyielding like he was talking to another soldier, "I don't want to go. I have to go, and I don't have a choice."

"Are you coming back?" Bailey asked between sobs.

Jake was shocked by her question and by the element of fear in her voice. "Of course I'm coming back."

"Do you promise?" she cried.

Wendy glared at him. Her eyes were weary and exhausted but there was something else, something succinct in its meaning. She was trying to communicate something unmistakable and disturbing in its implications. It caused Jake to hesitate. He understood the dangers he faced. Now he realized he wasn't alone. He could feel the stab. They were scared, frightened to death that he wasn't coming home. They understood his vulnerabilities. They knew he wasn't indestructible. They loved him but they didn't have the option of fighting harder. They had no real way to cope with the terrible stress of war. All they could do was drown in helplessness and pray, hoping that he was okay. The burden they were suffering was greater than his.

Jake dropped to his knees. While he now felt emotionally vulnerable, he also ceased caring about anything else except being their father. His little girl was frightened, and his son was crying. The questions ripped through his mind in rapid succession. What was he supposed to tell them? Was he supposed to admit that he could be killed in an instant in any of a million different ways? Was he supposed to admit that they might never see him again? No. He couldn't do that. Through their tears, through the lens of their innocence, Jake appreciated how terrible and foreboding the world really was.

"I will be back." Jake put his fingers under Bailey's chin. He lifted her face to his and wiped away her tears. "Do you understand? I promise you, Paul, and Mommy, that no matter what happens I'll be back. I need you to be strong just for a little longer." He kissed her head. "I give you my word that you're going to see me walking back through that door, and one day I'll be home for good." Bailey put her arms around his neck and he hugged her. She was still crying. Paul kept his face buried in Wendy's shoulder, his muffled sobs waxing and waning as he tried to catch his breath.

Jake stayed with the kids until late that night. They talked for a long time and he read some books, and they eventually fell asleep. When their eyes finally closed, the thought that bullied into Jake's mind was that they might never see their father again. But the thought brought with it a dark companion...if he died he wondered how long it would be before they would need a photo to remember what he looked like.

For Wendy, sleep was impossible. She lay awake staring at the ceiling and for the longest time, she didn't move a muscle. Something wasn't right. Something new at the far edge of her sixth sense was wrong. She perceived a churn of intense sadness. But it wasn't hers. It was nondescript, not really having any form. It was coming from Jake, but it was unusual... like it hadn't happened yet.

She could hear him breathing. It sounded so peaceful, so comforting. She very slowly reached over and lightly put her hand on his shoulder. Immediately, she gasped and pulled away. It was too much to bear and tears were again cascading down her cheeks. With a simple touch Wendy saw a vision of her husband. It was just his face swaying toward the sky. There was blood on the side of his head and at his lips. The muscles were clenching at his jaw and the strain in his eyes bore testament to intense pain and torment, but it wasn't physical, it was sadness and immense feelings of guilt. Then his life drained away.

It was a premonition, and Wendy believed it was the last night she would see her husband. She had experienced fear and sadness in the past, but this was different. She just couldn't explain how. She touched Jake again. Nothing. The vision was gone. She nestled in next to him and silently wept the rest of the night.

CHAPTER 25: THE WORLD ON A PRECIPICE

[JULY 17, AD 2379 (THE FOLOWING DAY)]
[ARRIVAL DATE MINUS 61 YEARS]
[LOCATION: SPRING HILL, TENNESSEE]

The small aerotransport was waiting when Jake opened the front door at precisely 0600. When he turned to Wendy, he felt the pain of two worlds colliding. Everything they needed to say had already been spoken. When he took her in his arms he felt her trembling. She felt firmness in his demeanor. His touch was powerful and resolute, and lacked the tenderness she had enjoyed over the last ten days. He released his embrace and stepped back into the war.

"Where are we going?" Jake asked the pilot.

"My orders are to have you in New Washington by 0700." The pilot was all business. When Jake finished securing his harness and attaching propulsar bracelets, the aerotransport turned away from the house. A moment later they were airborne.

After being transferred to a second transport in New Washington, the entire contingent of Alpha Group was taken to an undisclosed location in Northern Mexico. In a deep bunker, they were met by Delta Group, which had been flown in from operations in North Africa.

If tension was any measure, this mission was going to be unlike any they had ever experienced. Before the rumor mill had time to churn the overhead lights flashed on and off a few times. It was a signal that the briefing was beginning. Col. Fisk was at the front of the room. Next to him were Col. Anthony Ramirez and a contingent of the highest-ranking military brass. General of the Armies, Leon Montgomery, was front and center. His rank and responsibilities put him in league with only two other Americans in history—General George Washington and General John Pershing. The glint of the light reflecting off his five stars demanded everyone's attention and respect. While supreme authority over the military rested with the President, next in line was General Montgomery.

"Gentlemen. Have a seat." He motioned toward Alex. "Col. Alexander Fisk, commander of Alpha Group of the Special Operations Division, is the ranking field officer for this mission. Col. Anthony Ramirez, of Delta Group is second in command. Stand at attention for Secretary of Defense, Admiral Percy Bernard."

Admiral Bernard strode into the room with the aura that he was everyone's boss, including General Montgomery's. He was about five foot eleven inches tall with short gray hair. A wide dark scar ran obliquely from the middle of his forehead toward his left eye, and extended far down his cheek. He wore a sharp black civilian suit that matched the black patch covering his left eye.

"Gentlemen. Take your seats." There was a sense of urgency and the Admiral didn't waste words. "This is Operation Hades. You are going into the heart of the Persian Empire." His gaze around the room was met by a deadly silence. "This is a mission of vital strategic importance. The fate of the world is in your hands. If anyone in Alpha or Delta believes he is not fit for duty or up to the task leave now." When no one volunteered, he said, "Allow me to introduce Dr. Freidrich Von Meitchellgruber from the Ministry of Public Safety. He is a physicist and will be describing your objective."

A holographic image of the British Parliament appeared. It made international news when it had been blown up three days ago. "The footage you are seeing was taken from a security camera one block away," the doctor said. There was a brilliant flash of blue, red, and orange light. Then the camera went out. He continued, "Half the building and all of its occupants were vaporized. The rest of the building collapsed into rubble. The crater is over twenty meters deep." The hologram went back to the original scene. "This is the same image you just saw slowed down by a factor of one thousand." The image focused in on the point of origin of the explosion. A sudden white and yellow light emanated from a single spot at the base of the clock tower. "Now," the doctor said, "watch with care the spot of origin. The speed is slowed by a factor of ten thousand." There was nothing there, then out of nowhere, there was a black object. A large explosive device had suddenly materialized. No sooner had it materialized, it exploded.

The doctor went on, "Several months of security footage have been reviewed, and it has led to the apprehension of an enemy operative. He used a new type of technology to geographically mark the exact spot where the explosive device materialized. What does this mean? It means that we're next. There has been a substantial increase in similar explosions, mostly civilian and government targets, throughout Europe and Asia over the course of the last several weeks. Each time it happens, it is part of an ever-expanding radius with the explosions extending across Europe as far as England. Russia and China have been hit particularly hard. As we speak, these bombings are continuing to spread across Mongolia toward Japan. There is no defense against this type of attack. The question is… how are the Persians doing it?"

The holographic image changed to a harsh and rugged mountain chain. It rotated in the air between the soldiers and Dr. Meitchellgruber. "This is the objective. These are the Zagros Mountains that extend from Western to Southwestern Iran. Seventy miles south and east of Shiraz is Mount Kuh-e Kharman. Each bombing has been associated with a simultaneous diversion of tremendous energy to this mountain. There is a deep subterranean military research facility under this mountain that we have dubbed *Hades*. It is, of course, heavily guarded. As we speak, the world's top minds in multidimensional physics are working at the site, and sources tell us that for decades they have been working on devices designed to alter, or manipulate, time and space. In effect, what we believe is that they have developed a new type of transport device that is responsible for the explosions. Their capabilities are expanding as evidenced by the progressive increase in range."

To fully prepare the Guardsmen for the dangers they might encounter in the subterranean facility, Dr. Meitchellgruber went on to explain the basic physics of how they suspected the Persians were manipulating space and time to create wormholes. "I warn you that in the second phase of the assault, when the transport device is activated by our team of scientists, should a wormhole be successfully opened, it is of vital importance that it remain stable. Think of it as a living being…should it be traumatized, or become unstable, from a theoretical perspective, it will be devastating for life as we know it on this planet."

"Thank you, doctor," Admiral Bernard said after once again taking the podium. The rotating hologram switched back to the mountain and three-dimensional images of the subterranean facility. "This is it gentlemen. This is the objective of Operation Hades. Phase One: you will neutralize all resistance within the facility. Phase Two: get as many of the Persian scientists and as much of the computer equipment, paperwork, and files out as possible. Phase Three: extraction and destruction of the facility. When you successfully complete your mission, Mount Kuh-e Kharman will cease to exist."

The hologram blinked into an image of a vehicle. The Guardsmen had never seen anything like it. It looked like an odd submarine but with an exterior covered by what resembled old style tank treads. It was open down the middle like a donut. "This is the ST-17 Gopher," Admiral Bernard said. "This is how you will be getting in and out of the facility. You will be traveling underground."

The Gopher was the latest development from MST Global—a highly classified subterranean transport. They rolled out only a week before and even though the military hadn't had time to perform any sort of independent testing, under the circumstances they were the only hope United America had of reaching the Persian facility.

"What you are witnessing is the Gopher in action." The hologram showed the Gopher sitting motionless. The front suddenly glowed bright white and blue. The exterior began writhing like that of a worm, it twisted, and plunged downward at a forty-five degree angle. It disappeared below ground faster than a submarine could dive under water. "Keep your eye on the marker. It's exactly one mile from the point of entry. Roll the hologram ahead two minutes. The path the Gopher took in this test was through solid rock." No more than he said it, the Gopher came barreling out of the ground and took a short leap through the air. "It is capable of speeds up to twenty-five knots through solid rock. Faster through less dense materials."

MST wouldn't reveal exactly how the Gopher worked, and they went so far as to refuse to allow United American scientists the opportunity to examine the vehicle. MST provided their own pilots and crews, and offered their services with no strings attached. Under the circumstances, the government had to accept. It was the only way they could get Alpha and Delta Groups into the chambers below the mountain.

It was theorized that the Gopher traveled by somehow altering the molecular structure of the surrounding earth, converting it into a highly dense material that it then conveyed through the opening that ran the length of its hull, finally kicking the material out behind. There appeared to be no limitations as to what the Gopher could travel through, and it was equipped with the ability to reverse the process, to close down the tunnel behind them as they went.

Admiral Bernard turned the briefing over to General Montgomery who went on to detail how Alpha and Delta Groups were to be divided into their respective sixteen man teams. Along with science officers assigned to some of the teams, the Guardsmen were going to be transported by a fleet of ten Gophers. The drop point was off the Iranian coast. They would get that far by hitching a ride on the underbelly of a fleet of submarines. At the designated drop point, they would detach and burrow underground, rendezvous in a single tunnel, and proceed to predetermined points directly under Mount Kuh-e Kharman.

Once each ST-17 Gopher took its designated position two meters outside the primary structure, they would pierce into the facility and release XBJ-71—an odorless clear gas and the latest development in chemical warfare. By itself the gas was undetectable and inert. But when activated by a strong pulse of blue spectrum light, it would instantaneously undergo a chain reaction that would alter its structure, transforming it into a paralytic neurotoxin. It was unique in comparison to previous weaponized neurotoxins in that it didn't directly cause death, blindness, or other significant neurologic sequelae. XBJ-71 preserved the function of the victim's diaphragm, and the individual would remain conscious throughout an otherwise completely paralytic experience. The effects would only begin wearing off after approximately six hours. During that window of time, the victim was defenseless.

As second in command of Alpha Group, Jake would lead the assault on the large central structure, the area thought to house the transport device. The transport platform itself would be secured by Col. Fisk's team while Jake's would primarily function in an anti-personnel capacity, eliminating any and all enemy threats, and then loading the Gophers with Persian computers and scientists.

When the primary briefing was adjourned and everyone got up to leave, General Montgomery stepped in front of Jake. His voice was frayed on the edges and deeply hoarse. "Lt. Col. Gillean," he said.

"Sir. Yes, sir," Jake snapped to attention.

"At ease." General Montgomery extended his hand. Dark scars ran across the skin on the back of it, and he was missing a couple digits. His disposition was no-nonsense and blunt. "I read Col. Fisk's after-action report from Corinth and Portland. Also got a report from Lt. William McGuire…says you went above and beyond in risking your life to save his in Corinth, and that you eliminated several T7s single-handed in the process. Very strong work. You did the service proud."

"Thank you, sir," Jake said.

"Saw the fountain footage." His eyes narrowed and he maintained a grimace.

Jake's face flushed. "My apologies, sir."

"Don't be. The public has to support this war. Since Portland and that little walk you took in the water, the Treasury has sold over three trillion ameros in war bonds. That's your doing." The General appeared to be proud. "I trust the little girl is well?" he asked.

"With her parents, sir."

"I also have come to understand that you were the one who discovered some of the Persian SS had gone stealth, and you were responsible for securing the dome...an action that saved hundreds of lives." The General carefully studied Jake's response as he talked.

"I'm just part of Alpha Group, sir. The other men deserve the accolades, and Col. Fisk coordinated the op. Our success and every life saved is a reflection of his diligence."

That was the response the General was looking for. In his experience, the ability to handle praise appropriately was an indication of how a soldier's head was screwed on. He took Jake's response as a measure of his maturity. He furrowed his brow and leaned in, "You're too modest. I looked at your file. You graduated first in your class at the Special Forces Academy, you're a class five sharp-shooter, more than a dozen citations for valor, and two Silver Crosses. Son, you have a rare gift. You maintain a presence of mind in battle like few others."

"Thank you, sir."

"Col. Fisk has recommended you for promotion. I agree with him, and your promotion is being fast-tracked. Soon enough you will be Col. Gillean...with your own command."

"Sir?" Jake said. He was stunned. "And leave Alpha Group?"

"No, son," the General said. "Alpha Group will be yours. Col. Fisk is to make Brigadier General. He'll be placed in overall command of The Guard."

The news was shocking. It was good. It was beyond good. It was what Jake always wanted. "I'm honored, sir," he said.

"No," General Montgomery said, "the service is honored. Wish we had more like you. I saved the best for last. Based upon reports from the Guardsmen in Alpha Group and your superior officers, I have officially initiated the process...you have been awarded the Congressional Medal of Honor." The General watched the color fade from Jake's face. There were no current living recipients of the Congressional Medal of Honor. He slapped him on the shoulder. "You earned it." He laughed and added, "You know that I served with your father?"

"He spoke highly of you, sir, was proud to have served with you." Jake said. He felt like he needed to grab something.

"In South America. Among the bravest and brightest men I've ever known. If it hadn't been for his illness, he'd be doing my job. I know he'd be proud of you."

"Thank you, sir."

General Montgomery noted that Jake's expression hadn't changed. He leaned in, "Smile son," he said in a hushed voice, "you earned it."

Elation emerged across Jake's face, "Thank you, sir."

General Montgomery walked away, paused, and turned back to Jake. He cleared his throat and said with a half-quizzical half-complimentary expression, and loud enough for others to hear, "I failed to mention that I saw the footage at the hospital. Thank your mother. For all his talents, your father couldn't sing to save his life."

Jake accepted the compliment, turning a nice shade of red in the process.

* * * * *

Three hours after the briefing and intense closed-door meetings with the officers, Jake was busy conducting assault exercises with the men in a massive underground tactical holodome. They drilled through the day and well into the night with holographic mock-ups of the Persian facility. After all the preparations were made and Col. Fisk was satisfied that every eventuality had been accounted for, and the men knew what they were supposed to do, they were allowed three hours of uneasy sleep. The next day, they were on a transport headed for a rendezvous with the Pacific Fleet. A ten-minute window was open for text-only communications with family. It would be the last opportunity until after the mission.

HI BABY, Jake typed.

Wendy heard the familiar chime indicating there was an incoming message. The military's security system for dependents of service personnel used facial recognition technologies to verify her identity. Only then was she able to read the message. She hesitated. Grasping the counter with one hand for support, she brought the other up to cover her mouth. She bit down hard on her index finger, trying to muffle sounds of crying. Tears were again working their way down her cheeks. It was too much to bear; the feelings of frightened loneliness and loss were beyond her ability to cope. She wanted to scream out, 'Why? Why now?' She had always been so strong. Why was she suffering such intense fear, and why were her nerves being pushed to the point of a complete breakdown. 'Bailey and Paul are in the next room,' she thought, 'they can't see me like this.'

ARE YOU THERE? Jake typed. He patiently waited for a response.

HI…she finally responded.

HI, BABY!

I MISS YOU. Wendy typed.

When her words scrolled across his screen Jake responded, I MISS YOU TOO. IT'S HARD TO BE BACK.

She agreed. IT WAS THE MOST WONDERFUL 10 DAYS OF MY LIFE.

Jake sensed the tension in Wendy's words. He wanted to lighten the mood. He typed, I STILL CAN'T GET OVER HOW MUCH THE KIDS HAVE GROWN. AND BAILEY. SHE'S SO MUCH LIKE HER MOTHER.

YOU REALY THINK SO?

I DO. THERE WAS A TIME WHEN I WAS REALLY APPREHENSIVE ABOUT ALL THE SNOTTY-NOSED BOYS COMING AROUND. NOW I FEEL KIND OF SORRY FOR THEM. SHE'S JUST LIKE HER MOTHER. THEY DON'T STAND A CHANCE.

YOU CAME AROUND.

I WAS SCARED. STILL AM. There was a long pause. WENDY, YOU STILL THERE?

YES, she typed.

EVERYTHING OK?

NO. NO, IT'S NOT. A momentary lapse before she continued. JAKE, PLEASE COME HOME. WE NEED YOU. She considered her words and added, I'M SCARED. I DON'T HAVE A GOOD FEELING. She deleted the last sentence and continued, I NEED YOU.

Jake waited for her response. He read the first message. Moments later the second came through. He hesitated, not knowing how to respond. A third and fourth message came in quick succession. The final read, PLEASE PROMISE ME THAT YOU WILL COME BACK.

I PROMISE, he typed.

PROMISE ME THAT YOU WILL COME BACK, she repeated.

WHEN I CLOSE MY EYES I SEE YOU. SO MUCH JOY AND AT THE SAME TIME SO MUCH PAIN, BECAUSE I KNOW THAT WHEN I OPEN THEM YOU'LL BE HALF A WORLD AWAY. I PROMISE YOU, WENDY, I PROMISE YOU WITH EVERY FIBER OF MY BEING THAT WE ARE GOING TO BE A FAMILY.

Wendy tried in vain to keep her emotions in check, but she was sobbing as bitterly as anyone who discovered she was alone. She lurched with spasms of grief, and the communicator came in and out of focus. Something terrible was about to happen. She didn't know how or why...she just knew. I LOVE YOU, JAKE. I'M SORRY I'M NOT AS STRONG AS YOU.

Jake was taken aback. He read her words again – *I'm sorry I'm not as strong as you.* He experienced a tremendous squeeze of guilt. He felt his eyes trying to well up with tears. His next reaction was to look away, fearing that the men might see him and perceive it as a sign of weakness. He blinked in an effort to clear the building moisture. That's when he experienced a self-revelation—it had nothing to do with the men. That was just a convenient excuse. The problem was that he was scared of his own emotions. 'My God,' he thought, 'I've made Wendy feel like she's the weak one.' He realized that because he had deprived her the opportunity to share his heartbreaks, the trials and tribulations of his soul, and his deepest fears, she considered her own as being a sign of weakness.

'Damn, I'm so stupid,' Jake thought. He perceived a voice urging him, '*Why are you keeping her out? Let her in. You're completely safe.*' It was a watershed moment, and he was hesitating. It was so simple and yet the prospect was frightening beyond measure. To allow his feelings to escape the solitude of his mind, to escape the prison he built was against his strongest instincts. He closed his eyes and typed, I'M SCARED TOO. It was hard, but once he did it, he felt a weight being lifted. It was the first time he ever admitted to himself, much less anyone else, how he really felt. I'M REALLY SCARED. He paused to collect rogue thoughts that were going in different directions, and he began again. I'M SCARED OF DYING. I'M SCARED OF YOU LIVING WITHOUT ME. I'M SCARED OF BAILEY AND PAUL NOT HAVING THEIR FATHER. I KNOW YOU'RE SCARED. I KNOW YOU FEEL ALONE, BUT WE'RE SCARED AND ALONE TOGETHER. Jake found it impossible to go on. TELL THEM HOW MUCH THEY MEAN TO ME. I HAVE TO GO NOW. YOU WILL BE IN MY ARMS SOON. I LOVE YOU.

Moments later, on the opposite side of the world, Wendy took Bailey in her arms and lifted her into a hugging embrace.

"What Mommy?" Bailey had always been a happy and willing participant when it came to getting hugs, but she was also old enough to know when something was wrong. She could tell her mom was sad, that she had been crying, and that she was only pretending to be happy.

"Close your eyes," Wendy said.

"What Mommy?"

"It's okay. Close your eyes, sweetie."

Always the dutiful girl, Bailey did as she was told. She closed her eyes and nestled her face into her mother's shoulder and neck. She felt the arms around her, gently squeezing. It was clearly the most comfortable and the second safest place in her world.

"Keep your eyes closed," Wendy whispered as they swayed slow circles in the room. "Keep your eyes closed. I want you to think about Daddy. This hug is from Daddy. He's a world away, but he's sending a special hug just for you."

Bailey squeezed her eyes shut. She wrapped her legs around Wendy's waist and imagined her daddy swooshing into the room. He scooped her up and held her in his arms. In her mind, just for a few moments, she was in the safest place in the world…no needs, no wants, no fears.

"Paul. I just talked to Daddy," Wendy announced as she entered his room.

His eyes lit up in excitement, "Is Daddy home?"

"No honey. I talked to him on the Vintel." Paul's smile quickly faded into disappointment. He turned back to his toys.

"What are you doing?"

"Building a tower," he mumbled.

"Come here." Before Paul knew what was happening he was being given a bear hug. "Daddy told me you needed a big ol' bear hug. And this too," she kissed his cheeks several times. "And he also told me to give you this." She tickled the side of his neck. When he reached his hands up to stop her she reached down and tickled his armpits, then she tickled his ribs.

"Stop it!" He laughed. She tickled him some more. "Stop it!" He pulled away and rolled out of reach. He yelled, "You're not Daddy!" and ran off to find something else to play.

CHAPTER 26: CLOSING THE GAP

"The guy he's taking out is a trained fighter."

"Doesn't look like he's trained," Director Drum commented.

"Given what we're seeing, I understand that it doesn't look that way. He's been retired a few years, but he was a contender for the word heavyweight boxing title. He took Bulldog Brody ten rounds and lost by decision," Ludwig Arness said. He was the highly capable Director of the DSS's Domestic Counter-Terrorism Unit.

"Has he made a statement?"

"He's embarrassed. Says no one ever handled him like that."

"Boxing is about rules. The real world is different," Director Drum said. "Slow it down to half speed."

"Umm, it already is half speed."

"Really." She raised her eyebrows. "Impressive. Cut the speed again." They were in a classified meeting in her office, reviewing security footage from the gym in Reno. "He's fast. Definitely military. Did you run a recognition sequence through the usual systems?"

"I did. I ran him through all our databases and searched all our known covert groups. His identity is unknown. He's not part of our military, nor is he part of MPS or DSS. I even had some of our overseas contacts run him against foreign databases. The guy in this recording doesn't exist."

Drum pointed at the Vintel unit. "This suggests otherwise. Run the checks again using other features, tattoos, and facial structure. He's missing some fingers so run a hand profile."

"Already working on it," Arness said.

She shook her head and commented, "Hard to believe this is the same guy who was in New Bethesda a couple months ago." What she didn't say was she regretted that they failed to eliminate him when they had the chance. By the time she received the lethal directives, orders that took the operation from surveillance to elimination, he had disappeared from the hospital. Had she received the order an hour earlier, he would have been exterminated.

Director Drum answered directly to the shadow power behind the Egalitarian Party, the small group of elite bankers who controlled United America's economy. They promised political protection and were paying her well to accomplish a single task…the quiet elimination of Jake Gillean and Benjamin Murray. She understood that Zimmer and the Egalitarian Party wanted to investigate him, that they were interested in time travel, but her handlers wanted him dead. She didn't know why and didn't care. They only gave her enough information to accomplish the task.

Her time and DSS resources were being monopolized by the sudden wave of political assassinations, and the murders and disappearances of several agents. To avoid attracting undo attention, she could only sparingly pull DSS resources from the intense national investigations. She angled to develop her quarry as potential suspects and have them eliminated that way.

Drum stared at the image of Dr. Benjamin Murray. Her eyes were daggers. 'You better run you son of a bitch. I'm coming for you,' she thought. She studied Arness. He was as usual…cool and collected. "How far ahead are they?" she asked.

"The recording is from nineteen hours ago. We tracked several pods that moved away from the vicinity of the gym in the minutes after they exited the building. We tracked those that contained two passengers. Regression analysis has picked up some anomalies in the tracking systems. They are somehow manipulating the grid and swapping quantum signatures with other pods. If they stay in densely populated areas they are exceedingly difficult to track, but we are working out the math."

"You've implemented Protocol Eleven?"

"We have. It takes time, but so far, it's working."

When the President declared martial law, it initiated a series of national security protocols. Protocol Eleven gave the government the power to remotely deactivate any pod and hold its passengers for questioning. The DSS was coordinating efforts with local police departments to apprehend suspects at the moment their pods were deactivated. In this manner they were able to eliminate false tracking and navigate the complex anomalies they were seeing in the grid.

Director Drum turned back to the Vintel and watched the recording again. She said, "This was a big break. How did it fall in our laps?"

"The owner had been robbed and installed the surveillance systems. It was patched into the local police department database. We picked it up through a facial recognition scan."

"Good work. I want you to quietly divert as many resources as we can to this. We're getting close."

CHAPTER 27: INTO THE HEART OF THE PERSIAN EMPIRE

[JULY 18, AD 2379]
[ARRIVAL DATE MINUS 61 YEARS]
[OPERATION HADES: THE GUARDSMEN ARE BEING TRANSPORTED FROM THE UNITED AMERICAN MAINLAND TO THE STAGING AREA – LORD NELSON NAVAL BASE IN WESTERN AUSTRALIA.]

The muffled drone of the transport's engines made it easy for the Guardsmen to take a nap. By the time the plane completed its climb into the upper stratosphere, half the soldiers were asleep and the others were on their way.

"This seat taken?" Alex asked.

"All yours," Jake said. It was obvious he was distracted. Alex guessed it was his correspondence with Wendy.

"Did you reach Wendy before the shutdown?" he asked.

"Yeah," Jake said exhaling. He stretched and rubbed the back of his neck. The tension had given him a headache.

"Any new pictures?"

Jake reached inside his coat and pulled out a dozen shots.

Alex looked with a dreamy smile and chuckled. "I'll never understand how such an ugly son of a bitch ended up with such a good looking family."

"Lucky I guess. Wendy said this one's for you."

Alex studied the photo. "Thanks," he said. He lounged back, making himself comfortable. Given the stress of the mission, he needed a break from planning lines of assault and talk of the Persian transport facilities. Any other topic was welcome, even if it was just for a few minutes. "Have a good visit?" he asked.

"Yeah. Nice to be a family."

"I don't envy you when the boys start coming around. You have a few years though."

Jake laughed, "Just had that conversation with Wendy." He didn't really want to talk about it so he changed the subject. "Anything you want to tell me about? Did you meet any girls?"

"No," Alex admitted. "Not this time. Between my hobbies and trying to save the world...who has time? Besides, keeping you children from playing in traffic is hard enough."

"Well, what did you do for the last ten days?"

"Nothing as exciting as you. I went to a conference."

"A conference? What kind of conference?" Jake asked.

"I can't tell you that," Alex said. "It's classified." After another pause he added, "If I told you it might hurt my image."

"What image?"

Alex scoffed, "What do you mean, what image? The tough guy image."

Jake nodded and grinned, waiting for Alex to cave. He did the mental countdown – 'Five, four, three, two, one...'

"Fine," Alex said. "It was an economics symposium."

"What? You get ten days off, and you go to an economics symposium?"

"Yeah. It was fascinating. It focused on the history of banking and international corporations. The focus was from the founding of the New World to the present."

Jake's eyebrows furrowed.

"What?" Alex said, his tone clearly defensive.

"Actually, I think it sounds interesting," Jake admitted.

"Actually, it's fascinating," Alex retorted. "Social and political movements and even wars, don't occur in a vacuum. If you understand the money, who has it and the forces preventing or promoting other people from making more of it, history all of a sudden makes a lot of sense. I dare say that it becomes rather predictable," Fisk said. He was excited by his revelation and went on, "Take this war. It's fascinating. We now suspect that the Persians had been planning this war for the last thirty years. We just didn't act until it was too late. You don't have to be a scholar to understand that what got us through the first three World Wars was our financial system. A currency backed in something of tangible value such as gold has definite advantages over a fiat currency in many ways, but a fiat currency that's backed by a population's strong faith and trust in the power of a central government and its power to maintain order, and a currency that is managed well, you know...without issuing too much or too little into the circulation and the interest rates being appropriately controlled, has tremendous advantages, especially in war-time when spending not only outstrips production, but what you have on hand in terms of commodities of tangible value, like gold, silver, and platinum."

"Wait a minute," Jake said. "Go back to the Persians planning for war."

Alex couldn't hide his excitement. He rarely had the opportunity to discuss his true interests. "Okay, with the rise of Persian power," he said, "something remarkable happened—they created a climate of economic stability in the entire Middle East and across almost the whole of Africa. They lured in huge investments from all over the world. They set up the most elaborate Ponzi scheme in history. We now know that whole companies and markets were nothing more than illusions, others were single companies marketed under multiple names. They manipulated currencies and sold Persian treasury bonds to the West as fast as we could throw in our money. Everyone believed the Persian Empire represented the next great economic boom. Portfolios were growing, and no one wanted to believe it was a ruse. Greed clouded everyone's judgment. We have a long record of making the same greedy mistakes over and over again, and while financial ambition is one of our strengths, it's also one of our weaknesses. The Persians recognized that and we got played." Alex turned toward Jake and went on, increasingly animated and talking with both hands. "Then, when the time was right, they let international relations spiral out of control with an invasion of South Africa. They made war inevitable at a time when the people and the government of United America were the most financially vulnerable. When we were maximally invested, they pulled the rug out, and our markets collapsed. Half our banks went bankrupt overnight. You remember the statistics…well over a hundred million people lost their jobs in the first week. Retirement portfolios from coast to coast simply vanished into thin air. On the backside, turns out the Persians quietly cornered the world's supply of gold, silver, and platinum—using our money to buy it up. When war broke out, they issued a new fully-backed currency throughout their empire. The beauty of what they did was punctuated by the fact that they borrowed and borrowed and borrowed, and when they couldn't borrow anymore because war broke out, they declared all debts null and void. They played us for the fools we are and pulled off the greatest swindle in history. There's no better way of saying it than that. They understood what others didn't…that if they were to have any chance of winning a war against us they needed to hurt us financially first."

"You make it sound like what they did was obvious." Jake said.

"We have the advantage of looking back," Alex answered. "History isn't history until you're done living it."

Jake shook his head, "I still find it amazing we allowed them to pull it off."

"It's called greed my friend. If you're getting a 12 to 15% return on your Persian investments year after year, are you going to ask questions? Probably not." Alex moved forward in his seat, like he was ready to get up, "Let me ask you...did you eat okay when you were home?"

"We're getting by. Big garden and farmers in the family."

"Well, you can thank the Persians for the fact that you're just 'getting by.' We used to be the world's breadbasket. We were by far the largest exporter of agricultural products, and in less than thirty years, we became an importer. By taking advantage of free trade agreements they wrecked the agricultural sector of our economy. They did it by flooding the United American market with food they subsidized. Our farmers couldn't compete. The imports were far cheaper and undercut domestic production. Now we can't adequately feed ourselves. We can't even manufacture a decent tractor in North America. All things considered, it's amazing we've stayed in this thing and put up such a fight."

CHAPTER 28: UNDER THE PERSIAN EMPIRE

[JULY 19, AD 2379; LATE AFTERNOON]
[ARRIVAL DATE MINUS 61 YEARS]
[OPERATION HADES: THE UNDERWATER AND UNDERGROUND TRANSPORT OF THE ASSAULT FORCE]

Operations within the submarines were intense. Never before had they attempted a penetration so deep into enemy controlled waters with Nautilus Class subs. On several occasions they powered down their antimatter engines and waited in silence as Persian convoys skirted the surface of the ocean above them, and as Persian submarine patrols crisscrossed the deep. The majority of the journey from Australia consisted of the five primary submarines and smaller escorts traveling in separate groups in a fanned out pattern. Then they turned and passed single file over the drop point, with about two kilometers separating each group. The drop point was on the ocean floor approximately twenty-five kilometers off the Arabian coast—off Bushehr, Iran. While Alex's Gopher was the first in line, Jake's was the last.

"Drop in five." The announcement from the submarine came over the Gopher's com.

"Okay boys and girls," the Gopher's pilot announced. "Secure the hold and strap in. We detach in five."

Jake moved up one side of the hold and down the other. He checked harnesses and made sure the equipment was locked down.

"You doing okay?" The question was directed to one of the scientists.

"Yeah, yeah, yeah,' he nervously said. "I'm okay." His speech was fast and his face sweaty. "Given the danger I'm surprised we made it this far. Their systems should have detected us. Maritime stealth technologies are substandard and overrated. I'm sure they're watching. It's just a matter of time before they attack."

Jake secured the man's straps and moved down the line, thinking to himself that the scientist was going to be a danger to morale if he kept it up. Finally, Jake strapped tight into a wall harness on the back wall of the cockpit. Out the cockpit window, the gamma lighting technologies showed the ocean and all its associated sea life. It lit up the underwater darkness roughly two hundred and fifty meters in every direction. The depth gauge indicated that the submarine and its under-mounted Gopher were descending rapidly.

"The floor should come into view right about…now," one of the pilots said. She was right. The ocean floor materialized and once in view, it appeared to be approaching rapidly. When they were fifty meters from the bottom the quick countdown began. At twenty meters there was a soft clanking sound, the Gopher jerked, detached, and the submarine pulled away. For a moment, the underside of its giant hull could be seen as it pulled away. Jake felt his weight shifting further forward as the Gopher powered up and assumed a near vertical descent.

The pilots were relaying orders and status reports to each other. "All systems operational," one said.

"Tunnel entrance detected," another said. "We have computer lock. Boring apparatus activated."

"Rear tunnel closure systems online and operating at 100%."

At the moment they were entering the tunnel left by the other nine Gophers, a large explosion rocked the ocean. The Gopher lurched to the side but its systems compensated. The tunnel was now enveloping the nose of the craft.

A rapid series of voices from the submarine came over the com. "We're under attack. Shields holding. Evasive maneuver Delta Six. Launching holograms." Then nothing. The Gopher completed its descent into the tunnel and closed it down behind, cutting off all further communications.

"Holy…, that was close," one of the pilots said as he wiped his brow.

The female pilot remained cool and collected. "All systems operational. We are 2.27 kilometers behind number nine, and the lead is running straight and easy at 11.7 kilometers." She turned to the other pilots, "Focus on what's in front of you. The submarine crews are the best at what they do. If there's a way out they'll find it. There's nothing we can do to help them. I want a status update on the other Gophers, and Lt. Col.," she turned to Jake, saying, "We took quite a…" She stopped because he wasn't there. His straps were dangling as he had returned to the hold to check on his men.

Forty-seven hours had passed since the briefing, and the Gophers were approximately three hundred ten kilometers from their objective. For the next fifteen hours they would travel through solid rock toward Mount Kuh-e Kharman. It was an unnatural feeling, as though planet Earth was somewhere else, and they were entombed within an absolutely dark and unfamiliar world. It tested everyone's nerves to be traveling underground for so long with no avenue of escape except for the technologies carried within the Gophers. Their only communications would be with the other nine Gophers traveling in the convoy.

The Persians were unaware that the potential for an underground attack existed. Despite having spies embedded deep within almost every agency in the United American government, and in corporations throughout the country, MST Global's weapons development program was untouched. This meant that the Persians were unaware of the existence of the ST-17 Gopher and its remarkable capabilities.

There was nothing particularly comfortable about the interior of the vehicles. Just like an old cargo transport, the seats for the soldiers folded down from the sides of the interior compartment so that the men would have to stare at each other when harnessed in. Once the weapons were again checked and rechecked they were secured in compartments above, and on the floor below. Diagnostics were performed again on the exo-suits, and the BCD communications systems were calibrated. Operating deep underground, they would be without satellite relays and would instead be relying on direct communication between individual BCDs. It was sub-optimal but necessary given the circumstances. Once Jake was satisfied everything was ready, all they had to do was wait.

"Lt. Col.," one of the men said to Jake, "do you have your flute?"

Jake considered the request, and when several others chimed in with similar sentiments, he pulled it out. It was small and inconspicuous enough that he carried it in one of his exo-suit compartments, but when unfolded it was a metal tube almost twenty centimeters long and capable of producing sounds that were unexpectedly deep and full. The men found it mesmerizing. It was a good way to cope with the stress of waiting.

The drone of the Gopher's engines and a slight vibration lulled most of the men to sleep. There usually wasn't a lot of chatter before a mission. The boisterous personalities never made it this far. They were culled early, during training, or they got themselves killed in the field. The men who made it to the level of Guardsmen were different. They were tough as nails and tended toward being quiet.

A sudden bump jolted Jake out of sleep. He was in one of the deep and vague dream sequences that usually occur in the first half of the night, one that was hard to recall even though it was there a moment before. It was about family, but the rest of the details were gone. The interior of the cabin was dimly illuminated by red bio-luminescent lights running across the floor behind their feet, and more across the overhead. Jake unsecured his harness and walked to the front to check out what was happening in the cockpit.

The pilots were at ease at the controls. There were four separate Vintel units operating. The holographic displays were showing in real time the cabin, the exterior of the craft, the function of the engines with digital displays of dozens of different parameters, and still another showed all the Gophers and was monitoring the tactical group's progress relative to the surface. Lights in the front of the Gopher illuminated the inside of the tunnel, and at the edge of perception, was the rear of the vehicle in front.

Proud as peacocks, they showed Lt. Col. Gillean the controls, the novel monitoring equipment, and the redundant back up systems that were built into the craft.

"This is a geologist's dream," one of them said. "We've seen igneous and metamorphic rock, folds and fractures, coal, ore, marble, and we ran through a fairly large oil deposit about an hour ago. Right now what you see is limestone. Hard to identify anything smaller as we're moving pretty fast." What Jake saw looked like a train going through a very small underground tunnel. The walls were flying past at an unbelievable rate considering that in front of the lead Gopher it was sold rock.

Jake made his way back to the cabin. All the men were asleep, except for Captain Hammer. He was built like a fire hydrant with dark hair and a thick neck, which at a point no one could discern, turned into a head. There was a deep scar across his cheekbone. His real name was Rolf Wilder. He earned the nickname when he accidently hit himself in the head with a hammer. He had to go to the hospital to get patched up but decided he liked the scar. The guys convinced him that it made him look tough so he decided to keep it. He was in the rear of the craft pacing uncomfortably.

"Lt. Col.," he said as Jake approached.

"What gives?" Jake asked.

"Can't sleep. Tired of sitting." The truth was told in his pacing and incessant shifting of weight from one leg to the other. He couldn't sit comfortably because of his restless leg syndrome. Thus far he refused to see the doctor out of fear that something negative would end up in his file. Most nights, about an hour before he'd go to sleep, he found himself on the receiving end of tingling, aching, and crawling sensations through his entire body, but mostly his lower extremities. Occasionally they would extend to involve his arms. It felt better if he moved, rubbed, or walked around, but as soon as he'd try to lie still in an attempt to sleep, the sensations would come back to torment him.

Jake didn't say anything, but he did notice that Hammer kept rising up on his toes and back down. He figured it was just a nervous habit and left it alone. He planned to let Hammer talk if he wanted. Long ago he learned that an important part of being a leader was listening to his men, and they appreciated him for it.

"This one's going to be ugly, sir," Hammer said. He took a deep contemplative breath and asked, "How did it ever come to this? How did they get this far ahead of us in technology?" He wasn't expecting an answer, just venting his frustration. "The whole world is falling apart up there and here we are digging underground. Less than two days ago," he said, "I was sleeping with my wife. The day before, my mom was doting on me like I was five years old. She insisted on making hot chocolate from scratch, you know, melting the chocolate and mixing it so thick you can eat it with a fork. She put marshmallows on top. Have you ever had it like that?"

"No," Jake said. "Not the real thing."

Hammer thought about it for a minute and went on. As he talked, his facial expression indicated that he was seeing something other than the scenery in the Gopher, that his mind was elsewhere. "Would you believe she even made a peanut butter and jelly sandwich? She keeps the peanut butter cold so when she puts this huge glob of crunchy on it, it won't smear without tearing the bread. I keep telling her to store it in the pantry. She even cut the crust off and served it to me on a plate. It had this huge lump in the middle...looked like a mouse crawled in there."

"Best meal you've had in a long time," Jake said.

"It was," Hammer admitted. He continued staring into space as though reliving the moment—narrating for the benefit of everyone else. "Best meal I've had in a long time. I remember when I was a kid I'd eat around the edges until all I had was this big lump of peanut butter. Then I'd just bite into it. I'd complain that it was lumped up, but I'd judge the quality of the sandwich entirely on how thick it was. And I'd have this white mustache. It's impossible you know, to drink hot chocolate with marshmallows and not get marshmallow all over your upper lip."

"Sounds like a good memory," Jake agreed.

"I couldn't do it that way though...the sandwich. It was the strangest thing. I wanted to eat it like I used to but for some reason I just couldn't. Mom was watching. I could tell she was thinking the same thing. She had this look of disappointment. It was like she wanted her little boy back. But I don't think he exists anymore. This war's taken most of what's left up here." Hammer pointed to his head. "I should have just eaten it the way I used to, if nothing else just to give her some joy, but I couldn't do it." He turned slightly so that he was facing Jake. "Does that make any sense?"

"It does." Jake felt the same way. He longed for the carefree days of his past, a time before everything good became jaded by all his bad experiences. "I think we've all changed. We survive but little parts of us die every day. You don't realize it as much until you go back home. This war is making casualties of all of us." After a pause he asked, "Did you talk about it with your wife?"

"No. I wanted to but I couldn't. You'd think I could talk to her."

"Hammer, you have to give yourself a break. I don't think it's quite that simple," Jake said. "Look at how we live. We wake up in the morning and realize that through some miracle of God we've survived to see another day. Then we have to do it all over again, and again, and again. We pick out our weapons for the day with the realization that our life depends on making the right choices. And how many times have those choices actually proven to be exactly what sees us through the fight? It's a maddening cycle. At the same time, we have to place absolute trust in the men around us. I don't think that's a natural thing to do. It takes training and incredible discipline. I think it does something to the mind when a person constantly lives on the edge…to be constantly aware of your mortality and realize that any moment might be your last. How can you possibly explain to your wife what that's like? She wouldn't understand because she can't. No matter how much she might want to, or how much she might try, she will never, ever, be able to understand. And when you take a life, whether it's from a distance or up close and personal, no one except the guys who have lived it will ever understand."

"I suppose you're right," Hammer admitted.

Jake motioned around the interior of the craft, pointing at the other men. "This is your family. Every man here would die for you. The brotherhood runs deep. The uncommon experiences we share make for uncommonly deep friendships." After a pause Jake added, "My dad was special-ops. I remember that the strength of his friendships was something to behold. Mom was jealous because the guys shared a kinship with him, had a path to his heart that she didn't, and I'll admit that at the time I didn't understand. There was no way either of us could. So I don't think it's unusual at all that you couldn't talk about it."

"Think we'll get through this one?" Hammer hesitantly asked under his breath, almost embarrassed to voice his fears. He was more concerned for the rest of the world than he was for his own safety. The briefing really freaked him out. He believed, as did everyone else, that if they failed to take out the transport facility, the inconceivable was possible…the West as a culture might fail. It was Thermopylae all over again. When he thought about what it would mean to surrender to the Persians, the images were horrific in the absolute. While the odds of a successful attack were growing as the Gophers closed in on the facility, the odds of a successful extraction appeared remote. The Guardsmen were informed of that during the briefing. While they would do their duty, the deadly seriousness of the situation was not lost on Hammer. That's largely why he couldn't sleep. The memories of lumped up peanut butter were only a distraction.

Jake gave his assessment and his tone left nothing to question. "No soldiers in the history of the world stand a better chance of pulling this off. We'll do this one just like we trained, and then we get the hell out of Dodge. All in a day's work for Alpha Group, and when we get back I want to try some of that hot chocolate." Jake slapped him on the shoulder and said, "Take one of your seven hour tabs and get some sleep. I need you alert."

Hammer did as instructed. As he walked away, Jake couldn't help thinking that he was right to be worried…the next day was going to be hell.

On the surface of the planet the frequency of bombings was steady. Moscow, Paris, and Berlin were suffering, and London had not seen as much destruction since the bombings by the German Luftwaffe during the Second World War. Tokyo and Hong Kong, even though they hadn't recovered from the Third World War, were seeing their share of destruction. The Persians were primarily targeting fixed structures in civilian sectors. The ultimate objective was to spread absolute terror and bring the rest of the world to its knees.

Several hours had passed, and most of the Guardsmen were awake and moving around the hold. The stress of being in a confined place was nerve racking, like being in a tomb. The nervous scientist was prattling on about something. From the rear of the hold, Jake couldn't hear exactly what was being said but from the reactions it generated he correctly assumed the man was annoying in the extreme. He took a seat next to the scientist, who queried,

"Why do you think they're not transporting thermonuclear or dark matter weapons, or even biological agents?" He answered his own question, "Because there's some volatility. It's unstable. Once they solve that problem, Western culture will be eradicated. They think we have less inherent value than a diseased rat." He was wringing his hands and looking around with fear in his eyes. He wasn't talking to anyone in particular. "They didn't tell you about the other transport facilities did they? Yeah, you only know what the government is telling you. They're ready to come on line. One is in Northern Zagros Mountains, another in the Ahmar Mountains of East Africa, and there's a third on the ocean floor thirty kilometers southwest of Karachi."

"How do you know all this?" Jake asked.

"Because I was there. I was in the meetings when we were analyzing the tech. We're trying to reverse engineer our own transport facility on a ship so that we can move it around. The first thing we'll do is take out theirs. The concept is simple." The scientist nervously laughed between sentences. "The entire concept is grounded in ideas of theoretical physicists from the 22nd and 23rd Centuries. Yeah, yeah, that's where it all started. They were trying to solve problems with high-velocity travel through space. Their objective was to suspend time. Yeah, and the Persians got ahead of us. They had some breakthroughs." He started rubbing his thighs and laughing, "They discovered they could predictably manipulate the space-time continuum. They figured out how to make wormholes and how to control the location of the other end of the wormhole. That's how they're sending explosives behind our lines."

"What's your name?" Jake asked.

"Halbert. Halbert Trenton." He stood up and paced in a circle. Under his breath he began saying, "We're going to die. We're going to die."

Jake calculated the time and held up three fingers to Raul, who acknowledged. Jake wanted a pneumatic syringe loaded with a three-hour deep sleep sedative. Jake flashed a hand signal indicating that it should be calculated for a one hundred and fifty pound individual. Raul handed the syringe to Jake.

"So tell me, Dr. Trenton," Jake asked, "how does one go about generating a wormhole?"

"It's very complicated. Very complicated. You need a platform seventy-five meters in diameter and thirty meters in height. The fourth dimension… time, we pause it within the chamber. Distance is like a long linear rope. We twist it back on itself. Yeah, yeah, that's how we do it." He continued to pace nervously, increasingly out of his mind. He put his hands on the chest of one of the Guardsmen and grabbed at his exosuit. "Yeah, you enter a predetermined coordinate. The target site is juxtaposed over the transporter's platform." He laughed. "Theoretically, at that moment, the object on the platform is in two distinct locations. It's in a superposition of states…one bomb becomes two. We close the wormhole, and the bomb is transported to the target. Yeah, yeah, do you understand me? Linear time and distance snap back into place and pull the bomb along with it. The object is on the platform one moment and disappears, ha ha, it destroys the target at the other end."

"Let's get you strapped in," Jake said. He pointed to a seat. Dr. Trenton sat down. His eyes were wild.

"I don't want to die," he blurted out. "Location, location, location. They have to select a location. They need a spotter to select coordinates so the bomb doesn't materialize in a wall. Need a hard surface. The detonator is underneath. It falls and explodes."

Jake took a moment to get his harness on because the doctor was squirming.

"If they learn how to retain the bomb on the platform and send the theoretic duplicate to the target, they can use the same bomb over and over. Do you know what that means? We're going to die. No, no, I don't want to die. They have to reload a new bomb from outside the mountain each time. That's why they can only do a bombing every ninety minutes."

Jake brought the syringe up to Dr. Trenton's neck. "They're doing experiments with goats, trying to transport living material." There was a quick pulsing sound and the doctor's head fell limp. He was silent. Raul secured the head harness to keep him safe and immobile.

"Show's over," Jake said.

Everything the doctor said was true except he neglected to mention that the Persians were constructing an additional launch site under Mount Kuh-e Kharman. Heavy construction was taking place and higher levels of security were in force. It was with incredible misfortune that the arrival of United America's Gophers would coincide with intense Persian security drills.

CHAPTER 29: THE ATTACK

The ST-17 Gophers were running behind schedule. It was 0750 on the morning of July 21, 2379 before they made it into position. One was lost to mechanical failure five clicks from the objective. The crew was divided in half and transferred to other Gophers.

"Commander Saleed. We detected seismic activity." The emergency report came from one the Persian technicians in the control room. Many of the personnel within the mountain felt the low rumble. Being almost a mile under the surface it was a disconcerting sensation.

"How bad?" Saleed asked. He was the commander of the facility, responsible for non-scientific aspects of the transport facility, including structural integrity and its security.

"Enough to register a 1.4 on the scale."

"Do you have an epicenter?"

"No, sir. Triangulation failed. It was an unusual pattern though. It appeared to wander, if such a thing is possible. There was activity all around the facility. It built up to 1.4 and just stopped. It's been quiet ever since."

"Any aftershocks?" he asked.

"No, sir."

"Keep me posted. All transport activities are suspended until we conduct a full inspection," Saleed ordered. "I want the structural engineering teams on it now."

"I'll see to it immediately, sir."

Inside the Gophers, the pilots nervously awaited the order. It finally came from Col. Fisk. "Initiate boring procedure."

"Confirm. Initiating boring procedure," the female pilot announced. With a hand controller she guided a boring device through the two meters of stone separating the Gopher from the interior of the facility. With surgical precision it snaked its way around piping and bundles of wires, and punched several holes approximately five millimeters in diameter through the wall, high up near the ceiling. The final stages of the process, tedious work designed to prevent debris from falling inside the structure, consumed forty-five minutes.

With sweat soaking her uniform and beads across her brow, she gave a sigh of relief and carefully backed her hands away from the controls. "Insert the camera," she said to the co-pilot.

"Yes, sir. Initiating camera insertion," he responded. He took over the controls and, with Vintel-assisted guidance, advanced the camera until it was in perfect position. They were now obtaining real-time audio and video records of everything happening within the target areas of the Persian facility. The information was uploaded to Fisk's Gopher for general analysis and into the BCDs of the Guardsmen. Jake reviewed the recording with his men using a large hologram detailing the interior of the transport chamber. He finalized everyone's placement and the objectives for the assault. The process occurred simultaneously with Guardsmen in the other Gophers, with Jake coordinating their every move and verifying that everyone knew where everyone else was.

Once the cameras were functional, the pilots prepared for XBJ-71 nerve gas infusion. It didn't take long until all systems were operational and Col. Fisk issued the order, "Initiate infusion." The gas began streaming from storage tanks on the Gophers into the immense facility. Getting the concentration to adequate levels would take several hours.

In the interim, with the operation of the cameras, the Persian scientists were identified and marked for extraction. So far everything was happening as planned. Once the facility was secured and all resistance eliminated, the brains behind the operation were the next objective. As the information they possessed was valuable in the extreme, they were marked for extraction and would be transported back to North America for interrogation.

Jake synchronized his BCD with the rest of the Guardsmen and prepared for a long wait. At exactly 1100 hours the assault would begin with activation of the nerve gas. At 1101 the Gophers would barrel through the floors and walls, and the Guardsmen would emerge and fan out within the chamber. But that was three hours away. The wait required nerves of steel.

A team of computer scientists in the lead Gopher needed every minute of the time to hack into the Persian mainframe. They had a lot to accomplish, including the deactivation of any override protocols the Persians had built into the security system. They would shut down communications from the transport chamber and close the multiple thick osmium-carbon steel 8130 alloy gates that led in and out of the facility.

If everything worked perfectly, twenty minutes had been allocated for the collection of information and to apprehend the scientists. Another ten was calculated for extraction—for the Gophers to get far enough away before the mountain was blown to hell with dark matter weapons.

* * * * *

There were a number of Persian soldiers in place throughout the facility. Each carried a sidearm, gas mask, and a rifle that appeared to be equipped with guided munitions. Their black uniforms and gray belts were of a style reflective of loose fitting Arabic fashion and an indication that they were part of an elite command.

Sergeant Iqbar El-Santuri, Second Platoon, Company B, of the Second Regiment, Fourth Brigade, drilled his Persian troops relentlessly. "Again!" he yelled. "You'll keep doing this until you get it right!"

His troops quivered under his stare. He was the most feared, the most hated, and the most respected man in their lives. He paced up and down the lines, reveling in the fact that they were more scared of him than they were of the Western infidel. He took pride in being larger than most, standing six foot three inches and weighing two hundred forty-five pounds.

"What is this?!" he yelled at one of the soldiers. He picked him up off the floor by his uniform and turned him around so that he was facing the rest of the platoon. Through gritted teeth he said, "You're going to get this right, or I'll make you lash every soldier in this platoon!" He roughly set him back down.

The soldier was visibly shaking. To be forced to lash everyone else in the platoon because of your own screw up was considered the most severe form of punishment as it guaranteed lasting enmity and a short life.

The sergeant's demeanor fluctuated between angry and angrier. He had killed at least a dozen of his own men through the years with his bare hands by breaking their necks during self-defense training. The soldiers didn't dare protest.

The Fourth Brigade had recently been pulled from the northern front in Greece after having its ranks depleted, the result of eleven months of hard fighting. In the process of being brought up to strength, it was assigned guard duty at the transport facility. Vigorous training drills had been taking place all week.

"Take it off and do it again!" Sergeant El-Santuri yelled.

The weary soldier stood in front of his platoon. He was wearing a gas mask and was fully outfitted with biological warfare equipment. The mask was off center and failed to seal properly. He took it off, folded it, and placed it in a pouch attached to his vest.

"Now!" the sergeant commanded.

The soldier pulled the mask out of his pouch, and in one fluid move, with one hand only, it was in place. When the mask made contact with the chin and forehead simultaneously it activated and sealed itself to his face, enclosing his eyes, nose, and mouth. With the other hand he held his gun upright as if he were ready to fire at some invading force. In less than a second, the mask was functional, he was in complete control of his weapon, and was aiming with both hands.

"Good! Now everybody!" The sergeant bellowed.

* * * * *

Col. Fisk communicated a general announcement to all the Guardsmen. It was short and to the point. "Men, never has so much been asked of so few. We do this just like we trained. Synchronize BCDs. We activate on my mark plus thirty. For God and country…mark."

It was exactly 1059.30, and the nerve gas activation process was initiated. At nine separate locations throughout the facility, a burr hole used for gas infusion was widened. The instant the clock struck 1100 hours small rockets were fired into the facility. They exploded and emitted a rapidly flashing intense blue light. It happened so fast that by the time the thought registered within the unsuspecting workers' and soldiers' brains that they were seeing something unusual, the paralytic process was in full swing. Everyone in the facility suddenly found themselves falling to the floor. Their arms, legs, necks, and even their facial expressions were completely paralyzed. All of them were completely helpless, all of them…except a nervous soldier standing with his weapon at ready in front of Sergeant El Santuri.

The soldier was half a second away from removing his mask when he witnessed his Sergeant and everyone else in the room collapse to the floor. They couldn't have fallen harder if they had been slapped down by the almighty hand of God. Skulls and faces cracked on the tile floor. A second later there was no movement whatsoever. Everyone was either face down or crumpled over another body. Blood oozed from around the heads of several in slowly expanding arcs.

'By the grace of Allah, what's going on?' he thought.

The Sergeant, in all his military greatness, had been rendered completely helpless for the first time since his father beat him unconscious at the age of eight as punishment for watching his older sister take a bath.

The single remaining Persian solder, Private Mahatma Hagravan, at first forgot about his gas mask. He was panicking. His fellow soldiers were down. He couldn't make sense of it. They were entirely limp. They didn't blink. They didn't react. Through the mask he couldn't smell the foul stench that was emanating from the bodies, several had defecated, and all of them had urinated. He reached for his mask to remove it. That's when he noticed they were breathing. 'There's something in the air,' he thought. Without warning, alarm systems began blaring. Red lights were flashing. He backed against the wall, not knowing what to do.

"GO! GO! GO!" came the command. It was exactly 11:01. The ST-17 Gophers lurched forward and plunged through the walls. Jake's Gopher entered the main transport chamber on one side while Alex's entered on the opposite side. When the cargo doors slammed open, he was the first one out. His men scattered out behind him and took up aggressive positions to eliminate any Persian resistance. There was none. Gas masks on and guns in hand, they stepped over the defenseless personnel, quickly securing the chamber and adjoining corridors. In less than a minute, scientists were being dragged across the floor and were placed facedown in the Gophers. Computer equipment that could be loaded easily was ripped away and secured on board. Paperwork and anything else that was thought to have any inherent value was confiscated as well.

Jake moved through the main chamber. His soldiers gracefully turned, twisted, and stepped over the paralyzed, scanning with diligence for any signs of danger. Each team sounded off with similar status reports.

The computer team successfully hacked the Persian security systems so that on the surface they had no idea what was happening. The impenetrable doors slammed shut and from topside they couldn't override the system to get them back open. Further, all visual and auditory communications with the bunker went to static.

Once the Persian facility was deemed secure, the scientists streamed out of the Gophers. They swarmed over the transport device. They attached sensor equipment in and around the computer control panels, and other devices were placed both inside and outside the massive sides of the transport platform. Instantly, trillions of bits of information were being uploaded to satellites and redirected to receiving stations in United America and England.

The actual transport platform resembled two great rectangular satellite dishes facing each other. A similar high-tech panel enclosed its back and top. The floor of the device was made out of some sort of novel ceramic substance, but it was slightly soft, almost organic to the touch.

The scientists working at the control console activated the transport. A set of coordinates was plugged in and the machine began the process of twisting and manipulating the passage of time over the platform. A swirling and contorting mass resembling a semi-reflective, semi-transparent blob approximately twenty feet in width and fifteen feet tall materialized from a single central point within the confines of the platform.

It was mesmerizing. The swirl of deep blue and gray was rolling…almost breathing. It captured Alex's attention. It was as alluring and beautiful as it was dangerous. A low pitched hum and crackling sound like static electricity emanated not from the machine but from the mass within the chamber. Two of the scientists were sticking specialized sensory equipment in and out of the swirling orb, taking readings and recording the data.

Alex moved toward the transport platform. On top of a nearby monitoring station, he found what appeared to be a small black leather-bound case. He took it as though he expected it to be there. He casually put it into a pouch on the thigh of his exosuit.

Off to the side, there was another corridor. It was ten meters wide. Most importantly…it wasn't supposed to be there. It wasn't included in the schematics leaked by United American operatives. Jake carefully moved forward to check it out.

"There's an unknown corridor off the main chamber. I'm checking it out," Jake said. "Capt. Hammer. Position two men at the top and two more with me."

The guardsmen adjusted their positions. Two men followed behind Jake with pulsar rifles at ready, twisting and turning to meet any threats. Once inside the tunnel, Jake went about twenty meters and discovered that it opened into another large chamber. He spied the construction. "There's a second transport chamber," he announced. "It doesn't appear to have come online."

His sixth sense told him something wasn't right. Danger was lurking. Moving farther down the corridor, to the edge of the new enclosure, he noted approximately thirty workers lying motionless on the floor. The complete silence in the room was interrupted only by alarms wailing from the adjoining structure. While the sound waves echoed down the corridor, the alarms within the new chamber remained silent as they had not yet been installed.

One of the workers, a janitor, lay in a urine-stained white uniform. His mop ended up half under him and he clipped the edge of his bucket of water when he fell. The water spread out across the floor. He lay in the middle with his eyes open but unmoving, fixed on some nondescript spot on the ceiling. Operations were racing through Jake's mind, but he took a moment to consider the man…just some unlucky guy trying to survive, might have had a family, a wife, or possibly some children. Probably took the job so he would be able to feed them, to survive the frightening chaos around him. Jake knew he shouldn't think about the Persians as though they were human. While disgusting, giving Persians the dignity befitting members of the human race would do nothing except make the difficult job of killing them all the harder. It might result in hesitation. Even a fraction of a moment's hesitation could get him, or a team member killed. His mind flashed to the American soldier in Corinth, the one who picked up the small child and exploded as a reward for his compassion. If Jake hadn't hesitated, if he'd shot the child, that soldier would still be alive. Jake shook away the flash of compassion. If somebody had to die he'd rather have it be the enemy. Dehumanizing them was a natural coping mechanism.

There was a gurgling sound coming from the janitor's throat. He was choking on his vomit. The sound bothered Jake. It was the way his father died, a terrible way to go. Keeping his pulsar ready and simultaneously scanning the room, in a quick move he grabbed the man's shoulder and tossed him over onto his stomach. He was going to die anyway, but there was something vile about leaving him to drown in his own vomit.

There were tools, ladders, scaffolding, and computer equipment scattered through the chamber. What Jake saw next stopped him in his tracks. His eyes enlarged as his brain processed exactly what he was seeing. On a large palate were three guns. Not just any guns. These were really big guns. Damn near cannons. He noted an open panel on the ceiling, right where it met the wall. Inside was a gun that was in the process of being mounted. They were such that when the panels were closed, they would blend in with the surroundings and wouldn't be noticed. The compartments in the chamber were open, and they lined the entire periphery. Others were mounted in clusters across the chamber roof. There must have been forty or fifty in various stages of installation, enough to rake every square inch with fire.

Jake felt a surge of fear. A microsecond after his brain made the connection, his adrenal glands overloaded his system with a surge of pure and unadulterated adrenaline. The alarm system…it was likely on a timer. If security codes were not entered, the guns would activate and drop through the panels. They likely operated on a combination of motion and heat sensors. There would be no defense. He turned and sprinted as fast as he could while simultaneously announcing his find through his BCD.

"All teams! Persian cannons are in the ceiling! Take them out!"

Alex stood with his back to the large chamber and faced the transport platform. His eyes were uncharacteristically closed as if in some meditative trance. He didn't react when, without warning, panels in the ceiling broke loose. It happened at the same moment Jake's voice came across the BCD with the alert. His words were lost in the chaos. The mounted guns rolled out and began firing in rapid succession. The noise was deafening. Every room, every hallway and corridor, the entirety of the main transporter room, there wasn't a square inch of space within the facility that wasn't being decimated by the guns. The exosuits' shield systems helped, but they were soon overwhelmed. Many of the Guardsmen didn't have time to scream and were cut down where they stood.

The guns activated because of the actions of the lone Persian survivor— Private Mahatma Hagravan. Unimpressive so far in his training, in a crucial moment, he fought to overcome his cowardice. He remembered the secondary communications center. It was two hundred meters down a side corridor. He stayed away from the main passageways and by cutting through several side rooms he accessed the corridor and raced to the communications center. Its systems were still operational, and on the screens, he saw what was happening. Everyone was lying lifeless on the floor, he saw one of them being dragged by his ankles into a strange vehicle that shouldn't have been there, there were gapping holes in the walls, and the place was crawling with enemy soldiers.

Voices were coming across the communicator. "Is anyone there? Respond."

His hands were shaking when he pushed the button to transmit. "I'm here," he said.

"This is Commander Saleed. Identify yourself."

"I'm Private First Class Mahatma Hagravan."

"Status report. Give me a status report," he demanded, unable to hide the anxiety in his voice.

"I'm the only one left," Mahatma cried.

"What do you see? What's happening down there?" Commander Saleed asked.

"Enemy soldiers. They're everywhere. I don't know what to do."

After a pause, during which Saleed took in the gravity of the situation, he yelled, "Listen to me! Today you are a hero. We have been cut off. We can't get in, but you are going to help us."

"How? What can I do?" On every screen he imagined that he saw the enemy soldiers approaching his position. His heart raced and his hands were shaking with fear.

I'm going to give you a number sequence." Commander Saleed directed Mahatma to a separate computer system. He punched in a series of numbers and on the screen appeared the words…SELF DESTRUCT TERTIARY PROTOCOL.

Mahatma's eyes grew wide when he read he words. "It…it says this is a self destruct protocol."

"You will be safe and you can save all of Persia."

Mahatma could tell from the Commander's voice that he was lying. His voice was frantic, "What do you need me to do?"

Commander Saleed said, "I need you to enter a code." He calmed his voice, sensing that he risked losing the only hope he had of fending off the attack.

"Yes, sir," Mahatma agreed. He pressed the buttons, and when he came to the last in the sequence, he held his finger over the security console. He paused. With his eyes closed and his face elevated upward, he muttered a prayer. He screamed out, "Allah Akbar!" He pushed the final button. Two large guns plunged through the ceiling behind him. He felt no pain as the guns turned him inside out.

While he was entering the code, the pilot of Jake's Gopher was preparing to announce that they only had two minutes remaining. In that instant, everything changed. The cockpit shattered as though it was an elegant crystal goblet. Her head and body lurched backward. Several guns simultaneously killed her before she had any chance to comprehend what was happening. As designed, the guns were unmerciful, cold and mechanized in their killing. The motion detectors made no discrimination between friend or foe, and nothing larger than a bacterium would be left alive within the facility.

The Gopher pilot's entire upper torso was quickly torn asunder. With the initial lethal volley, her hand jerked backward on the controls. As a result, the Gopher lurched forward. Like a great Roman candle, sparks marked where each bullet glanced off its hull. Due to its mass and rapid movement, almost every motion-sensitive gun in the main chamber trained in on it, while the remaining Guardsmen fought valiantly, destroying as many of the guns as they could. The Gopher hit the sidewall of the inner chamber, partially climbed up it, and rolled onto its side. With the tracks along its sides, it continued barreling and spinning through the room, knocking over everything and crushing everyone in its path.

In a different part of the facility, the Persian Sergeant El-Santuri lay prone, with his head turned slightly to the side. The image of the far wall and several downed men fixed on his retina. It was blurred and out of focus. Several United American commandos had passed in front of him, and he was powerless to act. What he didn't know was how they pulled it off. There were so many layers of security protecting the facility that getting in or out was impossible. Yet here they were. Private Hagravan was their only hope. He counted down the minutes and felt a sense of satisfaction when the panels along the ceiling exploded downward. There was an immediate cacophony of intense firing, and the room was filled with smoke. Blood and shredded body parts filled the air. In the three seconds before his death, the sergeant felt the red hot pain of six different shots piercing through his limbs and torso. The seventh entered above the right ear. The next ninety-four served no real purpose.

Easily half of his team was already dead in the smoke filled and darkened chamber by the time Jake sprinted out of the corridor. Most of the lights had been blown out by the combination of fire from the Guardsmen and the mounted guns. The resulting effect on the chamber, because of the firing and the glow from the orb, was a scene from hell. The Gopher's wild path through the room was drawing the fire of most of the guns while the remaining men of Alpha Group took aim at the ceiling without real effect. One of them dove into the tunnel cut by the Gopher, he would survive for a few moments longer, but that would be all.

Without the benefit of time, in a place where a fraction of a second stood between life and death, pure instincts took command. Jake saw the silhouetted black outline of someone standing in front of the transporter. With the helmet and gun he recognized the outline as being that of a Guardsman. Two steps later he was diving through the air toward the figure. A bullet hit the heel of his boot. He was spinning in midair. With an outstretched hand he caught the base of the soldier's helmet and yanked him down. The momentum pulled them both into the transport chamber, rolling them into the heart of the undulating blue-gray orb.

The ST-17 Gopher smashed into the side panel of the transport device while the mounted guns continued their unrelenting and furious fire. The Gopher's cargo of dark matter explosives detonated. For a millionth of a second the entire chamber was bathed in a black light, but it only lasted for a moment.

CHAPTER 30: THE GREAT
TRAGEDY

[JULY 21, AD 2379 (12:06 A.M.)]
[ARRIVAL DATE MINUS 61 YEARS]
[LOCATION: SPRING HILL, TENNESSEE]

Wendy rolled over in frustration and glanced at the clock. It was just after midnight. Three and a half hours ago she was reading bedtime stories. It seemed like thirty. The kids were sound asleep and she was in a duel with insomnia. She lay on one side and suffered visions of Jake's death. Turning in frustration to the other side, she heard the rap of the military's Decedent Affairs officer on the front door. At that very moment, on the opposite side of the globe, eleven hours ahead of Spring Hill, Tennessee, Mount Kuh-e Kharman exploded. All at once the house started to shake. At first it was a dull vibration that lingered on the edge of perception, but it grew until the house began to creak and groan. Wendy sat up. The next moment her feet were on the floor. She could feel it moving up and down. She hadn't experienced an earthquake before. It wasn't violent enough to elicit fear, but it was sustained and relentless.

She put on her slippers and wrapped a light robe around her, debating if she should take the children outside. In a single burst, the earthquake grew more violent.

"Wake up. Wake up," she said, straining to keep her voice calm. Paul didn't respond so she picked him up. He was limp and remained in a deep sleep until a row of collectable antique pods rolled off his shelf. They crashed to the floor and startled him. He pulled his head up, and through confused eyes, he started processing what was happening.

Wendy ran from Paul's room and into Bailey's. "Bailey! Bailey! Wake up," she said. A picture fell off the wall and made a loud pop when it hit the floor. Bailey roused and began to sit up when Wendy grabbed her by the arm and pulled her out. "We have to go."

"My blanket," Bailey protested. Not realizing what was happening she pulled away and snatched it from its place next to her pillow. In the process she lost her balance and fell into the bed as Wendy's momentum carried her in the opposite direction, causing her to bang into the wall.

Wendy regained her balance and grabbed her. "We have to go! Come on!" she yelled.

"What's happening to the house?" she asked in excitement. She found her footing and followed behind Wendy.

"Mommy! Mommy!" Paul cried. He squeezed his arms around her neck, digging his shoulder into her throat and choking her.

"It's an earthquake! We have to go!" Wendy said. They made their way out of the room and down the hallway. The floor down its length was rising and falling like small waves. They passed by the dining room. The chandelier was swaying wildly and large cracks burst open in the walls. The furniture was bouncing across floor. Wendy had to dodge to the side to avoid being hit by the dining room table as it careened across the room. She made it to the front door, unlocked it, and pulled. It wouldn't open. The house had shifted and the frame squeezed the door tight. No matter how hard she pulled it wouldn't open, then the house shifted in the other direction and it suddenly sprang open. They darted through it into the night air.

Her instincts screamed that she should get away from the buildings and trees. She loaded the children in the pod and accelerated away from the house, steering it to the center of an open field. They came to a stop on top of a small knoll that offered a good view. The lights from Spring Hill illuminated the horizon to the south. To the north, at the bare edge of where the landscape met the horizon, were vague hints of light emanating from the city of Franklin. In the other directions she could see lights from neighboring farms dotting the darkness like tiny beacons. Wendy found it comforting to know that they were there.

The earthquake was steady and had lasted another ten minutes when a wave of undulating purple-blue light appeared along the entirety of the eastern horizon. Like a great rolling tsunami reaching miles and miles into the sky, it was frightening in every way imaginable, and it was coming fast, gorging itself on everything that stood in its path. Lightning shot out in all directions. Thick bright flashes shot upward to the heavens while the earth below was being scorched with vengeance.

"What is that?" Wendy asked as she peered through the windshield. As it grew closer, she screamed, "Oh no!" Gripped by fear, she didn't know what to do. Should they stay in the pod or get out and huddle on the ground? In a mere moment of indecision it was too late. The wave was sweeping over them. "Get down!" She launched herself over the children and shielded them with her body. "God help us, please help us," she repeated over and over again.

"Mommy, I'm scared! What's happening?" Bailey yelled. Paul was shaking and crying hysterically. The pod was shaking and the noise was deafening. Lightning was crashing and the hills were blanketed with explosions of fire. As continuous flashes of light were abusing the sky, they were jolted by a series of shocks emanating from the closest strikes. Then, within a minute, the great wave of electromagnetic energy passed over. It knocked out everything electrical and passed off into the west. In its wake were violent winds and rain that came down sideways. Within another thirty minutes, the rolling hills were bathed in darkness interrupted only by a crescent moon and billions of majestic stars that were now unveiled in a cloudless sky.

Scared and isolated, Wendy held the children close. They felt alone in the world, like they had been abandoned on a forgotten little hill. The air felt crisp and unseasonably chilly.

Beyond the dull rumble of the earthquake that was fading into the background, they could hear something else. Emerging across the hills was the eerie howling of coyotes. Its volume grew in intensity and converged all around. It sounded like they were in pain or suffering under the weight of madness. It caused the hair to prickle on the back of Wendy's neck and gooseflesh to erupt on her arms, and she experienced a vision. Something ominous had been disturbed from its slumber. Hidden within the frightening melody was a ghostly echo. It emanated from the nearby hills of Franklin, hills that hid within their bellies a long forgotten anguish. In her vision she saw a horde of wandering souls wearing strange blue and gray uniforms. They had suffered various degrees of mutilation. She saw men carrying their own severed limbs, others were missing parts of their faces, still others were dragging their entrails. She saw gnashing teeth, expressions of shock. In some she saw emptiness, and in others, tears of despair. Coming out of the fog, she saw Jake, mounted on a horse. He was reaching his arms out toward the heavens, crying in agony and loss. He was dying. He swayed in the saddle, and then in slow motion, he began falling. There was nothing for him to grab onto as he fell. He kept falling and falling into blackness. Wendy felt light-headed. Her arm flung outward for something to hold. Her fingers curled tightly around the door handle.

"Mommy, you're crying. What's wrong?" Bailey asked.

Wendy blinked back to reality and realized she was in the pod. She forced a smile and hugged her children. "I'm just so happy that we're safe."

CHAPTER 31: WHAT HAPPENED

"I just got a communication from Zimmer," Ben said. "He wants me to come in to get my communications systems fixed."

"What do you make of it?" Jake asked.

"I'm not sure. The situation is evolving nationally and internationally. It makes sense he'd want me closer. Sooner or later he's going to develop a hard suspect. He'll need me to do an interrogation."

"I think it's odd that he's waited two and a half months to call you in," Jake said.

"He thinks I'm protecting you."

"You're not the only one," Jake said.

"What do you mean?"

"Haven't you ever considered that there's another version of you somewhere, or even teams of agents trained to perform the same interrogations?" Jake didn't mention that he found the interrogation files from Ben's BCD. He came away with the conclusion that Ben was one of the cruelest human beings he had ever encountered. Cold-blooded and ruthless in the extreme, he was also a mystery. His personality was quirky and amusing, but when working, he went through a metamorphosis, a true Dr. Jekyll and Mr. Hyde. "Logic dictates," Jake continued, "they would duplicate their capabilities. Far too risky to allow you to exist in isolation."

"I hadn't considered that," Ben admitted.

"One of two things happened. They either made you feel like you were unique and indispensable, or you convinced yourself that you were."

Everything Jake said was making sense. He expected Zimmer would be calling him in, but he didn't. One day had rolled into the next and nothing happened, despite the fact that the world was falling apart. Granted, there were distractions, but Ben now recognized he had been functioning in a state of denial. There had to be suspects being interrogated. Every time someone turned up missing or dead the Egalitarian Party had to be rounding up spouses, maids, secretaries, and everyone in between. They were going to every length possible to expose the conspirators, to uncover the source of the information leaks and the abductions, and yet he hadn't been brought in. Numerous foreign nationals were known to be missing, and someone had to be interrogating them. That had to be it. He was assigned a task and would only be allowed to do it as long as he was useful.

"I think you're right. I'm expendable," Ben said. "If I go in, I don't think I'll be coming back." He felt the grip of real fear. It had been there since well before Zimmer's briefing, but now it was far more primal.

His heart was racing as he executed a series of multi-pod transfers, switching the grid identifications at random. He picked pods that were in front and flipped their identities. He also did it to some that were behind.

* * * * *

"Targets identified. We've got them," the DSS field agent said.

"Is it confirmed?" Director Arness asked.

"Yes sir, dark green pod fitting the description of the one from Reno. We've got visual. Looks like it's been in an accident. The front end is dented in. Units are converging. We've got two tactical teams of aerocycles, one is behind and the other is circling to come in from their front. They're executing grid transfers as we speak, but we're maintaining visuals."

"We move when everyone's in place."

"Confirming rules of engagement, sir."

Arness paused. "Take them alive, but if there is ANY resistance eliminate them."

"Rules confirmed." The senior officer in the field knew what Arness meant—identify the targets first, then kill them. "Sir. There's a tunnel up ahead. Two thousand meters and closing."

"Move in now," Arness ordered.

"Confirmed. All teams go."

The pod was deactivated from the grid and came to a sudden stop, snarling the flow of traffic coming up behind. Almost immediately, before Ben or Jake would have had time to react, the pod was surrounded by DSS agents. Some of them dismounted and carefully approached on foot, coordinating movements and aiming their pulsars at the vehicle. Others hovered in a circle, remaining on their aerocycles, centering their onboard weapons systems at the target. One of the agents on foot inched forward, opened the door, and dodged to the side…it was empty.

* * * * *

Ben and Jake had abandoned the pod in the busy downtown district of Phoenix, but before Ben left it for good, he programmed it to make a trip to Tulsa. How far it would actually get through the checkpoints he didn't know. It didn't matter. They walked fifteen blocks, carefully staying in crowded areas, and finally made it to Chinatown. They'd have to wait it out until MST provided a new mode of transport.

They went into a back alley bar and casually selected a booth where one could see the front door and the other the back. They ordered food and a drink and began again where they left off.

Ben gave a sigh of relief and asked. "Do you know what happened… as a result of the Gopher exploding?"

"I reviewed the files," Jake said.

"What files?"

"The ones I took from your BCD."

"Not those," Ben whispered. "Those are government files released for public consumption." As Ben talked he was already routing a request to MST headquarters for the real files on the Great Tragedy. He directed that they be downloaded directly to Jake's BCD. He said "Open channel E17 with Summit Alpha Omega 7 encryption, and you'll receive the real file."

Jake did as instructed and the file began streaming to his BCD. The origin was identified as unknown. He gave Ben a curious look. Soon enough he'd discover who the people were behind the file.

Jake opened it. It was labeled top secret and included footage of events within the Persian Bunker. "How did you get this?" he asked.

"It's not what you know…it's who you know," Ben laughed. "Soon my friend. We're almost there."

The computer modeling depicted the wormhole created by the Persian transporter and the programmed destination site over two thousand miles away. There was an explosion of the dark-matter weapons stored on the Gopher. The combination resulted in a catastrophe of unimaginable proportions. Jake's face turned ashen as he watched. A burst of electromagnetic energy surged upward from Mount Kuh-e Kharman, casting itself into outer space like a demonic flare. At the same time, a massive wave of energy surged out from the epicenter. Thousands of meters in height and depth, it churned everything with tremendous heat and energy. Rocks instantly liquefied and boiled. Atomic bonds destabilized and every complex earthly substance was reduced to its basic elemental form, a process not seen on such a vast scale since the primordial molten earth was born. What formed on the surface was a vast ocean of a sand-like substance that churned in the ground and air.

As the wave of electromagnetic energy swept around the planet every orbiting satellite was destroyed. The wave spread over the globe, knocking out everything electrical and casting the surface into darkness. The earthquake continued for hours. There were volcanic eruptions throughout the Middle East as the integrity of the tectonic plates was destroyed. The orange and yellow molten material shot upward, casting a glow within the undulating waves of black and brown debris. The energy wave spread outward from the mountain at tens of thousands of miles per hour, only to inexplicably slow and stop once it reached the other end of the wormhole.

Jake couldn't continue. He paused the program and leaned back against the booth. He perceived the coldness of the dark wood as it pressed against his spine. He was hesitant to ask but the words just shot out, "How many people died?"

"It's estimated at thirteen billion."

A horrified stillness followed. "How is someone supposed to comprehend that many lives?" Jake asked. He didn't expect an answer. He shook his head in dismay and restarted the file, continuing the terrible discovery of what actually happened.

The planet had suffered a near-mortal wound. It occurred in a circular pattern that in the end stretched out from the mountain in a radius of approximately twenty-five hundred miles. When the destructive energy spread outward from the mountain like tidal waves across water, when it reached its zenith, it suddenly stopped. It folded back on itself and then inexplicably flickered out at ground zero.

The details of what actually happened were numbing. At the epicenter winds churned thousands of miles per hour. Temperatures unseen in the life of the planet caused lakes, rivers, and vast portions of the ocean to boil. A great black cloud of vapor and dust expanded into the atmosphere and swept overland. At the same time, to fill the void where large bodies of water and land barriers vanished, great walls of water rushed inward. Initially, as fast as the water rushed in it was vaporized. It led to worldwide storms and flooding that occurred on an unprecedented scale. Great earthquakes and giant tsunamis devastated coastal regions around the world. Afterward, the sea and coastal regions were littered with the remains of trillions of dead fish, and agricultural production was decimated.

A million square miles were destroyed. No people. No birds. No insects. No bacteria. No organic matter of any kind remained. All that was left, as far as the eye could see, was sand and rock. Billions of people, without warning, were gone. They vanished as though they never existed, and along with them went all traces of the great Persian and Middle Eastern cultures of the past…everything replaced with dead earth.

When it finished, the geographic landmass of the Persian heartland was rendered unrecognizable. Mountain chains disappeared while volcanic activity, which erupted along specific corridors, created new ones. Massive bodies of water disappeared and new ones took their place. Tectonic plates shifted and raised the levels of land, and as the seas boiled off, thick salt flats remained as the only reminder of what once existed. The fragment that remained of the ruined Persian subcontinent was now connected to Africa. The largest parts of India were gone. Water spilled from the Mediterranean Sea into the Indian Ocean along a new pathway that was hundreds of miles wide.

"What happened at home?" Jake asked.

"Spring Hill and Franklin fared well," Ben said. "Less than ten people died as an immediate result of the disaster, and being tight-knit communities fortunate to be positioned in an agricultural region, they endured the wave of starvation that followed with minimal suffering."

"And my family?"

Ben paused, not knowing what to say. "Jake, I don't have any information about Wendy or your children. They're not in the record."

The Western Hemisphere fared well in comparison to the East. Even so, the damage was extensive. United America's infrastructure was devastated. The coasts were hit with giant waves, bridges were destroyed, and buildings damaged. But all things considered, there was minimal loss of life…at first. The next two years saw mass starvation, riots, and disease that directly and indirectly led to the death of up to ten million people.

In the end, United America finished in a position of world dominance. The transmissions received from the assault teams before the explosion were hidden away and classified. The official account was that the information was lost. But there was more to it than that. MST had built many of the satellites orbiting the planet, and they routed the streaming information to their lunar stations. The United American Government did receive versions of the transmissions, but they were highly edited and of poor quality. They only retrieved the data MST wanted them to have.

"Do the people really believe the government's official position?" Jake asked.

"That it was a dark comet?"

Jake nodded.

"Most accept the explanation," Ben said, "but rumors about Operation Hades and government conspiracy theories abound."

"Conspiracy theories? About what?"

Ben hesitated. "In the hours before the explosion, the United American military pulled out all along the Persian lines. They retreated wholesale, pulling millions of men and women out of harm's way. They called it a strategic realignment, but they didn't tell the allies. They redeployed outside the radius of destruction, into Western Africa, Northern Europe, and England. Same thing happened with the Navy."

"You're suggesting the High Command knew what was going to happen?"

"Not the High Command," Ben said. "They were screaming bloody murder. The President issued the order unilaterally…and there's good evidence to suggest that she knew, at least in some capacity. All I can say is that someone knew what was going to happen."

"No," Jake exclaimed. "You're suggesting that the President, President Evelyn Morgan, knew this was going to happen, that she sanctioned the death of billions of people by not aborting the mission?"

"It's not that easy," Ben explained. "She was found dead at the time of the Great Tragedy."

"What?" Jake was shocked. His emotions were fresh and raw. He had just been told that his President was dead. The pain stabbed deep even though the events Ben described occurred sixty years in the past.

"Right before issuing the order, she demanded privacy," Ben said. "Later she was found slumped over her desk. Her death was ruled suicide, but we have reason to believe the team that eventually emerged as henchmen for the Egalitarian Party actually assassinated her. Recordings of her voice when she issued the redeployment orders indicate that she was under great duress. We suspect she was being tortured when she gave the order."

"What?" Jake exclaimed.

"That's not the worst of it," Ben went on, "her grandchild was with her. It was ruled a murder suicide."

Jake was visibly upset. "Murder suicide? No way. Not in a million years. Do people believe it? Did they believe it?"

"I'm afraid so. You can get people to believe anything if it's said with conviction. The Egalitarian Party has proven that much over and over again.

"I don't…" Jake hesitated and asked, "Do you hear that?" He was suddenly alert, pointing his finger in the air.

"No. Hear what?" Ben said.

"Something's going on. Aerocycles. I've been hearing them. There are at least twenty in motion. The others are hovering. From the pattern, they're doing urban sweeps, moving this way."

Ben's eyes widened. "I think it's time we move."

At that moment, the front door opened. A police officer entered and took a look around. He spied the dozen patrons in the front of the establishment and announced in an official voice, "Everyone get up. You are instructed to move outside the building for facial scanning." When no one moved, he yelled, "NOW!" They scrambled away from their food and drinks and filed out the door.

Positioned next to the door, the officer held his pulsar at his side, scanning the main bar and dining area, and down the side with the private booths.

"Act casual," Ben whispered. "Let's exit out the back." They slid out of the booth and put their backs to the officer and started walking.

"Hey! You two! This way!" He thumbed toward the front door. They turned and walked toward the officer. The other patrons had already exited the building. As they walked past him, he grabbed Ben's arm and said, "Hold up there." He glanced toward the door to make sure no one was lingering. When he turned back he studied Ben's face, briefly turned his attention to Jake, and said, "Are you Ben…"

It happened so fast, he didn't have time to finish. Jake disarmed him, smashed his communications gear, and threw him against the wall. He was airborne when he hit, impacting it with his back, upside-down. He crumpled to the floor, rolled to his side, and moaned, "No. Stop."

Jake was standing over the officer when Ben intervened. Positioning himself between the two, he grabbed the officer's uniform and said, "Tell me what you know. What's going on out there?"

"I'm with MST," he whispered.

"What?" Ben helped him to his feet. He was in obvious pain, wincing as he held his neck. He favored his back and had a limp. "Why are you making a contact like this?"

"Orders. There's been a breach. Things are happening within the DSS that have been compartmentalized. We don't know what they know. We can't risk routing contact information through your BCD until it's resolved and we're sure we're not compromised." He turned his attention and glared at Jake. He exclaimed, "Bloody hell. Stupid goon." Ben chuckled. Jake didn't. The severe pain in the man's back and radiating down his leg was an unwanted memento of what happens on the business end of Jake's wrath. He wasn't happy about it. "Who the hell is this guy?" he asked.

Jake was serious and alert, scanning outside for signs of danger. His

BCD was collecting information from the environment and feeding it to his brain.

"Just a little local muscle," Ben said.

"I was instructed to bring these to you." He pulled a small package out of his pocket.

Ben unwrapped it and discovered two smart-polymer masks. The last time MST briefed him on the device it only existed in theory. That was a year ago and all that was available at that point in time was computer modeling. The fantasy had now become reality.

Facial-recognition cameras kept the country under constant surveillance. The system was originally designed, and society willingly accepted it, as a safety measure against crime and terrorism, but it evolved into a weapon of unprecedented power that was used to control society. The system's mainframe had the capability of picking out a single known individual within minutes from trillions of image captures per day, and it could additionally pick out unknowns who didn't belong.

Counter-technology was the answer. The masks were thin and transparent enough to be undetectable when deactivated. But they were uploaded with thousands of alternate faces and when activated the false images would be detected by onlookers as well as the security systems. From this point forward the only way they could move around would be with the masks. Ben estimated they needed less than a week. Once they had accomplished all of their tasks, they would find their way out of United America and head for MST Global's Island...but that was only if Jake agreed to help them overthrow the United American Government.

The officer handed an envelope to Ben. "These are your instructions. There will be a diversion on my mark that will draw the sweep off in another direction." He limped to the door and waited, holding one hand at the small of his back and wincing in pain.

The instructions directed them to a pod waiting six blocks away. Ben shoved the note into a glass of water where it immediately disintegrated. They put on the masks and left out the back door.

CHAPTER 32: INTERROGATION IN HAVANA

It took a day for MST's communications capabilities to be restored and for orders to begin routing to Ben's BCD. The level of encryption in the messages was now so complex as to cause a perceptible delay, giving the voice coming through, the voice of MST's leader, a more intense computer-like quality. It took another day for Ben and Jake to make their way from New Orleans to the Island of Cuba and into the city of Havana. At their destination, was a fully furnished house located in the middle of a rough, economically-disadvantaged neighborhood. According to instructions, Ben left Jake behind and proceeded to the Havana Maritime Museum. In a specified alley behind the building, he met the first in a series of drivers.

The accommodations in the safe house included bars on the windows, surveillance systems monitoring every approach, and a new epsilon grade Vintel unit. After Ben left, Jake activated the Vintel unit, and it sprang to life. He sped up the transmission so the data was streaming at an incredible rate, yet he caught every nuance. He reviewed the Egalitarian Party's version of world events and the escalation of tensions between United America and the rest of the free world. Regardless of the spin, it was easy enough to read between the lines…the military was on high alert, things were ugly, and hostilities could erupt into another war at any moment. He guessed that it would happen either in some God-forsaken corner of the planet as a result of sloppy discipline, or United America would launch a huge first strike.

Jake considered his options before conducting another search for Wendy,

Bailey, and Paul. Back when he was a patient in New Bethesda, he tapped the Internet Cloud with his BCD by routing a connection through one of the hospital's Vintel Units. What he found was terrifying in that it confirmed what the nurse had told him in the ICU. There was no record of his life, and his family didn't exist. He remembered the horrid feeling that squeezed him. Its grip was unrelenting, he couldn't breathe, and his mind was slipping away, descending into utter madness. He took a deep breath. Things were different now. He was on a more solid foundation and maybe he could handle it. He wanted to know about other things, like what happened in Spring Hill after the Great Tragedy, and what happened to his friends. He also felt compelled to confirm again that his life, the nightmare, was in fact real. Jake grasped the edge of the table and squeezed, his missing fingers trying in vain to participate in the agony as he was again tormented by a barrage of self-doubt. Was there a chance that his mind was confused? That he was a psychiatric patient and none of it was real…that the false reality existed only in jaded memories, that his family and his life were nothing more than a mirage?

Jake heard another voice creeping in. This time it was the voice of self-preservation and reason. It asked if he really wanted to endure the pain again. Did he really want to see the Vintel confirm that, because of him, all traces of his family were gone? Jake's fingers were shaking when he deactivated the unit and powered it down. He squeezed his fists tight and pushed away from the unit, realizing at the same time that if anyone was watching, his search parameters would have had the potential to alert the Egalitarian Party of his location. That alone was a good enough excuse to turn his back on the Vintel unit. He'd conduct the search later. No… he'd go to Spring Hill and see things for himself. When Ben got back he'd inform him of his plans. Until then, he took out his stress on the workout equipment, and an hour later, he disappeared into the city.

When Jake left the safe house and descended into the tangled maze of tenements, he was shadowed by agents from MST. They were well trained and disciplined, always keeping their distance, remaining in the shadows. They assumed, albeit incorrectly, that he was unaware of their presence.

* * * * *

Ben followed instructions to the letter. He found his way to the museum and into a pod. The door opened and it slowed just enough so he could jump in. What followed was a series of transfers designed to shake potential tails. One thing was apparent to him; whoever was coordinating the operation was leaving nothing to chance.

Ben eventually found himself in a small boat in the center of the Hazleton District. The wealthy neighborhood was designed to have the aesthetic allure of the ancient city of Venice; at least before the latter sank into its watery grave. His mind was wandering. He considered all the events that had transpired in his life to lead him to this moment. Everything he had done in his career with the military and with the MPS was to advance the interests of United America and the Egalitarian Party. There were no alternatives. He swore loyalty to the Fascists, and up until his thirties, he never really questioned the principles underlying his devotion. How could he? There were no alternatives, no competitors to offer an alternate vision. Until MST formally took him into their fold, the Egalitarian Party and Fascism were all he knew. The Egalitarian Party created the intellectual and psychological foundation he drew upon. They controlled what was taught in schools and the information received through the Vintel. Ben realized in retrospect that his brain had been masterfully programmed by the culture in which he lived all the way back to the moment he blinked into the world and the cord was cut.

It was a difficult transition. When MST first revealed an alternate vision of American society and the world, he was defensive and angry. He didn't want any part of it. But he began to see things differently. Looking back, it was easy to recognize what he didn't see before, that the mental paradigm he had operated within, the manner in which he thought about the world, was built in its entirety by the warped ideologues put into key positions of power. His patriotism was blind. He first became the perfect henchman for the Fascist system, then he became one of them. He always understood that he would remain useful only insofar as his thinking was right. He was told that he was elite. He even came to believe it. But eventually he saw the truth. There wasn't anything brave or courageous in what he did. Although there were moments of peril, his work as an interrogator with the MPS was exactly what he was designed to do. He always moved with the grain and in accordance to the dictates of the Egalitarian Party because that is what he was supposed to do. His life was no more his own than that of a marionette. But that was before he discovered who he really was. All that seemed so long ago.

The boat entered a tunnel, and in the brief cover of darkness, Ben was ushered into a second boat that passed in the opposite direction. He hunched down low under falsely painted floorboards to avoid detection while a decoy assumed his position in the first boat.

Ben felt the gentle sway of the boat rocking back and forth in the water. His reminiscences returned to the first confrontation with MST. When they exposed the truth of who he really was he wanted to lash out. His response was anger and intense denial. But then as he learned more about MST the intensity of deep personal conflict grew. It wasn't all about the Egalitarian Party anymore. Paradigms, visions of the world that were diametrically opposed in every way, became locked in a great duel. MST's vision for United America, their concepts of liberty and freedom, they were the antithesis of those he had been supporting, those demanded by the Fascists. Ben remembered questioning what exactly it was he had been fighting for as a member of the Party. He had conducted interrogations and killed so many people that he lost count, people whose only crime was to raise objections against the Party. It was all about the maintenance of power. Once he truly realized what he had been doing, he simply had to reconcile that against what he was willing to fight for.

Ben came to understand that he did have control over his choices and how he would live his life, and in the ultimate role he would play in ripping down the bulwarks of evil that had imprisoned one of the greatest countries the world had ever known. As the boat neared its destination, Ben thought back to the days of his inner conflict. He remembered how he felt. He wept in shame when he came to understand the Egalitarian Party and the role he had played in advancing its agenda. He believed he was fighting for a country he loved, but he wasn't. He thought his actions were serving the good of the people, but they weren't. That was just how he rationalized and came to morally accept his actions. Now he saw things differently. His actions were ones of pure self-interest and self-advancement in a system that worked to stifle the freedoms and liberty of an entire continent.

He shuddered at the realization that the human brain was so flawed as to allow men just like him to not only fail to object, but to find morally and ethically acceptable the sins of the Party. He thought about the great purges that swept through the military and the agrarian regions of United America. Those who were brave enough to object effectively threw their lives away. They didn't accomplish anything, because everyone else sat on the sidelines. The Egalitarians were allowed to cull from society its conservative and libertarian ideologies, and the lack of resistance encouraged them to remove the stain of criminal individualism from North America. Estimates of the number of deaths were hard to determine as the Party covered up the early waves of killing and told posterity that it never happened. In reality, between fifteen and twenty million people lost their lives, and even more were lost indirectly. The academics of the time applauded the effort as a necessary step in moving society toward a utopian dream, little realizing that they, along with religious institutions, were next on the Fascist menu.

The Egalitarian position was that the perfect social order required the elimination of all opposition and indoctrination from the cradle. They maintained that those who were already poisoned by self-love and greed, those who lived their lives motivated by personal gain as opposed to the greater good of society, needed to be quarantined and eliminated before the infection of their impure philosophies might contaminate another entire generation. Equality of outcome was the rallying cry. They maintained that just as skin color, height, or hair color were unacceptable determinates of social success, so too were IQ, DNA-driven personality and work ethic, and athletic prowess. All measures were driven by genetics and were unacceptable means by which social and economic outcomes should be determined.

After the brutality ran its course, a Fascist regime with strong undercurrents of Marxist-inspired socialism assumed unchallenged control over the North American Continent. In retrospect, the metamorphosis actually occurred in small steps over hundreds of years, but it took a giant leap during the period of time immediately following World War IV. United America turned into a nation unrecognizable. As Ben shook off decades of brainwashing and learned from MST, he was left perplexed by the question of how a people who for centuries enjoyed unprecedented freedom could so completely abandon their rights and liberties. They allowed the Constitution, their protection against tyranny, to be eroded and then systematically destroyed. The Right to Bear Arms was the first to go. Then it was Personal Property Rights and Freedom of Speech and the Press. After that the courts gutted the citizens' rights to a fair and speedy trial. Protections against illegal searches and seizures were stripped, and by the time that happened, the Fascists had gained complete control. The people were left without any means of legal resistance, and they couldn't hope to fight the indomitable power of the Egalitarian Party and the massive central government.

Ben killed in the name of United America, and in essence, to support the interests of the Party, but he had also witnessed what happened to individuals who were disloyal. They were imprisoned, tortured, and executed, and their families were left destitute. Family members were often imprisoned as co-conspirators. What was he supposed to do? Was he supposed to turn his back on Cecilie and his children? Was he supposed to leave them dangling on a limb, completely unaware of the danger they would be in because of his actions? He was risking absolutely everything for abstract ideals, for principles of freedom and justice that the New World lost. MST understood his dilemma. They promised his wife and children would be safe, that they were under constant surveillance, and when the time was right, they would be moved to a safe place. All Ben could do was take the risk and trust they would get it done.

The boat came to a stop inside a fully enclosed private dock adjacent to an old Twenty-Second Century stone mansion. Ben was escorted into the home, down a flight of stairs, and into a wine cellar. At that point his guide, an elderly man who had little to say, bid him good luck and walked out. He closed the door and Ben was left alone.

Racks of wine completely lined the walls of the beautifully adorned room. The ceiling was covered with intricately carved and skillfully finished wood. The floor was a grand wooden inlay depicting a scene that appeared to be of an ancient Roman vineyard. The walls of the room had no corners. It was a perfect circle. And there was only one door—the one he had come through. Something was about to happen, but he wasn't sure what. He looked around, half expecting that the walls were going to part, or that the floor was going to pull away to reveal a hidden stair.

It was at least a minute before Ben heard the clicking sound of the door lock being opened. Then he heard a quick knock. It conveyed an invitation for him to open it. Mildly apprehensive, he reached forward and grasped the handle. When he opened it, he was shocked to find, not the stairs he had previously descended, but a corridor with an armed guard posted at the entrance. The wine cellar had rotated so imperceptibly, he failed to perceive the movement. The corridor led into a large brightly lit room twenty meters away. He could hear voices. He carefully stepped past the guard and moved down the hall.

There were a dozen people milling around, five women and the rest men. Two additional guards stood motionless against the wall. While a couple of the guests appeared to be acquainted, none knew the ultimate connections they shared until this meeting. Ben scanned the room from left to right. When their eyes met, a look of astonishment betrayed their mutual surprise. It was Dr. Guy Stuart, the physicist who took part in the briefing about John Doe in New Washington, the one who challenged Director Zimmer. Ben was happy to see him. Of all the people he might have imagined being at the meeting, he never would have considered Stuart.

Following on the heels of his entrance into the room, Ben received another encrypted message through his BCD. It was the same methodical voice. "Dr. Murray," the voice said. He was looking directly at Stuart while the communication was being transmitted. "As you now know, Dr. Stuart is one of us. The mission objective is approaching critical. Meet with Dr. Stuart only when directed by the President. He has information you'll need." The message abruptly terminated.

They shook hands in the midst of the group. Ben was surprised at the level of pleasure he felt. It wasn't just Stuart though...he looked around the room and felt his stress rapidly diminishing. It was good. For a long time, Ben had felt as though the weight of the world was resting on his shoulders. Now he knew he wasn't alone. He had allies in the struggle, and if first impressions were accurate they appeared to be very capable.

The guards stepped outside the room and the meeting began. Speaking through a Vintel unit positioned in the center of the table, a set up oddly similar to the briefing about John Doe in New Washington, the same nondescript voice that communicated through Ben's BCD briefed everyone in the room. The person's face remained completely obscured and he, or she, only identified himself, or herself, to the group by the code name AF20. The next two hours of the meeting were spent outlining the objectives of the society and the current state of affairs. All of those present clearly understood that while each had been working independently, the society had been present at all points of their lives, hiding in the shadows, and assisting them when they needed it.

Not all of them knew the details of what came next. MST, a privately held company that had already fundamentally altered life on the planet, and which was attempting to do so again, was founded by Col. Alexander Fisk—Jake's friend and commanding officer. He lived in the Twenty-Fourth Century, traveled back in time, and lived out his life in the Nineteenth Century. All those seated around the table were direct descendants of Fisk. He set up the organization to stand unified in purpose and to withstand the tests of time. The only way he could foresee that it would survive and eventually see his objective to fruition was to allow only direct descendants to be part of it, and for its leader to execute coldness in culling the organization of weak links.

Fear and caution now owned the room. Each realized the importance of what they were attempting to accomplish. They were attempting to rescue an entire continent from tyranny and from under the heel of Fascism. At the same time, the Egalitarian Party had benefitted from over sixty years of unchallenged power, and they learned from history the importance of consolidating their gains, something they did in murderous fashion.

"We have secured Lt. Col. Jake Gillean," AF20 said. "He is physically recovered, but at this time, he doesn't know about us, or who he really is. Within twenty-four hours he will, and then he'll decide whether or not to join us."

"Is there any chance he'll say no?" one of the participants asked. He was a thin and nervous man, short and balding, with an aura of being obsessive-compulsive. The articles on the table in front of him were in perfect order, and at one point during the meeting, Ben spied him reaching over and slightly rotating his neighbor's napkin so that it would be perfectly parallel to his own.

"That is a risk we face," AF20 responded. "But I have every confidence that we are prepared, that we have done everything right, and that he will join us of his own volition. He will become the leader of the military arm of our revolution."

"And once we replace the government with an elected body?"

"Once we are successful, as his capabilities surpass our own, he will certainly play a role in rebuilding the country."

The man nodded. His mannerisms gave the impression that he had doubts, and suggested he thought Jake had the potential to become a threat. Ben shook it off as the product of anxiety.

AF20 went on to outline MST's role in the current state of world affairs, and the objectives that would have to be met over the next several days. What AF20 kept guarded were MST's black box research projects. One of them would help topple the Fascists and subsequently change life in North America, and the other would dramatically alter life on the entire planet.

For the time being, everything, absolutely everything, centered on putting Lt. Col. Jake Gillean back together again, determining how he ended up appearing out of thin air at the reenactment, and figuring out what went wrong to cause his family line to be lost. That was the burden Ben shouldered.

Near the conclusion of the briefing AF20 said, "Now more than ever, security and secrecy are vital." MST Global had repeatedly been the target of espionage from countries around the globe, but primarily from United America. It came down to two things...power and greed. Now it would be worse because it was about survival. Everyone knew the stakes. They were going up against not only the United American Government and the Egalitarian Party, but also the world's most powerful bankers, the power brokers within the military-industrial complex, the upper tiers of military leadership, and the fraction of society who had grown rich off the system.

After a moment of silence AF20 said, "There is a traitor among us."

"What?" There was a collective gasp. Heads turned and they began eyeing each other with suspicion.

"Because of the information that has already been betrayed, very soon the President of United America will be lobbied by very powerful forces to order the arrest of the John Doe from Director Zimmer's time-travel investigation...in other words, Lt. Col. Jake Gillean. MST will be under increased scrutiny. Any connections discovered between yourselves and MST will put you in immediate peril."

Expressions of fear were exchanged around the table.

"This contingency has been anticipated," AF20 said. "At birth each of you had a device implanted in your skull, at the base of your brain. It's designed to explode when activated, resulting in your instant and painless death. It can be triggered as a self-destruct device, activated by a combination of spoken numbers and Latin words." The expressions of fear around the table morphed into ones of shock. AF20 went on, "Each of you has a unique verbal code that when repeated three times, followed one minute later by the same sequence, will result in detonation of the implant. Each of you will be given your code along with a permanent deactivation code that you may use if so desired. The purpose of the device is to protect you in the event that you are compromised."

"Bernadette McMillan," AF20 said. "You have betrayed all of us. You turned your back on your family and a noble cause for financial gain, a gain that amounted to no more than a pittance."

Bernadette smiled. "The money had nothing to do with it." She was in her mid-fifties, a sharply dressed, good-looking redhead. She worked as an executive in the communications industry.

The group watched a recording of Bernadette as she revealed what she knew, which included MST's interest in John Doe and that his real name was Jake Gillean. She even outlined the company's designs to take over the United American Government. She gave up details pertaining to MST's investments in time travel research and expressed her belief that they actually had some breakthroughs. She described the company's possession of classified data related to Operation Hades and went so far as to suggest that the company not only had something to do with the foreign abductions of United American assets, but also the numerous domestic assassinations. She was considered a loyal and dedicated member of the team until yesterday, when she sought out and revealed the information to a government operative working for Director Zimmer.

"Why would you do this?" one of the other women, Irene Chalmers, asked. She was mad, as suggested by the clenched jaw and red face.

At first Bernadette was without reaction, then she smiled again. "Do you really think you can win? You're all going to die…and for what? This is a hopeless cause. You're a bunch of fools." Bernadette didn't bother trying to defend herself, but instead launched into an attack. "You recite your naive incantations about restoring liberty and freedom, that you want to impose some new form of equal access to justice. It's all a dream, a cute little dream without any foundation in reality." She was leaning forward in her chair, almost standing as she preached to the group, "When the Constitution was written, Ben Franklin said, '*We have given you a Republic, if you can keep it.'* Well those days are long gone. The people of United America rejected that form of government. They made a decision and elected the Egalitarian Party. They wanted Fascism and that's what they got. Why can't any of you see this? Look around you. The people of this country, of any country, are too stupid and ignorant to participate in any form of representative government. They always end up gaming the system for personal gain, and then they reject it. You're trying to re-impose something they have already rejected."

"You know what?" Dr. Stuart said. "You're right. But when people quote the Founders they usually fail to understand their meaning. If you want to quote one, Thomas Jefferson is as good as any. He said, *'Democracy will cease to exist when you take from those who produce and give to those who will not.'"* He pointed at her and said with fire in his voice, "That's what this is about…not your skewed and perverted version of history, the one offered by the Party, the one that's being taught in schools." Stuart made a fist and shook his head, finding that even looking at Bernadette caused him to feel nauseous. "What happened was that over time, people became dependent on the government, because of government policies. It was ultra liberalism and an unending growth of statism with its bureaucracy and regulations that led to the curse we have today. The great lie perpetuated by the ultra rich was that raising taxes and redistributing the wealth would level the playing field. It didn't. They were sitting on fortunes made over the course of centuries. They had armies of lawyers who made it appear they had no income. They fomented the cause of equal outcomes and succeeded in destroying the middle class. They grew richer in the process while the people became dependent on the government. The Great Tragedy pushed it over the edge. The people bought into the lie, and for personal benefits, they elected the Egalitarians. They in turn hijacked the system. Those ultra-wealthy became the Party insiders. That's how this monster was created…self-righteous greed and power on the one hand and increased dependence on the government on the other." He smashed his fist on the table. "That perversion is what you betrayed us for?"

"None of that matters now does it, Dr. Stuart?" Bernadette sarcastically laughed. "The ancestors create the democracy, and the grandchildren destroy it. Freedom?" Her tone was derisive. "You want to restore freedom? They had freedom and rejected it. The low sloping foreheads in the Midwest and South, even in the inner cities, they haven't evolved. They're ballast, an anchor holding society back from the next great phase of evolution. The Egalitarian Party is seeking perfection, and that's why you'll lose. You're looking to the past for answers. We're looking to the future. Project Darwin will change everything." Her expression hesitated as she realized she had said too much, yet her smile remained cold and malicious. The fact that she was family, that they shared a common genetic ancestor, didn't ease everyone's anger. In fact, it amplified the desire for revenge. "You can fight for a dream if you choose," she quipped, mocking the group. "As for me, I'm not going to die for your jaded fantasy of a ridiculous utopia filled with inferior genetic material. Yours is a lost cause no matter how you look at it."

The exchange having run its course, AF20 took command of the meeting "No, Bernadette. Rest assured, you are not going to die for a lost cause. You are going to die because you betrayed us."

Bernadette's face immediately went white. She looked around the room and seemed to realize for the first time the angry faces that were looking back. Her hands began trembling. The two sitting next to her rolled their chairs away, expecting the device in her skull to detonate. The door opened and two security guards entered, each of them big and as rough in appearance as pro rugby players. They took up position behind her and stood at attention. Not able to run or hide, she had nowhere to go.

"You ignorant bastards. You can't do this," she screamed. Bernadette turned and tried to run but the bulk of muscle blocked her path.

"Dr. Benjamin Murray," AF20 said, "I would like for you to demonstrate your talents for the group. We need to know what else she betrayed, and Project Darwin needs to be defined."

Ben calmly stood, his mind already focused and objective regarding the details of what he was about to do. Bernadette turned toward him, her eyes wide. Her expression was one of shock and fear, like a cow about to be ripped apart by a bear. Ben could have interrogated her without the audience, but AF20 obviously preferred that everyone witness. A pulsar blast to the head would have been less disturbing than what they were about to see.

The process that Ben was about to demonstrate and the equipment he would use were considered by the Fascists to be highly classified. The interrogation device, actually developed by MST through a front company, used a series of highly sophisticated quantum computers, sensors, and thousands of triangulating lasers. It was capable of simultaneously imaging anatomic structures within the brain while also detecting the finest nuances of neurologic activity…once the background noise was accounted for. It could detect the release of a single packet of neurotransmitter from the discharge of a single neuron across a single specific synapse in every area of the brain. Further, and this was the greatest breakthrough, Ben could actually manipulate and cause the discharge of a single neuron of interest without disturbing its neighbors. Other processes integrated with the equipment were designed to analyze activity within her neural networks and augment memory recall in some areas of the brain while inhibiting the conscious withholding of memories in others.

In its most simplistic explanation, Bernadette's mind, her thoughts, everything that made her special and unique, none of it was hers anymore. The unchallenged and willful control she enjoyed over her brain was about to be wrested away. There was nowhere left for her to go. She couldn't retreat into the sanctum of her mind. Her private thoughts and emotions, facets of her being that had always been hers, were now nothing more than cruel mirages. Sensing what was going to happen, she determined that she could resist, that she could fight Ben by bending her thoughts. That was her jaded fantasy. Her mind belonged to Ben, and it was about to be raped.

Simplified versions of the technology Ben was about to use had seen application in the medical community for the destruction of brain tumors. It had essentially rendered open brain surgery as obsolete as stone tool trephination. Another application was its use in modern interventional psychoneurology. By tapping into its ability to precisely map the three-dimensional hard drive of the brain, it could be used to destroy single networks of neurons that stored a person's traumatic memories; similar to the way a corrupted file might be removed from a computer. There were shortcomings though. Memories stored in a brain are highly integrated and exist in broad overlapping networks rather than being compartmentalized. Afterward, the subjects were aware there were blank spots in their memories, but blank spots with haunting shadows and intact emotions. If too much brain matter was destroyed, a fundamentally different person with an altered personality might emerge from the procedure. In mainstream medicine it was considered an aggressive and controversial form of treatment and was the last therapeutic resort, requiring the opinion of several doctors. Ben, on the other hand, operated entirely on his own. Within the Egalitarian Party and the MPS, and now with MST, there were no rules of oversight; he was judge, jury, and executioner.

Ben carried out his work with a level of precision and expediency that no one else he knew could duplicate. While he took no joy in it, he did his work like an unfeeling automaton, without external or internal reservation. He did what he had to do in a finite and perpetually cruel world. While this woman's transgression, her willful betrayal, was a great personal affront, and her political philosophies self-serving and profane, he couldn't bring himself to feel hatred or animosity. In this context, he simply didn't have the time or the energy to waste on fruitless exercises with his emotional self. He was completely indifferent, regarding her as nothing more than a brain gone bad. He had a job to do and that's all there was to it.

When Ben moved around the table, the attendees between him and his target scrambled out of the way like the parting of the waters. As he moved toward her, Ben pulled a weathered leather pouch from the inside pocket of his jacket. He carefully laid the pouch on the table, unzipped it, and folded it open. It was the interrogation equipment he carried with him at all times, its ultra-high tech revealed for the first time to everyone in the room.

Foreign dignitaries, military commanders, corporate executives, agents of espionage, three heads of state, and thousands of criminals had been interrogated with the very same device. Generally his targets were men, but not always. Over the course of his career, he had extracted information from at least two or three dozen women in the field, and at least a thousand in practice sessions. Prior to his first female interrogation, he thought it might be different in some way, or that at least his reaction would be different. But he was mistaken. Turns out it was just like all the others. He was objective, deliberate, and never cared one way or the other. A brain was a brain. Some had male bodies and others had female; all things considered, gender was nothing more than a trivial difference.

His method was quicker, easier, and cleaner than the primitive torture techniques MPS operatives utilized in the past. In fact, nearly every other country in the world was still using the techniques Ben rendered obsolete in United America, even though they denied it publicly. By his hand, untold numbers of lives had been saved, always in the name of United America, and it was all done through the technique he was about to demonstrate.

Ben put his hand on her shoulder and gently pushed downward. "Please have a seat," he said.

Bernadette collapsed into the chair, frightened beyond measure. She reached for the armrests several times before successfully clenching them in a death grip, her fingers clawing deep into the leather fabric to find refuge. Her lids were open wide while her eyes made quick saccadic movements from side to side. Her pupils were dilated. Her carotids visibly pulsated in the throes of a massive fight-or-flight response. Her heart was pounding as she watched Ben calmly prepare his tools. Her respiratory rate increased and deepened. Her body readied itself for a last dramatic battle. Survival was at stake. She bolted out of her seat, lunged forward, and tried to smash his equipment with her fist.

She had no chance. Ben blocked her wrist in the air with a quick movement while the guards snatched her from behind. "Please remain in your seat," Ben said. His voice was eerily calm and even.

Now overwhelming fear kept Bernadette in her seat, and she remained nearly catatonic when he moved in to start the procedure. He placed the device over her forehead and slid the posterior aspect over the back of her head. Its appearance was vaguely similar to a headband about five centimeters wide and three centimeters thick. It was comprised mostly of a metal alloy that had amazing properties. Individual folds of the alloy were slightly thicker than aluminum foil and equally pliable, yet it was strong enough to stop a projectile at point blank range. It was embedded with the most sophisticated technology ever produced. Ben activated the device and flaps immediately extended outward. Bernadette squeezed the armrests, tears flowed down her cheeks, and she emitted a high-pitched whine when the device folded up and down to cover her skull. Panels extended down the length of her nose. She began shaking when it went up her nostrils and pushed all the way to the roof of her nasal cavity. The device folded separate panels over the ears and deep into the ear canals. Others spread across both cheeks. Within seconds, it extended from her posterior ears and the base of her skull to the inferior aspect of her eyes, and it completely covered her scalp.

"Phase two activation," Ben said. Tens of millions of microscopic probes, each less than the width of a flagellum, painlessly embedded deep into the tissues of her head. The probes were so small and adroit that they met essentially no resistance as they passed through the soft tissue and bored through the bones protecting her brain. They stopped only after they were deep in the biomatter of her thoughts.

Ben placed a device over his eye. While looking much like an old-style magnifying eyepiece, it was in fact a highly complex quantum interface. Its purpose was to seamlessly integrate the systems, to provide a connection between his BCD and the interrogation device. Through this conduit he would not only be able to visually navigate through precise computer-generated images of Bernadette's neuronal networks, he could also manipulate neural activity and destroy whatever he desired.

As he wanted everyone to witness what he was doing, he produced a second interface and positioned it on the table. After he adjusted a few settings, an incredibly detailed three-dimensional hologram of Bernadette's brain appeared over the table. It was a meter in diameter. Next to it, suspended in mid-air, were a series of rapidly changing numbers and mathematical computations. It looked like a cockpit display but a thousand times more sophisticated.

"Bernadette. Squeeze your right hand," he said. No more than he said it, the hand fell limp. Her entire right arm was next, followed by her leg. Ben repeated the process on her left side. Inside of twenty seconds her limbs were paralyzed.

Her mind was screaming, panicking with abject fear. Her conscious control was being ripped away, and she had no means to resist. It was far worse than any other form of rape. The others in the room were horrified, many took a step back and covered their mouths. The hologram showed what Ben was doing, and as he shut down the motor area of her brain, Bernadette's body became completely limp, like a rag-doll. Her high-pitched whine continued until Ben said, "Please stop whining." He followed the activity in her brain to isolate the network pattern responsible for the whine and deactivated the pathway with the device's triangulating lasers. It worked by preventing electrical discharges from traveling through the neurons. The whine immediately ceased and she began making gurgling sounds in her throat with each inhalation.

Bernadette tried to wrest back control but her efforts were in vain. She cried out, "Help. Please help me."

"Oh my God," one of the others in the room breathed.

With volitional control of her limbs gone, Bernadette was in effect paralyzed from the neck down. From Ben's perspective…he didn't want her squirming around. Paralysis was always the first step. She was slouched in the chair with her head dangling to one side. Ben asked one of the security guards for his belt. He ran it behind the chair and secured it around her chest so that she would remain sitting up. He repositioned her head into midline and extended her neck so she would breathe easier.

"What's your name?" he asked. She didn't answer. "Please state your name." After a brief pause, "Is your name Bernadette?" Each question and her subsequent refusal to answer allowed Ben to hone in on the neural circuitry controlling her behavior. He inhibited the appropriate circuits and she began talking.

"Yes. My name is Bernadette," she said. Her voice was crisp and betrayed no resistance.

Ben made a map of the locations of some basic things and began the interrogation in earnest. As Ben worked, the men and women around the table were able to see exactly what he was doing. The holographic image of her brain twisted and turned in orientation and would quickly zoom in on individual neural networks and connections. They could see the patterns of neural firing change as the question and answer session progressed, and they saw how he was marking each area, down to the specific and intricate interneuronal connections and networks that stored unique and highly integrated memories. What the observers didn't appreciate was that those connections were being mapped for destruction.

While everyone was reduced to a state of complete fascination, much like children at a circus, Dr. Guy Stuart was studying the characteristics of the device. He had questions about the amazing degree of three-dimensional definition, the statistical analysis that allowed the device to isolate an individual discharge in a brain with billions of neurons and trillions of interneuronal connections. He understood that the electrical background noise in the central nervous system had to be incredible. There were also pressure fluctuations with every heartbeat and each breath. To isolate a single neuron buried in the deep structures was like trying to hear a pin drop on carpet from a hundred yards at dueling rock concerts while being blindfolded and wearing headphones. Yet the unit Ben was using navigated through the system and solved the mathematical equations with little to no apparent delay. He was impressed with the computer systems and the physics of the device and already had dozens of questions for Ben. He hoped that if he played his cards right, he might be able to handle the device and study it up close.

Ben was an artist as he navigated through the ultra complexities of Bernadette's brain. He was reading the activities of her neural nets and getting a feel for how her unique brain was operating in a process akin to a conductor driving ten symphonies at the same time, but instead of a single baton slicing through the air, his was controlled by subtle motor movements in all ten of his gloved fingers, each working independently of the others, yet all part of the same process. Every brain had its own distinct feel. Bernadette's was no different in that regard.

She was revealing codes, combinations, names, numbers, and events, all without hesitation. She described an affair she had with a Party insider and her subsequent introduction into the inner circles of Fascism. She proceeded to outline everything she had revealed about MST and her knowledge of Jake Gillean. Those pathways were mapped for annihilation.

"Tell me how you feel about the Egalitarian party," Ben requested.

"We are everything," she said. "The Party is the answer. We will make the world a better place, but obstacles, inferior genetic material, are in our way."

The pathways that lit up followed the pattern Ben expected. He turned to the others in the room and said, "If you look at the activity here," he lit up the area he was referring to on the hologram, "and here, and here… these areas correspond to what you could arguably call religious devotion. They are always intimately intertwined with the emotional centers of the brain. Humans are designed for religious belief. They always find something to worship—God, money, government, mother earth, take your pick. The focus of Bernadette's worship is the Egalitarian Party and Fascism. There's nothing we could have done to prevent this. She made her choice a long time ago and willfully potentiated all these neurological pathways. Her beliefs are strong and not open to debate. It's important that you understand that. It's just like a computer, but we can't wipe the hard-drive and start over. With a brain you can only wipe the drive. There's no starting over." He turned back to Bernadette and said, "Tell me about Project Darwin."

"Project Darwin is the Final Solution. We will rid the country of the genetically inferior, those who don't have the intellectual capacity to understand that Fascism is the answer. We will have the perfect race."

"How?" Ben asked.

"The food supply."

Bernadette went on to outline the Egalitarian Party's plan to sterilize vast portions of the country in an effort to halt the reproduction of undesirables. The food supply was going to be laced with chemicals that would accomplish the task. It was clean and perfect. No direct killing, the people would live out their miserable little lives, and the Party would aggressively offer to artificially inseminate any woman who desired a child in an effort to keep the population up. What they wouldn't know was that the babies would be from eggs and sperm cloned only from choice Party insiders, selected for Party devotion, intellect, athleticism, and beauty. The cause of the disaster would be blamed on a fungus contaminating the food supply and dairy products. The end result of the evolutionary stress would be a perfect society that had successfully shaken off its inferior DNA.

Ben was shocked by what he had just learned. "What's your role in Project Darwin?" he asked.

"I am one of a thousand women selected to donate eggs for cloning. I'm an Eve."

"How many men?"

"Another thousand," she said.

"How was the Party able to keep something this big so secret?" Ben asked.

"Only a few of us know about the Final Solution. The rest thought they were participating in a study sponsored by the Party to study the genetics of highly evolved people."

"When is Project Darwin going to be launched?"

"The first food shipments will go out on June 6. They will withhold the dispersal of food from the distribution centers for two weeks prior to June 6 under the guise of an international incident and supply problems. Then they will release the laced shipments hoping for rapid consumption."

After a few more questions, which produced the names of the lead scientists and politicians behind the plan, Ben was finished. In all, about twenty minutes had passed. The mining of information from Bernadette's brain was easier than downloading files from a computer. In a manner of speaking, that's exactly what Ben had done. While the brain is an astonishingly complex neural network, it is in essence an organic computer. Access to its information only took the proper technology and a means for the person being interrogated to communicate. The others in the room stood in stunned silence, not only because of the information she revealed, but by how easily Ben breached her brain's defenses and took what he wanted.

In so many ways, the brain was millions of years more advanced than anything that could ever be produced by man. It was the informational interface between the physical realities of life on planet earth and individual conscious thought. While the quest for the seat of the soul within the body was an intriguing historical sidebar, the brain was long ago found to be the seat of awareness, of personality, of consciousness, and of the conscience, and also…of the still mysterious subconscious. It was the throne not *upon which*, but *in which*, sat the sentient being. While Bernadette was at Ben's mercy and had lost temporary control of her throne, in a moment she was going to lose permanent control. Her kingdom was no longer hers.

Circumstances didn't require Ben to kill her outright. In other words, it wasn't the body or the heartbeat of the traitor he was worried about, it was the information encoded within Bernadette's neural networks. It was her memories. They had to be destroyed. Even though they were encoded within the substance of widespread areas of the brain, it was possible to erase them. It took all of one hundred milliseconds for the device strapped to her head to emit thousands of precise triangulated laser blasts within her neural network. Each blast exploded one or a couple specific neurons at the microscopic level. In that moment it destroyed every pertinent memory she possessed.

Bernadette didn't even flinch. There was no pain, just a tweak of sudden confusion and a conscious sense that something abnormal had happened.

Ben's final act was about to begin. He turned to the others and said, "Everyone realizes that she can't be allowed to walk away? She represents a danger for all of us. If we make her disappear, the Egalitarian Party will know. If we execute her, they will know. She has to be returned to her life in an incapacitated state. Does everyone understand why I am doing this?"

When no one responded AF20 announced, "Please proceed, Dr. Murray."

Ben shifted his gaze back to Bernadette. He considered that she appeared to be every bit in her fifties. As such, it was exceedingly unlikely that her damaged brain would have the ability to shift destroyed functions to other undamaged areas of the brain. This was a plasticity, a repair and recovery phenomenon that was observed almost exclusively in the young. At her age it was unlikely her brain would adapt and learn to communicate effectively. All Ben had to do was seal what remained of her memories into an inescapable cage. Put another way, if he forever destroyed her ability to integrate and communicate the information that was stored in her brain, she wouldn't be a threat to MST. It would simply appear as though she suffered an unfortunate massive stroke. It wouldn't raise any suspicions.

The areas he was looking for were usually located in the left side of the brain. He was looking for specific locations that for centuries had been called Broca's area and Wernickes area. They tended to be located in the frontal and temporal lobes, respectively. While many functions in the brain are divided equally on each side, the language centers tend to be lateralized to one side, namely...the left side. It was easy to permanently destroy these areas and the large networks of fibers that formed their interconnections. Additionally, one major cerebral artery provided blood to both areas. A clot or rupture had the potential to destroy both areas.

Bernadette only regained control over her movements when Ben released the inhibition. Her limbs tightened and sprang back to life. Her spine straightened and she sat up. "What did you do to me?" she cried. She held her hands up and worked her fingers, promising herself that she would never again take for granted conscious control of her muscles.

"I want you to sing." Ben said.

"What?"

"I need for you to sing," he repeated.

"I'm not going to..." Bernadette immediately scrunched in her seat and yelled out. She felt like her insides were being ripped out. Her pain resulted from Ben's stimulation of neurons in her pain centers. "Okay! Okay!" she gasped. "What do you want me to sing?"

"Sing anything. I don't know...sing *The Egalitarian Anthem.*"

Bernadette began singing the anthem, and what the others saw made them feel absolutely vulnerable. Some wanted to vomit. One of them did. Ben began making large sweeps with the lasers through her language centers. They watched the holographic image. It showed what was happening as he destroyed the tissue. Millions of neurons were being severed and destroyed like a tiller ripping through uncut grass. The brain tissue was instantaneously liquefied. As Ben tracked along the language pathways Bernadette's speech became nonsensical. Then it was garbled. Finally, all she could do was grunt meaninglessly. Then there was silence. It took about twenty seconds. Bernadette's eyes were wide, her expression one of bewilderment and surprise, mixed with panic.

The final act was to eliminate flow through the major blood vessels feeding the area. Ben focused on the details of his work. He was cold and objective and had long before dehumanized his target. He started a short distance from the origin of the left middle cerebral artery and began creating a clot. He worked along its course toward the internal carotid artery and the Circle of Willis. He took a sharp turn and eliminated flow through the left anterior cerebral artery, extending the vicious clot far enough to prevent collateral flow from getting through the anterior communicating artery. In effect, he cut off all blood flow, preventing the delivery of oxygen and other vital molecular materials to her left frontal and temporal lobes. Given the amazingly rapid metabolic rate of the brain and its inability to store materials for long-term use, it didn't take long for the stroke to become manifest. As he worked, Bernadette's right arm and leg went into a very brief spasm and fell forever flaccid and useless. Her eyes deviated far to her left and her head rotated in the same direction. Her skin suddenly seemed to hang loosely on her face and her mouth gaped open. Her lips became floppy and without tone. From Ben's perspective the stroke was complete, from hers it wasn't. The left side of her brain would essentially digest itself and scar tissue would form. She would spend the rest of her living days in the care of her immediate family, or a more likely scenario, the Egalitarian party would have her euthanized.

She began having a seizure. She whined and began shaking her left arm and leg. Ben pulled a pneumosyringe from his leather pouch. He injected the anti-convulsant medication into her carotid artery on the right side. It immediately terminated the seizure. She fell silent and didn't move.

The others in the room, with the exception of one, had never witnessed anything like the spectacle that had just unfolded. They were aghast and felt sick. The rape of Bernadette's brain was existentially disturbing but the manner in which her stroke was perpetrated represented something altogether different. Ben didn't kill her, but he may as well have.

They needed time to think about what just happened. Several of them looked at Ben differently, viewing this man, this doctor, as a henchman. Several wondered if he was a psychopath. How could anyone claiming to be a physician perform such a heinous act? But…he was on their side. There was at least some degree of morose comfort gleaned from that. The harsh reality was that life was brutal, and they were working against the odds. The Fascists were planning to destroy the progeny of hundreds of millions of people. They were going to kill life before it ever had a chance.

Bernadette was unconscious. Her body was limp and her breathing heavy and irregular. Rasping sounds emanated from her throat, sounding almost like a snore, a product of her neck being flexed with her head flopped forward and twisted to the side. Ben felt indifferent as he stepped away from his victim. It was her reward for betrayal. He turned his attention and studied the expressions on the other faces. Dr. Guy Stuart was pale, the blood having rushed from his face. Everyone in the room had been pushed to a state of revulsion…except for one.

The man's name was Derek Stowe. He was also a physician, the head of MST's immunobiomolecular research division, the same group that perfected the drug given to Jake to speed his healing. Derek rose from his seat and moved around the table. He brushed past Ben and knelt on the floor in front of Bernadette. He called out her name several times. "Bernadette. Bernadette. Can you hear me?" While he called her name, he performed a cursory exam, checking her pupils and assessing her reflexes. When he was satisfied that he completely understood the extent of what had been done he stood up and faced Ben. "You took an oath," he blurted. He poked a finger hard into Ben's chest. His voice was raised, just a few decibels short of yelling.

Ben took a step back, expecting that in the next moment he would be dodging a punch. Derek was bigger than him, and even though he had a potbelly, he appeared to be capable of holding his own in an altercation. Everyone froze as the scene played out.

Derek collected himself. It would have been easier for Ben had he made a closed fist and punched him as hard as he could as the expression of sadness and utter disappointment that was fully welled up in his eyes proved far more powerful. His voice cracked, "We stand for something better. What happened to you?" The question was asked softly, but it slashed like a knife. "What possibly could have possessed you to think that she deserved this?" Derek turned back to her and placed his hand gently on her head. He proceeded as though he was talking to her. She emitted a moaning sound but was otherwise completely unresponsive. A strand of drool was forming in the corner of her mouth, and her eyes were slightly open to the air. "Bernadette. You were brainwashed. You didn't deserve this. There's nothing we're fighting for that can possibly justify this level of immorality."

The room was awkwardly silent. One of the men was hugging the trash can after having thrown up.

Derek shifted his attention to the group. "This is not what MST stands for. If we're no different than the Fascists, what exactly are we fighting for? Before this meeting, I understood that we were fighting for a vision that life is precious, that every life holds within it a priceless value. We're engaging in a fight to restore one of the world's great Democratic Republics, a country that at one time was dedicated to ideals of freedom and equality, a country that at one time believed in liberty and justice. This was an act of barbarity worthy of our enemies…not us." He looked back at Ben and added, "If we reduce ourselves to their level, we accomplish nothing except to bridge the gulf between us and them."

The room remained shrouded in silence, no one daring to respond, not because of any lack of conviction but as a result of shock. They took in the site of Bernadette's body and the wreckage it had become, all the result of such a seemingly insignificant insult to the arteries. The brain was far more fragile than any of them appreciated, and at the same time it was far more powerful and amazing than any of them had ever dreamed. Written in plain sight in front of them; written in her flaccid extremities, her awkwardly inturned ankle, and in her sagging colorless face, were innumerable declarations of the power of the brain and its complete dominion over the function and actions of the body. During Ben's interrogation, more than one person around the table came to the astounding realization it was absolutely beautiful, that the human brain reached the apex of beauty in both function and structure, and that on another level entirely…it was nothing more than a complex organic computer. They also came to the ultimate realization that triumph over the Egalitarian Party would be more difficult than they ever imagined. The Fascists possessed a hundred million brains just like Bernadette's, brains that were programmed to be dedicated to their cause and to fight with all brutality to preserve their societal and financial advantages.

Derek took another shot at Ben. "Have you been with the MPS for so long that you fail to see the difference between right and wrong? Is your brain like hers in some respects? Have you been corrupted? Your actions are in direct contradiction to everything Col. Fisk believed in. It sullies everything we've spent our entire lives working toward."

Ben put up his hand indicating that he had heard enough. His anger was on the edge of an explosion. His heart rate was up. He could feel his brow furrowing and his jaw clenching. While nothing was to be gained from escalating the drama, he had been pushed beyond his ability or willingness to let the accusations go unanswered. "Thank you," he began. "You have succinctly expressed your opinion and now everyone knows where you stand. I'll consider your remarks in the good faith in which they were offered." He stepped forward into Derek's space. Derek slid back a step. "Let me ask you something. Did she talk to you before the meeting?"

"Yes. We did speak. She was very pleasant, very engaging. She didn't deserve…"

"She asked you about your research?" Ben asked.

"She did, but I don't see what…"

"You said she was engaging," Ben again forcibly interrupted. "Engaging because a beautiful woman took an interest in you and your research?"

"I resent the implication," Derek said, his face turning red.

Ben turned to the Vintel and asked, "Where is she keeping it?" The question was directed to AF20.

At first there was no response. When the transmission began, AF20 was finishing another conversation. They heard a rapid exchange of words, mostly inaudible—something about a decryption code and an urgent transmission, followed by AF20 saying, "…I need confirmation from eyes on the ground and send it to my station immediately." Only then did AF20 respond to Ben's question, "The top button of her jacket." Although AF20's voice was scrambled, there was no mistaking a heightened level of stress. Something big was happening. The transmission immediately shut down, terminating the connection.

Ben seized the top button of Bernadette's top. He cut it off with a knife supplied by one of the security guards and tossed it to Derek. "On that recording device, you'll find all the information the Egalitarian Party needs to find you and your family, and the means to steal all of your work, all the data you spent your life perfecting. You would have been tortured and killed."

Derek was dumbfounded. His ears were joining his face in turning red. He couldn't find words to say, stammering, "I…I…"

Ben ignored him and turned to the group. "We have to live in reality. These are dangerous people. They will stop at nothing to preserve their positions of privilege and power. Consider what you've seen here against the brutality perpetrated by this government. They have murdered on a massive scale, with an efficiency that would cause both Stalin and Hitler to blush. And you heard what their sick and twisted minds have conjured up with Project Darwin. Any day now they are going to put this all together and mobilize every resource they have to destroy MST and all of us." Ben pointed at Bernadette. His voice was louder and more aggressive. "She deserved her outcome. She is a traitor. She's guilty of sedition. She would have instigated the death of all of us and our families. Prepare yourselves for what's coming. This isn't going to be a debate. It's going to be a fight beyond your wildest imaginations."

Ben's anger raged. He couldn't shake Derek's accusations. They cut deep. They were the same indictments he made against himself when he looked in the mirror and he'd be damned if he was going to listen someone else saying the same thing. Ben pointed at the recording device and scowled, "You don't see those too often in the safety of your lab do you? I would offer a little advice…front lines or tucked away doing research, each of us has a job to do. When this is over, I'll take you on a tour of the government incinerators. You can look at the logs detailing the millions of people who have already been eradicated. Then you can teach me all about morals and ethics." Venting didn't help. Ben felt his anger building and it was only with extreme difficulty that he managed to hold back from decking Derek. He finally turned his back to him and addressed the others, his demeanor that of a college professor. From their perspective he was calm and the picture of control. "Does anyone have any questions about the interrogation or how the device works to harvest information from the brain?"

The security detail carried Bernadette out of the room. What was left of her would be placed in a park close to a hospital, but not in Havana, more likely it would be in New Orleans, where she lived. She would be positioned on a secluded bench. A Good Samaritan would anonymously notify local authorities, informing them that a lady in the park was having an attack of some sort. After an initial medical work-up, she would be admitted and cared for, until the extent of her permanent dysfunction became apparent. Then she would fall under the government's euthanasia protocol.

As soon as the security guards took her body out of the room, another came rushing in. "Hell's breaking loose all over the city," he excitedly said. "We have to evacuate immediately."

* * * * *

The housing tenements in the city of Havana were old and dilapidated, the smell a mix of sweat and garbage. As Jake made his was down one street and across another, he noticed that the city had an atmosphere of unease. He could hear an occasional dog barking against the background noise of the inner city neighborhood. It was a rough area of the city, burdened by drugs, alcoholism, and a high level of crime. In fact, most of Havana was this way, except for a small upscale area where the privileged class lived. Most United American cities had fallen into similar states of disrepair. The middle class had been wiped out to the point that society disintegrated into small groups of *haves* and large populations of *have-nots*.

A casual glance down the alleyways more than once gave him a view of rats crawling over and around homeless drunkards who were passed out and sprawled across pieces of synthetic cardboard. Empty bottles of booze glinted off shafts of sunlight and refuse collected in the corners. He passed an occasional work crew fixing the streets and the underground piping. Their nature was unhurried and bored.

"We have a newbie," Marco said. He was looking out the window of the bar when he spied a stranger. His finger indicated the direction. It pointed directly at Jake.

"Get the others," Ramsey said. "They were going over to 23rd."

"Do you think he has any?"

Ramsey grinned. "What do you think? Look at him. Get in front and start backtracking. I'll get behind him, and we'll roll him."

"Good times!" Marco yelled. He hurried out a side entrance and ran through the alleys to find his friends.

Unconcerned about the potential dangers of an unfamiliar environment, Jake continued his tour through the streets. He was dismayed. The people were lifeless, their spirits destroyed. It reminded him of past experiences in the Southern Confederacy, of a people utterly defeated, the spark of vibrancy dead and buried. He turned and stepped into a small grocery store. The attendant didn't offer a greeting. In fact, she didn't even bother looking up.

The shelves were half empty and what was available was basic, good enough to live on but not enough to make a gourmet meal. He inspected the half-stocked shelves and saw flour, bread, butter, pasta, and some other staples. There were containers of sauce, but when he looked at the plain white labels with black lettering, they all said the same thing—*Tomato Sauce; from concentrate.*

When he finished walking up and down the aisles, he returned to the register empty-handed. The clerk commented, "Used your quota already, didn't you?"

Jake took note of the retinal scanner on the counter. That was how the government tracked people and monitored their activities. Everything was controlled through central computers, and every citizen had a unique identifier. It was like the country had grown a nervous system with computerized tentacles and a human host at the end of each that needed to be controlled. There were no currencies being exchanged from one hand to the next...all of it, every transaction, went through the Egalitarian system. It was the ultimate form of control and the ultimate means to suppress a population. That was when Jake noticed the bars on the windows and the security camera above the door. "Do you own this store?" he asked.

"You trying to be funny? Of course I don't own the store."

"Well, who owns it?"

"The government owns it. Just like everything else."

"Can you tell me about the quotas?"

She looked up for the first time and made no effort to hide her annoyance. At first her expression was a glare. She eyed Jake like he was from another planet. He smiled in return and she started to soften. "You're not from around here are you?" she said.

Jake laughed. "I'm having a little trouble blending in." He raised his eyebrows, "What gave me away?"

She smirked, only slightly amused. Pointing at the retinal scanner she said, "The government tracks everything. Each month everybody gets a quota. It's based on age, height, weight, gender, medical conditions, and such. Every purchase goes through the retinal scanner. That accesses your allotment. You can draw from it, but once it's gone for the month you're out of luck. If a person has medical problems there may be certain foods that they can't buy."

"Really?" Jake was stunned by the revelation. "People don't make their own choices?"

"People aren't smart enough to make their own choices," she said, rolling her eyes.

Jake was still struggling with the idea. "The government controls what a person can and can't eat?"

"Well, yeah," she said, mystified as to why this stranger found it so objectionable. "If someone has diabetes, they shouldn't be eating foods with lots of sugar. So the government won't let them buy it. People with heart problems don't get foods with high salt content or cholesterol. And if someone is too old and sickly they don't get anything at all."

"Is there a black market for food?" He asked. She nodded her head in the affirmative. "What about alcohol and tobacco?"

"All of it," she said. "It's all smuggled in, mostly from South America."

Jake noticed several men loitering in front of the store. He kept them in awareness and went on. "Do the people get enough to eat? Or does the government use the food supply as a tool for control?"

An expression of fear took over. In a move that was smooth and subtle, like that of a prison inmate being watched by a guard, she motioned toward the security camera with her eyes and nonchalantly pointed to her ear. She meant to say that the government was watching and listening.

Jake walked underneath the camera, reached up, and snatched it off its mount. He scanned the serial numbers into his BCD and quickly hacked the system. He tracked back to the mainframe, deleted the previous five minutes, and created a feedback loop that would run for another two hours. He put the camera back and returned to the cashier.

Her face was ashen. "Tampering with one of their security devices is a crime punishable by imprisonment. I can get in trouble too."

"What's your name?" Jake asked.

"Millie. Millie Rosenthal," she answered.

Jake sized her up, curious about her fear. "Millie, do you know what it's like to go about your life, to make choices all on your own…without the government watching?" When she didn't answer he added, "Don't worry, I erased all the footage. I was never in here, and it's running a loop with earlier footage. For the time being you are officially off the grid."

"Who are you?" she asked.

"A friend…I think," Jake said. "You didn't answer my…"

"Yes," she emphatically blurted out. Her eyes suddenly were bright and her face alive. "I've dreamt of being free since I was a child. So does everyone else. I wanted to be an astronomer but they said I couldn't. Freedom is all we whisper about in the dark late at night." She began talking in a hushed tone, "But we hear them coming. We hear boots and banging on the doors. It's always between 2:00 and 3:00 A.M. When the sun comes up, another one of our neighbors is gone. We live in a state of constant fear that we'll be next."

"You said the government owns everything," Jake said. "Are any businesses owned by regular people?" Jake noticed there were now eight men in front of the store.

"There are, but only people who are part of the Party can survive in business. For everyone else it's impossible. The laws are harsh and the taxes so high that they always fail. The only hope is to sell out your family and neighbors and become one of them…if they let you. Then life is easier."

Jake motioned with his thumb toward the door and asked, "Who are they?"

"Local thugs. You'd do well to watch yourself and stay away from them."

"Thanks," Jake said. "I'll take that under advisement." He pondered for a moment and asked, "Millie, if the government is controlling everything so tightly, how do you survive?"

"Barely. There are times when there's nothing to eat the last day or two of the month, but I have it better than some. The government reduces the quotas so low for the old people, especially when their health begins to fail, that they can't survive. We do our best, but I'm trying to take care of my grandmother, and it's so…" Her words were interrupted by movements outside the store. "That one right there," she casually pointed to one with long straggly black hair and a dirty goatee, "that's Ramsey. He is the ring leader of the gang."

Jake nodded and turned to the retinal scanner. "Do you mind if I look at this?"

"Knock yourself out."

Jake was sickened by what she was saying, and he aimed to do something about it. He plugged the serial number and the address into his BCD, did a quick search and accessed the scanner's operating systems. He breached the outer defenses and snaked his way into the system, easily breaking through the Egalitarian firewalls and other security measures. He was leaning on the counter, concentrating on the codes and lines of data rapidly flashing through his BCD. He heard the door open and several men walk in. He counted the pattern of seven sets of feet. The eighth didn't come in and was likely outside keeping watch. From the pace of their gait and the spread pattern they assumed behind him, he assumed their purpose wasn't to rush an attack. He finished what he was doing, mumbling,

"These security systems are more rudimentary than they were sixty years ago," he said. When he found where he needed to be, he inserted several self-propagating viruses. They attacked the system, wiping out the control parameters and destroying the quota system. Until it was fixed, the people could purchase any food they liked without the government telling them what they could and couldn't buy. But he didn't do it just in Havana, he entered the heart of the data mountain and corrupted the system for the entirety of United America. Jake pushed away from the counter and smiled at Millie. "I entered my purchase. I want you to take the food I listed home to help with your grandmother."

Millie had backed away from the counter and was up against the wall. Her eyes were big, darting back and forth. They were centered on a figure standing behind Jake. In the chrome trim lining one of the displays sitting on the counter, Jake saw their reflections and determined their positions. As there was no sudden movement he turned slowly, as though he didn't have a care in the world. He came chest to face with the much shorter Ramsey. Six others stood behind. Jake scanned them with his BCD and counted eleven knives in total, and no other weapons. They were dressed in rough inner city gang attire, had greasy slick-backed hair, and none had shaved in quite some time. Three of them were nervous and scared, two were firm and ready for a fight, and one was smiling and bouncing up and down on his toes...a real psychopath. Ramsey stood in the center, cool and collected.

"I didn't come in here looking for trouble," Jake said.

The corner of Ramsey's mouth smirked ever so slightly. "Looking has nothing to do with it. You came into our neighborhood." Two of his men reached into their pockets and secured their grips on their knives, getting ready to flick the blades out for a fight. One held his behind his back.

"My advice is for you to back on out of here," Jake warned.

"We want everything you've got."

Jake considered the predicament. He would have preferred to walk away, but they weren't giving him a choice. "Are things so bad that you have to resort to this sort of thing to survive?" Jake shook his head and said, "You should have brought more."

Ramsey didn't react at first. He sized up his prey, grinned a mouth full of yellow teeth, and motioned to his friends that it was time. "Didn't ask your…"

Jake stepped forward, standing over Ramsey, and said in a loud voice, "Rule number one…shut the hell up and attack."

Ramsey's hand was coming out of his pocket, his switchblade in the process of opening, when Jake's finger jammed into his eye. The sudden blunt force ruptured the globe. He dropped the knife, yelled, and fell backward with his hands on his face. His motion momentarily blocked the path of two of the others. Jake moved to his left, dodged a wild slash from the psychopath, catching the tip of the blade across his forearm, and then he punched him. The motion of Jake's fist was so fast the thug didn't see it coming. His jaw fractured and his head ripped backward. He went airborne for a moment and fell unconscious to the floor. The others were on him now and in a flash of motion he side-kicked one of the others who flew backward against the metal shelves, sending them toppling over and food flying everywhere. The three who were scared backed out of range, leaving only one who was willing to fight. He had his knife out and was slicing it wildly through the air, yelling. Jake stepped back, dodged his weapon and grabbed a can of food that was rolling across the floor. He sized it up in his hand and went in for the attack. He faked a throw. The perp dropped back and ducked. As soon as he came up the can had already been launched. While his eyes were drawn to Jake the can smashed into the side of his head, giving off a disgusting hollow sound. He fell to the floor moaning. Blood immediately pulsated from a large gash over his temple. It rushed down over his ear and covered his hands.

Unimpressed, Jake stood over the four downed men. "Bunch of morons," he muttered. "How did you ever survive so long?" He pointed at the three remaining gang members, "Come here."

"We don't want any trouble," one of them said, his voice quivering. Jake motioned again and they slowly inched forward, holding their blades down at their sides. "Look…you win. We're done," another said.

When they refused to come any closer Jake said, "Come here and give me those pocket knives before you hurt yourselves." When they handed them over, he proceeded to break the blades off at the handle. "First off," he said, "you're holding them wrong, and secondly—go get yourself something respectable. These are pieces of crap, unstable, terrible grips, and weak at the base. If anybody gets hurt with these, more than likely, it's going to be you." The lookout opened the door and took two steps in before stopping. When he realized that his friends were down a sudden expression of shock took over, his mouth dropped, and he turned and ran as fast as his feet would carry him. Jake shook his head again in disgust.

"See this nice lady?" Jake said to the three cowards, pointing at Millie as he spoke. "She had this store spotless before you came in here. I suggest you get busy and clean it up." While they scrambled to put the shelves back in position and restock the food items, Jake confiscated the knives from the four downed men. As fast as he found their weapons he broke them in half.

The psycho regained consciousness and was writhing in agony, his jaw grossly deformed to the side. Jake picked him up by the belt as though he weighed nothing at all and deposited him outside the door. The other three, each battered in their on way, got up on their own accord. Jake pointed at Ramsey and said, "You're going to stay. You three," he pointed at the cowards who had just finished cleaning up, "better take your friends to the hospital."

When they left Jake got a bag of ice and tossed it to Ramsey. "Put that on it and it won't hurt so bad."

He did as he was told. The eye was dead. It was leaking a clear jelly-like substance and the aspects of the eye that used to be white were now an angry red secondary to hemorrhage. Because the tissues surrounding the eye were swollen, it gave the eye the appearance of being recessed inward. It looked every bit as painful as it was.

"Kind of a dangerous pastime, why do you do it?" Jake asked.

"What the hell is it to you?" Ramsey retorted.

"You've obviously got some talent in leading people," Jake said. "Otherwise your friends wouldn't follow you. Why do you do this? Are things so bad that you have to attack and rob innocent people to survive? Aren't there any legitimate means for you to earn a living?"

"You arrogant son of a bitch." Ramsey spit on the floor in anger. "What the hell do you know about things being bad? You don't live like the rest of us. Look at you."

Jake grabbed Ramsey's wrist and squeezed. The compression caused him to drop the bag of ice and scream out in pain. "Your first lesson is manners. You don't spit on someone else's floor. Clean it up." Jake pushed his wrist downward while he spoke. Ramsey collapsed to his knees in pain. When he wiped the spit up with his sleeve, Jake brought him back to his feet.

There was a commotion outside about a half-block down from the store. They heard a short burst from a police siren. All activity on the busy street came to a sudden stop. Two male officers got out of their pod and accosted a family on the street. They singled out a husband and wife and their daughter who was seven or eight years old. One of the officers waved the onlookers away while the other forced the family back against the wall. He started going through their bags and checking their identifications.

"What's happening over there?" Jake asked.

"Shake-down." Ramsey said. "Happens all the time."

It was difficult for Jake to discern everything that was being said as his BCD's ability to pick up and amplify sounds was diminished by the combination of the distance and the sound waves dissipating when they passed through the glass storefront. He was only picking up fragments of dialogue.

"Please," the husband said. "…No,…officer, please."

The little girl was crying.

"Before the Regional Magistrate," the policeman said. "Subversive activities."

"But…nothing...innocent," the husband protested.

The officer kneed him in the groin and he fell to the ground. The little girl started screaming. "Resisting….officer of the law," the policeman said. He kicked him a few times. Everyone else scattered, and the street was quickly abandoned by everyone except the family and the attacking policemen.

The man's wife was clutching her daughter. Both were crying and protesting. The second officer pulled the little girl away from her.

Inside the store, Jake grabbed Ramsey by the back of the neck and pushed his face toward the window. His tone was altogether different—it was ominous and aggressive. "That doesn't look like a shakedown to me. What is going on?"

"Questioning," one of the policemen said. He slapped the woman.

"No!" she pleaded. Her back was against the wall. Her long hair disheveled and in her face, sticking against wet cheeks. "Please no!…let them go!"

Jake pressed closer trying to catch what they were saying.

"Rot in prison…anti-government activities," the officer said.

The little girl broke free. "Mommy! Mommy!" Frantic and screaming, she rushed back to her mother and threw her arms around her. She held tight with the help of her mother as the officer tried to pull her away. The other officer began kicking and stomping the husband again. He pulled out his pulsar and pointed it at him.

"Stop! Stop!" the woman screamed. "I'll do what you want!"

The daughter was immediately ripped from her arms and handed to the husband. He was battered and could hardly hold her. He was crying while the little girl continued screaming, "Mommy! Mommy!"

"Going in for questioning." The officer laughed. He grabbed the woman by the hair and threw her in the back of the pod.

The other policeman was standing in front of the husband. He pointed at the little girl, "Keep her under control. We," then it was inaudible. Finally Jake heard, "lesson."

The pod pulled away, leaving the man and his daughter alone. She was frantic and screaming. He was on his knees holding her and crying.

"That's not a shakedown!" Jake said. He tightened his grip on Ramsey's neck and smashed his face against the glass. "What's going on?!"

"Those officers are vicious. They pick out a woman and rape her."

"What?!" Jake was incredulous.

"They threaten arrest and rape her!" he yelled. "They do it all the time!"

"And you do nothing?" Jake said through gritted teeth. He could still hear the little girl's screams for her mommy echoing in his head. The experience blended with so many horrible memories from his past that he couldn't take it.

"What can we do?!" Ramsey pleaded as he yelled out in pain.

"You can fight for what's right!" Jake said.

"It's hopeless!"

When Ramsey said it, it inflamed Jake even more. He pulled Ramsey around so they were face to face, his nose nearly pressed into Ramsey's destroyed eye. Spittle was flying out of his mouth as he growled, "Where are they taking her?"

"Parking garage on the corner of 43rd and Francis Galton! Security floor is on the lower level, in the basement!"

"How far?"

"Two kilometers that way." Ramsey pointed, his blood stained hand quivering in the air as he indicated the direction.

"You see this happening around you, and you do nothing," Jake scowled. "Instead you target innocent people. You make me sick! You don't know the meaning of hopeless. You're just a sniveling coward." He picked Ramsey up with one hand and threw him down on the floor as though he was discarding a piece of trash. He pulled out one of his pulsars and activated his energy shield as he ran out of the store.

By the time Jake bounded across the street and made it to the father and daughter, other people were emerging from hiding to help. They stopped in their tracks as Jake approached. His frame was huge and cast a shadow over them. He grabbed the man by the shoulders and brought him to a standing position. His voice was booming and sure, "Wait here." He made eye contact with the little girl. She was sobbing between efforts to catch her breath. "I'll bring your mother back safe." Then Jake was gone, racing down the street at incredible speed, chasing after the policemen.

As he ran, Jake blasted the security cameras positioned on the streets. They exploded in furious balls of flame and smoke. At the same time, through his BCD he tapped a backdoor channel to United America's military surveillance satellites. He rerouted the signals and took temporary control. All across the Caribbean Sector, level III alarms went off and chaos went up the military chain of command. Officers froze at their controls, not knowing what happened or what to do. Computer teams raced to figure out the cause of the failure. They were blind and all fingers pointed to the Brazilian military. For the moment, it was assumed that it was part of an attack.

The signals ripped from military intelligence were now being sent to Jake's BCD. Orbiting satellites altered their orientations and aimed their sensors at Havana. He scanned the route ahead of him and began receiving ground level information on his surroundings, the disposition of military and police units, and the schematics of the garage. He could see the pod as it pulled around the building and stopped at the security gate. It was going into the lower level just as Ramsey predicted.

The local police department was already releasing scores of hovering sentries to suppress what they surmised was a riot. Several of the city's surveillance cameras were already out, and it had to be some sort of coordinated attack. Jake picked them up. The first waves were coming in from three directions, converging to intercept his line of travel.

Jake hadn't run more than a kilometer when the first sentry approached from the left. This one was on routine patrol when re-routed. He adjusted the setting on his pulsar and lurched to the side at the last moment. The sentry fired and a sudden high-amplitude sound wave hit him as he turned. He felt the shock of its blast. Designed for population control, it was supposed to traumatize his ears and cause immediate deafness, but with his energy shield the signal was dampened to the point that it did no damage. He spun toward the sentry and fired an electromagnetic pulse, the blast frying its internal components. Its momentum sent it skidding and tumbling across the pavement. For his purposes it was useless. To hack into the system he needed to capture one that was alive. But it wouldn't be easy when every second was precious. Its weapons systems and visual tracking sensors were mounted underneath, he would have to avoiding them by capturing a unit from above. He picked up the dead sentry and threw it on the sidewalk underneath a second floor balcony. He purposely chose one that was facing the sun so that the reflection would hide his movements until the last possible moment. He raced inside the building, leapt up the stairs, and kicked down the door to one of the apartments. He bounded through a family residence, causing a family to scream at his sudden appearance. They fell backward and scrambled to get out of his way as he ran past. By the time he made it to the window, there were over a dozen hovering sentries scanning the immediate area and sending images of the downed device back to precinct headquarters. One of them was just outside the window. Without hesitating Jake raced forward. Just before impacting the window he blasted the unit, specifically targeting its rear mounted propulsion system. The energy pulse shattered the glass outward in a million small fragments. The sentry spun out of control. Jake leapt through the air and grabbed it. On the way to the ground he fired a series of electromagnetic pulses, hit the ground, rolled hard, and came up firing. The sentries fired several shots at him before falling lifelessly out of the air, careening into surrounding buildings and throwing sparks as the metal casings scraped across the pavement.

Through his BCD, Jake detected a second and third wave of sentries racing toward his position. ETA was less than a minute. At the same time, the military's surveillance satellites indicated that, in the garage, the officers were dragging the woman out of the back of the pod. Jake knelt on the casing of the shiny metal sentry. It was squirming, trying to get away. They were originally designed for use in urban warfare, and he knew them well in the battles against the Persians. Unfortunately, they were also perfect tools for a despotic government to control its population. He reached underneath and broke off the sentry's weapons array. He threw it to the side and with it flopping side to side and twisting, he hacked into the system. Lines of data were cascading through his BCD and within fifteen seconds he hacked into the Havana Police Department's computer systems. He wrested control of the nasty little weapons away from the city. He launched all the remaining sentries and altered the targeting systems. They began sweeping through Havana destroying all the surveillance cameras. As a secondary objective he turned the machines of tyranny against the local muscle of the Egalitarian Party. The police pods would be destroyed and the police officers subdued. With slightly over five hundred sentries sweeping through Havana it would take about fifteen minutes, and the entire city would be off the government's grid.

That accomplished, Jake got up and ran toward the parking garage. The schematics indicated his best point of entry, and the fastest way for him to get to the woman, would be to go in on the ground level. They were on the lower level, one floor below. They would be separated by concrete and rebar several feet thick. To get in on the lower level, he would have to run around the entire building, snake through the security gate, and make his way down the ramp. It would take precious time. He saw that the officers were forcing the woman across the trunk of the pod.

In the garage, the policemen were in cool and sadistic moods. Reveling in the power they wielded, they knew all too well that they could do what they wanted with impunity. The people were weak, too scared to respond. The woman had no means to resist and no recourse within a system where the police were members of the power establishment...loyal defenders of Fascism, soldiers charged with keeping order at the level of the city street. They could do whatever they wanted so long as they did the bidding of their superiors, and that bidding was to foment fear on the streets. It was deemed to be the best policy to keep the population under control.

The officers temporarily deactivated the pod's built-in communications systems so they wouldn't be disturbed. Without thinking, they removed their communicators from behind their ears, just like all the other times. They thought of what they were about to do as being no more significant than taking a break from their jobs to get a cup of coffee, and they fully expected to be back out on the streets within thirty minutes. The pod came to a stop in the usual spot in a secluded section of the garage where they were sure to be undisturbed.

"Get out," one of them said, his voice definite in its determination to maintain complete control. She cowered in the far corner of the rear compartment. "I said get out!" he yelled. She cried out while refusing to move, pressing her body harder into the opposite door panel. The second officer opened the door. She screamed and fell out onto the concrete. They laughed. "Ha ha, works every time. You should have seen the look on her face." They carried on until they were both standing over her, watching her as she gained her hands and knees and tried to crawl underneath the pod.

"I don't think so." The second officer grabbed her by the ankle. "Why do women always try to do that?"

"Do what?"

"Try to get under the pod." He laughed and pulled. Halfway under the vehicle, she screamed and kicked. Her heel caught his wrist and he lost his grip. He erupted in anger. "That's how you want to play it!" He pulled his pulsar, adjusted the settings, and shot her. A pulsating electric shock ripped through her body and she writhed on the ground as he kept firing. At first she was screaming, but when the shocks finally subsided, she was left crying and writhing in a fetal position.

"Easy," his partner said. "You know I hate it when they throw up or soil themselves." He stepped between them, pulled her out, and picked her up. He pressed her against the side of the pod and said. "Stop crying and quit squirming. This is going to happen, and you're going to cooperate. If you don't, I'll send your husband to prison. You'll never see him again. Or that pretty little girl of yours…how old is she? Maybe we should go back and get her."

"No! No!" she cried. "I'll do what you want!"

"Hell with it. Let's go get her." the other officer said.

"No! I promise. I'll stop squirming!" Her face was frantic with fear. The men were like jackals. There was nothing she could do. She was powerless to resist.

"Now see how easy this is." He led her to the trunk and laid her face down.

"No. Wait a minute," the other policeman said. "She's a mess. I can't stand it." He pulled her off the trunk and pulled her shirt off. He wiped her eyes and cheeks and moved the hair away from her face. "You know, once you get all the hair away, this one's kind of pretty." He looked at his friend. "There, isn't that better?" He turned and grinned at her. It was sick and evil in every way imaginable. He said in a hushed voice, "I hate crying. If you cry, we're going back to get your little girl."

They forced her face down on the trunk, ripping at the rest of her clothing. They stopped for a moment and began arguing. "Whose turn is it to go first?"

"Mine."

"Are you sure?"

"Yeah. Remember, earlier this morning you…."

Their exchange suddenly stopped. There was a quaking sound. They looked around for the source of the vibration. "What is that?"

"I don't know."

They listened as it grew louder. The vibrations grew more intense. Dust, pieces of gravel, and shards of concrete began falling down on the front of the pod. They backed up, one with his belt and pants undone. The woman pushed away from the trunk and ran a short distance. Her legs were still trembling with spasms from being shot with the pulsar. She tripped and fell, and then crawled behind a pillar.

The noise grew to a roar as larger pieces of concrete began falling. The pieces were now a foot in diameter. They rocked the pod and smashed huge dents across its hood and top, shattering the glass alloy windshield. The officers saw a hole opening up in the ceiling. Suddenly there was a loud explosion, and a bright white light flashed. The officers fell backward temporarily blinded. The hole was two meters across. The rebar was bent completely downward, out of the way. Jake jumped through the hole and landed on top of the pod, a pulsar in each hand.

He launched off the vehicle and was on one of the officers before he could react. A pulsar blast nearly took his head off, the momentum of the shot sending his dead and bloodied form rolling across the floor. Without hesitation, Jake turned to the second officer. He was still on the ground when Jake kicked him in the face. It was a glancing blow and when he attempted to pull his pulsar, Jake shot his hand. He yelled out as the weapon dropped. The skin and much of the underlying muscle was burned away from his hand. In the next fraction of a second, Jake was on him. He grabbed him by the collar and hollered out in anger, throwing him through the air. His body careened off the side of the pod and landed on the ground amid the concrete debris. For a brief moment the officer passed out from a concussive head injury.

"Never again! Never again will I walk away!" Jake said through gritted teeth as he shook the officer. "Look at my face...so you'll know who killed you."

The officer's eyes widened as Jake deactivated the facial polymer, revealing his true face. "No! No!" he screamed.

Jake grabbed him by the back of the head, turned him toward the pod, and smashed his face toward the surface. The officer managed to get his hands and arms in front to dampen the first and second blows, but Jake's strength and fury were overpowering. "Never again! Never again!" he yelled out. Each time he yelled he smashed the officer's face into the increasingly bloody metal. The bones cracked and splintered as Jake yelled out in a psychotic rage. Over and over he rammed the man's head into the pod until there was nothing hard left in his skull to absorb the impact. When Jake finally threw the body aside and stepped back to take in what his rage produced, he was covered in blood. He felt drunk. There was a deep twist of primordial pleasure, a feeling he wished wasn't there...but it felt so good. When it gradually fled into the background he turned his attention to the woman.

She was terrified after hearing the sounds of the stranger's wrath. Unable to move, she hid and tried to remain silent. Jake's BCD indicated that her position was behind a pillar. He could see her outline. He stepped wide around it so she could see him from a distance before he approached. "Did they hurt you?" he said, his demeanor had completely changed and his voice was compassionate and caring.

When she first laid eyes on him and beheld a huge stranger covered in blood and dirt, her expression was one of terror. But when she processed his words she started crying, "They hurt me! They hurt me!" She began rocking in a fetal position, crying, her body shaking in spasms.

"They will never hurt anybody again." Jake said. He found her shirt and handed it to her. He cautiously helped her sit up. "Grab around my neck," he said as he picked her up. "Let's take you back. Your family is waiting for you."

Jake carried the woman through the streets of Havana. Sirens blared for miles in every direction. The sentries were flying up and down the streets wreaking carnage on Egalitarian infrastructure, explosions and blasts were echoing off buildings, and trails of smoke were rising throughout the city. Jake remained in complete silence while the woman wept. He felt emotionally empty, neither positive nor negative, but more like a blank slate, numb and closed off after what he had just done. He carried her the entire two kilometers and returned her to her husband and daughter. The little girl was elated, and they wept with joy. Jake made eye contact with her. He felt something deep inside starting to burst but pushed it away. He forced a slight smile, but it was wrapped in utter sadness. He put his hand gently on her head; just barely touching it with the tips of his fingers... they were trembling, then he turned and walked away.

At MST headquarters, in the privacy of an inner office within the primary command center, AF20 watched a secret feed from Jake's BCD in stunned silence and admiration. Despite everything he had endured, the driving characteristics of Lt. Col. Jake Gillean had been preserved. The man was the computer genius and warrior they knew him to be. What he did couldn't be called hacking, he had actually smashed through the Fascist's security systems with complete ease. MST weapons programmers and computer espionage teams spent years of research trying to accomplish what Jake had done in minutes, and an entire city had been temporarily liberated.

AF20 pushed away from the desk, unable to contain a smile of satisfaction. It was a solemn moment. AF20 whispered, "It has begun."

CHAPTER 33: THE SEARCH

[APRIL 20, AD 2441]
[140 DAYS AFTER ARRIVAL; LATER THAT AFTERNOON]
[LOCATION: HAVANA, CUBA]

Jake returned to the safe house and showered. He discarded his clothing by burning them and dumping the ashes in a storm sewer several blocks away. He activated the Vintel and began exploring the details of the Great Tragedy. Blocking out the rest of the world, he was soon reliving his experiences in the Persian bunker. He accessed the file from his BCD and replayed the last minutes—the flash of light and his loss of consciousness. That had to have been the moment of the explosion and the terrible event that wiped out the Middle East and beyond. The number of lives lost was so high that he found it impossible to comprehend. The ferocity of the destruction was equally difficult to grasp. He carefully studied satellite imagery, looking for old landmarks he might be familiar with. He zoomed in and out, traveled across the barren landscape, and navigated around the still active volcanoes. It was hard to believe it was earth as it more resembled the landscape of a lifeless planet.

The door flung open and Ben rushed in. Excited and nervous, he quickly closed the door and peeked out the windows. He asked, "What are you doing?"

Casually pointing at the Vintel as though Ben was a moron, Jake sarcastically answered, "What does it look like?"

"Didn't you hear the sirens?" Ben asked, "Or the explosions? Something happened. All hell is breaking loose out there."

Jake shrugged as though it was nothing to worry about and went back to the Vintel.

"What did you do to your arm?"

Jake glanced at his forearm. The wound was on the extensor surface, not a normal place to get a cut. It was about five centimeters long, and although it wasn't deep, it still looked mean. "Just a little careless," he said.

Ben stared. He thought it was amazing that one man could be the source of everything they were doing, yet in a moment like this, he could be completely ignorant of what was going on around him. He thought it was like trying to protect a butterfly flailing in the eye of a hurricane… he made it halfway through, was in a temporary calm, and was naïve to the fact that there was still going to be hell to pay. But then he reminded himself that Jake was no butterfly. He may have lost his footing, but the last thing he would ever be accused of being was fragile.

"We have to go," Ben said. "The city is in chaos. People are rioting. The police lost control. The latest is that the military has been called in to restore order. Troops are landing as we speak. We need to get out before they establish a perimeter."

Jake turned off the unit and stood up. "Let's go."

As they were leaving Ben said, "In case you were wondering, we're going by submarine to an island just north of St. George's in Grenada.

Once they were on the vessel, it quickly submerged. It traveled east, hugging the bottom a few miles out from the Cuban coast. They were making good progress and were momentarily outside any imminent danger. There was plenty of room to move around inside the craft and its compartments; the bridge, the engine room with its fusion generators, a sleeper with several bunks, a galley, and a ready room with a variety of computers.

Ben pointed at the computers. "If there's anything of a more personal nature that you'd like to explore, you have a green light." What Ben didn't share was that MST wanted Jake to perform his search on those computers. They were controlling the feed, and there were certain things they wanted him to discover—and others they needed to hide.

"You're sure these are okay?"

"This access point, or address, doesn't exist. It's completely invisible."

"How's that?" Jake wanted to be sure before he began searching.

Ben explained that the signal was stolen from probably over two or three thousand random units from all over the globe, small fragments of signal were taken from each in a random fashion. The signal only delayed by a couple milliseconds despite utilizing other computers as intermediaries. The submarine was basically just receiving data; it wasn't sending anything back to the system. The intermediary computers were the ones interacting directly with United America's data mountains.

An awkward pause followed his explanation. Jake eyed the unit and shifted his gaze back to Ben.

"I'm going to get some shut eye. I'm tired," Ben said.

"About time," Jake sarcastically commented.

Ben didn't get it.

"All I could think of was get lost, or scram," Jake said, the tip of a southern drawl revealing itself in the comment. "You going to bed saves me the hassle, and you don't get your panties all bunched up."

"Oh," Ben said, happy to see that Jake was smiling. "I never understood grunt humor." He turned and walked away. Talking to himself but loud enough for Jake to hear, he added, "Few more blows to the head, and I suppose I'd understand the brute's jokes, but still doubt he'd be funny."

Jake chuckled, was going to say something about Ben's mommy coming to tuck him in, but he left it alone. He turned his attention to the Vintel.

Wendy was completely absent. He couldn't find any hint that she had ever existed. That part didn't make any sense. Paul and Bailey, and even his mother, Janet, were all gone. That made sense to him, but he grew increasingly confused when he discovered Thomas Gillean was also gone from the record. Why would he be gone? He wasn't part of the line that descended from the family farm. That line came up the maternal side of his family. Jake felt an overwhelming surge of melancholy as search after search came back empty.

He painstakingly searched the database for anything he could remember from his early life, things beyond his family. He searched his grade school, his high school, the military academy, and his friends. He did find reference to his friend Tom Wilson. He got drunk and died in a swimming accident in his late teens. How could things be so different? Tom was one of Spring Hill's successes and was the proverbial *picked himself up by his bootstraps* story.

The terrorist attack on the museum in Portland occurred but was completely different from the way he experienced it. Almost everyone died. The roof of the auditorium collapsed with the initial explosion and only forty people survived. Eleven men from Alpha Group died. He recognized several of his men. Tess, the girl Jake rescued as the building was coming down, was listed with the deceased.

His friends in the Guard were scattered, dying here and there. Alexander Fisk was listed. He actually was able to bring up a picture. He looked exactly the way Jake remembered. He was listed as having died at the time of the Great Tragedy, but nothing was mentioned about the operation in the underground bunker.

Jake again spent time studying the worldwide disaster. As the Vintel related a theory about a dark comet striking the heart of the Persian Empire, he considered what actually happened. He could see the ST-

17 Gopher lurching across the interior of the cavernous bunker. It was partially climbing up a wall, completely out of control. It was rolling and smashing everything in its path while at the same time being shrouded in flashes of light from the Persian guns. There was an explosion. Somehow that explosion, in combination with the activated Persian transport device, resulted in the Great Tragedy. Again, Jake couldn't wrap his head around the death toll—twelve to fourteen billion people; it was numbing.

Jake went back again to find information about his family. That's when he discovered that the farm in Spring Hill was gone, hidden under a housing development that previously wasn't there. After several hours, he couldn't take it anymore. The searches were nothing less than torture, and he couldn't bear discovering another consequence of his mistakes.

Jake tried to wrap his head around what had become of his life. It was now the year 2441. He was born in the year 2349. When he left his family in the year 2379, when he walked out the door for his last mission, he was thirty years old and second in command of the most powerful fighting force in the history of man. He was slated to get a promotion and was going to be the leader of Alpha Group. He was supposed to live out the bulk of his life in what remained of the Twenty-Fourth Century, but things went terribly wrong. He was thrust into the past—into the 1800s. He lived there for four years…four brutal years immersed in the living hell of the American Civil War. Then, at the moment of death, a death he welcomed, he inexplicably reappeared at the Battle of Franklin reenactment on December 2, 2440. It was now 2441. He was living in a time not meant for him. He didn't belong in the Twenty Fifth Century.

So much had happened between the moment he disappeared from under the Persian mountains and when he reappeared in Franklin. In the throes of the 1800s, he screamed out, he cried with unfathomable bitterness, in utter submission he tore at the vestments of his soul, then he embraced a seething hatred of mankind. He fought with all his might and somewhere in the process he lost himself…and then he lost everything.

Jake squeezed his hands into fists. His tension was one of shame and anger as he fully realized the nightmare revealed through the Vintel. Everything that changed was the result of his actions. Everything he saw was the consequence of his decisions. He knew from the letter he received after his father died, the letter he wrote to himself from the 1800s, that he was going to travel back in time. He knew it. He knew it, and yet he didn't take it seriously. He failed everyone who ever mattered. That realization was worse than hell.

Jake's head felt heavy as the weight of his crimes suffocated his conscience. He turned off the Vintel and turned away. Emotionally he felt catatonic, he couldn't shake the image of the Vintel indicating NO DATA FOUND in response to the inquiries he made about his family. That was punctuated by the lives lost in the museum in Portland. He knew that he had to do it…but he wished that he had never looked for his previous life.

Jake was at a porthole staring into the dark. It was 2:30 in the morning. The submarine was sliding through the water in complete silence. He was squeezed by the realization that he was alone. The world had no claim on him, or he on it. He didn't belong here. Just being alive, just being, was painful beyond measure. He wished he could just close his eyes and not wake up…just blink into nothingness.

"Not good?" The voice came from behind.

Jake turned to see Ben leaning against the doorframe. "No," he said. "It wasn't good."

Ben had been watching for a long time before interrupting Jake's solitude. Empathy wasn't his strong point, but he did suspect he understood what was happening. Jake was reviewing what had become of his life and was trying to find a reason to keep going, a reason to keep living. He also understood that from Jake's perspective, it would be hard to find a reason to keep fighting.

"Tomorrow," Ben said, "I would like you to tell me what happened after the explosion under Mount Kuh-e Kharman. It's going to be a long day, so I suggest you get some sleep." Ben held a pill out for Jake and offered a glass of water. "Tonight you won't have any nightmares."

Jake's facial expression was flat and exhausted. It reminded Ben of the first time they met. Jake had started to recover. He had been increasingly expressive and funny, and maybe there was a little hint of optimism, but all that was gone. Jake took the pill and swallowed it.

"Jake, I'm sorry," Ben pointed at the Vintel. "I know it's not what you wanted to see. Tomorrow we'll put it in perspective. We have a lot to talk about."

Jake looked at him with an expression that suggested they should talk now.

"Tomorrow." Ben held to his previous statement. "Go get some sleep. That pill's going to knock you down in less than two minutes, and seeing how you're too big for me to carry you, you'll be sleeping where you fall."

Jake was still in a long drug induced sleep when they arrived at their destination, a small island just north of St. George's in Grenada. Rather than emerge on the surface of the water, the submarine navigated through an underwater tunnel and came up inside a cavern hewn into the rock. Above them was one of MST's old weapons manufacturing centers and its harbor facilities for loading and unloading ships. As scientific development progressed, the factory became obsolete and fell into disrepair. The rats owned it now. However, underneath the ruins, the facility was as active as ever. It was a fully outfitted underground command center, the station for a team of computer hackers and the collection of information pertaining to the disposition of military resources in the region, and it was one of the locations where MST held abducted political prisoners for interrogation.

Once Jake awoke, he was given breakfast and a tour of the facility. Afterward, in the privacy of a comfortable office, he sat with Ben and revealed the next part of his story.

CHAPTER 34: A FLASH OF LIGHT AND THEN NOTHING

[JULY 21, AD 2379]
[ARRIVAL DATE MINUS 61 YEARS]
[OPERATION HADES: THE ATTACK ON THE PERSIAN TRANSPORT FACILITY UNDER MOUNT KUH-E KHARMAN]

All hell was breaking loose. Guardsmen were yelling out status reports, frantic orders were being issued, and the Persian guns were chewing everything up. The Gopher careened up the wall and rolled, crushing everything and everyone in its path. Jake and Alex were on the platform, inside the glow of the activated transport chamber. From their vantage everything was happening in slow motion. Suddenly there was an intense flash, and then nothing…just a deep restless sleep.

Jake's first real perception was the extra effort it took to draw in each breath. Every part of his body felt heavy. Before he could gather enough strength to open his eyes, he reviewed what he remembered. His BCD flickered and came to life. Still in a daze, he accessed the playback and reviewed what happened. The last thing was being in the transport chamber. After diving through the air, he rolled once, regained his footing, and readied himself for his next move. That was when he realized that the person he grabbed and pulled onto the transport platform was Alex. He was slow getting up. Bullets, hundreds and thousands of bullets were piercing the flowing orb-like substance that filled the transport chamber. They entered with finger-like projections, stopped, and fell harmlessly to the platform. From the vantage of being inside the Persian transport device they witnessed the unfolding chaos. His men were being chewed up. He needed to find a way to knock out the Persian guns. Then there was the flash of light, and it was all over.

Jake lay still for a while, feeling like he had been thrashed. When he finally raised his hand to his temple, every joint in his upper extremity screamed in protest. There was a repetitive pounding rocking his body, shooting up his neck and into his head. It was his heartbeat.

It was hot. He removed his helmet and felt the sun beating down on his face. As the world came into focus, Jake discovered he was surrounded by tall grass. The random buzz of a fly was the only notable noise. Otherwise the silence was deafening. He rolled onto his side and found purchase enough to get to his hands and knees. There was a pair of boots visible a few meters away. It was Alex.

Jake scanned the area. They were on the side of a hill in the middle of a grassy meadow, a clearing in an otherwise tree-dominated landscape. The sky was mostly clear and pale blue. The distant horizon was given up to haze, the result of high humidity. He could see several small fields off in the distance that were in cultivation. He couldn't be certain, but it appeared to be cotton.

His BCD failed to capture any signals from Central Command, or any other satellites for that matter. He rebooted the system. After a diagnostic check, he performed a routine sweep. It again failed to detect any signals. A secondary and tertiary sweep across every known channel and frequency indicated that the air was completely dead. It was odd. Jake ran another systems check. The BCD was operational and the system was working perfectly. He altered the visual function to magnification and scanned the area. To his amazement the fields were growing cotton, but it was an odd and mongrel variety he had never seen before.

Jake staggered over to check on Alex. There were no apparent wounds and he was breathing.

"Wake up." Jake shook him until he moaned.

Alex attempted to open his eyes. He was mumbling incoherently at first, "We made it. We survived." As he gained more of his faculties, he moaned and asked, "What happened?"

"I don't know. Better get up though." Jake was looking around for his pulsar. It was gone. Neither of them had a weapon. Other than standard issue knives strapped to their ankles, they were defenseless.

"What the hell?" Alex muttered as he scanned his surroundings. "Where are we?"

"I don't know. All I remember is a flash of light and then nothing."

"The rest of the men?"

"Just us." The thought that they were potentially the only ones to survive thumped them in the chest.

"How long have I been down?" Alex muttered.

"The time function says we've been out for about twenty-five minutes. Your BCD working?"

"Says no signal," Alex answered.

"Mine too," Jake said. "My exosuit's fried. Every function's been destroyed." He added, "We better get out of this field."

Despite each step being excruciating, they made it to the woods. They stepped under the canopy and went about ten meters into the woods.

"We should find some water," Jake said, noticing that his mouth was parched.

"That way," Alex pointed up the slope, "Let's get a better view." He was thirsty too and felt lightheaded due to dehydration.

A couple hundred meters through the woods and they reached the opposite side of the hill. They peered out from the edge of the tree line into a similar grass covered meadow. The small elevation they were on was the only one in a landscape otherwise flat and unmoving. There was a road a kilometer away. A pasture separated them from the road. There were several calves grazing lazily, while others sought refuge in the shade. The presence of animals meant there was water nearby.

They cautiously approached. As they got closer, Jake noticed that the animals he thought were calves weren't calves at all. They were not only fully grown, they were the raunchiest bovine specimens he had ever seen. One was pregnant and looked like it should have popped a week ago, her sides bulged disproportionately, and her utters were massively distended to the point that one was nearly dragging the ground. The heaviest weighed only six or seven hundred pounds, and the tallest was hardly more than elbow high. Mounds of flies rolled over one another in a perpetual mass of motion across their backs and in the corners of their eyes. The next thing Jake noticed was the wooden fence. It was of an old style and was hewn with an axe.

"This can't be happening," Jake said. His eyes were wide and his heart began racing.

"What is it?" Alex asked.

"I don't know," Jake said. He walked along the fence, his head turning left and right, taking in every detail of his surroundings. Again, he unconsciously muttered, "This can't be happening."

Alex followed a short distance away, scanning for any signs of danger.

Jake's anxiety heightened as he took note of the trees and the flora. There were thistles and Jimson weed. He saw an oak tree, a shagbark hickory, and a sassafras. Next he spotted a magnolia. He was walking faster, almost running, as he recognized several other types of trees. With his heart pounding against the burden of fear and anxiety he came to a stop under a struggling apple tree.

"What's going on?" Alex asked.

Jake couldn't speak. He held his hand up in a gesture indicating he needed a moment. His hands were on his knees. 'This can't be happening!' screamed over and over in his mind. Through the chaos of racing thoughts, he accessed the buried memory of the letter:

JAKE,
YOU'RE ALONE IN YOUR ROOM WATCHING DAD'S FINAL MESSAGE. IT IS DECEMBER 24, 2367. THE CLOCK SAYS 9:43 P.M.

I AM WRITING THIS LETTER TO YOU, TO MYSELF, FROM THE CONFINES OF THE PAST. IF OUR EFFORTS ARE SUCCESSFUL YOU WILL BE READING THIS LETTER FIVE HUNDRED AND THREE YEARS IN THE FUTURE.

IN AN ACCIDENT I CAN'T EXPLAIN YOU WILL BE TRANSPORTED THROUGH TIME – BACK TO THE NINETEENTH CENTURY. YOU WILL LIVE THROUGH THE AMERICAN CIVIL WAR. LEARN EVERYTHING YOU CAN ABOUT THE FARM AND YOUR FAMILY'S HISTORY… THEY MUST SURVIVE. IF THEY DON'T, EVERYONE YOU KNOW AND LOVE WILL CEASE TO EXIST. JOIN GENERAL NATHAN BEDFORD FORREST'S ESCORT AND YOU WILL BE WHERE YOU'RE NEEDED.

PROTECT JOHN AND ELIZABETH.

JAKE GILLEAN
NOVEMBER 30, 1864

"This can't be happening," Jake said.
"What?"
"By all the laws of physics this should be impossible," Jake said. "Time doesn't work this way. It's a linear process but only in one direction. You can skip forward in time only by traveling near the speed of light. You can't go backward. It's always a one-way trip forward. There has to be a logical explanation."

Alex pulled an apple off the tree and tossed it to Jake. "Better cut it first, unless you like worms." He grinned and bit a chunk off his own and chewed. "Reminds me of basic. Gotta get your protein where you find it. You know," he commented, "I've never seen the sky without a couple transports flying across it." He looked back at Jake and asked, "Now what are you yakking about?"

"I can't prove it yet, but I don't think we're in Kansas anymore. Actually, we could be...the point is, I don't think we're in Persia."

Alex took another bite. "What do you mean?"

"These trees," Jake pointed around him. "They grow in other ecosystems around the world, but I know for a fact they all grow together in the American South. And the air is heavy. Sure the hell feels like the South."

"I know. It's work just getting it in and out." Alex finished chewing his bite and spit out one of the seeds. He glanced at the apple and saw half of a green worm wiggling out of a hole, smearing its juices across the white pulp. "So you think this is the South. Have you lost your mind?" He took another bite.

"What? No. I'm serious."

"Did you get hit in the head?"

"No. I don't think so," Jake said.

"Then what are you getting at?"

"I don't know." Jake paused and strained to listen. "Did you hear that?"

"Hear what?"

"Listen." He waited a few moments and said, "That. It's a woodpecker. How many times have you heard one of those?"

"Don't recall ever hearing one before," Alex admitted. "Hardly proves your point though. Do you hurt as bad as I do?"

"It's getting better," Jake said.

"I'm getting too old for this." Alex closed his eyes and rubbed his temples.

They filled their pockets with apples and walked on until they found a stream. Both knew that it wasn't a good idea to drink fresh water without purification, but the real danger was dehydration. If their military immunizations held up they should be protected from any of the microorganisms that might be laying in wait.

Both felt an incredible wave of irresistible fatigue. They found a safe and adequately camouflaged spot and hunkered down. They took turns sleeping until early the next morning, their slumber breaking only when the sound of a rooster echoed across the landscape.

The pains of the previous day were gone, and they both felt energetic... and hungry. They moved off in the direction of the rooster.

Soon they were looking at small square-frame farmhouse. Its architectural style was early American. What gave them pause was that it was newly constructed, no more than a couple years old. It was roughly six or seven meters to a side, almost a perfect square with a basic porch on two sides. A chimney jutted out from the side of the house at ground level and ran up until it was about five or six feet above the level of the roof. The windows had functional wooden shutters mounted on the outside and half of the openings were without glass or a screen of any kind. The house was surrounded by a couple smaller farm buildings and a barn. They were also in good repair, and equally old in style.

There was a fence wrapping around one side of one of the out buildings. Inside were several pigs. A boy came out of a building with a couple ears of corn and some apples. He threw them in with the pigs. Actually he took aim and threw them, trying to hit the animals, aiming for their heads. He laughed and yelled out their names.

Jake and Alex were close enough to hear. The boy was speaking English. But his accent was exceedingly thick, enough to make the language hardly recognizable. He was Caucasian and appeared to be about ten years old.

"What do you think?" Jake whispered.

"At first I thought we should watch for a while, see how many people are in there," Alex said. "But he doesn't look Persian, and I swear that unless I've gone mad...he's speaking English."

"Pattern Alpha 1?" Jake suggested. It meant one person in the lead and the other about ten meters behind to scan for threats.

"Yeah. I'll take the lead," Alex said. He added, "Watch your head. He might be a soccer player."

"What?" Jake was confused. By the time he got it Alex was already ahead of him.

They approached the kid in the hope of getting some answers. The situation appeared to be reasonably safe, and it presented an expedient opportunity to figure out where they were. They emerged from the woods with about ten meters between each other.

It didn't take long for the boy to see them. "Who are you?!" he yelled. "Momma! Momma!" He kept a curious eye glued on them while he called out. As the distance between them decreased and the better they could hear, the heavier his accent became. It was recognizable as being a drawl from the Deep South, but it was far thicker than any they had ever heard. Given his incredibly fast rate of speech it was almost unintelligible. "You soldiers? Don't look like no soldiers I ever did see." He glanced at the house while keeping his eyes on the strangers. He called out, "Momma! Wez got some visitors come calling!" he said, "My daddy's a soldier. He's in the infantry. In the 2nd Alabama. He done went off to shoot some of the Yankee invaders. He's at Fort Morgan right now doing some training...marching and shooting and such. Took his own gun with him and everything. MOMMA!" he hollered again. "Left us with the best one though, and my momma's the best shot in these here parts. Could shoot a deer in the eye at a hundred yards and that's so, you better believe me, I don't tell no stretches. She's probably got a bead on you right now."

Alex motioned Jake forward and they were standing shoulder to shoulder in front of the boy. He was curious. He looked them up and down and cocked his head to one side as though he was trying to figure something out.

"Son, where are we?" Jake asked. His heart was racing. The boy looked at him like he was stupid. It was an odd question to be asking.

The boy wound up and let loose with a loud, "MOMMA!"

"What do you call this place?" Jake asked.

"MOMMA! WE GOT SOME VISITORS!" Then he said in a normal voice, "Done said so a whole slew of times. You heard me didn't you? Don't know what momma must be doing." He hadn't taken his eyes off them when he decided to answer Jake's question, "Ya'll are in Jackson County, Alabama. Don't you know nothing? You talk funny. Ya'll from England or something?"

Jake and Alex looked at each other. They failed to hide their sudden surprise.

"Did you say Alabama?" Alex asked.

The boy nodded.

"Bloody hell. We're in Alabama," he exclaimed. "How do you like that?" He glanced at Jake. The color was gone from his face, like he had just seen a ghost. "You were right," Alex said. "We're in the South." They took their helmets off and held them down at their sides.

"Ya'll come over from England?" the boy asked again.

"England? No." Alex said. He corrected himself, "Well, yeah originally. Yes, we're from England."

"Preacher come over here from England. He sounds funny too. Kind of just like ya'll," the boy said, proud for having guessed correctly.

"Son," Jake said, "I'm going to ask you a strange question, and I just want you to give me a straight answer."

The boy was confused...not knowing what the heck a *straight answer* was.

Jake took another stab at it, "I mean just give me your best and most honest answer." He paused, finding it difficult to actually form the words. He asked, "What year is it?"

The boy was surprised. His eyes went back and forth, studying each of them. He put his hands on his hips and looked them up and down as though he was conversing with a couple clowns, or a couple morons escaped from the traveling circus. "It's the year of our Lord 1861. May. May 24, 1861. Don't you know that?"

The matter of fact way the boy said it magnified the horror. It was 1861. Jake's hands began trembling; the world was spinning and coming in and out of focus. 'Oh my God,' he thought. 'I'm trapped in the past. I can never go back.' The revelation was a nightmare beyond his wildest imagination. He wanted to yell, to lash out, anything he could do to make everything stop, just enough so he could sort things out. He took a step back. All he could see was his family. Images of Wendy, Bailey, and Paul flashed through his mind. They were now without a husband and father. He was without a family, and there was nothing he could do. They would go on thinking he was dead. They wouldn't be able to hear his voice calling out for them. His legs suddenly felt weak, like he was going to fall on the ground. He bent over and put his hands on his knees.

The boy was peculiarly amused. He took pause to observe Jake's reaction, regarding it as an oddity deserving a penny for admission. At first he saw signs that Jake was horribly upset, then he suddenly gathered himself and stood erect and stony, like a statue. His eyes were firm and his jaw clenched. For a fleeting moment he thought about jumping in front of the stranger and yelling, '1861!' just to see what would happen, since that was obviously what set him off. But discretion won out and he elected against it.

From Jake's perspective he had to forcibly compartmentalize his feelings. So great was the emotional trauma that he couldn't face reality. As a soldier he was trained for this. He emotionally underwent a schism. He willfully suppressed everything, actively forcing his emotions into the background and closing them off, and at the same time focusing on being a soldier. It was the only way he could see to survive.

Jake thought about the Persian bunker. He focused on the theoretical physics of a wormhole manipulating the space-time continuum. The dark matter weapons must have exploded. Somehow it destabilized the wormhole and cast them into the past. Regardless, it was just like his letter predicted. But the date on the note was November 30, 1864. That meant that they, or at least he, was destined to live at least three and a half years. While his questions came in rapid succession…no answers were forthcoming.

Through the initial shock, Alex remained calm. After a moment of contemplation he said, "1861, huh? We are indeed a long way from home."

"Momma! We gots us some visitors!" the boy yelled again.

His mother was busy adjusting the hems on his good pants. In her concentration, she was ignoring him. The pair of dark brown pants had followed Ronald for the last two years but he just kept on growing. Once more they had become far too short. As they were the ones he wore to church on the Sabbath, and as it wasn't fitting or proper to have his socks and legs on display for the whole of creation to see, she was letting down the legs. This was it though. They were at the end of their length, and there was just a fraction of a hem at the bottom, just enough of a turn to accept an adequate stitch to keep them from fraying. From now on, any growth would come at the peril of showing off his socks again.

"Does that boy have his head stuck in the fence? Good Lord!" she exclaimed. She put down the needle and thread and got up from the table. In her aggravation, she thought he sounded like an ornery old goat bleating for nothing more than the sake of bleating. But once she caught site of the strangers, she understood what the ruckus was all about.

The woman's appearance stepping off the porch and walking toward them temporarily interrupted their psychological tumult. She was smiling, unafraid and openly curious in the way she studied them. Alex shifted his helmet from his right hand to his left as she approached. The boy pointed at Jake's with a look of intrigue. Jake handed it to him.

"Momma, they don't even know what year it is. I told 'em though... May 24, 1861." He put the helmet on and gave the outside a rap with his knuckles. "Is this a soldier's hat? It's kind of heavy." Without waiting for an answer he marched off to give it a test run.

His mother was pleasant, displaying a level of grace and proud dignity that weren't diminished in the least by her abundant extroversion. As the region was rather sparsely populated the prospect of gaining the acquaintance of new people, of having visitors other than neighbors, wasn't an altogether common occurrence. The men represented something new, and she wanted to get the most out of the opportunity.

"Good morning, gentlemen," she said. "My name is Gertrude. Folks just call me Gerty though."

"Pleased to make your acquaintance ma'am."

She gave a quick curtsy and smiled. "

"My name is Alexander Fisk, and my friend here is Jacob Gillian. We apologize for just showing up here on your doorstep unannounced."

"Nonsense Mr. Fisk. You are most welcome to any hospitality I might be able to offer."

"Thank you, ma'am."

They immediately noticed her teeth. They weren't reflective of her warmth of demeanor or proper behavior. They were yellow. A couple were turning black. One in front was fractured and another missing. Her hair was coarse but otherwise well kept. Her dress was simple and functional for the period. But on a day that was already getting hot, it was long sleeved and buttoned to the neck. They both imagined that it had to be terribly uncomfortable. Yet, despite all the superficial observations, they found her to be courteous, well spoken and educated, and exceedingly hospitable.

Jake introduced himself with a nod, saying, "Good morning, ma'am."

"Mr. Gillean," she exclaimed. "Please, just call me Gerty. Everything else sounds so formal and pretentious." She looked over to see what her son was doing. He had picked up a stick and was pretending to march through the yard as though it were a gun. He was wearing Jake's helmet and having a grand time. "Has Ronald been minding his manners?"

"He has," Alex said. "Very good boy."

"Things have been hard for him since he lost his little brothers."

"I'm so sorry. What happened?"

"Last winter. Doctor says it was typhus," Gerty said. "Had a bit of an outbreak in these parts, and they weren't as strong as him. They fought hard but didn't make it. Was a sad time for all of us, but our faith in the Lord remains strong. Every day we pray for strength and understanding." Gerty was talking about it with a matter-of-fact quality that spoke volumes. Life in rural Alabama in the Nineteenth Century was a hard and brutal struggle. They were hacking a life out of the wilderness and there were no guarantees. Extreme hardship and loss were omnipresent aspects of life.

"You would be proud of Ronald," Alex said. "He was mannerly and most helpful. We were just about to ask him where we are exactly. You see, I'm embarrassed to admit it, but I think we might be a little lost."

"You mean you all don't know where you are?"

Alex sheepishly grinned. "Seem to have lost my map."

"I'd be happy to help get you back on track." She picked up a stick and used it to etch out a basic map in the dirt. She indicated that they were in Northern Alabama. She showed them where the major roads were and described the distance to the closest towns.

"Suppose we wanted to go all the way to Spring Hill and Franklin, Tennessee. What would be the best way?" Jake asked.

"Now that is a long way to go. Have to admit that I don't know exactly, but if I recall, those towns are south of Nashville. Could travel by train to Nashville by going here," she indicated the town on the dirt map, "and then make your way to your final destination."

They studied the map and asked a few more questions to solidify in there minds where they were exactly. They pulled up maps from the log files in their BCDs and overlaid their position, based on her description. They reviewed the distances and were able to estimate what they would need in terms of provisions.

"May I be so bold?" she asked. She seemed to take a keen interest in the material used to make their exosuits. She felt Alex's sleeve, pressing it with her fingers. "What is this made out of? I do declare, in all my days I have never seen or felt anything quite like it."

"It's a new material. Comes from the Orient," he said. "It doesn't wear well though. It's hot and doesn't breathe. Very uncomfortable."

"I'm so sorry to hear that," she offered her response in earnest, as she understood their predicament. "That is indeed a struggle we all contend with during the summer months."

"I would like to offer you a business transaction if I may," Alex said. He turned to Jake. "Do you mind if I speak to Gerty alone for a moment."

"No sir. By all means," Jake responded, unconsciously slipping back into military formality. He stepped away and walked toward Ronald in order to ask some more questions.

Alex and Gerty strolled casually toward the house. "I have some money and a couple hours of our labor that I'd give in exchange for food and some clothes that might be more practical for our purposes."

He reached into one of his pockets and pulled out a wad of money. Her eyes widened. He had thousands of dollars. He peeled off a $500 dollar note of Confederate States of America currency. "Will this be enough?"

"No. I can't accept that. It's way too much. I can't in good conscience accept that. I can't provide you with anything close to that value."

"Okay. I understand." He folded the bill back with the others and pulled off two $100 notes.

"Are those Dixies I see there?" She was referring to $10 notes he had on the outside of the wad. They were issued out of Louisiana and were backed.

"You know your money," Alex laughed.

"Those Confederate dollars are new issue. Don't know if I trust 'em yet."

He put the Confederate currency away and pulled out five Dixies. He smiled and offered them to her.

She grabbed the money and said, "Only if you let me feed you a nice meal too."

"Deal," Alex said.

The price was still oddly in her favor but not so much that she found it disagreeable. For $50 in Dixies she'd supply them with two sets of regular clothes and shoes, two pairs of socks apiece, two hats, some old newspapers, enough food in a gunny sack to get them by for a week or two, and a hearty meal. Eventually, the deal turned into two meals, breakfast and a late lunch. The clothes belonged to her husband. He was a rather big man himself for the time, but for Alex, and especially for Jake, the fit was off—well off—short in the legs and tight across the chest and arms.

She agreed to a second exchange. She'd let out the hems as far as they would go and make all the appropriate alterations if they would agree to perform more odd jobs around the farm. She needed them to shovel manure and spread it in the garden, mend a fence that one of the cows knocked down, a job that necessitated setting two new posts, fix some shingles on the barn roof that blew off in a recent storm, and chop some wood. They readily agreed, and in return, Gerty made sure to take just enough time making the alterations so that the work would be done.

When Ronald was out of earshot Jake asked, "How did you get her to help us? She can't be giving us all the clothing and food in exchange for just doing some work."

Alex leaned over, supporting himself on the axe. "Did you know this was going to happen?"

Jake was surprised at the question. "Yes."

"So did I," Alex said.

"How?"

"It's complicated. We'll talk later and I'll fill you in on all the details. How did you know?"

Jake gave a quick look around to make sure no one was listening. "Wrote myself a letter and buried it on the family farm. Got it when I was a teenager."

"What did you bring with you to prepare?"

"Nothing," Jake said.

"Nothing?"

"No. I didn't know when it was going to happen. All I was told was to learn everything I could about this war and about my ancestors on the farm. Did you know?"

"To the minute. All the details up until we took the leap. Was told to bring lots and lots of money and to learn everything about the banking systems and financial movements of the era."

Ronald arrived with drinking water, and the conversation abruptly terminated. Jake took great comfort in the knowledge that Alex also knew that they were going to travel back in time.

A few minutes passed when Jake abruptly said, "Wait a minute. When I first alluded to what I was thinking you accused me of getting hit in the head."

Alex raised his eyebrows, "There's a big difference between knowing something and believing it."

"What are you talking about?" Ronald asked.

"England," Alex said. "Do you know that in England you get to say everything twice…like here here, and that we will make any excuse we can to use the word jolly—like he's a jolly good fellow."

"Jolly good fellow," Ronald imitated. He laughed, "That's funny."

By mid-afternoon and with a half-day of hard labor under their belts, the men had full bellies and clothes that turned out to be respectable enough to pass without notice. Alex was rather proud of himself. Securing proper clothing was a formidable hurdle given their circumstances, and now they would be able to blend into primordial America's southern society.

Before they left they had to destroy the exosuits. They considered burying them in the woods but that wasn't good enough. They needed to burn.

Gerty protested. "No. Why would you want to destroy perfectly good clothing, especially material that came all the way from the Orient?"

"The material is terrible in this climate," Alex said. "The best thing is to burn them."

"I'll buy them. Cloth is a luxury. I'll turn them into something else."

"Lincoln is buying the same type of clothing. He's going to be putting it on Yankee soldiers. It wouldn't be proper to use the same clothing as Northern soldiers. In the Great State of Alabama it might lead to confusion and potentially dangerous accusations," Alex said.

Gerty considered his lie but had to agree, "I have read that Lincoln may be calling up volunteers in the near future." She suspected that her visitors might be fugitives from the law. They obviously didn't understand Northern Alabama. She went so far as to correct them on what had the potential to be a grave mistake. "I would be amiss if I didn't inform you that in these parts support for Alabama's secession from the Union has been far from unanimous. Although Alabama has seceded and become part of the Confederacy, Union sentiments run strong in this part of the state."

"Ronald suggested that your husband is fighting for the Confederacy."

"For the Confederacy…no. He's fighting for Alabama."

Gerty gave up her appeal for the clothing. She came to the conclusion that as far as foreign travelers go, the eggs of these two birds had seen some shaking before they hatched.

Jake and Alex said goodbye and put the farmhouse to their back. They began the long trek to Spring Hill, Tennessee. It would take time to fully comprehend the realities of their predicament. There were so many things to consider—in 1861 there was no running water. There were no hot water heaters, no batteries, no refrigerators, and no climate control devices in the homes. There were no computers, airplanes, satellites, pods, paved roadways, or service robots. Even the radio, long made obsolete in its primitive form, hadn't been invented yet, nor had the light bulb. They used candles, oil lamps, and lanterns for light. There were no antibiotics, no high-tech surgical techniques, and no reliable means of anesthesia. They used coal and wood driven steam engines for transport. Human slavery, something that evolved into a historical footnote, was alive and on full display in the South. Secession had already occurred in all the States that would leave the Union, except for Tennessee, which would declare on June 8th. The bombardment of Fort Sumter and the war chatter dominated the news, and what the Southern Confederacy didn't appreciate was that it was about to be torn apart by four years of brutal warfare.

It would have hardly been less dramatic had they been transported to another planet. Nothing Jake or Alex experienced in their lives, other than the English language, could have prepared them for the Nineteenth Century. They had been cast into a world that was fundamentally different from their own in almost every way. They had nothing in common in terms of life experiences or upbringing with the people of the South or the North. The soil was the same American soil they loved, but they were strangers, as completely foreign and out of place as any two people had ever been while walking across North America.

Over their first days of travel, they did find a couple things that were familiar. The language was the same. As a spoken language, English hadn't changed as much in the five hundred years after the 1800s as it had in the five hundred years before. Regardless, the accent and the regional slang in the South were strong to the point that it required effort for them to communicate effectively. The other familiarity was books. They were highly valued possessions in the 1800s.

On the first day of travel they poured over every detail of Jake's letter. He explained the details of the family farm, the urn, and how his father found it, and how the letter eventually came into his possession. It established an objective...to protect his ancestors so they would survive the war. It also gave a date—November 30, 1864.

"We'll go to Spring Hill," Alex said. "I'm interested in meeting your ancestors. Maybe it'll explain some things. We'll see for ourselves what rogue DNA got injected into the Gillean family tree to create the stick. Play our cards right we might be able to fix it before it happens." Alex laughed, amused at his own effort to lighten the mood.

"What are you talking about?"

"You know…the stick. The one you sat on."

Jake chuckled, even though he wasn't in the frame of mind for banter.

"Jokes aren't funny if I have to explain them," Alex complained. He looked up at the clear sky and took a deep breath. The dirt road stretched out in front of them as far as they could see. The next town, Bridgeport, Alabama, was another fifteen-miles. After that they'd make their way to Chattanooga and hop a train to Nashville.

"Tell me how you got your letter."

"I never said anything about a letter."

"I don't understand," Jake said.

"If I would have told you this a month ago, you would have thought I was insane."

"I already think you're insane," Jake said.

"That little fact notwithstanding, what I'm about to say is going to sound bizarre. About twenty years ago, I was on a joint training mission with England's finest. Urban warfare. We were using some of the bombed out neighborhoods in Belfast. I was on the point, and we were working out an interdiction scenario after an electromagnetic pulse bomb attack. Involved a lot of hand signals and line of sight coordination of ground forces. Hostiles were around every corner. Like I said, I was on the point and charged with developing intel on enemy positions. I'm moving from building to building with my team when we see a hostile make tracks into a culvert. It's just over a meter in diameter. They take post outside while I go in. What I didn't know was that as soon as I went in they were taken out. Rules of engagement means I'm on my own.

When I get through the tunnel I never did find the hostile. The tunnel opened up into a room filled with rubble. It's lit and there's a table. I mean it's a table decorated to the hilt. There's food on it, a silver service, and everything. There's an old man, well dressed, sitting at the table looking at me. He was expecting me. He said my name and asked me to take a seat."

"He said your name?" Jake asked.

"Called me Alex."

"Who was he?"

"This is the part that gets weird." Alex stopped walking and squared himself to Jake. "It was me."

"What?" Jake was confused.

"I know. It sounds crazy but it was me. I was about ninety years old. It was surreal. I was looking at him, and I saw myself. He confirmed that he was exactly who I thought he was and handed me a piece of paper. On it was a date. The same date we attacked the Persian bunker, the date we traveled back in time. He talked and I listened. He said things that only I knew and he went on to predict all the major events of my life up until that moment in the bunker. He told me I was going to end up here, but that's all he gave me. When I asked questions about what exactly I was supposed to do all he would say was, 'in due time.' He told me that I needed to learn everything I could about investments, finances and banking, and all about world economic history, and that when I travel back in time I should take as much money with me as I could. And that was all."

"What did you do?"

"I was a little freaked out. I didn't know what to do. The crazy thing was that he didn't mention that I was going to end up here with someone else. That's what I find confusing. Either it wasn't supposed to happen or he had a reason for not telling me."

"So you knew the date. That's why you asked me if I was prepared. What did you do to prepare?"

"Standing before you right now is one of the richest men in America. I'm carrying several million dollars in perfectly forged currencies and enough gold to impress a king. I have enough to build something. I just don't know what. Once we get settled, I'll start investing and will grow it into something bigger. Other than that I wasn't given an objective. Guessed that I'd figure it out as I went. The only thing close to an objective right now is what was outlined in your letter. I think it's a puzzle and we're supposed to figure out how to fit all the pieces together."

"What happened then?"

He told me to stand a short distance away then he and the table just disappeared. There was a snapping sound, and they were gone," Alex snapped his fingers, "vanished in thin air."

"Did your BCD record the whole thing?" Jake asked.

"Didn't have a BCD back then."

They walked on a heading due east. If they kept a reasonable pace they would easily make town before nightfall. At first they were talking a lot, but eventually that gave way to long periods of silent contemplation.

Jake was ravaged by feelings of guilt and loss. He painfully relived again and again the last moments he spent with Wendy. The night before had been difficult and the morning fared no better. She had been pushed beyond her capacity to control her emotions.

When the alarm went off she was already awake. Actually, she hadn't slept at all. She could hardly speak and only a few words passed between them before he had to leave.

"Baby, what's wrong?" Jake asked.

Wendy kept crying. She couldn't answer. Her tears were bitter and violent. It had never been like this before. Jake packed the last few things in his bag and placed it next to the door. He turned, hoping to hold her in an embrace, to share a moment of grief and affection. He wanted to console his beloved wife and be consoled in return.

The moment Jake's hands touched her shoulders Wendy had a look of fear. Her eyes widened and for a fleeting moment she was horrified. The transport was waiting in front of the house. Jake felt pressured. Why couldn't she understand that he didn't want to go? That it was hard for him too?

"Wendy, I love you," Jake said. He put his arms around her and she responded with a spasm of shaking. Her legs buckled. He was taken aback. He was confused and felt the sting of rejection. He continued to hold her so she wouldn't fall, but she wouldn't put her arms around him. He could feel her drawing away. He responded with frustration. He wanted to scream. Leaving was hard enough without his family piling it on. The next moment, he turned and left. He was out the door, walking briskly toward the transport in the belief that it offered refuge from his torment, an escape from the emotional trauma. He was muttering under his breath, something about wanting to leave, to get the hell out of there. He didn't mean it, but it came out. As angry and frustrated as he was, he immediately felt ashamed. He was ashamed for having allowed such terrible thoughts to not only find refuge within him, but that he actually gave them a voice. That was how he left home, how he left the love of his life. It was unforgivable.

On top of that, he didn't bother to wake Bailey and Paul to tell them good-bye. It was a purposeful act of omission. Wendy urged him to wake them. She said they deserved to see their father before he left.

"It's too early," Jake said. "They need their sleep. I spent a long time telling them goodbye last night."

Everything he said was true, but it was also a lie. It would have been hard. There would have been tears, but any sane father would have awakened his children. If not for them, which should have been his focus, he should have done it for his own sake, especially knowing how dangerous it was. Now, as he took one step after another on the dirty roads in Alabama, fixing the mistake was impossible. Bailey and Paul's last memory of their father would be that they woke up and he was gone…that he didn't even bother to say good-bye.

Jake ruminated over the experience for hours. Within the gloom of his contemplations he felt the physical manifestations of guilt. It pierced his soul with the strength of a spiritual rebuke from God. He felt the stab of the mistakes he made and heard the gavel crashing down its verdict…to his dying day these would be the demons haunting his soul.

"I promised them," Jake said. The comment came from nowhere.

Given everything Jake left behind, Alex knew where his mind was. "Promised what?" he asked.

"I promised Bailey and Paul that whatever happened…they would see me coming back home. That I would be with them." Jake could hardly get the words out. The guilt was just too much to bear. His insides were unraveling.

Alex didn't know what to say except, "I'm sorry."

CHAPTER 35:
NOTHING IS AS IT SEEMS

[APRIL 22, AD 2441]
[142 DAYS AFTER ARRIVAL]
[LOCATION: ISLAND JUST NORTH OF ST. GEORGE'S IN GRENADA]

Ben was alive with energy but anxious at the same time. His relationship with Jake had reached its Rubicon. Jake's story had been revealed through his first time travel. Now it was time to come clean about the connections between Jake and MST Global. The information he was about to divulge would change everything. After that, the decision belonged to Jake. They would drive ahead and fight in an attempt to deliver United America from the bondage of the Egalitarian Party and Fascism, or they might part ways as enemies.

Jake's demeanor was cold. Reliving the loss of his family and the emotions he felt those first days in 1861 left him exhausted and depressed. Now, as agreed, it was up to Ben to deliver.

From Ben's perspective, it was impossible to ease into the discussion they were about to have. It was going to be abrupt, it was going to be brutal, and the exchange would undoubtedly push Jake's anger to the brink.

"Let's do this," he said. "There's something I have to show you." Ben went to the desk and opened the top drawer. Inside was a large manila envelope. He took it out, held it in a brief moment of contemplation, and handed it to Jake. "Take a look. We have a lot to talk about."

When Jake finished telling his story he had been leaning against the side of a set of book shelves. He pulled out of the position and took a few steps toward Ben. He took the envelope, flipped it over, undid the metal clasp, opened it, and pulled out a photograph. "Oh my God," he gasped. Suddenly his knees felt weak, unable to support his weight. He reached for the back of a chair for support, missing it twice, catching it on the third try. His eyes welled with tears. He burst away from the chair, turned, and paced the room. "Oh God! Oh God!" He repeated the phrase again and again. So focused was he on the photo that he had no conscious realization of what he was saying. His eyes momentarily shifted back to Ben in search of answers. With confusion and a magnified realization of the losses he experienced in his life, he went back to the photograph.

Several times Jake paced the room, stopped for a moment, turned, and resumed pacing in the opposite direction. He came to brace himself on the bookshelf. His eyes were still full of tears and for brief moments his facial expression softened as though he would weep. A spark of something long suppressed, something normal and human was finding itself. It was the first time Ben had seen this side of Jake. The real and raw was still there. It found a way to survive under the weight of a lost soldier's rage.

Jake's knees buckled. He was ready to collapse. An even greater tidal wave of emotion was battering him under the surface. He tried valiantly to suppress the emotions but they erupted. It was uncontrollable. He was on his knees, in one hand he held the photo, the other was clenched in a fist. He was crying.

It was brief and with a deep breath, Jake reigned in his emotions and rose to his feet. "What's going on?" he asked. "Ben, what's going on? What does this mean?" and then, "How did you get this?" The questions were coming in rapid succession.

"Jake," Ben extended his hand. "Show me what you have there." He took the photo and examined it. "Who are these people?"

"It's my family," Jake said. "It's my family. It's been so long." He pointed, "That's Wendy, Bailey, and Paul. This is the picture I gave to Alex right before Operation Hades."

"Who's that ugly bastard?" Ben asked.

"That's me," Jake laughed while choking back sobs.

Ben held the photograph up and studied it, then Jake, and then back again. A grunt and shrug of agreement, and he handed the photo back to Jake.

"It's been so long. I can't begin to describe how much I miss them. Ben, how did you get this picture?"

Ben placed both of his hands on Jake's shoulders. "I asked you once to trust me. I'm asking you again. Parts of the story you told me I knew twenty years ago. You see…there's something very important that I'm about to tell you. If you follow my family tree back far enough, twenty-one generations to be exact, you'll find a very familiar name."

Jake was confused.

"The person I'm talking about," Ben said, "was a friend of yours. He's my grandfather removed by roughly six hundred years. His name is…Col. Alexander Fisk."

"What?" Jake was taken aback.

"Six hundred years ago," Ben went on, "the seeds for this moment were planted. They were planted by you and my grandfather. Do you understand what I'm saying?" Ben squeezed and shook Jake's shoulders. "Alex survived the Civil War, Jake. He survived and went on living with no thought other than how to help you and how to change the world. He loved you like a brother. He thought you were the most talented soldier and leader of men he ever met. Your friendship was the greatest fortune of his life. He loved you and your family. He also took seriously his oath to protect those under his command. As a soldier, he vowed that he wouldn't leave anyone behind. That's why we're here today."

As Ben talked, Jake was trying to reconcile what he was hearing against everything that had happened—all his traumatic experiences, the limitless sorrow and pain he saw everywhere he looked, the feeling that the world was drowning in a sea of unending war…all of it culminating into the breaking of his spirit, to his belief that life had no meaning, his ultimate failure and the loss of his family. It didn't make sense.

"After the Civil War, Alex created a society," Ben explained, "a very secret society. Today that society is known as MST Global."

"What?" Jake exclaimed, "MST came from Alex?"

"Yes. The entire operation is his brainchild. Since its creation it has been controlled by his blood descendents."

"But why?" Jake asked.

"It began as a rescue operation. He wanted to rescue you. But, and you know this better than anyone, Alex was what would be best described as an idealistic pragmatist. In the process of rescuing you, he also wanted to change the world into something better. He recognized that one source of international conflict has been energy resources. He challenged MST to meet the world's energy needs in a practical, benign, and non-manipulative way, and he wanted the achievements to be shared with the rest of mankind. What he didn't know at the time was what United America would become. You took your leap through time during World War IV. That was before the Egalitarian Party took over and before the Fascists solidified their grip on the nation. What started out as a rescue operation for you has evolved—now it's a rescue operation for an entire nation."

Jake considered what Ben had to say. He ran his fingers over the photo, gently over the cheek of his wife. "When Alex met the older version of himself, the older version knew all this?"

"He did," Ben said. "He was devoted to the concepts of liberty and justice. He knew you to share those same beliefs."

Jake's thoughts raced through one memory and into the next. He thought about the challenges they faced, the battles, the times they spent carousing, and Alex's quirky sense of humor. With review it was painfully clear how much everything in his life had changed, and how far his downward spiral had taken him. Jake allowed his mind to become poisoned by a continuous stream of hatred and anger. He abandoned mental discipline and eventually lost his grip on hope. At the same time he forgot, and then with vehemence, rejected his spiritual beliefs. At that point he was a marionette, a marionette whose conscience had been violated so often that it no longer offered any resistance.

"If you're not overwhelmed already, you will be," Ben said. "There's something I need you to see." He sat behind the desk and slowly drew up an object. Jake didn't react as Ben placed it on the top of the desk. It looked like a necklace, but there was a high degree of sophistication to the device. It came to life and sprang outward on its own, forming a perfect circle about half a meter in diameter. It was surrounded by a glow and it hovered a few centimeters above the surface of the desk. Ben leaned back in his chair as a crystal clear holographic image appeared over the desk. It was the shadowy image of MST's leader. AF20 was standing, very slightly leaning against what appeared to be a table. The holographic projection hovered over the desk and was approximately a meter in height. The voice was heavily encrypted and sounded exactly the same as it did when received through Ben's BCD. Ben was surprised. He had never seen a full body image of AF20. For no particular reason he always envisioned that AF20 was a man. The shape of the holographic image suggested otherwise. AF20 was a woman.

"Hello, Lt. Col. Jake Gillean. It's nice to finally meet you. As you have discovered, we have been looking for you. In fact, we have been searching for you since the date of the Great Tragedy. My name is AF20. I am the 20th surrogate leader of MST since the passing of our founder, our grandfather, and your friend, Col. Alexander Fisk. Please excuse the masking of my identity. I assure you that in the very near future, we will have the opportunity to meet in person. But for security purposes my identity has to remain guarded."

"I understand," Jake said.

"You have just been told what happened to your friend after the Civil War. I trust that you received a copy of the photograph?"

"I have," Jake said.

"Col. Fisk preserved that photograph, and it was one of his prized possessions. It has been handed down and great efforts have been made to preserve it. What you have is a reproduction. I have the original, and it's yours when we have the opportunity to meet. Until then there is so much that you need to know. Lt. Col. Gillean, your direct ancestor at the time of the Civil War was John Stuart, was he not?"

"He was," Jake said.

"He had a sister by the name of Amelia."

"Yes."

"Seven years after the war, Amelia married my grandfather, Col. Alexander Fisk."

Jake was confused. He said, "She was only..." he quickly did the math. She would have been eleven at the end of the war. Seven years later, they married, when she was eighteen.

"I know it must sound strange to hear this, given the fact that Amelia was just a small girl when you saw her last, and Col. Fisk was thirty years her elder. But I assure you, they shared a wonderful and full life. He treated her like a queen and their romance never faded. They were happily married for fifty-three years when Col. Fisk died in 1925. He was 101 years old. They had three sons, the oldest of whom became AF1. This means that not only are the current descendants, the people of MST, genetically linked to Col. Alexander Fisk, they are equally linked to Amelia Stuart, and are accordingly linked to you, albeit by an indirect route. All those who are working within MST, including Dr. Benjamin Murray are in effect your very distant cousins. The sense of kinship that comes with genetic linkage is something Col. Fisk believed would be essential in order for MST to ultimately survive, and requisite for it to fulfill his objectives. He clearly understood, and everyone at MST agrees, that you have a vital role to play. We are at an impasse and can't proceed without you.

"You will become very familiar with MST. We have been at the forefront of technological development for the last four hundred years. We have revolutionized the use of energy and space exploration and have started a colony on the moon. We have revolutionized the material sciences, we develop medications and vaccines, and we have moved three generations beyond the rest of the world in the application of energy shield technologies and in the development of novel means of propulsion. We will show you everything...and everything we have is not only at your disposal, it is yours. At the same time, we're asking for your help. For reasons that will soon become apparent, we need to know every detail of what happened to you during your time fighting in the Civil War.

"Do not take this decision lightly as your agreement to join us comes with risk. As you already know, the United America you fought for no longer exists. As a country, it is unrecognizable. It has fallen into the hands of a ruthless ruling elite. They govern with an iron fist and will use every means at their disposal to preserve their positions of privilege. There are powerful interests within the government and the banking sector aligned against us. At this time they are studying time-travel. They will weaponize the technology, and they must be stopped.

"We ask that you join us in our efforts, but the ultimate choice is yours. There are many things for you to see, but there are also some very important things you need to know before you make your decision. At that point, if you choose, you can walk away with the knowledge that we will continue to do everything we can to help you.

"At the conclusion of this message, you will have a visitor. Her name is Dr. Annette Ratzlaff. It's important that you hear what she has to say before you make any decisions. Please allow her the opportunity to fully explain everything and answer all your questions. Do you have any questions for me?"

"I have so many questions that I don't know where to begin," Jake said. "But in due time."

"Very well. Lt. Col. Gillean, it has been a pleasure to make your acquaintance. I very much look forward to meeting you and for the opportunity to talk about my grandfather."

Jake nodded and the transmission terminated.

Without delay there was a quick rap on the door. Its manner conveyed a significant degree of familiarity. The next moment, as soon as the door started to open, a woman burst into the room. She rushed past Ben even as he was extending an invitation to enter. She was a spry energetic woman in her mid-seventies. She marched into the center of the room, made a quick scan of the surroundings, locked her eyes on Jake, and made a beeline toward him.

"What a fine specimen you are," she said. She made a circle around him, looking him up and down as though he was a commodity to be bought or sold.

She made him self-conscious and uncomfortable. She inadvertently reminded him of what he saw in the 1800s at the slave auctions. It was a dark side of humanity that he loathed seeing then, and he didn't appreciate now. At the same time, he reasoned that she seemed harmless, quirky as hell, but otherwise harmless. He left it alone and would hear what she had to say.

Dr. Annette Ratzlaff's gray hair was pulled back into a loose ponytail, and her glasses were far too large, giving the impression of a large bug. She was medium height and thin, and her shoulders were ever so slightly stooped forward. She planted herself in front of Jake and stared at him with a big, delighted smile. "You'll have to forgive me," she explained. "I have been looking forward to meeting you for a long time, and when I first heard that you were found I was absolutely elated."

Jake glanced at Ben, not quite knowing what to make of her. "I understand that you have some things to tell me."

"Yes. Yes," she said, "let's get right down to why I'm here. In order for what I'm about to tell you to make sense, I need to build it up, to explain it from the beginning. Let me start by explaining who I am. My name is Annette Ratzlaff. I'm a geneticist. I am the director of MST's Biotech Division. My specific research interests are primarily in genetic therapies and DNA modifications in humans, and the reason we need to talk is because you, Lt. Col., are a perfect working product of similar work that was accomplished by my predecessors."

"What?" Jake said, startled by the revelation. "What are you talking about?"

His response was exciting. While it was exactly what she expected, there was an edge to his agitation that scared her. She took a step backward and said, "You are your parents' child. Rest assured that you are the genetic product of Thomas and Janet. It's just that the DNA residing in your cells is slightly altered from what they would have naturally been able to give you."

"What?" Jake said again. He was shocked. "Altered? What do you mean…altered? How? What did you do?" Jake's whole body tightened as he waited for her answer.

"Your mother's contribution to your genome is 100% natural. But your father's contribution…it was genetically modified."

"Modified?" Jake was taken aback by the indifference of her crass delivery. "His contribution was modified?" He looked at Ben to assess whether he knew. He was equally stunned, but more by her delivery than the content. "Exactly how? And how much of me has been modified?" Jake demanded.

"Less than 1%. Over 99% is exactly the way he would have given it to you anyway." She fumbled over her words and said, "I'm getting ahead of myself. Please, allow me to start from the beginning. It will make more sense that way."

She took a deep breath and began. Her speech was rapid and she went on as though her purpose was to avoid being interrupted. "It all started in 1953 with one of the most monumental discoveries in the history of man—the discovery of DNA, or deoxyribonucleic acid, and the DNA double-helix." As she went on she was pacing and using her hands in overly expressive gestures for added emphasis. "The basic chemistry hiding deep inside every living thing, from the smallest bacterium to the largest whale, the smallest shrub to the largest tree, all the way back to the ancient dinosaurs…the basic chemistry and genetics are the same." She carried on for twenty minutes describing the historical high points of DNA and genetics research. She was so excited about her work that she failed to recognize she was being a brute, demonstrating all the subtlety of a punch in the face when it came to informing Jake he was the product of genetic manipulation, that he was designed in a laboratory.

"The bottom line," she said, "is that after hundreds of years of trying, it became apparent that the time to manipulate DNA is before conception. The genetic material present the moment sperm and egg join is everything. If genetic therapies are going to last, they must be present at that moment. In your case we used the progenitor cells, the cells that actually make sperm. We took them from your father, removed the nucleus, eliminated the genes we were after and replaced them with engineered sequences, and the nucleus was re-inserted into the cell. The cells picked right up where they left off, none the wiser that they had undergone a major operation. Isn't that amazing? We learned to deconstruct and reconstruct life. We were performing microsurgery at the level of DNA."

"Wait a minute. Stop," Jake said in exasperation. He exhaled and ran his fingers through his hair.

Ben felt sorry for Jake. He didn't ask for any of this, and he certainly didn't deserve it. He made careful study of Jake's body language and the subtle nuances of his nonverbal behavior. He was tight. Enormous amounts of tension were swirling just beneath the surface. The more she talked the more it grew. His muscles were prominent, like they were heaving and squeezing his frame. But so far Jake was keeping it together. His external features were those of a warrior, weathered and worn but still well within his prime. The cut of his goatee, the scars from wicked injuries across his face and arm, and the missing fingers—all of it bore testament to a life that was one long series of brawls. As a result of the time they had spent together, Ben understood how accurate, and yet how deceiving, Jake's external appearance was. The Jake Gillean who first saw the light of day in Spring Hill, Tennessee, born as the only child to parents who loved him, the football player who liked fishing with his friends, the husband of Wendy and father of Bailey and Paul, the officer second in command of Alpha Group…that man was a gentleman from beginning to end. He was a force fighting for everything that was right. He was introspective, caring and compassionate, stalwart, and honest to a fault. While he was subject to all the pressures and failures inherent to being human, he was also filled with faith and reason. But something terrible had happened when he traveled back to the Nineteenth Century, something that erased and destroyed his family line, and nearly destroyed him in the process. Exactly what it was he didn't know. But soon enough, should Jake choose to join and fight with MST, his entire story would be laid bare.

There was something else. It took Ben a while to recognize what it was that he was seeing in Jake's eyes. Then it struck him…it was discovery. Jake was suddenly making sense of things in his life…things that hadn't made sense before.

"What changes did you make?" Jake's tone was aggressive. He was fixated on the thought that central events of his life may have been related to MST's genetic experiments.

"Some of the modifications were to turn specific genes off," she said, "or to down-regulate the expression of specific genes. Other modifications were to up regulate gene expression. In many cases, we changed the actual version of the protein being produced. But that isn't where it stopped. The bacteria that live in your bowel were genetically modified to break down chemical compounds in food that have often been associated with cancer, and they've been equipped with the machinery to elaborate essential vitamins and to maintain their colonies over extended periods of time, to survive disease, and to overwhelm any competing bacteria or parasites.

"What changes did you make?" He asked again. "How am I different from the person I otherwise would have been?"

"Philosophically speaking…you are you, Jake." She paused momentarily to let the thought take before she went on, "There is no other Jake Gillean. There is only one original and there was never another. You and your perception of consciousness would not otherwise exist." Dr. Ratzlaff's face was filled with curiosity and wonderment, as though she thought he would not have come to such a realization without her guidance. "Your consciousness and your conscience…neither would exist. Without the modifications we made an entirely different person with a different life experience and a different consciousness would exist. You're as human and as natural as anyone else. What we did is on the same par as a mother who chooses not to consume alcohol during pregnancy for the sake of having healthier offspring. It's not much different than selecting a mate based on a certain set of characteristics, for beauty or brains. What we did is just more direct and predictable."

"You're not answering my question. The modified genes, what exactly did they control?" Jake's hands were clenched into fists.

"Okay," she said. "Given our presumptions regarding the challenges you would face, it was determined that several genetic characteristics, if altered, would improve your odds of survival. Your intelligence, analytical and non-analytical, your ability to store your experiences in long term memory, and your ability to process and recall them were all enhanced. Your immune system was modified so that you would fight off infection with greater vigor, be more resilient against disease, and rid your system of precancerous and cancerous cells. Your muscle strength and speed were increased. Your ability to digest and extract needed micronutrients from your foods was increased. Your vision and hearing were enhanced. You are more resistant to DNA mutations. We made some psychological modifications. Your bones are stronger and more resistant to fracture and degeneration."

"Stop!" Jake said. His heart was pounding. She was confirming his greatest fears. "Psychological modifications? What exactly do you mean by psychological modifications?"

"Nothing to be overly concerned about," she said. "Just some modifications to tweak this characteristic and that."

"I asked you a question, and you're being evasive! What the hell did you do to me?"

Dr. Ratzlaff was fidgeting and avoiding eye contact.

Jake was ready to explode, "Answer the damn question! What did you do to me?!"

"I'm sorry, but…just that, I'm afraid."

Jake didn't understand.

She pointed at him. "Just that." Her finger was trembling and she took a step backward. "That's what we did. We found that certain genes were related to levels of assertiveness and aggression, and those areas of the brain are interconnected with other areas of the brain that give…." she hesitated and added, "pleasure. We found that there is a substantial interplay between those emotive experiences and a person's perception of pleasure."

"Oh my God!" Jake almost choked. He brought his hands up to clench the hair by his temples. He began to pace. "Because of you I experience more anger and aggression?"

"Yes."

"And these connections to the pleasure centers in my brain…you messed with those too? I experience more pleasure during acts of aggression?"

"Yes," she said.

"Oh my God! Do you have any idea what you've done?!" Jake yelled.

"What we did was…"

Jake held up his hand indicating that she should stop. The morose coincidence of his right hand missing the fourth and fifth fingers, the mangled hand of MST's DNA experiment looming in the air in front of her, caught her attention. The connection was made and a little pang of guilt tweaked its way through her. It marked the first moment she ever felt an emotion other than pride in her work.

Jake turned his back to her. His mind was screaming. The anger he felt was powerful and overwhelming. He wanted to lash out and strike something, but on another level it never felt so pathetic, so tangible, so contrived, so manipulated by genetic modifications…and so unworthy of respect.

He thought about how he would wake out of terrible nightmares when he was in the hospital. A nurse would come running in to check on him. How things have changed. Now his whole life was just one big nightmare… and this time there was no waking up to escape the torment. Nothing he thought was real in his life was actually real.

Dr. Ratzlaff looked to Ben for help. He shook his head indicating that she should do nothing. Silence was the proper course of action.

Jake picked up the photograph of his family. He sat down and quickly got up to pace the room. His emotions were violent and extreme, all negative and all dark. Any joy that might have been found in the wonderful memories of his wife and children was being suffocated by a sense of loss and a sense of complete powerlessness. Then there was another emotion, it was squeezing everything else, it was absolutely indomitable in the carnage it was wreaking in his heart…it was simple and all of his own making… it was guilt.

Jake needed to escape the wrath of his mind. He needed a distraction. As difficult as it was, the information Dr. Ratzlaff was giving him was less painful than what was waiting in moments of silence. He said, "And I passed these traits on to my children?"

"Insofar as the modified DNA is incorporated into your sperm… yes."

Jake recalled Paul's explosion of anger when he saw Bailey and his mother crying on the night he told them he had to leave. Jake saw himself in his son then, and even more so now.

"He didn't have a choice in this. He didn't deserve this."

Dr. Ratzlaff and Ben were confused, not understanding what he meant.

"I didn't have a choice either did I? Hard to raise my hand to object when I hadn't even been conceived yet. But why? Why go to all the trouble? Why not use a willing subject, someone fully informed and willing to take the risks?" It was futility on display. Jake was grasping and he knew it. He also knew there was no way he could have been the first. "What happened to the others?"

She hesitated. "What we did wasn't easy. You can't just shotgun…"

Jake held up his hand again and glared, "What happened to the others?"

"You're the only one who survived. You're the only one who successfully controlled the emotive or psychological aspects of our modifications. The others fell victim to crimes, usually of the violent sort, combinations of substance abuse, and/or extreme mood disorders. As we went along and studied our outcomes we learned what to look for. Fortunately, your father displayed the perfect combination of traits required to control the modifications we deemed necessary. You are a proverbial super-soldier, the perfected offspring of your father. But I can't overemphasize how complex the brain aspects of this are. No single gene is responsible for any specific psychological trait. It's a combination of thousands of genes, billions of neurons, and trillions of neuronal connections, and the choices you make in your life to potentiate the connections."

"You should have considered my mother," Jake said. "If you did you might have noticed her problems with anger management."

His comment met with silence. Dr. Ratzlaff wasn't aware that they ever considered that angle. Maybe MST hadn't been as thorough as she believed.

"Wait a minute," Jake said. He made a connection that was shocking in its implications. "You genetically modified my father. Did that have something to do with his illness?"

"Yes," she said. "Unfortunately multiple sclerosis is a risk."

Jake's eyes glassed over. He dropped his head and said, "My God! Do you have any idea what you've done? Do you have any idea how much he suffered? His life was a living hell. It was hell for all of us. Do you know what it's like to watch your father die?" Jake was now looming in front of Dr. Ratzlaff, staring straight into her eyes, "Do you know what it's like to pray so hard that it hurts, to pray that you could trade places?" Jake was coming unglued. He turned and lashed out, hitting the side of the bookshelf, splintering the wood and sending a row of books flying across the room. He turned back to face her. "Do you know what it's like to have all your prayers ignored!" he yelled, "and to think God doesn't care, and now I learn it was all part of some elaborate experiment! Do you have any idea how much I…?!" he stopped. His teeth were gritted. He was going to say how much he wanted to kill them for what they had done. But he didn't. He finished with, "Was Mom in on this?"

"No, and there were a couple reasons," she said. "We needed the Y chromosome, and have you ever met your mother?"

Jake couldn't believe what he just heard.

"I don't mean to be disrespectful," Dr. Ratzlaff said, "but there is no way she would have agreed to any of this. She hated the military and was distrustful of advanced technologies. Given that some degree of secrecy was warranted, Thomas elected not to tell her. The only reason he agreed was because he found the urn you buried. Jake, I'm sorry. But you're father knew everything."

Jake paused and stared at her. She didn't flinch from her statement.

"What do you mean…the urn? What do you know about the urn? He found the urn after I was born. What are you talking about…he knew everything?"

"He knew what was going to happen to you, and he knew exactly what would happen to him. He sacrificed himself for you. There are two things you should know. First, he found the urn before you were born, before you were conceived. And second, there were two letters in the urn. You know for a fact that you buried a second letter in that urn. In that letter you told him everything that happened. He read that letter a thousand times, and he burned it in the fireplace. You were sleeping right down the hall. He destroyed the letter you wrote him right before he died. Jake, he wanted to give you every advantage so that you would survive your ordeal. He was the most willing and the most dedicated subject we ever had. He was fully informed and knew everything that was going to happen. He knew what his future would be. Thomas Gillean is the bravest man we have ever known. He loved his son so much that he sacrificed himself, and he did it before you were conceived."

"No. No, it's not possible." Jake ran through the scenario in his head. He knew exactly what he buried in that damnable urn, and it didn't include a letter to his father.

"You're father possessed a remarkable mind," she said. "He was controlled, disciplined, introspective, and exceedingly insightful. He gave you all the equipment necessary to control the modifications we made to your DNA."

"Control it?" Jake was standing just a few feet in front of her. He shifted his gaze to Ben and back again. "I didn't control it. I couldn't." He tensed up and yelled, "IT ABSOLUTELY CONSUMED ME! MY WHOLE FAMILY IS DEAD BECAUSE OF ME! Oh, my God," he put his face in his hands and nearly slumped to the floor. "What have you done? What have I done?" He looked to Dr. Ratzlaff and again at Ben, "I couldn't control it," he repeated. He was almost pleading, "I couldn't control it."

Dr. Ratzlaff was taken aback. Not knowing how to react, she motioned to Ben to intervene. Once again he refused.

"I understand," she offered, "that he tutored you, he trained you so you wouldn't lose yourself. Your survival has only been possible because Thomas was such a remarkable man. I'm not saying this because I'm trying to manipulate you, Jake. I feel like I know your father because I saw the recordings."

"The recordings?" Jake said. "What recordings?"

"Your father made a series of recordings with the scientists who were working with him."

"Can I see them?"

"Yes," she answered. "All of them. They're yours. In a sense, what happened to your father occurred before MST ever existed. It happened long before you ever met Alexander Fisk or traveled back in time. MST's existence is possible only because you traveled back in time. Who knows what the first event was that started the whole sequence. I know that when you reappeared, your family history was changed, and there is no record anywhere of your life or the people you loved, but MST's records prove otherwise. We know the truth. We just need to figure out what went wrong."

Jake approached Ben. When he was no more than two feet in front of him he said, "I don't have to involve myself in this convoluted scheme."

"You can do whatever you want. I'll support you regardless," Ben responded. "If you want to crawl away and hide...go ahead. But you have to face who you are. You are a warrior. You're a soldier and a fighter. You know better than anyone that you cannot exact change in this world by being soft and tender. A soldier knows the costs, understands there will be sacrifice. There's a lot happening Jake, and beyond the capabilities of anyone else, you are designed, destined to stand absolute and firm, and when the chaos dies down and everyone else is bent and their will destroyed, Lt. Col. Jake Gillean will be the last one standing. You are resolute. Just as in the past, people will come to you for strength and protection, and they will follow you to the very gates of hell."

"You don't know what I've done," Jake said. His words were blunt and factual, but deep in the delivery, buried in the tone there was a crack.

"It doesn't matter what...," Ben was in the process of trying to make a point when Jake shouted over him.

"YOU DON'T KNOW WHAT I'VE DONE!" He exploded with an anger that skirted the edge of madness. He walked a few feet away and turned back as though he was in the midst of battle. His eyes were dilated and his frame loomed large. Boiling violence ripped his insides while Centurion-like stoicism commanded his facial features. The only outward signs of perturbation he betrayed were his raised voice, a barely perceptible twitch of his right hand, and the rhythmic contraction of his masseter muscles as his jaw clenched.

"Before you make your decision, I have something you might be interested in seeing," Dr. Ratzlaff interjected. She brought it with her as an insurance policy just in case Jake broke down under the strain of the meeting. "Here," she said. She handed a memory chip to Jake.

"What is this?" He held it with defiance, tight in his fingers.

"It's a recording from your father. I haven't seen that one. There's a series of security questions at the beginning that only you would know how to answer. He meant this one just for you."

Jake began to soften. He scrutinized the memory chip, considering what it might contain. At first he wondered if he should watch it. In the end, he really had no choice.

"Look," Ben offered, "there's more going on here than we've been able to put together, but five months ago you showed up nearly dead at a Civil War reenactment. You were covered in blood—forensic evidence revealed it was blood from more than twenty people. You were wearing a Confederate uniform and riding one of our horses."

"What do you mean...one of *our* horses?"

"I'm sorry, Jake," Dr. Ratzlaff said. "I haven't gotten that far yet. Balius is one of MST's horses. If you like I will take you to see him."

Jake was confused.

"Patience," Ben urged. "It'll all make sense." He grabbed Jake's wrist and closed his hand on the memory chip. "But first I think you need to see what your father had to say."

* * * * *

"How many days before all assets are in position and ready to move?" President Martinez asked.

"Four days. Then we'll be ready to launch the invasion," General Toby Wayne said.

The President was pleased about United America's plan to launch an invasion of Brazil. The goal was to take out the South American power before the rest of the world would have a chance to mobilize their resources.

The other generals were motionless, their silhouettes outlined by the walls of computers that lined the periphery of the room. The circular military command center was buried deep under New Washington, connected to the other centers of government through the labyrinth of tunnels. By decorum, the other commanders remained a step back from the holographic platform, only stepping forward if specifically asked for their opinion. They were careful to remain stony, to avoid betraying emotions. Some thought it was insane to launch the attack, recognizing it as the prelude to another World War. History had proven that no matter how powerful a country was, it could never stand alone against the rest of the world. This was especially true given United America's problems with the food supply. All the technological advantages they enjoyed would be useless if the people were starving. But they kept their thoughts private. They were cowed into silence by circumstances; by the rush toward war, by ideological enthusiasm, by the desire to avenge missing diplomats and assassinated politicians, and by fear for their careers and personal safety. As a result, the march toward war progressed without a voice of dissent.

The sole purpose of the military establishment was to offer advice regarding strategies that would be used to accomplish the President's objectives. Some desired nothing more than to avoid the snare of internal politics, others would do anything to curry the President's favor and gain advantage over perceived rivals. The tension in the room was thick and pasty.

"What's the intel?" the President asked. He was calm and calculating, his eyes darting from one part of the holographic projection to another as he processed the information.

"All indications are that our plan is working. We've taken advantage of the recent leaks in our communications and security systems and between the false information we released and our movement of assets in the Gulf and Atlantic, they are actively pulling men and material out of line." General Wayne indicated the troop movements on the holographic map. "They're shoring up their northern border and northeastern coasts as we speak. We'll smash through Peru and roll up their western defenses."

"Good, very good," the President said. With a smile of satisfaction he smashed his fist down on the railing. "The Peruvians are a cunning bunch."

"South American Union be damned, they've hated each other for centuries, Mr. President. We're just using it to our advantage."

"How many men do we have?"

"Upward of six million will be used in the initial wave. Gaps will undoubtedly open in their coastal defenses when they respond. We have a second lightning wave ready to take advantage when that development materializes."

"Time estimates?"

"Simulations range from ten days to three weeks, assuming they don't have any tech we don't know about."

President Martinez shifted the map to Cuba. "Anything to report?" He was referring to Havana.

"We threw a division in to restore order. We're still trying to sort out what happened."

"Any evidence the Brazilians were behind it?"

"None."

The President turned to face General Wayne. His eyes suddenly burned with anger. He was going to have his revenge. He said, "It was an overt act of war, and the Brazilians are responsible. The fact that you haven't found anything only means that you haven't looked hard enough."

General Wayne understood the implication. "I'm very confident sir. We will find the link."

* * * * *

NAIA Director Carl Zimmer paced nervously in his office. He couldn't believe the President called in the old man. He had to be pushing a hundred years old. What use could he possibly be at this point in time? The man was a dinosaur that had been buried ten years ago. He should have stepped aside twenty or thirty years prior to that, but he had such a lock on power that he couldn't be forced out. The secretary buzzed in, "Director Zimmer… Director Marshall has arrived."

'Damn,' Zimmer thought, 'he shouldn't be here. He's an ornery old bastard, and now I have to deal with him. This investigation requires intellect and subtlety. Marshall's answer to everything is to start killing people. He's an ape. It was a great moment in evolution when he decided to retire.' Zimmer pressed the com and said, "I'll be right there."

He moved across the office, paused to take a breath, and opened the door. Director Jorge Marshall was waiting, angry that he had to wait ten seconds, scowling that his departure from the intelligence community and his quiet life had been interrupted because of the incompetence of his successors.

"Director Marshall. Good to see you, sir. I appreciate you coming back to help sort things out," Zimmer said. He could feel his indigestion starting to kick in.

Marshall ignored him, brushed past with a limp, which he determined wasn't going to slow him down, and selected a seat. He pointed his cane at the desk, indicating that Zimmer should avoid wasting his time with feigned niceties. His posture was slightly stooped, and there wasn't much hair left, but his persona and brusque nature hadn't changed in the least. He scanned the room and noted the artwork on the walls with a disapproving glare. In his day, the walls were covered with information pertaining to NAIA investigations. He said, "I seem to recall that everything was in order when I handed you this office."

Zimmer's face was turning red. "We have had some unique challenges of late."

"Challenges?" he scoffed. His gaze shifted for a moment in contemplation before he came back to stare at Zimmer. Then he chuckled and said, "Interesting use of the word." His tone bore a vicious edge of sarcasm. United America had suffered missing diplomats and undercover agents all across the world, numerous assassinations had occurred on home soil, and Zimmer referred to it as a *challenge*. "Buried in that word," Marshall said, "is the implicit implication that someone is actively trying to resolve the dilemma. Let me ask you, how many people have you relieved of duty since this began?"

"None," Zimmer said.

"As I suspected." He shook his head in disgust. "You're leaking information like a sieve, and you leave everyone in position."

"We've completely revamped all of our security protocols," Zimmer said. "We've added layers of additional security and surveillance on all communications. We are using a new encryption protocol, and we carefully monitor the movements and actions of all our people."

"How many have been brought in for level III interrogations?"

"We don't do it that..."

Marshall raised his hand. The gesture was menacing and immediately accomplished its intended purpose.

Zimmer backtracked, "We've brought in and questioned thousands of people with no credible leads. A couple dozen have undergone level II interrogations. No useful information has thus far been obtained. I assure you, Director Marshall, that I've read everything you have ever written and I've reviewed your work—the problems facing us are unprecedented."

"Then you failed to learn the most remedial lesson." He rapped the Vintel platform several times with his cane like an angry schoolteacher while saying, "Stop over-relying on technology. The problem doesn't dictate success or failure...you do."

Zimmer lost his patience. His voice rose and he began, "There have been..."

"No need for that," Director Marshall interrupted, completely disregarding Zimmer as being worthy of an equal argument. "I was sitting in that chair when you were still on your mother's tit. In order to run these agencies you have to apply common sense." He stared at Zimmer for a long moment, reveling in the fact that his successor was squirming.

"Behind every action is a motivation for gain. To find answers, you have to deconstruct the problem and determine who gains. Cases that rise to this level are never as they appear on the surface. Further, cases important enough to come to this desk never occur in isolation. I told you that once didn't I?"

"You did," Zimmer agreed.

"Tell me about the cases you've worked on in the last year or two that have been compartmentalized. The ones you've treated as though they were unique and unrelated to the current...*challenges*."

"We have a couple cases," Zimmer regrettably admitted.

Marshall waved a finger, indicating that Zimmer should talk.

"There's a case of large amounts of food being diverted from Central Canadian distribution centers into the black market. Another involves military transports being used to funnel narcotics. There's a counter-cyber attack program developed in response to increased attacks on the Data Mountains. We're creating mirage Data Mountains in an effort to isolate sources. The system is integrated with orbiting satellites, and weaponized lasers will be used to eliminate individuals or teams of hackers in real time. There's another involving a potential case of time travel."

"Say again," Marshall said.

"Time travel. A John Doe showed up at a Civil War Reenactment."

Marshall's reaction was immediate. At first he looked away in thought, confused, then his eyes widened and his features froze, "Did you say Civil War?"

"I did."

The old man stiffened and rose to his feet. The color was gone from his face. Having stood up too quickly, the room momentarily began to go out of focus; he was off balance and fell forward, hitting the edge of the desk with his arms and upper chest. His bad knee smashed down hard on the floor. He realized a bolt of pain, fought through it, and staggered to his feet, breathless. He leaned forward over the desk and locked eyes with Zimmer. "Do you have him?"

* * * * *

DSS Director Jerica Drum kept a rapid pace as she moved through the corridor of the Havana Police Department. It was active with the military coordinating efforts to secure the city with local PD. "Does his story check out?" she asked.

"It does," Ludwig Arness said. "After we lost their trail in Phoenix, this is the first break we've had. We've made a positive ID. I pulled all the surveillance data, and we were able to piece together at least some of their movements. It looks like the whole show here in Havana was our target's doing. And you know what the odd part of it is?" Arness stopped walking. "By all appearances…it wasn't planned. He did it on a whim."

"You're telling me he took down a whole city simply because he decided it would be fun?" Drum made no effort to hide her doubts.

"Not exactly. I think he did it because he was pissed off. We have an eyewitness who has an interesting tale to tell."

They weaved their way into the overworked holding area and were soon looking at a feed from one of the interrogation rooms. A DSS agent was conducting a level I interrogation. "Who is he?" she asked.

"Name's Archibald Ramsey," Arness said. "A two-bit thug. Runs with a gang of low-lifes in the hood, mostly muggings, gambling and sex rings, drug dealing, that sort of stuff. This piece of work has a penchant for rolling drunks and targeting out-of-towners. MO is to work in teams, outnumber the victim by six or eight guys. Learned that little pearl before being dishonorably discharged from the military."

"Looks like he bit off a little more than he could chew," Drum said. Ramsey was wearing a dressing over one eye, a cervical collar, and a brace on his arm.

"Three of his friends were hospitalized, one with a head injury, one with a fractured jaw and a bleeding brain, and the other with broken ribs and internal bleeding."

"That makes four."

"Made the other three clean up the place. Took all their knives and broke them in half."

"Do we have it?"

"No. He deactivated the surveillance before they attacked."

They listened in on the ongoing interrogation. "I already told you everything that happened. Look what he did to me," Ramsey whined. "I never saw anyone move so fast. I was minding my own business when he jumped me for no reason. I tried to fight, but he had a knife. Once he got the drop on me there was nothing I could do."

Drum turned off the audio. She motioned to a side room where they could talk freely. "What do we have so far?"

"Gillian and Murray were in Havana. We located the place where they stayed, but it was completely destroyed by fire. Don't know if they or the riots did it. We have footage of Gillian and a person we suspect is Murray moving around before the riots."

"What do you mean?"

"His face was different. Both of their faces were different, completely unrecognizable. They were wearing some sort of masks. We were only able to recognize Gillian because he is missing the two fingers on his right hand. We tracked the movements of the presumed Murray, but we have nothing after the surveillance systems went down. Looked like he was sightseeing."

"And Gillian?"

"He took a stroll through the neighborhood and entered a store. A short time later the food quota system went down. According to the woman working at the counter, Gillian messed with the surveillance system and tampered with the retinal scanner. The whole system collapsed after that."

"Do you have a team on it?" Drum asked.

"Yes. But we don't have anything yet. Can't figure out how he did it. She denies having anything to do with it and claims she told him not to mess with the systems."

"Do you believe her?"

"She's the one who initiated contact with local authorities, and she's scared. But yes…I think her story is legitimate. As he was messing with the retinal scanner, Ramsey and his boy scout troop came in and tried to earn a merit badge. Gillian waylaid the whole bunch. Now here's where the story gets interesting. Afterward, according to Ramsey, two cops accost a woman on the street right in front of the place. They take her off for their own purposes. Gillian gets mad, pulls out a pulsar, a pulsar unlike any weapon Ramsey has ever seen, and chases after them on foot. That's when all hell breaks loose. The hovering sentries go berserk and start knocking out the surveillance system and targeting local PD resources. After that the riots broke out. Local PD recovered the bodies of the two officers in question. Scene looked like it was straight out of a war zone. One was killed by a pulsar blast, and the other's head was beaten to jelly."

"What about the woman?"

"No sign of her at this point," Arness said.

"Your theory is that Gillian did all this? That one man on a whim took out an entire city?"

"Yes, ma'am. That's the way it appears."

Drum considered the facts. She mumbled under breath, "Who the hell are you?"

"Will you take this higher?" Arness asked.

"I will but no one's going to listen. They'd never believe it. The President is screaming about the Brazilians. Havana is their justification for war."

* * * * *

Ben and Dr. Ratzlaff left Jake so that he could be alone and immerse himself in the holographic recording made by Thomas. Jake was immediately struck by how young and vibrant his father looked. He guessed that it was made several years before his death, before the illness took most of his strength. His gaze was as penetrating as Jake remembered, and his voice was just as disarming.

"Hello, son," Thomas said. "It's been a long time since we last sat down together. I want you to know that I am so very proud of you. The fact that you're with me now is an indication that you have found a way to survive a terrible ordeal. It means there is still hope." He smiled, "We have so much to talk about…"

Ben and Dr. Ratzlaff were in the bunker's central control room. For almost an hour they watched the movement of United America's military assets across the Caribbean and in the Western Atlantic. United America was building up an incredible force, and by all appearances, war was imminent. MST was feeding the information to the Brazilian High Command through a backdoor channel and they, in turn, were deploying their numerically inferior forces to meet the threat.

Ben's BCD indicated an incoming message. It was from Jake. He was ready. The pivotal moment for MST and the world was upon them. Ben was apprehensive when he entered the room, not sure what to expect. However, he discovered that Jake's persona was entirely different. He was commanding and yet at ease. His eyes were alert and emotionally neutral. He smiled and pointed at the destroyed bookshelf. The books were neatly stacked to one side. "Sorry. Won't allow that to happen again. I'll pay for the damage."

"Okay," Ben said, not quite sure what to make of Jake's mood.

Jake's thoughts were clear and precise. He recognized that his story was far from complete. He wondered if, just because Ben was a descendant of Alex, if he owed him anything…or if he owed MST anything for that matter. His answer was now clear.

"The cut on my forearm. I got it in a fight with an inner city gang in Havana."

"Oh," Ben said.

"And the whole thing with the city security systems and the riots. I am responsible."

"I know. I saw the recordings when you were sleeping in the submarine," Ben said. "For a guy armed with only a pulsar and an energy shield you sure made a mess of things. Do you mind if I ask why?"

When Jake looked at the world only a few things were certain…it was a world that had passed him by, it was a world in which he didn't belong, and it was also a world that needed him.

"Injustice," he said. "I did it because of injustice." Jake's expression was hard to read. He made eye contact and subtly nodded. "I'll never stop fighting. It's what I'm designed for."

It was enough of a statement to convey that he was going to cooperate. Ben grinned. "Will you tell me what happened to you during the Civil War?"

"If you'll listen."

"Lt. Col. Gillean, it's an honor to meet you," Ben said. He slapped Jake on the shoulder. "We don't have much time. The battle for United America is beginning. Things are about to get dangerous."

CPSIA information can be obtained at www.ICGtesting.com
Printed in the USA
LVOW041925150112

263987LV00002B/3/P